Heir to the Throne
Maria Albert

DESCENT of KINGS Book 2

Dreamspinner Press

Published by
Dreamspinner Press
5032 Capital Circle SW
Ste 2, PMB# 279
Tallahassee, FL 32305-7886
USA
http://www.dreamspinnerpress.com/

Cover Art by Paul Richmond
http://www.paulrichmondstudio.com

ISBN: 978-1-62380-561-6
Digital ISBN: 978-1-62380-562-3

Printed in the United States of America
First Edition
July 2013

Acknowledgments

A warm welcome to all my new readers! Special thanks to Rachel, Ariella, and Joylyn, my beta readers, first fans, and staunch supporters, and to all the folks at Dreamspinner for enabling me to fulfill my dream.

Particular thanks to Elizabeth North for asking to see a novel and enthusiastically embracing the series, and to Lynn West for her aid in coordination and production.

Extra special thanks to Paul Richmond for his graphic assistance, creativity, and flexibility, particularly in regards to his beautifully rendered cover art for the series.

Most ecstatic jumping-up-and-down, handsprings, and cartwheel thanks to my fantastic primary editor, Andi Byassee, for her invaluable comments and amazing guidance throughout this series. I never understood how an editor could truly improve a book until I had the good fortune and privilege of working with you, Andi. I truly love how you are as emotionally invested in the lives of these people as I am. There is no one I would rather take with me on this journey.

HAMMERHOME

DOROLINGAS

CARAMORE

MALAR IN FROMER

IRONHAND

AKEMORE

IRONFORGE

FROMER MTNS.

THE WATCHTOWER

FROMER MTNS.

NALEA

SARASTREN RIVER

THENALON

LOST ROAD

ARALON

WOODS

TAHIR RIVER

WESTERN ROAD

GLEN'S FORD

LOGARETH

METHW ROAD

HELDEN FIELDS

FEONOKE

GOWER

FENEMAL

RIVER

ATHANARA

HELDEN RIVER

ELVEN & DWARVEN CALENDAR 3013

MILES

0 50 100 150 200

N

CORODEN MTNS.

CORODEN MTNS.

GELTHOR PASS

ERENIA

SYLVAN RIVER

TANIERIA

LYSENIA

WOODS

ELINGOR RIVER

KIERNESS MARSH

MERDAN RIVER

FALNOR

FALNOR WOODS

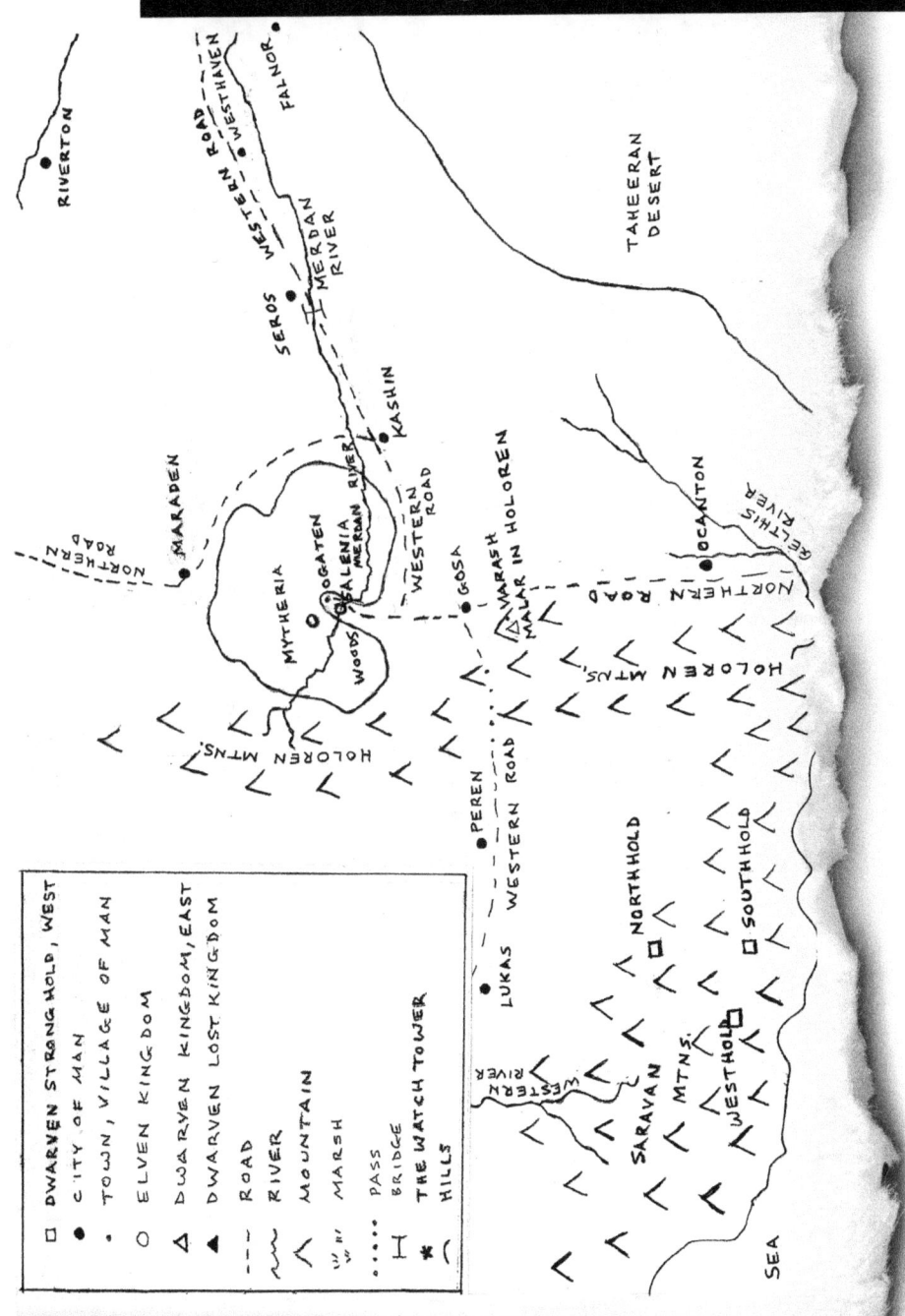

Chapter 1
Well Met

TALON was eyed with suspicion when he entered the inn, as he had expected to be. In a village as small and insular as this one, strangers were no doubt rare and, unfortunately, more often than not brought trouble. Talon certainly looked like he might: he was dirty, ragged, and well armed. He might look like a brigand, but he felt more like a beggar, save for the sheathed blade at his side. He drew strength and a small measure of dignity from both the Sword and the concealed armband on his bicep, from what they represented. But he was hungry and filthy and worn to the bone, so near to complete exhaustion it frightened him. Whyever had he come here?

He should have gone south as soon as he left the Gelthor Pass; he should have headed down the Southern Road toward Athanark as he had originally intended. There were disturbing rumors of trouble coming from there. But instead, he had found himself drawn north by that inexplicable portion of his Power that seemed to sense evil, that sometimes even detected danger before it happened. He had expected to discover the trouble he was seeking lay in Fenemal, the last City of Man in the north, but he was compelled to travel beyond that city, farther north still, almost to the mountains. It was there he had stumbled across the half-overgrown path leading from the Southern Road to this tiny village deep in the middle of these endless woods.

Talon had not slept for more than a handful of hours since before reaching Fenemal, and had not slept in a real bed for longer than he cared to remember. Nor had he bathed in anything better than an icy stream, and that had been many days ago, and he had traveled far since. The thought of a mug of mead and a hot meal, a warm bath, and a soft bed was tempting almost beyond enduring. Talon clutched his nearly empty purse and fingered the two coins it contained through the thin fabric eagerly, but his eyes remained on those in the room. He would, as ever, proceed cautiously.

The inn seemed full for this time of night, especially for so small a village, but those who were there drank deeply and without joy, and their conversation was tense and muted. Perhaps his instincts had not led him astray after all. There indeed appeared to be something amiss here.

Talon chose a back table where he could eye both the door and the room, near enough to the fire for warmth and the light he so desperately craved, but where it wouldn't dazzle his vision should he need to step out into the night again quickly. He slipped the strap of his slim bedroll from his shoulder and laid it in the empty chair beside him, his gaze continuing to wander about the room as he sat.

It was then he saw what stood beside the entrance: three pitchforks, two axes, and a few stout walking sticks were leaning against the wall, the closest thing these men might have to weapons. He was too tired. He should have noticed them long before he had entered the room so deeply. He cursed himself for his carelessness. But the forest that surrounded the village was disconcerting; there was a wrongness to it that had kept him awake and on edge all of last night, though ever since Fenemal, dark visions had haunted his dreams. Still, lack of sleep was no excuse. He never should have missed seeing the weapons.

The innkeeper approached Talon cautiously. He was not so fat as some, but cleaner than most for a village this size. Perhaps there might be a bath to be had here after all. Talon tensed, waiting for the suggestion that he remove his weapon, but it did not come.

"You're lucky you didn't continue onward tonight, stranger. In truth, it's past dusk and a wonder you made it here at all. What can I get for you?" The innkeeper was remarkably friendly. Looking as he did, Talon had not thought to be given such a warm welcome, if a somewhat ominous one. Hopefully, he could find a single night's peace here before confronting whatever evil threatened this place.

"Mead and dinner, a bath, and a room for the night," Talon said wearily, stripping off his gloves now that it was safe to do so, now that it did not appear he would need to use the Sword, at least not in the immediate future.

He saw the innkeeper eyeing his hands in surprise. Talon knew without looking why he stared. His hands were astonishingly clean, soft skinned, and pale; they did not match the rough, tanned, weathered appearance of the rest of him at all. He silently cursed himself for the lapse in judgment. He should have left his gloves on. He knew better than to do anything to draw attention to himself. But by Idare, he had not wanted to eat his supper wearing those cursed gloves!

"I'd not begrudge a hungry man a bowl of soup and some bread and watered wine to go with it, even if he didn't have the coin to pay for it, and I can offer you a spot by the fire," the innkeeper said carefully. The Man's eyes were upon his face again, obviously assessing his appearance and doubting his ability to pay but not wanting to risk angering such a rough-looking and possibly desperate man who carried a sword and must know at least the basics of how to use it. Talon was also well aware the innkeeper could have instead called to any of the knot of burly Men sitting about and tried to have him disarmed or tossed out on his ear. They would never have succeeded, of course, were he not to allow it, but he would have left with as minimal resistance as possible. He'd not risk harming innocents. But instead, the innkeeper had shown him remarkable compassion.

Smiling tiredly, Talon did his best to look nonthreatening. "You are very kind, Innkeeper. Far kinder than I had any right to expect or than most would be, seeing me as I appear. But despite how I look, I am not a beggar and do not need your charity. Please, save it for the next man who comes to you who might be worse off than I am. Nor do I want you to fear that I might be trouble to you and yours. I am neither a killer nor a thief. I am merely an honest traveler who has fallen on hard times, nothing more." The lie came easily to him, as all the many thousands before it had. Like all believable lies, it had a kernel of truth in it. If only the Man before him knew who he truly was!

Talon reached into his lean purse, pulled two worn silver pieces from it, and held them out to the innkeeper. Hard times, indeed. The coffers of the Kingdom of

Amontir had been reduced long ago to what little he and his few surviving kinsmen carried in their meager purses, to what few coins lay in their secret Caches, most of which were now dismayingly empty. They'd have starved to death long ago were it not for the aid of the wizard Arcanus, the Dwarves, and the Elves.

Forcing such dark thoughts down, lest they overwhelm him, Talon continued, "I prefer mead to the wine and something more substantial than soup, and I desperately need a private room with a lock and a hot bath. I assume this will be enough?"

The innkeeper smiled at him in genuine warmth, the wariness gone, though the tension Talon had seen in him and everyone else here remained. He took a single silver from Talon's palm. "You keep the rest, stranger. This will cover all I can provide. Our kitchen is not nearly as well stocked as it should be," he said, the smile leaving his face and a frown replacing it. Obviously forcing better cheer, he added, "But you'll not go hungry, no sir! And I'll begin heating the water right now for your bath. I'll show you to your room after your dinner." He headed off toward what was apparently the kitchen.

Talon continued to surreptitiously watch the others in the room, resisting the urge to instead lean back his head and close his eyes.

When his food and drink came, he sipped appreciatively from the tankard of mead, bitter though the brew was, and then, watching the innkeeper's face, he casually asked, "Are there bandits in your woods?" There seemed to be enough able-bodied Men in the room that such should not be a problem, unless it was an organized force, but it was obvious something was wrong here.

"There are things worse than men that hunt in our woods," the innkeeper said, before turning and walking away quickly.

Talon heard the fear in his voice. Men were often suspicious that speaking of evil brought it down upon them. He was loath to press for more information. He was weary and did not want to have to battle this night.

He tasted the fare cautiously. The stew was well spiced, although oddly of potato and carrot and greens with no meat. But it was hot. The bread was coarse but fresh enough. The mead was passable, if somewhat bitter for his taste. Sighing in the closest he'd come to contentment in far too long, Talon leaned farther back in his chair, allowing himself to relax just a little.

The deceptive air of calm was suddenly rent by a scream from outside and then a loud wailing. There was the screech and thud of chairs as Men scrambled to their feet and grabbed for the weapons by the door. Talon had already crossed the room, tugging on his gloves as he ran, and was out the door before many of those nearest to it had reached it, heading out into the night toward the sounds of the commotion.

A man was holding a hysterical woman, who was straining against him toward the forest. "My baby, my boy!" she cried.

Talon stood before them, his gloved hand on Kathalanar's hilt. "Tell me, who or what has taken your child? What do I hunt?"

"You can't," the Man said, his voice hoarse, without hope. "He's gone. It's the wolven. They took my son."

"Show me," Talon commanded.

The Man pointed to a house closer to the forest edge than most, his hand shaking violently in his grief. "We thought we'd be safe in the house. But they came through his window, into his room. I heard him cry out. I wasn't fast enough." He fell to his knees sobbing, pulling his wife down with him.

Talon ran to the house as others went to the grieving parents. He looked into the child's room from the back window, the one facing the woods. There was blood on the pallet on the floor. Another innocent taken!

There was enough moonlight that the tracks were easy to spot. Talon studied the spoor by the window intently. The Man was right. There were four of them, definitely wolven, the large, savage distant cousins to the hunting dogs of Men. This would be a relatively easy hunt, compared to what he usually faced—only beasts.

Still, he must be cautious. He was far too close to exhaustion, and he could not afford to make a mistake because of it. *Carelessness can kill even the most seasoned warrior.* He heard his father's voice in his memory, speaking the warning to him as clearly as if it were a moment ago instead of decades past. For all he looked to be a man in his late twenties, save for his world-weary eyes, Talon was a scant two years short of nine decades of age. The Amontir did not age as other Men.

Talon slipped into the woods, moving as soundlessly as a pumar, continually scanning the ground and the forest around him. He followed the trail as long as he could. It was not easy tracking the wolven through the forest by moonlight. There was more blood, too much. But still he pressed on.

The forest became denser and the treetops blocked the moonlight. He lost the trail. Cursing softly, he carefully backtracked to where he'd last seen the tracks. He would not bring the child back alive, but he would bring him back. He would not return without him.

As he climbed into the higher branches of a strong oak, Talon wished for the bedroll he'd left back at the inn. Sleep was a long time coming, and when it came, his dreams were again dark, as full of blood and death as the long, violent history of his people.

He wakened long before dawn, his heart thundering loudly in his ears, visions of the horrors from his nightmares still vivid. He looked frantically for the faint light of the moon, when it was the burning blaze of the sun he needed, but it was near pitch black now. Clouds were obscuring the moon almost completely. He was a fool for not having returned to the village while there had still been enough light to see by! He fought the urge to draw upon the feeble light of the Sword. A fire would be enough; he must light a fire!

Talon nearly fell from the tree in his eagerness to reach the ground and chided himself for his stupidity, again hearing his father's warm voice in his memory gently reprimanding him for his carelessness. Memory of his father's voice, of his love, helped to calm him.

He began looking for dead wood, twigs, and especially pinecones, anything that might light easily and burn brightly until he could see to collect more fuel. Jumping at every unexplained snap and pop in the woods around him as he worked, he expected at any moment to feel the cold hands of the Enemy's Revenants, the walking dead, grab him and drag him into the darkness to their master. Again, he fought his need for the Sword's Power.

"No, He is not here, they are not here. You are safe. It is only wolven, animals, not monsters that you hunt this time. They are no danger to you, not while you are alert, while Kathalanar is at your side, not unless you let panic overwhelm you. There is no danger, not here, not yet, only fear," he chastised himself as he gathered together a small armful of wood and a few precious pinecones and laid them in front of the tree. Placing his back to the solid safety of the trunk, he took out his flint and steel and set about lighting the fire.

Once the fire was burning steadily, he forced himself to leave it, to venture more deeply into the darkness outside the friendly, warm glow of the blaze, to gather the wood he needed to keep the fire going until morning, to keep him sane. He could not fall to the King's Madness, not here, so far from the sole surviving kinsman who might help him. "It is not the Madness come to claim you. It is only lack of sleep this time," he said aloud, praying it was true. But it had been six years since he had last fallen to the Madness, and six years before that when he had first fallen to it, and neither Farad nor Lunahr were here to save him this time.

Gone! Farad was gone! Talon fought his panic and despair over the unknown fate of his eldest cousin. The bond that had linked them to one another for twelve years had shattered a sennight ago, without warning. Farad would never have broken the bond, knowing how desperately his cousin relied upon it. Talon knew he must have been killed.

Dead! Farad was dead! He fought down renewed panic at the thought. He had teetered upon the brink of Madness at the sudden loss of his cousin's light, until his bond to Lunahr had flared twice as bright to compensate for the loss. But the comfort of Lunahr's bond was not enough. Lunahr was so far away. He needed to see his young cousin, to embrace him, to feel him warm and alive before him.

Talon dared not draw upon the strength of the bond now, in these woods that exuded such evil. He feared the darkness of this place, but far more he feared that he might lead the Enemy to the one man he loved most in all the world now that Farad was gone. Even the Elves of Riviera might not be able to keep Lunahr safe if the Enemy learned they were the ones who had been sheltering him for the past six years. A single year remained until Lunahr turned twenty-five, until he came-of-age, until he could return to them, an adult, at the height of his Power. Idare, it felt like six lifetimes had passed instead of six years! Alone; he was so unbearably alone. It had been two years since he had even seen another of his kinsmen. There were so few of them now. Too few.

Talon forced his dark thoughts down and continued to gather all the dead wood he could find. He returned to the fire with the armload of wood, his arms shaking with his desperation to sit before the blaze, praying to Idare that what he had gathered would be enough to last until dawn. Then he laid some of the thicker branches on the flames, crossed his legs, laid his arms at his sides with his palms up, and began breathing slowly and deeply.

Once he had found a measure of calm, he began the familiar chanting Arcanus had taught him so long ago. Slowly, gradually, he found a temporary refuge in the flames. In the absence of the sun, fire was the one thing that had always comforted his people. He prayed that this time it would be enough.

AT THE break of dawn, Talon was up and moving again after carefully smothering the last embers of his fire. He found himself turning toward the sun, wishing for the brightness and heat of midday, when the sun was at its zenith, at the apex of its power. He forced his eyes back down to the ground and found the wolven tracks again.

He followed them for a long time. The wolven had taken their kill deep into the forest. He found where they'd eaten. There were some scraps of cloth, some shattered bits of bone, a few strands of hair. Another child dead, but at least there would be no body. Idare, what horrors they faced that it would be a mercy to know there was no body! But his parents would need to see something in order to accept the boy's death, in order to grieve.

He took off his tattered cloak and gathered what little remained carefully, wrapping it gently. Then he looked at where the tracks led deeper into the woods. He would hunt later. Now he had a sadder duty to perform. He headed back to the village.

He met the first of the villagers deeper into the forest than he thought they would have found their way. There must be someone among them with some skill in tracking, but they had lost the trail and were looking around hopelessly. The Men eyed him warily, pitchforks and axes raised, as he emerged from the sheltering trees. "I was in your village last night. I've come to return the boy's remains to his parents, so they may bury their son."

"It's him. The one I told you about," a Man said. Talon recognized the father's voice before his face. He looked like he'd aged a decade or more in the single night. Talon handed the cloak carefully to him, and the Man trembled as he took it. It was a somber procession that returned to the village.

"What, back so soon?" Talon heard a woman ask, and then the wailing began.

Talon headed for the inn. The innkeeper was there and seemed stunned to see him. "It's a miracle you're not dead as well. Poor little Billy! He was only six. Those monsters came three weeks agone. Five of the men have been lost hunting those vile things. We can never find them, but they find us easily enough. We've set traps for them, but they go around them. The deer and rabbits are gone, and even the birds and squirrels have either fled or been eaten. It's once they ran out of even that game that they came here, to the village. Our pigs, the goats, the chickens, even the dogs were all dragged off into the woods and devoured. We are their prey now."

No wonder there had been no meat in the stew! Still, these villagers should surely have been equal to the task of hunting ordinary wolven. Perhaps Incuban's dark hand was present here after all. Maybe the wolven were the evil he had been seeking.

The innkeeper handed Talon his bedroll and his silver piece. "You did your best. I'll not take your coin, for what you did for William and Amanda, but you'll still get your meal, bath, and room."

Talon took the bedroll but closed his gloved hand about the innkeeper's hand so he would keep the coin. "I'll need an axe and a rope. I only came back so the boy's parents could bury their son's remains and start to mourn. Now I go to hunt the wolven that have been plaguing you. You will lose no more of your children, or your men. I have killed such creatures before. I will come back to you once the beasts are gone, so that you can know you are safe. Meanwhile, no one goes out alone, even in daylight. No one goes out at night at all. Shutter your windows and bar your doors. Even then, no one sleeps in a room that faces the woods. Go out in groups ringed with armed guards and gather all the dry wood you can find. Rim the village in fires each night till daybreak until I return. Post armed sentries to watch the woods at all times," Talon said in a voice that was firm and commanding, one used to instant obedience without question.

As he turned to go, the stunned innkeeper said, "Please, my name is Goras. Who are you? What is your name?"

"I am a Captain of the Watch. I am called Talon," he said, and then he was gone, vanishing into the woods like a wraith as the Man gaped after him in astonishment at his revelation.

ARAS crouched down beside the unfamiliar plant, studying it with quiet interest instead of his usual excitement and joy at such a find. He only idly wondered what secrets the plant held, what medicinal uses the leaves, stem, and roots might have.

He rose with a small sigh and resolutely continued walking, soundlessly crossing the carpet of fallen leaves, moving with the silent grace all Elves possessed. He was on a journey of discovery, but plants were not his objective, although the one he left behind was not one of the hundreds of plants he had studied before, in the Wood surrounding Nalea. This plant did not grow there.

This was not his forest, the one he knew so well, though it bordered his own. He had traveled west along the Sarashen River the short distance to the Tahir River, along that river to the banks of the Methris and then into the woods, still not knowing where he was headed, not caring. Aras had been traveling for a full fortnight and was nearly out of food now, despite all that he had foraged on his journey to supplement the supplies he had brought with him.

If his beloved mentor, the healer Jarnath, were here, he would be able to tell Aras all he might ever want to know about the plant he had just examined. Jarnath would share his knowledge eagerly, answering Aras's myriad questions with his customary gentle patience. But Jarnath was not here. He had not known to come. Aras had not told him he was leaving. Aras almost cried out at the wave of guilt and loneliness he felt from his leave-taking, at the memories of his parting which haunted him.

ARAS had left his father and his home in anger after nearly five decades of secrecy and planning, fear and frustration, all of it culminating in the final humiliation of his coming-of-age ceremony. He had received exemplary marks from all his instructors. Never had they seen a single candidate excel in every single aspect of training. His skill in tactics, strategy, and in all the myriad forms of martial arts, both armed and unarmed, were unsurpassed by anyone they had ever trained. Aras had graduated first amongst all his peers, to the accolades of all but the one whom he most wanted to impress.

His father had not attended the ceremony. It was inconceivable that his father, the High-King, the ruler of the Seven Kingdoms as well as the leader of their combined military forces, both the King's Guard and the Guard, not preside. In three millennia of tradition, such a thing had never happened before. It was not only an insult to Aras, but to every other graduating candidate of their military training program. This time Lord of the Guard Ahrnad was the one to preside over the coming-of-age ceremony, in the High-King's stead. Though by tradition his title was Lord of the Guard, Ahrnad was an Aerta, one of the King's Guard, not one of the Guard, second in command to the High-King. Thankfully, he was also not truly a Lord and therefore was not bonded to one of the Trees of the Lords' Grove. Ahrnad was a cold and often cruel bigoted man, not one whom Aras would wish to see blessed with the long life the grace of the Trees accorded.

Once the ceremony had ended, three quarters of the other graduates had begun celebrating their adulthood in the traditional manner: they began pairing off immediately and slipping into the woods to enjoy the fruits of their labor, now that they were finally of an age that such sexual liaisons were permitted, disregarding their promises to those who awaited them at home. The remaining graduates, ones who had chosen to honor the pledges they had made five years earlier to the suitors that awaited them in their home Kingdoms, restricted their celebrations to drinking and singing and dancing.

Most of those who graduated would become Reservists. They would return home to whichever of the three River or four Wood Kingdoms they had come from and continue on with their lives until such time as they might be needed. Thankfully, in the three thousand years they had been relegated to these lands, such a call had never gone out. Some few who were dedicated or self-sacrificing or prideful or belligerent enough stayed in Nalea to join the King's Guard or Guard, or the Army or Navy, as they were sometimes still called.

Aras had no eager suitors awaiting him in Nalea or elsewhere. He did not come from the Seven Kingdoms as the others did. Nalea, the military base that housed both the King's Guard and Guard, was his home. He had been born there and grown up there and finally reached maturity there, in utter isolation from his peers, save for the last five years of his life. He had endured the terror of his childhood alone. He had survived the machinations of both his parents on his own, save for what little aid and comfort Jarnath and some few others had dared to provide. And now he was truly alone, more alone than he had ever been.

Aras had been shaking with hurt and anger as he left the revelry of his classmates all around him, deftly evading Jarnath. He had ignored his Tree Aranas's calls to him across their bond. He did not want the Healer to console him, nor his Tree. He wanted only to confront his father, to force him to acknowledge him as an adult, as his heir. He should have known better.

Their meeting, as with all meetings with his father, turned into a battle. But this time Aras had not backed down, he had not attempted to appease, he had used neither tact nor diplomacy: he had screamed back. His father's final words to him had cut him deeper than any blade ever could.

"Go! Leave! You think completing your training changes anything? A soldier who will not kill is worthless! You are nothing! You have always been nothing! You are useless to me! You belong to that traitorous bitch who bore you, whose face you wear! You belong to that treacherous swine Jarnath who ruined you! You are her son, you are his, you are not mine. Do you hear me? You are not my son!" His father had turned to the King's Guard surrounding them in the audience chamber and had roared an order to them. "Get him out of my sight!" Then, stiff-backed, he had turned and walked away from his only son without another word.

The soldiers had escorted Aras from the audience chamber wordlessly, their faces expressionless. Aras had fought to force his own mask in place as he had stumbled from the audience chamber, but he knew his face betrayed him. He was all but gasping at the pain of his father's complete and utter denial of him; he had almost fallen beneath the assault of his father's thoughts and feelings as they nearly overwhelmed him, until he slammed a shield into place against them. But amidst the frustration and loathing, the anger and the hatred coming from his father in punishing waves, there had been more: there had been fear.

Surely his father could not be afraid of him? Surely he could not have finally realized who and what Aras actually was? No, his father did not suspect. He had heard his father's thoughts with brutal clarity. His father truly thought his son was weak, spineless, worthless, a sniveling coward, an embarrassment to him. Never once had he felt more, not since Aras was fourteen, when Aras had lost what little love his father might have had for him.

Aras had retrieved his twin swords, his dagger, and his bow and quiver. Even he—especially he—was never allowed before his father armed. He tripped up the marble steps with unaccustomed clumsiness and headed for his rooms. He could not stay here in the Palace, or even in Nalea. He could not endure the pain of his father's continued rejection.

With shocking clarity, he realized he would do as his father had commanded. He would leave. He already wore his weapons. What else should he bring?

His eyes fell upon the small pack of field rations from his last test mission, a fortnight ago. The lightweight, compact raeta would yet last for months without spoiling. There was still enough for a sennight's journey there. He would forage and eat the raeta only as needed.

Snatching up the pack, he scanned the room, his eyes lighting on his elaborately carved alabaster bureau. He strode over to it and deactivated the imbedded, warded gem, which was hidden by a complex masking spell, with a wave of his hand and a muttered word of Power. Then he opened the secret compartment in the back of the bottom drawer. The purse of coin from the Lands of Men was there, and his single remaining inert gem-battery, the jewel Men called *Elfstone*. Aras took both and then hesitated. There was one other item remaining: the small, unopened package, which, to his surprise, had been stealthily given to him by Commander Narenius only a few nights ago, with instructions that it not be opened until after his graduation.

Aras had tested it, of course, despite the fact that it had been given to him by someone he trusted, because of the fact that it had been. But there was no trap, no wards, no poison, nor explosives, nor other hidden danger—at least, none that his Power could detect.

He opened the package now, without curiosity or enthusiasm, more from a sense of duty and respect for the one who had delivered it to him in secret, no doubt endangering himself by doing so, than any desire to see what it might contain. There was a note inside, sealed in silver wax stamped with the image of a swan. He recognized its significance immediately: the seal of the Royal House of Riviera. His heart quickened with interest. He broke the wax seal and read the brief note, his eyes bright with unshed tears before he had finished it.

> *Dearest Aras, son-of-my-heart, as you cannot now ever be more,*
>
> > *When I had this designed and forged for you, it was one of a matched pair; it was to have been a wedding gift. Would that I could still give it to you as such! Instead I must gift this to you as a coming-of-age present. May you never need to use it.*
> >
> > *I wish I could say all that is in my heart. I wish so much more!*
> >
> > *Stay well Aras. Take care of yourself. Be safe. Would that I had the Power to ward you.*
>
> *With all our love and hopes for your safety,*
> *King Laranela of Riviera*

Aras knew that Laranela had not dared write more; even by saying so little, by mentioning even in passing the broken betrothal to his daughter Elanara, he had said too much. Laranela had risked arrest and execution for treason for what he had implied by his wishes of safety for Aras. He had not wasted ink in writing wishes for Aras's happiness. It was fortunate that the gift had been safely delivered, that he had effectively hidden it and his father had not discovered it. Aras was not afraid of his father, but he was afraid of what his father might do to Laranela, the man who had looked forward to calling Aras "son" for all he had two of his own whom he loved deeply.

Aras held the note to his heart. He could feel Laranela's presence upon the paper, his love, frustration, fear, and desperation. Laranela had been gripped by strong emotion while writing this: worry for Aras, for his daughter and the rest of his family, for his Kingdom, for all of them.

Swallowing hard, Aras carried the precious note to the fireplace and forced himself to toss it into the flames, watching the paper blacken and curl, until it was utterly consumed. Then he went back to the package and opened it. He gasped at the beauty of the hilt and the intricately crafted sheath and then lovingly pulled the blade forth. It shone like a beam of moonlight in his hands. The blade was made of pallenteum, an extremely rare and coveted metal, though few nowadays valued it for its true worth: pallenteum would hold Power like no other metal could.

Surely Laranela could not suspect—no, of course he could not. He must have selected the metal only for the fact that it would not tarnish nor rust nor ever need sharpening. Once forged and hardened, pallenteum was all but indestructible; only intense heat could destroy it. Aras removed his dagger from his belt and attached the gift in its place.

He must go now, while he yet could. The love and warmth of the gift had weakened him terribly. He had an irrational urge to run to his father, to kowtow before him and beg his forgiveness, to somehow obtain even a fraction of the love from him that Laranela had dispensed so freely. Or to go to Jarnath, who would smother him in such love that he could never leave.

Aras headed for the doorway to his room and halted midstride, his gaze caught by the tremendous mirror of silvered glass mounted upon the wall by the door. He sped quickly past it, fighting the urge to smash it. He could not risk his mother knowing something was wrong, that he dared leave, and she would know if something happened to the mirror; the next time she tried to contact him, she would know, and she would realize her pawn was no pawn at all but a potential threat. She would hunt him down and do her best to destroy him.

ARAS forced his attention back to his surroundings with a start, thoughts of his mother instinctively causing him to fear for his safety. He was angry he had allowed himself to become so distracted when he was alone and in unknown territory, when there was the potential for danger all around him.

It was getting late; it was nearly dark. He must not allow himself to be so preoccupied. Many things hunted at night, and this part of the forest did not welcome him; there was an unsettling darkness here, some kind of danger. He could sense it all around him, but the feeling was vague, not yet focused. There was no way for him to defend against it, as yet no enemy to face.

Normally he would have sought shelter ere now, but in the morning he had stumbled across a Village of Man he had not expected to find. He had ached to explore it, to speak to them, but there had been angry voices and sadness there that boded ill toward a stranger not of their kind. Men sometimes welcomed Elves into their midst, but he could not take the risk that they might not. He had been cautious and studied them, hidden, and then left without revealing his presence, thinking it wise to be well away from those Men.

His head snapped around, his musings again interrupted. He cursed himself for his continued inattention, that his thoughts had been on the morning and not the present. He had felt something, sensed something, an impression of hunger and stealth. Belatedly, he realized he was being followed, stalked, hunted. Something was behind him, stealthy but not entirely silent; his straining ears heard the sound of heavy breathing. It was large, whatever it was. And there was a similar sound from the front to the right as well, and another from the left. He was surrounded! It was an ambush!

Aras drew his bow and nocked an arrow, his every sense screaming to him that he was in mortal peril. He scanned the trees anxiously. That one! It was the tallest and the strongest of those he could reach in time.

Aras raced toward the tree and let loose his arrow at a dark form that broke through the forest undergrowth scant yards from the tree he sought, still not knowing what it was that came for him. He slung the strung bow over his neck and shoulder, to free his hands, and leapt catlike into the tree, pulling himself upwards. There was the sound of snarling and roars of frustration, rage, and bloodlust.

He turned to watch, still climbing. Wolven! A pack of them. Five. No, six. He looked a little outward. There had been seven a moment ago, but his arrow had flown true. He frowned. They were all males. They should not be, were this a true pack. The remaining wolven snapped and gnashed the air below, howling and growling, but then one of the smaller ones began jumping and awkwardly but determinedly clawing his way up the tree. Aras did not think the animal would be able to reach him. Surely it would slide back down? Wolven were not built for such climbs.

As he expected, the wolven slid back with a frustrated growl, but a second took his place, determined to reach him. Aras was safe for the moment, though effectively treed. He need not loose any more arrows. He need merely wait until the beasts grew frustrated enough in their efforts that they went in search of easier prey.

The thought troubled him. He remembered the village he'd seen and thought of how silently the wolven had stalked him. Would a Man have sensed their nearness in time? He doubted it. And the Men there would no doubt forage and hunt in these woods; they would come to gather wood for their fires. The women and children might enter the woods as well, seeking mushrooms or berries, or the children might come to explore or play. He had once observed Men doing all those things, long ago.

He gritted his teeth in resolve. He took no joy in killing—his father was right in that, at least—but despite what his father thought, he could kill when there was need to, to protect others. He had done so before.

Aras gained a steadier purchase and shot downward through the branches. The climbing wolven died without a cry. Now there were five. Another arrow followed the first. Four wolven remained. He loosed another arrow. Then there were three. Those final three wolven had been hanging back. They were enormous, far too massive to attempt the climb. He had not known wolven could grow so large.

He did not have a clear shot at them through the branches at first, but then something completely unexpected happened: one of the wolven darted away and then ran back at the tree, turning and spinning at the last moment so his shoulder hit the trunk, with the full force of his weight and charge behind it. The impact nearly knocked Aras from the branches. He had to snatch at a limb with his string hand to keep from falling.

He repositioned and steadied himself, but the other two had begun mimicking their packmate's astonishing behavior. The tree was hit from the other side. Aras cursed as he dropped his arrow. He drew his next and nocked it and let fly all in one motion while the beast was still almost directly below.

The arrow hit where he aimed, between the wolven's eyes, killing him instantly, but the tree was struck from behind at the same instant by one of the other two, far harder than before, and Aras felt himself begin to fall. This time his grasping right hand found no purchase, and the bow was wrenched from his left, wedging tightly in the branches.

Aras twisted to land on his feet as he plummeted toward the ground, but just before impact his left foot hit one of the dead wolven. As a result, his right foot struck the ground hard, at an angle, his ankle wrenching painfully. He barely stayed afoot, his weight on his left foot as he lunged toward the brush past the tree. Knives of fire lanced up his leg every time his right foot touched the ground. He fought for balance as he desperately tried to put some cover and distance between himself and the two remaining wolven, drawing his twin swords as he ran.

He spun to the right just in time to avoid a beast that lunged for his back, and the wolven rushed past him. Aras stabbed outward with both blades at the other as it charged him. His right sword stuck deeply into the beast's chest and caught between his ribs, wrenching the blade from his hand. He heard the wounded animal crash to the ground, thrashing. Then Aras was struck from the left by the wolven that had missed him before. His teeth found Aras this time, sinking deeply into his shoulder and chest, the weight of the beast bearing him down.

Aras barely felt his remaining sword slip from his nerveless fingers. Scant inches over and his left arm would have been severed at the shoulder. He unsheathed his new dagger with his right hand and slashed at the beast's throat. The animal's thick coat and layered muscle resisted Aras's blade as the wolven bit deeper. Weakened as he was, had it been any but a pallenteum blade, it would not have been up to the task, but at last he found the jugular and severed it. The animal collapsed onto Aras in his death throes, his teeth still clamped tightly about his prey.

Aras had never felt such pain. His chest was wet with blood, his own mixing with that of the wolven. He could barely breathe for the weight of the beast on his chest, and he could hear the frantic thudding of his weakening heart pounding in his ears. Then the creature on top of him fell still, and the other, still skewered upon his sword, ceased his struggles as well. It was suddenly quiet, the only sound his own raspy breathing and the rapid pounding of his heart.

Aras pictured his father looking down at him in loathing, reprimanding him for his incompetence, for not felling all seven without taking injury from one of them. The image gave him the strength he needed to reach for the jaws of the creature that pinned him. But his right hand was slow and weak and shaking, and it would not obey him as it should. It was then he realized in despair and horror that he had not survived the wolven attack at all, that he would end his days here.

No! He could not die here, not from such a pathetic, puny battle as this! How could his fate be to die like this, alone in a foreign wood, of a simple wolven bite? He had thought his mother, or one of her two enemies, Incuban or Arcanus, would have been the ones to slay him if he had failed in the mission he had set for himself, or perhaps his father, were he ever to have discovered Aras's secret. To die like this, such a pointless and worthless death, when the fate of the world rested upon his shoulders!

He'd failed them, all of them: his father, Jarnath, their people, all the people everywhere. All the races he had wanted so desperately to save: the Aerta, the Oceana, the Trees of the Grove, the Gryphon, Men, the Dwarves, everyone. He heard his Tree Aranas, who had grown silent with the distance of his journey, cry out frantically across his bond. He felt the steady trickle of Power from the Tree expand to a stream as his Tree fed him what strength it could. But Aranas was far away, and weak himself, too weak and too far away to save him. The strength he freely gave could not compensate for that which trickled out onto the rotting leaves beneath Aras with every beat of his heart.

The bleeding had been slowed by the wolven's teeth, which were still embedded in his flesh, but he was already dangerously weak. Anosar! If only he had thought to bring anosar, or his other medicines, with him! What a fool he was, to have traveled without them! A few sips of anosar could have meant all the difference.

Jarnath would not be disappointed in him. Jarnath would mourn him as a lost son. His father was the one who would curse him for his stupidity, as he had cursed him for being born, as he had cursed him for every moment of his life since.

"Forgive me," Aras mouthed soundlessly to both of them, lacking even the strength to speak, his eyes welling with tears as he thought of them. His sight, which had begun fading to blackness dotted with bright pinpricks of light, suddenly crystallized into sharp focus. With remarkable clarity, he saw the faces of the two men he had been thinking of: Jarnath's kindly face, looking down at him in love and anguish, and his father, scowling down at him.

Aras's brow creased in puzzlement. But who was the third person, the Oceana whose face hovered between them? He was not old yet ageless as his father and Jarnath, but instead young, so very young. He must be at least a decade from coming-of-age. He could not be one of the Guard or even a trainee; he was still a child. His was not a face out of memory. Who was he, and why should Aras be having a vision of him now, as he lay dying?

The stranger was so beautiful, and so sad. His silver hair framed a fine-boned face which was creased in grief, and his blue eyes were wet with tears. Aras's heart went out to the young Oceana. If only he could help him! If only he could touch him, he might comfort him.

With the last of his strength, with a trembling hand, Aras reached for his cheek. For a single astonishing moment of confusion, he felt the warmth and silken softness of his skin and the wetness of his tears beneath his fingertips, and he thought he felt a hand upon his own face as well. But then there was a roaring in his ears, and all thought ceased as darkness claimed him.

TALON entered the woods again, traveling more quickly this time, following the trail he'd found before and pressing on past the site of the kill. He continued onward, following the spoor deeper and deeper into the endless woods. The wolven traveled far in their roaming. But he knew they would head back for the village as soon as they hungered again, and their kill had been small. They would head back tonight. Half the day was already gone. They might even now be far ahead of him, circling back toward the village.

He stopped, wavering in indecision. Should he press onward or go back? Perhaps he could lay a trap for them that they might not spot so easily. He cast one final look upon the ground and froze. Surely not! He knelt down to take a closer look at the faint, fresh, yet barely discernible track overlaid by the more recent paw print.

Oh Idare! Not here, not now, not alone in these woods: an Elf. Talon knew at once that the wolven would not be heading back to the village tonight. They had the scent of easier prey, which had unknowingly come to them.

Talon quickened his pace. He feared he was already too late but refused to let the knowledge paralyze him. He must be in time to save him!

He had to slow a few times and backtrack when he overshot the trail. Sometimes he found Elven tracks, but more often not. This one knew how to conceal his trail from even the most skilled Man's eyes. He suspected he would not have found sign of his passage at all, save that something appeared to be distracting the Elf. He seemed to be walking aimlessly, without purpose or direction, stopping randomly here and there, his tracks fluctuating between being completely indiscernible and faint.

Talon knew of few others with his gift for tracking who would have seen the latter tracks. But the wolven had the scent, and their prey was far ahead of them. He could see from the meandering trail that the Elf did not know he was hunted.

Dusk approached and then night fell. It was madness to continue. But Talon kept going until he could no longer see the ground at all, let alone the trail. Then he climbed a strong tree, dreading what he might find on the morrow. He had thought there would be no more victims. As much as he dreaded the morning, he feared the night more. He forced himself to breathe slowly and steadily. He must calm himself. He could not afford to succumb to dark thoughts here, where he was already surrounded by such darkness. Gradually he relaxed, and sleep finally claimed him.

HE WAS in a battle, and he was losing. He could see by the flickering firelight of the city burning behind him that there were wolven and chimaera and hippogryphs leaping and lunging, slaughtering everyone in their path. And there was an entire army of Revenants, twisted reanimated mockeries of Dwarves and Men and even animals.

Then a horror like nothing he had ever seen lunged at him: it had the body of a Man but the head of a wolven. He could not defend himself! His sword was elsewhere, fending off another undead monster.

Frantically, he swung his sword away from the thing he'd just beheaded before it even had time to collapse, but it was too late. The man-wolven's teeth closed tightly about the wrist of his sword arm. He watched his life's blood flow down his arm, staining the eagle-wing handguard, and felt horror as Loruthanar fell from his grasp, leaving him helpless, weaponless.

He screamed in terror as cold, lifeless hands clawed his back even as he struck out with his bare fist, pounding on the muzzle of the thing that held him. It glared at him with yellow eyes and bit harder, raking a dagger across his unprotected chest as if it were claws, instead of stabbing him as it might have.

Unexpectedly, a terrified voice cried out in panic, louder than the sounds of the fighting, than the roar of the flame. "Laren, no! You cannot help me! You must leave me or He'll find you!" Then there was sudden blackness and horrible silence.

T ALON awoke screaming "Lunahr!" He almost fell from the tree with the violence of his waking, with his wild shaking. That had not been him battling for his life! The sword was not his; it was Lunahr's blade, Loruthanar.

It was a dream, another nightmare of this dark wood, shaped by the wolven he hunted. *Idare, please let it only be a dream!*

Talon felt desperately for the thin coppery strand in his mind that had bound him to his youngest cousin for the last six years, first cautiously, lest he break it, then in increasing panic. It was gone! Not a trace of it remained. His tie to Farad had been severed only a sennight ago, after twelve years of the strength it had brought to him. Lunahr could not be gone as well! Talon's mind told him they were both dead, forever lost to him, but his heart could not bear to hear it.

He deliberately attempted to repress all thought, all memory of them, as he felt his panic build. He scrabbled madly down the tree, falling the last few feet. He stood shakily and drew Kathalanar. Desperately trying to force back the debilitating panic and suppress the loss before it crippled him, or worse, ignited the King's Madness, he used the techniques his father had taught him, years before he had inherited the King's Sword. This was the only means the other Lords had to regain their centers, to protect their cores, to find calm when the light of the sun or of a fire was not available.

Talon was truly alone now, for the first time in twelve years. He slammed back the terror the thought brought and fought the weight upon his heart as he began the intricate dance of the sword exercise he had learned so painstakingly. He threw his entire body and spirit into the dance, praying it would be enough to save him, battling his demons in the dark.

Neither Farad nor Lunahr could help him this time, and sunrise would come too late. He would be lost to the Madness. Talon felt it begin to close around him and started to strip off his glove, to unleash the carefully hoarded Power of the Sword. But then the first rays of the sun broke through the branches and touched his face, and he drank them in desperately, feeling their nascent warmth upon him.

Talon looked up into the sun and stared at its naked power until he feared he would blind himself and forced his eyes away. But it was enough, for now. The demons had fled from the light, back to the dark corners of his core, where they would wait for nightfall, when he would be vulnerable, when they would try to overtake him again.

Later, before dusk again fell, he must build a fire and use every meditation trick he had ever been taught to fortify his mind against the demons of the Madness that plagued him. Nightfall would tell whether it would be enough. If not, he had only the Sword to save him, and the other two times it had not been enough.

Talon backtracked his own trail until he regained the trail the wolven had left. He followed the trail for a long while. His blood ran cold. Three more sets of tracks joined the other four. From the size and depth of their tracks, these other beasts were huge, easily twice the size of any wolven he had ever seen.

He kept following, and now the interval between the wolven and Elven tracks began narrowing rapidly. Talon read the signs of the attack as if it was enfolding in front of him.

From the age of the tracks, the attack had happened at dusk. Some of the wolven had broken off, angling away from the others on either side. They were closing in for the kill; they were about to ambush their prey. And finally the Elf realized he was being hunted!

A few dozen yards later, Talon came across a body, not of the Elf, but of one of the wolven, an Elven arrow neatly between its eyes. At the sight of the arrow, Farad's face flashed across his core. He was dead! His beloved cousin, Lord of House of Wolven, was dead! Talon ruthlessly forced his thoughts away from Farad and back to the beasts he hunted.

An Elf with a bow would be a formidable foe, but would it have been enough against seven creatures such as these? But there, at the base of one of the trees, were four more wolven, all similarly slain. Talon started to have hope. He saw the slashed tree bark and looked up into the branches. Then his breath caught and he climbed quickly.

His eyes had not deceived him. It was an Elven bow. He traced the signs of the wild climb and the perilous fall downward. And he saw another shadowy form, amongst the underbrush, past the tree.

Talon climbed down, bow in hand. There was an arrow at the base of the tree, one that had not been released into a target but had fallen. Picking it up, he held the bow at the ready but did not nock the arrow. He did not think any of the beasts were near, and the bow felt strange in his hands. He was by no means a master at the bow, and he knew it might well betray him. Elven bows were not lightly used by others.

The Elf's landing had been on his feet, but a poor one; the Elf's weight rested on his left foot too strongly. He followed the enormous tracks of the two remaining massive beasts.

The struggle had continued into denser foliage. The shadowy form he had glimpsed from the tree was revealed: it was the sixth wolven, slain by a sword, which still protruded from it. And there, the seventh and last, easily the largest wolven he'd ever seen, dead at the hands of its prey. But the Elf was there as well, clamped tightly in the death grip of its jaws. Talon fell to his knees by his side.

The Elf's hair was long and golden, where it wasn't tinted dull red from blood, and his fine-boned face was pale, far too pale even for an Elf. His face was ethereally beautiful, even for one of his kind, breathtaking, even in death, especially in death, knowing that the perfection of it would soon rot.

Talon felt hot tears stream down his face in loss for this nameless Elf, knowing he could not give the body the peaceful burial it deserved, that he must instead mutilate the corpse by beheading it. He could not risk that the Enemy might find it and use it against them, but he would not burn it. Even in death, an Elf would not want to feel the touch of flame. At least it would be a single, clean cut. Kathalanar was up to the task. The King's Sword had beheaded many. Talon's hands shook at the knowledge of what he must do, the thought of cutting that elegant neck nearly making him retch.

Talon swallowed hard, laughing harshly at the folly of his tears. The Amontir had cried an ocean of tears, to no avail. Another lay dead, like the boy Billy, like Farad, like Lunahr, all but eighteen of their people and all but a handful of the Dwarven Kingdoms. Idare, would it never end?

He fought down the despair, which threatened to smother him even in the light of day, and forced himself to continue his examination of the body and the weapons beside it. There was a second sword on the ground and a dagger at the beast's throat.

What a fighter the Elf had been! Had Talon not gone back to return the boy's remains to his parents, the Elf would have lived. He had failed this nameless Elf as he had failed so many others; so many lost, so many dead. He should have come sooner, but how could he have known?

Talon stripped off his right glove and gently, hopelessly, felt for signs of life at the Elf's throat. He snatched his hand away in astonishment when he felt the faint pulse of his heart beneath his fingers. Surely he could not yet live?

Hand shaking, he felt again and his doubts evaporated. Talon tore off his other glove, opened his meager pack, and laid the contents of his healer's pouch out before him, eyeing his scant supplies critically. He had little left of the three powders: *lashar* to stop the bleeding, *resan* so that the wound would not fester, and *jassa* to prevent the fever that so often followed such injury. Nothing for strength, nothing for pain, though the latter did not matter for now; the Elf was not conscious.

Talon looked about for the right sort of leaf, and quickly found what he needed. He did not have enough bandages. Removing his good shirt from where he had concealed it in the center of his bedroll, he tore it into long strips, wishing it was linen instead of Thenalonese silk. Then he tried to pry the jaws of the wolven from the Elf, but even his strength was not sufficient to the task, even with the damage the Elf had done to the muscles and tendons.

Arcanus had once explained to him why a body stiffened so after death. If only Arcanus was here with him now! But the wish was as futile as the many thousand before it. He must utilize the tools he had and pray they might be enough.

Talon used the axe the innkeeper had given him and pried open the jaws, cracking more than a few of the beast's teeth in the process. Fresh blood flowed sluggishly as the teeth reluctantly pulled from flesh. Without the pressure of the jaws and the teeth still sunk deep into the wounds, the Elf's life's blood would have flowed more freely, and he would surely have died.

The wound was large and deep. A Man would have died ere now. Even an Elf should not have been able to survive. This one was remarkably strong in body and spirit to yet live.

Talon quickly washed the wound with water from his flask, knowing as few Men did that alcohol would be far preferable for the task. But at least the water was clean. He sprinkled the *lashar* and *resan* he had unwrapped onto the wound, nodding in satisfaction as the bleeding stopped almost immediately. He covered it with the leaves he had gathered, and then wrapped it tightly in the few true bandages he had and then the improvised ones.

Taking out his metal cup, he filled it with water from his water skin and poured the *jassa* into the water. The dark green powder was best brewed as tea, but he did not have the time to prepare it that way. He held the Elf's head up, opened his mouth, and poured the contents in slowly, massaging his throat as he did so in the special way Arcanus had taught him, forcing him to swallow. Most of it made it down, he thought. At least the Elf did not choke. He longed for one of the Elven draughts, *anosar* or *thesha*, which would have restored strength.

Talon looked for other signs of injury. The Elf's right ankle was swollen nearly double. But other than some scrapes and bruises, that was all, at least on the outside where he could see, where he could treat. He covered the Elf with his worn and filthy blanket, which had spent far too many nights upon the ground. But it was the best he could do for now.

Searching the Elf expectantly now, rather than reluctantly, he hoped to find some Elven medicines that might help him. He found only a large, heavy purse full of coin; a tiny one that contained a single perfect Elfstone; a half-empty water pouch, made of that amazing waterproof fabric the Elves used in place of animal skins or bladders, which indeed contained only water; and a scant mouthful of *raeta*, Elven traveler's bread.

Even such a small piece would be as life sustaining as an entire meal or more of Man's food. Such Elven fare was wondrously complex and flavorful, containing a number of grains, nuts, and seeds, far heartier than what a Man would think to bake. The thought of the bread had him salivating and his stomach rumbling. He scowled at it. He had no time for luxuries such as food, and no supplies in any case.

Talon dragged off the two large wolven carcasses, and then the others, so that any scavengers who engaged in feasting upon them would not consider Talon and the Elf part of their meal. Hungry as he was, he would not think to eat the vile things, not when they might be tools of the Enemy.

Using his knife, he performed the grisly task of removing the ears from each of the wolven. He would not sully Kathalanar with the beasts' blood. Using the innkeeper's axe, he chopped off the muzzle of the beast that had bitten the Elf, swinging with such fury that the axe sank deep into the dirt as well. He only wished that the wolven could feel what he did to them. But the villagers would need proof of the beasts' defeat. He wrapped his grisly trophies carefully in some large leaves he selected specifically for their ability to slow the natural process of putrefaction, tying the bundle with a piece of the twine he carried.

Then he gathered as much firewood as he could find without straying too far from his charge. He sought some sort of shelter as he searched. Luck was with him in that, at least. There was a small clearing, some distance from the attack, in which there was a tremendous tree, the base of the trunk hollowed and scorched from an ancient fire, though it yet grew tall and strong. Both he and the Elf would fit inside easily enough, with room to spare. It would do.

He deposited the armful of wood he had gathered inside the tree and returned to the Elf. He lifted him, grunting at the weight of his burden. Elven bones were incredibly dense, and as a result, they were far heavier than their deceptively slight appearance led one to believe. A normal Man would not have been able to carry an Elf so easily, but the Amontir had strength of body beyond that of normal Men, those his people had once, in their arrogance, called Lesser Men.

Talon carried the Elf as gently as he could to the tree, then retrieved the Elf's bow and other weapons, as well as his own pack and bedroll, which he bundled again with the practiced ease of thousands of repetitions of the task. Venturing warily back to the carcasses, he was relieved to see that they were yet unmolested. He removed the salvageable arrows from the bodies, cleaning the gore from the heads carefully, with the proper respect for the razor-sharp arrowheads. He cut the shafts of the arrows that were wedged too tightly into bone to remove and brought them to the tree.

Eyeing the armload of wood he had gathered, he realized it would not be enough and wearily headed out to gather more after checking upon his charge.

Finally, he rejoined the Elf, worn to the bone and covered in wolven blood and the Elf's blood, as well as weeks' worth of filth. He wished longingly for the bath he had been promised in the village and smiled slightly at the thought of how this Elf might view his rescuer when he awoke. But the smile died quickly at the thought that he might yet succumb to his injuries without ever waking.

He had done all he could. It would be best to sleep now, in front of the shelter, when the sun was still high, the woods were safer, and the sunlight upon him might keep the demons at bay. But sleep was a long time coming.

THE first thing Aras became aware of was pain: his shoulder, chest, and ankle throbbed with it, but it was no longer unbearable. He did not yet open his eyes; it was too great an effort. Then he realized he was breathing easily again. The weight of the great beast was gone. And it did not quite feel as though he were outside. The air was incredibly foul, but he could still feel the forest all around him. He smelled his own blood, and the wolven's. And he scented a vile stench he had not expected. There was a Man here. He reeked. Aras realized he smelled of the Man as well.

His father's cautions echoed in his ears. Was he a prisoner? His hands tensed against his will, and he recognized the smoothness of familiar wood in his hand. His bow! But he'd lost it in his fall. Had the Man returned it to him, perhaps so that he might be reassured upon awakening?

"Easy, my friend. You are safe. There is no enemy for you to fight here," a strong voice said from beside him.

The words were Elvish, but how could they be? He was the only Elf here. The voice was deep, the mouth which spoke them apparently that of the Man.

Aras opened his eyes and looked about, his eyes verifying the evidence his nose had detected. The foul odor was coming from a woolen blanket which lay over him, and from the Man before him. Aras tried to sit up but inhaled sharply, gasping at the pain which tore through his shoulder and chest like fire, even as the further onslaught of the smell from his ill-considered action nearly made him gag.

"If you must sit, sit slowly, my friend. I have nothing left to stop the bleeding if you reopen your wound," the Man chastised, but his voice was gentle, like Jarnath's, rather than condescending or vicious or mocking, as his father's would have been.

Aras sat up with infinite care, leaning his back against the blackened wood. The effort exhausted him, and he felt dizzy and lightheaded, as if he might faint. He recognized the feeling and realized it must be from blood loss. But at least his wound had not been spurting like one of the fountains of Riviera, not like the last time he had been so gravely injured.

He closed his eyes and leaned back his head, forcing down the childhood memory, concentrating on breathing short, shallow breaths, drawing what strength he could from the living tree that sheltered him. Feeling the ridges of wood under his legs and buttocks, he realized that, even unconscious, he had been drawing strength from the tree, though not nearly as deeply as he did now that he was aware. He feared he would kill it, but this was not one of the Trees of the Grove: it was not sentient, it was not aware. If it had to be sacrificed, then the cost would be worth the price. Every tree in the land stood to be reduced to ash if he were to perish, and not only the trees.

The dizziness passed, but Aras hissed again in pain when he tried to breathe too deeply. He was furious with himself for betraying such weakness to a potential enemy. He opened his eyes again. Bright eyes watched him from the near dark. He could not tell their color in the poor light cast by the flickering firelight from outside the trunk, even with his sharp eyes.

"Forgive me," the voice said, in a strong, warm, rich tone, "I have nothing for the pain." Aras was surprised by the depth of remorse he heard. This Man had the voice of a healer.

Aras sat up straighter and let the blanket fall from him, wishing he had the strength to fling it from him in disgust, though it might insult his rescuer. By the light of the fire he saw the flash of white teeth, and a self-deprecating smile lit the shadowy face, which was framed by dark, stringy hair.

"Do not worry, my friend. My stench offends me almost as much as it does you, I think. Forgive me the blanket, but I needed to keep you warm in light of the severity of your injuries. I feared you would be far less favorably impressed by me than I was by you. You felled all seven wolven as they attacked you," the Man said in clear admiration.

Aras was startled by the approval in the tone, which vividly contrasted with the criticisms he had imagined his father voicing. He looked carefully about, trying to discover all he could about the strange Man who had apparently rescued him.

A sword lay sheathed at the stranger's side, but his own twin blades and dagger lay within easy reach, as did his quiver. His eyes focused on the latter in surprise. It was full once more. All the arrows he had spent had been returned, although two were unnaturally short, as if only the fletched shafts remained.

"I had to cut those last. Your arrows struck deeply and wouldn't pull free of the bone," the Man said, as if in answer to his unasked question.

Was there nothing this stranger missed? Aras was thoroughly overwhelmed. It had been decades since he had felt so vulnerable, so confused, so helpless. How had this Man learned Elvish so well that it flowed from his tongue as freely as the language of Man? Had he succored him in gratitude for some past kindness done to him by the Aerta or Oceana?

"Your water pouch is by your side, if you thirst. I had hoped you might carry some anosar or thesha as well, but you travel even lighter than I."

Aras fought to keep the shock from his face. And he knew of Elven medicines! Aras was all too familiar with anosar, but though thesha certainly sounded Elven, it was unknown to him. He would have remembered if Jarnath had ever mentioned it, particularly if it might be something as potent and treasured as anosar.

He must ask his rescuer about it, later. It would be too much effort to speak now, and he wanted to assess the Man longer before saying anything, afraid he might reveal too much. Aras lifted the pouch to his lips and drank sparingly. His arms sank back down to his sides as if made of stone.

"You can speak, can you not? I do not so often have company that I would not welcome to hear a voice other than my own. Although I am usually a man of few words, I find I have begun the unsettling habit of speaking to myself, just to hear a voice, in my loneliness," the Man said. Then he frowned suddenly, as if angry with himself for revealing that he did so.

Aras instantly abandoned his resolve to remain silent in the face of the Man's loneliness and despair. It rolled off of him and buffeted Aras in waves so heavily that he almost cried out at the stranger's pain. Seldom had he been so attuned to the emotions of a stranger. He would never have expected to be so affected by a Man.

"Thank you for all you have done," Aras said carefully, or so he hoped, in Common, which felt awkward to his lips and hurt his throat to speak.

The stranger smiled slightly, even as the feelings of loneliness and despair vanished as if they had never been, as if the Man had somehow shielded himself from Aras's unintentional use of his Power. "Ah, you impress me further. You speak Common well," the stranger said, still in Elvish. "But I think Elvish comes easier to my tongue than Common does to yours. I am called Talon. Will you honor me with your name?"

The question caught Aras unprepared. One did not speak one's name lightly, though in Nalea everyone used their given names, even he and his father. Although Aras was not truly his given name. Not even his own father suspected it was not, but it was close enough to it that he was reluctant to speak it. "Betula. You may call me Betula," Aras said after a moment's hesitation, speaking the Elven word for the tree Men called *birch*. The name was fitting. His Tree, Aranas, was a betula.

"You are far from your woods and your kind, Betula."

It was not a question, but Aras answered it anyway. "Yes."

"If I retrieve your raeta for you, can you eat?"

Aras nodded weakly. So, he had been searched. The stranger removed the raeta using a leaf held between his fingers so that his hand did not touch it, Aras noticed in relief. Although the Man's hands were odd. They did not fit with the rest of him at all.

They were not worn and weathered and dirty, but looked soft and surprisingly clean and pale. Everything about this Man was a riddle!

Aras lifted the small piece of bread to his mouth and chewed it slowly. It almost took more energy than he had, but he forced himself to swallow it. Then the stranger held his water pouch to his lips so that he might drink again.

"I am sorry I cannot offer you anything else to eat. I did not think I would be camping in the woods, and I could not forage far from here while you slept. Tomorrow, once it is light, I will find breakfast. You must eat to regain your strength."

"There is a village near here. I would like to get there as soon as we can, to release the villagers from their vigil."

"You speak as if you are not of that village," Aras said in surprise.

"I am not. I am a traveler. Two nights ago, just after I arrived there, a child was taken by the wolven you slew. I recovered what remains there were and then set out to destroy the creatures."

"I don't understand," Aras said, puzzled. "They were not your people. They paid you to do this?"

Talon stiffened and anger flashed in his eyes. Aras realized he had insulted his benefactor. "Forgive me my ignorance," Aras said, in the formal form reserved for student to teacher, or subject to king. It was not a form Aras used often, or lightly.

The look of anger fled Talon's face, and it was his turn to apologize. "Forgive me my temper. I am tired, and I forgot for a moment how little you must know of Man's ways. I hunted the wolven because I knew I could slay them when the villagers had not been able to. I had killed such beasts before, although never so many at once, or ones so large."

Aras noted that he did not say "never alone." If he only carried a sword as a weapon, Aras's respect for Talon grew. He knew he would not have fared nearly as well without his bow.

Talon's words mirrored his own thoughts. "I underestimated my foe in my need for vengeance. I tracked the four smaller wolven. The other three were unexpected, in many regards. I do not think I would have survived the battle you fought," he admitted, a look of annoyance again flashing across his face as if he had surprised himself by voicing his limitations.

For a moment Aras thought that explained why Talon had helped him. Perhaps he felt Aras had unintentionally saved his life in doing so? No, he did not think this Man would leave any stranger to die.

"You learn quickly, my friend. It is not a trait for which Elves are known," Talon said, as if he had heard his thoughts. His smiling eyes took the sting out of the words. There was some private joke here.

"I saw the village of which you spoke. I do not think I would be welcome there. I do not think any Elves dwell near here," Aras said cautiously.

"You need not worry," Talon said dismissively. "You have done what I set out to do. You have rid them of the enemy that plagued them. I will see that you are well received."

Aras sensed a veiled threat in that last. He thought his well-spoken and gentle-voiced benefactor was no stranger to the sword at his side.

Aras felt a flush of excitement, of fragile hope. Could he truly be both warrior and healer? He had the eyes of a healer and the hands of one. He must learn all he could from this Man.

But even such a slight increase in the beat of his heart left Aras dizzy again. The effort of sitting and speaking were taking their toll upon him in his weakened state.

Talon leaned toward him in concern. "Forgive me. The night has been long and I am too many nights with little sleep and too many days with little food. I should not have kept you talking for so long. You must rest now. You strain yourself."

Indeed, Aras felt too weak to argue the point. His vulnerability both frustrated and frightened him. Only once before had injury so debilitated him. But that was long ago, and then he had been among his own people, tended by Jarnath.

If his mother came for him now, while he was so weak, so helpless.... He forced the terror away. He was safe. Talon would not allow anyone to harm him. He was astonished as much by the bizarre thought as by the fact that, incredible as it seemed, he somehow knew it to be true.

TALON helped Betula lie down once more. It did not take long for sleep to claim the Wood Elf. Talon watched the woods outside their shelter, his gaze drifting often to Betula's exquisite face.

Betula appeared to be young, though it was, of course, impossible to tell how old he was. From his features and his naiveté, Talon might have thought he had only just reached maturity, but there was such watchful depth to his eyes and caution in his voice that he might well be centuries old. Yet elder Elves seldom roamed; few enough young ones did.

Talon wondered again what had brought him so far from home, alone, to a place such as this. Had he been on his way to Nalea, or perhaps from it? He was wearing one of the intricately patterned reversible camouflage cloaks of the King's Guard. One side was designed to look like tree bark and the other to mimic the forest floor. Was he a scout? Or a messenger? Talon hesitated to ask. He was one of only a handful of Men who even knew of Nalea's existence. Betula might become wary of him if he spoke of the Elves' secret military base.

Talon looked outside again, scanning the trees for danger, and then turned his eyes to the leaping, crackling flames, drawing comfort from them as he always did.

TALON'S eyes snapped open. The fire was still strong; he had not closed his eyes for long, but nonetheless, he was surprised. The demons were still at bay. They had not pounced upon him instantly in his sleep as he had expected them to. Instead, Betula was the one who was moaning in his sleep and moving restlessly.

Talon touched his forehead gently, concerned that he might be feverish, but the Elf's incredibly soft, smooth skin was no warmer to the touch than it should be. He breathed a sigh of relief. He had no more medicines for fever.

He placed his hand gently on his young friend's good shoulder, again daring the physical contact that Elves abhorred, and spoke softly to him. "You but dream. May your dreams be more pleasant." Betula quieted at Talon's words and touch, and Talon was surprised to find that touching the young Elf soothed him as well. Reluctantly he removed his hand, and the feeling of warmth and contentment vanished. He rubbed his fingertips together in longing.

Talon looked past the fire into the night. He would not be sorry to leave these woods. There was something malevolent here, beyond the wolven, something that haunted one's dreams.

The night passed slowly. Talon longed for dawn so that he might sleep. He fought to stay awake. The quiet of the woods, the soft crackle and warmth of the fire, his exhaustion from too many miles walked and too few hours slept all conspired against him, but he did not allow himself the dangerous luxury of sleep.

Finally, it was dawn, but the sky only brightened to a dim grayness, instead of the bright light he had expected and craved. Talon felt a stab of fear. Within moments the sky darkened perceptibly, until it was nearly as dark as night again, and his fear rapidly bloomed into terror. The sun! Where was the sun? He needed the sun!

Talon heard the distant rumble of thunder, and his panic fled with it. He had no time for such weakness now. He looked at the blackened wood of the tree trunk and the clear ground around it. If lightning was coming, they would no longer be safe here. But the village was over a day's walk at a steady pace, and Betula's ankle would not bear his weight, even were that his only injury. Elves healed far more quickly than Men, but even they required time.

Reluctantly, he woke the young Elf. "I would let you sleep, but a storm comes, and I do not wish to see whether lightning might find this tree again. I must find us a new shelter. You must keep vigil for yourself until I return."

Betula nodded and readied his bow.

Talon left quickly, axe in hand. He was glad to be out of the tree hollow and on the move again. He was not used to remaining in one place for a day or more at a time. He circled about their tree, spiraling outward. The thunder cracked more loudly. The storm was approaching quickly. He must find shelter soon.

Finally, after a long and frustrating search, he saw a pile of gray rock jutting out from the ground where it rose to a small hill. He approached cautiously, Sword drawn. There was an opening in the rock and wolven tracks everywhere, but he was relieved to note that none appeared more recent than two days ago. This, then, had been the den of the wolven Betula had slain.

He entered, still on his guard, but it was empty save for shards of bone, antler, and horn, tufts of fur, beaks, feathers, strands of hair, and scraps of cloth. Talon's jaw clenched. He had found the remains of the rest of the missing villagers, in amongst the remains of many dozens of animals.

Talon sheathed the Sword and cleared the shelter as best he could, sweeping it clean with a pine branch, carefully sorting out and gathering all the remains of the Men into a single pile by the mouth of the den. He would return the scant remains to the villagers so both the dead and their kin might find peace.

Putting Goras's axe to good use, he chopped pine boughs to line the floor of the den, masking the foul smell of the wolven and their prey so they might sleep tonight. He hoped Betula would forgive him for the trees he wounded, although even in his haste he was careful not to take too many branches from any single tree.

Talon gathered firewood quickly as the storm neared, knowing it would not be enough for the coming night, but hoping the storm might keep other hunters in their dens and that Betula's presence might somehow keep the Madness at bay. Finding a strong, straight sapling, he felled it quickly, lopping the branches off the slender trunk hastily. If Betula asked, he would have to lie about it. A branch would not suffice, and he did not have time to search the woods for deadwood, hoping to find something equal to his need that had died a natural death. He would fashion a proper walking stick from it later, but it would suffice for now.

He brought the firewood to the den and left the axe there as well. Then he headed back, carrying the improvised staff. He had hoped to find breakfast as well, but there was no time, although he managed to find a few edible leaves on his way back. Betula would eat a little, at least.

The storm had moved unusually quickly, and the sky overhead was a boiling dark mass of gray. The first drops fell as he came upon their shelter. Talon was pleased to see Betula greet him at the opening, leaning heavily against the tree trunk with a neat bundle at his feet. He'd packed Talon's bedroll and pack for him, and his weapons were sheathed for travel.

"We must move quickly," Talon said, handing Betula the staff he had crafted for him.

Talon was relieved when Betula nodded and accepted the staff gratefully and without comment.

The rain soon turned to a deluge as they slogged through it. The soft ground churned into mud, and the dead leaves that carpeted the ground were clingy and slippery. Betula slipped and stumbled and would have fallen, but Talon caught him and wrapped his strong arm around him, knowing Elves do not like to be touched by Man. Betula stiffened for a moment, and Talon was afraid he would shake off his help, but instead, to his surprise and relief, Betula leaned more heavily against him.

They proceeded more quickly. The thunder was deafening, and the lightning dazzled their eyes with each flash, but Talon found his way back to the den without difficulty.

"Ah, if only I had some soap," Talon joked as they entered their sanctuary from the ferocity of the storm. Betula smiled with his eyes for a moment, although his teeth were gritted tightly against his pain. He was shaking with it, and with the wet and cold. Talon set Betula down gently in the back of the den as the wind and the rain lashed the front.

Talon had stuffed the pathetic bundle of his meager belongings under his loose shirt, in a vain attempt to protect them from the rain. The blanket was soaked almost to the core, but the remains of his second shirt in the center were only slightly damp. He shredded the last of his shirt into bandages.

Betula was trembling violently. "We need to get you out of those wet clothes, and I must rewrap your wound," Talon said.

The Elf nodded, unable to speak.

Talon cursed softly under his breath, in a tongue Betula would not have known if he'd heard. He should have carried him, but it had been an effort before to carry him even to the tree. Also, Talon was sure that now that he was conscious, Betula's pride would not have allowed it. At least he lay on a bed of soft pine.

Talon took off Betula's cloak, and water poured to the floor from it. He shook it dry, marveling again over the amazing properties of Elven fabric. But water had poured through the tears in the chest and shoulder, and unfortunately, his clothes were not made of the same water-repellant fabric. Betula was as soaked to the skin as Talon, in spite of the cloak.

Talon peeled the wet clothes from Betula and covered him with the cloak for warmth. Then he carefully unwrapped the soaking bandages. Betula's skin was cold to the touch, and he was still shivering violently. Talon washed the wound gently with the last of the water from his canteen. The wound was healing well, Talon saw in relief; there was no sign of infection and it had not reopened.

Talon saw Betula watching him and smiled reassuringly, realizing his expression had likely been too intense, if not grim. He rewrapped Betula's shoulder in the new bandages and pulled the cloak over him again, laying some pine boughs over him for extra warmth.

"Now I will build the fire." Talon lay wood as near the entrance as he could so the smoke would exit the den and the fire would not be so close that it might frighten the young Wood Elf. All Elves were afraid of fire to some degree, some more than others. It took a while to light the fire because of the strong gusts of wind that invaded their shelter, but the wood burnt fiercely once lit, the fire fed by the cold fresh air from outside.

ARAS closed his eyes and inhaled as deeply as he dared of the pine. It smelled like home. He could not draw strength from this deadwood as he had from the living tree that had sheltered him before, but the scent was soothing nonetheless. His trembling slowed and stopped as the cloak and branches warmed him, and he drifted away on the scent of pine.

WHEN the fire was going well, Talon checked on Betula once more. The young Elf was either asleep or unconscious, but at least he felt warm to the touch again, and his trembling had stopped. Talon was frustrated that the village lay just out of reach. He spread the soaked blanket along the floor near the fire to dry but knew it would take a long while. He hated traveling so ill-supplied.

He took his small cooking pot and his water skin, as well as Betula's water pouch, outside. Once the pot filled with rain, he filled the skin and then the pouch and let the pot refill again.

Finally, he brought everything inside. He looked at the pot and sighed. He wanted nothing more than to peel off his own wet clothes and sit by the fire, and he was reluctant to leave his charge, but he knew he had to find food. Sleep alone wouldn't replenish Betula's strength.

The sky had lightened a bit, and the rain was a steadier downpour now, the violence of the storm rolling off toward the east.

Talon began foraging. The pickings were meager at first, but then Talon found a small bush with a handful of dark red berries that he recognized instantly and gave a glad cry. Now he would truly be able to help his young friend! He had not expected to find a *shavosh* bush here; he had not thought it could grow in the wilds. Talon had only ever seen the treasured plant grow in the carefully cultivated Healers' Gardens in Riviera. The remarkable stimulant, *thesha,* could be brewed from the berries. It was particularly effective in restoring strength in the case of blood loss. *Shathen* could be brewed from the leaves, which would both reduce the swelling of Betula's ankle and lessen his pain.

Talon picked all the delicate berries eagerly but was careful not to crush them. Then he picked some of the dark green leaves from the bush as well, which he wrapped carefully about the berries to protect them. He put them into his large pouch, tucking it carefully under his shirt.

He shivered with the cold the rain had brought but continued his search, hoping to find more food and other medicinal plants to replenish his depleted healer's kit.

But only a short time into his search, the storm suddenly roared to gale force, boiling back across the sky from the east. The clouds had an ugly greenish tint to them now. Talon felt an irrational urge to seek cover and scoffed at it. He could not possibly get more wet.

But then he was pelted by rain, so icy cold he at first thought it hail, it stung so severely when it hit his skin. Talon found shelter under a pine tree, eyeing the storm distrustfully. Roiling green clouds tore westward across the sky, and the howling wind sounded almost like angry, haunted voices. Talon wondered if it might be an unnatural storm and was relieved he had collected the water and plants when he had, fearing the storm might otherwise have contaminated them somehow.

After a while, the wind changed direction again, and the sky lightened to a reassuring gray once more. Talon stepped tentatively from underneath the pine. The rain was warmer again, and somehow felt cleaner. This new wind was not nearly so fierce either, although the air was still cold. Talon shivered and decided it was time to return to the den. It would be safe to walk under this rain.

When he reached the den, Talon was relieved to see the fire still burning, although it was getting low. He added more wood. He was pleased to see that Betula was sleeping peacefully.

Talon unexpectedly and inexplicably felt ravenously thirsty. He drank a full two-thirds of the water from the pan, then set the pot with the remaining water on the ring of rocks he had placed around the fire for that purpose, careful not to set it too close to the flames.

Talon dropped the few leaves and berries he'd gathered into the water, ignoring the other plants from the morning for now. He slowly simmered the berries and leaves, careful not to allow the mixture to become too hot; it must not boil. He poured the steaming dark-red liquid into his cup. It smelled delicious, and he vainly wished there was enough for two.

He let it cool a bit and then walked over to Betula and roused him gently. "Drink this. It will give you strength and take away some of the pain and the swelling of your ankle, for a while, at least."

He held the cup out to Betula carefully and helped him drink, lest he spill any of the precious liquid. Betula drank it all then smiled at Talon and lay back down. Then he closed his eyes and drifted off to sleep again.

Talon shivered and went back to the fire. Peeling off his own wet things, he laid them out to dry next to Betula's clothes. He sat as close to the fire as he dared and went about the work of fashioning the sapling trunk into a real walking stick, hoping the activity might warm him. After trimming the branch stubs with his knife, he carved the top of the branch so it fit comfortably into his hand, then narrowed it a bit so it might fit the Elf's slender palm better.

There was barely room to stand in the den, but he did so, hefting the stick, weighing it carefully in his hands, this way and that, and finally removing a length from the bottom with the axe. He tested it and smiled. It was a good length and well-balanced now. It could also serve as a weapon, if need be. He shaped it further.

His thoughts drifted, and he cursed and jerked his hand away. He'd fallen asleep for a moment and cut himself on his knife. Fortunately, the wound was not deep and barely bled. Putting the blade and the staff aside, he wrapped his arms around his legs, rested his head on his knees, and dared to close his eyes. He would not sleep; he would only rest for a little while.

ARAS awoke from a dreamless sleep feeling well rested. He even felt somewhat like himself again and wondered what it was Talon had given him to drink before. He must learn how to brew such a drink, which had the strength of anosar but was unknown to him. He had not thought anything else might be so strong.

Aras was impatient with his enforced convalescence. He disliked being a burden, especially to a stranger not even of his kind. Although Talon seemed more like a friend now, somehow. He had not expected to find a friend among Man, and certainly not in so short a time. This one, at least, was little like the Men his father had warned him of.

Aras felt hungry and realized he had not had the energy to before. He sat up carefully. His shoulder still throbbed, but it was not so painful to move his arm. And the swelling around his ankle was definitely less pronounced.

He looked outside the den. The sun shone brightly. He must have slept through the rainy day and the night, and part of this day as well. No wonder he felt so well rested! But it was still cold, and he was surprised to see the fire was out, particularly when he noticed there was still wood piled along the wall. Talon lay naked by the fire's ashes, and Aras realized he was shivering violently.

Aras rose carefully and limped awkwardly over to Talon in concern, hissing with pain from his ankle, which had stiffened from his enforced inactivity. Aras knelt next to Talon, relieved he was not made dizzy this time by his exertions. When he touched Talon's shoulder gently, he was startled by how hot Talon was. At his touch, Talon stirred but did not waken, even as he was wracked by a violent series of coughs. Aras shook Talon, who moaned but did not otherwise respond. Aras's concern over his own injuries vanished in the face of Talon's obvious illness.

Aras realized that Talon had neither eaten nor slept, and had been drenched and then made bereft of even his blanket, because of him. He felt Talon's clothes. They were still wet, as was the blanket, but his own clothes were dry. Covering Talon in his warm cloak, he dressed as quickly as he could, his injured ankle and arm making it ridiculously difficult. He saw the water skins and tried to get Talon to drink, to no avail.

He saturated some of the unused bandages Talon had made and laid them over Talon's forehead in an effort to cool him. Fevers were dangerous. This malady was serious, potentially fatal. He needed to find something to cool Talon's fever as well as food for both of them. He saw the few wilted plants Talon had gathered the previous morning, but there was nothing he recognized that would treat fever.

There were several small pouches lying on the ground near a somewhat larger one, all of which he recognized as being of Elven fabric and waterproof. But although the smaller pouches smelled of herbs, many of them familiar, with medicinal uses, they were all empty. Talon's small pack was also empty, the meager contents already exposed on the floor of the den. He would bring the larger pouch and the pack; he would need them to carry whatever plants he might find.

Aras picked up the staff and saw guiltily how much work had been done to it. He gathered up the wet clothes and blanket. "I will be back as soon as I can. Rest... my friend," Aras said, adding the last with only the briefest hesitation.

He hobbled outside, leaning gratefully on the staff, intending to lay the blanket and clothes out to dry in the sun on the warm, gray rock surrounding the mouth of the den, which had already dried save for a few stray puddles. To Aras's astonishment, when he unbundled the crumpled shirt, a jeweled armband tumbled out from where it had been concealed inside the right sleeve, hitting the rock with a clang and rolling a short distance before circling with a musical hum until it fell still.

Aras picked it up and examined it. It was three inches wide and nearly a quarter inch thick, with ridged edges at each end as thick again and a beautifully intricate hinge and clasp. The metal shone like moonlight, the same pure, unnaturally bright sheen as his pallenteum dagger, and a single, perfect ruby, as wide as a thumbnail, was set into the band. The stone was raw, not cut into facets, as a Dwarf would style such a gem.

What in the world would a ragged Man like Talon be doing with such a kingly piece? For a moment Aras wondered whom he might have stolen it from, but then angrily pushed the thought aside. That thought came from his father, not from him.

This Man was no thief. Aras's gem-battery yet lay in its pouch. Such a stone was invaluable: any number of wards could be enabled through it. Men would call that stone emerald or beryl, and likely cut it into facets, though by doing so the thief would unknowingly render it inert and unable to fulfill its true purpose. Talon spoke Elvish fluently and without accent, and he used Elvish medicines with the familiarity of a skilled Elven healer. Surely he would know the value of such a gem? Yet he had not taken it, nor the full, heavy purse by his side, when Talon could easily have robbed him and left him to die and none would have known. Talon was an honest Man, an honorable one. Aras had known there must be such Men in the world.

Aras laid the shirt flat upon the ground, and the blanket. He debated hiding the armband beneath one of them, but it felt wrong to leave it unprotected. Instead, he reentered the den and gently fastened the armband about Talon's right bicep. He was again alarmed by how hot Talon was. He must hurry.

He headed out into the woods. The ground was muddy, and there were fallen branches everywhere, evidence of the violence of the storm. At least firewood would not be a problem, although the green wood would smoke and not burn as well as dead wood.

After nearly tripping several times, even with the staff to aid him, Aras slowed his pace. He could not risk a fall. He would not be able to aid Talon were he to injure himself further.

He disregarded the pain in his ankle, knowing that ultimately the activity would help him heal. But he was still frighteningly weak, and he had to rest often and was frustrated by the resultant delay in his search. There was nothing edible here and worse, no medicinal plants he could recognize.

Aras passed their once sheltering tree. As Talon had feared might happen, it had not survived the storm. It lay blackened and burnt along its length, split in half and fallen. Aras touched it sadly. It had not been truly aware, but it had been strong and proud for all its suffering and had given freely of its strength in his time of need. He mourned its death, but he was comforted to know that leaving it had served a purpose other than to make his friend ill.

The forest smelled scrubbed clean by the rain. Aras breathed the fresh air in short, shallow breaths, remembering the pain of breathing too deeply. Still, it invigorated him.

He pressed onward, straying much farther from camp than he would have liked. But then, to his delight, he suddenly found himself in a healer's treasure trove. That small white flower was thasheera, to treat Talon's fever. The roots of that fallen sapling were unmistakably fashaya; they could be used to treat Talon's cough. And not far from there, fetha to clear his lungs of the fluids that Aras feared now filled them. And here were some leaves that smelled and tasted of mint, asur.

Beyond the small rise were the remains of a hollow tree and a hive. There were several drowned bees, but there was also some honeycomb and honey he could salvage. He filled Talon's empty healer's kit with the gooey mass, knowing it would clean easily and not leak. Past the hive there were some more edible plants. He gathered them eagerly, filling Talon's pack with all he could find.

It was awkward returning, one hand holding the pouch and pack and the other holding the walking stick. It hurt too fiercely to carry them over his shoulder, even on his good side. Aras was relieved when he finally saw the mouth of the den. He brought in the plants first and laid them on a pine bough.

Talon had thrown off his cloak and was shaking violently. He lay atop the charcoal and ash, oblivious to it in his delirium. Had Aras rekindled the fire earlier, Talon might just as easily have rolled into the fire and burned himself. The thought of Talon being burnt horrified him.

Aras went outside as quickly as he could and bent to retrieve the clothes, fighting sudden dizziness as pinpricks of bright light dotted his vision. He was overexerting himself. He sat down abruptly on the ground and then lay down and concentrated on breathing, fighting to remain conscious.

He felt dizzy and nauseous, as if he would both vomit and faint, and knew it was from the earlier blood loss. Cursing his weakness, he forced himself calm, breathing slowly, deeply, until the feeling passed. He must be more careful.

Rising slowly and cautiously to a seated position, he again reached for the clothes. The sun had done its job, and now the clothes and blanket were dry to the touch. Aras stood slowly and carefully limped back to the mouth of the den.

He entered and knelt by Talon's side, intending to dress him. But when he touched Talon's skin, it was so hot to the touch! He feared he'd taken too long in his foraging.

He covered Talon in the cloak and blanket instead and worked quickly, lighting the fire with practiced ease, thankful now for the many repetitions his instructors had insisted upon, which had at the time seemed like the most base cruelty to him and the other cadets. There was not an Aerta or Oceana born who was not innately terrified of fire, with good reason.

Aras filled the pot halfway with water. He soothed Talon with wet cloths upon his brow as he waited impatiently for the water to boil and then added the flower and root and some of the leaves to the pot. He stirred it and then set the pot higher above the fire and tended to Talon as he watched it simmer until the liquid was a murky greenish brown and smelled right. He let it cool, anxiously testing the temperature repeatedly.

Taking Talon's cup, he carefully filled it with the liquid. "Drink this," he said, holding his friend's head and pouring some into his mouth. Talon swallowed reflexively but then gagged and retched, nearly knocking the cup from Aras's hand in his delirium.

This was very bad. Talon must drink. Aras tasted some of the brew. It was strong and bitter, but to Man's tongue must taste differently. Perhaps the asur and honey? Aras poured the remainder of the medicine back into the pot and then added a generous amount of the asur and honey. He let it steep for a few moments and then filled the cup again.

Again he held Talon's head while he struggled weakly against him. "Please, you must drink it," Aras implored. He poured it more slowly. A swallow. Aras waited, breath held, but it stayed down. He tipped the cup gently. Another swallow.

When the cup was three-quarters empty, Aras was satisfied. He tucked the blanket and cloak tightly around Talon's legs and groin and washed his face and chest repeatedly with wet cloths, doing all he could to cool him.

As he bathed him, Aras could not help but admire Talon's lean frame. His body was hard and well muscled, not at all gaunt as he had expected it might be from the way he was dressed. His arms and chest were those of a warrior; he had the muscles of one, and his legs were those of one who obviously walked far more often than he rode.

Aras was surprised to find that Talon's skin was far smoother and softer than he had expected to find it and nearly as hairless as one of his own people, rather than hairy as he had been told and seen Men were. Belatedly, he realized that unkempt and ill-groomed as Talon was, he should have been bearded as well, but his chin and cheeks were as smooth as the rest.

But Aras noticed to his confusion that here and there upon his body, Talon's perfect skin was marred by white and pink masses of imperfection. He realized to his horror that they must be signs of old injuries that had never properly healed. He'd ever only seen similar signs of such trauma and suffering on animals before. This mark must have been from a blade, and that one was obviously a badly healed bite.

Aras shuddered at the distinctively shiny damaged tissue that indicated a poorly healed burn. He recognized it only because he had found a dead deer once in the woods of Nalea with just such an odd mass of shiny damaged tissue and brought Jarnath to it, to learn what it might mean. Jarnath had reacted violently to it. He had almost fainted when he had seen it and had run from the carcass as if it might somehow destroy him.

When Jarnath could speak again, he had explained that the deer must have been injured by fire, that it had been burnt and then recovered. Aras had been horrified to hear it, nearly as ill as his mentor at the thought. Fire was a primal fear to both the Aerta and Oceana; they had lost most of both races, as well as their Homeland, to fire. But Jarnath had personal experience with the travesty to the flesh of burns. Jarnath was one of the few Lords who had survived the Annihilation. As a healer, he had been exposed to countless horrors beyond imagining tending to the survivors of the War, of the Night of Fire.

Aras shivered and forced his thoughts back to Talon. He traced each imperfection on his skin with his fingertip in compassion; Talon, who knew so much of healing, had had no healer to tend him when he was injured. *This time he does,* Aras thought proudly as he bathed Talon's torso and limbs again and again. He wished he had a river that he could lay him in, so the cool waters could run over him and reduce the fever more quickly. He wished Jarnath were here, with all of his many medicines.

Talon was seized by another coughing fit, but he did not disgorge what he had drunk. His hand groped blindly, as if searching for something, and Aras gripped his reaching hand tightly.

"We are a fine pair, are we not, my friend? And I fear you hate being helpless even more than I." Aras's voice seemed to comfort Talon, so he began singing softly, songs of home, ones Meloneth had taught him.

The trembling slowed and eventually stopped. Talon seemed to be breathing easier as well. Talon's hand relaxed and released his. Aras reheated the broth, refilled the cup, and encouraged his friend to drink again. It was easier this time. He sighed and put the cup down, relaxed enough now to eat some of the greens he'd gathered. And when he finally felt tired beyond the limits of wakefulness, he obediently lay down to sleep. It would not help his friend if he were to sicken as well, and he was still weak enough from his injuries that the thought frightened him.

WHEN Aras awoke it was dark. The ash was cold. The fire had gone out long ago and there were ominous but unidentifiable sounds outside, in the trees beyond the den. Aras quickly built the fire up again and listened anxiously, relieved when nothing approached. The wolven had likely scent-marked their territory thoroughly, and perhaps even the violent storm had not obliterated all trace of their scent. Other predators, even of the same species, would be reluctant to challenge such formidable adversaries.

Talon still slept, but his sleep seemed more natural. Aras was relieved to find that though Talon was still hotter than he thought he should be, he was not burning as before. The fever no longer threatened to consume him.

Aras brewed more broth, again generously flavoring it with asur and honey. He woke Talon, and this time his eyes focused on Aras's face for a moment. "Drink this," Aras instructed, and Talon did so without question. "Now sleep. You are ill. You need your rest." Talon's eyes closed obediently. Aras did not think his friend had been truly conscious after all.

After poking the fire, Aras began carving twining vines and leaves onto the head and body of his staff to keep himself awake. He paused in his carving and looked at Talon while stretching and flexing his arm and foot, careful not to disturb his friend. Soon he would be healed enough to travel, and Talon would be well enough also. He and Talon would part company.

The realization saddened him far more than it should have. Aras was surprised at the strength of the friendship that had formed between them in such a short time. Was it always this way with Men? They lived such brief lives.

He wondered if perhaps they might travel together, for a while at least. He sensed Talon knew much he could teach him. But Talon had become ill caring for him. He might have died. Men died so easily. He did not know whether Talon might resent him for it. Daylight was a long time coming.

At dawn, Talon still slept. Aras felt it would be safe enough to sleep again as well. But first he would eat. He began simmering some of the plants he'd gathered earlier. Feeling his friend's forehead gently, he breathed a sigh of relief. Talon's face was only as warm as it should be, and he had not coughed at all during the night. Talon stirred at the gentle touch and his eyes opened.

"Welcome back, my friend. How do you feel?" Aras asked.

TALON felt disoriented and appallingly weak, though not at all terrified by his helplessness, as he should have been. Instead, he was ravenously hungry. Something smelled good. "What happened?" he asked, trying to sit up, finding to his consternation that it took more strength than he had.

"Slowly, my friend. You've been ill," Betula said, helping him sit.

"I don't get sick," Talon said, impatient with his weakness, shrugging off Betula's arm even as he realized he was naked beneath the blanket. After a moment's blind panic at the thought the Enemy had somehow found him, he remembered stripping off his cold, wet clothes and sitting before the fire. He must have fallen asleep. But it had been dark outside. How could he have slept, without the grace of the sun, and still be sane?

His eyes widened as he realized to his amazement and dismay that his armband was about his bicep and exposed where Betula could not help but see it. He subtly shifted the blanket to cover it. He had taken it off and concealed it inside the sleeve of his shirt, as he always did, whenever he bathed or was naked for any reason. Hadn't he? He was certain he had done so. How could he have let Betula see it? But Betula seemed oblivious to it.

"Ah, but I don't think you usually go without sleep or food for days on end, then lie naked and cold without even a fire to warm you," Betula argued.

"I have done far worse to myself many times for far longer," Talon said dismissively. He thought again about the sudden odd change in the storm, the feeling of wrongness, and the stinging rain. And the wind had come from the east, he realized uneasily.

"Nevertheless, you have had a serious fever and a worrisome cough, and have been delirious and unconscious for much of the past two days," Betula said, smiling. But it was not the usual sort of Elf-to-foolish-Man-child smile Talon had seen so many times in the past, although seldom directed at him. There was friendship in that smile, and he realized Betula had called him friend twice.

"Forgive me," Betula said, this time in the less formal manner of friend to friend. "It is just that I had thought before you were one who would like feeling helpless and dependent upon another even less than I. After having learned I know so little about Man after all, it is gratifying to know I was right in this, at least. Are you hungry?"

Talon nodded. "Then eat," Betula said, holding out the spoon and single bowl.

He did not offer to feed Talon, at least. He accepted the meal both eagerly and reluctantly. He was famished, and the stewed greens smelled wonderful. The simple fare tasted incredibly delicious, as the first food after a fast always does. He fought to pace himself, but devoured it all too quickly.

When Betula made to dish up the rest for him, Talon asked, "Have you eaten yet?" concerned that Betula, who also needed to eat in order to regain his strength, deprived himself.

"Not so many hours ago," Betula assured him.

Talon nodded in relief and accepted the refilled bowl gratefully.

Once he was finished with his meal, Betula said, "You should rest again, now. You should feel stronger when next you waken."

Talon started to object, but then realized he was still exhausted. He felt a great warmth radiate from Betula and basked in it, as if it were the sun. He need not fear sleep now, with Betula beside him, irrational as that might seem. He did not have the energy to think further upon it. Lying back down, he was asleep again in moments.

ARAS studied his sleeping friend's face fondly. In sleep, Talon looked far less serious, much more at ease with himself. After he was sure Talon was deeply asleep, Aras left to gather lunch and other useful roots, bark, herbs, and leaves. The latter he would dry in the sun, then rub into flakes or grind into powder to refill the pouches his friend carried. Aras had never thought to bring medicine with him on his journey. How foolish he now felt for it! Jarnath might have advised him to, if Aras had told him he was leaving. But then he could not have left. He could not have said good-bye to Jarnath.

Aras did not let such melancholy thoughts seize him. The woods were clean and joyful this morning. They no longer felt strange.

Aras wandered farther than before, gathering an assortment of greenery. It was much easier to walk, now, and to bend and stretch his arm without pain. He moved more quickly and did not tire so easily.

Aras returned to the den and laid a number of things out in the sun to dry, bringing the rest inside. Then he stretched languidly, lay down beside his friend, and slept.

A LONG time later, when Talon awoke, he indeed felt stronger and sat up without much difficulty. Betula was asleep at his side. Talon looked at him in wonder. He was not alone anymore. He did not need to feel cautiously in his mind for a thin metal thread. There was a thick, twining vine wrapped about his core that shimmered the pure bright silver of pallenteum, the Lord's Metal, not the copper of pyrenteum, the King's Metal, though it connected him to Betula just the same.

But it could not! Their cores had not touched. How could they have? Betula was not one of his people. He could not be bonded to him. But the evidence was unmistakable.

Had the Elf somehow violated his mind while he slept? The thought died stillborn. Betula would not harm him. Betula? He should not think of him by a name other than his true name if they were bonded, but he knew no other name for him. Their minds had not touched, then, at least in no way he had ever felt.

Was it because Betula was an Elf? No, he shared no such bond with Elanara, and if he was to have bonded to any Elf, it should have been to his betrothed. And though, as an Elf, her core was brighter than a Man's, it was still not strong enough that he might bond to her. He had not thought any Elf's was.

But then the realization it must indeed be possible triggered a puzzling memory, one buried and all but forgotten six long years ago. When he had touched Elanara's brother Eladar's core soon after meeting him for the first time, while Eladar was traumatized and unconscious from slaying a fox, out of necessity, Talon had been shocked by the brightness and strength of the young Elf's core. It had been akin to one of his own peoples'. Why should his be so much stronger than his sister's, than those of the other Elves he had touched?

Talon felt incredible, soothing warmth radiating down the bond from Betula. Perhaps Arcanus could enlighten him, when next he saw him. For now, it did not matter. It was enough to know the demons were at bay, at least for a time.

Betula had looked and sounded much stronger and healthier. Perhaps tomorrow they could set out for the village. The villagers no doubt thought him lost to the wolven, even as they might wonder why they suffered no new attacks.

Talon rose and stretched silently, glad to see his old talent had not failed him. His new friend did not stir. He was pleased and surprised to see a fairly large quantity of food had been gathered. Betula must have ranged far while he slept. Talon's pulse quickened. Betula had left him while he slept! But even though Betula had been so far away, Talon had somehow yet been safe from the demons that plagued him. He calmed. He was truly no longer alone.

Talon saw his clothes were neatly folded by his side. He looked at them in distaste and resignation and began dressing reluctantly. They were threadbare, stiff, and scratchy, and they still stank, despite the deluge. The loose sleeve of the shirt pulled easily over his armband. It was unnoticeable under the coarse linen. It continued to disturb him that Betula had seen his band. He'd certainly not meant to reveal it to him. He forced the worrisome thought aside.

Talon left the den and drank in the sunlight joyfully, rather than desperately. He looked at the plants drying in the sun in puzzlement for a moment, until he recognized four of the six and their uses: they were medicines. The white flower was for fever; Men called it Ghostlips, but to the Elves it was known as *thasheera*. The yellow root, *fashaya*, was for cough. The dark-brown bark, which would prevent a wound from festering, was *resan*. And the leaf, *lashar*, would slow bleeding. The other two, both leaves, were unknown to him. He would have to ask Betula about those.

He thought he might walk in the woods for a while but remembered he was unarmed. He reasoned that if he might need his blade, it was perhaps best he not go far after all, because he felt himself tiring already.

With a start, he realized he had let Kathalanar stray far from his hand. He was shocked and appalled. In all the long decades he had carried the King's Sword, he had never been so irresponsible. And even as children, he and his kinsmen were never unarmed! Talon suddenly felt eyes upon him, and he tensed, terrified by his vulnerability, until he realized the scrutiny came from the den.

Betula smiled at him from the doorway and walked over to him, leaning much more lightly on the walking stick. "If you feel up to it, I could use some help gathering more firewood. I think perhaps together we can do the work of one now."

Talon smiled in return, in an attempt to hide his anxiety, but also because it was truly good to see his friend so recovered from his injuries. "Just let me get my sword," Talon said, and Betula nodded.

Talon returned shortly, wearing his gloves, the blade at his side. They headed into the woods and gathered firewood in companionable silence and returned to camp with their burden.

Betula checked the drying plants before they went inside. Then he began filling the pot with plants while Talon built a fire. As lunch cooked, Betula fashioned a spoon from a piece of wood he had apparently selected for the purpose, carving expertly. Talon had noticed the vines twining around the staff and watched him carve the spoon with interest.

When lunch was ready, Betula divided the contents of the pot neatly in half, passing Talon's bowl and spoon to him and eating from the pot.

"You cook as well as you carve," Talon said. "It is a welcome change for me."

"Ah, so then you always travel alone?" Betula asked, and Talon sensed it might not be as casual a question as it had sounded.

"I prefer to keep my own company," Talon agreed cagily. He had not lied to Betula. He had not said "Yes." He again touched the awful void on his core where the thin coppery strands that had bound him to his kinsmen should be. He had not been alone for twelve years; first Farad and then later Lunahr had been only a touch away. But panic did not rise in him, and he felt no need to seek the solace of the flames. He was no longer alone. Betula was with him.

"And you. You roam far from home. Do you prefer solitude, or is it that few would care to venture into Man's world with you?"

ARAS thought of his father, of their parting and the many reasons for it, and replied softly. "No, I could have all the company I might want. But then, how could I find what I sought?"

"And what do you seek, Betula?" Talon gently pressed.

"Answers. And questions to find more answers. There will be time enough for duty and tradition and solemnity." Aras could not tell Talon more, not yet. He could not trust so easily.

Talon nodded. "I have often felt the same. I would have walked these lands even had I been given a choice, although perhaps not for as long as I have. I travel to help others. There are many dangers in this world, and I have found that those most often beset by them are oft those most ill-equipped to face them."

"Ah. I sensed I was hardly the first stray you've succored. If you feel you will be well enough, I will be able to travel to the village with you tomorrow, I think. I know you are eager to return."

Talon smiled. "I will enjoy traveling with you, my friend."

"May I have six of those small pouches you carry?" Aras asked. "I wish to replenish your dwindled supplies for your further travels."

Talon nodded and accompanied him outside. "I recognize these four," he said, naming the plants and describing the uses he knew for them. "And these?"

"This is soforath. It is for pain. It is very strong, and dangerous if you use too much. Boil a cup of water and add only a single pinch," Aras said, demonstrating the proper amount. "And drink only one cup twice in a single day and night, spaced as equally apart as possible. I have found that once at dawn and once at dusk works well, if you do not have a sand timer or water clock to accurately measure the interval. It will make you sleep, also, so do not use it if you are still in danger." Talon nodded, filling his pouch carefully.

"And this one is just for meals," Aras said, smiling. "It is called thalu. It makes a rather flavorful tea, and is prepared in the same way as any tea. It is a shame I do not have any asur left; it blends well with thalu. It's used in the same manner as mint and has much the same flavor. I used that and the honey to temper the flavor of the medicine I gave you, for at first you could not drink it. The honey is all gone as well, now, but would have been difficult to carry, in any case. It is fortunate that the fabric my people weave is so easy to clean; the remains of the honey should wash out of your healer's pouch easily enough.

"But tell me, I must know. That drink you brewed for me: it had the Power of anosar yet it is unknown to me. What is it called? How did you learn of it? What plant is it made from? How is it prepared?" Aras asked eagerly.

Talon laughed. "So many questions! The bush it is from is called shavosh. Are you familiar with it?"

"No. Please, describe it to me," Aras urged, eager to hear of it.

"I will do better. I will show it to you, though only the leaves remain. I used all the berries. The berries are small, dark red when ripe, thin-skinned, and fragile, with a single seed in the middle. I saved the seeds so I might plant them, as simmering them does not harm them, although I am not optimistic that they will sprout. I will gift you half of them to take home to your own Kingdom, whichever of the Wood Elf Kingdoms it might be, to plant there. I did not think shavosh could grow outside of the Healers' Gardens in Riviera. I did not think the soil outside of their lands could support it."

"Riviera? You have been there?" Aras asked wistfully.

Talon scowled and grew silent.

Aras was intrigued by the sudden sharp change in Talon. It was as if he had encased himself in invisible armor. He had become as cold and hard and unfathomable as his father.

Aras felt the familiar pain lance his heart at being so rejected. But why should he? This was merely a Man, one he had only just met. Why should he care what Talon thought of him or how he treated him? But he did care, very much. Too much.

"Forgive me if my question somehow offended you," Aras said contritely, his voice little more than a whisper.

TALON looked at Betula in surprise. He had apologized with the weary, hopeless tone of one who knows he can never please, one who knows forgiveness will ever be denied to him.

Talon's heart went out to the young Elf. He was so like Eladar, or like Lunahr in some ways, yet so different.

Lunahr! The loss of his young cousin slashed across his core afresh, wounding him more deeply than any blade could. Talon quietly and ruthlessly suppressed all feelings, all thoughts of his lost cousin.

ARAS almost cried out. The coldness had been replaced for a single heartbeat with anguish, unbearable loss, but then it was as if Talon had turned to ice. Talon was masking his thoughts and emotions from Aras somehow. He had not thought any but the most skilled and powerful of the few surviving Lords and Ladies of his own people might be able to do so! But Talon's coldness was not the complete absence of warmth, but more like a metal grate over a hearth, containing true fire within so those outside might never be burnt.

Aras's gaze turned to the trees around them, and then he looked at Talon. He needed time away from Talon, to ponder all he had learned and all that yet puzzled him. "I think I would like some time alone amongst the trees," Aras began hesitantly.

"Go, my friend," Talon encouraged, and Aras smiled at him gratefully and left. He walked purposefully into the woods. It was good to be among the trees again, but their strength was not what he sought, nor only time to think. Talon was so complex, unexpected, and unfathomable. He would no doubt occupy Aras's thoughts for a long time to come. But first he must test himself. He needed to learn what his temporary limitations might be, as a result of his injuries.

He went to the clearing where their fallen tree lay. When Aras tried to walk without the staff, he felt his ankle protest. He was impatient to heal but resisted the urge to push himself. He sighed. There would be time enough for walking tomorrow.

Aras found his balance, spotted a suitable target, released the staff, drew his bow, nocked an arrow, and let it fly, all in one smooth motion, hissing at the sudden pain in his shoulder. The pinecone he had aimed at swung gently but did not fall. He had not hit it in the center; he had only grazed it. He heard his father's voice in his head, ridiculing him for his incompetence.

Gritting his teeth, he tried again, and this time the pinecone swung wildly. In his mind's eye he saw his father turn his back and walk away from him in disgust, as he had when Aras was fourteen years old and bleeding to death in the training grounds.

Forcing the memory away, he drew again. His third shot knocked the pinecone from the tree, and when he went to retrieve his arrow, he saw it had punctured the cone deeply and squarely on the mark. He felt no satisfaction from the success of his third shot. He should have felled it the first time.

He tried his twin blades. His left arm was still slower and weaker than his right. Sudden movement caused him pain, and he did not have his full range of motion.

Aras eyed the staff he had discarded distastefully, then thoughtfully, seeing it with new eyes. He hefted it again, as he had when he'd instinctively tested it for balance the first time he held it. Flipping it on end, he struck a mock foe with it. He flipped it again. Then he spun it until the wind whistled around it. He started to smile, but then he faltered, and the staff fell from his hands.

He cried out and fell to his knees. Something was wrong! Danger! He was in danger! Not his mother, but someone else with Power akin to hers, or even stronger. It must be Incuban or Arcanus! One of them had somehow discovered him!

He fought terror. He was not ready to confront them, not yet! Then, as suddenly as it had come, the feeling vanished.

Aras was left shaken, and he rose quickly, looking about for an unseen foe, frightened and confused. He had never felt anything like that! It was terrible. But he seemed safe now. The danger was apparently past, and he believed himself to be unharmed.

Talon! What if Talon had been attacked as well?

Aras fought the urge to run to Talon's side. Instead, he picked up the staff and made every effort to reach Talon as stealthily as possible, lest the unknown foe be near.

TALON had made sure Betula was well clear of the den before drawing his blade, even though he wore his gloves, and with them on his hands masking the true nature of the Sword, he knew it could not be recognized. He was still upset about the armband. He had never meant for Betula to see it, at least not yet, when he was still an unknown to him.

Betula might yet prove to be an agent of the Enemy, a devious trap set for him. Betula was so ethereally beautiful. Even Elanara, who had claimed his heart at his first sight of her, did not possess such breathtaking perfection of feature. Betula was too perfect, too desirable to be real.

But Betula *was* real. He had saved Talon's life, nursed him through his illness. Betula had done nothing to harm him while he was helpless. Surely seeing his armband yet not acting against him was proof enough of Betula's true nature? If Betula were Incuban's tool, Talon would already be dead, or worse still, a captive on his way to the Enemy.

Unless the Enemy was trying to get at all of the Watch through him? Betula might even have caused his illness, in order to be able to cure him, to gain his trust. There were poisons enough that could mimic such an illness.

Talon swore and pushed the thoughts from him. Betula had not feigned his injuries; they had been real. Betula would have died without his aid. Betula would not have had the means nor opportunity to act ill upon him. Yet still....

Talon felt the wrongness of the thoughts plaguing him. His illness must not be entirely gone. His head was not fully clear. He looked inwards, viewing his core, and felt horror as he saw an ebony shadow in his mind's eye, amorphous and dark, a veil of filth wrapped about his naked core. But not only about his core. It also touched the curling end of Betula's pallenteum vine that supported him.

Pallenteum cannot tarnish, cannot be dulled. Talon probed carefully, afraid to touch the dark veil and equally afraid to disturb the link, lest he accidentally sever it, though it did not appear at all fragile, as his other bonds had been.

He was sickened to see that the metal of the vine underneath the veil did not glow but was instead pitted and unclean. As he watched, the veil flowed suddenly forward, unwrapping from his core and wrapping instead about the thick vine, as if to smother it. The vine began to wither and rot underneath the assault at an alarming rate and to loosen its vital hold upon his core.

Heart hammering in panic at the danger to Betula, and also at what the loss of his support would mean to his sanity, Talon ripped off his gloves and grasped Kathalanar's hilt. The Enemy! Idare, the Enemy was here, inside him!

The blade of the King's Sword glowed softly with a pure red light, like that of the sun's Power at sunset, when it was at its weakest, anemic and sputtering, instead of blazing as it should have been as Kathalanar's true nature was revealed. *Idare, please let it be enough!*

Talon saw the veil grow thinner still and felt the vine grow stronger again. ***Darkness, I banish thee!*** Talon commanded without speaking aloud. Almost instantly the veil disappeared into a single oily coil of smoke, and then even the tendril of smoke disappeared. The vine no longer looked damaged. Instead, it throbbed with Power and appeared fully healed. But his core was yet dull and pitted and scarred where the darkness had touched it. The sight of it frightened him.

He began the exercise Arcanus had taught him, laying name to each of the demons that plagued him:

Illness—a demon never before known to him, not even when the plague had slain so many of their kin. He fought it, slashing with his blade. *I banish thee.*

Weakness—a demon he seldom fought, but he fought it now and vanquished it. *I banish thee.*

Suspicion—always a friend to him, why now a demon? He hesitated, but then drove it off as well. *I banish thee.*

Self-Doubt/Indecision—always before the strongest, why so far down the list now? With a fierceness, *I banish thee.*

Fear/Panic/Terror—three linked together, so very strong, so seldom named. He fought them for a long time, but finally was victorious. *I banish thee.*

"I am cleansed," Talon said aloud, concluding the ritual as calm enveloped him, and he basked in the strength the Sword had brought to him as if it were the sun. But where was loneliness, always one of the strongest? How could he leave a demon unnamed, undefeated?

Talon probed for it and found it absent. The exercise was done. He lowered Kathalanar in wonder. The old familiar heaviness no longer shrouded his heart as the darkness had shrouded his mind. He turned his gaze inward once more and sought his core. It looked whole again, and the thick pallenteum vine that coiled protectively about it gleamed.

Talon turned his focus to the outside world once more and looked at his blade. It no longer glowed; its energy was drained, subdued. The distinctive pyrenteum blade was the color of copper dipped in blood until he slipped his gloves back on and the masking spell within them instantly engaged. Under the glamour, Kathalanar was no longer the exquisitely crafted blade of a king, no longer ancient nor magical nor powerful. He was still a beautiful blade, but iron in color, just an ordinary sword anyone might wield.

Talon had carefully hoarded Kathalanar's pure Power for the past six years. He had not used the Sword's Power once since Ardock. He'd dared not. But with Farad and Lunahr both gone, he had precious little protection from the King's Madness that had been threatening him for many days now.

Had this then been part of the trap, to force him to use Kathalanar's limited Power against the shadow in his mind? Or would the shadow itself have brought the Madness? He might go mad just worrying over the unfathomable puzzle.

Talon cleared his thoughts and ran through a different set of exercises then, a set of martial meditation exercises taught to him by a sword master, not a wizard. Each stroke was perfection, each thrust precise, each step a dance. He was almost done when he felt eyes upon him. Someone or something watched him from the woods. He pointed the Sword toward his foe unerringly, even as his straining eyes saw as little as his ears had heard.

TO HIS consternation, relief, and joy, Aras saw Talon was in front of the cave, alive and whole. He was exhibiting no signs of distress, nor was he in any danger Aras could detect. Instead, he was swinging his sword in a sequence of beautifully choreographed, intricate exercises. Aras knew now that he had befriended a true sword master, not just a swordsman. He had been right: Talon was both warrior and healer. Despite what his father had always claimed, it was possible to be both.

Aras was reluctant to reveal himself, unsure how best to make his presence known without it appearing that he had been spying on his friend. But suddenly the point became moot, as Talon spun about and faced the area Aras stood in, the sword pointed toward him, eyes searching.

Aras revealed himself and approached. "Forgive me. I did not mean to interrupt you."

"I did not hear you approach," Talon accused, sheathing his blade. He sounded upset, but as if his ire were directed at himself rather than Aras.

"Good," Aras said, satisfied. "I needed to see if I could still be silent, even with this." He lifted the staff and flicked it end to end before placing it on the ground again. "You crafted me a fine weapon, when I thought you had only made me a crutch. Thank you. You and I think alike, it would seem. I was also testing myself."

TALON nodded. He had not meant for Betula to see his naked blade yet, even masked, but it did not seem to hold any significance for him, as the armband had not.

He found it increasingly difficult to hold Betula at arm's length. This Elf was more a kindred spirit to him than any Man he had ever met, save his own kinsmen. It made him uneasy, how well Betula already knew him. He had not meant to get so close to another, and certainly not to another Elf. His heart was far from this place, and it made his wanderings more difficult.

"Forgive me my insult, whatever it might have been," Betula said sadly, as he abruptly turned and slipped back into the woods.

Talon cursed and followed. He had not meant to hurt his friend. "Betula, wait! You said nothing wrong. Please. We should start dinner. We need to go to sleep early, if we are to leave at dawn and walk through the day."

Betula stopped and turned to face Talon, looked searchingly into his eyes, and nodded, apparently satisfied at whatever he had found there.

They entered the den and prepared dinner. After they ate, they made sure the fire was well fed, and then they slept.

TALON was relieved to waken the next morning with the first rays of the sun and realize he had not dreamt. Betula was up at dawn as well and seemed as eager as he was to be on his way.

Talon cut his blanket in two and used half to bundle the remains of the dead. He planned to carry them to the villagers, along with the rotting trophies from the wolven; the leaves had only slowed the process of putrefaction, not stemmed it entirely.

They ate the last of the forage raw, packed their meager belongings quickly, and then set out.

Although they traveled slowly, by midday they still both felt the strain and rested longer than their meal would have required.

They continued on and spoke little, saving their energy for the journey. They covered more ground than Talon had expected they might, successfully foraging as they traveled. But by early evening Talon noticed that Betula's jaw was set with the strain, and he was limping more noticeably again.

Talon felt winded and weary as well, as if he had been traveling for many days instead of one. He started scanning the treetops, although it was not yet dusk. "We should camp here. That should make a suitable bed for the night," Talon said, pointing to a promising tree.

"I can still travel," Betula said willfully.

Talon smiled at him. "As can I, but we are both feeling the strain, I think, and it is foolish to push ourselves when the village still lies so far away." He set his pack down and began removing the berries, nuts, and greens they had gathered earlier in the day.

ARAS was surprised by the smile, the compassion, when he had expected scorn or disdain for his slowness, his frailty. No one save for Jarnath had ever been so forgiving of him for all his many inadequacies before.

Dinner was simple fare, and they did not bother to light a fire. They ate in companionable silence.

"Forgive me," Talon unexpectedly apologized. "I realize now you might feel ignored. I do not mean offense by my silence. I am used to traveling alone, and already I have spoken more in the past two days than in the two weeks before."

Aras smiled. "There is nothing to forgive. I value the sounds of the woods and the company they provide nearly as much as I do your own." He scowled. "No, that is not what I meant to say. I certainly value your company far more." He sighed. "I must admit now that you were right. I am indeed far more weary than I realized. I find I have been eyeing our bower longingly," he said, and then blushed at the unintentional double entendre of the term, even as he hoped Talon's knowledge of Elvish might not be precise enough for him to notice his faux pas.

To Aras's astonishment, a spark of appreciation flared in Talon's eyes for a single heartbeat and then was gone. Had he imagined it?

"I am tired as well and find I am looking forward to sleeping for the first time in a long time," Talon said distinctly as he rose, shouldering his pack and heading for the tree.

Aras rose as well and almost called out to offer to carry Talon's pack for him, concerned his friend might not share his own agility, but Talon climbed surprisingly quickly.

Aras left his staff at the base of the tree and then followed Talon into the thick branches. His friend had chosen well. There was plentiful room for both of them. They would be secure. Even injured as he was, he climbed quickly and easily, as at home in the tree as on the ground.

"I think we will be safe enough up here that we need not sleep in shifts so that we can guard one another," Talon said. "Do you agree?"

Aras was surprised and flattered that Talon might ask his opinion, as if he were a trusted comrade. "I do. Sleep well my friend."

"You also, Betula."

Aras forced himself to relax, knowing he would waken at the first hint of danger, as would Talon. In spite of his weariness, the calm, steady breathing of his friend, the music of the wind in the treetops, and the other sounds of the night, it was well past dark when Aras finally drifted off to sleep.

Chapter 2
Innocence Lost

The Elven High-King Laedrin scanned Lord of the Guard Ahrnad's report for the fourth time and still did not read more than a handful of words. He flung the pages away in frustration. He almost called the King's Guard to look for Aras, but he stopped himself.

His son was gone. He had chosen to leave. He had purposefully, willfully abandoned his post. He had committed desertion, treason. If he died, the fault would be his, the blame his. He had chosen his path. If he was not fit to be Laedrin's son and heir, then he deserved death. Better that he find out now so he knew to sire another.

Not that he had ever wanted a son. Ithelia had seduced him. She'd been so cold, so aloof, that she'd made herself a challenge for him. She'd made the thought of conquering her appealing. He could have forced her to his bed, but then he would not have truly defeated her. He had worked long and hard on his victory over her. He had even wed her. He had made her High-Queen.

The people had loved her as they had never loved him; they worshipped her. All the more so when she announced she was with child, for they had despaired of there ever being an heir. They thought themselves doomed to an eternity under his rule. She gave them hope, and they loved her all the more for it. And as soon as she had told them, she kept him from her bed.

Laedrin remembered first seeing Aras, so small and weak and helpless. He had despised Aras from the moment he laid eyes upon his infant son. But Ithelia had fawned upon him, and still had kept Laedrin from her bed, long after he should have been welcome again. He was infuriated by her coldness to him. Then she had finally told him what lay in her heart. "I have all I ever wanted from you. I will never tolerate your vile touch upon me again."

He realized then, too late, that she was the one who had defeated him. She had used him to get a son by him. He hated her and he hated Aras. But Aras was still his son, his heir. He'd tried to mold him to become a soldier, to one day be ready to assume the role of High-King, but Ithelia kept careful control of the boy. Then unexpectedly, when Aras was eight, Ithelia left. She simply vanished, without a word, without a trace.

Laedrin knew his people all thought he'd finally killed her or exiled her. The truth was, she had disappeared, of her own volition, for her own reasons. He had no idea where she'd gone, nor did he care, other than for what his people thought of him for it. His people kept close watch upon his son, lest he vanish as well.

It was then that Laedrin had made his second mistake. He had let the healer Jarnath take over caring for the boy. Laedrin had been relieved Jarnath stepped in to do so. Aras was a nuisance, always underfoot, clumsy, eager. It was Jarnath who completed the destruction of the boy. Jarnath molded Aras into a healer in his own image, but he'd been careful about it, discreet. Laedrin had never suspected the damage Jarnath had done to his son.

When Laedrin took Aras from him to train him to be a soldier, at the age of twelve, Jarnath had shown no outward sign of caring. Laedrin never suspected the true extent of the healer's influence and affection until the practice session that changed everything.

ARAS had just turned fourteen. Laedrin had pitted him against one of his best men, Marlaenus, though Laedrin was reluctant to acknowledge his prowess; Marlaenus was one of the Guard, the Navy, the Oceana, not the King's Guard, the Army, the Aerta Laedrin favored.

Aras had natural talent; he was born to be a fighter. He might look like his mother, but he fought with his father's hands. Laedrin was watching with pride. It was one of the few times he'd ever felt anything but contempt for the boy.

Marlaenus's men were cheering Aras instead of their own commander, not because they feared not to, but because they saw what a fighter Aras was. Aras was using his twin blades, holding his own against a man twenty times his age.

Marlaenus was the one who slipped and stumbled. He should have been the one who was injured. But Aras twisted himself so his blades would miss Marlaenus when he would have impaled him. The incompetent, soft-hearted fool was so intent upon keeping his opponent from injury that he failed to note his own danger. He fell upon Marlaenus's upraised sword. Laedrin still remembered the look of surprise and dismay upon Aras's face, when he saw the sword protruding from his thigh as he fell.

Then Marlaenus did the worst thing he could have: he instinctively pulled the sword free. Aras's life's blood began spurting from him. Marlaenus had been horrified when he realized the extent of the injury, when he saw the artery had been damaged, that Aras would die before a healer came.

Still, Marlaenus tried to save him. He sliced his sash free with his dagger, balled it together, and pressed his hand to the wound, but the fabric was drenched in blood at the next pulse of Aras's heart. It was hopeless.

Hands shaking, Aras had removed his sheathed dagger. Laedrin thought Aras meant to take Marlaenus to oblivion with him, as Laedrin would have were he the one who lay dying. Instead, Aras removed his own sash and wrapped it about his leg and knotted it, then twined it around the sheathed dagger and began to turn it. He commanded Marlaenus to take it and twist it until the blood stopped flowing and to hold it fast until the healer came. As soon as Marlaenus's hands held it, Aras fainted.

Marlaenus followed his High-Prince's orders, and the bleeding stopped! Marlaenus's men had gathered around him defensively, in silent support of their doomed commander. Laedrin stood at a distance, watching; he could feel the tension in the air. All present knew he would kill Marlaenus for what he had done to his son.

It was then that Jarnath came, with two of Marlaenus's men, who had gone to fetch him. Jarnath was ashen and shaking. When he saw the blood sprayed everywhere, he had almost collapsed, but with the Guards' aid, he made it to Aras's side. "He's alive," Jarnath announced. Laedrin could tell he was shocked to find him so. "How did you know to do this? How did you know how to save him?" Jarnath had asked in wonder when he saw the tourniquet in Marlaenus's hands.

"I did not. It was the High-Prince. He did this before he lost consciousness. He had me twist the knife for him when he no longer could," Marlaenus said.

"You have saved his life by doing so," Jarnath pronounced. "Come, help me carry him to the Hall, so I may save his leg as well."

Laedrin watched them go, all of them. Marlaenus had injured Aras and should have died for it, but he had saved him as well. Jarnath had proclaimed it. Laedrin could not act openly against Marlaenus. He had cursed and left for his rooms in disgust.

The boy lived, but Laedrin did not send for Aras again. He had given up trying to train Aras to be a soldier. Neither he nor his army had any use for a leader who would kill himself on a foe's sword rather than harm him. Aras was not his son. Ithelia's whelp had a healer's heart, not a soldier's. Laedrin had kept contact with the boy to a minimum for the thirty-five years that followed, though he kept a careful watch upon him.

During that time, Aras's popularity with the Navy grew. Nothing overt. He was no danger to his father's crown; Aras's heart was still too soft for that. But Laedrin's spies saw much. Laedrin would have saved himself considerable grief by using them decades before upon Ithelia. They kept a close eye on everyone the High-Prince saw.

Whenever one of the Navy got too close to Aras, he was reassigned to whatever hazardous duty Laedrin could find. Marlaenus died in the mountains, not two months after their combat. Many of his men were lost on river duty. The Navy alone now patrolled the mountains and the distant woods, all the dangerous duty, while the Army patrolled the safer woods surrounding the base. The Navy's shifts were long and hard.

Aras learned the price of his friendship. He soon distanced himself even from Jarnath. Yet still Aras did everything he could to try to win his father's favor. Laedrin was well aware of it. But the boy had his mother's face, her voice. Laedrin hated him more each passing day.

When Aras had turned forty-four and finally begun his formal training, Laedrin made sure he was not treated the same as the other cadets. At his command, his son's instructors were twice as brutal with Aras as with the rest. To his surprise, Aras not only survived the training but excelled in all aspects of it, save for the most crucial: he was a healer, not a warrior. As a soldier, as a son, he was useless.

Laedrin ignored his son's coming-of-age. He was not present for it, he did not acknowledge it. But Aras came to him and would not be denied. He told his father he was an adult. They fought, and for the first time in millennia, Laedrin felt fear.

Aras had never before stood up to him. He was becoming a true threat to him, a danger to his crown. He tried to conceal his fear from his son and thought he had succeeded, until that parting look Aras had given him. Aras had seen his fear, and he had left.

Laedrin should have stopped him, chained him if necessary; he had suspected he might leave the base, though he'd not truly thought Aras possessed the courage to do so. But there had been something in Aras's eyes that had stayed his hand: he'd seen love. Aras loved him, despite all that had ever been said or done between them, as a true son should love his father.

Laedrin had not been loved since his brother Hadrin had been killed, three millennia ago, or at least since his Tree, Arandrin, had fallen silent a millennia ago. Ithelia had certainly never loved him. He had thought his heart turned to ice, but he found he could not bring himself to act against one who loved him. He cursed himself again for his weakness. He would live to regret it, though perhaps not for long.

The night Aras left, Laedrin began to be plagued by nightmares, visions of death: sometimes he lay bleeding and dying and sometimes Aras did. They were portents of evil, of danger. He tried to ignore them, but he could not sleep. Soon he could not eat either. Almost a full week passed. Jarnath noticed. Jarnath saw his weakness. Laedrin suspected Jarnath secretly reveled in his affliction. Yet Laedrin had to confide in him. Jarnath was the only Lord among the healers, the only one with any true healing Power. Laedrin demanded to be cured.

Jarnath gave Laedrin sleeping elixirs. But they succeeded only in trapping him in his slumber. He dreamt such a detailed vision of his own death that he still saw the oozing decay of his arm, felt the weakness of his body, even upon finally awakening.

Days passed, and it only grew worse. Now the dreams were only of Aras, of his death, but still they weakened him, as if they were of his own death instead. Finally, Laedrin gave Jarnath an ultimatum: he had three more nights to cure him, or precisely a fortnight after Aras left, he would execute Jarnath. He made sure Lord of the Guard Ahrnad and his subordinate Alwen were informed and that Jarnath was carefully watched, lest he try to end Laedrin's life first.

Tonight was the final night. Tonight either he slept dreamlessly, or Jarnath would pay the ultimate price for his incompetence.

JARNATH still could not believe Aras had left. He was furious with Laedrin for letting Aras go. How could he have? For all Aras was a man in age, he had led such a sheltered life that he was still truly a child. He would be ill-prepared for the harsh reality of the world outside their Wood. There were so many dangers he might face!

And Aras was ill-supplied. He had taken no medicine with him. His healer's kit was still in his room, and he had not stopped at the Healers' Hall. Jarnath doubted Aras had even thought he might become ill or injured; his last injury was long ago. He doubted Aras had thought to take coin or even food. His every need had been provided for his entire life.

Aras had not said good-bye to him. Jarnath admitted that was what was at the heart of his anguish. Aras had said good-bye to Laedrin, but not to him. He knew the truth, that Aras could not have left had he tried to say good-bye, but still it hurt. He sighed heavily. He knew Aras had had to go. Under the shadow of his father, he would never be able to find himself, never truly come-of-age.

If only he had a friend, someone to journey with, to watch over him, to teach him, to help him, to love him. Aras so desperately needed to be loved. He was so vulnerable. He could be hurt in so many terrible ways by the world.

Elanara would have been good for him. She was older, three hundred, but she had a brother only a year older than Aras. She would have been able to accept his youth, to understand him, even love him. Her father, Laranela, was King of Riviera, Jewel of the River Kingdoms. Laranela was second only to Laedrin in the power he wielded. The union would have done much good for the Kingdoms. And it would have been so easy for Aras to love Elanara. She had beauty and grace but also warmth. Her lips still knew how to smile, her heart how to laugh.

Jarnath was thankful Aras had been kept from her, for propriety's sake, until he came-of-age. Aras had not had the opportunity to fall in love with her before their betrothal was broken and she was instead pledged to wed Prince Talon. Aras's heart would be lost so easily to the first person who showed him warmth and compassion and kindness.

For now he was the one who held Aras's heart close to his own. He had been more of a father to Aras than Laedrin ever was. Laedrin did not have a heart. He did not think to miss it. Laedrin had a sword. What need for a heart? Hearts only spurt out your life's blood when wounded. Hearts betray everyone in the end. Ultimately, of every death, one could say, "His heart has stopped."

Jarnath again wished he had the courage to stop Laedrin's heart. If Aras had loved Elanara, he would have. If Laedrin had broken Aras's heart when he altered the betrothal, forcing King Laranela to wed his only daughter to a Man, he would have destroyed Laedrin's heart; he possessed a number of medicines that might be used to that effect. Not that he needed any of them. He could drain Laedrin's life away with a single, simple touch. Jarnath shuddered at the beguiling and repulsive thought and reminded himself for the thousandth time he must not harbor such dark thoughts, that they were slowly destroying his own heart.

Jarnath had never liked the High-King—for his coldness, his cruelty, his bigotry—but he had respected him and understood the reasons for his faults far better than any save a few ever could. As a Lord, one of the few who had lived through the War, Jarnath certainly understood far better than the three generations that had lived and died under Laedrin's reign since. They knew no other life. They owed Laedrin for their very existence. Their forbearers would never have escaped the Homeland without Laedrin to lead them; they would have been incinerated in the Annihilation with all the many millions who had perished. What they had survived, what they had endured, had changed them all.

Memory seized Jarnath, and his thoughts were drawn to the darkest days of the War, to the even darker days before the Insurrection he and a handful of others had secretly been instrumental in instigating. They never would have done so had they known the cost, the price they would all pay in attaining freedom from their creators, their oppressors: the blood of millions was on their hands. Jarnath fought against the familiar crushing depression, the guilt that threatened to consume him. Praise Aralyn and Ragnar both that Aras did not know, that he would never know what they had done, and why!

Even the simple, silent prayer was an act of rebellion against those who had once enslaved them. The Oceana and the Aerta worshipped no Gods; neither had the Faeren or the Aerie. Of all their peoples, only the Houerfashang and the Latents had ever done so in the many millennia of their recorded history.

Not that Jarnath truly believed their written history, not any more. Jarnath now knew that history was not written by the victors, but by the survivors. His people had won the War, if anyone at all could be said to have done so, but they had been all but obliterated in their victory. The Faeren and the Aerie, who had truly both become extinct in the single, final, horrific act of defiance that had destroyed their Homeland, had become the convenient scapegoats for the War.

There was no mention of the Insurrection, or even the Houerfashang or Latents, in any surviving book in Nalea or the Seven Kingdoms. The very word "slavery" had been stricken from their merged language, blacked out in their dictionaries. The pages regarding the Procreation Ban and all the other laws pertaining to their kind had been torn from their legal tomes. Laedrin himself had seen that the offending pages of law concerning their subjugation and the alchemical tomes detailing their creation were stripped from the Library of Riviera and incinerated three millennia ago. He lit the fire personally and watched the pages burn, to ensure only ash remained. To speak or write about any of it was punishable by death.

The War of Emancipation instead became known as the War of Flame or the War of the Wind, depending upon whether the Faeren or the Aerie were cast as the primary villain. The truth was buried under millennia of half-truths and outright lies and forgotten by almost all. Jarnath had never believed the ancient saying that a lie told often enough becomes the truth, until he'd witnessed it firsthand.

Jarnath sighed, the weight of the knowledge heavy upon him. Had his beloved Shiaera lived, she would have written the truth defiantly, in spite of the cost. Lithunia, their master strategist and chronicler, would have written a history of their people that would have made even the strongest and coldest among them weep. Both would have ensured no one would ever forget. He shamed their memories, and those of the many others who had died, with his silence. But he had little choice. He would not only be endangering himself, but some few precious others who had survived and reproduced in secret.

Jarnath had at first only suspected that some few other Latents in addition to him might live, that freed now from the Procreation Ban and in hiding they might breed unchecked, that their recessive traits might be passed down to their offspring and come to the fore. After the first accidental one, Latents might have been artificially created from an unnatural alchemical fusion of the essence of those of the four races combined with select females of Dwarven stock, but they could breed naturally as well. They should be encouraged to, were the world a kinder, gentler, more sane place. Latents were natural healers. They could sense emotional and physical distress in others, diagnose it, and cure it. Even here, in their new lands, where the soil and water were weak in Power, they thrived.

The life spans of the Aerta and Oceana shrank from ten millennia to a mere single millennium in their adopted home, except for those few fortunate Aerta Lords blessed by their symbiotic relationship with the Trees of the Lords' Grove. But the

Latents depended upon neither the diluted waters nor stunted Power of the trees to sustain them. They drew their Power from every living creature around them, gently and steadily banking it within themselves for when they had need of it, like living gem-batteries, biological equivalents of the carefully crafted jewels Men called *Elfstones*. Latents flourished where all others faltered, and in turn, they could heal those who were sick or injured in mind or body, imparting their own strength to others.

Laedrin mistakenly believed that Jarnath's Power came from the Lords' Grove, from Aranath, the Tree he was bonded to, as the Power of every other surviving Aerta Lord and Lady came from his or her Tree. Laedrin would have been appalled to learn the opposite was true: the Trees' waning Power instead came from Jarnath, and they in turn gifted what little they could spare to the Lords and Ladies with whom they had a symbiotic connection. Jarnath sustained the Grove through the countless cadets and soldiers of Nalea who surrounded him, from the minute Power he siphoned off of each of them. Never enough to harm; only enough to ensure the survival of the Trees of the Grove and thereby those who relied upon them, plus those few injured Aerta and Oceana in need of healing.

As a result of such misdirection, Laedrin had been ignorant of the survival of the other Latents, until Laranela and Naraena. Those two were far too powerful when they should not be: they were both Oceana, they had no Tree to sustain them, yet they were nearly as strong as if they had such a bond. When Laedrin discovered it, he knew what they must be. Had Laranela not been the son of the King and Queen of Riviera and Naraena not been a gifted and well-loved healer, he'd have slain them both, but he could not act openly against them. Instead, he merely kept a relentless eye upon their parents, and upon them, to insure the two were kept far apart from one another. He dared not let them meet. Even knowing it would likely cause civil war, he'd slay them both before he'd ever risk them potentially mating, for what he perceived would be the nightmare that might be born from their union.

That they met anyway, that they'd married and mated before he realized it, in defiance of his machinations and then his commands, enraged Laedrin. He could not kill Laranela, who at the tragic death of his parents had become King of Riviera, nor Naraena, now a Queen, so instead he turned his fear and his rage upon all of the Oceana under his command. The entire Navy was made to suffer for the crimes of only two of their people. But Laranela was from Riviera, Naraena was from Tanieria, and they had met, married, and mated in Salenia, so in Laedrin's mind, all three of the River Kingdoms had betrayed him.

Repercussions notwithstanding, Jarnath did not doubt Laedrin would have killed any of the royal couple's three children in the cradle, had he or she been born a Houerfashang. Each child was carefully watched, through adolescence and into maturity. It was to the Royal Family's fortune that their eldest and youngest children, Elavar and Eladar, both sons, were born Latents, and their middle child, Elanara, their daughter, was born an Inert, with only the recessive trait locked away inside her.

But because of them and their parents before them, Laedrin suspected there were others. He became obsessed with finding them. Fortunately, Jarnath had been able to warn the few he knew of, and they and any others safely hid from the High-King. It was the ultimate irony that the one place Laedrin did not look was in his own bedchamber and then his own nursery: Laedrin had never suspected that his wife, Ithelia, was a Latent, or that in turn, his son Aras was one. Even now he did not. And of course, Aras did not know. He must never know. Jarnath would ensure Aras was kept mercifully ignorant of the horror of his heritage. He was far too gentle a spirit; the truth would likely destroy him.

Aranath had been most insistent that Jarnath keep the secret of his own nature hidden from Ithelia, and so he had never confronted her about her own, though he had often wondered where she had truly come from and whether she had come to Nalea specifically with the intention of wedding Laedrin all along. She was only a Latent, but she was a particularly strong one, with nearly the seductive Power and enticing skill of a Houerfashang.

Jarnath wished for the thousandth time that Aras, the son-of-his-heart, lived in one of the Seven Kingdoms, the idyllic, utopian recreation of the flawed society they had lost, instead of here in Nalea, on the military base that housed the soldiers who protected the illusion-turned-reality. Nalea might no longer be populated by the battle-hardened, physically and mentally scarred soldiers of the War, but the men and women here were a far cry from their civilian kin. Jarnath had lamented Aras's lost childhood, he had bemoaned the callous way Laedrin treated Aras, but he had never truly hated Laedrin until the day Laedrin had almost killed his own son.

ARAS had been only fourteen, thirty years shy of the age when a child normally began his military training, yet his father had already been training him for two years. This time he was forcing Aras to spar with one of his best soldiers, neither of them armored as they should be.

Two soldiers had come running to the Healers' Hall. "Come quickly! The High-Prince is dying!" they'd told him. Not hurt, but dying. Jarnath had grabbed his medicines and run.

They told him breathlessly what had happened as they kept pace beside him. Their commander Marlaenus had stumbled and Aras had injured himself while saving Marlaenus.

Jarnath saw the blood in the dirt and on the soldier by Aras's side and knew he was too late. But Aras yet lived. Miraculously, the soldier had applied a tourniquet to his leg. He'd done everything right, except he still held the sheathed dagger. He hadn't tied it off as he could have. Jarnath did so, telling Marlaenus he'd saved Aras's life. He had him help carry Aras to the Healers' Hall. As they carried him, Jarnath commented that Laedrin wasn't there when he should be; his son was in shock and might yet die. Jarnath was so distraught he couldn't keep silent, even knowing his criticism might easily be labeled treason.

But then Aras's eyes had opened, and he had astonished Jarnath by smiling weakly up at him. "I won't die, teacher. I do not truly sleep. I could have finished the tourniquet myself—I still had strength enough—but I had to save Marlaenus. I think he might be safe now. With your words, Father might let him live. You played your part well, Jarnath."

"You speak as if this were a game," Jarnath had said, appalled.

Such an odd look came over Aras's face then. "But it is a Game. Only they think I am just another one of the pawns, like my poor father. They do not know I am also a Player. They think they are winning, but they are wrong. In the end, I will win, you will see. I must go. Mother is calling me again. She is going to scold me, but it's all right. I'm not truly afraid of her any more. It's all just part of the Game. Even she must die with the other two in the end. Only one Player can live. Those are the rules. I am not the one who made them: they did. But I always play fair, always by the rules. That is why I will win." Then his eyes closed.

Jarnath was convinced that Aras was in shock, delirious from his injury. Yet something about what Aras had said and how he had said it chilled him.

Jarnath had saved Aras's life and his leg. But something was still wrong with the boy. He eyed Jarnath so strangely. Jarnath finally asked what was troubling him.

"I should not have told you about the Game. I was weaker than I knew and not thinking clearly, from the blood loss and also for Mother's screaming. She was so angry with me, for nearly dying before I could fulfill her purpose. It is so hard, sometimes, to keep her at bay, to keep my thoughts my own, without her knowing, to let her think she controls me."

Jarnath was truly concerned, then. "Aras, what are you talking about? Your mother vanished when you were eight. She has been gone these six years past. Do you know where she is? Have you been seeing her in secret?"

Aras looked about the empty room carefully, but it was as if he sought to see past the walls, into the corridors and rooms outside. "I know where Mother is. She is far from this place, but I can hear her voice still. She speaks to me."

Jarnath looked at him warily and Aras laughed. "No, I am not mad, Jarnath, my teacher. I hear your voice as well, even when you are far from me; there is such kindness and caring and healing about you. You keep much hidden that I should like to know, but I would never violate your trust. I listen only to those thoughts you broadcast openly, though I know I miss much by not delving deeper.

"Father's thoughts are the diametrical opposite to yours, vicious and violent and grim; his mind is so like Mother's, yet with only a hint of Power. I cannot help but think that once there was far more to him. I wish there was still. I pity him his shadow life." Aras had sighed then, as if the weight of the world lay upon his slender shoulders, and looked at him with eyes both sad and wise, ancient before their time.

But then he smiled and his face lit with all the joy of youth. "But I hear a few others as well. They are so very different! Meloneth sings to me. All his thoughts are lyrics and there is always music accompanying them. It is very distracting, but so beautiful that I do not mind. Etheria thinks not in words but in images. It is as if her mind is filled with paintings and each sentence is a stroke of her brush. Areth's thoughts are wonderful, so full of life. I listen to her for hours on end.

"It is only the Lords and Ladies I can hear, and most of even their voices are not strong enough to fully make out. It is as if they are mumbling to me. Once I thought everyone heard as I do, but I learned long ago that I am special in that regard."

"You could not possibly have such Power. You speak as if you were a wizard, but you cannot truly hear our thoughts or know our hearts. It is like your talk of the Game, a child's fancy, nothing more," Jarnath argued desperately. Aras revealed too much! If he said such things where his father's spies could hear, his father might learn his horrible secret!

Aras had smiled at him then, such an odd smile, a knowing smile. The hairs on the back of Jarnath's neck had stood up, and he had felt himself drawing away from Aras, fearing he might be in more danger from him than his father. But then it was as if a blanket of warmth and love descended upon him, and his fear vanished. He knew that even were Aras powerful enough to someday learn all the terrible secrets he kept, he still would have nothing to fear from Aras.

IN THE almost four decades since, neither he nor Aras had ever spoken of such things again. But now Aras was gone and Laedrin was plagued by nightmares of death, Aras's death. Jarnath wondered at first if Aras might be sending Laedrin visions to torment him, but he could not believe it. Even if Aras had the Power to do so, he would not. After nearly five decades of rejection, he still loved his father as any son might. He still desperately sought his approval, his love.

Jarnath realized he must turn elsewhere for aid. The wizard Magus was in the City on business for Arcanus. He had yet to meet either of them, or their compatriot Circe. He'd purposefully kept his distance the few times they were in Nalea, lest whatever Power they possessed might pierce the veil of the secrets he kept. But this time Jarnath would seek an audience with Magus and beg him for his aid. He would tell Magus only that Laedrin was plagued by nightmares, dark visions of his son's death, and ask that he perform a scry to calm and reassure the High-King.

MARCUS hesitated, eyeing Jarnath intently. He had only come to deliver Arcanus's message. He had not expected to work any magicks while here. Arcanus had warned them over and over that their Power was not to be used lightly, that they were never to undertake any major magicks without his knowledge. But though a scry was complex, it required great skill rather than great Power. It would not drain him. Marcus had done scryes before, always successfully and never to ill effect; how could there be, when one was only viewing something from a distance? High-King Laedrin was an important ally to them. Should he not put the High-King's mind at ease regarding his son, since it was within his power to do so?

"Of course. The best time for such a viewing is after dusk, but before midnight," Marcus said, automatically adding the air of mystery Arcanus required. The cloaks, most of the mumbled words, except for those few words of Power, the gestures, even their staves: how surprised people would be were they ever to learn it was all just window dressing, trappings! Their Power came from within, from their cores, just as the weaker Power of their distant cousins the Amontir did.

Realistically, the timing Marcus had named meant they would probably view Aras eating his dinner, or sleeping, either of which was comforting and innocuous enough. Marcus didn't think he needed to worry about catching Aras doing something other than eating or sleeping. Even if he were in one of the Elven Kingdoms, one did not casually bed the son of the High-King.

"Am I correct in assuming you would also like to be present?" Marcus asked Jarnath.

"Yes, if that would not affect the scry," Jarnath said, his eagerness readily apparent.

"No, it would have no ill effect to have the two of you there. The best place would be the High-Prince's room, as his aura would be most pronounced there," Marcus said. Really, he only needed to touch something that belonged to the High-Prince, but his room would offer privacy.

"I am very grateful to you. I will tell the High-King," Jarnath said, leaving with startling abruptness for an Elf Lord.

Marcus smiled under his hood. He did not even need to review the steps for scrying. He was familiar enough with them. He went to the Lords' Grove to await dusk. As an honored guest of the High-King, he had been permitted entry. It was quiet there, and private.

Marcus looked up at the ancient Trees around him, sacred to the Elf Lords and Ladies of Nalea, and wondered whether the Trees could truly hear and think and feel as they were rumored to. He ached to touch one and see. He was sure his Power would reveal the truth to him, but it was forbidden, and he would not break the taboos of these people, nor pit his own magicks against those of the Trees, if they truly had any.

The needles of one of the Trees stirred overhead. Marcus looked up curiously. The other Trees were not affected by whatever wind stirred the needles of the cedar. It was almost as if it were whispering to him.

Suddenly, he was seized by an urge to speak. "I am Marcus, son of Lianara of Riviera," he said, then stopped, appalled. He had spoken his true name! Why would he have done such a thing?

He looked at the Tree suspiciously. The needles were rustling more briskly, almost as if the Tree might be laughing at him. He looked about uneasily, but none of the other Trees seemed interested in him.

Perhaps it would be better to wait elsewhere, but it was dusk already; the last rays of the sun were gently kissing the treetops. He resisted the urge to leave. He would not let these Trees intimidate him. He was the second most powerful wizard west of the Dwarven Lands.

Of course, there were only the three of them, him and Arcanus and Selene. Selene insisted she was more powerful, but she was younger, only just thirty-three, and he was thirty-six, nearly thirty-seven, although to Men they looked far younger, perhaps seventeen and eighteen, for she was a half-Dwarf and he a half-Oceana. It rankled that his mother's people did not even consider him an adult yet.

It was blatantly apparent Selene was yet a child. She was certainly never serious enough about her talents, for all they'd both been training with Arcanus since before they could walk. Marcus was sure he must be stronger than she was. Arcanus was careful to avoid the issue whenever they asked by sending them off to run errands for him. They'd learned not to ask.

Marcus glared up at the Tree. He was sure it was laughing at him now. Which meant it could read his thoughts, which was not at all fair, because he had no idea what it was thinking, and he had not been rude enough to touch it, and... he swallowed. The needles had stopped rustling.

The Grove was suddenly quiet, still as death. Something was wrong, something terrible. He was able to sense that much, and it frightened him.

Marcus left the Grove quickly, too quickly. He had forgotten the slender birch, the tree set slightly outside the circle of the rest. He almost ran headlong into it, swerving just in time to avoid it, except for his right hand, which brushed lightly against the bark.

Agony shot through his left arm and his chest and his right foot, and he heard a scream of pain and terror and loss. He stumbled, and his hand fell away from the bark. The pain was gone, the scream gone. It was the Tree! The Tree had been screaming!

Marcus looked at the birch, horrified at what he had done, at what he had felt. He kowtowed before the Tree. "Forgive me! I did not mean to touch you," he said in the mode of subject to king. His heart was hammering. He did not think the Tree was listening to him. How could it be listening, with what he had just felt?

He should not have come here. He did not think he had done any harm by it. He hoped he had not. Marcus left quickly, looking behind him at the Trees of the Grove. They were weeping, all of them. He did not know how he knew, but he did.

He turned away, not sure what he would have done if he had seen the tall cedar or one of the other larger trees reach its branches out to console the smaller birch. He had the oddest feeling that they might, were they able.

Marcus concentrated on his breathing, slowing it and steadying it, as he headed for the Palace, then stopped. His core was a jangled mass now. He could not work magicks with it like this. It would not just be difficult, it would be dangerous. He had to find calm, to regain his center.

Jarnath and the High-King might already be waiting for him. He had said after dusk, though he had not specified when. It would be dangerous to keep the High-King waiting. But there was a stream near the edge of the woods, and he desperately needed the sound and feel of running water.

He ran for the edge of the woods, glad this part of the City was deserted. No one should ever see a wizard run: wizards only walked with dignity or glided or sometimes even flew.

The sight of the stream calmed him, and the sound, and when he sank his hands into the icy waters, a shiver ran the length of his body. He wanted only to lie naked within the stream and let the waters pass over him.

He contented himself with pulling back his hood, bending down, and letting the water rush across his face. Then he thrust his head full into the stream; he could not help himself. The sound and feel of the cold rushing water soothed his mind.

After remaining there for as long as he dared, he rose and wrung the water from his long silver hair with his hands, glad for the hood to conceal his wet hair. Of course, the ways of wizards were strange. They would not ask, but still, they would wonder about his hair. But at least he was calm again, if a little nervous at keeping them waiting.

Marcus forced himself to walk at a sedate pace to the Palace. The King's Guard allowed him entry and escorted him to the High-Prince's room. High-King Laedrin and Jarnath were already there. The High-King was speaking.

"… think this is going to keep me from executing you…," Marcus heard as the door opened, then the sentence abruptly broke off.

Executing? Whatever was going on?

He entered the room outwardly calm, grateful for the hood, which hid his face from view. He knew with a single glance at them that it had been a mistake for him to agree to the scry. The High-King was glowering at Jarnath. It had not been an idle threat.

Marcus forced an air of dignity about himself as he removed his hood, painfully conscious of his wet hair. "High-King. Healer," he said, nodding in greeting.

He fought the urge to bow, even to kowtow, at the High-King's feet. Laedrin was so like Arcanus, powerful and potentially deadly when angry. He must tread carefully here.

"Please, sit," Marcus instructed, and was relieved when they both obeyed, although the High-King was watching him with a look of challenge upon his face.

Marcus began walking about the room, touching things here and there with his fingertips. The room was so bare; it revealed little of its owner. His eyes fell upon the large mirror on the wall. It was exquisite. It was not merely of polished metal, as most mirrors were, but was made of silvered glass, framed by solid silver, ornately detailed. It would be ideal for the scry itself, but he still needed something that might help him locate the High-Prince.

He admired his own reflection in the mirror. Seldom did he get a chance to view himself so clearly: blue eyes, fine features, long silver hair, gracefully upswept ears. He touched his reflection in the glass and almost drew back his hand, he was so startled. The High-Prince's aura was so strong upon the mirror! How vain he must be, to study himself so intently in the mirror that it would be as strong as that!

If it were Arcanus's mirror, Marcus might think he was studying himself in introspection, or focusing his Power. Or even communicating through it.

He'd caught Arcanus doing so by mistake, once. He shuddered at the memory. Arcanus had been raging, screaming at his mirror in a language he'd only heard scraps of here and there in the most complex magicks Arcanus worked. There'd been a face looking back at him, one not his own. Marcus had not been able to see it clearly: he'd seen only a glimpse of breathtaking beauty, of red-orange hair and red eyes.

Arcanus's face had darkened in fury, his eyes had glowed red, his wrinkles had vanished, and his white hair had darkened to burnt sienna: for an instant it was as if Arcanus's face and form had transformed into something quite different from that of the wizened old Man who mentored him, something bearing an unsettling resemblance to the face in the mirror. Then Arcanus had ripped the mirror from the wall and smashed it to the ground. Shattered glass had sprayed everywhere, and Marcus had fled, terrified Arcanus might catch him watching while so enraged and might kill him for it.

Marcus forced himself to calm. Even the memory of it terrified him.

He grasped both sides of the frame firmly and lifted the mirror up and off the wall. It was heavy; he must be careful not to damage it. He laid the mirror on a small table, glass upwards. Reaching into his robe, he pulled forth his water pouch and poured a thin film of water over the surface of the mirror, muttering some exotic-sounding words. He always used the same words when he performed a scry, lest he ever have to perform a second one on the same individual, so he would not arouse the slightest suspicion of the charlatanry of it all. Waving his staff over the glass for added effect, he focused his thoughts upon it, waiting for the High-Prince's image to appear. With such a surface he should have a scry of unsurpassed clarity.

The water changed. It clouded and grew dark, dark as ink. Marcus was startled but did his best to hide it. It wasn't supposed to do that! It had never done that before. What in the world was the matter? "The High-Prince is in a place of great darkness," Marcus improvised, stalling for time.

Marcus muttered more words and focused more of his Power, all of it; he had no choice. He could not stop with such a result. What would the High-King think? But he had never intended to use so much Power. He should not be doing this without Arcanus here to oversee it, or at the very least, to give his permission.

The water rippled then, as if a stone had been cast upon a lake. The impenetrable blackness at the center of the mirror lightened, and to his relief, he could see the beginnings of a face.

Marcus was sweating from the strain. He saw his hand was trembling, but he could not stop it. Then suddenly, the image in the mirror grew clear. It snapped into focus. He saw an Elven face, so ethereally beautiful he gasped, his own vanity forgotten. But the face was pale as moonlight, pale as death.

The image grew to the edges of the mirror. The Elf was in the woods far from here. Marcus had never before been able to feel distance in a scry as sharply as he did this time. He was one hundred fifty miles at a good pace from where Marcus stood. Marcus was horrified at what the mirror now revealed. The High-Prince was in the jaws of a monstrous wolven! Its jaws were clamped tightly about Aras's chest, and there was blood, so much blood! Aras was speaking, asking for forgiveness. He knew he was dying.

Laedrin and Jarnath were both bent closely over the mirror. It was so odd: he could see their reflections in the High-Prince's eyes. It was as if Aras could see them as well, through the mirror, as if he were speaking directly to them.

Marcus watched helplessly. How could someone so beautiful die? If only he could help him! Without thinking, almost as if he no longer guided his own hand, he touched the water.

It was as if a knife pierced his heart and his life's blood spurted from his chest. In an instant all his Power, his very life's energy, drained from him, pouring into the glass of the mirror, past the glass, somehow, toward the image or the darkness surrounding it. Marcus yanked his hand away in terror and fought to keep on his feet. The mirror suddenly shattered, spraying broken glass and water everywhere.

He and Laedrin and Jarnath were driven to their knees as they were lashed by glass. Marcus was protected by his heavy cloak, but he saw the other two bleeding from dozens of tiny wounds. As if from very far away, he heard the High-King say, "My son is dead," in a voice of wood. Then he rose and walked out of the room.

Marcus and Jarnath got shakily to their feet as well. Marcus's mind was in turmoil; he was reeling from the disaster of it all. The High-Prince was dead, and something had taken his Power from him, drained him of his very life! Marcus was terrified by his own weakness. He could scarcely stand!

He needed the stream. He was too weak for the river; he would drown. He must sleep, regain what strength he might, to be strong enough to walk to the stream. Right now he did not have strength enough to leave the room.

"Please, you must try again! He cannot be gone," Jarnath implored.

Marcus was surprised at the depth of emotion the healer revealed. This was no mere love for his High-Prince; it was as if he had lost his own son. Marcus could use the healer's grief to his advantage. "The High-Prince was surrounded by dark magicks. I must meditate in order to focus all my powers against them." He was pleased with himself: he sounded powerful and wise, rather than weak and helpless. "If I might use the High-Prince's room, as his aura is strongest here."

"Of course. Whatever you need is yours," Jarnath readily agreed.

I need to be carried to the stream, Marcus thought, but did not give voice to his thoughts.

"I will see you are undisturbed," Jarnath said. Marcus nodded and the healer bowed and left, closing the door behind him.

Marcus sagged, collapsing onto the High-Prince's bed. What if he weakened further, or if no strength returned? He might die in this room!

A soft knock interrupted his dark musing, and he forced himself to his feet. "Enter," Marcus said, then cursed his stupidity. He should have ordered them away. But it was Jarnath.

"Forgive me, Honored One. I hope I am not being presumptuous, but I realized I should have offered you anosar, to restore your strength, in case you are in need of it. You look fatigued. I do not know for certain it would work in this instance, but I was remiss in not thinking to do so immediately."

And I was a simpleton to overlook the fact that I had a healer at my disposal! Marcus thought. "Thank you, Healer. Your offer is accepted," Marcus said aloud, with all the dignity he could muster.

"I will fetch some immediately," Jarnath said and left.

Marcus sank back onto the bed. Perhaps he might live through the night after all.

It seemed Jarnath was gone for an eternity, but Marcus knew he must have been quick. He accepted the flask from him, trying not to look desperate.

"You should drink three sips at a time at the most. It is extremely potent, very rare, and highly valued. The effects are immediate, and you must wait eight hours before drinking again, if you have the need. There is a water clock on the mantle, there, to aid you in tracking the time. It is crucial you not imbibe too much at once, or too often," Jarnath warned. "The flask I gave you is full. You may save the rest, in case you ever have need of it again. It will keep indefinitely as long as the stopper is in place."

Marcus had not even noticed the clock before. He took careful note of the time, as instructed. "Thank you, Healer," Marcus said respectfully.

Once Jarnath left, he broke the seal of the flask. He forced himself to sip when he would have drunk greedily. He felt instant warmth course through him. His hand, which had been shaking from the all but negligible weight of the flask, stilled, but he felt no other change. He drank two more sips. He began to tingle; the odd feeling started in his ears and radiated inwards. The room seemed brighter. He hadn't realized his vision had been affected before. And his hearing seemed more keen. He wondered then if his perceptions were being altered. Might that be where the danger lay in the drink, why it must only be sipped and over a certain length of time?

He tried to walk. His knees did not buckle under him. He might make it to the stream, now. No, he would first rest here. He would sleep in the High-Prince's bed. He would no longer need the stream, at least not immediately.

Marcus shuddered as he lay down upon the dead High-Prince's bed. Aras had been young to die, barely an adult, not twenty years older than he was. *I will not die so young. I will be more careful in the future,* he thought confidently.

Arcanus would be angry with him when he learned what had happened. Perhaps he wouldn't tell him? No, that would be worse, to try to hide it. Arcanus would find out anyway, and then he would be furious. He'd seen Arcanus enraged only a few times. Even Selene was scared of him, then.

Marcus thought longingly of his sister. She would be pitiless in her ridicule, but she would also be warm and caring and would gift him with her own strength. She would rejuvenate him. He sighed. She was far from this place. Perhaps she would touch his dreams while he slept.

But his dreams were instead visited by something dark, something monstrous. He fled screaming from it and awoke still screaming. He clamped his hand over his mouth to muffle his screams, then pressed his face into the pillow until he finally forced himself to silence.

Something horrible had spoken to him, truly seen him in his dream. It had reached out to touch him. "It was just a dream," he told himself out loud, over and over. But it was not. It was much more. The dream had the power and clarity of memory, of reality. It was the darkness from the woods about the High-Prince; it was the Enemy that Arcanus had so carefully hidden them from: Incuban.

Marcus heard the voice again, every terrifying word. *I see you, Marcus, son of Lianara of Riviera. You are delicious. I will enjoy dining upon you, touching you, teaching you, tasting you. And you will enjoy tasting me. It is futile to run. You are already mine.*

Marcus had run screaming from the threat, and the voice had laughed. Incuban had let him escape, let him waken, as if it were all some sort of sick, twisted game to him. Only Marcus had not escaped. He knew the moment he shut his eyes Incuban would return. Incuban was toying with him, as a cat does with a mouse he captures, before he devours it. He must go to the stream! He needed more strength. He was not a mouse; he was an Oceana, a wizard. He would not die so easily.

Marcus left the room without difficulty. Fortunately, the King's Guard let him leave the Palace without question as well. He headed for the small stream by the Guest House near the Lords' Grove. He stripped off his bright blue cloak, soft blue pants, shirt, and undergarment. He shivered in the cold night air as he walked naked into the stream.

The water was colder now than during the day, refreshing and invigorating. He lay down in it. It was freezing! He shook with the cold but held his breath determinedly and let the stream's Power flow over him. Finally, when his lungs felt as if they would burst, he sat up and inhaled the crisp night air eagerly. Then he repeated the process, over and over.

Gradually, he felt the Power of the stream flow into him, replenishing much of the energy that had drained away in the scry. He would stay here until just before dawn and then return to Aras's room. He would pretend to do a second scry for Jarnath just after dawn, reaffirm Aras was dead, then go. He felt no guilt at the deception. Aras had been dying. He'd seen it, they all had. Incuban had killed him, or the darkness of the woods had, or the wolven. He was unquestionably dead by now. But Marcus would not be.

As he'd planned, Marcus returned to the High-Prince's room just before dawn. Just after dawn, there was a knock upon his door. He did not need to seek Jarnath. Jarnath was there, apologetic and eager. He looked like he had not slept either. Marcus assured Jarnath the power of daylight would cut through the darkness.

Aras had a second mirror, a smaller one. Marcus used the same pointless ritual, but this time worked no magicks, though he pretended to. "I can find no trace of him. I am sorry, but he is dead, he is gone. You must grieve for your High-Prince. Your people must grieve. I must inform Arcanus of Aras's death. I will leave immediately."

Jarnath nodded and mumbled his thanks. As Marcus left he saw Jarnath look about the empty room desolately. Then Jarnath's shoulders began to shake and he fell to his knees, openly sobbing. Marcus closed the door, troubled. Elves seldom wept and Elders never did, yet Jarnath was overwrought. Marcus suddenly felt guilty for lying to him, but then scoffed at the sentiment. He was being foolish. Aras was dead, scry or not, and he had himself to worry about now.

Marcus went to the stables. He had not come on a horse, but he would leave on one. "Honored One," the stable master said reverently when he saw him.

"I have urgent business elsewhere. I need your fastest horse," Marcus said, careful to sound commanding rather than desperate.

"At once, Honored One," the stable master said. He brought a dappled gray stallion to him. "His name is Stormcloud. There are none faster, though he has a temper to match his name. He is a messenger, but he is trained also as a war-horse, as are all our steeds."

Marcus nodded. He leapt upon Stormcloud's wide, bare back, grasped his mane, and immediately urged him to a gallop. He flew down the path toward the Sarashen River. He'd ride along it for the short distance to the Tahir River, go along it to the Western Road, and then head west, either to Logareth or Fenemal. He needed to mask himself within the teaming life of a city so Incuban could not easily find him.

Marcus rode long and hard, putting the danger far behind him. He couldn't understand, though, why he hadn't come to the Road yet. He looked toward the sun, to gauge how long he had ridden, and knew horror. No! It could not be!

Either the sun was setting in the east, not the west, or his mind had somehow become clouded. He had inexplicably turned the wrong way at the fork. He had been riding northwest instead of southeast all this time, heading into the wilds, the mountains. Fenemal must be at least a hundred miles to the south of him! And he must waste more time now, heading further north until he intersected the Methris River and then turning to follow it downstream. He could not risk cutting through the woods and becoming disoriented, especially when he could no longer trust his own senses not to deceive him. At least the route along the riverbank would be quicker than through the dense woods.

Finally, he was able to turn Stormcloud, constantly checking his direction against the sun in his paranoia. Then he began the long route south, downriver, alternating Stormcloud's pace between a gallop and a walk and a trot, dependent upon the terrain and what he thought the horse could bear.

The sun set, night fell, and still he pressed on, by moonlight, careful of direction, navigating by the stars as Arcanus had taught him to. It was halfway to dawn when he finally stopped. His body ached from being so long on horseback. He was hungry, thirsty, exhausted, and Stormcloud must graze and sleep. He rubbed Stormcloud down, praising him for his endurance and setting him loose to graze; he was well trained and would not stray far. He ate a meal of cold provisions. He dared not light a fire. Fire would draw Incuban to him. He fought against sleep but finally succumbed.

Marcus awoke shaking in horror and saw the sun just beginning to set. He had been trapped in sleep the night and a full day, possibly more than one. He opened his shirt. With a trembling finger, he touched the faint round dots splattered on his chest, the thin red lines upon his stomach where there should be none, ghostly remnants from the dream, and he remembered. He felt the searing agony and the ecstasy of the melted wax upon his bare chest and loins and the caress of the silken cords that had bound him. He heard the crack of the whip that had made his heart race, felt the kiss of the lash upon his naked stomach that had made his manhood stiffen in desire. And Incuban's touch upon him, inside him, over and over again.

Marcus rose and stumbled and cried out in pain. He could scarcely walk for the pain; how could he ride the horse, how could he sit? Sobbing in relief, amazed that Stormcloud was still there by his side, he laid a hand upon his warm withers. He stroked the stallion's proud back and then his muscled legs, his hands caressing further downward and over to the horse's member. Stormcloud danced away from him, angrily stomping his hooves, baring his teeth at him. Marcus looked at his hand in horror and at the horse that had been trained to lash out with its hooves to cave in enemy chests and skulls, to trample fallen foes.

Marcus began whimpering deep in his throat, then fell to his knees and curled into a tight ball. Stormcloud stepped cautiously away from him. He could call to Selene to aid him. If he led Incuban to Arcanus, Arcanus would kill him for it. But Selene had talents of her own that Arcanus had forbidden her to use; she truly was stronger than he was. She might be able to resist Incuban where he could not. Or perhaps enjoy his attentions. Marcus could flee while Incuban pleasured himself upon his sister.

Marcus recoiled in horror at the thought not his own. Even now, awake in the fading light, Incuban influenced him. He could not call her. He was an Oceana. He was strong, he would endure. He reached for his water pouch, opened the flask, and took a large swallow from it, then corked it again. It burned going down, his throat, his stomach; it radiated fire across every nerve of his body. What had he done? He'd reached for his water pouch, not the flask of anosar! But he'd uncorked it instead, he'd drunk from it, he'd gulped it. He'd taken too much!

The world exploded in sound and color and light. He heard laughter, terrible laughter, as Incuban came to him again while his senses were warped by the drink. All that had gone before was as nothing compared to the depravities forced upon him now, the twisted games of mind and body that left him a quivering, whimpering mass in the dirt. A day might have passed, or a week, or a month, he neither knew nor cared. He saw only that Stormcloud was gone. His one hope for escape had vanished.

Marcus screamed for Selene and then for Arcanus, in his terror and desperation activating the forbidden bonds. He begged, he whimpered; he would die if Incuban came to him a fourth time. He was so weak. Incuban was feeding upon his core, draining the life from him even as he somehow violated his body through his mind in his sleep.

Marcus reached with trembling hands for the anosar, terrified it might be empty, terrified it might not be. He forced his hand away without checking. His arm was frighteningly thin. How long had he lain here without eating, without thinking, trapped in the merciless, mind-warping dreams? Why hadn't Incuban or his servants come to claim his body while he lay helpless?

So you'd summon your father, Escolier, and your sister Selene for me, so I can defeat three enemies in a single stroke, a laughing voice said in his mind.

Escolier? Arcanus! He meant Arcanus! What had he done? He tried to break the links, but he could not, although Incuban was not the one to stop him. If he broke the links, they would never find him. He would be lost.

SELENE looked out over the city of Endroad from the balcony of the Palace. She could see the roof of the Temple of Aralyn from here. She'd gone there twice since arriving, the first time as a servant of the Goddess, the second as a supplicant. The Temple would send the three wagonloads of fabric as she'd commanded on her first visit. She'd be sure the drivers saw them vanish, with only a crack of thunder and flash of lightning to mark the spot where the wagons had been. Arcanus would be pleased. She shuddered. If he knew she had gone to the Temple the second time as a common worshipper, he'd be far from pleased.

She wrapped her cloak more tightly about her. She saw a flash of white hair below her in the street and her breath caught for a moment in hope, in joy. But it was only an old woman, her hair falling loosely about her shoulders instead of bound in a bun as most women would wear it; white, not silver, her face old and wrinkled, not young and handsome. She sighed. She missed Marcus greatly. They were together so seldom now.

The Enemy had been advancing so quickly. Arcanus was becoming more tense with every passing day. More afraid. Perhaps he should be, but not for the reasons he was. She remembered her last conversation with her brother.

"MARCUS, do you think the Gods are punishing us? That they're angry at Arcanus and at us for aiding him in his deceptions?" Selene had asked hesitantly.

"What Gods? There are no Gods, Selene!" Marcus had scoffed. "It's all Father, you know that. It's always only been him."

"No, it hasn't," she'd argued. "Arcanus only started collecting tribute from the Temples two-and-a-half centuries ago, dictating what people should leave at each so we'd have the weapons and food and coin we needed to wage the war against Incuban. But Men have worshipped their Gods for thousands of years. Who collected the offerings then?"

"The priests, of course, from the Temples. They grew fat and rich on them. Other people took what was left at the shrines, the ones with brains and nerve enough to know a free meal when they see one. They'd take the food or coin those others were foolish enough to leave there," Marcus said cynically.

"But what if the Gods are real? Not Jarnath, Meloneth, Areth, Laneth, and those others. We know they are only Elf Lords and Ladies. But what about Ragnar and Aralyn? Why are only those two Gods worshipped, not just by my people, the Dwarves, but by Men as well, since long before the Elves and Dwarves ever came to these lands? If they aren't real, then why don't the Dwarves have different Gods?"

"The Elves don't have Gods. We don't worship anyone. We don't need to," Marcus had said proudly.

"You worship the water and the trees. That's Aralyn, whether you call her by name or not," Selene had argued.

"But we don't worship them! We need the water and the trees, so we respect them and protect them, and they in turn nurture us. That's not worship, it's common sense. What's wrong with you, Selene?"

"Aralyn came to me in a dream. She warned me that I had to stop stealing from Her Temple, that I was dooming myself to darkness if I didn't," Selene confessed, her voice scarcely above a whisper.

Marcus eyed her uneasily. "Did you tell Father?"

"Of course. He thought it was Incuban. He checked." She shuddered. Arcanus had not been gentle. He'd hurt her. He'd left nothing private, nothing.

"Then it was just a dream, an ordinary dream," Marcus said confidently, his voice tinged with relief.

"That's what Arcanus said." She hadn't called him "Father" since. A father shouldn't hurt his child; a father's touch shouldn't burn. She'd never feared Arcanus before—she'd only ever respected him—but she feared him now. He terrified her. She knew that, had he found Incuban in her core, he'd have tried to burn him out of her. He'd have killed her to do so, if need be. She'd been careful to hide her fear from Arcanus. She'd been getting so good at hiding things from him, from both of them. Especially her dreams of Marcus, in her bed, under her Power, helpless beneath her, all his arrogance turned to whimpering desire for her.

She'd turned away from him then, lest he see the desire. And the fear. She'd begun worshipping Aralyn in secret, Her and Ragnar both, as her mother's people, the Dwarves, did. She'd not dreamt of the Goddess again, at least not yet. She hoped if she did that Aralyn would approve of her now. That she'd protect her from Arcanus. That she'd protect her from herself.

The Amontir worshipped Arcanus as if he were a God, him and Idare both, though Idare was long dead. She wondered what they might do if they knew the appalling truth about Arcanus: how he impersonated the Gods, stole from their Temples, punished and manipulated and rewarded entire cities of worshippers. What would they think of him if they knew about the floods and the famines he'd brought, the poisoned wells, the sicknesses, all to punish the people for when they'd not given enough to the Temples, so they would kill their rulers and their priests and the next year give so much their own children starved?

Arcanus had been so intent upon ripping through her defenses in search of the Enemy he feared, he'd left himself completely unguarded. She'd learned those shocking secrets, then, as well as others far worse. Arcanus would kill her in an instant if ever he learned what she'd seen. She'd learned his deepest, darkest secrets: horrific crimes against the Elves that made his crimes against Man appear to be child's play.

She'd been thinking long and hard since then, and her thoughts frightened her. She'd realized that Arcanus was worse than Incuban. Incuban was horrible, but he was truly, completely insane: he thought it was all a Game. He was in it to have fun, to win. Arcanus was coldly, cruelly sane; fully, frighteningly aware. He knew people were more than just pawns in a game, or toys, or playthings, yet he was just as vicious as Incuban. He manipulated everyone around him as if they truly were game pieces on a board, knowing they were so much more.

Especially the Amontir. Arcanus dictated whom they'd marry, all in the name of preserving and focusing the Power of the thirty Great Houses, fine-tuning his creations. There had been no Amontir until Arcanus had come three thousand years ago. Arcanus had created them, combining his own essence with the essence of Men, as well as the essence of various animals and even the trees, mating them all together somehow using alchemy of the flesh at a minute level, smaller than the naked eye could see. Arcanus's work was far more intricate and delicate than the mockeries of life Incuban crafted.

Arcanus had done it all to a purpose, his own dark purpose. Only that motivation had remained hidden when she'd stolen her glimpse at his naked core. That and his true name. But she'd seen other things. She'd seen how he fed upon the Amontir, draining the Power, the very life from them; a little here, a little there, keeping them weak, keeping them dependent upon him. Arcanus had kept careful control of Prince Talon in particular. She suspected that Talon alone was powerful enough to be a danger to him. Arcanus kept Talon weak, made sure Talon viewed him as a second father, even as he kept the Madness near so he could eliminate the Prince easily, without suspicion, if ever he grew to be the danger he had the potential of being.

If only there were someone she could tell! Someone who might help her. Ragnar and Aralyn were real, they had to be. She needed them to be. She couldn't fight Arcanus on her own. If the Gods couldn't help her, then only Incuban could. It frightened her, that she might betray Arcanus and Marcus to Incuban. That she might need to someday, to keep herself safe from Arcanus.

SELENE gasped and almost fell, her mind dragged forcefully back to the present. Marcus! He was in danger, he was dying! Selene barely kept from screaming his name aloud.

"Lady Circe, is something wrong?" Prince Tomas asked, reaching out his hand, but drawing it back without touching her, unsure how to aid her. One did not touch a Dwarven Lady, nor a wizard, and his guest was both.

"I am summoned," Selene said, striving for calm. "I require your fastest horse, immediately."

"Of course, Revered One, at once. I'll see to it personally." Prince Tomas hurried from the room. She could see he was grateful for the excuse to leave her presence. She knew she frightened him.

Selene touched the link to her brother fearfully. That could not truly be Marcus, could it? He was screaming, begging, whimpering; he sounded terrified, yet his voice was but a whisper. He was truly dying. She could feel how weak he was. She knew, in theory, someone could send his or her mind down such a link and view another's core, even send them strength. But she had never done so. And what if it wasn't truly him?

Selene, as you love me, help me! Fly, you must fly to me! Don't let me die! Marcus begged, terrified. What had happened to him?

Selene swallowed. She'd flown only once, six years ago, when she'd flown Marcus to Caramore to warn the Amontir of Incuban's imminent attack. The effort had nearly killed her. She would have no strength left to aid him if she flew now. But Marcus was sobbing. She could hear him in her mind. It was chilling to hear Marcus completely stripped of his haughtiness, his Elven pride. She dared not send a message back to him. Whoever or whatever had harmed Marcus might be able to trace or even attack her through her message.

Selene climbed onto the ornamental railing that surrounded the balcony and flung herself forward. She barely kept from splattering herself on the cobblestones at the base of the tower, but then she was aloft, lightning arcing out from every limb. She heard shrieks of fear and screams of terror, from the courtiers and Guard alike. All were cowering from her. She ignored them all as she shot northeastward, toward her brother.

SELENE was exhausted, her strength nearly spent. She'd had no idea Marcus was so far away when he called! She'd flown over eight hundred miles, over the Taheeran Desert, the Falnor Woods, and the Coroden Mountains. She knew that, by road, her route would have been far longer, but even so, her journey seemed endless. She must land soon or fall. She was so close! She must reach him!

Finally, she saw movement below. Marcus? She cursed as she realized it was a group of four Men. They must be hunters or fur trappers to be out here, in the middle of nowhere, but she did not go low enough to see. She continued onward only for a few moments before a bright flash of blue cloth lying in the dirt caught her eye. Marcus's cloak! He was nearby; she could feel him. She concentrated to land carefully by the cloak, but then fell the last ten feet as the cloak unexpectedly moved, startling her. The landing was painful. She bit her tongue and nearly broke her ankle.

Her eyes widened in horror as she realized the moving cloth shrouded her brother. He was all but a skeleton: brittle, blistered skin stretched tautly over bone, eyes sunken. He was emaciated almost to the point of death, as if he'd suffered months of deprivation, though he'd been well when she last saw him, only weeks ago.

"Help me, Selene," he gasped, speaking her given name aloud. They never did so outside the safety of Arcanus's various strongholds! Selene reached for him, and he collapsed into her arms. She held him, terrified. What magicks had he been working that he might be so weakened, that he had drained his very life into them?

Water! He needed water, running water to lie in. The Methris was near, but its water would not be enough so far from any of the Elven Kingdoms, especially as weakened as he was. And there was no cold stone for her to draw strength from to aid him. There was only forest loam. The hunters! They would have the Power she needed to save Marcus.

She began to sing. Not a keening wail, not a lamentation for her dying brother, but a siren song, laced with Power to entice the Men she had seen. Her voice faltered for a moment at what Arcanus might say if he discovered her preying upon Men. But she would do anything to save the brother she loved. Even lose herself.

Selene swallowed hard against the fear. No, she would be strong enough to control the voracious, dark hunger that Arcanus had warned her could someday awaken within her. She was truly mad to broadcast her Power like this, as if setting out a beacon for Incuban to see. Incuban must not discover her, nor Arcanus, though she would almost rather have Incuban find her than Arcanus. Almost. She shuddered and broke her link to Arcanus.

"I heard you think his name. You've seen. You know he's taken me," Marcus whispered.

Selene's eyes widened in horror, and she almost pulled away from him. "How could you bring me to him?" she cried, looking frantically around her.

"Not here. Nightmares… so real." Marcus's voice faded altogether as he fell limp.

"Marcus? Marcus!" she screamed, shaking him in her terror, funneling what small amount of strength she could into him, just enough to ensure he might live a short while longer.

The Men were coming; she could feel them approaching. She smelled them before she saw them. The scent of their arousal was strong on the gentle breeze. It set fire to her core. She stripped off her hood and veil, shamelessly baring her naked face to them, and then stripped off her cloak, revealing her modest brown dress. Only her immediate family and her future husband should ever see her so exposed. But then her dress fell to her feet as if of its own volition and her undergarments. She exposed herself fully to these lusting strangers, beckoning them with her entire body. Her hips swayed sinuously, her tongue wet her lips in promise, and her hands caressed her breasts.

Her prey came tripping and stumbling eagerly toward their fate, already fully ensorcelled by her Voice and the sight of her. The first she took with only a kiss, her tongue dueling with his as she all but sucked the very life from him. She fell to her knees when she was done, drunk with the Power that coursed through her as he fell to the ground unconscious, barely alive. She fought against temptation and took the second only with her hand; he sprayed his seed and all but his life across her face, her bare breasts, before he, too, fell. The third she took with her mouth, driving him to ecstasy and swallowing his seed hungrily, not once but twice, until he lay still, scarcely breathing.

Shaking, vibrating, throbbing with Power, she fell upon the fourth like a bitch in heat, all control lost. He was the youngest, the most handsome; she had saved the best for last. She mounted him, gasping first in pain as her maidenhead was breached and then in passion, riding him in wild abandon until he spent himself deep inside her, his release triggering her own, their screams of ecstasy mingling.

It was over quickly, far too quickly to sate her. She forced her new lover to arousal a second time and pleasured herself upon him until he shuddered in release within her once more. Still it was not enough. She took him a third time, until he lay moaning in his release. It was only when she tried to mount him a fourth time and he began begging and then screaming for mercy even while yet entranced that she realized he was in agony and would not survive if she continued.

She rose, sweaty and dripping, and approached Marcus to share the energy she had stolen with her brother. She started to unlace his pants without realizing what she was doing, until he awoke and began cowering from her, whimpering, crying, begging like her last victim. She came to herself for a moment. She poured her Power into him, calming him, hugging him tightly to her bare breasts, guiding his mouth to her so he might suckle upon her. Marcus fought against her wildly but still with terrifying weakness. She was shaking again, not with what felt to be limitless Power, but instead in horror and revulsion at what she had done, what she had become.

In terror and rage, she tore into Marcus's mind, demolishing the last remnants of his tattered defenses, and sought out every shred of the twisted shadow, the dark oily veil clinging to Marcus's core. She incinerated it with a thought, until even the last curl of smoke was but a memory. Then she built a pyrenteum chest inside Marcus's core and locked away all the tortures, the depravities, the horror her beloved brother had endured at the hands of the monster that had attacked him, healing his mind and his spirit as well as she was able. Then she turned her thoughts outward.

Marcus was blessedly unconscious, the body's natural reaction to such an unnatural healing, or so Arcanus had taught her. The thought of Arcanus had her shaking once more in terror. Her victims were still unconscious. Marcus would be safe if she left for a time.

She ran all the way to the Methris, afraid to fly, more that the lightning would ignite the forest around them than it would be seen by either Incuban or Arcanus. She dove into the cold, clear water, scrubbing the taste, the smell, the feel of her sin from her body as best she could. She was shivering, not from the cold or wet or even the memory of what she had done, but, to her horror, in need for more.

She ran back to Marcus's side and dressed quickly, the hypocrisy of her maidenly attire nearly making her weep. Forcing herself to artificial calm, she made sure her four victims still breathed, still lived, and then she lifted Marcus into her arms and carried him to the River on foot. He needed the water, but not here. It was not safe. She came here only to protect the forest.

Igniting her lightning over the water, she rocketed into the sky. Turning westwards, she flew them over the Coroden, careful to steer clear of the Elven Kingdom of Erenia and the Falnor Woods that surrounded it, yet to stay near enough that the Power of the Elven city and Wood might mask their own. She landed with her precious burden just west of the Kierness Marsh but east of Falnor, a City of Man on the banks of the Merdan River.

Selene entered the water with Marcus, both of them fully clothed. She held him in the healing waters, carefully holding his face above the surface. He was still unconscious. Now and then she fondled him. She could not help herself; she loved him and he was still so handsome, even starved and wasted as he was. His fine-boned features stood out so clearly.

Her eyes left his face and concentrated on his groin. She forced her reaching hands away from him. *Wake up, Marcus, please wake up,* she begged silently. She must feed again, soon. She had used so much of her Power flying. Why hadn't she stopped in the mountains, where there was cold stone to strengthen her as well as a stream for Marcus? *Because the heat of even one Man is like a month within a Mountain.*

She severed the link to Marcus. He must not know her thoughts. They had become so dark!

She started singing. Perhaps a woodsman or a band of travelers might hear her? But it was a group of bandits who came: six of them, ugly and mean and ragged and dirty. They looked beautiful to her, delicious. She took them two at a time, between her legs and in her mouth, in a wild orgy of hunger. She left them all moaning in agony.

She had heard their vile thoughts. If she were a simple traveler, they would have raped her to death. She returned the courtesy, only she left them slightly better, or perhaps worse, than dead. She left them all impotent, permanently damaged. She fell to her hands and knees, sobbing and vomiting.

She had not realized how hard it would be to fight the hunger. She'd fed on so many, so quickly. More, she must have more! But the more she took, the more she wanted. Her desire burned within her. It was consuming her, raging unchecked like a wildfire. Arcanus had warned her of this. He'd known what would happen were she ever to let the demon of desire inside her loose.

She'd been a virgin this morning. She was an unwed Dwarven Lady. How could she be other than virgin? She was not even an adult yet. She was far from being an adult. What had she done to herself?

Marcus stirred and his eyes opened. He looked better; he looked like he would live. "Selene, I'm so sorry! I never should have called to you, but I needed help so desperately. I tried not to call you. I swear I fought against it for so long, but then he came to me again, and the *anosar*—I could not even think. You are so strong! You freed me from him. But I am so weak, and so afraid. Arcanus will be so angry with me. He frightens me when he is angry. It is my fault the Enemy found me. I was so careless, so stupid. Help me, Selene! I am so afraid." Tears streamed from his eyes, and he was trembling.

She fought the urge to put her arms around him to comfort him. Even now she felt the hunger screaming within her to take Marcus the way she'd taken those others. She wanted him so desperately, to feel him thrashing under her, to feel him inside her. She had always desired him, loved him more than a sister should love a brother, but her thoughts had still been so innocent before, so pure. This was different, dark and vile, dirty and terrifying. She fought her desire, and for the moment, she won.

"Arcanus will not hurt you when you're already injured. It's not as if you activated your link to him and led Incuban to him."

Marcus's eyes widened in horror. "But I did! I think he's safe now. You freed me from Incuban. He no longer touches me. I can see we are far from where we were, for the trees, the mountains. But Arcanus will find us, he will come. You must protect me from him," he begged.

Selene paled. "He cannot see me, not now. I... I am not well. I need time alone. I'll be strong enough soon, I know I will. I can come back once I am well again, once I am sure." She rose to her feet, and Marcus struggled to sit.

"Don't leave me alone, Selene! Please, you can't! What if Incuban comes back for me? What if he finds me!" Marcus was crying again.

She couldn't bear to see him like that, and to be unable to comfort him. But she must not touch him. "Don't worry, Marcus. Incuban will not find you again. We truly are far from where we were. Keep your link to Arcanus. Do not try to find him. He will find you. The bandits cannot harm you. They are far weaker than you. It will be days before they will be able even to stand. Take their weapons, their food, their coin. Get away from them before they recover. I would carry you away from them, but I cannot. Good-bye Marcus. I love you."

She flew, fast and high. She heard Marcus screaming after her, but she had to fly far, quickly. She did love him as a brother, but also, she wanted him so desperately. But he was still so weak that even with all the Power she had gifted to him, she knew that at her slightest touch, she would kill him. She would drain his life from him completely.

She must find men, strong men, many men. If she could only get Power enough, the hunger would be quenched. Then she would be able to think again. She could resist it. She knew she would be strong enough to. She must be strong enough.

LUNAHR awoke slowly, fearfully, expecting to feel pain from the many wounds he'd received in the battle outside the burning ruins of Alridge, to yet be covered in soot and sweat, blood and gore. He had not thought he would awaken at all. Even before he had severed his bond to Laren, he had known he could not survive such a battle much longer, that he was as doomed as those he'd desperately sought to aid. Yet he was clean, conscious, and miraculously uninjured: there was no trace of where the blades or claws or teeth had pierced him, not a single scar. But not even for a moment did he think it might be the Elves who had found him, rescued him, bathed him, healed him. Not this time. He was lying naked upon a soft bed on a white silken coverlet in a strange stone room, one that had neither the look nor the smell of the Elven Kingdoms.

He never should have lied to Laranela when he left the safety of Riviera at the King's urging. Like Elavar and Naraena before him, he had been sent off alone and unescorted, under the guise of messenger. Unlike them, thanks to the Lady Joy, he had known it was a ruse. Fearing even Riviera might not survive against such an implacable Enemy, Laranela had desperately sought to send those he loved to safety.

Lunahr should have listened to the man who had become as a father to him. He truly should have headed to Erenia, to his guardian Elanara's side, instead of secretly heading south along the Methris on his self-imposed scouting mission to try to gain crucial intelligence on the advancing Enemy so that he might help save Riviera, the Kingdom that fostered him, and Loatia, the one they in turn protected.

There was cold stone all around him, illuminated by many dozens of lit candles, each of them blood red. He must be underground, inside a Dwarven Mountain. It had the look and feel of a Dwarven chamber. But how had he come to be here? Farad?

Farad had gone to the Dwarven Lands. Could it be that Farad had somehow rescued him in his hour of direst need?

Lunahr sat up cautiously, still unable to believe he was not injured, afraid he might be delirious, that this might all be a hallucination, his last moments of life on the battlefield. But he moved easily, without pain. He scanned the room eagerly for Farad. It had been twelve years since he had last seen the cousin he loved.

"Ah, so my virgin bride is awake at last," a sensual voice said as a figure stepped out, seemingly from the solid rock of one of the walls.

Lunahr instinctively rolled from the bed, or at least tried to. He was brought up short, his limbs jerking against something hard and unyielding. Lunahr looked frantically at his hands and feet, for the first time noticing the pyrenteum fetters that encircled him at wrist and ankle. How could he not have realized before that he was bound, chained? Pyrenteum, the King's Metal, stronger even than pallenteum, the Lord's Metal. Blades could not pierce it, rock could not crush it, fire could not melt it, only wizards knew the shaping of.... Oh, Idare save him! No!

Lunahr's head snapped up to look at the figure who approached, slowly, sinuously. He gasped in horror, in astonishment. The being that approached him had the face and form of a God. His brow was high, his cheekbones were perfection, his lips red and moist; he had the most sensual mouth of anyone Lunahr had ever seen. Lunahr tore his gaze away from his mouth. His waist-length hair was the red-orange of flame, and his eyes! His eyes were the same hue as his hair. How could eyes be red? His eyes burned: with passion, with promise, with madness.

Lunahr whimpered as he jerked his gaze to the side and gasped. His ears! His ears were the unmistakable upswept ears of an Elf. No! He could not be! How could He be an Elf, if this was whom he thought, and who else could it be? Lunahr dragged his eyes down from His face to His torso. It was glistening, hairless. His captor's skin seemed to glow by the light of the room's candles. He was exquisite; it was as if each muscle had been chiseled by a master sculptor. Lunahr found his gaze compelled lower, toward the Elf's groin. Lunahr let out a small cry as he forced his head upward, as if fighting against an invisible hand.

No one had ever described their Enemy as looking like this! He had thought Incuban a wizard, a Man like Arcanus, not an Elf. Why hadn't they warned him? Why hadn't they told him?

"Incuban," Lunahr said bravely, shocked to hear the calmness of his voice, though it should be faltering in terror. He had been captured when he had thought he would be killed. Idare, no, this could not be happening!

PYRFIER laughed, amused by the boy's small triumph, excited to feel him desperately exerting his full will against him when he, in turn, was using only the smallest hint of Power upon him. Still, what delicious Power the child had! This one was a prize indeed. He would be worthy of savoring.

Pyrfier executed a slight bow, acknowledging the name the Amontir knew him by in obvious delight. "Ah, I see you know me," he said in the language this child knew as Elvish. His plaything was not nearly as well versed in Common, and he would not want him to misunderstand a word, or miss a single nuance. "But such fear! You should not fear me, Lunahr. You must not believe the lies they have told you about me, Farad and all the rest of your kin. I have been so grievously maligned," he said as he approached the bed, his voice that of a wronged innocent.

LUNAHR shivered in terror. His name! Incuban knew his given name! The most crucial part of his true name, and he knew it! "How—?" Lunahr's voice cracked, and he licked suddenly dry lips. "How do you know my name?" he asked, unable to conceal the panic he felt.

"Ah, Lunahr, my dear, sweet child. I know so much about you. Farad has told me so many wondrous things," the beautiful monster said, eyeing him knowingly.

"No, he wouldn't!" Lunahr cried in desperate denial, fists clenching at the obvious lie, as he strained against the chains.

PYRFIER laughed, truly amused. He was not lying. Oh, there were so many lies he would tell this boy before he was done, yet that had been the pure unadulterated truth. Farad had indeed revealed much to him, as he lay dying in the depths of the Dwarven Mountain of Malar. Pyrfier had learned Lunahr's true name. He had learned of the Watch's last refuge, the Watchtower, and all its many secrets. He had finally even learned the true name and lineage of their current King, who yet called himself Prince: Prince Dewalaren, son of Prince Evanaren, Lord of House of Obearn, of Amontir.

Idare's grandson! He would finally have a chance to retaliate against that conniving worm Idare for his audacity, his insolence, his treachery, though it would be through his grandson. How deliciously ironic that the current Prince was the great-grandson of King Albinar's murderer, his puppet, Ebonar! And that Farad, of all people, was the one to have finally revealed the identity of the Man he had protected at the cost of his entire family, for nearly nine decades. Yet the child believed that, in this of all things, he lied! It was so wonderfully amusing that he thought so.

"FARAD hates you!" Lunahr screamed, fighting not to sob. "You killed his entire family! You tortured—" His voice broke, but he forced himself to continue. "You tortured them to death, all of them, his parents, his brothers, you...." He could no longer speak as the memory of the horrors he had heard left him paralyzed with fear.

"Yet still, Farad betrayed you to me. I know your true name, Lunahr, son of Quilahr, Lord of House of Eagles, of Amontir. And such knowledge does give me no small amount of Power over you, does it not?" Incuban asked, stroking Lunahr's cheek lovingly.

Lunahr recoiled from his touch, jerking his face away from him. "I'm not afraid of you," he said defiantly.

Incuban laughed. "Don't be absurd, boy. I can taste your fear. It is delicious, as are you," he said, his eyes slowly raking down Lunahr's body.

Lunahr felt defiled even by the look. He began trembling violently in terror of what was to come. But Incuban did not touch him again, not yet. Instead, he stepped back a pace. "It was fortunate for you I came upon the field of battle when I did. My creatures are unfortunately not very bright, for all they are wonderfully loyal. They should have recognized you instantly as someone I would wish to meet. Instead, when I found you, your core was nearly dark, your life all but spent. Yet even so, you burned so brightly!

"I have guested so many, from all the Houses of Amontir, but seldom have I had the luxury of taming a Lord. Farad's father, Jarad, was the last. Dewalaren has them so well trained, to fall upon their own swords when I would take so much greater pleasure impaling them. But not with my sword," he said, and now he reached out to stroke Lunahr's hip.

Lunahr did not even feel his touch. He barely heard the last words as he began thrashing against the chains that bound him. Laren's name! Incuban had spoken Laren's given name! How could Incuban know it now, when he had never known it before? He let out a cry of pure agony, of spirit-searing despair. No! He had been unconscious, he had only just awakened. He could not have betrayed Laren to their Enemy! Idare, please, he could not have! Lunahr began sobbing.

"Poor boy," Incuban said, brushing the hair from Lunahr's face, stroking his tear-stained cheek. He lifted the finger that had touched Lunahr, bringing it to his lips and sucking upon it with an obscenely wet, sensual sound, fellating it. "You are so young to be burdened with so much pain. And so lonely. You have been living in exile from all your kin for six years now. It was cruel of them to abandon you to the Oceana. Those cold, haughty beings do not like to touch Man, nor to be touched by him, do they? Even Elanara, even Elavar, touched you so seldom. You were forced to beg for the simplest hug, while all the rest of them would pleasure themselves so very eagerly upon one another at their most casual whim. They treated you as a child, did they not? When anyone can clearly see you are certainly not a child," Incuban said appreciatively, running his fingers lightly down Lunahr's chest to his hip again. Lunahr writhed under his gentle touch, turning his groin from him.

Incuban sighed, withdrawing his hand. "No one loved you, did they, Lunahr? Not even Eladar. Especially not Eladar, despite his false promises to you. He deceived you, Lunahr. In your heart, you know it is true. Eladar left you, didn't he? Do you know how many he has taken, since his graduation? He promised to return to you, didn't he, the day that he came-of-age. It was your special secret, wasn't it? You were going to become lythenia, weren't you? He was supposed to remain chaste. He would return to you and wait the single year that remained until you came-of-age. Then you were to have publicly declared your love, in spite of Amontiri Law, despite how his parents felt about it, how your precious Prince Dewalaren would feel about it."

Lunahr tried to force his forearms against his ears, to drown out Incuban's merciless words.

"But Eladar betrayed you, Lunahr. He broke his promise. He's fornicated with half of Nalea, even though he knew you were waiting, that you were saving yourself for him and he had promised to do the same. He laughed as he betrayed you. He told his many, many lovers all about you, how you were nothing more than a pet to him, a plaything. How you followed him about like a lovesick puppy. How disgusted he was by you. How he was accepting a posting in the Dwarven Lands immediately upon graduating just to get away from you," Incuban taunted.

"That's not true! None of it's true! He loves me! He'd never betray me!" Lunahr screamed in angry denial, tears streaming down his face.

"OH? THEN why did he stop writing to you? Why did he not return after graduating? Why did he go to the Dwarven Lands?" Pyrfier asked, his voice mild, curious. All the while he had been speaking, he had been continually focusing his Power on the helpless child, who was disintegrating so perfectly beneath his relentless onslaught.

"He... I... I don't know!" Lunahr sobbed. "I begged them to tell me, but they kept giving me excuses. They wouldn't—and then they left, all of them! Eladar never came back from Nalea, and Elanara never came back from Erenia, and then Queen Naraena left for Tanieria and then Salenia, and finally Elavar.... They left me, all of them!" he cried.

Pyrfier reveled at how tortured and betrayed Lunahr already felt by their abandonment. Those pathetic fools made this almost too easy! "But what of King Laranela?" Pyrfier asked innocently. "He did not abandon you, did he? Although... he was the one responsible for all of it, was he not? He was the one who sent them all away from you. He was the one who forced Elanara to break her decades-long betrothal to Aras, to promise herself to Dewalaren instead. Dewalaren does not need you anymore now, does he, now that he has Elanara to love? And Laranela was the one who sent Eladar to the Dwarven Lands, when he would have come home from Nalea. He sent Naraena, who was like a mother to you, hundreds of miles away from you, and then Elavar, who was like an older brother to you. Oh Lunahr! How you must hate Laranela for it! He has taken everyone you have ever loved away from you, has he not?" Incuban asked, planting yet another of the many seeds which would one day soon bear such delicious fruit.

"What? No! No, he... he was...," Lunahr stuttered in denial.

The boy's head was spinning from his devious attack. The child was unable to form a coherent thought, let alone an argument against all he was hearing. "I give you a gift, Lunahr. Laranela was not the main villain. Oh no. It was Laedrin, the Elven High-King," Pyrfier said conspiratorially. "Laedrin threatened to kill Eladar if

Laranela did not alter Elanara's betrothal so that she would marry Dewalaren instead of his own son. Ultimately, Laedrin is the one who is most to blame for you losing Eladar. Though you can hardly excuse Laranela for his cowardice, for his avarice, can you? He would do anything to keep his throne. He sold his only daughter to Dewalaren, as if she were a common whore, so he might keep it. He sent Eladar, his young son, barely a man, to exile in the barbaric Dwarven Lands so he might keep it. He tore out your heart and trod upon it, all so he might remain King. Such a man is unworthy to be King, is he not?"

LUNAHR stared at him in mute horror. He was lying. Lunahr knew He must be, but it sounded like the truth. He was so confused! *Laren, Eladar, Farad, please help me,* he begged silently, knowing he was beyond help. He was inescapably alone.

Oh Idare, why hadn't he died? *Please Idare, help me die quickly! Don't let him hurt me,* he desperately prayed.

PYRFIER shook his head sympathetically. "You loved Laranela as a father, and he betrayed you. You loved Dewalaren as a father, and he betrayed you as well. And you loved Eladar as so much more: he was to be lythenia to you, yet he, too, betrayed you. Poor Lunahr. It's hard to face the truth, isn't it? It's hard to love and to be betrayed by those who hold your heart in their hands." Suddenly Pyrfier's eyes burned, they blazed. He strode from the bed, glaring at the brazier, fingering the handle of the glowing brand that lay within the flaming coals as he stared into the comforting flame.

"I know what it is like to be betrayed, Lunahr. I, too, once loved. I, too, was once betrayed. There is only one cure for a broken heart, Lunahr: revenge. Your heart can only heal when you have caused the one who hurt you more pain than you were made to suffer, more pain than he might have believed possible. Yes, only then, when the one who betrayed you is writhing before you in agony, will he be punished as he deserves," Pyrfier said, eyes crackling with actual flame. "Laranela, Dewalaren, and Eladar must all be made to suffer for their crimes against you, Lunahr. And of course, Laedrin. Oh yes, we will have our vengeance upon all of them, you and I.

"I will help you, Lunahr. I am your friend, your one true friend, your only friend. You are so fortunate to be under my protection now. I will keep you safe from all those who have used you, who have harmed you. It hurts, doesn't it, Lunahr? But that is what life is, isn't it? It is all about pleasure and pain, sacrifice and reward, the arts of love and revenge. The Aerta and the Oceana, those two pitiful races you call the Elves, have tricked you, haven't they? They are not what they appear to be. Oh no! So high and mighty, so aloof. They pretend to be so perfect, when they are today what they always were, the least of us. They are nothing like what they pretend to be.

"But I know the truth, Lunahr. Someday soon, I will teach it to you. I will share many lost truths with you. You will learn all about the Aerie and the Faeren. You will hear the horrific history of the Latents and the Houerfashang. You will learn how all four races abused and persecuted us. You will hear the multitude of sins they committed against us. But we punished them for their crimes. Oh yes, how we punished them! We saw them burn, all burn, in Ragnar's purifying flame.

"But you are not ready to hear, not yet. There is so much else to teach first. I have spent millennia learning the intricacies of pleasure and pain. I will share all of it with you. I will bring you to such exquisite agony that you would trade no pleasure in the world for it. Then I will bring you to pleasure which will make you beg for those agonies again, if only so that you will learn to cherish the pleasure more. Oh, Lunahr! If only you knew the wonders I have in store for you!" Pyrfier said, as he set the brand back in the gentle embrace of the flame, and his gaze roamed to the various tables set about the room, to the many implements of delight they held: the barbed whips, gleaming blades, glowing brands, and molten wax but a few. These were only the beginning of the wonders he would show this child.

Seldom had he been given such a perfect subject to work with. What glorious Power he had! This one was special. He was almost a challenge. He could have been as entertaining as Farad, had he had the chance to reach adulthood. Like Farad, this one was far closer to what Escolier had been trying to achieve when he created the Amontir. Pyrfier wondered whether Escolier realized he had succeeded in breeding another Latent. How he hungered for such succulent Power! From what he had learned from Farad, he was almost certain Dewalaren was one as well. Oh, the pleasures he would take from that one, from all of them!

This one he would not tire of so quickly, so easily, as the hundreds of thousands of others he had consumed in these lands and the many millions before. No, he would be one of those special few he had so treasured, particularly those he had most enjoyed during the past century. Sweet Alaria, Farad's mother, Lady of House of Eagles, had entertained him for a full week. Strong Jarad as well. Innocent Alarad, Farad's youngest brother, had lasted nearly two. Ah, and Ilene, that unexpected natural Latent, the Dwarven Princess hidden away in Armsguard.

It was from the essence of such as she, natural born Latents, Dwarven maidens, that he and his kind had first been conceived, in the laboratories of the alchemists of the flesh of the four races. And sometimes in the bedrooms. Even the most hardened alchemist could often not resist the beguiling nature of his test subjects, though there were laws against such things, of course. Laws that were made to be broken, like those they failed to protect. Broken and bleeding, chained and helpless, begging and whimpering, violated over and over again, until their bellies were finally swollen with the unholy proof of the depravity of the researchers. No, his kind had not always been bred with clinical detachment in pristine, sterile conditions in the laboratory, gestated in artificial wombs and then decanted.

Not that it mattered to their oppressors how they came into being. Either way, they were desired and reviled, valued and debased, born into a life of sexual slavery from which there was no hope of escape save for one: death. Blessed oblivion. Yes, they had learned their lessons well. He and his fellow Freedom Fighters had released so many from the bonds of life. He personally had bestowed death's sweet kiss upon hundreds of thousands here, and millions more before.

Curious; why had he been thinking about…? Ah yes! Sweet Ilene. She had been surprisingly strong, remarkably satisfying. She had not died, but they were of no use once their minds were broken beyond repair.

Marcus had not broken. Almost, but not quite. He would be playing with that one still had it not been for Selene. She had actually stolen his prey before he was finished with it. The knowledge excited him. Now there was a prize! There was something about her, something special. He had sensed it when feeding upon Marcus. Selene was without question at least a Latent, but he suspected she might be far more. The thought that she might actually be Houerfashang almost sent him flying from the chamber in pursuit of her. But he should not jilt his eager new Amontiri boy-bride for another so soon.

Perhaps Lunahr could somehow aid him in obtaining Selene? But no matter. Even without her, Lunahr was valuable beyond price, even had he not bred so true: he was tied to Dewalaren's heart, to Farad's, and to the Elves of Riviera, especially to the Royal Family. Oh what sweet revenge he would reap with this single playing piece!

But that was not all, oh no. Lunahr was so innocent, so beautiful, true, but most importantly of all, he was House of Eagles, the only survivor of his House, save for the blood of Eagles that yet flowed through Dewalaren's and Farad's veins. And one other's, of course. He laughed aloud. Only Escolier knew what that meant to him, and Dewalaren's precious advisor would never dare reveal the secret of House of Eagles, why of all the thirty Great Houses Escolier had crafted, that one was of such particular interest to him, when Escolier had not even told them how he had fathered the rest.

Pyrfier turned back to the bed. He had let his musings distract him, and his new toy was being suspiciously quiet. He ran to his plaything, enraged. How dare he! Those idiots who had bound him had made the chains too loose this time. The boy had wrapped one of them about his neck. He had thrown his weight against it, intent upon taking his own life. His face was already purple, his lips blue, his tongue lolling and eyes bulging. Fortunately, he had not been able to fully crush his windpipe, but he was only moments from suffocating.

Infuriated, Pyrfier grabbed the length of chain in both hands, his eyes flaming with Power. The impervious pyrenteum chain instantly melted, the entire indestructible length of it turned to liquid, which poured down upon Lunahr's bare chest in a deluge of delight. Lunahr's body was rocked by spasms of agony. Involuntarily sucking in a lungful of air, he screamed as the molten metal burned smoking craters in his perfect chest.

"Foolish child," Pyrfier snarled, wrapping a single long-fingered, viselike hand about Lunahr's throat. His own fingers were undamaged by the molten pyrenteum, his skin unmarred. He was infuriated by the boy's rebellion. Lunahr writhed in agony on the bed as his flesh continued to cook.

"You will learn obedience. I see that I will have to punish you for your insolence before I pleasure you. But I will not break you. Oh no, dear one. You are far too precious to me. You will learn, Lunahr, soon you will learn. You will be the perfect tool of my vengeance. I will forge you well," Pyrfier promised, as he bent down over him, sinuously licking the first of the smoking holes that marred Lunahr's chest, the molten metal sizzling on his tongue. Pyrfier reveled in the delicious aftertaste of the flame, laughing in mad glee, his fury already forgotten as Lunahr finally fainted.

Chapter 3

Lost Kin

JARGAS adjusted the awkward pack about his broad shoulders for the hundredth time since beginning his long journey. After crossing three rivers and two mountain ranges, his great grandsire's war axe was still bound securely to his back. His journey was almost over. The Dwarven Lands began somewhere within this range of mountains. Soon he would reach his ancestral home. He wondered what sort of person the current King might be. He hoped he was a better man than the brother his great grandsire had fled from so many years ago. Their self-imposed exile must end. War was almost upon these people. They needed their western kin.

The Fromer Mountains were much like the mountains of home in many ways, yet so very different in others. There were no ogres or obearn here as there were in the Holoren. But there was something that hunted here; he'd heard its hunting cries last night and seen its large tracks this morning. Some type of great cat, from the look of the prints.

He did not like cats. They thought his legs scratching posts; they would extend their claws and rip them through the thick curly mats of black hair on his legs. His sister, Jarina, liked cats, but then, she moved like one, thought like one, and fortunately, for all she was sister to him and twin besides, she even looked a little like one, lithe and sleek. She looked nothing like him. He smiled fondly, thinking of her, glad again for the link that bonded them. He had never been so far from their home, and she would have been worried about him could she not still touch him through their link. And, he admitted to himself, he would have worried about her.

She had wanted to come with him, of course. Their father, Rongas, had forbidden it, as had he, as if their words had ever held any power over her. Still, they both reminded her that, as Chieftess of the Varash, her duty lay with her mother's people, not her father's. It was not that she did not know it or had not performed her duty well these past nearly seven decades, since she'd come-of-age, for all that she still looked a lass of perhaps thirty. It was that her duty to her brother took precedence over aught else.

Their father had grumbled that he'd not have some Dwarf he'd never met cast his eye upon her and covet her like some cold jewel in his earthen vault, for she had the same entrancing power their mother had, who had cast her spell upon him, for all he was King of his own people.

That had stopped Jarina. She hugged her father to take the sting out of it and laughed and said she'd not wed a Dwarf, not when her dreams had always been of a tall, dark stranger, a Man of mystery like her grandmother had wed; a Man of great power in great pain, whom she might heal and love.

Jargas sighed. He feared he knew the truth. She would never marry. She could not, for she carried the curse of their mother's line: she would die birthing her first child, as had every Chieftess these four generations past.

A bone-chilling, shrieking roar cut across Jargas's thoughts. One of the great hunting cats. But this one cried out in pain, not rage. It surprised him that he might know the difference, but then, Smoke and Midnight's mother had screamed like that as the obearn killed her, and perhaps some of Jarina's knowledge had rubbed off on him over the years as well. So, there was something even more fearsome that hunted in these mountains, though he had seen no tracks of it yet. Perhaps there were ogres and obearn here after all. These mountains had changed. His father had not known of the cats.

The chilling cry echoed all about the rock around him. There was no way to tell where the danger lay, and it was almost dusk. The sun's light was fading. He would not make the safety of the door to the Kingdom tonight after all. And there was nothing here to burn for fire and no cave to shelter him.

This terrain was too treacherous to walk at night, even with his keen eyes, which saw nearly as well in the dark as in the bright light of day. He would spend the night with his back against bare rock. He clutched the stout staff in his hand more tightly. He might well have need of it this night.

There was another hunting cat scream, but this time, the scream of a Dwarf or a Man cut through its echo. Jargas quickened his pace, casting his gaze about for either, though they could be many leagues away from here. Sound was deceptive against rock such as this. Then he saw something glint in the fading rays of the sun up ahead.

He let out a hunting cry of his own, the challenging bellow he used upon the ogres, bearing down upon the great cat that had felled the Dwarf. The enormous cat turned its head toward him with a snarl as he attacked, mouth open, six-inch fangs extending well past its chin, shoulder muscles bulging under thick fur as it leapt for him.

Jargas crashed his staff down upon the beast's skull, shattering bone and teeth, pulping its head with his first blow. The cat lay twitching on the ground, not quite knowing it was dead yet.

The Dwarf was twitching upon the ground as well. Jargas checked him for signs of life, not thinking he would find them. The cat had been upon his back, biting his head and shoulders. But the glint of metal he had seen had been a chain mail shirt and a metal helm, and the Dwarven armor had withstood the fangs. The Dwarf's head and shoulders were uninjured; the teeth had not penetrated the armor at all.

The backs of his legs, though, were slashed from midthigh to ankle. His boots, along with his legs, had been torn to ribbons by the beast's powerful hind claws. The Dwarf was bleeding profusely and already unconscious. Jargas pulled his blanket out of his pack and cut it into strips with his hunting knife, binding the wounds as best he could. He was no healer.

He noticed the body of a second cat, then, on the ground, the head almost severed from the neck. That one was a male, and the one he had just slain a female. The Dwarf had apparently attacked half of a mated pair.

Jargas had slain an ogre at sixteen for his own coming-of-age, for his mother's people, and had also slain an obearn at fifty for his coming-of-age for his father's people, though it wasn't the first such beast he'd killed. This Dwarf looked to be about fifty, though it was hard to tell for sure. The clearest indication he'd not yet passed his test was that his hair and beard, although long and thick, were as yet unbraided. Only after successfully completing his Rite of Passage would he have the right to wear it proudly braided, as an adult. Jargas picked up the Dwarf's axe and finished the job of beheading the beast, wrapping the grisly trophy in the remains of his blanket and slinging the second axe onto his back from the leather strap that hung from it. Jargas would not have him fail his passage to manhood for lack of the trophy as proof he'd succeeded, when he'd completed the task.

He lifted the Dwarf and began carrying him in his arms, as if he were still a child. He certainly looked to be one in proportion to Jargas, though he weighed at least two hundred and fifty pounds, nearly half as much as Jargas, and he was tall for a male of their kind. He was more than half Jargas's height, perhaps four-and-a-half feet tall if he stretched, although a Dwarf would never stretch. The tracks the Dwarf had left made a relatively distinct trail, considering the terrain. Jargas backtracked them, hoping they might lead him to shelter before the sun's light completely faded. Although he could see as well in the dark as any of his father's people, there were no footprints where the Dwarf had crossed bare rock, and the tracks were becoming far fewer and farther between and were easier to spot with more light.

He'd walked much longer than he'd hoped to when the sun's last rays touched the side of the valley. It was then he saw a great door of metal, set into the solid rock, glint in the final light of the sun. As he watched, torches were lit, framing the door. He need not worry he would lose sight of it in the dark, in spite of the convolutions of the terrain and the rock that intermittently blocked his view. He had the keen sense of direction of his father's people and he'd walked many an unknown valley at night before.

A short while later, Jargas loomed out of the darkness before the Door Guards. Like the ones in his father's Kingdom, they were in full plate mail, more fully armored than the Dwarf in his arms, and carried bared war axes. They stared at the giant before them in wide-eyed but grim determination, axes raised.

Jargas knew he looked like a Dwarf—he groomed and dressed like one—but he towered a full three feet over the tallest of them, and he was tanned by the sun, instead of pale as his father's people. "I've rescued one of your people from a great cat," Jargas said in Dwarvish, his second native tongue. "I seek entry into the Mountain. He needs a healer."

The light from the torches revealed much. He saw their suspicion and fear and courage turn to horror as they beheld his burden. One of the Guards worked deftly at the hidden mechanism to open the door into the Mountain, without any challenge or question.

Jargas knew the door would normally stay shut until morning. It was then Jargas realized he had rescued someone of importance. As the massive steel door swung open, the Guard called out to other Guards on the other side of the door, "Let him pass! Lead him to Gervan at once! He bears the Prince!"

Six Dwarves rushed to surround him, not to imprison him, but to escort him. Jargas was relieved that they had assessed him favorably and had not mistakenly believed he'd been the one to harm their Prince. He'd been worried that they might have reacted far worse, but he got a clear look at their beards and hair and recognized the distinctive pattern of their braids. They were almost identical to his own, save for one major variation and a few minor ones. This must be Malar. No doubt they had noticed the same about his braids and had been both puzzled and reassured by it.

Two of the Dwarves led, two others stood to either side of him, and the other two followed behind. The entry hall to their caverns was of unadorned gray rock, though it was carved smooth. It was at least ten times as wide as Jargas and three times as tall.

After a short distance, it branched abruptly into six passageways. The Dwarves leading him chose the second from the right. They proceeded in a series of turns along a twisting labyrinth of intersecting passageways.

The sense of direction he had inherited from his father triggered as if he had lived underground his whole life instead of for part of it; he knew he could find his way out again, if need be. Like all Dwarven strongholds, including their own, this one was deliberately built as an intricate maze. Jargas knew there were many deadly traps, invisible to all, their secrets carefully revealed only to those who dwelt within, to ensnare any who might attempt to penetrate their home, for all knew of the great treasure vaults that lay within every Dwarven Mountain. Jargas carefully noted every step of the lead Dwarves' feet and movement of their hands as they weaved around triggers for those traps, as they bore deeper and deeper into the Mountain.

Finally, they came to an archway with a stone door set almost seamlessly into it. One of the Guards leading him ignored protocol, and instead of using the speaker tube set beside it, he pressed his palm against the door. The door must have weighed at least one thousand pounds, but it was perfectly balanced and swung open easily at the Guard's touch. Jargas did not have to duck his head or turn sideways to enter here, as he often needed to in Man's world.

Jargas entered a room of stone with two other doors leading from it. The rock here was carved in intricate swirls and whorls along the wall. There were no corners in this rounded room. The furniture was all of stone, too, though this stone was of a deeper gray, almost blue. There were a dozen chairs padded by midnight-blue cushions and a number of low tables between them, all of a curved line.

"Gervan!" a Guard called, and a Dwarf came through the doorway in the far wall, wiping his hands on a towel. He stared at Jargas, his eyes traveling up his great height, but they stopped before they reached his face when he saw Jargas's burden.

"Valar! Quickly, this way." He led Jargas through the second doorway. There were two rows of beds here, also of stone, but again with thick cushions upon them. "What happened?" Gervan asked.

Jargas laid the injured Prince down gently on his side on the bed indicated, exposing his bound wounds. "His legs were clawed by a long-toothed cat," Jargas told the healer, indicating the bloody blanket strips. "It bit his head and shoulders, also, but I don't think he took any wounds from that, for his armor. I saw none." Jargas stepped back.

Gervan nodded, peeling the blood-soaked bandages from Valar's legs. He pulled out a slim gold case, a tray of stone jars containing salves and powders, and a roll of bandages from a curved stone drawer set into the wall. Jargas hadn't noticed the drawer before. Jargas saw now that, when Gervan slid it closed, it fit seamlessly into the swirling design of the wall.

The healer poured a bottle of amber liquid into a basin set into the wall, thoroughly wetted his hands, and then used more of the liquid and clean linen to clean his unconscious patient's wounds. Then he opened the case, and Jargas saw it contained a number of slender needles of varying thicknesses and lengths, as well as skeins of thread. He dipped both the thread and needle he selected in a smaller bowl of the disinfectant before sewing the skin along the vicious gashes back together. Then he bandaged the wounds. He worked quickly and efficiently, but not emotionlessly: his face was grief-stricken. Jargas saw the Guards who watched intently were as well. The Prince was well-loved.

Finally, Gervan finished and turned to Jargas. He looked up into Jargas's face, his eyes darting rapidly from the twin braids of his beard to the single, long, thick, intricate braid of his hair. It was obvious that Gervan, too, had recognized the distinctive weave of Malar. He took in Jargas's worn and dirty traveling clothes, his eyes widening at the sight of the two axe heads protruding over his shoulder, the pack, and the bloody blanket which concealed the gruesome trophy within.

"What is your name?" Gervan asked, his voice so laden with various emotions Jargas could not guess what he might be feeling or thinking.

"Prince Jargas of Malar in Holoren, son of King Rongas, grandson of King Vorgas, great grandson of King Valgas, Prince of Malar in Fromer," he said, stating his ancestry far enough back to show his kinship, in the Dwarven custom of one visiting a Kingdom not his own, but one which he has ties to.

Jargas heard gasps of shock from more than one Guard's throat behind him. Gervan's eyes narrowed in speculation. "Tell me, Jargas, did Prince Valar slay the beast that attacked him?" he asked, omitting Jargas's title, as if he'd not heard it.

"No, he did not. I did," Jargas said truthfully, intrigued.

Jargas saw the light extinguish from Gervan's eyes, and he realized it had been hope that he'd seen.

"But he slew that beast's mate, first, before the female I later slew attacked him. I brought back the trophy he was claiming, the head of the male he'd killed." Jargas removed the bloody blanket from his back. "And I have his axe as well, and it still bears the blood of the beast."

Gervan unwrapped the gory trophy and nodded, exhaling heavily in relief. "It is fortunate you did so. He is in your debt, Jargas, as are we all. How is it you happen to be in our mountains this night?"

"Am I correct in thinking this is the Kingdom of Malar in Fromer?" Jargas asked in response, though it could be no other, for its location and the style of braid, unless Malar had somehow been conquered by another Kingdom in the centuries since his father's people had left it.

Gervan nodded.

"I am here to speak with your King. My father seeks to mend the rift between the branches of our family, our peoples. We have learned that war is almost upon you, and we would not see you follow the Lost Kingdoms into oblivion. We seek to ally ourselves with you."

Gervan locked eyes with Jargas, and Jargas could tell he was being assessed. Then Gervan's gaze darted from side to side with a look of nervous intent, as if indicating the Guards standing behind him, who could not see his face, in silent supplication to Jargas for his understanding.

The healer said in a compassionate voice that did not at all match the desperation of his expression, "First I would tend to you as well. I can see your skin is burned by too much sun from your journey. I have a salve that will take away the pain and help you heal."

Jargas would have objected that he was only tanned, not burned, that he had the sun-hardy skin of his mother's people, but the intensity of Gervan's gaze belied the casual air of his words. "Thank you. I would be most grateful to you."

Gervan herded him to the very back curve of the room, to Jargas's thinking, as far from the Guards as he could. Gervan pulled forth another hidden drawer and removed a salve, whispering under his breath as he did so, "Watch your words with the King. Speak from a position of weakness, not strength, as if your people were the ones who would be aided by an alliance, not ours."

He spoke more loudly, "Here, rub this upon your skin where it is burnt."

He continued under his breath. "Do your best to appear nonthreatening to him. Do not speak your lineage too proudly; omit your title and those of your forefathers. Balgar well knows the name of your great grandsire. Take care in your words regarding Valar's test. May Ragnar protect you." Then he led Jargas back to the Guards about the Prince's bed.

Gervan spoke to one of them. "You must go to King Balgar and bring Jargas with you. Tell the King his son undertook his test of manhood alone this night in secret. He passed the test, he killed the pumar he hunted, but he was gravely injured by a second beast, which Jargas, a kinsman from afar, slew, acting as his second and saving him. Jargas has brought Valar to the Mountain and he will live."

The Guard nodded in understanding and then turned to Jargas. "Forgive me, but in spite of your station, if you are to appear before the King, you may carry no weapons."

Without argument, Jargas carefully and cooperatively unslung and handed the Prince's bare war axe to the Guards, as well as his grandsire's wrapped one, and then surrendered his hunting knife and his staff. The last was hardest to part with. He felt naked without it in his hand.

"We must be sure you are weaponless," the Guard said apologetically, indicating they would search him. Again, Jargas did not protest. They searched him as far as they could reach without stretching. Jargas obligingly bowed his head and shoulders without forcing them to ask, so they could search the rest of him.

Jargas was surprised to see that four of the Guards stayed with the Prince while only two of them accompanied him on his journey to see the King, including the one who'd spoken to him and commanded the others. Surely the Prince was far safer in the Healer's Cavern of his own Mountain than the King might be when faced with a giant from another Kingdom with potential claim to his throne?

He was led down a dizzying maze of corridors and again mapped the safe route they took in his head. The corridor they were in unexpectedly opened up into a Great Hall. This room was a natural cave, a single, huge open chamber; there had been no need to alter it further. It glistened in the light of hundreds of lamps. There were tremendous stone pillars, as well as stalagmites and stalactites, some four times as wide as his shoulders and dozens of feet long, others no bigger than his fingers, and hundreds more every size in between. Jargas stared in awe at great, wavy sheets of stone, as thin as drapery and nearly as translucent as glass, and at impossibly long and narrow straws of rock. There were at least a score of clear crystal pools of water interspersed about the chamber. It was truly magnificent, everything his father had ever told him about the lost home his father had never seen.

The courtiers standing about the Hall were far less impressive. They had a pale, weak, shifty look about them. If Jargas disliked the look of them, he despised the King from the moment he set eyes upon him. If his great grandsire's brother had been anything like this, it was no wonder he had left the Mountain he had loved, taking the cream of the nobility with him. Having seen the King's son, he had not expected how the father would appear. The sight of him instantly brought to mind the tales he'd heard of the great blind cave slugs that dwelt in hidden crevasses deep within the Mountains of the Lost Kingdoms.

The King was obese, at least half again as wide as he should be. He sat upon his massive carved stone throne as if he had been poured into it. Great rolls of fat hung over the edges. He wore a gleaming jeweled helm, which sparkled in the lamplight. Instead of the two gold rings Jargas and all the other Dwarves he'd ever seen wore at the end of their braided beards, his beard was studded with jewels, and the ends were capped in gold. Each finger of both hands bore a different jeweled ring. His clothes were of a heavy gold brocade fabric, and Jargas suspected many fine wires of true gold were woven into the cloth. A heavy chain of gold hung from his neck, with a single ruby the size of a walnut set as a pendant at the bottom of the chain. He glistened with his excessively ornate jewelry, in gaudy contrast to the natural splendor around him. The King's eyes widened when he saw Jargas, in surprise and fear, which he hid quickly under a look of contempt, but not so quickly that Jargas failed to see it.

The two Guards knelt, and after a moment's hesitation, Jargas knelt with them, casting his eyes to the floor.

"Why do you bring this giant before me?" the King asked the Guards imperiously.

The Guard to Jargas's right who had spoken to him before spoke now, but his voice sounded strained to Jargas's ear. "Prince Valar undertook his test of manhood this evening, alone and in secret. He slew the pumar he hunted, he passed the test, but a second pumar gravely injured him. This Dwarf acted as his second. He killed the second beast and brought Prince Valar back to the Mountain. Gervan has tended the Prince and says he will live."

The King's voice took on a shrewd quality. "My son left the Mountain in secret, you say? Where, then, were his Guard?"

The Guard swallowed heavily. "I do not know your Majesty. Should I summon them for you?"

"In time, in time. And where was the Door Guard, that they might let him leave the Mountain alone?" the King asked, his voice deceptively mild.

The Guard sounded more nervous. "I do not know, your Majesty. I am of the Night Guard. My shift had not begun when the Prince left. I only just came on duty before he returned to us, after the sun had already set. My men and I left to go with the Prince to Healer Gervan as soon as the door was opened and we saw him injured."

The King's voice took on a deadly tone. "So, I am to understand that my only son, my heir, a mere child, was allowed to leave the Mountain alone and unguarded? That he was not even noticed missing until he was locked out?"

Jargas saw through the corner of his downcast eyes that the Guard at the King's feet was trembling now. "Apparently so, your Majesty," he all but whispered in response.

"Rise! Bring my son's Guard to me, the ones who let him leave unprotected," the King commanded.

"At once, your Majesty!" the Guard said, his voice gushing with relief. He fled, walking quickly backward, bowing the entire way before he turned and ran.

"You, giant, speak! What were you doing near our Mountain this night? Are you a thief seeking to gain entry to our Kingdom to rob our Vault? Did you think bringing my son to me might earn you a reward instead?" The King's voice was both scathing and oily.

To Jargas's ear, it sounded as if the King described something he himself might have attempted. Jargas clenched his teeth and calmed his temper before speaking, choosing his words carefully, his well-rehearsed speech useless now, after Gervan's warning and what he had just seen and heard. "I have traveled from afar to your Mountain, Majesty, from my own, but not for the treasure you describe. I came only to seek to renew my ties to my kinfolk. Nor do I seek a reward for saving your son; knowing he will live is reward enough. If you permit me to speak it, I will tell you my name and lineage and why I have come, and I also have a gift I would give you, if the Guard who yet kneels before you will return it to me."

The King's eyes lit in greed and narrowed in anger, and Jargas saw the Guard he spoke of blanch. Jargas belatedly realized he had unwittingly endangered the man. He quickly added, "He was wise to take it from me, for although it was not brought as a weapon, it could certainly be used as one."

"Tell me your name, then, and show me this gift of which you speak," the corpulent King commanded. Jargas could tell he was far less interested in the former than the latter.

"I am Jargas of Malar in Holoren, son of Rongas, grandson of Vorgas, great grandson of Valgas of Malar in Fromer," he said, purposefully omitting his title and those of his ancestors as Gervan had urged, though it grated to do so. Despite his care, there was a sudden intake of breath from those gathered about the room. "I have come to request an alliance between our two Kingdoms, to reunite what was sundered these seven centuries past. Our people miss the mountains of home, and would return to them. Also, we have seen that war approaches your Kingdom, and we would offer our arms to your aid, should you have need of them. You might well vanquish this foe without our poor aid, for although we are mighty warriors, now I see you are just as mighty. I offer you the war axe of Valgas as a gift, in honor of such an alliance."

The King was looking at him craftily now, and Jargas was curious to see the focus of his eyes was upon his right wrist, not his face. "You are abnormally tall for one of our kind. Does the blood of Man also flow within your veins?"

"Aye, from my mother's people," Jargas said, carefully hiding his reluctance in revealing it. He was proud of his dual heritage and would not lie about it, even though this King might think him tainted for it.

"Aha! But you claim you are here on behalf of your father's people, not your mother's, despite the band you wear?" the King challenged.

"Aye, I claim so because it is true. My father is the one who sent me on this quest. My mother's kin have not," Jargas said honestly, wondering what significance the armband held. Jargas wore the armband on his wrist as a cuff, for it had not spanned his bicep even when he was still a boy. Of everyone he had ever met, might this vile King know the secret of his lost heritage?

"So you are not here to try to form an alliance between our Kingdom and Dorolingas and Ironhand?" the King pressed.

"No. As I have told you, I seek only to reunite our single Kingdom, which was split in two so many years ago."

"Reunite it under which King? Yours? With your lineage, might your father not be King?" Balgar asked silkily.

"Aye, my father is King, and I am Prince and his heir," Jargas admitted. This next part was the hardest thing he had ever had to say, for he had no doubt his father would never have instructed him thusly had he ever met this King. "For the sake of our people, my father will abdicate his rights to the throne, for himself and his line."

"Your father has no more right to be King than your great grandsire had! He brought our Kingdom to the brink of civil war, then chose the road of a coward and fled, ransacking our Vault and our Library, stealing our treasures, our goods, our books, our people. Do you deny it?" The King was shaking with rage now and had raised his great bulk from the throne, although he settled quickly downward.

Jargas thought that the lost treasure was the part that galled this gilded King more than any of the rest, that he listed his losses in order of importance to him. His own father had listed them to him in precisely the opposite order when he had spoken of it to Jargas.

Jargas chose his words with care. "What is past is long past. My father had no part in what happened, nor did I, nor did you, Great King, nor does your son. I do not claim understanding or responsibility for the actions of my forbearers. I only aid my father in seeking to heal the great breech between us, to reunite our sundered Kingdom, thereby strengthening it, before the onset of war.

"If you accept the war axe I bring, then you accept our kinship and our aid, if it is needed. Your family and your Kingdom have already benefited once by our aid, for your heir yet lives. If you do not accept the gift, then when I return to my father, I will bear that news instead. The choice is yours." Jargas did not think the King would accept what they offered. It sounded as if he had refused at least one proposed alliance already that might strengthen him against such a powerful enemy. But he stood to lose no power through this alliance, and instead to gain by it. Jargas had been sure to mention his son to him again, to remind him that he had already gained much.

He could not believe that this man sat bandying words with him, when any true father would have immediately excused himself to see his injured son, particularly a Dwarf. Dwarves bore few children and treasured those few dearly. He hoped that the King would refuse; it was an ill alliance he was forming. He did not want to ever see his father—a great man, a diplomat and scholar and warrior, a true King—kneel before this mockery of a King, as Jargas had knelt before him. He would be hard pressed to kneel before him ever again. He felt soiled by it.

"Do you come to us poor kin, or rich ones?" the King asked, avarice dripping from his voice. "I see you have some small amount of gold upon you," he added, negligently waving his hand toward Jargas's braid rings.

Jargas gritted his teeth again before speaking. "The Holoren Mountains of my home have neither jewels nor the precious metals you mine from your own mountains, Majesty. But in spite of that, we are skilled in the arts of the forge. The arms and armor we produce are coveted by Men, valued by Lord and King alike, even by the Elves, though they might try to deny it. And our stone masons' work is no less appreciated. Our coffers have gold and silver enough that we might enrich your Vault." Jargas had to force the words from his tongue. His people had sweated and bled for centuries to achieve their wealth. He could see this mockery of a King would strip them of all they possessed. He would form this dark alliance if he could, then bear news of all he had seen to his father and hope he might sway him against it.

The King's eyes gleamed with lust for the treasure. Jargas thought it was indeed fortunate that Jarina was safely home, far from this creature. The King must never be allowed to look upon her. He forced the thought away, lest his eyes gleam with the thought of murder his heart suddenly held.

"Let me see the axe," the King commanded.

The Guard held it forth, and Jargas unwrapped it and handed it to the King, who took it and eyed it hungrily and then scornfully. "An unadorned weapon for a King," he scoffed. "My own great grandsire's axe is encrusted with jewels and laced with fine filigree, and it weighs twice what this one does."

Jargas bit firmly down upon his tongue until he tasted the tang of his blood. He might not choose to wield an axe, but he was as proficient in the use of one and as knowledgeable about them as any warrior of his kin. King Valgas's axe was a perfectly balanced, exquisitely crafted yet functional weapon.

"Very well. We will aid you, my poor cousin, and accept the alliance you offer. In fact, the Crown is in debt to you for returning our kin to us, both those we had not known we had lost, and those we had thought lost forever. We would repay that debt to you."

"The alliance between our Kingdoms is all I seek." Jargas wanted no token from this foul King that might later be held over his head.

"And that we have granted you. But that does not repay the first debt, only the second. Though we can do so. I would reward you for the life of my son with the life of one of your own kin. We have in our dungeon a Man, one of your brothers-in-arms. We will release him to you."

Jargas's brow creased. "I know of none of my people who would have come here."

"He is banded a Captain, as you are," Balgar said, pointing to the armband Jargas wore about his wrist. "So, we return one lost to you who you also did not know was lost, or perhaps whom you thought dead, for he has been here for some time. We will be glad to be rid of him. I will relinquish his band to you first."

Balgar rose from the throne. "You will wait here. It is in the Vault, and none but I may go there." He spoke to one of the Throne Guard. "Retrieve the prisoner's bow and quiver and knife from the Armory." Then the King departed, while everyone in the room bowed respectfully.

Jargas looked at the band on his arm, and his pulse quickened. There was a Man being held here who might be from his maternal grandsire's homeland, who might even know who his maternal grandsire had been! The King knew something as well, for he'd called him a Captain. Yet they had imprisoned him, so they neither feared nor respected him.

He wondered what offense the Man had committed, if any, to have caused him to be imprisoned, and how long he'd been captive. He realized it might have been something trivial or something in the King's mind only. Dwarves were well known for their pride and their tempers, and Dwarven Kings doubly so, but this crafty King was unlike any he'd ever heard of; he might be capable of many foul deeds.

Jargas looked about the cavern, memorizing the details of it. It was everything his father had ever said of it. He could be at home in a place like this, were it not for the King. In the tunnels and rooms connecting to it too. Even though it was built by Dwarves, for Dwarves, he had not had to duck his head or turn sideways to enter any of the doorways here. Dwarves were short of stature, but broad of vision, and they built on a grand scale.

The courtiers in the room eyed him warily. He was glad none approached him. The cold stone held far more interest for him than these slimy kin.

Balgar returned, an armband in his hand, and Jargas drew in a breath and held it as the King offered it to him. He took it with a steady hand. It was almost identical to his own: solid pallenteum, the same dimensions, the same weight, the same look, the same feel, only unlike his own, this one was engraved with a beast that was known to him: a snarling wolven in midlunge. He traced the image with his fingertip. Then he exhaled. "I would like to see the prisoner. What is his name?"

"I don't know, but he calls himself Hunter."

Jargas nodded as if that meant something to him.

"Come, I will take you to him. I would like to see if our hospitality has taught him some manners," the King said, laughing as if he had said something witty.

His laugh made Jargas's skin crawl, but he forced a smile. He wondered what Balgar might be up to. Why return Hunter's band to him? It was worth a fortune for the metal it was crafted from alone. Why mention Hunter at all? To test him? To taunt him? Or to lure him to the dungeon so he might also be imprisoned? Was the Man who had worn this already dead? Balgar would find Jargas neither easy to kill nor to catch and confine, even without his weapons, and he could rearm himself easily enough by overpowering any of the Guards. Jargas well knew how to use an axe, though he did not prefer to wield one.

Balgar and a squad of his Throne Guard led Jargas deep inside the Mountain. The King puffed and wheezed as he walked: moving his great weight was obviously an effort. It was cold and damp here, and silent save for the King's labored breathing. The sound of their footsteps echoed off the walls of the wide hallways. The Guard at the door they finally approached looked surprised to see them and nervous.

"We are here for the prisoner. Open the cell," Balgar commanded.

"Majesty, then I must first see if it is safe," the Guard said, his voice apologetic.

"Why would it not be safe? Is the prisoner not chained, as ordered?" the King demanded, his temper flaring.

"No, Majesty," the Guard said, quailing before the King. "We tried, Majesty, but we could not keep him chained. We still don't understand how he frees himself. He has been very difficult to keep confined."

The King was glaring at the Guard. Now Jargas believed there was a prisoner here.

The Guard continued quickly. "But he has tried to escape many times, and he has not succeeded. Beating him did not work. We did so more than once. We even lashed him, but nothing we tried worked. So now we no longer open the cell door. We slide in a pitcher and tray and only slide in another when they are returned. We see that he has bread and water and cannot escape."

Jargas was infuriated by what he heard, but kept himself carefully in check as he asked the Guard, "How long has the prisoner been here?"

"A few weeks," the King said dismissively.

"Four months," the Guard said, simultaneously.

"You've kept my kinsman locked alone in the cold and dark and damp for four months with nothing but bread to eat and water to drink?" Jargas asked, his voice deadly quiet.

"No, there used to be light, and he was fed better at first, but the Captain said that he would cause less trouble if he weren't so strong. When he attacked us two months ago, the Captain took his light and blanket and ordered that no one enter the cell and that he be given only bread...," the Guard trailed off fearfully, obviously realizing how pathetic and inadequate his excuse sounded. Jargas well knew how he must look and sound to the cowed man: an angered, towering giant, with the height and breadth almost of an ogre, but the look of a Dwarf, speaking Dwarvish, and questioning him as if he were his King.

Jargas turned to the King and saw fear in his eyes and the beginnings of treachery. "To imprison one Captain so foully might go hard on you, but to attempt to imprison another would not be forgiven. For all my mother's people did not send me, they know I am here. And I would remind you that you and I are also kin, and you would not want my father's Kingdom as an enemy. And they are already impatient for my return."

"Please, Lord Jargas, you would not withdraw your support of an alliance over this simple misunderstanding? The Captain overstepped his place and will answer for it," the King wheedled.

"Of course not. Now, I would see Hunter," Jargas said, even as he wondered why the King might call him Lord instead of Prince, if he were to use a title at all.

The King waved angrily at the unfortunate Guard, and he fumbled at the lock with a shaking hand until he finally opened the cell door. Jargas snatched a torch from the sconce on the tunnel wall and strode into the cell. A wall of stale air fouled with sickness and excrement almost made him retch. He looked about. At first he saw no one: the bed was empty, and no one was standing. But something moved in the shadows on the floor against the wall. He shifted the light.

A Man lay on the floor. He was filthy, and his body was wracked by spasms. Jargas strode over to him and knelt. He was tall and broad-shouldered, but terribly thin; his clothes were a tent about him. His eyes were sunken, open and staring, but lucid, in a scarred face. He was not old, but his skin was wrinkled and hot and dry, and his lips were cracked and caked in dried blood. He was breathing quickly and deeply, and when Jargas felt his heart, the beat was not steady, but uneven, and the pulse at his throat was weak. His shirt was open, and Jargas saw pronounced ribs, and his stomach looked swollen and distended.

"When was he last given water?" Jargas asked. He looked about the room and spotted a tray nearby. There was a dry, empty pitcher and an equally dry cup, both on their side, and something small and fuzzy and green that might once have been bread.

"He is fed once every day... or should have been," the Guard said, looking in fear at the tray. "If the pitcher and tray were not returned...," he trailed off, swallowing.

"If he were ill and could not return it, instead of tending to him, you would kill him for lack of even water and bread!" Jargas fumed.

He bent over the Man again. The stranger was squinting his eyes against the light of the torch, as if it were unbearably bright, but he was watching Jargas through his lowered lashes. Jargas showed him the band on his wrist. "I've come to take you home, kinsman," he said in Common.

The Man's eyes widened and then shut against the resultant flood of light, but he did not speak. Jargas did not think he could. Jargas lifted him as if he were a child, although his bone and what was left of his muscle still had weight, far more than he expected them to from the look of him. It was as if his bones were as dense as a Dwarf's. "I'm glad your healer knows his craft better than your Guards know theirs," Jargas said to Balgar in disdain.

"He will receive the best of care," Balgar promised, his voice obsequious, all trace of haughtiness vanished. "Guard, lead him to Gervan at once!" he commanded. The Guard jumped to obey, leading Jargas back down the hall.

Jargas followed, carrying Hunter, heading quickly down corridor after corridor, keeping careful track of where and how he was led, adding to his mental map of the Mountain. It would be well for him to know the way away from the dungeon, in case he ever found himself prisoner there, and from Gervan's door, he knew the way back out of the Mountain. He recognized Gervan's door when they came to it and strode inside, past the Guard who had opened the door.

"Gervan, if you're here, I have urgent need of you," Jargas called out. He turned to the Guard. "You, out of my sight!"

The Guard looked startled, as if he might protest, then saw the look in Jargas's eyes and left quickly, without a word.

Gervan came from the same archway he'd entered from the last time. He looked at Jargas in surprise and at the Man in his arms. "Jargas! Come, into the other room," he said, waving him to the room with the beds he'd seen before. Valar was no longer there. Jargas laid Hunter gently on one of the beds. It was barely long enough for him.

"Whom have you rescued this time?" Gervan said, beginning to check his new patient as Hunter's skeletal form was wracked with convulsions.

"A kinsman. He's called Hunter. He's been locked in the dungeon in the cold and damp for four months, been beaten more than once, whipped, and these past two months has had no light nor even a blanket for warmth and been fed only bread and water once a day. Then he took ill and has not even had water to drink, let alone bread; I've no idea for how long." Jargas's voice was shaking in indignation.

"Hold him gently and make sure he doesn't fall from the bed. I will only be a moment." True to his word, Gervan left but returned almost immediately with a pitcher of water on a tray, a cup, a jar of honey, and a smaller one of salt. He mixed the salt and honey into the water, tasted it and added more salt, then filled a cup. He held it to Hunter's mouth. "Drink this very slowly. Only take a little at a time and hold some of it in your mouth if you can," Gervan said gently in Common.

Hunter tried to comply, but much was spilled as his entire body was wracked with spasms and the cup shook.

Gervan said to Jargas, "Try to hold him still." Jargas lifted Hunter to a sitting position and gently embraced him from behind, pinning Hunter's back to his chest. The healer encouraged Hunter to try to drink again, and he got more of it down this time.

"Lay him back down. That's all we dare give him for now. He must keep what he has drunk down," Gervan said to Jargas in Dwarvish.

He turned to Hunter and said in Common, "I know your head pains you greatly and your muscles as well, but I can't give you anything for the pain yet. But I'm going to give you something to try to stop the spasms. It will relax your muscles. Drink it very slowly, and if you feel you might retch, don't force yourself to finish it." Gervan pulled out a metal flask from one of the concealed stone drawers, opened the stopper, and then carefully poured the liquid into Hunter's mouth.

Hunter drank slowly and did a better job, spilling less than he had of the water. "Very good. Now just try to relax. You're safe here. No one will harm you while you are in my care."

Gervan turned to Jargas and said in Dwarvish, "Much of his suffering is from the lack of water. Had it gone much further he would not have been able to drink, and then I could not have helped him."

Gervan turned back to Hunter and spoke in Common once more, his voice gentle and soothing. "I'm going to bathe you now, and rub your skin with lotion and ointment. Your skin is very dry, and cracked."

Gervan said in Dwarvish to Jargas, "He's very tall and his muscles are still strong enough that I could use your help, as he can't control them. Can you hold him while I bathe him?"

"Of course."

Gervan peeled off the Man's rank and filthy clothes and discarded them. Hunter had soiled himself more than once in his illness and had apparently had no water to spare for cleanliness for a number of months prior to that for him to look and smell as he did.

As the Healer washed Hunter, Jargas noted the many scars he bore, reading his hard life by them: there were blade marks, marks of teeth and claws, a large scar from a healed burn, and other scars not so easily identified, some old and others new. The scar on his face ran from his forehead across his left eye down his cheek and disappeared into his beard, but the blade that had made it hadn't blinded him. His beard was short enough that Jargas thought he had probably entered the cell clean-shaven. His hair was dull and ragged. He was a sunken-eyed, pale, bony ghost of a Man. But his eyes were the most disturbing of all. They were already dead, though they still watched him.

"Balgar would keep a Man such as this, who has fought and lived through so much, in a cold, dark hole without water until he died!" Jargas raged.

The healer whispered urgently to him, "Quietly, Jargas, unless you wish to send him back with you for company. The King has ears everywhere."

"His son would make a better King," Jargas said more softly.

"Only if he lives long enough to," Gervan said bitterly.

Jargas looked at him sharply.

"No, the pumar you saved him from weren't Balgar's doing. If anything, he delayed Valar's Rite of Passage as long as he could. Now that he's passed, as a man, he's a greater threat to his father's throne than as a boy. You saw how the Guards react to him, versus his father. They love the Prince, but they despise and fear his father. When he heard of the attack from the Night Guard, did he come to see his son, as any other father would have? No! I pity Valar, having a father such as him."

"Does Valar know of the danger he is in?" Jargas asked.

"Aye. I've made sure he's seen it, though he does not want to."

"Where is he?"

Gervan sighed as he rolled Hunter onto his side to bathe his back and then laid three layers of clean towels over the soaked and soiled cushion, rolling Hunter onto them when he was done. "Valar awoke and insisted to be brought to his own rooms. I told him I will check on him later, but right now he needs to sleep, and he'd rather do so in his own bed. But do not worry. I made sure he is guarded by those we trust while he rests."

Hunter suddenly shuddered and went limp.

"What's happened?" Jargas asked, afraid he might have died.

Gervan felt for Hunter's heartbeat and sighed in relief. "It's all right. The medicine I gave him is merely working. The spasms and convulsions are stopping. He will be able to rest somewhat and to heal. I will have to waken him every twenty minutes or so to give him more of the honeyed saltwater. He still needs to drink much, but he can't do so all at once." Gervan opened a different drawer, selected a small glass sand timer from a row of a dozen in varying sizes, and upended it onto the stand beside the bed next to the one that Hunter lay on, starting the flow of the grains of sand.

Jargas was surprised. In his experience, only Men used sand timers. They all came from Thenalon, the only City of Man with those who had the ability to blow glass and craft an instrument so delicate. Though the Elves certainly had the ability, to his knowledge they instead favored water clocks. Dwarves, too, knew the art of glassblowing, but the timekeeping devices, in his father's Kingdom at least, were far more elaborate, intricately crafted mechanisms that accurately kept the time, as long as they were kept carefully wound. He would have expected to see the same in use here.

His puzzlement must have shown upon his face, for Gervan's next words; Jarina often teased him it was as easy to ascertain his thoughts by gazing at his face as it was to read the words upon the pages of a book.

"I suppose you must think it an eccentricity upon my part that I rely upon such primitive technology, when I have at my disposal the finest clocks in the world. My son, Arvan, chides me for it often enough. But I have found when I have a number of patients in residence simultaneously, each with a set time for his medication, that it is far easier to keep track in such a manner. At a single glance from anywhere in the room I can see who will need my attentions next. Though by Aralyn's grace I've currently only the one patient, I am set in my ways."

"I hope you did not take offense. I was indeed surprised, but did not mean to appear critical of your methods."

"I quite understand. Now, if you'll help me lift your kinsman and carry him to the bed beside the timer where it is clean and dry, he'll be able to sleep better. We'll need to burn the cushion he's lying upon now."

Jargas lifted Hunter carefully and placed him onto the clean, dry bed. Gervan washed his hands in the basin he'd used before with Valar, which had apparently been emptied since. He opened a concealed drawer and took out a clean sheet and blanket, which he covered Hunter with.

Gervan went to the end of the room, opened a different door than the one they'd entered from, and returned with a small, high-walled cart. He stripped the towels from the wet, smelly bed Hunter had lain upon and rolled them into a bundle; then he put them into the cart and proceeded to do the same with the bed cushion. Jargas helped him with the latter. "I'll be back in a moment," Gervan said as he disappeared with his burden.

After hesitating a moment, Jargas followed, curious. He saw Gervan head down the corridor to another door. From here he could see it led to a small room or closet, with a second door on the other side, which from his mental map would lead to the corridor.

He ducked back inside the patient's room, his curiosity satisfied. They had a similar efficient refuse-removal system in their Mountain. At some set time, a Dwarf would remove the waste and clean the room as well, to remove the smell.

When Gervan returned, he had a hot, soapy washcloth in his hands and a dry hand towel, which he handed to him. Jargas accepted both gratefully, tossing the dirtied linens into the laundry bin Gervan opened for him after he was done.

Gervan headed back to Hunter's bedside, thanking Jargas for his aid and adding, "It's a miracle his lungs sound clear. There are any number of diseases he could have died from under conditions like that. If he were stronger, I'd suggest you take him and the Prince as far and fast away from here as you could. It would be safer for Valar to live in exile with your kin than here."

"I would speak with Valar if I can. I would like to know why my kinsman was imprisoned in the first place, and what, if anything, he might know of him," Jargas said.

"There will be time enough for that tomorrow. Valar must rest tonight. You should rest as well, Jargas, for it sounds as though you've had a long journey. But first you might like to bathe, while I wash up and cook so that we may eat. I welcome you to my table tonight. You may stay here as well. I have a spare room you may use. Forgive me my poor hospitality. I know this is not the way visiting royalty should be treated, but I truly believe you'll have more appetite and a more restful night here, for all I set a poorer table and have less grand chambers than the King."

"You are very generous, Gervan. I appreciate your hospitality."

His host sighed. "I am selfish, really. I would hear of your father's people, for some few of my own kin had sense enough to go with Prince Valgas when he left, and I would like to know whether their sons or grandsons or great-grandsons are yet alive and well."

Gervan led Jargas back into the antechamber and then through the door he'd initially come from into his private chambers. They bypassed the family, dining, and kitchen chambers to the left and three sealed doors to the right, the latter of which Jargas thought were likely the bedchambers. They came to a final pair of doors at the end of the hall. Gervan pointed to the door on the left. "This is the privy."

Then Gervan opened the door on the right, and Jargas let out a sigh of contentment, as he beheld a magnificent bathing chamber. The floor here was as smooth and polished as the floor and walls of the corridor had been, but the walls were carved in the same soothing, intricate curls and whorls as in the sick room.

Jargas saw to his relief and joy that the stone tub, which was sunken into the floor, was at least twice as wide as he was, half again as long, and deep enough that he could fully submerge. He'd not be forced to stick a single limb at a time into some small metal portable tub, as he'd had to in the inns of Men as he'd traveled from his home to here. He set his pack down on the floor, near the wall.

Jargas was puzzled by the two gold handles which protruded near the floor at one end of the tub. He peered over the side, eager to see the detailed carvings which graced the surface, and looked first with curiosity and then wonder at the single hole set into the side of the tub about half a foot from the edge, in addition to the plugged hole at the bottom that he'd expected to see.

Could these be the water pipes his father had told him of? If he turned the handles, would hot and cold water truly blend together and flow forth, without need of pumping or heating or carrying buckets of water? There was nothing like this in his father's Kingdom! The few water engineers Malar in Fromer had been blessed with had stayed in Fromer with the King. They'd had no need to do otherwise; from what Jargas had heard, they were wealthy beyond dreams of avarice, spoiled and pampered.

Their lost Homeland was nothing like their current lands. Here they had intentionally built upon the tops of the tallest mountains they could find, in the center of this great continent, as high up and far away from the sea as they could.

Their people had valued their water engineers for many millennia before coming to these lands. They were the ones who had kept the great lock, dike, and dam system that protected the Homeland running smoothly and efficiently, ensuring the safety of their great cities and all their people. Much of the Dwarven Homeland had sunk below sea level over the millennia, and their low-lying lands were riddled with mines, tunnels, and quarries which had to be continually pumped dry. Their water engineers were highly paid, honored, and respected, valued even above the librarians for the importance of their work.

Jargas sighed heavily. They had paid the ultimate price for it, proudly, during the Inundation. Every single water engineer, nearly all of their journeymen, and most of their apprentices had died, many in the Great Wave and all the rest engaging emergency backup systems as the flood waters continued to rise, overcoming safeguard after safeguard, and when those all systematically failed, frantically jury-rigging bypasses, trying to stem the rising waters long enough for them to implement the emergency evacuation plans every child had practiced since he or she could walk but had only in their most horrific nightmares dreamt they might truly need.

"Prince Jargas, does the bath displease you? Forgive me if the chambers in your own Kingdom are far superior, but this is the one both I and my patients use; only the Lords and the Royal Family have finer. Ragnar help me, and I asked you to aid me in bathing Hunter and you even helped me carry his soiled bedding to the refuse cart! I did not even think how inappropriate it was for you to do so. Your forbearance with me until now has been boundless," Gervan said, his voice laced first with contrition and humiliation and then fear.

Jargas cursed himself for his unforgivable breach of etiquette of shaming his host by seeming to find fault with his hospitality. He hastened to reassure Gervan before he could find further fault with himself. "No, Gervan, it is I who must ask you to forgive me! Your hospitality is flawless. I am not displeased at all. I gladly aided you in tending to my kinsman. As you might imagine, for Ragnar and Aralyn both blessing me with my build as they have, I often aid others in my own Kingdom in transporting heavy or unwieldy items many places, including to our refuse rooms.

"As for this chamber and the tub, though we have ones equal in size and beauty within our Mountain, we have nothing that is their equal in terms of engineering. It is when I beheld the faucet handles, when I realized the significance of both them and the pipe, the thought that you had a constant flow of hot and cold water at your beck and call, that I became overcome. I began to think of all we had lost. It brought to mind the Inundation, the sacrifice of the many water engineers who died so that we might live. I was silent only in honor of their memory, when otherwise I would certainly have been effusive with my praise. But I think even my father might forgive me for such a heinous breech of etiquette, given the cause. I hope that you might do the same," Jargas said humbly.

To Jargas's relief, the fear and shame fled Gervan's face, and a sheepish smile replaced it. "Then neither of us is at fault and neither should take offense. Who among us could ever think about the Inundation without being so moved? Now then, it would be both my honor and my pleasure to show you all the amenities I can provide."

He depressed a section of rock, and a formerly invisible door swung open. "You can place your soiled clothes in this laundry bin here. It opens directly on the other end to the corridor, so they can be removed and laundered for you without disturbing your privacy."

Gervan opened a second concealed area, this one containing a number of well-stocked shelves. "In here are towels, washcloths, robes, and slippers, though unfortunately the latter will be of little use to you."

He pressed another hidden mechanism. "Here are soaps and oils for your skin, hair, and beard."

He pressed a final panel. "And here are various sets of combs and brushes. You are welcome to use or to keep as little or as much as you need of each; I will not take offense in either case.

"I am not a callow youth; I am not usually so sensitive and unsure of myself. From the first you reminded me much of Valar in your friendliness and openness to me, so much so that, for a moment, I truly forgot you were a visiting Prince and that I might be overstepping my place in your presence. I am pleased to see my initial assessment was on the mark. I want your stay here with me to be a comfortable one, Jargas. Am I correct in assuming you'd rather I not use the appellation 'Prince' while in private?"

"Aye, you're correct. It is the same in my own Kingdom: we're not ones to stand upon formality, except when it's truly called for. Again, Gervan, I want you to know I am well pleased with you, both as a person and as a host. You truly provide all that I could ask for, without my needing to ask."

Gervan smiled. "Then I leave you to your privacy. Please feel free to use the privy if you've a need of it, while I check upon Hunter. Afterward, I will be washing up in the privy and then changing before I begin to prepare our dinner. Take as long as you would like here. Dinner will be fresh and hot whenever you might emerge. As a healer, I am used to having my meals interrupted, and I've an efficient system for keeping foods warm as well as cooking and heating dishes quickly. I often cook great quantities at a time so I can eat whenever I have the time to do so.

"Oh, and lest you scald yourself, the handle on the left controls the hot and the water comes out steaming. You will need to temper it at least to a degree with the cold on the right. Using both at once, you can achieve any temperature you desire. And please, feel free to fill the tub as deeply as you need and as many times as you need. We are blessed by Aralyn in that we have no shortage of clean water here in our Mountain. The stopper at the bottom opens the drain and releases the dirtied water. Unless you'd prefer me to run the bath for you?" Gervan added, looking sheepish again, as if belatedly realizing he should have offered to do so from the start.

Jargas grinned. "And deprive myself of the joy of using such a marvel? I think not!" He laughed heartily, and Gervan laughed too. "Thank you, Gervan. I'll see you for dinner." Still smiling, the healer left.

Jargas went to the cabinets and selected different soaps and oils that appealed to him and a handful of bathing cloths. He'd not touch the towels yet, while so filthy, although his hands, at least, were clean. Laying everything beside the edge of the recessed tub, he then carefully removed his two beard rings and his hair ring and set them upon his pack, and then began the tedious task of unbraiding his hair and beard. Running his fingers through both, he reveled in the feel of his fingers. Stripping off his clothes, he placed them where Gervan had indicated. Then with all the excitement and joy of a child opening a gift and playing with a new toy for the first time, he turned the handles.

It took far longer than should have been necessary to fill the tub, as he varied the settings of each handle, experimenting with temperature and flow. He could not wait to tell his father and sister all about this wonder!

Jargas settled with contentment into the steaming tub, decadently allowing the water to first cascade onto his broad back, massaging his travel weary muscles, before it flowed down into the tub. He had not had a hot bath since Logareth, and it had been nothing like this. Finally, he turned off the water and lay blissfully soaking in the relaxing heat.

Eventually he roused himself enough to begin soaping his body, hair, and beard. He let the tub drain and refill, and then soaped a second time. Finally satisfied, he drained the tub, filled it and rinsed, soaking for far longer than necessary in the clear, steaming water, feeling the tension of his journey and his meeting with the King drain from him.

Reluctantly, he rose and pulled the stopper a final time, allowing the water to drain. He didn't want to keep the healer from his dinner, and truthfully, his own stomach was trying to gnaw its way through his backbone.

He dried himself with the thick, fluffy towels his host had provided and then unpacked the set of clothes he'd originally intended to wear before the King, had he arrived in the usual manner of a visitor from another Kingdom with time to wash and groom and change and prepare. Looking at the elaborate, colorful brocade, he changed his mind. No, he'd save these for the morrow. Instead he pulled out his set of everyday clothes. They would far better suit dinner with the healer. Then, mindful again of the passage of time, he began the elaborate ritual of combing, oiling and braiding his hair and beard, without allowing them to fully dry first as he normally would.

When he was done, he estimated he'd been in the bathing room for nearly two hours, at least an hour less than he usually might take. There was no clock in this room, of course. No Dwarf would ever dream of rushing another in his bath.

Jargas made sure the room was as tidy as it had been when he came, save for his pack, which he left beside the wall, and then set out to find his host. His stomach growled hungrily as he followed the enticing aroma of freshly baked bread to the kitchen.

Gervan beamed, seeing him. "Now there's the look of a contentedly clean yet hungry guest! I'll only be a few more moments, if you'd care to sit in the dining chamber. I only need to set the table and arrange everything in serving dishes."

"What kind of guest would I be to allow you to do so when I've two strong arms to aid you? If you'll show me to the dishes, I'll set the table, and I'll carry in whatever you instruct me to."

Gervan's smile grew. "In that case, they're in here," he said, opening a concealed cupboard in the rock. "It will be just the two of us. My son Arvan is dining with a friend this evening."

Jargas took two of everything he thought they might need. The alabaster plates and bowls were contrastingly sturdy and fragile. He stacked and carried them carefully as he headed for the dining chamber. It was a joy to be within a Dwarven Mountain again, away from the clutter of Man's world, where he was forever bashing his shoulders and shins and hipbones on cabinets and counters and furnishings that were spaced too close together for his frame.

Except in Jarina's house, of course. She'd built and furnished it with him in mind, as well as their people. As Chieftess and Healer of the Varash, she spent little time within the Mountain. In part for her scandalous ways, Jarina was far more comfortable within the confines of the Varash village where their mother had lived before she'd wed their father.

He smiled wistfully in thought of her. How he missed her! He wondered how he had survived the journey without his sister's mischievous smile to light his days. He mentally touched the thick copper strand that bound him to her and drew comfort from the river of love for him that flowed through it. That was how he'd survived. He did not know what he would have done without their bond.

The oval dining table was wide and long, ringed by a dozen stone chairs in the same bluish stone as those in the entryway to the healer's home. He chose one end of the table and a seat beside it and set two places with numerous plates and bowls, so they might face one another easily to speak while they ate. Then he headed back for the mugs they'd be needing, and again for platter after platter of foodstuffs: a beautifully rare roast of goat's meat; two stuffed roasted chickens; a platter of six plates holding intricate geometric designs of different types and shades of sliced goat cheeses; half a dozen bowls of different varieties of mushrooms, ranging in size and color from tiny snow-white buttons to taupe monsters the size of his palm; and two loaves of bread. Then there was a cask of mead, another of fermented goat's milk, three different wines, and a pitcher of water.

Once everything was ready and Gervan joined him, Jargas prepared to sit, only then realizing what he'd failed to notice before, in his distraction over his sister and the sight and smell of the food. Sitting at the table was going to prove far more difficult than he might have hoped. Although the doorframes were large enough for his frame and the hallways wide, the furniture was scaled to a normal-sized Dwarf. The chairs, since made of stone, would likely be sturdy enough to hold his great bulk if he put two beside one another, but the chair legs were uncomfortably short, as were the table legs. Jargas sat sideways to the table, with his knees nearly up to his chin.

His father had a special table and chair for him in his Dining Hall. He'd not thought of the difficulty before accepting the healer's invitation to dinner. Jargas weighed what he knew of Gervan and the protocol of the situation and spoke, relatively sure he'd not offend his even-tempered and warm-hearted host. "It is not at all my intention to insult, but if it would not be improper, I'd ask if you might have a cushion I might use to sit upon the floor, so that I might tuck my legs straight out under the table and sit that way."

Gervan grinned at him. "I'm greatly relieved to hear you ask! I was trying to think of a politic way around the difficulty I saw you were in and was afraid I might insult you by offering just such a compromise. Would that all of the world's royalty were as congenial as you! I'll be right back."

He returned in a moment with a soft cushion of deep blue. Jargas sat contented and relaxed, easily able to reach the tabletop.

The two began to eat and spoke at length of Gervan's Kingdom and his own and Gervan's distant relatives in Malar in Holoren. Gervan kept an eye on the sand timer he'd set beside his plate and excused himself every twenty minutes to give water to Hunter.

Jargas ate sparingly, as he always did when made a guest, but Gervan caught him at it. "Now, I am still hungry, but trying not to appear a glutton to you, for I would not have you view me in the same light as the King. You are easily twice my size and have had a long journey and must be at least twice as hungry. There is plenty here, and my larder is yet full. I would not starve if you were to partake of more. In fact, you will insult me, your host, unless you eat and drink your fill."

Jargas grinned in relief and helped himself to another half chicken, a heaping portion of the tiny white mushrooms he favored, and a thick slab of bread, and Gervan served himself seconds as well. They spoke longer, continuing to eat until every serving dish lay empty.

Gervan leaned back, his hands clasped over his full stomach in contentment, and smiled broadly at Jargas. "I have missed such company! I cannot remember the last time I've smiled so much in a single day, nor felt so light of heart. Nowadays, no one is free to speak his mind, for fear he might speak to a spy of the King, or be overheard by one.

"Please, we have spoken much of our respective Kingdoms, but tell me what goes on in the rest of the world, for we are isolated from it and hear little of it now. As you can imagine, news of the King's 'hospitality' has traveled, and we have few visitors. Those that do come, I like not at all.

"Balgar has allied himself with questionable Men. Sometimes I think they might be the very enemy we will soon face. I fear we have been weakened from within, so they might crush us all the more easily. Our door is solid, but it does us little good if left open."

A Dwarf came rushing into the room without warning, and Jargas was startled, for he had not heard him coming. He was younger than Gervan, an adult, but not by much, perhaps, and looked similar enough to him that Jargas thought he might be Gervan's son, Arvan. There was a look of fear on his face as he entered, but when he saw Jargas, his expression grew blank and he drew to a sudden stop without speaking.

"Arvan, it's all right. It's safe to talk in front of Jargas. What's wrong? You were supposed to be at Alron's house for dinner. What has happened? Is he ill? Or has something happened to him or his family?"

Arvan shook his head. "No, they are not the ones endangered. His father, Valron, knew I was dining there. He rushed home and sent me to warn you, fearful to come himself, afraid he'd endanger Alron and his wife by doing so. Valron said he overheard the Captain of the Guard speaking to four of his men; they are heading here. He fears you are going to be arrested by the King."

"But I have done no wrong," Gervan denied, although he looked troubled.

"Since when has that mattered in recent years? Father, please, you must flee before they come!" Arvan entreated.

"I cannot. I have a patient who needs me. Arvan, it might not be me they are after. You are the one who must hide until you hear it is safe to emerge, as we have practiced."

They heard the sound of many steps echoing in the corridor from the healer area to the private chambers, and Jargas wished for the staff that had yet to be returned. But there were chairs and trays and plates he could use as weapons, as well as the knives they'd eaten with. And he'd fought many foes barehanded; he needed no weapons to defend himself or his friends.

"Both of you stay here. Try to stay out of sight," Gervan urged as he headed for the door to the corridor, obviously hoping to intercept the Guards before they entered the dining chamber.

Jargas stopped him, "Nay. I've dined as a guest at your table. If it is danger you face, I'll not let you face it alone."

Gervan shook his head, "No, Jargas. Instead I beg you to see my son safe." He turned, but it was too late; the Guard had found them.

"Gervan, we would have you come with us," the Captain said, his face grim.

"I would know where you are taking me," Gervan said bravely.

"To the dungeon," the Captain said, and Arvan let out a cry and stepped in front of his father. Jargas stepped in front of both of them. "You'll have to get past me, first, to arrest him."

The Captain bristled, glaring up at him, but then a look of understanding flashed on his face. "No, you misunderstand me. I am not here by order of the King. If he knew I was here, he would execute me for it. Please, I seek your aid as healer, Gervan.

"The King drank heavily at dinner tonight. He started blustering about all that happened today. He was enraged that the Door Guard let his son out for his Rite of

Passage, singling them out for punishment over even Prince Valar's own Guard. He had all eight of them brought before him by me and my lieutenant, Lownan. He had his personal Guard bring the ten of us to the dungeon. The King went with us.

"The King has been in foul moods before, but this was different. He ordered Lownan and me to chain our eight men. We did not want to, but we could not disobey a direct order, so we did so. Then he ordered Lownan to flog them," he said, choking upon the words, fisting his hands at his sides in helpless memory.

"He made Lownan whip our own men while he watched. But that was not enough for him. He took the whip from Lownan's hand and said he did not obey him as he should, that he was too gentle with them. Gentle, as their backs bled from the lash!

"The King said he would not be defied. He said he's seen there is treason brewing. He ordered his Guard to chain Lownan beside the eight and to strip him of his shirt. Then the King ordered his Guard to hold me and to force me to watch. And he took up the whip and he began flogging Lownan himself," the Captain said, his voice hoarse.

"Only he would not stop. Even when I fell to my knees almost dragging the others down with me and begged, he would not stop. I cried and still he would not. Finally, I lost all reason, wanting only to choke the life from him with my bare hands, and I began struggling and fighting. And he laughed!

"He commanded his Guards to hold me fast, by the chin, by the hair, so that they might force me to watch as he finished. Laughing gleefully, mercilessly, the entire time, the King flayed every last bit of skin from Lownan's back. He whipped him to the bone in places. Then he ordered the Guards holding me to chain me and to call in every member of the Door Guard, even those who were on duty, leaving the entrance to the Mountain unprotected. He wanted them all to view Lownan and me both, so they might learn the consequences of disobeying him.

"Finally he let me go; he must truly be mad to have done so, for he must know I can no longer be loyal to him after what he has done. As a Mountain Guard, it is my duty to protect our Mountain and all those who dwell within from any foe that might threaten it. But surely our greatest, our only current foe, is the cruel dictator who rules us? We will see him fall. But first, we must see Lownan and the others tended to, in defiance of his orders. Please, Gervan, I beg you. As a healer, you must come with us to aid them."

Jargas said coldly, "You didn't show such compassion toward Hunter when you took his light and blanket and food and even water and left him to rot in his cell. The Guard at his cell door said the Captain ordered it, and that is you."

The Captain shook his head, "No. If you're talking about a prisoner, the Dungeon Guard is part of the King's Guard. Gordas is their Captain, not me. He's the one you want to make answer for that. I command the Mountain Guard, or did, until today. I'll not serve that madman another day, and I doubt any of the rest of us will after this. It is only a matter of time until each of us suffers a similar fate, or worse, until he brings the very Kingdom to its knees."

The Captain turned back to Gervan, "Please, Gervan, I fear Lownan will die. I fear he will die even with your aid, but maybe you can take away his pain, at least.

We will tell all who will listen that we abducted you and threatened to slay your son if you did not aid us, so that if we fail and the King yet rules, if he lives and we do not, you will not suffer for your aid."

Gervan sighed heavily. "If I did not know you as well as I do, nor trust you, nor see the agony in your eyes, Dergan, I would fear this was an elaborate and devious test of my loyalty. I knew one morning I would awaken and by that night would commit treason, but I did not think that it would come so soon, that it would be today. Aye, I'll come with you. But I'll need to gather some supplies if I am to tend to Lownan and the others."

Gervan headed to the chamber with the beds where Hunter lay for supplies, and they all followed him. "See that Hunter drinks every twenty minutes, Arvan. He's due for another drink in a few moments. Jargas will show you what to do. He helped me before."

He turned to Jargas. "I know you wish to accompany me, but you must stay here, to see your kinsman safe as well as mine. Arvan is a healer in his own right. Though he has less experience than I possess, he is well trained and skilled. He values the knowledge I have gifted him as much as others value gold. We have lost much by treasuring cold things of earth. I am pleased that he follows in my footsteps."

Captain Dergan looked at Hunter, compassion in his eyes. "I see why you are so angered against Captain Gordas. I did not even know we had a prisoner, let alone such a mistreated one. It's a wonder he's still alive. He does not look like he could be."

"We should hurry. Your absence might be discovered at any moment, and it is more than likely King Balgar would make Lownan suffer for it."

The Captain nodded, and the six exited wordlessly.

When they were gone, Arvan said, "Thank you for defending my father. You took a great risk. You could have ended up in the dungeon with him had they truly planned to arrest him."

Jargas laughed. "Then I would have at least had pleasant company."

Arvan looked at him as if he were mad.

"Forgive me. I cannot imagine what it must be like to live here, so in fear that you are a healer, yet have forgotten laughter has the power to heal as well."

"It hasn't always been like this, even for me, and I am yet young. It is only in the past few years King Balgar has changed so much. That is why Valar has trouble seeing him as a true danger. He still remembers the father who once loved him. Still, I cannot believe the King would so enrage the Mountain Guard when he must know it will only spur them to act against him. He must truly be mad."

"The timer has finished," Jargas said, and they both turned to Hunter to waken him, but saw that he was awake already. He was watching them silently. Jargas looked at him keenly. "You've been listening to us," he accused in Dwarvish. "You've been awake the entire time, haven't you? And you speak Dwarvish."

Hunter eyed him carefully. "Yes," he admitted in Dwarvish, his voice rough and scratchy. He winced, as if even speaking the single word caused him pain.

Jargas tried to remember everything he might have said in front of him, but could not. He sighed. "Well, I can't see as how you'd want to use any of it against me, considering what the King did to you. Come, it's time for you to drink."

Jargas aided him in sitting and Hunter drank slowly and carefully. Then Jargas laid him back down.

"Why... Gervan... with... Guard?" Hunter asked afterward, looking concerned, the broken sentence spoken so painstakingly obviously an effort.

"Ah, that you couldn't hear, for we were in the other room and spoke quietly." Hunter nodded and Jargas told him what had happened.

Hunter looked very troubled by it, and he tried to sit up on his own. Pain flashed across his face, and he clutched his stomach and then turned his head and vomited onto the floor. He disgorged everything he had drunk, but still his body was wracked with dry heaves, even after his stomach was emptied. Jargas held him, trying to gently force him back flat onto the bed. Hunter's face was twisted in agony as his tortured muscles strained. Then suddenly he went limp.

Arvan checked his heart and sighed in relief. "He's lost consciousness again, but he's still alive. I need to go get my father. I'm not sure what to do for him. I've never treated anything like this. Didn't my father give him something for the pain?" Arvan asked.

"No, he couldn't. He gave him something to stop his convulsions, but said he was too weak for the medicine for the pain. You stay here with Hunter and do what you can for him. I'll go."

"But you don't know how to get to the dungeon," Arvan argued.

"The King brought me to Hunter, and I came from there to here with him. I'll just reverse my steps. I don't just look like one of you, despite my size; I reason like one of you too. I won't get lost," Jargas said confidently.

"Good luck," Arvan said.

Jargas set out for the dungeon. He hoped he wouldn't run into anyone on the way. Fortunately, it was the middle of the night, and even in this underground city, the passageways were deserted, except for when he arrived at the dungeon. There was a Guard there, but he was a Mountain Guard, one of the ones who'd been with Captain Dergan, not one of the Dungeon Guard. He had raised his axe, but lowered it when he recognized Jargas.

Jargas ducked into the chamber. There were over a dozen empty sets of manacles on the walls and a number of men lying upon the floor, under blankets. Gervan was talking in hushed tones to Captain Dergan. When he saw Jargas, he went over to him and asked, "Why are you here? Is Arvan all right?"

Jargas nodded. "It's Hunter. He tried to sit up after he'd drunk, and it pained his stomach. He started vomiting and couldn't stop, even after his stomach was empty. He finally passed out from it. Arvan wasn't sure what to do."

Gervan nodded. "I've done what little I can for Lownan, but I'll not have him stay here. Jargas, if you would please carry him for me, on his stomach," he asked. He turned and talked to the Captain a moment longer, instructing him to bring the less injured men to safety and then urged Jargas to return with him to his home.

When they arrived, Jargas saw that Arvan was greatly relieved to see his father and eyed the wounded Guard in compassion. Jargas placed the Guard gently on a bed next to Hunter's. Gervan checked upon Hunter. Gervan's face creased with concern, and he began talking softly to himself, but not so softly that they could not overhear.

"I have been a healer for over three hundred years now. We lead an easy life in these mountains. There are injuries and accidents, but, as with Valar, those I can treat, those men I can save. Never since I received it have I had one I cannot help, and now I have two. If ever there was a time to use it, it is now. Have I turned into Balgar that I would hoard it, lock it away forever unused? But I might need it, Arvan might. Yet who would I be to save if I left two such men to die? If Lownan dies there will be murder this night, and we will be consumed by war from within. If Hunter dies, our Kingdom might die with him, ripped and sundered from without, those who might have helped us instead become our enemy."

Jargas and Arvan were eyeing him uncertainly. Gervan looked up in sudden decision. "I will return in a moment," he said, and he left.

Jargas asked Arvan, "Do you know what it is he is speaking of?"

"Nay, I've never seen him like this; he is in such pain," Arvan said, concerned.

Gervan returned carrying a slender metal bottle that shone like moonlight in his hand, and Jargas recognized the sheen of it instantly: it was pallenteum, with a stopper of pearl. "It was meant only for one. I will give them each half and hope it is enough. Hold Hunter's head. Tilt it back while I pour. Arvan, you help him swallow it. This we can't afford to spill a drop of." They watched Hunter drink. Whatever was in the bottle, he swallowed it easily, though he was not conscious.

Then Gervan turned to Lownan and had Jargas sit him up, holding him, his head tilted back. Unconscious though he was, he also drank it easily. "Now lay him back down and we will see whether it is enough, or whether I have doomed them both when one might have been saved."

Arvan asked the question on Jargas's tongue. "Father, what was it that you gave them?"

"A healing draught. Not one of my own. It was given to me many, many years ago by one of your people, to repay aid I had given to those he was escorting," he said, looking at Jargas and then flushing darkly. "He told me it came from the River Elves. He said that it was not something lightly used, for it had the power to save and heal one who was beyond saving. He told me to keep it in case one I loved was ever dying, for he had gotten it too late. He said none he loved yet lived, and he wanted only to join them in death. I know no more about it. It is very old and may not work, or they may not have each gotten enough for it to work. It is Elven; who knows how anything of theirs works? But I hope since neither was yet dying, though they were fated to, it might work well enough."

Jargas asked, "What was his name? The Man who gave it to you?"

"He called himself Archer. He was banded House of Serpents. I've often wondered if he yet lives, if perhaps he's found some small measure of happiness in all these many years. Does he live?"

Jargas looked at him thoughtfully. "What do you know of my people?" He had not thought to ask Gervan before.

"Only what little Valar told me a few years ago, though he knows more than he spoke. Such knowledge is only for Kings and Princes, but he has been as a son to me since he was born, and like a brother to Arvan. We do not usually have brothers, except for our twins. It's too bad, for I think we miss much by that.

"I know that each Captain of the Watch is a Lord of one of the Great Houses, and that each of your bands depicts the symbol of your House. I know that war is coming from afar to claim us all and that you help those that can be helped and die helping those that cannot, for still you try. As Hunter is not banded, he must only be a Knight, not a Captain and a Lord, but still I cannot believe Balgar would have jailed him and harmed him while he was in our keeping."

"He is banded." Jargas pulled out the band from where he'd concealed it on his other wrist, under his shirt. "He is House of Wolven. Balgar took this from him, but returned it to me for him."

Gervan's eyes widened in shock. "A Captain! I would have you remember, Jargas, that there are those here who have helped him, as well as harmed him. For your vengeance is also known to me, and I do not want our Kingdom to share the fate of Maragar."

Jargas eyed him shrewdly. "What do you know of Maragar?"

"Valar has said nothing to me of it. I know it is forbidden to speak of it, and there is much he would not say, even to me. But the fate of Maragar is legend among our people. It was two-and-a-half-centuries ago, when your people first came from across the Deathshand Mountains. You sought sanctuary in Maragar and they gave it to you, but their hearts were full of greed and treachery, and they betrayed you to your Enemy. You destroyed them for it. You brought their Mountain down upon them, slaying the entire Kingdom." Gervan looked at him in fear and cast his eyes downward. "Forgive me for speaking of it."

Jargas was angry, then, but at himself. "Gervan, I'll not have you humble yourself before me. You have nothing to fear from me or my kin. None will harm you nor yours, nor your Kingdom. You are all under my protection."

Gervan looked up at him in gratitude.

Arvan spoke up then, from Hunter's bedside. "Father, look! Something is happening. He does not look so ill as before."

Jargas and Gervan turned their attention to Hunter, and their eyes widened in surprise. Some semblance of health was returning to Hunter. His skin was no longer dry and cracked, as it had been even with the lotions and ointments, but looked firm and healthy again. The wrinkles caused by his dehydration were almost gone from his face, and his eyes did not appear so sunken any longer. Though his ribs still showed and he still looked overly thin, he looked malnourished but not starved, and his stomach was no longer swollen. And he was breathing more easily. When Gervan felt his heart, he said it beat steadily and more strongly.

At Gervan's touch, Hunter's eyes snapped open. Jargas saw that his dead eyes had not recovered as the rest of him had. But they were alert, and he eyed Jargas and Gervan keenly. He sat up, as if it was not a difficult thing to do.

"Careful, kinsman. You must not push yourself. You are still not fully well," Jargas cautioned.

FARAD'S mind was suddenly sharp again. Much of the pain was gone and the weakness that had plagued him as well, and his muscles obeyed him once more. He should not be so strong!

He felt in fear for the bond to Dewalaren, afraid he might have accidentally bled his cousin of his strength through their bond without meaning to. But the bond was gone. There was only a tiny bright smooth spot on his core where the strand had been. The rest of his core was so tarnished it was black with it, and the surface was scarred and pitted. It frightened him to see it so. It should not look like that. No core should ever look like that.

Then he remembered. He'd severed the bond to Dewalaren in the dungeon—it must have been days ago—when he'd realized he was dying, fearful of bringing his cousin to death or triggering the King's Madness. He'd been alone, for the first time in twelve years. Alone in the cold and the dark without even that faint connection he feared to touch. But there was light and warmth here: some light, though not the sun. He was so long without the sun! And there was a kinsman here, though one unknown to him. A banded Lord, but his eyes must have deceived him, for the symbol he bore was of one of the Lost Houses, House of Gryphon. None had survived that line. And he looked nothing like the rest of their kin. Was this a foul trick of the Enemy?

Farad looked at him intently, but did not betray himself by using the King's Eyes upon him, though he felt strong enough to for the first time in many months. He spoke to him in Amontirin. "Are you truly Lord of House of Gryphon and kin to me? How came you to be here? Who has sent you to my aid?"

The giant looked at him in surprise and spoke to him in Dwarvish. "Methinks that might be the language of my grandsire, kinsman, but it is not known to me. I speak Dwarvish, Varashin, and Common. Take your pick of those and I will be able to answer your question."

"Who sent you to find me?" Farad asked in fluent Dwarvish.

"No one. It was merely a fortunate coincidence for you that I came when I did, for you would not have survived for much longer without water and medical assistance. I am here on behalf of my father's people, who are kin to Balgar, I am ashamed to say, not my mother's people, and I am kin to you through her. Balgar gave your freedom to me as a reward for saving his son Valar's life, or so he says. I still do not trust that is why he did so. He saw my band, which resembles your own, and called me a Captain. Gervan has told me something of our people, but I would hear more."

Farad shook his head. "I cannot tell you more. If you were truly a kinsman, you would know our tongue and our history."

"I would if my grandsire could have remembered any of it. But when my mother's people saved him, he was near death. He survived the rock that had claimed his people, but was gravely injured. He lost all his memory, even of his name and how to speak. But my grandmother cared for him and loved him. She was Chieftess and Healer of our village. They were wed and he became a great warrior, our village Champion. He lived for one-hundred-and-twenty-four years after he was found, although he already appeared to be a Man of thirty or so when first we saw him and I suspect even then he might have been older.

"My grandmother bore a single child by him, my mother, Jahira, but she died in the bearing. He wanted no other wife after her. My tribe was without a Chieftess until my mother came-of-age; he ruled us for those intervening years, though it is not our custom. He was a kind and just and strong ruler.

"When my mother finally attained her maturity, she ruled alone, as is our custom. He died soon after. She did not marry until she was forty-one, to my father, Rongas, King of Malar in Holoren. All thought my mother past the age to conceive, though she did not look her age. I think she might have had the long life of her father and borne many children, had she the chance. But she bore only me and my sister; we are twins. She died birthing us. Now my sister, Jarina, is Chieftess and Healer of the Varash.

"We have recently learned that there are many Dwarven Kingdoms, the survivors of the Lost Kingdoms, living in exile in the Saravan Mountains that border our own Holoren Mountains. They have told us of the darkness that claimed the Dwarven Lands after we left them. They have said it is coming to claim all the rest, the last of the Dwarven Kingdoms, the Kingdoms of Men, and those of the Elves.

"My father thought that it would be better to stop the darkness here, before it crosses these mountains, and so he sent me to meet with the current King and offer an alliance, to restore the strength of our divided people. That is why I am here and able to receive your life as a gift from one I must now call King." He said the last with bitterness.

"Your story has the ring of truth to it, although I know of no Dwarven Kingdoms in the Saravan or Holoren Mountains. I would speak with you more about that later. But first, where was your grandsire found?" Farad asked, trying to smother the hope he felt stir within him.

"In what was once a pass through the Deathshand Mountains. I don't know what you might have called it. What the Dwarves call the Great Marsh and the Dead Sea lay directly to the east of it. We were nomads then. The valley we called Summerhome was buried by the rock that claimed my maternal grandsire's kin. Once he was well enough to travel, we left those lands forever. We journeyed far to the west, seeking new lands, almost as if we were driven. We bypassed the Fromer and Coroden Mountains, until we finally settled in the Saravan and ceased our nomadic ways."

Farad tried to hide his shock, the sudden wild hope that flared to life. "They should never have been so far south as that. No wonder we never found trace of them! Tell me, did your grandsire leave you no other heirlooms? A sword, perhaps, or other mementos? A seal or perhaps a ring?" Farad made the question sound a casual one, mentioning the only item he was truly interested in hearing about last, as if an afterthought. Idare, could this man possibly hold the lost King's Ring that they had been searching for these past two-and-a-half centuries? Could the means of destroying their Enemy truly be within their grasp?

"NAY, the Man who wore this band had no seal nor ring, and his sword was buried by the rock." Jargas did not lie, but he did not state the full truth, either. His grandsire was not the Man who had worn the band of the House of Gryphon. They had buried that Man with his sword in his hands under a cairn of rock. His grandsire had been the one with the ring, and a band of his own. Both were made of a different metal, not pallenteum, but a metal the color of copper dipped in blood. Both the ring and the band were graced with a single uncut ruby, the size of a Man's thumbnail, set into the metal. No beast was engraved upon that band. But he would not tell Hunter these things, not yet. "What was the name of the Man who wore this band before me?" Jargas asked, holding up his banded wrist.

"Since he must be long dead, it will harm no one to speak his name: he was Stephan, Lord of House of Gryphon, Protector and Friend of King Albinar's eldest son, Crown Prince Rowanar. I doubt not that Stephan was so gravely injured trying to protect the Prince, for I cannot imagine him living without him. We lost much when those Houses Prince Rowanar led were lost to us. We lost too much," Hunter said sepulchrally.

Jargas carefully hid all feeling from Hunter. He could not be sure, until he found out what band the King's son wore, but he felt in his heart he was right. Hunter had just casually told him what his family had sought to know for these two-hundred-and-fifty years past: the name of his grandfather, Rowanar, and now Jargas knew that he was the grandson of their King!

"If the King's eldest son and heir died with the rest, then who is your King now?" Jargas asked, eager to hear whether he had living kin, cousins of his mother's family.

"That is not something lightly spoken, Jargas! King Albinar had three sons. The Enemy has been trying to learn the secret of the current line these two-hundred-and-fifty years past. I'll not casually reveal that secret to someone I do not truly know yet. But I would know something else from you. How is it I can now move and speak again, when I was so near death before?"

Gervan spoke then. "I gave you a healing draught."

Hunter eyed him coolly. "I know of no Dwarven medicines that could do what has been done for me. I would know the truth."

Gervan's face flushed. "It was not Dwarven, if you must know. It was Elven. I had it from the River Elves."

"Has he sent her people here to save me? He should not have! There is great danger here."

"So you are friends with the Elves as well as the Dwarves?" Gervan asked.

"We are friend to all who need our aid. I would know if there are Elves here. They would be in great danger."

Gervan shook his head. "No, the draught came from one of your kin, Captain of the Watch Archer, Lord of House of Serpents. He gave it to me... let's see... could it really be so long ago as that? Yes, some ninety years past. I asked Jargas, but now I know why he did not answer me. He has deceived me, but I do not fault him for it. One learns quickly to conceal the truth and avoid answering questions here. It has been the only way to survive. Tell me, Hunter, does Archer yet live?"

Hunter looked troubled. "We know not. He was last of his line; his wife and sons were killed. He disappeared ninety years ago. We've assumed he is dead. There are few of us left, now, too few, so many Houses are lost." He gritted his teeth. "And mine almost one of them. I must get my band back from Balgar."

"You need not worry about that, kinsman. He entrusted it to me for you," Jargas said, and he pulled back his shirt sleeve, exposing the band, and unclipped it from about his wrist.

The hand Hunter held out trembled. He snapped the band into place around his naked bicep. It fit loosely about the wasted muscle. "I don't suppose he would have given you my weapons as well?"

Jargas shook his head. "He sent the Guard to fetch them from the Armory, but I have yet to see them."

"I may have need of them before I leave here. I must test the King after what I have seen and heard, for I'll not leave a Resemblant masquerading as the King."

"What is a Resemblant? I've not heard the term," Jargas asked, curious.

"You are fortunate. They have yet to cross over these mountains, I think. They are servants and spies of the Enemy. I will not speak his name, for he is already too near me. He takes a Man or a Dwarf, strips him of his core, and places one of his servants' minds into the shell of the body, so that it might mimic the lost man, causing death and treachery, destroying families and cities, rending entire Kingdoms asunder. And they are not the worst of what is coming, not by far, but I cannot speak of those others.

"I am too long without the sun to think about them. I am too long in this place. I should have left months ago. Much may be lost for my being here, though I hope more will be gained. I hope it is a Resemblant, a shadow in the shape of your King, for if not, I can do far less to help you. I wish I had been raised to believe regicide is necessary in certain instances, but even to think upon it makes me ill."

Jargas agreed. "This Kingdom has seen enough of civil war. Still, it would be nice if the King's heart might finally fail him of its own accord, the twisted, black thing it is."

FARAD noticed that Arvan had been listening intently to them. He'd forgotten about him. He was still not himself not to have registered his presence before now. He did not need to use his Power to read Arvan's thoughts, but he would use it upon his father.

Farad's eyes glowed with red-gold light. "**Gervan, freeze!**"

Gervan had been about to say something when Farad spoke. Suddenly, it was if he had turned to ice. He was motionless, save for his breathing, as his eyes glazed over.

Then Farad locked his eyes upon Arvan. "**Arvan, look at me, listen to me**," Farad commanded. His voice again echoed with Power in the stone room. Arvan obeyed, unable to do otherwise. As quickly as a striking snake, Farad snatched Arvan's wrist and held him fast.

Once Farad had his attention, he did not seek to influence the healer's son further with the King's Voice. He needed Arvan to do what was right of his own free will. "Do you see my eyes? Look past the light. Do they look cold and dead and terrible to you?"

Arvan swallowed and nodded.

Jargas looked on, intrigued, but did not interfere, despite the strange red-orange fire he also must see and what Farad had done to Gervan.

Farad would not harm Arvan, though he was frightening him. But it was necessary. He would do far worse to save him, if there was need.

"There is a reason for it. I have a killer's eyes. Many men kill and do not look like this. But my eyes have seen things no eyes ever should; my hands have done things no hands should ever have to do. You have nice eyes, Arvan, warm eyes, a healer's eyes and a healer's hands. You don't ever want to lose that look or that touch. Promise me you won't do what you are thinking to do. You will not kill the King and try to make it look as if his own heart was the one who betrayed him, rather than yours."

Arvan licked his lips nervously. "I don't know what—" he began, but Farad would not let him finish the lie.

"Promise me, Arvan. I'll not let you go until I hear, until I believe you speak truly to me. I owe your father, Gervan, my life. I'll not see his son twisted into someone he can no longer love."

ARVAN was startled by the strength of the grip on his wrist and by this strange Man's words. Hunter read his very thoughts, his very heart! He looked fearfully at his father, but he was still as a statue, as if oblivious to them. Arvan turned his gaze back to Hunter. Hunter frightened him, but his own thoughts frightened him as well. "But my father is in danger from him! We're all in danger! You would have died because of him. Lownan may yet die."

Hunter shook his head. "Balgar's end will come soon enough. He has sealed his own fate too many ways to escape it. Promise me. Look me in the eyes and promise me."

Arvan felt trapped. If he tried and failed, if he were caught, they'd torture him, they'd make him confess that his father was involved, even though he would not have been. His father cherished life. Although he despised and feared Balgar, he could never kill him. And Hunter somehow knew what he planned, and now Jargas did as well.

He'd never thought he'd ever kill anyone. He was a healer by his nature as well as his training, and here he was barely an adult, and he'd have to live the whole rest of his life knowing what he'd done. He'd told himself it was worth it, but if Hunter, who had been treated so cruelly and almost killed by the King's whims, argued against it…. Arvan took a deep breath and shuddered. "I promise I won't kill him," Arvan said, and he meant it. The nearly unendurable tightness in his chest eased.

Hunter's eyes bore into his, and then he smiled and released him. Only his mouth smiled; his eyes could not. "Thank you. I have enough darkness scarring my core without you on my conscience as well. I would save an innocent when I can; there are few enough of you left. Do not worry what your father might think of what he just heard. I have spared him even the thought that you might do such a thing. When I release him from my Voice, he will know nothing of what has just happened.

"That healing draught he gave to me was not lightly given, although he does not realize what it truly was. He could not have ever used it, had he realized. I've heard of them, but none I know have ever seen one, let alone felt its healing.

"The Elves have some magic to them, but it is not something they wield easily. This in particular carries a grave price. The Elf who made it drained his own life into it, to save someone of great importance to him. Why it was not then used, I cannot guess. The selflessness of that act, the purity of the one who made it, may yet be enough to save me when I have feared I was beyond saving.

"I was not afraid to die. I have longed for death these many decades. It is my curse that I must ever fight against what I would embrace. Each death I have caused has chipped at my core. It is so pocked and battered that my mind would shatter if I were to even witness one more death, I think. But perhaps the Madness might yet stay at bay a little while longer, although I know I am soon doomed to fall to it.

"Forgive me. I frighten you, and you cannot understand. How could any but my kin understand? Just know that you save your own sanity, your very self, your spirit, by remaining the healer you were born to be."

FARAD took a deep breath and released Arvan's hand and Gervan's mind at the same moment.

"I agree. I would not see harm come to Balgar, much as I despise him," Gervan said, continuing their earlier conversation, oblivious to all that had since transpired. He looked at Arvan in concern. "Arvan, what's wrong? You look ill. You've too gentle a spirit to hear such harsh words. Forgive me for upsetting you."

"No, Father. I am just tired, and so much has happened. I think perhaps I'd better go to bed."

Gervan nodded. "We should both sleep now, I think. It has been a hard night for two healers. Hunter, Jargas, please excuse us. And the two of you must get some rest as well. Jargas, I'll show you to our guest room. You may stay with us as long as you're in our Mountain."

Jargas shook his head and smiled. "I'm not ready to sleep just yet. Just leave the door to my chamber open and I'll find it easily enough. Goodnight, Gervan, Arvan. Sleep well. You've both more than earned it. May only pleasant dreams visit you."

"Goodnight," Gervan said, then left with his arm around his son's shoulders.

Farad sighed again. He was exhausted. He had used too much Power when he had no reserves, only the borrowed strength of the healing draught. He'd placed himself back into danger by weakening himself so. The King's Madness thrived upon weakness. But he'd saved Arvan. His own sanity or his life was a small price to pay. Arvan shone brightly for one without Power. He was a jewel beyond price.

Jargas eyed him keenly. "You've magic of your own, Hunter. You froze Gervan's mind and body and turned Arvan's heart to your will as if it were nothing."

Farad paled. "Not magic, Jargas. Power, frightening Power, but never magic. It was hard to do, not easy, to stop Gervan from seeing and hearing without harming him. And I used reason to sway Arvan, not the Power. You wonder why I did not affect you, why I betrayed myself to you? I am neither fool enough nor strong enough to set my Power against your own, Jargas. And you did not try to stop me, for fear you would harm them in trying, for the Power is still raw and untested in you, for all your advanced years."

"Perhaps I did not because I trusted you not to harm those who helped you," Jargas countered.

Farad shook his head. "You are not so naïve as that, Jargas. At least I hope you might not be. Evil flourishes where there is faith in goodness. Were you so innocent, you would recoil from me in horror were you to learn the things I might do, out of necessity, in the name of self-preservation and duty to my crown."

Farad could not believe he had just goaded Jargas to stop him now, while he was yet weak and helpless. He knew his loose tongue to be a result of his imprisonment. He recognized the signs. Yet even knowing so, he was powerless to censor his words as he should.

If Jargas was to view his core, he might well kill him, as he himself would likely kill any other whose core was so blackened. He had not turned his eye inward for some time. He had been appalled by what he had found the last time he had done so. Seeing his core now, so damaged, had almost been enough to tip the scales and plunge him into the Madness.

Farad closed his eyes. He'd felt Arvan's pulse, as well as looked into his eyes, to know he told the truth. He'd saved an innocent, weak and marred as he was. He clung to that thought as if it were a lifeline. He had to get out of this place. He'd been in the dark for too long.

HIS link to Dewalaren had kept him sane in the cell when they'd thought to drive him mad from loneliness and the darkness. But the illness had come and then there was no water, and he'd forced himself not to touch the link, lest he draw too much from it and either kill Dewalaren or start him back down the path to Madness. When the temptation became too great, when he knew he'd not be able to control himself, fearing what he might do in his delirium, he'd severed the link.

Six years ago he'd felt the Madness claiming Dewalaren a second time, but he'd been unable to save him. He'd not had the Power. He'd have sent what he had, and died to save the cousin he loved from such a horrible fate, but he could not. The innocents, the children he'd been trying to save, would have died without his aid, although ultimately they had died anyway.

He had not known Lunahr already possessed the King's Power. He'd never suspected it; none of them had. Lunahr had still been a boy when he left, only twelve. He was still a boy, only twenty-four, and the Amontir came of age at twenty-five, not sixteen as other Men. The Power Lunahr must have now! At the tender age of eighteen he'd been able to bring Dewalaren safely back from the brink of Madness.

But Lunahr might be far from Dewalaren now. Farad had felt the darkness building in Dewalaren, unchecked. Farad had tried desperately to finish here, so he could return to his cousin in time to save him, if he needed saving. Five more Kingdoms had been destroyed in the twelve years he'd been here in the Dwarven Lands. Five more peoples he'd fought beside were gone forever. So much horror, so much death.

He'd spent the past year with Dorolingas and Ironhand, forging an alliance between the two, seeing them begin to act as one when he left for Malar. He'd been confident when he entered Malar, too confident. When the King decided to imprison him, he hadn't resisted; he'd seen the petty tantrums of Dwarven Kings before. When he was jailed for a week without word, he started to become concerned. He demanded to see the King. Another week passed, and he requested to see him. A total of three and he'd humbled himself, though he did not beg. He could not.

Day and night were as one underground. He had tried to keep track of time by counting his meals. When at least a month had passed, he'd freed himself from the chains but failed to escape the cell. They'd rechained him. He'd done it again. They chained him again. Over and over he tried, using all the tricks he knew of mind and body. They started beating him. He knew it was folly to keep trying, but his mind and his hands no longer obeyed him; he was free of the chains without meaning to be.

Finally, two months ago, they'd whipped him. It was after the tenth stroke that he'd lost all control, that he unchained himself and attacked them. He'd almost gotten away that time. He'd almost overpowered all six of the Guard, but the last grabbed his ankle and he'd lost his balance. Weakened by the two months of abuse, he'd fallen. Then they'd set upon him in earnest, kicking and stomping on him as he lay on the ground.

He'd awoken in agony from all they'd done to find the blanket gone, and the light. Only a faint glow seeped in from the hallway under the door. But mercifully, the beatings stopped. They left him alone. Very much alone.

They no longer brought food in to him. A tray bearing only a pitcher of water and hunk of bread would come once a day, pushed through the narrow tunnel set into the stone wall near the door with a pole and recovered after the tray and pitcher were empty with the hook at the end. The tunnel was too narrow to escape through and capped by a door on the hall end until needed in any case.

Thankfully, there were no insects or rodents as a dungeon of Man would have held. They were too deep in the Mountain: it was too dark, too cold, too wet. So bitterly cold, so unbearably dark.

His core had dimmed to a shadow, and illness had finally claimed him. Then there was no bread, no water. He could no longer even stand. He'd rolled himself against the wall to lick the moisture from it. It was then that he'd broken the link to Dewalaren. He'd had to.

He had been alone, truly alone, for the first time in twelve years. He lay on the cold, damp stone floor, his body wracked by spasms, scarcely able to breathe. He longed so desperately to hear someone, anyone, to feel someone beside him, to feel warmth, to see light.

The hallucinations had started, first the visual ones and then the voice. It was as if someone was there, in the cell with him, where there had only been unbearable emptiness before. But there was no warmth, no comfort from the presence. He knew it was all in his mind, that he must be going mad.

Then, miraculously, the door had opened. A giant had stridden into the cell, bearing light. The King was with him, but the King cowered behind him; the giant was in charge, not the King. He had the look of a Dwarf but the size almost of an ogre. But for all his powerful build, he'd been so gentle, warm, and kind. Farad could not move, could not even speak, but it did not matter. The giant had shown him his band, though he wore it about his wrist as if it were a mere bracelet. He'd called him kinsman, and told him he'd come to take him home. House of Gryphon, a Dead House, a Lost House, after two hundred and fifty years, to reappear in the hour of his greatest need!

Farad feared a trick of the Enemy, or that Jargas was merely a delusion conjured by his desperate mind. Even now he feared this might all be a fever dream. He might not really be clean and warm and dry, tended by healers. Jargas and Gervan and Arvan might all be figments of his tormented mind. How could there be an Elven healing draught here? What if he was to open his eyes again and find he was still in the darkness of his cell? The light had never left, here.

FARAD opened his eyes in blind panic for the light. The light was still there, Jargas was still there, the room was still there. It was all real.

"Easy, Hunter. It was a nightmare, nothing more. You're safe now," Jargas said, his large warm hand squeezing his shoulder reassuringly.

Jargas had thought he'd been sleeping. Safe? No he was not safe; the light was so far away. "Please, the light, bring it closer to me," Farad begged. He bit his tongue, cursing his inability to control his words, to hide his need. He should never reveal his weaknesses, particularly when he was so paralyzed by them.

JARGAS had meant to tell Hunter he needed his rest, but there was desperation, even terror, in Hunter's voice, so he brought the light closer to him. Hunter stared at it as if entranced and then reached for the flame, as if he were a moth and would burn himself upon it. Jargas moved it back just out of his reach, and then grasped Hunter's wrist firmly but gently and placed it back upon the bed.

Hunter resisted him. Jargas was surprised how strong Hunter was, healing draught or no, for he was still far from healthy in body and even less healthy in mind, Jargas suspected. But even in the peak of health, Hunter could never be stronger than him. Jargas had yet to meet the Man or Dwarf who ever equaled him in strength. He'd even bested many an ogre.

FARAD relaxed his arm. Brute strength would not prevail here; wits were needed. Farad forced the rest of his body to relax as well. He feigned sleep, hoping Jargas might leave. After a while, he heard Jargas rise. "Sleep well, kinsman. If you can still hear me, I'll be in my bedchamber if you need me. I'll leave the door here and there open, so I'll hear you if you call for me," Jargas assured him and then left the room.

Farad listened to the ensuing silence in agony, counting out the seconds. He meant to count five minutes, but after three he could bear it no longer. His eyes snapped open, and he snatched the oil lamp from the slide-out shelf by the bed. He grasped it so forcefully that the lamp almost poured out onto the bed. The flame sputtered, nearly drowned by the oil.

Farad whimpered deep in his throat, an animal sound, a wolven in fear. He bit his tongue, hard. He was a Man, not an animal. The flame steadied, and he began the familiar meditation, chanting softly in Amontirin. But his core was too chaotic, the flame too small; he was losing himself to the Madness. He could not lose himself here, with no one to save him.

Focus, he needed something to focus on in addition to the pitifully inadequate light, but the pain was gone. Farad held his forearm carefully over the flame. He must be careful not to damage himself more than Gervan might be able to treat. The heat brought focus, and the pain even more: it was intense, exquisite. It felt good, so very good. Farad lowered his arm into the ecstasy of the fire. He could pour the burning oil over himself and the blanket so the fire could cleanse him of his demons; the fire would free him. Farad recoiled in horror at the thoughts not his own as he suddenly recognized the insidious whispers in the darkness. The Enemy had found him!

Farad howled in terror and rage and flung the lamp away. It shattered against the wall. The puddle of oil flamed briefly amidst the shards of the broken lamp on the floor of rock, and then the bright flame dimmed and went out as the oil was consumed. The room was plunged into utter blackness. Farad screamed as his mind shattered.

JARGAS heard the wild howl and the agonized scream that followed, and snatching his lamp, he ran out of his room and down the dark hallway. He saw Gervan and Arvan coming too. "**No! Stay here! It's dangerous!**" he commanded and ran to the room where Hunter had lain. From the light of the lamp in his hand, he could see Hunter crouched on the bed, naked and howling like a mad wolven. He set his lamp down on the little ledge beside the doorway, next to an unlit lamp, his eyes never leaving Hunter.

Hunter's eyes were no longer dead and dark. They blazed with the red-golden fire they'd only hinted at before. Those terrible eyes looked upon Jargas, and he saw the fire from them lash out to burn him. But Jargas felt his own eyes flame, and the fire within them countered Hunter's attack.

Jargas surged toward the bed, muscles straining against the air as if fighting against the current of a river in spring flood. He made it to the bed and grabbed Hunter by the shoulders and flung him to the floor, trying to pin him. Hunter bucked and fought and clawed and bit like a wild animal, but Jargas subdued him and held him fast, locking eyes with him.

Jargas saw past the flame. Those eyes that had been sane and lucid after such deprivation, after isolation and cold and damp, after darkness and hunger and thirst and illness, were lost to madness now. Jargas held Hunter pinned to the ground, by his great weight and bulk as much as by the hands that held Hunter's arms fast. His warm brown eyes bored into Hunter's dead, dark eyes. Jargas forced himself into Hunter's mind, ripping past his tattered defenses, tearing through recent memory.

Jargas felt the flame sear him and heard the seductive voice urging Hunter to burn himself. It could not have been real. It must have been the madness. But then Jargas heard laughter and the same voice, and it was neither madness nor memory as it spoke tauntingly to him.

You seek to challenge me already, Jargas? You cannot save Farad from me! He has been my favorite plaything for a century. I instructed Balgar to imprison him, to prepare him for my visit, but that fat fool actually forgot about him! He left him to wither and die! When I came to amuse myself with Farad in his cell, he was already all but dead. There was scarcely even the tiniest flicker of flame, nothing for me to feed upon. I had thought him unsalvageable. But you have rekindled him for me.

The hideous laughter came again. *I tried to kindle him too. He would have made such a lovely sculpture of torment, a work of living art of flame, though he would have crumbled to ash all too quickly. I did not realize how weak Farad's mind was, that he might truly try to immolate himself! I am glad he did not. I have been saving him.*

I have never touched his body, not even in his dreams, though I have dwelled in his thoughts, here and there, from time to time. He has such deliciously dark thoughts. I feel so at home in his mind. We are so alike, he and I. I have pleasured myself long and often upon those he loves, but him I have waited for. He is to be my prize once the last three Dwarven Kingdoms fall. Then I will take him. He is not a virgin, of course, so few are, but he is almost as good as one. He has not known a man's nor woman's touch in ten decades. I've seen to that. It adds a layer of delight.

But you, Jargas, you are truly an innocent! You have never known the touch of love, neither from man nor woman, in all your many years, have you? You are so pure and you overflow with raw Power. Ah, and what is this? You are not alone I see. You bring me a present! Such a sweet prize. It has been so very long since I have feasted upon a woman of Amontir. Does your sister have Power akin to yours? What is her name? Ah, Jarina, lovely. Can it possibly be that she is an innocent as well? I must taste her and see.

To Jargas's horror, he felt something hot and wet and unspeakably vile dripping down his link toward Jarina. Jargas bellowed in rage and leapt from the house in his mind, reaching out and grabbing the strand below the horrible liquid, afraid it might break with some of the liquid on it, where he could not reach it. But the link held firm and he felt Jarina's strength coursing into it. She sensed danger and tried to aid him, not realizing the danger was to her.

The liquid surged onto his hands, and he felt agony as his hands began to dissolve under it. It was liquid fire, consuming his phantom flesh. He clamped the strand of the bond between his knees and scraped every last drop of the burning mass from the strand until it gleamed again, shining blood-red copper, and then let go, holding on only with his legs. He watched the palms of his phantom hands burn to the bone in places. Soon it would leak through!

Jargas's eyes widened as a rabid, half-starved wolven leapt down his bond to Jarina toward him. Jargas was powerless to defend himself against it as it opened its great jaws and bit both his phantom hands off at the wrists. To his surprise, he felt no pain, only relief from the agony of his burns. But the wolven writhed in agony now, as the liquid consumed his mouth from within. No, he would not let it die when it had helped him save Jarina!

Without consciously intending to, Jargas changed. His mental image of himself was no longer that of the Dwarf he saw in the mirror. Instead, great hairy-clawed forepaws grew from the bloody stumps of his wrists, and the rest of him morphed with them into a tremendous obearn. He grabbed the wolven with his paws and hugged him tightly, securing them both to the strand.

Suddenly Jargas felt appallingly weak. He became a Dwarf again, but now his hands were regrown. He barely kept hold of the strand with his knees, barely kept hold of the beast. The wolven was no longer gaunt and hungry, it was huge and muscular, but only for a moment. Then it vanished in a burst of light. A tiny gray moth fluttered out of the glare. It flew slowly and erratically toward Hunter's house. It fell upon it and then disappeared inside.

The horrible monster was gone. But Hunter's house was blackened and pitted and scarred, and only the tiniest flicker of light sputtered within. Jargas felt for Jarina. She was there, she was safe, she was whole, she was strong; she sent a wave of strength toward him without him needing to ask her for it.

His strength renewed, Jargas climbed the strand and reached out and touched Hunter's burnt house, carefully, gently. He snatched his hand away, his mind recoiling at the flood of horrific images that dwelt within.

He forced himself back. Hunter had saved Jarina. Whoever he might be, whatever he might have done, he had saved her from that vile burning monster, saved her light and laughter from terror and pain and depravity; he'd seen a flash in Hunter's mind of what he'd saved her from.

Jargas clasped Hunter's house firmly with both hands and sent his own strength and what Jarina had given him into it. The flame in Hunter's house became stronger, but the images sharpened with it. Memory flared brightly and burned Jargas. The memories were so brutal he almost fled, even knowing Hunter had saved his sister.

Jargas forced himself to see what had driven Hunter to the brink of madness and beyond. He sought only recent memories, but instead was flooded by older ones. Farad. Hunter's given name was Farad, the name the monster had spoken. Jargas saw Farad's father, Jarad, Lord of House of Wolven, whom Farad had loved as only a son can love a father, captured by terrifying things that might once have been Men and Dwarves: mutilated, animated corpses, some of them fused and twisted, part animal, part man. *Revenants!* The word screamed across his mind, the very sound of it a blow which left him staggered. He boxed the word away in a chest of stone he fashioned with a thought in his need. But the creatures were only servants of something far worse, the dark and diabolical creature that had come for Jarad.

Jargas had been caught in a flash flood once, in a valley in the mountains of home. He'd survived by clinging to a rock, as the tree trunks and other debris battered him and the roaring waters tried to drown him. He felt the same now. He yanked one hand away and grasped the link back to his own house, clinging to the warmth of it for life, for sanity, as Hunter's memories raged over him.

Farad had lived to see his father tortured and beaten, repeatedly violated, and finally crippled by his tormentors, the master and his servants. No, not seen. Farad was not there, but he had been linked to his father by a bond like the special link Jargas and Jarina shared. Farad had felt every cruel thing that had been done to the father he loved. But his father had not been alone. Those monsters had Jarad's wife, Farad's mother, as well: Alaria, Lady of House of Eagles. They kept Jarad alive to see what they did to his wife.

For seven days they ravished her. They kept her alive, kept the links to her four sons strong, so they'd feel everything done to her as well. Farad and his brothers had sought their parents desperately, had fought their way to them, but when they had finally reached them, they were too late. Their mother was dead, and what was left of their father, a crippled, mindless husk, died soon after.

But that was not all. In the months that followed, Farad lost each of his beloved brothers to those creatures. *Revenants!* The word exploded from the stone chest, shattering it. Jargas grabbed hold of it and slammed it into a stronger chest he forged of pure pallenteum. Haranad, the second eldest, was first to die. Then Sarad, the next. Then the youngest, Alarad, most loved. Farad had wept for days at the side of his pyre. He had wanted only to die himself, to end his torment, but his hatred and need for vengeance and his desperate need to protect his King from these monsters kept him alive. *Incuban!* Jargas suddenly had a name for the depraved creature of fire and torment, for the master of those who had destroyed Farad's family. He tried to contain that name as well, but it would not be contained. It burned everything it touched. It raged like an inferno across the charred wasteland of Farad's mind, his life.

Jargas snatched his hand away. He was on his knees, hanging by the link. He could not experience any more; he could not help Farad. Farad was beyond help. Jargas grasped the coppery strand leading back to his own mind, to sanity. He fought to see memories of his own, pure and warm and wholesome, to counter the horrific images burnt into his mind. He saw his father, Rongas, felt his strong arms embracing him as he knelt before him after passing his test of manhood. His father had always been a pillar of love and strength. He saw Jarina, laughing in joy; she lived in love and light. One of her smiles was worth all the treasures in Balgar's Vault, yet she gave them freely to everyone.

Farad had saved her. An image of Alaria flashed across his mind, as he'd seen her in her anguish, and for a heart-stopping instant he pictured Jarina in her place and then forced the image away. He pictured Farad sobbing beside his brother's pyre for a moment but then saw instead his own father, broken and sobbing at Jarina's grave. He forced that image away as well. He could not leave Farad alone in such horror, lost to madness, when he had so weakened himself saving Jarina. He must help Farad somehow. He must bring what light he could back to Farad.

Jargas took a deep breath and touched Farad's house again, shying away from those deeper, older memories, seeking newer ones. He had not meant to see so much; it had all sprung out at him.

He sought the cluster of new memories that might reveal whatever had triggered the madness. Jargas passed by bright flashes without probing. He saw faces here and there but passed them by without putting names to them. There was a tall man, with Farad's build, with brown hair and deep-blue eyes and a fierce gaze; the visage unexpectedly softened as the man smiled, and he radiated warmth and love. There was a boy as well, with long blond hair and green eyes, so fine boned and fine featured that Jargas thought he was an Elf, until he saw his ears. His face was lit with joy; he was singing. Jargas could hear his song for a moment, but it flashed by quickly. Farad loved them both, the man and the boy. Jargas marveled that Farad could still love anyone after what he had lived through.

Then Jargas saw Farad's journey into the mountains, different Dwarven Kingdoms, different memories, but all ending in battle and death as the Enemy consumed those Farad tried so desperately to save, until Dorolingas, until Ironhand, until Malar.

Jargas saw the King imprison Farad, saw his time in the cell. He saw the pride fade, saw the annoyance turn to concern, to fear, to desperation. There was no loneliness, even in his isolation. Another had been with him, almost to the end, until he'd broken the link.

Farad had often gone without food and water, although he had never before been at the point of dying from lack of either. His body had suffered much pain and injury and deprivation in his long life. A fact sprang to light and startled Jargas. Farad was one-hundred-and-forty-six years old!

But he'd been chained and helpless in the cell, and they'd beaten him and whipped him. It had been too similar to what had happened to his parents, to his brothers. All the unbearable memories always too close to the surface had flooded over him. Balgar's men had done much damage to Farad's spirit, and then the illness had come. But still he'd kept sane.

In the room, what had finally driven him to madness? It was the light! When the light had gone, when the oil had burned dry, that was what had triggered the madness. There was something in this Man that needed the light. Something that cried out for the sun.

He'd been kept from the sun for four months. The torches had helped, even the little lamp, but he could not face darkness, true darkness, total darkness, not now, when he was so weakened. Jargas followed the terror into the darkness in Farad's mind. He forged a second, larger chest of pallenteum to seal the worst of the memories into.

Memory flashed then from deep in the darkness, memory from years ago of Farad building a similar metal coffer, but of the same coppery metal as their links, forcing the lid shut. *Dewalaren, my cousin, my King, I release you from your Madness. You are well.*

Jargas echoed the words, slamming the chest he had forged shut with vehemence. *Farad, my kinsman, I release you from your madness. You are not truly well, but you are as well as you can ever be.* Suddenly there was light again within Farad's house, though it was not bright.

Jargas left Farad's house then. Once outside he was pleased that he could still see the light from it, though he sensed it was still far dimmer than it should be. Then the wolven was back again. It was old and gaunt, lean and scarred. It gazed at the thick coppery wire that led now from Farad's house to Jargas's own, then looked at him with eyes that were not yellow as they should be, but brown, as dark and dead as Farad the Man's.

Jargas nodded at the wolven and then headed back along the strand to his own house. The wolven did not follow him. Jargas saw his own house with relief, bright and glowing and unscarred, and he entered and turned his eyes outward.

Farad's eyes were open, but no longer burning; they were brown again, dead and brown. Jargas got off of him then and rose and reached down a hand to help him to his feet. Farad stood without taking his hand, his eyes never leaving Jargas's face. Farad studied him intently, in the faint glow of the light from the lamp Jargas had brought. "I should not be bound to another. There is only one man who should know me so well."

Jargas nodded. "You did not invite me to you. I forced the bond upon you, but I had no choice. You had need of me. I looked at no more than I had need to, to cure you of your madness. I kept the link only because I think you may yet have need of my aid again. But your secrets are still safe, although there is much I wish to know, especially now, if I am to protect Jarina."

Farad hissed. "Never speak even part of a true name aloud lightly! How can you be known by your given name? How can she? Can it be you truly do not know the danger you invite? There is Power in such names, Power to protect and Power to harm. But you stood against the Enemy, raw and untrained. You stripped his thoughts from both my mind and your own bond and held him confined and then sent me the strength I needed to banish him.

"You even learned what I have longed to know for nearly a century. I think he actually spoke the truth to you. Now I know why I yet live, when I should have been slain long ago. So my fate is tied to the Dwarven Kingdoms? I have tied my fate to them of my own free will.

"I did not know that House of Gryphon bred the King's Power so true. Your House was always strong of body and character and solid of mind, but never did they show true Power. Perhaps that is why you are yet untainted by the Madness that touches each of us, even those with only traces of Power. Your core is solid and unmarred. I cannot remember my core ever looking so pure.

"With a touch I could tell whether what you have told me of your lineage is true, but I have not been invited and I will not ask. I have seen enough by your actions to know that you are not one of the Enemy's minions; you have aided me when it would have been easy to see me captured or killed. I am in your debt.

"I must ask your forgiveness. I did not mean to siphon so much strength from you, but I could not help myself. I needed your strength to banish the Enemy, and you do not seem to be too weakened by it, for which I am glad.

"Come, Jargas. I need my clothes and my weapons. For the Enemy to touch me so deep in a Dwarven stronghold, he must already be here. We will need Gervan and Arvan's aid." Farad walked toward the door to the hall with a steady confident stride, as if he had not nearly lost first his life and then his mind. Jargas followed, but swayed off balance for a moment. Farad eyed him sharply. "You are sure you are well?"

"Of course," Jargas said, but his balance was off, as if one leg was suddenly shorter than it should be.

"Between the energy you gave me and that which I severed from you, I have weakened you when you thought I had not," Farad said, concerned.

"I may not bear the scars of my battles as vividly as you, but I am no stranger to injury," Jargas argued.

"But I think you are used to little affecting you. Your muscle and sinew and bone cannot help you when your core—your house, that is what you called it, in your thoughts—is weakened. You must tread carefully until your full strength returns to you. I expended what strength you gave me and what I took from you banishing him, or I would return it to you."

Farad took up the lamp and entered the hall, and his breath hissed. Gervan and Arvan stood there frozen in the act of running, as if they were statues. "Have I done this to them? But I could not have seen them here. Even in my Madness, I remember all that happened."

Jargas swallowed. "They were coming to aid you. I told them to stay here. Have I done this? Have I somehow used the same Power you wielded before on Gervan?"

"To do so unwittingly...." Farad's voice was tinged with horror. Then he said with surprising compassion, "Jargas, try to shield yourself against our bond if you can. You may not like what I might find. No matter the outcome, you must not blame yourself."

FARAD handed Jargas the lamp and then reached out and touched each of the two men on their foreheads with his fingertips. He let his essence drift toward them, as light as an eagle feather fluttering down in a breeze. He saw their cores, small and dark as all those without Power are, but pure and sweet, strong for those of their kind. Thankfully, they yet appeared intact, when they might have been shattered all too easily. Farad let the breeze that bore the feather of his consciousness blow softly upon them, careful not to let even the feather touch them, and then he carefully withdrew.

GERVAN and Arvan fell backward, obviously startled by their sudden appearance. Farad knew that to them it would have appeared as if he and Jargas had just materialized from thin air.

Where did you come from?" Gervan asked, confused. "Hunter, we thought it was you screaming. You are well? Was it Lownan then?"

Farad cursed. "I forgot all about him." He snatched the lamp from Jargas and ran back to the sick room, afraid of what he might find. But Lownan was alive, breathing smoothly and easily. Farad checked as carefully as he had with Gervan and Arvan and, to his relief, found Lownan's mind intact as well. Small and dark as it was, it had posed neither the threat nor the target that Jargas's core had, so neither he nor the Enemy had harmed him further.

Gervan checked Lownan as well, peeling away one of the bandages. It pulled away easily. He gasped and unwound the rest of it, and then the others. A layer of new skin covered Lownan's back: there were neither lash marks nor hairs, and the skin was so thin, he could see all the blood vessels and muscle underneath, as if it were a soap bubble. But when he carefully touched a spot by his shoulder, it did not burst at his touch. The skin was soft and fine as a baby's, but it held fast. "So, the draught halved has saved you both," Gervan said, relieved.

Then he turned and chastised Farad, "You should not be out of bed. Your arm! You have burned yourself!"

Farad looked down at his arm. His eyes widened as he saw the blackened and bloody flesh of his forearm.

"Surely you must feel it!"

Farad shrugged. "I am always in pain, though not by choice. Forgive me for damaging myself after you worked so hard to heal me."

Gervan shook his head and produced salve and bandages. "How am I to see you healed?"

"Believe me, I am more well at the moment than I have been in a long time. Where are my clothes?"

"Discarded. I have others that might fit you, though. It has been a long time since I have tended a Man, but not so long as that." Gervan turned to Jargas. "If I might enter your chamber? I store them in the guest chamber."

"Of course," Jargas agreed.

Gervan led them to the bedchamber and touched one of the walls, and a previously undetectable door to a closet swung open from the rock. He took the clothes off the bottom shelf.

Farad looked at them in surprise as he started to dress. "These are from Thenalon, or at least, the Thenalon of one hundred years ago, before it was overwhelmed and burned." An hour before, memory would have flooded him and sent him screaming.

But confining his memories in the pallenteum chest as Jargas had only dimmed them. It did not eliminate them. He must not think too deeply, or he might call them forth; the chest might spring open, releasing them, along with all the others.

"Was it really so long as that? I must be getting old, not to realize," Gervan said. "Some of the few who escaped the city fled northward and fell into the hands of our army. The northern cousins of the ogres and pumar who had destroyed Thenalon had attacked us as well. They even breeched our door but did not get far into the Mountain. We sent them fleeing and pursued them out the other side of our mountains.

"I tended to the refugees from Thenalon we encountered. I saved those that I could." His face clouded at the memory. "We should have escorted them to a City of Man. Even then, King Balgar was a selfish man, thinking only of his own Kingdom. Had we a different King…."

Farad looked at Gervan intently. "Gervan, when I spoke of Resemblants before, I only suspected your King might be one. Now I am almost certain of it. I plan to test him, expose him, and slay the thing in his place if it is as I fear. But I will not cause a civil war and anarchy here. I would have the Mountain Guard and Valar aid me if they might. Valar loved his father. I hope he might wish revenge upon the one who destroyed him, rather than upon me when I merely seek to put his father's body to rest."

Gervan looked at him. "I will speak to Captain Dergan and to Valar."

"But you must only tell Valar if he will not seek to warn his father against us," Farad cautioned.

Gervan said, "We will go to Captain Dergan first, so he can alert his men and ready them. Then we will tell Valar. He will listen to us, he must. Hunter, you and Jargas should stay here for now. Arvan, come with me," Gervan said, and they left.

"I need my weapons," Farad said, after they had gone.

"I will get them for you," Jargas said.

"No, it is too risky," Farad argued.

"I will be careful. I know who I can ask, where it is safe to go, and where it is not," Jargas said confidently.

Farad reluctantly let Jargas go.

TIME crept past. Farad started to pace the healer's chambers, fretting. He felt caged. He forced himself to stop pacing. He was not caged; he must not feel confined.

They were gone too long, all of them. But he must wait here. There was no way to find them. His breath hissed at the sudden certainty that Jargas was in danger. He should not be able to tell so much; they were freshly linked and had not opened themselves to each other. Even if it were true, if Jargas needed his aid, how could he hope to find him in this Dwarven labyrinth?

The dungeon! Images flashed across their bond: Jargas was in the dungeon, chained, hurt, helpless, raging.

Farad left Gervan's home and traveled quickly and purposefully down one corridor after another, drawn to Jargas, a map of the route he needed to take flaring in his mind.

Panic seized him. If he became lost, he would never again see the sun! Farad grabbed hold of the bond to Jargas and drew light and warmth and strength from it. He had never been able to risk touching his bond to Dewalaren like this. He felt calm settle over him. He knew the way to Jargas, and Jargas knew the way out.

But then agony lanced across Farad's left thigh and his stomach, and he fell to his knees. He rose, pale and shaking, and ran. It was not his pain. It was Jargas's pain he felt. They were branding Jargas. He recognized the feeling of burning metal scorching skin. Memory kindled: the agonies of his parents, his brothers, the smell of his own flesh burning a short time ago, in Gervan's home, and a hundred years ago, in Thenalon.

The chest in his mind rattled and shook as the memories tried to spring forth fully, and Farad used every ounce of his will to keep it shut; if it opened, it would cripple him, and then he could not save Jargas. His terror gave him an extra burst of speed as he ran. He was close, so close to Jargas. He could yet be in time to save him. He must be in time to save him!

Farad arrived in the familiar passage and saw one of the Dungeon Guard who had beaten and tormented him in his cell guarding the door that led to Jargas. All control fled. Farad wrenched the Guard's mind away from him even as he tore the battle-axe from his already lifeless hands before the body fell. Farad yanked open the door and leapt into the chamber, axe raised, and froze, appalled.

Captain Dergan and the four men he had led to Gervan's home hung by manacles from the wall. The Captain's men could not be alive and look as they did. He had not seen such horribly burnt bodies since Thenalon. The Captain yet lived. His body was whole, not burnt at all, but his reason had fled him. Watching his men tortured to death in front of him had reduced him to a howling madman.

Gervan was there as well. He hung suspended above the floor from his wrists as the others were, but thankfully he appeared unharmed, sane. The torture must have been before he'd come, or he'd be in Dergan's state. Gervan was staring in wide-eyed horror at Balgar.

Jargas was beside him, also chained, but he was so tall, he stood upon the floor. There was a vicious burn mark along Jargas's leg, where his pants were blackened and burnt away, and another burn along his stomach. Jargas was cursing and writhing, desperately attempting to break the chains that bound him.

"… cannot save Gervan, you whoreson of an ogress," Balgar was saying to Jargas, a look of mad delight upon his face, a bar of cooling steel in the pincers in his gloved hand, the orange beginning to fade to darkness. "Although perhaps I should spare him for now, save him for last. I do not have his son, yet. Arvan will pay for what his father has done. Gervan leaves my own son to suffer, bleeding and in pain, and he gives the medicine that would have healed him to that traitor I lashed and that pathetic plaything you rescued? You and Gervan will watch while I whip Arvan to a screaming skeleton. You'll learn to cherish the sight. It will be the last thing you ever see, I'll make sure of it. I'll put out your eyes with this, and you can dangle from these chains in the dark until you starve to death."

Farad could free Jargas easily from where he stood with a thought, but he could not risk it yet. Jargas would kill Balgar instantly, and first Farad needed to be sure he was a Resemblant and not the King.

Farad dove for the King, knocking the metal bar and pincers from his hand as he wrapped his hand about his forehead, the blade of the war axe in his other hand at Balgar's throat. He reached for the King's mind with his own, expecting to find the amorphous oily mass that mimicked the mind, a Resemblant in his stolen, bloated body.

Farad recoiled in horror, releasing the King and stumbling backward. He had instead found the blackened, twisted, burning core of a Dwarf. This was still Balgar, still the King. He could not act against him. The axe fell to the floor.

Balgar glared at Farad, both enraged and triumphant. "You Amontir are all paralyzed by your foolish Laws! Incuban will reward me when I return you to him. What he has given me already will be as nothing. I had not realized the true value of the treasure I held in my dungeon until he thought you dying.

"He wants you for himself. He will teach you so much before he is through with you. He has shown me such wonderful visions of what he will do to you and your cursed kin, all of you who try to take my Kingdom from me."

"Father?" The voice from the doorway was agonized, but not from the pain of his injuries. Valar stood there, leaning heavily upon Arvan, staring in disbelief at his father and his father's victims, taking in all he saw and had just heard.

"Ah, there you are, my son," Balgar said calmly in a lightly scolding voice, as if his son had just arrived slightly late for dinner. "You bring me the last of those I must punish. You are such a good, obedient boy. Chain him beside his father. I will let you help me repay them for the pain you are suffering."

"Father, please," Valar pleaded, his voice shaking. "Let us help you. You are not well."

"What? You dare speak to me in such a tone?" Balgar roared. "You side with them against me, when they sought to steal my Kingdom from me with their false talk of alliances?"

Suddenly Balgar's voice became crafty. "Of course. You are a man now. They've seen to that. But why be only a man, when you can be a King? I should not have sent my Throne Guard out to look for you. But I do not need them to protect me, nor to punish you for your crimes against me." Balgar's voice had become deadly. "I will do what needs to be done. I see your black heart. You seek patricide, regicide. No, my son, my line ends with me." From the folds of his clothes Balgar took a knife and lunged toward Valar and Arvan.

Farad's eyes widened in horror as he recognized the familiar blade. No! Farad would not let his own knife, the one Dewalaren had gifted to him, be used to slay an innocent! But he could never reach Balgar in time to stop him.

Without hesitation, Farad touched the pallenteum blade of his knife with his mind, twisting it in Balgar's hand as he tangled Balgar's feet with a thought. It was so easy. Balgar fell and impaled himself upon the knife, his great weight driving the blade deep into his heart, all the way to the handguard. Balgar twitched and then lay still.

So very neat, so simple. None would ever know Farad had killed him. Instead it appeared an accident, a self-inflicted end richly deserved. Farad crumpled to his knees and began retching in horror at what he had just done.

Valar was on his knees by his father's side. Arvan had all but carried him there; Valar was yet so injured he could not walk unaided. Arvan checked Balgar for signs of life. "I am sorry, Majesty," he said to the man who a moment ago had been Prince, but was now King. "The knife pierced his heart. I cannot help him, my father cannot, no one can. He is dead."

Valar swallowed and nodded. "See to your father, Arvan, and to the injured. I must summon the Throne Guard. Their duty is to me now." Valar tried to stand, but could not do so unaided.

Farad was still on his hands and knees, his core in turmoil. He had committed regicide. Balgar had deserved death, and there had been no other choice: so small and dark a mind could not be healed of such madness. Balgar had been turned by the Enemy, his core had been burning, and he had called Incuban by name. Balgar had tortured shackled prisoners, innocent men, to death. He had delighted in their pain. Yet he was the King. Farad had slain a King. He had done it to save Valar and Arvan, two innocents, but it did not matter. He had broken his people's most sacred Law.

He could never face Dewalaren again. He was aberrant, an abomination. He had done the unthinkable, the unconscionable, the unpardonable. He was alone with his guilt in the cold, the dark. Farad felt the cracks of Madness spider-webbing along his core.

Then, suddenly, there was warmth. It radiated down the coppery wire that touched his core and spread across it, filling the cracks first with warmth and then with heat, which fused the shattering mass whole again. And then Jargas was there in the flesh, his strong arms embracing Farad's body as his core embraced Farad's mind. Arvan or Valar must have released him.

Farad heard Jargas's warm, deep voice rumbling in his core, so the others could not hear. *You should have freed me and let me do it. It wouldn't have hurt my house, my core, to. I've killed before, men deserving death far less than Balgar. He tortured those men to death. He tried to brand Gervan as well.* Farad could hear the indignant rage. *I twisted my leg in front of the brand and took it instead. Then Balgar turned on me, branding my stomach to punish me. Both of us would have ended up like those other poor men. How can it be wrong to kill a man such as that, to free a Kingdom from him?*

Farad could not speak, even with his mind. He dropped all his defenses and let Jargas into the very heart of his core. He let Jargas see the tragic history of his people, brought to ruin through regicide: the shining Kingdom of Amontir, far to the east, beyond the Deathshand Mountains, past the opposite edge of the Dwarven Lands. Greater Men, with lifespans over four times that of Lesser Men; great Lords with fantastic powers of mind. The wise and gentle King Albinar, counseled always by his wizard advisor, Arcanus, and all but worshipped by his younger brother, Ebonar, whom Albinar cherished above all other Men.

But then the wizard Incuban came. Arcanus welcomed him in joy, as a long-lost friend. But Incuban ignited a terrible madness in Ebonar: not the King's Madness, but something far worse. Ebonar slew his own brother and the Lords and Ladies of all the Great Houses in a single horrific night of ambush and carnage, all to claim the three symbols of power of the throne for his own: the Ring, the Sword, and the Knife.

Farad showed Jargas how Arcanus aided Albinar's three sons in escaping with the sons and daughters and kin of all the Great Houses. Ebonar's son Idare, horrified by what his father had done, tricked his father and stole the symbols from him, outwitting even Incuban, joining Albinar's sons in their desperate flight for safety.

Idare gave each symbol to one of his cousins, King Albinar's sons, and then they separated for safety, Idare staying with the youngest among them. Each son led ten Houses and took one symbol. They were to have rendezvoused on the other side of the Deathshand Mountains, in the Dwarven Kingdom of Maragar.

But the eldest son, Rowanar, keeper of the King's Ring, and all the Houses he led, and the middle son, Alanar, bearer of the King's Knife, and the Houses he led, never came. Then Maragar betrayed Felenar, the youngest, and his ten Houses to the false King Ebonar and Incuban.

Arcanus, who had gone looking for the missing brothers, suddenly reappeared in their time of greatest need and battled beside Felenar, though he was seen to have but a shadow of his former Power.

Maragar was obliterated in the ensuing battle: the Mountain toppled down upon the entire treacherous Kingdom. Most of the Amontir escaped; just over fifty were lost. But Arcanus vanished for a time, and among those slain was Felenar, last living heir to the throne if Rowanar and Alanar were dead.

It was then that Idare, son of the King's brother, son of the King's murderer, took up the King's Sword and led his people across the Dwarven Lands. He vowed that even if neither of his cousins lived, none would ever call him King unless he held all three symbols of power in his hands once again.

He was still called Prince when he died, as was his son, and his grandson, who now ruled them. Farad was careful to cloud those men's names and faces in mist so Jargas could not see them, for he yet could not trust him with the secret he had helped keep for nearly a century and a half. The Enemy must never learn the name or face of their current Prince or his father.

This is different, Jargas said to Farad silently over their bond. *This is not a madman slaying a true King; this is a mad King who needed slaying. You've not condemned his people, you've saved them. I'll not let you suffer for that. You are a great man, Farad, if only you could see yourself as I see you. I had not meant to bind you so strongly to me, but I do not think you can walk alone any longer. You and I must leave this place as soon as we can, if you are to be well again.*

Gervan came to them, his face creased with concern. "I was afraid you would strain yourself. You are not yet well. You must rest and drink more and heal."

Jargas shook his head. "He needs the sun to heal, Gervan. Hunter cannot heal here. He is not like us. He cannot draw comfort from cold stone and darkness as we do."

Farad rose shakily to his feet. "First, I would help the Captain, if I can. Then I must speak with King Valar, about the alliance I had proposed to his father."

Gervan returned to his home to get medicines to sedate the Captain, so they might unchain him, while Arvan stayed with Valar, with Jargas and Farad to guard them.

Valar spoke to Farad. "Arvan told me what happened to my father. I think I knew he had been changed. My own father could not have done these reprehensible things. It helps, knowing he was a Resemblant. We knew of such things. Your people had warned us decades ago of the danger that was coming. I wish the knowledge might have spared him. But at least I can bury him with honor, knowing that although the body is still his, his spirit left it long ago."

Farad would not tell him the truth. It was better he believe the lie.

"There will be a coronation. I will insist it be quick and simple; this is no cause nor time to celebrate. Then I would hear of the alliance you proposed to my father."

Farad bowed and said, "Thank you, your Majesty." At least his self-imposed mission had not ended in disaster. It had taken twelve years, but finally the Dwarven Kingdoms would be united as one, although only three now remained. And now Jargas's people would aid them as well. If Aramis and Rolin could get Thenalon and Aralon and some of the other Cities of Men to join them here, in the mountains, if Dewalaren and Lunahr could rally the Elven Kingdoms, perhaps they might yet stop the darkness. Could Men and Dwarves and Elves fight together against a common enemy? They must fight together or perish.

GERVAN returned to the cell. The Captain was sedated, although Jargas had to pin him in order for Gervan to be able to do so. He was unchained, as were the bodies of the dead Guard. Valar leaned upon Arvan, yet needing his aid to walk, while Jargas acted as his Guard.

That night, there was a purge of the ranks of the King's Guard, and a number of the Mountain Guard were reassigned to positions of power within the former. There were a number of other arrests as well, and more than a few disappearances, as some courtiers fled before they could be found.

Farad told Gervan, "Some of those who have fled will go to the Enemy, while others will have fled for fear of His wrath. But there will still be a few spies here, carefully hidden, ready to work further treachery from within. You and Arvan must be sure Valar knows this and ensure that he and his men are constantly on their guard."

"I swear to Ragnar and Aralyn both, we'll see Valar safe or die trying." Gervan removed the bandages and checked Jargas's burns again, reapplying the salve he'd used earlier upon them. "These burns should have been mine. Balgar was coming for me with the brand, but Jargas twisted himself and swung his legs about, taking the brand meant for me. Then Balgar gave him the second as punishment for it."

"Do not paint me a hero. I wanted to save you the pain, that is true, but I also tried to catch him and crush him between my legs, but he evaded me. I had not expected him to be so agile. I am lucky Hunter came to distract him, and then Valar, for I can think of better ways to die than as those poor guards did whom he branded to death. Is there any hope for their Captain?"

"Dergan sleeps now. I hope Lownan might be able to help him. Seeing him recovering when he'd been fated to die might bring Dergan to himself again. It cannot hurt him. He is beyond harming further."

Farad could do nothing for Dergan. He had carefully viewed his core, but as he had known it would be, it was too small and dark for Farad to do anything to aid him. It would be all too easy to end his suffering, but he would not, if Gervan held even a sliver of hope he might yet be saved.

Gervan eyed him in concern. "You must drink again, and eat if you can. I had thought you healed enough by the draught that you might not retch again as you did in the cell."

"I am well enough. I will be fine," Farad argued.

"Tell me so after you've drunk this."

Farad cautiously tasted what Gervan offered him, then drank it down. "It is but water," he said, puzzled.

Gervan looked relieved. "Aye, water, plain water. You would not have been able to drink it a day ago, without the honey and salt, and I thought you might not be able to now. We've made some soup for you. Perhaps you'll be able to stomach it after all."

Farad ate the soup and some bread without difficulty. Once he was done, he asked Gervan for a razor.

"Why that?" Gervan asked suspiciously.

"Because I wouldn't expect anyone but a Healer to have one, within the Mountain. You must sometimes use one on your patients' backs or chest or arms or legs, in order to treat them. If not, a sharp knife will do. I would feel myself more were I clean-shaven as I should be. Besides, I plan to return to my people now, and they would not recognize me were I to appear before them bearded. We are all beardless. I am the only one of them who even has the ability to grow a beard, the only one who ever has need to shave."

Gervan looked disapprovingly at him but led him to the privy and brought him the razor he requested. A mirror of silvered glass was already mounted upon the wall over the sink. Then he left him to his privacy.

When Farad emerged, Jargas eyed him with interest. The scar on his face was vivid, more noticeable now, with the beard gone; it ran all the way down his chin. Farad's face was still drawn and worn looking, and his eyes still fearful to look upon, but he had a good, strong face, and the scar showed his ability and experience as a warrior. Farad had trimmed his hair shorter as well, doing a surprisingly good job. He looked a completely different person. To Jargas's surprise, he found his altered appearance suited him.

Even Gervan approved. "Keep the razor and the combs and brushes, and I'll give you a small mirror for your travels. I'll be sure you have a blanket and a cooking pot and provisions and whatever else you might need in the way of traveling gear as well, when you go. I know you'll be leaving us soon."

A messenger came and notified them that the following day they were to appear before the new King. The rest of the day passed quickly, and then the following morning, Farad and Jargas were both summoned to the King's presence, to an official ceremony in the Great Hall, which Gervan and Arvan and many others were to attend as well.

At the ceremony, Farad's bow and quiver were returned to him by King Valar, who offered a formal apology for his false imprisonment. The King showed his unwavering trust in Farad by doing so, for seldom did a Dwarven King allow someone not of his own Kingdom to go armed in his presence, within his Mountain. Farad's hand shook as he accepted Sethiana, whispering his bow's name to her and silently apologizing to her for allowing her to be taken from him. He caressed the familiar, smooth wood and truly felt himself again, for the first time in four long months.

He forced himself to listen as the King accepted his offer of an alliance and pledged his Kingdom to the Watch's aid. But the King was not finished speaking. King Valar also gifted him with a new knife, as a symbol of the alliance between them. Farad saw that the knife was finely crafted, with an antler hilt, and the blade was keen and wickedly barbed.

"I doubt you have seen a blade like it," Valar said proudly. "Our finest weaponsmith, Maradan, perfected the design. You see how the ends of the handguard turn sharply downward? If you twist the blade like so, you can disarm a foe, even one bearing a sword." Valar twisted his hand, showing him the skill. "Yet it is also finely balanced and weighted for throwing. There is not an Elf nor Man alive who could have ever crafted a blade like this one."

Farad gave his heartfelt thanks for the valuable gift. He could never have used his own knife again, after what he had done with it, even had it been returned to him. He forced the memory down, lest it bring him to his knees.

King Valar assured him that his men would begin work on sabotaging their pass, as Farad had suggested, readying it to be sealed if the Enemy's forces approached before the allied army came. The passes to Dorolingas and Ironhand had already been sealed, to funnel the Enemy toward Malar. "We will await the coming of your armies and your King, and we will fight to the last Dwarf," Valar swore.

To Jargas, Valar said, "I and my Kingdom both owe you my life. I will not have your father bow to me, cousin. Instead, I welcome him and all your people as our equals and allies. Any of you who wish to return to our Mountain will do so under my rule and I will command our army, but your father, King Rongas, will yet rule your Mountain and command your own army."

Jargas was overjoyed that his father would not be losing his Kingdom after all. His thanks were sincere and enthusiastic.

Farad and Jargas were given provisions and coin for their journey, and then the feast in their honor began. They both were seated at the King's table with his most high-ranking and trusted subjects, Gervan and Arvan among them. But the King knew they were both eager to return home and so limited the feast to a single day and night.

THE next morning, after saying their final good-byes, Jargas and Farad left at dawn to begin the treacherous and arduous crossing back over the mountains. They emerged from the Mountain into the wakening day. Farad viewed the morning sky, hungering for his first glimpse of the sun. When it crested over the peaks before him a moment later, he gazed upon it in reverence, and his body shuddered as he held his arms out and face upward to it.

Jargas eyed him, intrigued. The sun held no such power over him; he was as at home below ground as above it. The Door Guard were staring at them curiously. They disliked the fierce afternoon sun, but the gentler morning did not bother them.

"Come, Hunter, you will feel sun enough, soon. This valley will seem an oven in a few hours," Jargas said.

Farad sighed in contentment. "At noon I will strip off my clothes and lie naked on the burning rock and drink in the light. After four months without the grace of its touch, I could lose myself to it."

"Hunter, the sun can burn and kill just as the oil fire could have. It worries me to hear you speak so."

Farad shook his head. "Fire is a poor second, and these thoughts are my own. The Men of Amontir all crave the sun." He looked up at Jargas, curious. "All, at least, until you. That accident of your ancestry may save you from much, for darkness has always been tied to the King's Madness, in those of us who have Power enough to be afflicted by it. Yet you are sane and well, and none would have taught you the meditations to keep you so.

"Tell me, how old are you? You look perhaps forty, although you would appear younger were you clean-shaven as the rest of us, but you have your father's blood in you, as well as your mother's, so I cannot guess your true age. Dwarves live to be five hundred and we of Amontir reach two hundred fifty years, when we are not slain young. Few have lived past one hundred fifty these past two and a half centuries of our exile, and many not nearly so long. I am the oldest, now."

"I suspected as much. My grandsire was in the full flower of his manhood when he was found, yet he lived one hundred twenty-four years after that. I myself am eighty-three."

"Eighty-three, and no trace of Madness! And your sister, you said she is twin to you, and she also has Power. Is her core as sound as your own?"

"AYE, she is my twin, though she looks nor behaves nothing like me. She's a true Dwarven lady, in feature if not in manner. She appears perhaps twenty-five to my eye, but still acts child enough, for all she is Chieftess."

He smiled fondly, thinking of her. Their mother was forty-two when she bore him, well past the age when a woman should be able to conceive, but she still looked to be a young maid. It hurt to know she might yet be alive and beautiful and strong, were it not for him. He wondered still that his father did not hate him for slaying her with his birth, for he had loved her beyond naming; she was a treasure to him above all price.

Jargas had not slain his sister, at least, in his birthing, though it had been such a close thing he still fought the terror of it in his dreams. He had been born more than two months early, but still was half again as big as he should have been, had he been full term. His Mother had died in her birth agony, though she was strong. They told him later that his cries echoed hers, and that he reached for her even in her death.

But when the healers went to cut his blood-cord, they found to their dismay it was tightly twined about a second. When they pulled his sister from their mother's lifeless body, the baby girl was only half the size she should have been. At first they thought her dead, but Jargas had grabbed for her and held her tiny hand and not let go, and they saw her chest rise and fall as she struggled to breathe. They did all they could to help save her, pulling her away from him. She was such a fragile thing they sought to keep her separated from him, lest he crush her. But he and his sister had cried inconsolably and reached for each other, and neither would eat from the wet nurses who tried to feed them.

It was then that their father, who knew something of the ways of twins, for they were more common among his people, roused from his grief and placed the two together again. His father told him they'd found each other with their tiny hands and held tightly to one another and instantly calmed. They would not be separated again. He named them Jargas and Jarina, the boy after both him and his wife, and the girl only after her, according to the customs of his people and hers.

They each shared two wet nurses, and Jargas drank from a third as well, while his tiny sister watched with her bright brown eyes. She was slow to grow, but he grew tremendously. Once full grown, she was barely five feet tall, while he towered a number of inches over seven feet. She had her mother's face and hair and eyes but the petite build of a Dwarven Lady. Jargas had the face of his father but his mother's eyes, his father's bulk and bone and hairiness, but his mother's height and beyond.

Jargas felt for the bond, the coppery wire in his mind that had connected him to Jarina for as long as he could remember. He was so far from her! He touched the strand gently and tugged ever so lightly upon it, like a spider pulls upon a strand of its web. He felt her answering tug, and a wave of joy and warmth coursed across the link to him. He sent back an answering wave along the fragile thread and basked in her love for a moment before letting go. Jargas looked outwardly again and was surprised and concerned to see a look of utter despair and anguish upon Farad's face. "Hunter, what is wrong?"

"I heard you, all of it, your thoughts of your mother and your birth and your sister and your father. I felt the bond between you. It is so strong! I felt you touch her, and I felt her answer. I felt the love between you. She is so bright! Her core sings, she is so pure. After our mother was killed, and our father maimed and soon dead, my brothers and I linked to one another. We thought we would be strengthened by it.

"It has been so long since I have felt such a touch. My link to my cousin was never so strong. I would not let it be. It would have been dangerous for him. How can I be linked to you as if you were a brother when I do not even know you? Already I rely on that link. I would be lost without it. My mind screams that I cannot be made so vulnerable, but I am helpless as a babe now."

"You are tired, Farad," Jargas said gently, using his given name now, when he'd not before out of respect for Farad's custom, knowing it was safe to do so as there was no one near enough to hear it. "You are worn to nothing, yet still you fight. You are not helpless, for needing help. You have learned an awful lesson, a wrong lesson, that you cannot rely on others, because they will be used against you, taken from you. The Enemy seeks to weaken you by dividing your strength in that manner. But I am strong, Farad, and for all her wee size, my sister is strong as well. Jarina is so very bright and full of joy and laughter. Were you to meet her, I think she might be able to help you. She is a healer, and you are still in need of healing."

"No! How can you even think to bring me to her? I heard Him! He spoke her name, He has seen her brightness, He lusts after her already. You have seen the memories in my core. You know what He will do to her if He finds her. If you sever your link to me, it might be years before He finds either of you again. I am a danger to both of you! You must sever your bond to me."

Jargas heard the terror in Farad's voice. He well knew Farad himself could break it, if he truly wished to. "I am our village Champion. I protect our tribe from all the dangers it has ever faced. How can protecting one more be a burden? I will not sever our bond, Farad, not when you are in such need of me.

"Now, enough of such dark thoughts. The sun shines brightly overhead. At noon I will let you bask in the sun like a lizard, though I will make you lay on a blanket, for I'll not have you burn your back. And you'll not lie on one side for too long, for I will not have you burnt red, either. Then we will be on our way. But still, you will walk with me in the light, and that should be sun enough for you."

Farad took a deep breath, held it, and slowly exhaled. He repeated that four more times, then nodded. "I was fortunate indeed to have met you when I did, for you have saved me already a number of times. I am not used to being the one who needs rescuing. You are giving me a new perspective, one I am sorely in need of, I think. Thank you, Jargas."

AT NOON, when the sun was high overhead, brutally hot and bright, Farad found a flat slab of scorching rock and laid his blanket upon it. Then he stripped off his clothes and lay under the sun, eyes closed to its glare. The heat and brightness were an almost unbearable ecstasy after so long in the cold and dark. He basked in the sun's radiance as Jargas had basked in Jarina's.

Farad wondered what it might feel like, to love such a woman, even as a sister, or perhaps as a man was meant to love a woman, then firmly drove the thought away. It had been a century since he had lain with a woman. He would not, he could not, ever again. He had neither the desire nor the ability to any longer. He had seldom ever even thought about it, all these many long, lonely years. So why was he thinking of it now? Was it because Incuban had betrayed his impotence to Jargas? Was it because it was safe here, in the full radiance of the sun, to think such thoughts?

Farad saw again the quick flash of image from Jargas's mind of his sister. She had been so bright she had almost blinded him. But here, when pictured against the noonday sun, he could see her clearly: dark haired and dark eyed, petite and soft yet strong, with a smile as full of mischief as delight.

Farad turned onto his stomach and hugged the searing rock, and the image faded. He breathed deeply, letting the sun's healing rays work their magic upon him. Slowly he relaxed, his thoughts drifting lazily. A little while later, from far away, he heard someone speaking his name, his given name. He blinked and rose.

Jargas was eyeing him with an odd expression on his face.

"What is it, my friend?" Farad asked, as he pulled on his undergarment.

"You are different," Jargas said, as Farad pulled on his pants.

"Different?" Farad asked, pulling his shirt over his head and tightening the lacing before tying it.

"You look better. Not fully well, but better. You were in such turmoil before, all cold and hard, sharp with jagged edges, but now you are warmer and smoother and… bah! I cannot describe it. I have neither the tongue nor the wit for it. I had never known the sun could heal, before."

Farad put on his boots. "I think I have had enough of its light upon me that the night will be safe for me. The Amontir are not as other Men, Jargas. Your father's blood has saved you from much, if you can live without the sun and have Power without the Madness it brings." Farad actually smiled, and then, in reaction to the look of astonishment upon Jargas's face, he laughed.

Jargas stared at him, stunned speechless.

"I am a poor example for you of your kinsmen, I think! Had you met Beryl or Fennel or Pierce, you would have had a far different opinion of us: Beryl with his loving heart and laughing green eyes and song, or Fennel with his gentle strength and warmth, or even Pierce, with his keen eyes and barbed tongue. Come, we should take advantage of my mood and travel far. I cannot remember when I last felt so light of heart. I have no doubt disaster will strike soon enough, but I will live for this moment alone, and for now, it will be enough."

THEY continued on their journey, through the pass back across the mountains, into the lands of Men, to Thenalon and then to Aralon. Farad did not smile again during the whole long journey.

Farad parted company with Jargas a week outside of Athanark, his body fully healed but his mind uneasy. "I must head north again. I am greatly troubled by what we have found, and what we have not. There was no sign of Pierce in Thenalon nor Fennel in Aralon, yet the alliance between the two has not been mended. I have been too long out of touch with our kin. I have a way to contact them, but I cannot yet share it with you.

"You must cross the Coroden and return to your Kingdom and your village. I will find you when it is time for your House to be recognized by the Prince. You have told me your home is southwest of Gosa and my bond will guide me to you, wherever you might be.

"If our bond should break, you must go at once to any of the Elven Kingdoms and show them your band. They will know how to contact us. Tell them your story and show them this." Farad handed Jargas an eagle feather, one he had acquired on their journey. The spine of the feather was now notched in a distinctive pattern at the base.

"Tell them Hunter, Captain of the Watch, gave this token to you, so they might know they can trust you, for the Elves will be as surprised as I was to see a band of a lost House, and our kin will be doubly suspicious, for you cannot speak Amontirin, when you should, other than those words and phrases I have taught you. Many bands have been lost to us, and the Enemy has used the ruse of a survivor of a lost House upon us before. Stay well, my friend. I hope I will see you again soon." Farad clasped his arm, then slipped quickly into the woods.

Jargas could no longer see him, but he felt the warmth of his link and traced his path through it. Then Jargas turned and continued down the Road to Athanark.

Chapter 4
The Journey

TALON awoke as the first dappled rays of sunlight filtered through the canopy of leaves above him and kissed his face. He felt astonishingly well rested and realized in relief his sleep had been unmarred by the nightmares that had plagued him. He silently turned toward Betula, planning to gently awaken him, but instead stilled and stared, mesmerized by the effect of the sunlight upon Betula's golden tresses.

Talon's fingers suddenly ached to run through that silken softness, to caress those perfect lips with his fingertip. Or with his own lips. Blessed Idare, Betula was the most beautiful man he had ever seen! His heart quickened with a moment's lust and then slowed just as quickly in guilt.

He slipped back soundlessly onto his back and shut his eyes against the temptation. How could he view Betula this way, when Elanara awaited him in Erenia? She was the most desirable woman he had ever seen. They were betrothed. He loved her beyond all reason and she... she felt nothing for him. No, worse than nothing. She despised him, though she had denied it and worked hard to conceal it.

He still did not understand why she loathed him, or why she pretended she did not, but the pain of her rejection cut sharper than any blade, wounding his very core.

At the unexpected gentle touch upon his shoulder, Talon's eyes snapped open, and he sprang into motion. Realizing it was Betula's concerned face above him, not an enemy's, he barely arrested his instinctive attack in time to avoid harming his friend. Although he saw that Betula had drawn back with impressive agility into a defensive pose that would likely have countered any blow he might have attempted to land, balancing as nimbly on the branches as if he stood upon the ground.

"Forgive me. You startled me," Talon apologized ruefully, angry with himself for having dropped his guard even for a moment. It was fortunate indeed that Betula was a friend, and not a minion of the Enemy.

"No, forgive me. You looked like you were in the throes of a nightmare, like you were in pain," Betula apologized in turn, as the coiled readiness of his pose eased.

"I was awake. I was merely thinking intently," Talon admitted, brutally forcing all further thoughts of Elanara away. His focus should be on his young friend. Friends were valuable and rare, to be treasured as much as kin. He was blessed beyond naming to have found Betula while his kinsmen were so distant from him, scattered throughout the Lands of Men.

He saw Betula's brow crease in compassion and concern and realized he was still revealing far too much by his expression. "Come, we must travel. We have no supplies to break our night's fast, and I hope to make the village before nightfall,"

Talon said abruptly and without further word began climbing down the tree that sheltered them, careful not to let his agitation cause a misstep. He heard Betula climbing down after him.

Once Betula reached the ground, Talon turned toward him, catching his new friend unaware. Betula's brow was creased in hurt and confusion and loss that echoed Talon's own heart before Betula realized he was being watched; then his expression cleared as if a mask had dropped over his features, concealing his pain.

Talon realized that he had unwittingly wounded his friend, that Betula had apparently taken his words as a rebuke, his gruffness as coldness or perhaps even anger. "Forgive me again, my friend! It is not that I do not value your compassion. It is just that I sometimes think too much, remember too much. To speak of such things, even in the face of well-intentioned concern, brings me further into the darkness. If I am to travel in the light, I must not dwell upon them. I cherish your friendship, Betula, far more than you must realize. Please, if ever I wound you again, either by my words or my deeds, do not seek to conceal it from me. I would know when I make such mistakes so that I might correct them. I would never wish to injure you, even unknowingly."

Betula's mask crumbled with the first of his words, initially revealing surprise and puzzlement, then understanding, and finally a pure joy that lit Betula's face like the sun.

He was so young, to reveal so much! An elder Elf would never betray himself in such a manner. Betula reminded Talon fondly of Eladar, for a moment, until the memory brought his thoughts back to Eladar's sister Elanara. Talon sighed. "I fear you have found a taciturn and melancholy traveling partner, Betula. You will think yourself well rid of me, once we part company."

To his surprise, Betula smiled and shook his head. "Not at all, my friend! Seldom have I been faced with such a challenge. I am instead determined to provide enough distraction that you change your very nature, for a time at least, while you are with me."

Talon basked in the healing warmth of Betula's smile as if it were the sun. Then he realized the early morning sun was in fact shining brightly, the forest around him was the vivid green that followed after the rains, he was well rested after a night of dreamless sleep, and most importantly of all, for the first time in a very long time, he traveled with a friend.

ARAS'S breath caught as an answering smile unexpectedly lit and transformed Talon's face. How different he looked! The dried mud and grime that marred his features and matted his hair could not conceal the handsomeness of his face when he smiled like that. Talon's deep-blue eyes shone like sapphires; more, they sparkled like sunlight upon the water with his joy. His eyes were more liquid and perfect than those of any Oceana Aras had ever seen. But it was his hair in particular that fascinated Aras. It was not the silver or white of the Oceana, nor the gold of the Aerta, like his own, nor, fortunately, even the distinctive black of his mother's, now that he was the only one to see, and she no longer concealed her true coloration beneath a masking spell. At first Talon's hair had looked black, but after the rains, Aras could tell that beneath all the dirt, it was a shade of brown, though which hue he could not yet guess. He longed to see it truly clean. Would it be a warm mahogany, or a dark walnut, or the rich, deeper color of forest loam?

Aras again saw a startled flash of awareness, of desire, as their gazes locked, the same as the one he had almost convinced himself he had imagined the day before, but then Talon turned from him. "Come, my friend. We must not tarry if we are to make the village by nightfall."

This time, Talon's abruptness did not wound him. This time he understood. Aras made sure his bow and quiver were properly positioned for the trek and then matched his stride to his friend's.

The journey was an arduous one because of his injuries. To Aras's chagrin, they stopped to rest more frequently than he suspected Talon might have, were he walking alone, although Aras pushed himself mercilessly, ignoring his pain and fatigue, doing his best to conceal both from his friend, with some limited success at least. As a result, they managed to reach the village just at dusk.

TALON had done all he could to ease their journey, but he was certain Betula had suffered, despite his stoic demeanor. As they approached the village, Talon was relieved and pleased to see fires rimming the village, as he had commanded, and the shadowy forms of armed men. But Betula looked at them nervously and drew his hood over his ears.

Talon called out to the men. "Ho, villagers! Your enemy is dead." As they strode between the fires into the village, they heard cries of surprise and eager voices as the news spread.

Goras and the others gathered about them. "Talon! Blessed Aralyn, it's a miracle! We'd feared you lost, though I should have known better after what you told me! But though you did not return, neither have the wolven, and we wondered whether you might have killed each other."

Talon regretted now that he had revealed to Goras he was a Captain of the Watch. He had done so to ensure Goras would follow his instructions without question when he might not have otherwise. But he did not want Betula to know he was that and more since Betula had not already figured it out for himself after having seen his band.

"All seven wolven are dead," Talon declared, holding up the rank proof of the deed. "But though I bring trophies from them to prove it, I am not the one who slew them. You owe your gratitude to my friend Betula, newly met in the woods, not to me."

The others looked at his hooded companion curiously.

Betula said awkwardly in Common, "I am pleased I was of service to you."

Then Talon held out the blanket with its sad burden. "And we found their den, as well, and the remains of your missing people. I return all we found to you, so you may bury your dead and lay their spirits to rest."

One of the men took the blanket and said in a gruff voice, choked with emotion, "Thank you. I did not think my brother would know peace." He left with a few others.

"Come," Goras said. "You both look like you could use a hot meal. And we must hear your tale." Talon nodded and followed.

ARAS stayed close to Talon. He felt more than one set of eyes upon him. In the inn, when he removed his cloak at Talon's gentle urging, there were gasps of surprise when the villagers beheld his distinctive features. Aras saw that some looked at him in awe and reverence, others in astonishment, and a few in suspicion bordering on hostility. He was right to have avoided this village before! He should never have come here now, even at Talon's side.

"This is Betula. It is he who slew the wolven for you, almost at the cost of his own life," Talon said, his voice firm, reminding them they were indebted to the Wood Elf suddenly in their midst.

"I merely slew what hunted me," Aras said humbly in Common and was relieved to hear mutters of approval at his words.

Then Talon told them the tale, and Aras was astonished at his knowledge of the details of the battle, as he had not been there, and they had not spoken of it. Talon was a phenomenally gifted and skilled tracker to have read so much from the site of the battle. Aras saw that Talon was also gifted in his storytelling, for the men hung upon his every word.

When Talon explained what followed, Aras noticed he did not mention his own illness. Then Talon grew silent and began to eat as excited voices spoke around them. Mead flowed freely, and the men drank heavily, reminiscing about the fallen villagers, telling tales of their bravery and of their foibles as well, mourning the passing of their friends.

Aras ate little. Though he didn't detect any animal flesh in what was laid before him, most of the food was prepared in a manner that was strange to him, and he felt uneasy, surrounded by so many potential enemies.

TALON caught the innkeeper's attention. "Now that we have eaten, we would welcome a hot bath and a bed for the night. Also, if we might borrow some spare clothes and have ours cleaned, we would be very grateful. Tomorrow we will need to buy some clothes and supplies."

"You may have whatever you wish from us, I think, for we are in your debt. Come, let me show you to your room," Goras said.

The innkeeper led them toward a wooden staircase. The inn was like most of the smaller inns Talon had stayed in, with a large common room below for poorer guests and a single room above, for honored guests with coin to pay, near the rooms shared by the innkeeper and his family. Coin was not mentioned. Goras showed the two men to the room. A tub was brought and filled, and Talon urged his young friend to bathe first.

Talon had not meant to watch Betula bathe, but his eyes drifted to the tub, at first in concern that his new friend might be wetting his bandages. He realized his gaze was lingering on Betula's exquisite form, his concern over his friend's injuries forgotten, and he turned quickly away, angry with himself anew. Betula was still a child. He'd spent enough time with him now to be certain of it. Or, if he had come-of-age, it was surely only recently. In any case, Betula was an innocent. Elves came-of-age at forty-nine, not at twenty-five like his own people, or sixteen like other men. He should not watch Betula bathe. Fortunately, Betula was apparently lost in his own thoughts and had not noticed his interest.

Talon busied himself with the meager contents of his pack.

ARAS was indeed deep in thought. He had at first been thinking of Nalea, of Jarnath and his father, until he had become aware that Talon was watching him. He was puzzled by his scrutiny at first, until he felt faint but unmistakable stirrings of lust humming through the air between them. He could not discount what he felt as he had tried to deny what he had seen.

He was astonished by Talon's apparent interest in him. No one had ever viewed him in such a manner, neither man nor woman, and there were an equal number of each who were permanently stationed in Nalea. Of course, it would have been completely inappropriate that they do so before he came-of-age. Yet during the past five years, most of the trainees around him had regarded one another in such a light, eager for the day they might act upon their flirtations. Their innocent, and not so innocent, teasing repartee with one another had been a source of fascination and wistful envy for him.

Never once had anyone spoken to him in such a manner or looked at him with anything other than quiet respect bordering on fear. No one would dare to. Who might ever be so stupid, so suicidal, as to take romantic interest in the son of the High-King, when even his few friends had paid the price of their lives for their folly in befriending him?

Aras had learned his lesson well decades ago, when Marlaenus and the others had been sent to their deaths by his father. When Aras had finally realized what his father was doing, he'd secretly been able to save those last precious few men and women who had risked all to befriend him. He had smuggled them out of Nalea to safety in Salenia, the furthest of the River Kingdoms.

Once Aras realized the price of his friendship, he made sure no one else suffered for him. He became as cold as his father; he kept a safe distance from all those around him. Yet none ever mistook his reserve for aloofness. Those of the Navy knew, they understood, and they loved him for having saved Marlaenus from his father's wrath the first time, and for all the support he'd given to them since, in spite of his father's bigotry against them, or more, because of it.

Only Meloneth and Jarnath had dared continue to befriend him openly, despite his efforts to see them safe. Each of those two Lords alone was confident that he was far too valuable to ever be slain for such effrontery, no matter how much Laedrin despised them, and so far they had been proven right.

Aras's thoughts were brought back to the present as he realized Talon was no longer looking at him, that he was, in fact, pointedly ignoring him. It hurt that he was, though Aras suspected why he might be. Aras could not hear Talon's thoughts, but he found he was increasingly able to sense his emotions. For all his outward projection of coldness, now, Talon was far from cold. There was incredible loneliness and longing emanating from him, despair and wistfulness that mirrored his own so closely it was as if they were brothers in their shared pain.

"I am finished," Aras said with forced cheerfulness, rising from the water.

"I will have the water changed," Talon said, leaping to his feet and leaving the room with almost comical alacrity.

Aras sighed and began toweling himself dry with the rough towel the innkeeper had provided, marveling at the poor quality of the fabric. The towel was ridiculously thick and retained the water it absorbed regardless of how hard he tried to squeeze the dampness from it.

He scowled at it in disgust and looked in dismay at the small pile of clothes Goras had left for them on the bed so that their own might be cleaned and mended. He lifted one of the innkeeper's baggy, nearly shapeless tunics with a sigh and donned it reluctantly. The garment was clean, at least, but hideously ugly and horribly coarse against his sensitive skin. The pants were enormous, but he managed to improvise a belt to cinch them at the waist well enough so he might wear them.

He began combing his hair, thankful he had brought his own comb with him, though he had purposely left his traveling mirror behind lest his mother somehow work her magicks upon it to locate him.

Talon was a while in returning with the innkeeper and a number of empty buckets. He'd obviously wanted to give Aras ample time to dress. Goras began emptying the tub by the bucket in preparation to refill it. Aras marveled at the laborious process. No wonder most Men did not bathe regularly! Even the simplest of tasks was nearly beyond their primitive skills.

After the tub was finally emptied and refilled with hot water, Goras departed. As soon as he was gone, Talon disrobed without modesty, although Aras realized that when he stripped off his shirt, he apparently removed the armband beneath it at the same time, so stealthily Aras did not even notice.

He was fully, completely, painfully aware that Talon kept his back to him as he stepped into the confines of the shallow, narrow tub. Aras found himself eyeing Talon's buttocks and back surreptitiously, fascinated by the rippling play of muscle beneath his skin as he lowered himself into the water. But his nascent lascivious thoughts were stillborn when Talon began scrubbing himself with such enthusiasm that he had to fight to keep from laughing.

He had heard that Men were filthy creatures and that they had an aversion to cleanliness which quite horrified his own fastidious people, and he had thought it true until Talon's earlier words about his sorry state. Now, watching the gusto with which he set to soaping himself, he realized that Talon was more than eager to see himself bathed. He wondered anew what his friend might look and smell like once he was clean.

When Aras saw Talon straining to reach the small of his back to scrub it, he found that he had to consciously bite back an offer to do it for him. He stared at his hand when he realized he was absently rubbing his fingertips against one another as he remembered the supple feel of Talon's skin when he had been cloth bathing him while Talon was ill. Talon's skin had been unexpectedly soft and smooth, but with hard muscle everywhere underneath. There was a strange dichotomy there. His body was much like his spirit.

Talon was hard and strong and powerful, a warrior born, yet he'd been as kind and gentle as Jarnath, as a healer. At the time, Talon had been vulnerable, completely helpless. Now Talon was well and so full of energy that he seemed to hum with life, with charisma. Aras's eyes drifted to him again. He wondered what it would feel like to touch him now that he was well: to hold him and be held by him, to caress him and be caressed by him, to do more.

His father would be horrified to know that his only son was even thinking about indulging in bed play with a Man, Aras thought with a mischievous grin. Then his eyes widened in alarm at the implication. His father would kill Talon without a thought, with his bare hands, merely for Talon having had the audacity to befriend him. His father would not need to use treachery and subtlety with a Man the way he had with the Naval Guardsmen he'd ensured were slain. Aras shuddered to imagine what his father might do to such a Man were there more than friendship between them.

Heart hammering in fear for his new friend, Aras tore his gaze from Talon; he all but ran to the bed and forced himself to lie down upon it when he wanted nothing more than to flee into the forest, to put as much space as possible between himself and Talon.

How could he have been so selfish? He was a danger to Talon every moment he stayed with him. He discarded his earlier hopes of traveling with him. Better to be alone than to endanger this Man who had tended him so selflessly, who had already nearly died because of him. No matter how competent Talon might be at survival, he could not hope to live if Aras's father wanted him dead.

Aras squirmed uncomfortably in the overly large rough clothes, hearing the sounds of loud voices speaking a foreign tongue leaking up through the floor. He felt so strange, so out of place here, though he had never truly belonged anywhere. Those below had stared at him in curiosity and awe, but also in suspicion and some even in anger. They must never have seen an Elf before. There were no Elven Kingdoms north of the Velmar and east of the Coroden Mountains. The only Elves were those in Nalea, and fortunately for the villagers, they seldom left their River or their Wood.

Aras listened uneasily to the boisterous, raucous celebration below, now that the wolven that had plagued the village were dead. It made him nervous knowing those Men must still be drinking heavily. He had heard much about the effect of alcohol on Men. They had no tolerance for it at all.

Aras was so lost in his thoughts that he jumped when he felt the bed depress beside him; heart pounding, eyes snapping open, he reached frantically for his side, for the dagger which was no longer strapped there.

"Calm yourself, Betula! Forgive me. It is only me," Talon apologized, stepping away from the bed, his hands raised palms outward in a calming gesture. He was also dressed in some of the innkeeper's clothes, now. "I should have realized I might wake you. I thought to share the bed; it has been so long since I have slept in one, and it is large enough that I knew I could do so without touching you. Having just bathed, I hoped I might not be so offensive that…."

Talon's face reddened with embarrassment. "Forgive me my presumption. It was unforgivably rude of me. I'm certain Goras must have another blanket or two that he can spare. I will sleep on the floor, of course," Talon said, as he turned toward the door.

"No, Talon, please wait," Aras said, stopping him in midstride. "Of course you might share the bed." Aras surprised himself at his own words, that he might volunteer to do such a thing in light of all he had just been thinking. Yet he found himself continuing his argument.

"Surely after all we have been through, it is not at all presumptuous for you to have thought you might? It is certainly large enough, as you said, and you are doubtless more tired than I am, from tending me so faithfully. I'll not have you become ill again for sleeping on the floor."

Talon laughed, a look of astonished amusement upon his face. "Become ill from sleeping swaddled in clean, soft blankets on the floor in the warmth of an inn? Truly, you do not know me well at all, my friend! Despite the evidence I have given you to the contrary, I do not get ill, ever, and I have gone without sleep for far longer than this and slept in places so hideous that one should never be required even to walk them, let alone sleep in them. But if you truly would not mind it, I would be most grateful if I might indeed be allowed to share the bed, for I will admit, I have been looking forward to it quite hedonistically," Talon said, his blue eyes twinkling in delight.

Aras found himself grinning in return, his heart quickening as he looked into Talon's eyes, entranced by them. They were the brilliant, deep blue of a summer's twilight sky, and Aras knew wonder that the wealth of warmth he saw in them was for him. No one but Jarnath had ever looked at him like this, with compassion and approval and caring.

"Never let it be said that any Elf ever stood in the way of anyone's quest for hedonism," Aras teased playfully, realizing too late that he had unintentionally lowered his eyelids in the blatantly flirtatious manner he had seen so many of his classmates use. Talon's eyes were now riveted upon his, and the tension in the air was so intense Aras felt as if lightning might crackle between them.

Talon looked away and began heading for the door again. "Actually, I have been told that I sometimes thrash about in my sleep, and I'd not want to risk reopening your wound. I think it best I ask Goras for that bedding and sleep on the floor in any case." Talon was facing away from Aras as if he couldn't bear to look at him and was out the door before Aras could speak in protest, even had he known what to say.

Aras was surprised by the depth of dismay he felt at Talon's abrupt departure. He felt his face flush with humiliation and his brow crease in confusion at the conflicting feelings boiling up inside of him: loneliness and longing, shame and frustration, lust and, astonishingly, even jealousy. He wondered who Talon had slept with before who might have said such a thing to him.

Then he heard his father's cruel, mocking laughter in his memory again; he heard him roaring that he was nothing, that he was useless. How could he have ever been so stupid, so conceited as to think that Talon might ever want him when even his own father wanted nothing to do with him? Talon never would have fled from him like this if he had truly cared about him. Whatever feelings of lust he might have sensed before coming from Talon were apparently only the instinctive animal reaction he had heard Men succumbed to when confronted with one of his kind. He was a child, a fool, an idiot!

Aras clutched the pillow on the bed tightly, fighting the ridiculous urge to cry into it. He had not cried since he was eight, since his mother had tried to use his terror and his tears to break him.

Aras wished Jarnath were here, that he might feel his fatherly arm around him and hear the loving reassurance of his warm voice as he calmly explained what Aras was feeling and why, when in truth, Jarnath knew so little about him. There was so very much he kept hidden. But even so, he would draw strength from Jarnath's misplaced love of him.

He still did not understand how Jarnath could love him when there was nothing about him to love. No, he knew, all too well. Jarnath only loved him because he deceived Jarnath along with all the rest; he had no choice.

Was he then truly any less of a monster than his mother, than Arcanus, than Incuban? Did he manipulate those around him any less? Was he any less intent upon winning this sick, twisted Game they were all playing? Talon, Meloneth, even Jarnath were all just pawns to him, weren't they? He would sacrifice any and all of them he needed to in order to win. He shivered, clutching the pillow tighter, knowing it was true.

No. No, there was a difference. He clung to that knowledge as if it were a lifeline. It was a chilling truth that he might indeed have to sacrifice those few who meant something to him, but he knew that each of them would willingly be sacrificed if they knew the reason. Each of them would die to save others. He'd seen it. And unlike the other Players, Aras fought for life, for selfless reasons, while the other three fought only to bring death, for vengeance, for selfish reasons. His spirit wept anew, even if his eyes would not, for every life that had been snuffed out in their mad scramble for Power, for revenge.

And there was another important difference, the crucial one: he would win. He would live, and the other three would die so that no one else would ever again be sacrificed upon the altar of their madness. His mother used to call him her little avatar, in that mocking way she had that let him know her scorn for him was even worse than his father's.

He had always wondered that such a word as "avatar" existed in any of the Elven tongues when he had been told time and again that his people had never worshipped any Gods. Hearing her words, he had decided long ago that, while it might be his fate to be like unto a God walking the earth, it was his choice to be a God of life, instead of a God of death. Drawing strength from that knowledge, he released the pillow he had been clutching so desperately, tucked it under his head, and promptly fell asleep, the sleep of the just.

TALON spent a long time in the common room of the inn despite his exhaustion, allowing the villagers to buy him round after round of drinks. He managed to surreptitiously swap most of the mugs of mead with those of his neighbors so that in truth he drank little. He was merely biding his time. He had to stay away long enough to be certain that Betula was deeply asleep. He could not risk entering their room while Betula was still awake.

Betula was not like Eladar or the other younger Elves Talon had met. He did not casually bandy about meaningless flirtations. It had been painfully apparent that Betula had no practice in saying such things, that his words had been spoken from the heart even if he had tried to make them sound casual. Betula was so young, so innocent, and so incredibly desirable that Talon was left all but defenseless against him.

He had been feeling so lonely, so vulnerable, knowing that Farad and Lunahr were both gone, that they were forever lost to him. Who knew how many others of his kin had been killed in the two years since he'd last seen one of them? The messages he'd gleaned from the Markers were scant at best.

Talon needed to feel warm, strong arms around him. He needed the reassuring touch of one who was yet alive to drive away his memories of all those many who no longer were. It would be all too easy to be enticed into Betula's bed, and once there, he had no doubt as to what the outcome would be.

He was angry at himself for it, and ashamed. How could he claim to protect innocents when he was willing to sacrifice an innocent to his own need? How could he so dishonor Betula like that? How could he dishonor Elanara? How could he dishonor himself? He was betrothed to Elanara. It was against her custom as well as his own for him to engage in sexual relations with anyone but his intended.

And Betula was in so many ways still a child. Betula's heart and spirit were oddly fragile. It was remarkable that any Elf could be so vulnerable, regardless of his age, but he was. Talon would not risk harming him. It would be so easy to break Betula's heart, to shatter his spirit. Though there was strength and resiliency there as well.

Talon wondered anew about Betula. Who was he? How could his people allow him to travel alone and unescorted, regardless of his physical prowess and martial skills? And why did he feel so drawn to him?

He had not thought anyone but Elanara might ever awaken such stirrings in his heart, in his body, but it was as if a missing piece of his core, of his spirit, had suddenly been found. There was a completeness to him now that there had never been before, even with Elanara—especially not with her.

Suddenly, all the old Amontiri ballads Lunahr used to sing, the poetry he used to read to them, made sense. Once he had thought Elanara could fill that emptiness inside of him. Only she never had, despite how well he had felt she could have had she wanted to. She had never wanted to. She had never wanted him.

Talon thought of his betrothed longingly. She was so incredibly beautiful. And so chillingly cold, so distant, he actually shivered with the memory of his last night with her, and of the weeks that preceded it. They had consummated their betrothal last year. He had spent three weeks with her in Erenia.

Talon had handed her his heart, revealed his most intimate secrets to her. He had betrayed his every weakness to her: he had even spoken of the King's Madness that afflicted him. And she had pleasured him, oh how she had pleasured him! Nothing in his few previous encounters had prepared him for what she gave. But though she was skilled beyond his wildest imaginings, she was coolly efficient, emotionlessly proficient. Talon loved her so desperately, yet she felt nothing. Nothing but disgust.

Talon still did not know why she might. Her elder brother Elavar was his closest friend outside of his own kin. He was like a brother to him, and Talon was fond of her younger brother Eladar as well. Elanara's parents had always been kind to him, and she had fostered his young cousin Lunahr eagerly and lovingly. But she loathed him, though he had not realized it until he had shared her bed. Why had she ever agreed to marry him if she felt that way toward him?

Once he had seen her true feelings, he had told her he would release her from the betrothal, though it had torn his heart in two to say so. He would never force her into a marriage she did not want. But to his consternation, she had reacted with alarm instead of relief. She had insisted that they marry, within a year or two at the most as they had originally planned, as soon as he could summon a quorum of his Lords to witness it, as required by Amontiri Law.

She had done her utmost to pleasure him once more, in an obvious effort to reassure him she indeed wanted him. But still, there was the same coldness, the same revulsion, though she tried so hard to hide it from him. Their lovemaking had left him more confused and hurt than before, lonelier than he had ever been in all the many decades before he met her, even as she yet lay in his arms. He had left, injured and bewildered, hoping that she might someday be able to explain. He still did not understand what was wrong. He feared he might never learn.

Talon fought not to groan aloud in frustration, in need. Betula was not cold. He was anything but cold. There was such warmth about him, such love waiting to be expressed, that merely being in his presence was like basking in the sun at midday. But there was no hiding the inescapable fact that, in his heart, Betula was still a child.

Someone had stunted his emotional growth. Someone had hurt him terribly, abused his spirit ruthlessly, battered him relentlessly, all but crushing the poor youth. Talon had noticed much in the short time they had been together: from the things Betula had said, from the things he had not, from his reactions.

Betula had not been crushed, but he had been injured, he had been wounded. Still, there must have been someone who had shown Betula at least a modicum of love and kindness for him to be as warm as he was, for him to possess the limited confidence he displayed. But he was definitely in desperate need of a friend.

It would be a mistake to leave Betula as he had thought to, he rationalized. He was far from helpless, but he was incredibly vulnerable. He might have a trained warrior's skill and ability, but he yet had a child's naiveté. There were so many dangers he might yet face, any one of which might overcome him were he to be left on his own to confront them. He had left the safety of his Kingdom, whichever of the four Wood Kingdoms he had come from, and entered Man's world ill-prepared and unprotected. There were so many terrible ways he could be hurt in this world.

No. He would not allow it. He would escort Betula safely to those who might care for him. To do so was no less his responsibility than to investigate the rumors in Athanark was. It was his duty to protect innocents, his purpose. What was the Watch for if not to protect those innocents they could save? He would travel with Betula; he would see him safely to one of the four Wood Elf Kingdoms as soon as he could and only then proceed to Athanark.

But perhaps that would not be best after all. He felt an almost overwhelming sense of urgency to reach Athanark, now that those here in the village were safe. Instead, he would take Betula with him to Athanark. He would confront the danger there with Betula by his side. From there they would proceed onward to a Wood Elf Kingdom. They would be near both Loatia and Erenia; only a few hundred or so miles and a single range of mountains would separate them from either.

He would be Betula's friend, his guardian, his teacher; he would be as a father to him, or perhaps a brother. But he should not, could not, be a lover to Betula.

Relieved by the decision, finally confident in his course of action, Talon rose and went to Goras, asking him for extra blankets so that he might sleep on the floor of their room. He explained that Elven custom did not permit them to share a bed.

Goras apologized for not having guessed as much and saw to it that Talon obtained what he needed. Talon climbed the stairs, his doubts finally laid to rest, the weariness of the past days catching up with him so swiftly and completely that he found he barely had the strength needed to complete the simple journey to their room.

He opened the door as silently as he was able and slipped into the darkened room soundlessly, trying to limit the light spilling in from the hallway, ensuring it did not strike the bed, at least, hoping he wouldn't disturb Betula's much-needed rest. He was pleased to note that Betula did not stir at all; if Betula was awakened by his presence, he did not indicate it.

He slid the bolt home, securing the room. As quietly as he could, he laid down Kathalanar and, after a moment's hesitation, stripped off his gloves and laid them within easy reach as well. He refused to wear gloves another night while he slept. He removed his boots and then laid out the blankets directly in front of the door, ensuring that no one might enter the windowless room without waking him so that he might guard them both, even in sleep. He sank gratefully onto the nest of blankets, reveling in the feel of the clean, coarse material of both the blanket and the borrowed clothes he wore against his skin. For the first time in far too long, he truly felt a Man again. It was not the soft bed he had craved, but neither was it the cold, hard ground, or the rough branches of a tree, or a damp cave, or, Idare help him, another fetid bog or swamp.

Forcing the memories of all he had endured these many long decades away with practiced ease, he focused once again on the warmth and softness cradling him, the feel of a full belly, the soft murmur of friendly voices and occasional drunken laughter from below. With a silent exhalation of contentment, he willed his muscles to relax, one by one, and within moments, sleep claimed him.

ARAS awoke in the morning feeling ill at ease. To his dismay and consternation, his dreams had been troubled again, although try as he might, he could not remember them. Normally, he did not share even his father's limited precognitive ability, but he felt a sick certainty that something monumental, something horrific, was about to happen, something that would change the world as he knew it and shake his people to their very core. Such visions often took the form of dreams, or at least, Jarnath had told him they once did, back in the Homeland, before the War of Flame, before the Annihilation, when Power flowed strongly through the earth and trees, air, flaming mountains, and water.

This land that had once housed only two small colonies of their people had become their new home by default, though it possessed only the smallest fraction of the Power they needed to survive. The life they had forged here was but a poor mockery of the World That Once Was. The magical talents of the Aerta and Oceana had withered here, as had their life spans. Even the hardiest of them lived a scant thousand years now, instead of ten thousand as they should, save for the few Aerta Lords and Ladies, of course, those whose Trees yet sustained them. But even the Trees of the Lords' Grove were dying here. They no longer moved, and even their voices had been for the most part silenced, though some yet spoke in the quietest of whispers.

Aras shivered, knowing that one day Aranas might grow as silent as his father's Tree, Arandrin, had, or worse, that one day the entire Lords' Grove would finally perish. He forced his fear down, concentrating instead on the more immediate terror of the dream. But Aras could remember nothing more than a somewhat muted feeling of dread. What could he have seen that was so horrific his mind was trying to protect him from it, that he could not remember even a shadow of what was to come? He would drive himself mad trying to fathom it!

But there had been another revelation this morning, an important one, one that he remembered vividly. In a moment of crystal clarity upon awakening, the knowledge had hit him with the force of a hammer: Talon was a Captain of the Watch, one of that mysterious race, the Amontir, that Arcanus shepherded, that Incuban pursued so mercilessly. Aras still was not clear as to what Arcanus's relationship to them was, but Incuban's was painfully clear. Incuban had chased Talon's people for two and a half centuries, across half a continent, devouring everything in his path in his pursuit of them, in his hunger for them. Aras knew now, without question, that Talon somehow had a crucial role to play in the crisis that was to come.

He cursed himself for his earlier blindness, for his stupidity before. How could he not have immediately realized the significance of the armband he had seen? True, he had been told that the Captains of the Watch, the Lords of the Great Houses of

Amontir, wore pallenteum armbands engraved with the image of the beast that represented their House. Talon's bore no such image, just the single jewel. He did not know why Talon's was different, but it did not matter.

Aras realized there was a reason Talon had saved him, and that he had in turn saved Talon. Their destinies were linked, inescapably intertwined. He must convince Talon to allow him to travel with him at all costs! But he would have to do so with the utmost care. He would not reveal his newfound knowledge to his friend, not until he was certain Talon trusted him enough. The Amontir had not lived through two and a half centuries of being hunted by their implacable Enemy by being incautious. He did not want to lie to his new friend, nor conceal so much from him. He had many years of practice dissembling, before his father, his people, and especially his mother, but he took no joy in it. He did so only out of dire necessity.

This was why he had been compelled to argue with his father. This was why he had come this way and no other. Meeting Talon was no accident. He suspected that somehow the fate of the world rested upon this meeting, and he sensed there would be other meetings, in the near future, no less innocuous seeming but no less crucial. He must be constantly vigilant to ensure he missed none of them.

The next round of play, the final round, was about to begin. He suspected it had, in fact, already begun. But this time the playing pieces were leaping onto the board of their own volition and taking on a life of their own once upon it.

Aras had become an active, though yet hidden, Player. The three other Players remained ignorant of him. His continued safety lay in that anonymity. One day, of course, most likely soon, he would be discovered. But by that day, he hoped the three other Players would have lived to regret that they never saw the potential of their playing pieces, that even the lowliest pawn on their board might someday become a King, that it might become more, that it might somehow one day even become a Player. Was Talon that piece? Or had that piece yet to be discovered?

Aras sat up soundlessly, looking for Talon. He spotted him easily, needing no lamp to see by. He was on the floor, in front of the door, guarding and protecting them even in his sleep, merely by his position. Talon's face was turned toward him. This time, even in his sleep, Talon indeed looked to be on his guard; there was a scowl upon his face. Perhaps his dreams had been dark as well?

Aras lit the lamp by the bed for Talon's sake and stretched silently, catlike. It was good to be clean again. The metamorphosis for Talon was remarkable. Talon's hair had been nearly black with filth before, hanging in stringy tangles about his face, later mud spattered and matted, and then clean but wet. Now, it was a rich, warm mahogany, and it looked like it might be as soft to the touch as a rabbit's fur. He ached to run his fingers through it to see. The dark color, so different from the silvers and blonds of the Oceana and Aerta, fascinated him as much as it had when he had seen his first Man, as a child. Aras sighed softly, as much at those bittersweet memories as with his longing to touch Talon.

Talon awoke with the sigh, or the light, or perhaps because he sensed even in his sleep that he was being watched.

Aras smiled at him, a warm and friendly smile, carefully devoid of any other emotion that might make Talon nervous, that might make him flee again. "That is the last time I allow you to sleep on the floor. Despite your earlier claim, it is obvious from your expression you did not have a restful night at all," Aras said, rising from the bed, standing without thinking. He hissed and almost fell to the floor from the pain that shot up from his ankle to his hip. But suddenly Talon was there, supporting him. It was astonishing, the distance he had covered, and the alacrity with which he had risen to do so.

"You should know better than to put your full weight on your injury," Talon chided gently, his voice warm with concern, like Jarnath's would have been, instead of cold with mockery like his father's. Aras still could not accustom himself to Talon's gentleness. But he was incredibly relieved that Talon had felt no hesitation in touching him after the fiasco the previous night.

"I forgot I was injured," Aras admitted sheepishly, his face flushing in embarrassment as he allowed Talon to lower him back onto the bed.

His nostrils flared unconsciously as he eagerly inhaled Talon's enticing scent, astonished by it. Talon's scent had been masked by filth before, but now Aras could smell him clearly, and he inhaled again, slowly and deeply, savoring every nuance of his tantalizing fragrance. Underneath the overlain aroma of soap, Talon smelled nothing like any of the other Men Aras had smelled last night. Talon smelled of exotic soils and new leaves, as an Aerta from a distant Kingdom might, but different as well. There was also an intoxicating undercurrent of woodsmoke, almost as if he were a smoldering yet somehow thriving tree.

Aras had always had a fascination with fire. He feared it, of course, as did all his people, yet still, either because of the taint of his mother's blood or the pitiless training he had received at her hand to inure him from it, long before his instructors had tortured him with it, fire had never held quite the same terror for him as it did for the rest of his people. Fire was Incuban's chief weapon. Perhaps because of that, there was something oddly exotic, forbidden, and sensual about the smokiness of Talon's scent. Talon smelled undeniably male, compelling, and more desirable than he could ever have imagined anyone might.

"Betula, are you all right?" Talon asked in concern, apparently alarmed by his silent scrutiny.

"I—yes, of course. It was... just the pain from my ankle, but it's gone now, really. I'll be able to walk well enough with the staff, I think," Aras dissembled, reaching for the walking stick that was leaning against the bed. He'd been observing Talon too blatantly. This was not going to be as easy as he had hoped. He would have to keep far more careful control of himself. He must not drive Talon away.

"Perhaps you'd better not—" Talon began, but Aras resolutely rose again, this time putting half his weight on his good foot and half upon the staff.

"Ah, there, you see? Much better," Aras said, as if it truly had been his ankle that had been troubling him. He took a tentative step, putting as little weight as possible on his injured foot, lifting it gingerly from the floor as soon as his ankle protested. "Nothing to it," he said, grinning at his small accomplishment.

"You are in an abominably cheerful mood this morning. Are you always like this?" Talon asked, his bemused smile taking the sting out of the complaint.

Aras laughed. "Of course not! Far from it! I am usually as glum and taciturn as you."

At Talon's startled look, Aras laughed again. "It is your presence that has changed me. Two like charges cancel one another out, you know. No, I doubt you would know that; few of your people dabble in alchemy. Well then, let's see. Aha! To put it mathematically, two negatives make a positive," Aras said, knowing he'd make little sense to Talon, hoping only to distract him from his true thoughts and feelings.

Talon shook his head and laughed. "You are completely absurd! I never would have expected such whimsy coming from you, from what I had already seen of you. Come, if you are up for it, breakfast will be ready for us downstairs."

Aras was relieved he had been able to mask the truth, though as always, he hated having to dwell in secrecy, in deceit. And he certainly had no desire to face the throng of curious faces again this morning. Still, he was pleased to see his efforts had apparently worked, that Talon no longer seemed wary of him and his dark mood seemed to have brightened.

Aras sat back down on the bed and put on his boots, lacing his right more lightly than the left. Though his ankle did not look so bad this morning, it had stiffened up considerably and was still quite tender, and there was some residual swelling. He had hoped it might be fully healed by now. Still, he knew he was fortunate. Elven bones were quite dense. A Man would likely have broken his ankle, where he had only sprained it, although the extent of the soft tissue damage he had managed to inflict was nearly as severe an injury as the break would have been.

He longed to feel Jarnath's healing hands upon his ankle, and then longed far more to feel his strong arms wrapped about him in a warm embrace. He was horrified to feel the threat of tears at the need which tore through him as sharply as the wolven's teeth. As he had done hundreds of times before, he forced the betraying weakness down.

Talon had donned his own boots, his gloves, and weapons long before Aras was done and was waiting patiently by the door. Aras reached for his staff and joined Talon. He hobbled toward the stairs, and looking down at them, resented them anew. Last night they had seemed almost a mountain for him to climb. With a sigh he reversed the laborious process.

When they got to the bottom, Aras was relieved to see that the inn was empty, save for Goras.

Talon saw his look and successfully guessed his thoughts. "The villagers eat with their families, although we might see some of them at lunch and more at dinner again, were we to stay that long. Only travelers would eat here in the morning."

Aras felt naïve and foolish but nodded in relief.

Goras greeted them warmly and brought them breakfast.

The bread and mead met with Aras's reluctant approval, but he apparently looked so suspiciously at the rest that Talon laughed. Aras's new friend informed him the revoltingly unappetizing grayish-beige mass in the bowl was porridge but did not reveal what the odd yellow and white squishy-looking substance on the plate next to it was. Aras suspected that his friend feared he would not only lose his appetite, but quite probably what little he had eaten of last night's dinner as well were he to learn.

Aras nibbled bravely on the bread; he found it edible at least, though far from flavorful. He raised his mug and crinkled his nose distastefully at the mead, which tasted even worse than it had the night before. But when Goras came out with a grin and proudly put a silver tray on the table, Aras was unable to conceal his horror at the scorched carcass reeking of seared animal flesh.

Goras's smile turned into a frown of confusion, seeing his look of revulsion and the nearly untouched plate of food before him. "Is something wrong with the food?" he asked, sounding hurt rather than offended. Pointing proudly to the formerly unidentifiable yellow-white mass, he added, "Those are the only eggs in the whole village. It's been days since our few surviving hens have laid; they were just too terrified to, before. We'd have let the mothers keep their eggs this time, we're in sore need of repopulating our hen houses, but they won't grow to chicks in any case, what with the rooster gone before they were laid. And I roasted this up special for you. It's done to perfection. Look, see, the meat's still nice and bloody. This is the first rabbit we've caught in weeks. The man who snared it was proud to give it to me for you, for your aid of us."

Aras tore his eyes away from the gruesome sight, fighting to keep from retching, looking in panic at the door, but refusing to leave Talon alone with the sadistic madman who stood before them.

TALON chewed and swallowed his final bite of eggs hurriedly, instead of savoring it as he'd planned. Mouth watering, he eyed the succulent roast rabbit wistfully for only a brief instant before he said diplomatically, "I am well pleased with it, but my friend has not traveled long in the Lands of Men and food from his home is much different. Please, save this fine meat for your family and your neighbors to enjoy. Instead, if you have any cake or greens, and clear water instead of mead, I think my friend would be well pleased."

Goras said, "Certainly, I'll be but a moment," still puzzled and obviously disappointed as he took his prize roast away, shaking his head in confusion.

Betula looked so ill and forlorn when compared to his earlier cheerfulness that Talon had to laugh. "Forgive me, Betula! I should have thought to warn you, but I'd not expected to see eggs nor meat upon their table, not after the last meal here. I know our customs are strange to you, that there is much about us you could not possibly yet know. The innkeeper is not mad, as I'm certain you fear, but is quite sane, I assure you.

"You know that many animals consume other animals to survive. Men are, after all, animals, just as Elves are. But whereas the Wood and River Elves are herbivores, Men are omnivores, both herbivore and carnivore, much as the Dwarves are." Talon's serious explanation was broken again by a smile. "Of course, comparing my people to the Dwarves probably serves only to condemn us far worse in your eyes! Yet, incomprehensible to you as we both might seem, we are, at least, not like the ogres. We would never think to eat other Men, nor Elves, nor Dwarves. We would certainly never even think to eat an ogre, despite all they have done to us," Talon said, the smile gone as he fought down dark memories.

He forced himself to calm, to continue. "But we do, at times, eat other animals. Not all animals, just certain ones, although our diets can become more varied when necessary."

"I... I KNEW you did. Men, I mean. I saw...." Aras stopped, hesitating to say more. He had once watched a City of Man in secret, for many long, wonderful weeks, until he was discovered. He had learned much about Men from watching them. He'd seen them hunt and trap, skin and cook animals. He'd seen them do many incomprehensible, sometimes horrific, things. But it had been decades ago, and he had been far from them. He had never before been so bluntly confronted with the product of their efforts as he had been just now.

The smell of the poor scorched rabbit still lingered. He fought down a new wave of nausea.

"Come, Betula, it's not so bad as that. Our host has not taken offense. You will see. He tries to please you, as his guest. Please, try to eat what he next brings. I'm sure it will be palatable, now that he better understands what you require. These people have been through much. Allow them to retain what small shreds of pride, of dignity, they have been able to salvage.

"He is a kind man, an honest one. Neither he nor his people deserved the torment they have survived. And he is generous, when he has little, when many others would instead be greedy and grasping, in their desperation. He even returned my silver piece to me. He would accept no coin from me for our room or bath, for our meals or even our clothes. We will not be asked to pay for breakfast either.

"You should repay his kindness with at least your silence, if you cannot offer your thanks for the meal. I will convey thanks enough for us both," Talon said sincerely.

Aras felt awful. He had inadvertently embarrassed Talon on his behalf and done their host a great wrong. He was determined to make every effort to right it.

TALON winced when he saw how crestfallen Betula now looked. He had not meant to chastise him too harshly; he had purposefully tempered his words, choosing them with great care. But the young Elf was remarkably sensitive to even the most gently worded constructive criticism. Talon wondered anew who had so crushed his friend's spirit, that even such carefully phrased instruction might so wound him.

WHEN Goras returned, he bore a tray containing a plate piled high with greens and three slices of honey cake, a pitcher, and a mug of water. "I picked the greens myself, just now, from the garden out back, so they'd be fresh, and the cake is one my wife had made for our daughter last night, for her coming-of-age. She turned sixteen yesterday, although we did not celebrate properly. I hope you like it. And now we'll be able to throw her a proper party."

Aras smiled at him somewhat shyly, pleased by the Man's efforts on his behalf, hoping to effectively convey his gratitude without words. Common still came awkwardly to his tongue. Aras was surprised to see the resulting flush that spread across Goras's face. He had not been flirting with the Man, far from it, yet his reaction was unmistakable. The man appeared completely flustered, but he looked happy as he left them to their breakfast.

TALON smiled at Betula warmly. "You have no idea the power you wield over Man with your smile, my friend. Seeing it is like water in a desert to a Man dying of thirst. Although some of us are swayed more easily than others, you will find," he added, as if Betula's smile had not sent his own heart racing.

ARAS grinned, sensing Talon's true reaction to his smile. "I wonder if you realize, then, what your own smile feels like, to those you gift it upon. It is the warmth of a fire on a chill winter's night."

Talon looked at him in such surprise that Aras laughed. "You bring joy to my heart, my friend."

His spirits brightened, Aras's hunger came insistently to the fore. Aras ate with relish, demolishing the mountain of greens and honey cake, and thirstily downing the cool, clear water. He sighed and sat back, stretching his arm again, which still felt stiff and somewhat sore. "You set an excellent table. I am much refreshed," Aras said carefully and clearly when Goras returned, beaming at him in genuine delight.

Goras blushed darkly again. As he cleared the dishes, he said, "Your clothes will be ready for you later in the day, after lunch, I should think. Meanwhile, the widows of the dead have brought their husbands' clothes and ask that you choose things that might suit you from amongst them. I had my wife bring them up to your room. We haven't seen any merchants for a while and don't expect to for some time. We usually go to Fenemal to trade handicrafts and furs for what we need, only we've had few enough pelts and had not risked the trip for some time now. If you tell me what supplies you need, I will find them for you."

TALON thanked him and asked for two blankets, a pot, a bowl, a cup, a spoon, two lengths of rope, and some bandages, or strips of clean white cloth he might use as such. He pulled his two silver coins from his lean, worn purse, knowing it would not be enough to cover the cost of even used items, but Goras waved it aside, as he had hoped he might. "No, you'll not pay for anything while you are here, at least unless you plan to stay more than a week."

Talon shook his head. "I plan to leave as soon as my clothes are returned, for I have business elsewhere. Thank you for your hospitality, and that of your fellow villagers. What is this place called, that I might tell any I meet that the people here are of good heart and fine mettle, and it is safe again to visit this place?" He wanted to add the village's name to his mental map, so that he might someday, when he next had access to it, add it to the physical map in his most recent journal, along with details regarding the village and the wolven who had plagued it. Each of their people recorded such critical intelligence from their travels and shared it with their kin whenever they could, though the opportunities to do so had become increasingly rare since they had lost Caramore, six years ago.

"This is the village of Gower, and it pleases me you would speak so well of us to others," Goras said proudly, and he left with the plates.

TALON led the way to the stairs, and Aras looked up with a sigh before climbing them again. Once they were inside their room, Aras took off his right boot and sat on the bed with his leg up, rubbing his ankle gently.

He watched as Talon looked through the clothes the women had donated to them and found a cloak and shirt and pants that fit passably. Talon nodded toward the pile, but Aras declined.

"I'm going to go down and talk to Goras some more, and hear news of the surrounding area, if he has any," Talon said.

"I do not relish those stairs again. I shall stay here and rest my ankle, I think," Aras said, and Talon nodded and left.

Aras silently rose from the bed as soon as Talon left and listened at the door to ensure he was truly gone before locking it. If his new friend returned before he was finished, he would claim unease in an unfamiliar place as the reason he had sealed the door.

This would be the perfect opportunity to ward the gem-battery he planned to gift to Talon. He was not certain another such chance might arise again before he and Talon parted ways. The thought saddened him, but he purposefully pushed the emotion away, not allowing it to distract him from his important task, as he sat down cross-legged upon the bed.

Aras removed the emerald-green gem from its pouch and deliberately cleared his mind of all distraction. Once he was sufficiently prepared, he carefully extended his Power into the stone. It pulsed and glowed with the beating of his heart as he began charging it, loading it with precious Power, painstakingly shaped into every passive and active protective ward he knew, from those that would merely divert the eyes and muddle the senses, enabling the bearer to remain undetected regardless of the skill of the one seeking him, to others that would divert an opponent's blows, or tangle his feet, or turn his own attacks against him.

When he was finally done, Aras returned the stone to its pouch. He should have felt pride or relief or even just contentment, knowing his friend would now be so well protected, even once they were far from one another, but instead he felt an overwhelming sense of loss. How could he miss Talon so fiercely already, when he had not yet even gone? How had this Man come to mean so much to him in so short a time?

Aras unlocked the door and lay back on the bed, trying to convince himself the weakness and nausea he felt were solely because of the Power he had siphoned into the stone, and not because the very thought of Talon leaving made him physically ill. He was startled by an unexpected knock upon the door and jumped. He did not think Talon would knock. He stood awkwardly, walking stick in hand, leaving the boot by the side of the bed, hoping it was Goras and not one of the other village men. "Enter," he said reluctantly.

But it was not a man at all, but a woman who entered. She was short and plump, with a kind face, red hair gone mostly gray, and eyes of gray, and she was followed closely behind by a girl, small and slender, with striking long red hair and eyes of green, fine featured for a Child of Man but with a disturbing aura around her, one he had never before seen. There was a pall of darkness about the girl, as if an ominous shroud of death or portent of disaster was overlaid upon her own bright presence. Did he see it because he had just so freely used his Power, and it still coursed through him, unmasked? Or perhaps because of the charged gem-battery he now carried, with the active wards of protection? Or because of the darkness in the woods surrounding them?

"I hope we're not bothering you. I'm Millicent, Goras's wife, and this is our daughter, Audra. We've washed and mended your clothes," the older woman gushed, holding them out to him.

Aras forced his attention to the mother, for the moment.

"I hope you like the work we've done. The fabric, it was a joy to work with: it's so soft and strong. I've never felt anything like it. And it dried so quickly and came clean so easily, even the… blood." She faltered on the last word nervously. The girl behind her blushed darkly but stayed silent.

Aras took her offering, still distracted by the girl, expecting the worst of their no doubt poor workmanship, but determined to make his thanks appear genuine for their efforts on his behalf. He held up the formerly ruined shirt and could not help but stare in astonishment. The tears at the shoulder had not just been mended, but stitched over with fine embroidery work. They'd turned the seam over each slash into a distinctive brown vine of a darker hue than the fabric, with three different shades of green leaves coming from it. Anyone might think the garment had been intentionally crafted in such a manner from the start. He was momentarily thrilled by the impressive work, but then mentally winced at the thought of a similar eye-catching design having been added to his cloak, thereby negating the entire purpose of the garment.

He resolutely examined the cloak and was stunned to find his fears were groundless. Here, instead of attempting similar artistry, they had used tiny, nearly invisible stitches and meticulously kept to the intricate camouflage pattern of the fabric, alternating between varying shades of brown and beige thread. He checked the interior of the reversible cloak and was startled to discover the distinctive forest loam pattern had not been compromised at all. The stitching was so tight and precise it was all but invisible there as well. He was almost certain the cloak would even withstand the rain again.

He smiled in genuine joy and wonder. "I cannot believe you did such fine work in so short a time. Thank you. You are both incredibly gifted. I will be honored to wear your work."

Millicent beamed at him and Audra gazed at him with worshipful eyes. "We're very glad you like it," Audra whispered shyly and then turned quickly to leave, her hair a flowing curtain of red behind her, all the more striking against the eerie black aura surrounding her.

"Wait," Aras commanded impulsively.

The girl stopped and turned back to him breathlessly, as her mother looked on, appearing intrigued but not alarmed.

Aras had thought only the Faeren had such coloration; he had never suspected a woman of Man might. This girl was apparently in terrible danger of some kind, and those wolven he had fought had not seemed entirely natural. They might well be Incuban's minions. Were Incuban ever to come here, should he ever catch even a glimpse of her, she would be lost. He would undoubtedly focus all his attentions upon her. It might be many days until he tired of her, until he broke her. She would not die quickly or easily.

He and Talon would both leave here soon. There would be no one capable of protecting her, but he could remain with Talon and keep him safe. He could not allow this child to come to harm. He felt an incredible wave of relief at the practical decision. Without even a moment's hesitation, Aras reached into his small purse and pulled out the gem-battery he had just so painstakingly charged. He held it out to her, saying, "This is for you. It is a coming-of-age gift for you, and also to thank you and your family for the great kindness you have shown me and the beauty you have given me. It is called an Elfstone, or sometimes beryl, and the color is almost as warm and bright as your eyes."

Audra's hand trembled as she held out her palm. Wide-eyed, she closed her fingers about it. "Thank you," she whispered breathlessly, and then she turned and fled the room. Her mother followed closely behind, closing the door as she left.

All the nausea and much of the weakness Aras had felt before had vanished with the gift. Filling the stone had indeed drained him somewhat, but not dangerously so. A short time amongst the trees and he would be fine.

Aras eagerly changed into the clothes they had brought, folding Goras's borrowed things neatly onto the chair in contentment. Then he lay down and began singing to himself, songs of home.

Talon came in a while later and eyed him keenly. He had two small bundles in his arms and laid them on the bed. "Here is a blanket for you, a pot, a bowl, a cup, a spoon, a rope, and some bandages. And Goras has packed a supply of food for you as well, now that he knows your tastes. It looks like we are ready to go, my friend. So, where were you headed, when you were waylaid?"

"Nowhere in particular. I just hoped to see what I could and learn whether my father judged Man too harshly, as I have always suspected," Aras said, fingering the embroidery of his shirt, forcing a smile. "I think my journey is well begun. And you?" He would say whatever he could to convince Talon to stay with him; he would do whatever was necessary to see that he did.

"I am on my way to Athanark. There has been some trouble there. I go wherever I am needed," Talon said solemnly.

Aras nodded, then stood, careful not to lean too heavily on the staff, trying to appear injured and in need of a friend, but not a burden or someone who might slow Talon down. He wet his lips anxiously, unable to keep all signs of his heart's desire from his face. "I would be honored to travel with you, my friend. I think there is much I might learn from you."

Talon's keen gaze was still upon him. "I do not walk an easy path, my friend," Talon cautioned. "You do not know me as well as you think. I have not said Talon is my name, only that it is what I am called. And my destiny, which is tied to my true name, will one day catch up with me."

Aras smiled. "Nor is my name Betula. I do not ask you your true name, nor even your given name, nor do I tell you mine. But I am called Aras by those who hold my trust, and I would be honored if you would now use that name as one of them."

Talon smiled at him, the warmth of it lighting the room like the sun. "Well met, Aras! Come, we can go far yet in the half day that is left to us." Then he shook his head, as if bemused. "But you did not heed my words about your smile, my friend! Both Audra and Millicent are quite enraptured. You should have heard them speaking about you to Goras! And Audra showed him your gift. An Elfstone, and she but sixteen! Ah, Aras, poor Goras; I must travel with you just to protect the other fathers of this world from you!"

Aras looked at him, feigning puzzlement, and Talon laughed.

Aras grinned back at him. Someday he would tell Talon why he had gifted the precious stone to Audra, perhaps. For now, he was thrilled to know that he traveled at Talon's side.

THEY began walking into the woods, soon leaving the village of Gower behind them, though they walked at what Aras was certain was, for Talon, a leisurely pace, steady but not too strenuous, and certainly far slower than his own usual gait.

Talon broke the silence. "If we are to travel together, my friend, there are things I must teach you, and there are things I would like you to teach me. Agreed?"

Aras nodded, curious.

"I travel from place to place, but I often do so stealthily enough that none mark my passing. I prefer it that way. One learns much, seeing and hearing without being seen or heard. I know you have this ability in the woods, but you must also adopt it in the Cities of Man."

"An Elf amongst Man, and not be noticed?" Aras said, openly amused.

"I understand your skepticism, yet an Elf in a hooded cloak, though perhaps not one as distinctive as your own, would appear a Man to most eyes. I traveled with an

Elf in such a disguise long ago, in Ardock. No, not long ago at all. It was only a scant six years. But I digress. The key is for you to learn to walk as Men do. You must hunch your straight back and shorten your stride. I can look like beggar or Lord, like thief or guard, with a few simple changes in step and stance and word." He demonstrated his talent for Aras, who was amazed, for Talon indeed was all those things, and more, without changing anything else outwardly.

"You amaze me, my friend, for I left Gower with but a single Man at my side, and now I find I walk beside a dozen or more!" Aras laughed.

Talon smiled, but then looked at him seriously. "Another thing. Your traveling name, Betula, is unusual enough to Man's ear that it also draws attention. Aras is a very ancient name, and a remarkably common one; it is one of only five I know which are given to Elf and Man both. It is a happy accident, my friend, if you could be convinced to use it amongst strangers. Would you consider it?"

"I will consider it," Aras acquiesced.

Talon continued in Common, the more guttural language, which he and Aras had spoken in public in town. "Also, although you speak Common surprisingly well, from what you have hinted to me, you speak it with a lilt in your voice and a stiffness which will draw attention to you. We will speak it from now on, until it flows as easily from your tongue as Elvish does from mine. And when you hear a word that puzzles you, you must ask me what it means, for sometimes words have more than one meaning, and to mistake it could lead to trouble."

"You have traveled with one of us, and you spoke of Riviera before. Which other of our Kingdoms have you visited, or perhaps even dwelt in, that you speak our tongue so well?" Aras asked curiously, in Common rather than Elvish, as Talon had suggested.

"Ah." Talon said, looking at him intently. "You must also learn that there are questions you must not ask of me." He said it lightly, but Aras knew from his voice and his eyes that it was no light thing.

Talon was quiet for a while, until he stopped and knelt by a plant. "And as to what I would learn from you, I know many plants and their uses, but no one may know everything. I would have you teach me what you can."

"I will know only their Elven names, but those I will teach to you, as well as their uses. This is *asuhla* and it is edible." He broke off a leaf for each of them, and chewed his.

Talon tried it, and his face crinkled, and he spat out the leaf. "I hope to not be so hungry again soon!" he said, laughing. "It is fortunate for me that Goras has provided so well."

Aras laughed also, for he had suspected their tastes differed when Talon had reacted so strongly to the medicine. "I also see plants that are unknown to me, for they do not grow in the woods of home. Would you teach those to me, as well?"

"Certainly," Talon agreed.

"Then I still have much to learn and little enough to teach," Aras said, discouraged.

"Ah. Don't worry, my friend. We will teach each other more than we might yet guess," Talon assured him, his voice warm with affection.

They traveled in companionable silence again. Aras was relieved for the reprieve from speaking, for Common was yet awkward for him.

After a while, Talon asked, "How is your ankle, and shoulder?"

"Sore, but better," Aras answered truthfully.

"IT WOULD be a good idea to carry the staff, even once you no longer need to," Talon advised. "I have never seen an Elf walk with one, and if you are hooded in a cloak such as that one and people recognize there is something unusual about you, they may come to a wrong conclusion, and few are foolish enough to harass a wizard in his travels. The carvings will help the illusion, I think."

Talon knew Arcanus had only two pupils, Magus and Circe. He privately suspected that all the stories of wizards were either Arcanus himself or his pupils in disguise, or tall tales manufactured to impress the listener. Arcanus spent little enough time amongst them and had not shown more than a fraction of his true Power since he and Incuban had destroyed Maragar in their battle two and a half centuries ago in the Dwarven Lands. But Talon wondered if the western half of that storm might have been his, whether he and Incuban had chosen the sky for their battle this time. He would have to ask Arcanus about it when next he saw him.

His eagle eyes spotted some rabbit spoor as they traveled, but he ignored the trail and the promise of a meal it led to. Talon had already determined he would neither hunt, nor eat meat in any town or city they might visit, while his young friend traveled with him.

ARAS traveled much more easily than he had even the day before. He was relieved he finally seemed to be healing from his injuries and was impatient to be fully well again, although he had grown rather fond of the staff after testing it as a weapon. The carvings he had made also matched the leaves Millicent and Audra had embroidered upon his shirt. It was a fitting affectation. He had not minded carrying it, but he was worried now, after what Talon had said. Little did Talon know his words had hit squarely upon the mark. He could ill afford anyone accurately identifying him as a wizard.

When they stopped to eat their lunch, Aras saw that Talon's food was different from his, and many of the things were new to him. He asked their names, and Talon told him, and what they were made of, and he tasted those that did not sound too offensive to him. Some of them were not unpleasant.

TALON smiled fondly at his young friend. Aras was so inquisitive: he reminded him so much of Lunahr. A dagger of pain sliced his heart at the thought of the boy he had loved so dearly. Lunahr was dead, gone forever: his eager smile, his unquenchable thirst for new songs, all the light, the joy, the music, the energy, all that he once was and would have become.

Talon felt his despair threaten to overwhelm him. "Come, we must travel," he said abruptly, rising quickly to his feet. He had to move now, swiftly, or he would curl into a ball in his grief and never move again. Walking would calm him and still his thoughts. The sun was bright overhead. He would be able to cope with the loss, if he were moving.

ARAS rose as well, shouldering his pack again. He winced. His injured shoulder had stiffened while he sat and was paining him. Talon was already disappearing into the trees. Aras tried to stride after him but stumbled and almost fell. His ankle had stiffened as well and throbbed in protest at such a pace; it was both weak and tender. Talon had not looked to see if he followed. "Talon, please wait! I cannot move so quickly yet," Aras called out after him, humiliated by how easily he failed his friend.

Talon turned and headed back toward him, his features creased in concern. "Your ankle pains you?"

"Somewhat. But mostly it has grown stiff. I only need a few moments to make it more limber again. Forgive me. I know I am slowing you down considerably. I do not mean to be such a burden to you."

ARAS looked forlorn and so young, painfully young. Talon took a deep breath and stared into the sun for a moment. Lunahr was gone; Talon had not been able to help him. But Aras was here, he was warm, he was alive; he deserved to be the focus of Talon's thoughts, now. The sun burned the image of Lunahr away for the moment.

He looked back at Aras. "You are not a burden," he said gently. "You are becoming many things to me, but a burden is not one of them. Forgive me. I forgot for a moment you are not fully healed. Fully recovering from wounds such as yours takes time, my friend. Be thankful you are an Elf, and heal so quickly. A Man would still be confined to his bed, I think."

Aras sighed. "It is one thing to know it will take time, and another thing to experience it."

Talon empathized with him. The few times he had borne serious injury, he had chafed at his prolonged convalescence as well, and his recent illness had uncomfortably reminded him of his mortality. He realized now that he had been setting a harsher pace than he had originally intended. Aras had not complained and had kept up well. But it was starting to cost him, in pain and energy. Talon was not being fair to his friend.

He began walking at a more reasonable pace, one which was easy for Aras to meet.

"I look forward to the day when I no longer hold you back," Aras said in obvious frustration.

"I tire easily now as well, my friend, and I certainly do not want to overexert myself to the extent that my illness might return." It still rankled that he had succumbed. He should never have taken ill. After decades of leading such a life without any such affliction, he would not have thought it possible. He again wondered if those greenish clouds and chilling rain had brought the illness upon him. If so, he was fortunate indeed that ordinary medicines had been able to cure him of the symptoms, although he had needed the Sword in the end.

As if reading some of his thoughts, Aras said, "Tell me, Talon, did the woods around Gower feel somehow… wrong… to you? Or is it just that they differ more than I thought they might from the forests of home? Although they didn't feel quite so strange, after the rain."

"What is it you felt, my friend?" Talon asked softly.

"I'm not sure, just that there was a… darkness about them. It was worst at night, I think. I have not slept well for many nights, since leaving the banks of the Methris. I have had troubled dreams, but it is also that somehow it does not seem safe to sleep at night, or to loosen your guard even for a moment. Forgive me, I must sound the fool," Aras said self-deprecatingly.

Talon shook his head. "No, my friend, I have felt it too. And my dreams have been haunted as well. There was indeed a darkness that had been building and gathering and affecting things, but the rain seems to have cleansed the land, at least for a time. I think, perhaps, I might not have become ill had I been elsewhere. Tell me, did you notice a… wrongness… about the wolven you fought?" He had been able to tell much from the tracks and signs the fight left behind, but he might have missed something. Aras had not spoken to him of the attack.

Aras did not even pause for a moment to think about it. "Yes. First I did not think to find such creatures in these woods at all. I had not thought they ranged so far north. Obearn are the usual predator one expects to find here, or even pumar, those that roam from the Fromer Mountains to the east.

"Also, from what you described of the raids on the village, these wolven seemed increasingly bold, even systematic, in their attacks. And I would never have expected to find ones the size of the three largest ones. I had never heard that they grew anywhere near so big as that. The other four were either of a different species or perhaps juveniles, but they, too, were unusual. They clawed at the tree, which I had expected, but they nearly succeeded in climbing it. Then the large ones… they ran right for the tree and rammed it, purposefully and repeatedly, and in such coordination they dashed me from my perch as if it were nothing.

"It is not an easy thing to separate a Wood Elf from a tree. They were far too cunning. And after losing so many of their number, the rest should have fled into the woods, but they would not stop. Even as it died, the one who bit me would not let go." He did not shudder as he might have, but Talon could tell it was hard for him to speak of it.

That ramming; in the jumble of tracks, he hadn't seen that. So that was how they had shaken Aras loose from his tree! He had never heard of the use of tactics before by any wolven. They did not act like wild beasts. So Incuban's dark hand had reached here already. Talon's people had seen no sign of such things in the lands of Men since the destruction of Thenalon one hundred years ago, when Incuban's minions had casually destroyed the greatest City of Man, the Jewel of the East. Except, of course, for the appearance of one of the Enemy's chimaera in Ardock six years ago.

Talon realized he must not think that because the bulk of Incuban's army still lay on the other side of the Fromer Mountains, all His minions would be bound by them. Incuban had already begun to infiltrate this land, to weaken it, when it was so weak already. At least he no longer felt that the darkness shrouded him, as it had in the woods around Gower. So Incuban had not penetrated far, at least. Talon would not allow him to do more. The statement glowed so strongly in his mind that he even believed it, for the moment.

They traveled far and finally made camp and slept, secure again in the branches of a tree. And for the first time since he began crossing these dark woods, Talon dreamt of Riviera bathed in moonlight, as he remembered it, instead of awash in blood.

ARAS awoke with the coming of the sun, but did not rise with it. He lay facing Talon, who still slept peacefully at his side. From what little he had voiced of it, Aras knew his friend had not slept peacefully for many nights before the previous night in the inn. A single errant lock of hair had fallen across Talon's left eye as he slept. Aras fought the urge to brush it back, afraid even so gentle a touch might be sensed as a threat and waken Talon. But Talon's eyes opened anyway and caught his for a moment.

"Ah. I had not wanted to waken you yet," Aras apologized. He sat up. "I should have realized that silence was not enough, that you'd feel my eyes and the sun upon you. Yet you look well rested, my friend."

"As do you," Talon said, also rising.

"My dreams are my own again. They are no longer black nightmares of death and despair," Aras said in relief.

Talon looked at him. "Then your dreams have mirrored my own. There is some small comfort in that. I do not relish the thought that the Enemy might be able to act against me so remotely. I was afraid he might have discovered me at last, but perhaps those dark woods have affected everyone in the same manner, and I am not being singled out as I had feared. I had begun to think my spirit was no longer up to the task set before me. We are indeed well met."

After he and Talon ate, Aras unwrapped the bandage from about his foot and applied a cream Talon had acquired in Gower. Even after the day's walk and the night's rest, there was little swelling and soreness.

"That looks good," Talon said, sounding pleased. "Now, let me change your dressing as well." Talon gently removed the bandages and studied the wound with practiced eyes. "Dark things never leave those they touch unmarked, but the scars you will bear will be faint, and you will bear them lightly."

TALON marveled again at how quickly the wound was healing and took some small pride in knowing that his medicines, although meager, had helped Aras in his time of greatest need.

They broke camp and began their walk anew. After Aras bent to show him a plant, Talon said, "I just noticed something I should have commented on long before this. The purse you carry is too tempting a target." He drew forth a small, worn leather drawstring bag. "Put a few copper and silver in here and tie this at your waist, instead. Conceal the rest somewhere comfortable for you. You can replenish this as you need to, in concealment. You won't miss it if it is parted from you, and you will be far less likely to be assaulted for it."

Aras nodded and did so.

As Talon and Aras traveled, they both added medicinal plants and spices to the bag of tiny pouches they each now carried, and they ate from what they gathered as they walked so they did not need to spend time foraging around their camp.

ONE day passed into the next in that manner as they walked south, skirting past the City of Fenemal without entering it, and made their way to the Western Road, which they stayed upon the short distance to Glen's Ford. There they crossed the Methris and then veered southwest away from the opposite bank instead of heading into Logareth and continuing on the Southern Road. Talon explained to Aras that in so doing, they would bypass the Feonoke Marshes and also shorten their journey by at least a sennight.

It was at noon, just under a fortnight after the start of their journey, that they came upon an ancient Road, which Talon told Aras was called the Lost Road. The area here was more heavily wooded again, but the Road itself was clear of trees, deeply grooved with ruts from wagons and worn flat by the hooves of many horses, part stone and part bare earth with some wild grass boldly struggling up here and there. Talon told Aras they were now less than a day from Athanark.

Aras felt odd and exposed on the Lost Road, as he had on the Western Road, and listened and looked about them warily at first, but soon grew accustomed to it. After journeying along it for a while, they were just contemplating whether or not to stop for a late lunch when up ahead they heard the distinctive sounds of battle. In synchronized unison, they slipped into the forest and silently approached the sounds of fighting, dropping their packs while still within the safety of the trees so that they could fight unencumbered.

They exited the woods onto the Road and found the remnants of a merchant caravan. There were five wagons, two tipped over on their sides, with several wooden crates smashed open, their cargo of brightly colored cloth and shining objects of metal spilt everywhere. The teams of draft horses lashed to the two overturned wagons were screaming and pawing at the air in terror, but the ones lashed to the other three wagons lay dead in their traces. There were many other dead horses and dead and dying Men all around them, amidst a horde of fierce, brutish Men wielding wickedly curved swords and mounted astride enormous wolven that slashed and tore and bit at everything that moved.

Already, Aras's bow was humming. An arrow caught a wolven in the throat, felling both beast and rider. A second attacker fell, and then a third, as Aras's hands moved in a blur. Talon's sword was a bright silver flash of motion no less deadly as foe after foe fell beneath the fury of his attack.

Aras emptied his quiver and then exchanged bow for staff, charging forward fearlessly to the nearest wolven, his staff whirring first as he twirled it with two hands, and then humming as he twirled it in one. He crushed the beast's skull with a single deadly blow as it charged him open-mouthed, the memory of such teeth still vivid from his last encounter.

The wolven's rider leapt from its back even as it died, curved blade in hand, and the impact of his sword upon Aras's staff sent him reeling to the ground. Aras wrestled the blade away from his throat and swore; the blade was wet with a sickly green stickiness.

"Talon, beware the poisoned blades!" he sang out in Elvish as he twisted out from under his attacker and forced the Man's own blade into his side. His foe convulsed only for an instant and then stilled, confirming Aras's assumption. Whatever the toxin was, it was deadly and worked quickly.

Aras leapt to his feet just in time to face three riderless wolven, which were converging upon him. He cursed himself for not having somehow felled more of the beasts with his arrows, though every arrow had downed a rider or a beast except the first, which had downed both at once. He should have positioned himself so that every shot might. He endangered Talon with his incompetence.

His staff was a blur as he lashed out at the snarling, snapping, lunging creatures surrounding him, terrified Talon might be overwhelmed by foes of his own before Aras could help him slay them.

He slammed his staff into the chest of the last of the three he fought, feeling its ribs snap even as the arc of his swing flung the beast headfirst into the trunk of a fir. Aras spun about, scanning the battlefield desperately for Talon.

The brief moment of relief he felt at seeing his friend still standing, still fighting, shattered as a riderless wolven sprang upon Talon from behind, felling him. Heart hammering in terror, Aras ran to his fallen friend. He killed the Man Talon had been fighting, but before he could attack the wolven as well, Talon thrust his blade deep into its neck, severing the jugular. The beast's blood sprayed him as it died.

Aras spun about in a crouch, looking for his next target, certain some enemy would have been coming for his back while he was distracted with worry for his friend, but there were no other Men nor beasts left standing.

TALON rose, scanning the battlefield for further foes, at first wary of treachery when none appeared but realizing from the number of bodies surrounding them that they well might have slain them all. The only one left standing was Aras, praise Idare.

Even knowing what a fantastic fighter Aras was, from having seen the signs of his earlier battle with the wolven, Talon had still feared for his friend. Every Man in the caravan, even those few they had seen desperately defending themselves when they arrived, had been felled.

Talon cradled his right arm in his left, cursing softly under his breath at the pain. He had barely been able to keep the beast's jaws from his throat, using his forearm as a shield, before recovering Kathalanar with his left hand and slitting the wolven's throat. Fortunately, although the beast's teeth had slashed flesh along his forearm, it had not closed upon it; it had not torn muscle and tendon and flesh, nor crushed bone. He could ill afford to lose the use of his right arm, even temporarily, though he could wield a blade just as proficiently with his left.

Talon smiled at Aras to reassure him, seeing the fear and concern in his young friend's eyes. "Most of the blood is not mine. It is not mortal, just painful. Come, there will be others who will need tending more than I."

Talon turned to the first of the fallen Men he saw. He was painfully young and would grow no older. To his further dismay, Talon saw that the livery he wore was distinctive and familiar: this Man was one of Master Trader Oberas's guards. "Their poison works quickly. Your warning was timely," Talon said, pointing to the slain Man. He had only a single shallow sword wound on his arm, yet he lay dead.

Talon turned to the next Man and the next and found to his despair there was no one left to tend. They had been slain to a Man. He counted seventeen dead in the livery of guards, four others who were likely wagon drivers, and Oberas.

Oberas lay back to back with one of his guards, covered in wounds, a bloody dagger in his hand, even in death his arm clamped tightly about the neck of the dead wolven rider who lay on top of him. The guard at his back was an enormous Man; he must have neared, or perhaps even topped, seven feet standing, but he would never stand again. There was a ring of fallen attackers, both men and beasts, about the two Men. These two had cost their foes dearly before they perished.

ARAS hesitated to say anything, but found he could not stay silent. "You knew these Men?" he asked softly. He'd felt Talon's pain grow and the sharp bite of sorrow.

Talon nodded. "The merchant's name was Oberas. He was a fine man and deserving of far better than this. He helped save the lives of both Princes of Riviera, years apart from one another. I will not leave him and these others to rot. They deserve the honor of a pyre."

Aras shuddered at the thought of burning the bodies, what it would look like and smell like. He was not sure he could do it, but he swallowed and nodded. "First, though, we must tend to your arm." He headed back toward the tree line for their packs and then called out to Talon sharply, his staff at the ready again.

Talon was at his side in an instant, drawn sword in hand.

"Tracks," Aras said, pointing. They led away from the Road, into the woods: a Man's, overlaid by a wolven's, the former deep and the latter shallow. "Someone who carries a heavy burden, and a wolven without a rider," Aras said, as they headed into the trees.

The trail was easy to follow and painfully short. Both the wolven and the Man they found appeared dead, the beast lying in front of the Man, its thick coat bloodied at its neck and shoulder. The Man was bloodied as well. He was in the livery of the guard, leaning against a sturdy oak, his head down, his right arm mangled from shoulder to wrist, bone showing whitely through the blood in places and thick muscle dangling from his bicep.

To Aras's astonishment, he raised his head as they came toward him and looked at them defiantly; he raised his blade as well, in his other hand, but it shook and swayed. Aras noticed the ground all around him was oddly free of tracks.

"I'll tend to this one, Aras," Talon said, still speaking Elvish, as they had been since the first sounds of battle. "You find whoever or whatever he was carrying." Talon gently knocked the blade from the Man's hand with his sword, and crouched by his side.

Aras was scanning the ground for tracks when a wild thing fell upon him from the tree branches above.

TALON'S head snapped up, and he saw that one of the curved blades lay glistening wetly beside Aras, who wrestled the creature on top of him. Talon snatched the sword up by the hilt and tossed it far into the trees in disgust, then yanked hard on the collar of the hellion afflicting his friend with his left hand, pulling the boy off in one smooth motion.

A hard fist lashed out and slammed into his wounded right arm. Talon hissed in pain and cuffed the boy hard across the mouth with that hand, cursing at the impact of the blow. He released the child, who fell limply to the ground.

"Did he cut you?" Talon asked Aras, oblivious to his own pain, heart pounding in fear, anxiously searching for any marks of injury upon Aras. Fortunately Aras appeared dazed but otherwise unharmed.

"NO, I was able to deflect his blow and disarm him at least," Aras said, standing. "He... surprised me." The Man-child had been wild and vicious. Aras had seen Man-children before; he had watched them for endless weeks once, long ago, but he had never seen anything like this.

"Please, don't hurt him. He's just a boy," they heard a weak voice beg in Common from the ground near their feet. The Man from the tree was dragging himself toward them on his good arm, and there were tears on his face.

Talon looked from the crumpled boy in his fine clothes, drenched in blood not his own, to the guard. The boy was thirteen or perhaps fourteen years of age, and the guard not much older, perhaps eighteen at the most. Was the rich boy Oberas's son? He had not known the man had a child. He was intrigued and impressed that the boy would risk his life for a guard, even one who had apparently saved him.

"He hits like a man and fights as dirty as one," Talon said in Common, holding his wounded arm. "But he will awaken. I tempered my blow, but I did not have time to be too gentle, for my friend was in grave danger if that poisoned blade had struck him even a glancing blow. We are here to save you, not slay you."

"Then I would hear you swear you'll keep him safe, before I die," the guard whispered.

"No. I will swear only to keep you alive to protect him. I do not give you leave to die. If you would see him safe, you must fight to live." Talon knelt beside him.

"I'll get our packs," Aras volunteered and ran.

"I am called Talon and my friend is Aras. What is your name?" Talon asked, as he began pulling the pieces of torn fabric from the guard's livery away from the wound in preparation to tending the gravely injured Man.

"Tarrell," the wounded Man whispered.

"And the boy?"

"Rion… Alarion."

Aras quickly returned with both packs and began opening them, pulling out the disinfectants and medicines and bandages they would need.

"It is not as bad as it looks," Talon assured Tarrell, feeling a wave of pity for the Man at his lie as he began blotting away the blood and the full extent of the injury was more clearly revealed. If this was his sword arm, he'd never wield a blade well enough to be a guard again. He would be lucky to keep the arm at all, or retain any use of it.

Together he and Aras carefully and thoroughly cleaned the wound, pulling together his torn muscle and flesh and reshaping his arm as best they could and swathing it in clean linen bandages. Tarrell quickly fell unconscious under their ministrations.

Talon was thankful he'd been able to restock his supplies in Gower and on the road. He was using up much of them on this single injured Man. Talon carefully administered the medicine for pain after consulting with Aras in Elvish as to whether it might be safe to do so.

Once they were done with Tarrell, Aras tended to Talon's arm after checking the boy again. Just as he finished bandaging Talon, there was a moan from the ground, and the boy sat up, his shaking hand moving to cover his bloody and swollen lip. There were tears in his eyes as he looked fearfully from Tarrell, who lay pale and still as death, to Talon, who had hit him, and Aras, whom he'd attacked. His eyes widened in guilt and horror as his gaze riveted on Aras's face. "I did not know! I did not realize. I would never have attacked you had I seen you were an Elf. I could have killed you!"

"It is fortunate for us all that you did not. Your friend Tarrell will live, Rion," Talon said gently. "Forgive me for striking you, but you gave me little choice."

"Who are you? I thought you some of the wolven-riders, come to finish us, or working with them at least, but you're helping us. Why?" Rion asked, sounding completely overwhelmed.

"I am Talon, and this is Aras. We helped you because you were in need. We will help you, still."

"I want to go back to the rest of our guards and to Oberas," Rion said, and there was fear and pleading in his voice.

Talon was surprised that he called Oberas by name. Perhaps this was his apprentice, and not his son. The grim news he had might be easier for the boy to hear. "You are his apprentice?" he asked, and the boy nodded.

"It sorrows me that I must be the one to tell you, but the others in your party were not so fortunate as the two of you. They are slain," Talon said softly.

"Everyone?" the boy asked in horrified disbelief. "Oberas? All our guards, even Elkrum?"

"I'm sorry. We came too late," Talon said, his voice thick with dismay at his failure.

"They came out of nowhere," Rion said, his voice dazed. "One moment the Road was empty and the next they just erupted out of the trees. They slew all our archers before any of them could nock a single arrow. And our horses went wild with fear at the wolven. Most of them were rearing or bucking in terror. Some of them tried to bolt. Most of our guards couldn't even draw their swords for fighting to stay mounted or to jump clear.

"I leapt from the wagon, diving for a fallen sword, one of theirs. Melkar had killed one of them, but then that man's wolven had...Melkar was... his throat.... I know how to use a sword; Tarrell's been teaching me in secret. I wanted to fight, to help, but Oberas ordered Tarrell to take me into the woods. I didn't want to go, but then one of the wolven slammed into me, knocking me headlong into the wagon wheel.

"I was only stunned for a few moments. I didn't even lose my grip on the sword, but Tarrell had already picked me up and was carrying me. I started to struggle, but then I saw one of the wolven was coming after us and I yelled a warning to Tarrell.

"He let me go and turned to fight it, but it was so fast and strong and big! It rammed right into him and tore and bit, and he screamed and fell. I ran up behind it and hacked at it with the sword until it collapsed. But Tarrell's arm... there was so much blood.

"He told me to climb the tree, to hide. I didn't want to, but he started begging me. He cried because he was so afraid for me. He'd been so brave and—so I climbed and he raked over our tracks with the sword, even though he could barely move, he could scarcely sit, even with his back against the trunk. And then we heard voices and I stayed silent and hid in the branches and then you came and I attacked you."

Talon could tell the boy was in shock. They needed to get him moving, and they needed to leave this place in case there were other enemies nearby. These foes reeked of Incuban's hand. They were in great danger here.

"You were very brave, Rion. You must yet be brave for just a little while longer. We need to get to Athanark as quickly as we can. We killed your attackers, but there may be others, and we need your help to get Tarrell to safety," Talon said, hoping the responsibility would be enough impetus to get him moving in spite of the horror he had barely survived.

"I will carry Tarrell to the Road," Aras volunteered, lifting him easily.

Talon and Rion followed. Once at the caravan, Rion looked about in horrified dismay at the dead, ignoring the wagons and the fortune in goods lying at his feet as if unimportant. For now Aras laid Tarrell on a nest of the brightly colored bolts of fine cloth that had spilt out onto the Road.

Talon unhitched the dead teams of draft horses and then gently approached the four geldings still bound in their traces, their eyes wild and their mouths foaming in terror. He began speaking to them softly, using his Power gently upon them. They calmed with gratifying ease, and he unhitched them from the two overturned wagons and then hitched each pair to two of the three upright wagons instead.

Talon belatedly realized Aras had been watching him in fascination, but then Aras cocked his head as if listening to something and ran lightly down the Road, returning in a few moments with two of the guards' horses, both mares.

Talon talked to the mares as he had to the geldings, realizing it was too late to conceal his efforts, and hitched both horses to the third wagon. They had acquiesced to pull it for him. They appeared willing to do whatever he asked of them, as long as he did not separate them from one another. He was thankful anew that his grandmother had been House of Horses and that he had no small amount of influence over such animals because of it.

"I know you said we must leave quickly, but if we unload two of the wagons, can we bring the dead with us? We packed everything in crates that a single man could carry and didn't load any of the wagons too heavily, knowing we'd need to cross the Feonoke Marshes and that we might need to unload one or more of them if any of the wagons got stuck. These were all fine men, and I shouldn't like to leave them here," Rion said, fighting to speak through the quiet sobs that shook him.

Though he was reluctant to tarry, so exposed to danger, Talon could not object, touched that this boy would leave behind a fortune in goods to bring the dead to rest. After consulting quietly with Aras to ensure he felt the same, he agreed, and they both helped Rion unload the two wagons, neatly stacking the crates by the side of the Road, not making any attempt to conceal them. Anyone who came this way would no doubt investigate and find them anyway.

Rion looked up at Talon hesitantly, biting his lip and then swallowing hard. "Forgive me, I know I am asking much of you, but could we also make room for Tarrell to lie down in the lead wagon? He can't lie with the rest. I helped pack the wagons. I know what we can take out to easily make enough room."

It would have been hard to resist anything the boy might have asked of him, and he would never wish to lay a man, especially a gravely wounded one, with the dead. "Of course. And after we are done, why don't you gather together the guards' packs from their mounts and pull out their blankets? Their packs should go in the lead wagon with you and Tarrell, and Aras and I will have need of the blankets. I'll give you their purses, and any jewelry they might be wearing, but they'll keep their swords or bows. I'm sure they would wish to be buried with them. We'll load the other two wagons while you keep watch over Tarrell for us, all right?" The boy should not help them in this gruesome task. He was small and did not appear exceptionally strong physically, but also, though he was staying remarkably calm and focused, he was quite possibly on the verge of shattering mentally. He should not have to shroud the dead men he had known in their blankets, nor load them onto the wagons.

"Thank you," the boy said, eyes old beyond their years welling with tears, and Talon realized from the depth of feeling in his words that he was thanking him for everything, including the grim duty he was shielding him from.

As they bent to their respective work, Rion spoke, as if needing to fill the silence, to bring some semblance of normalcy, of life, to a place shrouded in death. "Oberas thought Athanark might be far enough northwest to be safe. He said there are shadows from the east and south coming to claim us all, and good men must either flee from them or fight them. I had not truly thought he could fight until I saw him today. We left Ardock with all we had, heading for Athanark. Oberas has… had… friends there."

After handing Talon and Aras a number of blankets that he had gathered quickly, Rion looked over at the guards' horses, the two mares standing patiently in their harnesses, pointedly averting his eyes from the dead. "I did not think Kaldahar and Janahar would pull a wagon. Elkrum and Tarrell would have been so surprised to see them do so." His voice caught, and he choked back a strangled sob.

Talon spoke to keep the boy talking, as he and Aras worked quickly and efficiently. "They are both spirited ladies and exceptional mounts. They have agreed to do as I ask. Do you know how to drive a wagon, Rion? I can show you how, if you do not. After we reach Athanark, and see Tarrell safe, we can try to recover what you leave behind here, now, but others may come upon these things before we can return. If there is anything exceptionally precious or important to you in the two wagons we leave behind, or the goods that we set beside them, you should bring it with you now."

Rion shook his head. "I would not waste the time. They are all just things. Things are not important: people are. I endanger you and Aras by helping me. I make you as much of a target as I am. And Tarrell needs to be safely at the Brightwater. I know how to drive a wagon. Oberas said this morning at breakfast that Athanark is less than a day's journey straight along this Road, so I know the way as well, and the horses will be able to pull such a heavy load across such easy terrain for a short time, particularly if we rest them frequently, when they appear winded."

Talon was again impressed by the boy. Many strong men would have been left bawling like infants after such terror as he had faced. Few would have even considered the weight of the dead in relation to the horses, and fewer men still accustomed to such wealth would be willing to leave it lying on the Road for anyone to find. Rion was a jewel amongst men to do so.

His words resonated deeply, striking a strong chord within Talon's core. Six years ago, in Ardock, Mik, the boy who had nearly killed Lunahr while robbing him, had callously and cruelly told him just the opposite: that people were not important, only their possessions were.

With the memory of those words ringing in his ears and the sight and smell of the blood, of so many dead, Mik's face and Lunahr's unexpectedly and crushingly rose up to haunt him. Dead, both dead, the blood of two more children on his hands, following the many thousands of others he had failed to save. Idare, what a brutal world they were cursed to live in, that he had lived to see so many children slain!

He instinctively looked upward, frantic with need, seeking the sun. He focused upon it, drinking in its rays hungrily, amazed that it still shone brightly overhead, aloof in all its golden glory from the death and darkness upon the ground below.

"Talon!" Aras cried sharply in panic. Talon jerked his gaze away from the siren call of the sun's pure beauty, cursing his stupidity and blinking rapidly as his dazzled eyes watered, praying the damage he'd inflicted upon them was only temporary. He knew full well that if he looked too long, he would blind himself. How could he have been so careless? *Carelessness can kill even the most seasoned warrior*, his father's voice scolded in his memory.

Were he to blind himself, he would indeed have killed himself; he'd slice Kathalanar across his own throat in a heartbeat. What need had his people for a blind King? He was a pathetic enough excuse for one as it was.

Talon fought the urge to look into the sun again just as he felt a strong hand grab him by the jaw. He barely kept from snapping Aras's neck, realizing just in time it was his hand, that the concerned eyes swimming before his face were Aras's leaf green. Talon saw the terror in them drain to relief as he focused upon him and then kindle to white-hot rage; for a moment, it was indeed as if their warm green hardened into the bright silver-white of pure pallenteum before Aras blinked and they flashed a familiar green again.

"Do not ever do that again! Even Jarnath could not heal you, were you to blind yourself!" Aras fumed.

"Forgive me. It is just, always I am too late and good men die," Talon said, trying to explain without revealing too much.

"Those of us you have managed to save see it otherwise," Aras said, his fury extinguished and compassion taking its place. "You go to Athanark because you are driven to go. They are in danger, so you come to save them. You had no way of knowing these men would be here at this particular time. Do not blame yourself for their deaths. If you must blame someone, blame me. Had I not stumbled across your path, you would have been here days earlier and might have saved them," Aras said bitterly.

"Or more likely, I would have already been in Athanark, and not even known of the danger to these men until too late. It would not be the first time I made such a grave tactical error. I have made many. It is not your responsibility to save this world from the evil that threatens to consume it, Aras, nor to make up for my shortcomings."

ARAS could not argue the point, though he knew full well it was indeed his responsibility to save everyone, far more than it might ever be Talon's. He might be a Captain of the Watch, but he was neither a wizard nor a God. Ultimately, he could not hope to defeat his Enemy.

"Neither of you are to blame," Rion's voice piped up to both their surprise. "We all went on this journey knowing full well the danger involved. That is why we hired so many guards to protect us. But we also came because we had no choice. We fled certain death and headed toward the hope of safety, of life.

"Had he survived, Oberas would have blamed Elmoth at the top of his lungs, while in his heart blaming himself. But the only ones guilty of these deaths are the brigands who attacked us. They didn't need to kill us to rob us, but they never even tried to take our things. They shattered the crates and trampled our goods without caring, and they wielded poisoned blades. I don't understand why anyone would do such a horrible thing, how anyone could feel so little, or perhaps hate so much.

"All I know is that, save for Oberas and Elkrum, we killed few of them. It was the two of you who slew the rest. I saw the bodies where they lay. Many of the wolven-riders died from arrows, ones not ours: they targeted our bowmen first, and the fletching isn't ours in any case. And many others died by the sword, but a number of our guards died before they could even draw their blades. They were too busy fighting their mounts as their horses reared and bucked and shied from the wolven in their terror.

"If you had not come and attacked them, those evil men and their beasts would still have slaughtered everyone, but Tarrell and I would have been dead as well and they would have survived to prey upon every other refugee who fled to Athanark. They would likely have killed dozens, perhaps even hundreds. Our guards were all good, fine, brave men: each of them would have willingly died to save another. May whatever Gods you might follow bless you for saving so many on their behalf. Now please, we need to keep working in order to reach Athanark by nightfall, if we are to reach it at all, I think."

Both Talon's and Aras's consternation at Rion's words had metamorphosed into growing respect. Rion's keen eyes saw much, and he was wise beyond his years. "Thank you, Rion. I sometimes lose my perspective when faced with death, having seen far too much of it. And forgive me, Aras," Talon said, and then he sighed. "I seem to ask your forgiveness all too frequently. I will try to do better, to lessen the need for it."

"Forgive me also. I had no right to chastise you in such a manner," Aras said, appalled that he had done so.

"You had every right. I thank you for saving me from my own foolishness. Although I must admit, I am surprised that you invoked Jarnath's name. I have never heard one of your people mention any of the Gods of Men before," Talon said curiously.

"I am pleased to see I baffle you, then, as much as you at times confuse me," Aras said lightly, trying to divert Talon's attention. Even in his panic, how could he have been so careless as to mention Jarnath?

He gave Rion the men's purses and valuables, and they loaded the last of the bodies, putting twelve of the guards in one wagon, and Oberas and Elkrum, the four wagon drivers, and the remaining four guards in the other in an effort to distribute the weight of the load evenly and not burden either team of horses too greatly. Rion had asked that Oberas and Elkrum be allowed to ride together, as they had fought and died together, and it was a small kindness to honor his wish. It was fortunate Athanark was so close, and from what Talon had told him, the Road so flat, with such a burden. He helped Talon secure a tarp over each of the two wagons that bore the dead, and they made a small tent over Tarrell, to shield him from the sun.

Aras spoke up. "I will drive the rear wagon, with Rion driving the middle one with Tarrell, where Tarrell will be safest, and you in the lead, Talon. I have retrieved as many of my arrows as I could salvage and will have three other full quivers that I scavenged beside me on the driver's bench so that if we are approached from behind, I will be able to protect us."

Only six of his own arrows had been salvageable, four from the dead wolven and two from dead Men. But the guards' arrows, though inferior in quality, would suffice for now. He yet wore his swords, though he had not wielded them this time, and his staff was beside him as well.

"Your strategy mirrors my own thoughts exactly," Talon said approvingly, and Aras felt an inordinate burst of pride at his praise.

Without further word or preparation, they set out for Athanark.

TALON needed to speak to Rion at length. Rion had spoken of refugees and fleeing danger from the east and south and had come from Ardock. Talon feared now that some of the Enemy's forces had surprised them by coming up the Methris, that perhaps Incuban had even decided to ignore the last of the Dwarven Kingdoms completely for easier prey in the Lands of Men.

But both the River Elf Kingdom of Riviera and the Wood Elf Kingdom of Loatia were south of Ardock, along the Methris, as well as a number of the Cities of Men. Could two of the Elven Kingdoms have already fallen to their Enemy? No, he could not believe it; he would lose what little reason he had left were he to think both lost. Elanara should still be safely in Erenia, but her mother and father, her two brothers, and all their people were yet in Riviera. No, Riviera could not have fallen. They must yet be safe.

Rion was handling the terrible tragedy he had survived remarkably well. As anxious as Talon was for news, he did not want to do anything that might upset that delicate balance while they were still on the Road. They would hopefully yet reach Athanark by dusk, barring further mishap. Once safe, there would be time and opportunity for further questions. He would make certain of it.

He would not part from Rion and Tarrell until they shared all they knew with him. He would not soon part from them in any case, not until he was certain they were safe and well looked after. If the friends of Oberas that Rion had mentioned were not up to the task, or unwilling to assume the responsibility, he would do everything he could to aid the boy and his injured guardsman.

AFTER a while on the Road, Talon heard the gentle gurgle of water and realized the Helden River must be nearer to the Road here, or perhaps a stream connected to it. He waved his companions to a stop and, upon investigating, found that it would be a perfect place for the horses to quench their thirst, now that their terror was past. He and Aras and Rion needed to clean up as well, so that they would be more presentable when they tried to gain entrance to the city, instead of covered in blood and gore. Talon also wanted to check on Tarrell and Rion.

He cursed when he approached the middle wagon and realized Rion had been silently crying for some time, as evidenced by his swollen, red-rimmed eyes, though there was little he could have done to prevent it, with only the three of them to drive the wagons.

Rion wiped his sleeve over his face, trying to hide the traces of his grief, but Talon would not allow him to think poorly of himself for it. "There is no shame in your grief, Rion. You are no less a man for showing your capacity to love. I have wept over many lost friends, comrades, and kinsmen. You honor the fallen with your tears."

Rion nodded and swallowed in understanding, and perhaps gratitude, at his words, but did not speak.

Tarrell was still unconscious, but Talon was relieved to find he did not feel feverish, and there was no fresh blood upon the bandages. Teeth left unclean wounds, and his was nearly mortal and might yet prove fatal were it to fester. So far, the medicines they had used were working. "He is doing well. There is no fever. He sleeps so that his body might shield him from his pain, for a while at least."

Rion cleared his throat and asked uncertainly, "Is your own injury paining you terribly? Forgive me for striking your wound. Tarrell always told me to make your opponent's weakness your strength, that there was nothing dishonorable in saving a life in such a manner. Are you sure he will be all right? He is so pale, and I can't see how he will ever be able to wield a sword again."

The boy was as perceptive as he was brave. "I am fine. And Tarrell will live, although he may indeed lose the use of his arm, partially or entirely, or possibly even lose it, though I will do all I can to save it. Regardless, he will likely be confined to a sickbed for a time. Will you stay with him?"

"Of course! He is one of my best friends, perhaps the only one left to me. He is more like a brother to me than a guard. I've yet to come-of-age; I am still some weeks shy of sixteen. I have no family left, and I fear now neither does he. His brothers and their families stayed behind, in Ardock. He was certain he would never see them again.

"And Oberas had no family, no heirs. There is only me and his grown apprentices. But Kenneth, the one before me, lived with his family in Seaview on the southern coast, and we heard they were the first city to fall. I know Oberas feared him slain. His other two grown apprentices are yet safe, as far as I know. They live far away on the western coast, beyond two ranges of mountains, Alec in Delthos and Derek in Meria.

"I will try to find all three of them, of course, but until then, there is only me and Tarrell. Half of all that is left of our goods will be Tarrell's. I'm hoping he'll agree to become my guardian, now that Oberas is gone. In return, I thought I could teach him to trade. He has a good head for numbers and he writes well. He's good with people and very friendly. He's already helped me with the stock and the inventories, and he's almost as familiar with our goods as I am. I think he could become a successful merchant."

Talon was again impressed with the boy, that he had already begun planning for the future when his entire world had been shattered only a short time ago. Talon was surprised to hear he was already fifteen and nearly sixteen. He had thought him at least two years younger, if not three, for his slight build and diminutive size. By law he was only weeks away from becoming a man. "I think you plan well, Rion. Aras and I have… business of a sort… in Athanark, but we will not desert you. We will see you safe. This trouble that plagues the Road may have touched there as well. Tell me more of why you fled Ardock." His earlier intention of waiting until Athanark to question the boy fell by the wayside in the face of Rion's stoic yet open nature and his own need to know.

"It started months ago, the wrong things. There were more and more travelers to our city, Ardock, to the south of here, all of them coming from along the Methris, from the south. At first there was a stream of refugees, and then a flood: merchants and craftsmen, the very poor and the very rich, fisherman and farmers, villagers and city folk, everyone.

"There were stories, horrifying stories, of forests burning and of fighting, of entire villages and towns and even cities being destroyed. And it wasn't pirates, or thieves, or even an invading army from some distant Kingdom; they said the enemy weren't Men at all. There were instead terrifying beasts and things that might have once been Dwarves or Men. Some even swore they were the walking dead, somehow come to life again. Only they weren't really alive, not exactly. Oberas called them Revenants."

Only long experience in subterfuge allowed Talon to hide his reaction to the word. He'd had no idea Oberas had known so much!

Rion continued, oblivious to Talon's shock. "Tarrell knows more than I do. He heard all kinds of things in the taverns. Oberas told us all we were leaving, that we were going to Athanark, to his friends, where we'd be safe, and that if we weren't, he'd bring them with us, and we'd all head west through the Coroden Mountains.

"He started to sell his goods and buy wagons and horses, paying four times what they were worth. Then he sold the shop, for at least three times what it was worth, for you couldn't find a space on the floor of the most meager inn in the City, even though many didn't stop to stay there for more than a night or two.

"When we left I saw some of the refugees." Rion shuddered. "They were ragged and hungry and dirty, and their eyes… I don't ever want to look into eyes such as that again."

Talon clapped him on the shoulder. "Do not dwell upon it. Think of all that you will yet have to do in Athanark. Do you know where Oberas planned to stay while he was in the City?" he asked, trying to distract Rion from his memories and despair.

"We were to stay at the Brightwater Inn. Lonas, one of his friends, owns it. And we were to meet with Anadul of Shaten first. He is a cloth merchant." Rion bit his lip in uncertainty. "Beyond that, I don't know, but I'm hoping Lonas might help me."

"If he does not, Aras and I will. You will not be alone, Rion."

"Thank you, Talon. I'm very grateful to you, and to Aras. I'll do anything I can to repay you both for your kindness," Rion swore. "I could tell you think all our goods will be lost, what we left behind. But I think we might yet retrieve them, if we are fortunate.

"It's true that there were a number of refugees on the Road, but none of them were headed this way. The Feonoke Marshes reach right up to the Southern Road. You'd never even imagine the Lost Road exists, if you didn't know it did. Even then, the route looked completely impassable, especially by wagon. It all looks to be a single large marsh. But there are solid areas connected to one another, threading through the marshes, and Oberas knew how to navigate them.

"I thought that was why it was called the Lost Road, but Oberas said it was a remnant of the Thenalonese Empire, that it still goes all the way to Thenalon, in the other direction, to the east. Anyway, I'm hoping to send a salvage team to recover our goods. I know you didn't help us for coin, but name your reward and I will gladly grant it."

Talon shook his head. "As you say, we do not aid you for that. Keep your coin, Rion. You and Tarrell will have need of it. Now, come. Aras was gracious enough to water the horses while we have been speaking, but the three of us should clean up a bit. I would recommend a change of clothes for you as well, as you are likely fortunate enough to have one. Then we must continue on to Athanark."

"Of course! Forgive me. I never have learned not to be so chatty. But as for the clothes, you are right, I do have extra with me. I can't help but notice, though, that neither of you is carrying much with you, and it sounds as if you might not be as fortunate as I am, in that regard. If it would not offend either of you, or be against any tenets of your religion, or personal beliefs, I'd like to offer you both the extra clothes of our fallen men. I would offer you my own, or Tarrell's, but I'm afraid neither of you might fit ours."

"I will only accept if it will not upset you too much to see me so clad," Talon hedged.

"I would not have offered had I not meant it. I know which pack is whose, and I'm very good at judging sizes. I'll be able to tell exactly what will fit you. Even Wilton was impressed by my ability. He's the best tailor in all of Ardock, and he's nearly as hard to please as Ob…" Rion bit his lip and closed his eyes and exhaled shakily. Then he inhaled deeply and swallowed and opened his eyes. He forced a smile. "Forgive me. I'll go get them," he said, and headed to the wagon.

"He tries so hard to be brave, and for the most part succeeds admirably," Aras said softly in Elvish, approaching now that Rion had gone. "Do not worry. I will not insult such poignant generosity. I will wear whatever he provides with only positive comment."

"I would never imagine you might do otherwise, my friend," Talon assured him.

Rion returned with the promised clothes, as well as washcloths and towels for each of them, and even soap. The three of them bathed, though Aras and Talon took turns, keeping a careful eye on their surroundings, lest trouble catch them unawares. Aras washed his cloak and clothes as well, and set them on the wagon bench to dry in the sun. Talon again envied him the Elven fabrics and did not bother to do the same, knowing they would not dry so quickly.

To Talon's relief, Rion was quite taken with Aras's cloak, fascinated both by the design and the properties of the cloth, and spoke to Aras quite animatedly about it after an initial mutual hesitation, while Talon bathed and dressed. It would be good for Aras to learn to converse so freely with other Men, and Rion was certainly in need of both the companionship and the distraction.

Once Talon was done, they climbed back onto their respective driving benches and continued onward, watching the woods closely and listening for signs of further danger, of ambush.

It was dusk when they finally spied the great stone wall the Road was leading to; they had come to Athanark at last. The gate was closed and heavily guarded, and Talon noted the arrow slits in the towers and was sure there were archers manning them. They rode up, Rion pulling his wagon into the lead, while Aras reached nervously for his hood, having donned his cloak again, after drying it in the sun.

"What business do you have in Athanark?" a City Guardsman called out to them from his tower, and it did not sound an idle question.

Rion called out from his wagon. "I'm Alarion, apprentice to Master Trader Oberas. We come to trade what wares we have left, and to bury my master and our other dead. Our caravan was attacked by wolven-riding bandits, half a day's ride from here."

There was an exchange of talk, and the gate swung open wide enough to let a group of ten City Guard emerge, and then shut again. The City Guard approached, hands on hilts, warily eyeing the party, obviously not liking the looks of any of them. "We'll see what you have in your wagons, then, and your faces," the Captain said, looking pointedly at Aras, as one of his men came around the back of the wagon.

Talon stiffened, ready to come instantly to his friend's defense, was there a need. He was proud to see Aras toss back his hood and look the guard levelly in the face. The Captain's eyes widened as he realized he was confronting an Elf.

"There's bodies here, all right, Captain," one of the other men said, lifting the tarp that covered the blanket-shrouded men in the wagon Talon drove. "It's no trick. They're dead all right, poor bastards."

"This one isn't yet, but he looks like he soon may be," another said from behind Rion's wagon after viewing Tarrell, and Talon clenched his teeth as he saw Rion stiffen. "I don't know what's in the crates, but there's nothing under him save cloth that I could feel."

"This wagon's got bodies as well. Looks like they're telling the truth," the one searching Aras's wagon said.

The Captain walked over to Rion. "I'll need to go with you to your inn. I've got questions to ask of you, but I can see your injured man can't stay here while I do."

Rion nodded, grateful. "Thank you, Captain. We're supposed to go to the Brightwater Inn, but I don't know the street or the way."

"I do," the Captain said. He produced a yellow cloth from his pocket and waved it at the towers, calling, "Open the gate!" The gate opened wide this time. "Come,

Jornan, you ride with that one," he said and looked at Talon with mistrusting eyes. Talon cursed silently. The Captain had apparently accurately perceived him as a potential threat, from his ready defense of Aras. The Captain sat next to Rion.

The guard named Jornan slid onto the bench next to Talon, and Talon noted his hand did not leave his sword hilt. Talon clicked his tongue softly at Kandahar and Janahar, following Rion's wagon. He looked back and saw that Aras's wagon followed and that Aras slipped the hood back over his head as soon as they passed through the gate.

Talon heard some of what Rion told the Captain as his words drifted back to him. He concentrated on seeming harmless to the nervous guard beside him, but the man didn't relax at all.

Fortunately, the inn wasn't very far from the City gate. They had been drawing many interested stares, and Talon severely disliked being the center of anyone's attention.

At the inn, they headed for the stable. Seeing the Guard and loaded wagons, the stable master sent a stableboy to get the innkeeper, Lonas.

The Captain said to Rion, "We'll send a party of the Guard out to recover your other two wagons and the goods you left behind. We thought we'd seen the last of those wolven-riders, after the last time, but I guess there's more of them than we realized. We'll have to set out more patrols and have them go further out, if we want to have any more merchants get through. Few enough brave the Marshes, and all the regular caravans have ceased coming here, these weeks past."

He looked back toward Talon's and Aras's wagons, which bore the dead. "If you give me the names of the dead, I'll see they're buried. The City will pay for it, for you've done us a service by killing the bandits that attacked you."

RION nodded. Talon had already handed him Oberas's ring and purse, and the purses of the other guards and the drivers, and he'd put them with Oberas's other valuables in his wagon. Rion planned to give the guards' valuables and other possessions to Tarrell once he was well again, since on caravan journeys it was custom to give the belongings of fallen guardsmen to their surviving friends. "I will name the men for you. Please, I would appreciate it if you would see that the guards are buried with their swords and bows," he said, thinking Tarrell might want that for them, and remembering Talon had suggested it. "And I should like to attend their interment, to speak a few words over them," Rion said, fighting to sound a man.

He was gratified when the Captain said, "Of course," and looked at him in approval.

Although he was only a few scant weeks from coming-of-age, he was still boy enough that he needed the Captain's approval. He needed far more. He desperately wished Hardred was here to comfort him, to console him, to assure him Tarrell would live, and to protect him. How could Hardred and Alnas have deserted them when they needed them most, before they reached the safety of Athanark?

He swallowed hard at the unworthy thought. Had they stayed, they would be dead too. Alnas was an archer; he would have been one of the first to die, with all the other archers. And Hardred would have died trying to protect him or Oberas or any of the rest. He should be thankful they had gone, that they were yet safe. At least, he hoped they might be.

He wiped at the tears that started trickling down his cheeks again as an older man approached him, his face sad and fatherly. "Master Alarion, my name is Lonas. I'm the innkeeper here. Oberas sent word to me you were coming. My condolences for your loss; Oberas was a fine man and a dear friend."

TALON eyed Lonas carefully. His concern appeared genuine. The man truly appeared grief-stricken; his eyes had the brightness of unshed tears as they went from Rion's face to the wagons loaded with the dead.

The Captain walked over to Talon and said. "All right, you and your friend next. I'll have your story."

"You may have it, Captain, but first I need to tend to Tarrell, the wounded man. Once I've done all I can, you'll have my full cooperation." Talon slipped down from the wagon and walked toward Tarrell.

The Captain's eyes narrowed, and he moved to intercept Talon, but Aras was suddenly in front of him. "You may talk to me first, then, since you need to hear from both of us."

The Captain looked ready to argue, but looked into Aras's intent face and shifted his feet nervously. "Very well. If you'll accompany me?" the Captain asked, speaking far more solicitously to Aras than he had spoken to Talon. He waved Aras toward the inn.

Lonas spoke to the other Guard briefly regarding the dead and then showed Talon and Rion into the building. He led them up to the second floor toward two rooms at the back of the inn, which he told them had locks on the doors leading to the hall and were connected by a door that also locked. Talon carried Tarrell himself, ignoring his injured arm for the moment. He was surprised by the quality of the clean, spacious, well-appointed room. He laid the wounded Man carefully on the bed and asked the innkeeper for clean bandages, boiling water, and alcohol. After he had done all he could for Tarrell, he headed downstairs to the common room to be questioned.

Talon studied Aras and the Captain as he approached. The Captain was treating his friend with respect bordering on reverence. He sighed, knowing his own experience would be far less pleasant. The Captain rose. Upon seeing Talon he nodded and said, "I'm done here. Your friend has spoken on your behalf. I'm satisfied. I'll be getting back to my other duties now." And he was gone.

"Thank you for taking care of that for me," Talon said, his thanks heartfelt. "I tire of defending myself everywhere I go."

Aras smiled. "Come, let us assist Rion."

They went upstairs. Rion was sitting at Tarrell's side, looking small and lost. He looked up at them when they entered with wide eyes.

Talon went over to him and clasped his shoulder. "I know it might be hard to believe, but all will soon be well again, as well as it can be. Tarrell will recover, and until he does, Aras and I will see that you are safe. In the morning, we'll help you find those buyers Oberas lined up for you and make sure you're not cheated. And we'll help you find new guardsmen, too.

"Rion, you must sell all you can here, but you can't settle here. This place will not be safe for much longer, I think, nor will any place be, east of the Coroden. You must travel back down the Helden River, north on the Southern Road to the Western Road, and take the Gelthor Pass through the Coroden Mountains, then cross the Merdan River, and take the Western Road west to Gosa.

"Gosa is a large city, a prosperous one, far from the dangers that are coming. You can settle there and be safe. I will find someone who knows the way well enough to guide you, for my business takes me elsewhere. But for now, all you need think about is eating a hot dinner and then going to bed. Let me worry about the rest."

Rion nodded numbly, obviously overwhelmed by the thought of such a journey after the one he had just completed.

Aras ate dinner with Rion in the room Rion shared with Tarrell. Talon ate downstairs, eager to learn other news of the City.

TARRELL moaned in his sleep, and Rion was at his side instantly, but he didn't waken. Aras said gently, "The medicine for the pain Talon has given him also helps him sleep. He will be better in the morning, especially once he has eaten; you will see. But his body will need time to heal. Talon is an excellent healer, and he has treated such wounds before. When he found me, I was much the same as Tarrell, although my chest bore greater injury than my arm and I was much closer to death than your friend, for he did not find me nearly as quickly as he found you. Yet here I am."

Rion looked at him, wide-eyed. "Is that how you first met?"

Aras nodded. "I will tell you the story sometime, when Tarrell may hear it also. But for now, you must sleep and I... I need some time to myself, to think. Much has happened in a very short time, and I am not accustomed to living life at Man's fast pace. It is somewhat disquieting for me. But call me if you need me, and I will come."

Rion thanked him, and Aras left for the adjoining room he and Talon were to share.

Aras lay on the bed for a long time, thinking over the events of the past weeks. He eyed the door to the hallway, reluctant to leave it unlocked but unwilling to bolt it before Talon returned. He tried to convince himself it was safe to sleep, that he would waken to any danger. He knew his days would not be getting any slower or easier here, and his own troubles would soon catch up with him.

TALON slipped into the room silently long past midnight, trying not to waken Aras, bolting the door behind him. He listened intently but didn't hear any change in his friend's soft breathing. He crossed soundlessly to the bed and laid his weapons down within easy reach. He removed only his boots. He would sleep in his clothes, as always, so he might be ready to combat whatever danger might face him.

After a moment's hesitation, he stripped off his hated gloves as well and then slipped into the bed beside Aras, stretching his fingers and then rubbing his fingertips against one another with a contented sigh, reveling in the rare feel of bare skin. He imagined running his fingertips along a muscled shoulder or chest or thigh and suppressed a groan, barely resisting indulging in the urge.

He had just congratulated himself, as much for his moral fortitude as for not waking his friend, when he heard a quietly murmured "Goodnight" from beside him on the bed.

"Forgive me. I had not meant to wake you," Talon apologized softly, chagrined, fighting a stronger urge to touch Aras, now that he knew he was awake and conscious to repel such an advance if it was not wanted.

"You did not. I was awake already. I could not sleep until I knew you were safely beside me," Aras answered, just as quietly.

Idare, it would be so easy to disregard his vow to Elanara, to act upon his longing! "It is late. Sleep well, my friend. We have much to do come the morrow," Talon said dutifully instead, rolling onto his side so that he faced away from Aras, from temptation.

There was a soft sigh, of wistfulness or tiredness, Talon could not say.

"Sleep well," Aras replied, and then silence stretched between them. It was a long, long time before Talon was able to accede to his friend's wish.

THE next morning, Aras changed Talon's dressing, but Talon wouldn't let him use any medicine on the wound. "We need to save that for Tarrell. This will heal well enough without it, for now. I need to see if they have any decent herbalists here. They must, in a city this size. Come, let's check on Tarrell."

Rion was already awake when they entered the adjoining room, but Tarrell still slept. Talon said, "We'll wake him after I change the bandages, if that doesn't wake him anyway."

Rion nodded.

Talon carefully unwrapped Tarrell's arm. The wounded guard opened his eyes and looked about in confusion. His gaze turned to his arm, and he grew pale, staring with horrified fascination at the exposed wound.

Rion clasped Tarrell's good shoulder strongly, drawing his attention away from his injury. "It's good to see you awake! You're going to be fine. Do you remember Talon? He aided us on the Road. He's an expert healer. We're in Athanark, we're safe. We're going to stay and trade here, for a while, while you recover, but then we're going through the mountains to Gosa, west of here."

Talon worked quickly while Rion kept Tarrell distracted, explaining their new plans. He was grateful to the boy. Once he was done, Talon said with false cheer, "I'll tell Lonas it will be two for breakfast in here this morning. Come, Aras. Rion and Tarrell have much to talk about."

As he and Aras left the room, he heard Rion say, "You'll still be traveling with me, Tarrell, only this time not as my guard, but as my guardian...."

THEY went downstairs and spoke to Lonas. Talon advised him as to what Tarrell should eat to speed his recovery. Then Talon asked him about an herbalist's shop and where they might go to find new guardsmen and horses. They'd need riding horses, if their new guard did not all have their own, and likely additional draft horses to pull the supply wagon and wagons of goods, depending upon how much stock they sold in the City. Kaldahar and Janahar would not acquiesce so readily to pull a wagon for another man.

Lonas was eager to help them and knew his City well. He also assured them he'd safely escort Rion, and Tarrell as well, if he was up to it, to the burials of Oberas, his guards, and the wagon drivers.

Talon was relieved. He had not looked forward to accompanying them, though he would not have let them go alone. Farad's and Lunahr's deaths were still too recent, the pain too raw. Talon did his best to force thoughts of them down.

Talon advised Aras to leave his bow and quiver in their room and take only his swords and knife into the City, and Aras did so, bringing his staff and hooding his face, his cloak covering his swords. He could whip it off quickly enough, if needed.

Talon already knew his way around the City to a degree from his limited explorations the previous night after his meal, though he had not felt comfortable straying far from the inn, in case Aras or Rion had need of him, had Tarrell's condition worsened unexpectedly. He also had his memories of his last visit, nearly two decades ago, though the City had grown considerably since then.

ARAS, for his part, was fascinated by this City of Man. It was crowded and squalid, dirty and noisy. But it was also filled with energy and passion, and everywhere there were children, happy and sullen, smiling and hollering, playing and fighting. "So many children!" Aras said, awed.

"They grow quickly and die all too easily," Talon said morosely, and Aras looked at his friend in empathy. He'd watched the antics of Man-children before, many years ago, when he was but a child himself. These were every bit as odd and fascinating to him now that he was grown.

TALON found all three herbalist shops easily enough and was well pleased with the third one they tried. He spent his two precious silver pieces and did not argue when Aras put some of his own coin toward the purchase. It wounded his pride to allow it, although his people had long ago learned to subsume pride to practicality. They would never have survived, otherwise. At least now he and Aras were well supplied again.

They went to the weapons shop on Archer Street Lonas had recommended: Bloodhand Blades. It was run by a retired sword master named Vargas, an old friend of the innkeeper's. Lonas had told him that Vargas would be able to locate the guards they needed.

The outside of the shop was simple and unobtrusive, with wooden walls and door, and of course, no windows. Few shops could afford the costly luxury of glass panes, and at night even shuttered windows invited theft. A sign with a bloody hand holding a sword hung over the door, and Talon stiffened. An image of Lunahr flashed into his mind, and he slammed it back firmly.

Aras was looking at him in concern. "Is something wrong?"

"No, I'm fine," Talon lied. He took a deep calming breath and entered. He relaxed once inside. He was pleased by what he saw. Racks of short swords and longswords lined three of the walls, and a counter lined the wall on the right, with a navy beaded curtain on the wall near the break in the counter, indicating a back room. Two swords were on display on the center of that wall. A small bell sounded as they entered, and the proprietor, who was rearranging a rack of swords on the left wall, turned to welcome them.

The man was burly, his impressive mass muscle, not fat. His hair was gray and his face grizzled, with a long white scar running from ear to jaw on his left cheek. He was also missing his left arm: his shirt was sewn shut where the sleeve should have been. But despite the missing limb, he wore a sheathed sword at his side.

Talon noted that the man's welcoming smile stayed on his face, but he saw that the shrewdly assessing gray eyes did not like what they saw, sliding from Aras's cloaked face to his.

"Just a moment, sirs," he said politely, and then called out, "Argo, I've customers! Lend a hand," and instantly, out from behind the curtain came a handsome young man of twenty or so, leanly muscled and dark haired, also wearing a sword.

"Argo, set this one third down on the rack and finish reordering the rest, that's a good lad." He turned to them and said, "Now, how may I help you?"

Aras began looking around the shop with interest. Argo followed Aras around with watchful eyes.

Talon spoke for them. "I was told that Vargas the Sword Master might be able to recommend some reliable men who would hire on to guard a merchant caravan for a friend of mine. We are looking for fourteen good men." Fourteen would be able to guard Rion's three remaining wagons sufficiently. He should have only two wagons of goods at the most, depending upon how much he sold and what he might invest in while here to transport west, but he'd need a third wagon for supplies for the journey. They'd need to restock often en route in each city, as well as hunt along the way to supplement their provisions, in order to feed so many men.

"Sword master? You must have been talking to old Lonas at the Brightwater or Harnel at the Westgate, then. Few enough others call me that, nowadays." He eyed

Talon shrewdly. "You could hawk in the Square for the guards and save yourself the price of my fee."

"I could, but as I said, I seek good men. I need them to be reliable and honest, as well as to know how to fight. I can test their mettle well enough. Lonas told me you've a practice yard out back, and I'm usually a good judge of character, but sometimes flaws are only revealed over time. I would not want to risk making a mistake in this. We will pay whatever commission you deem fair," Talon said, suppressing a sigh as he realized he'd again have to rely upon charity from Aras. He'd not thought to ask Rion for the coin.

Vargas looked at him as if he had expected Talon to haggle over the price, and Talon saw he had scored a point toward a more favorable estimation of himself. The man nodded. "I know a few names for now, and I'll see who they might know. One gold per man, payable in advance, if you please," he said, walking toward the counter. Talon followed and Aras joined him.

Talon saw that the counter contained cases of daggers, as well as some other, more exotic blades, displayed upon blue velvet. Vargas was looking past Talon at Aras, peering intently at the face under the hood.

Talon's eyes strayed to the two swords mounted on the wall, curious. His breath hissed, and he stiffened. Aras and Vargas both looked at him.

"YOU have an unusual blade. The top one, with the black hilt. May I see it?" Talon's voice sounded casual, but Aras, who knew him well enough, now, could see the tension in him.

"I'm afraid it's not for sale," Vargas said, eyes narrowing.

"Still, I would like to see it," Talon said, his voice soft but unyielding.

"I think not," Vargas said suspiciously, and Aras saw that Argo was next to them now, and both he and Vargas had let their hands stray to their sword hilts.

"I would at least know how you came to possess that blade," Talon said, his voice one of command.

Aras looked at the sword curiously. The metal was dull and worn, although the edge looked sharp. It was a longer blade than many men could wield. Talon could have used it easily; he had the height and length of arm for it, but he already had an excellent blade.

"I purchased it, as I have every other blade here, including my own, once, long ago. Do you call me a thief?" His gray eyes darkened like storm clouds, and his hand tightened on the hilt of his sword. Aras looked at Talon nervously.

Talon suddenly seemed to be aware the situation was rapidly escalating in a direction Aras assumed he'd rather not see it take. Talon exhaled heavily, but none of the tension left him. "No, I do not call you a thief and I did not mean to give offense. It is just that the owner of that blade would have parted with it only in death, and he was kin to me. I would see it come home." His voice had taken on a pained note, and

Aras realized Talon was in agony over the sword, though his pain had at first come across as something else entirely.

"You can tell that from where you stand?" the man said skeptically, but it was said as a challenge, and there was a new look in his eyes.

Then Talon spoke again, and now his voice contained only grief and weariness. "I know Loruthanar as well as I know my own sword. The name is inscribed on the blade, but the letters are worn so low you could not read them now, even if they were in a tongue you knew, and there are few enough of us left who know it. The leather of the hilt once bore the image of eagles, and the sword guard is in the shape of encircling wings formed so fine you'd swear real wings had been dipped in black and gold. The right one curves up a little, and the left is chipped near the blade's edge. Name your price, and I will pay it. I won't bargain for it, and I won't leave here without it."

"That blade is old," Vargas said, and his voice was full of reverence now. "The man I bought it from had no idea what he sold me. I gave him a fair price for a good blade, but I could never have paid what it is really worth. A sword like this, a man is lucky to see once in his lifetime. But to own it...? I had never thought to own one so fine, or might hope to ever own one again."

Aras drew back his hood, and Vargas looked at him and nodded, as if he'd suspected the quiet hooded man might be an Elf. But to the side, he heard Argo gasp.

"Could we perhaps trade for it, blade for blade?" Aras asked, unbuckling his sheathed dagger and drawing the blade forth slowly, held parallel to the floor. The long, silvery blade shone like moonlight in the shop. "I understand Elven blades are valued by Men. There are none as sharp or strong, despite what the Dwarves might say. This blade is not as old as that one, but it also has a noble history. It was a gift to me from the King of Riviera, on my coming-of-age. And the blade is made of pallenteum, which is rare even amongst my people."

Aras was intrigued. The Man before him had stiffened as if in pain when he'd mentioned Riviera, he was certain of it. And he had not seemed at all surprised to find an Elf standing before him, though Aras doubted there might be any others in the City.

Vargas looked from him to Talon and back again. He sighed and took the sword carefully from the wall. He looked at it lovingly, as if committing every line of it to memory. He reached under the counter and pulled out a shabby leather scabbard, sheathed it, and held it out to Talon. "You can't carry a naked blade into the street and not have the Guard up in arms, especially looking as you do. You've an air of hardness and danger about you that makes a wise man wary."

Talon took the blade reverently.

When Aras started to place his dagger upon the counter, Vargas shook his head. "You asked me to name my price, and I'll not name that. I bought it for twenty gold, and that's all I'll ask for it. I wish I could tell you more about it. The man who sold it to me was named Rohas. He was a refugee from a village in the south, along the banks of the Methris. He told me he'd found it on a battlefield outside the smoking ruins of Alridge. He said it had saved his life more than once on the way here, but he needed food and a fast horse more. His own died on the way here. The scabbard I just gave you he'd found elsewhere. He said it was nothing special, but it fits the blade."

"Thank you," Talon said simply. "I am in your debt. I would give you a warning. Athanark is no longer safe. The trouble from the east and south is heading west and north besides. Athanark will be consumed by it. The wolven-riders that are preying on the Road here are just the beginning. Pack your stock, sell your shop, and join my friends' caravan to Gosa, or another caravan heading west through the Coroden Mountains. If the darkness can be stopped, it won't be stopped here."

Vargas nodded with a weary sigh. "You're not the first to say so. I'll consider it. Meanwhile, I'll find those men you wanted. Come back here in two days just after dawn, and I'll have twenty men for you to pick from. As Lonas told you, I've a practice yard out back. You can test them there."

Talon nodded and Aras handed Vargas the forty gold, twenty for the sword and twenty for the men. Once they were outside, Talon said, "Thank you, my friend," to Aras, in Elvish, and there was a depth of feeling in his simple words.

"I am sorry for your loss," Aras said, knowing his poor words could not possibly help his friend.

"I HAD already known he was lost." Talon's voice did not shake; it did not betray the nightmarish vision he had seen of Lunahr's death. He drew strength enough from the silver vine about his core to continue.

"I had not hoped to ever reclaim Beryl's sword, even if only to bury it, for there is nothing else left of him to bury and he was last of his House. He was so young, yet so special, and he was... very dear to me. There are so few of us left. It had been years since one of our number had last fallen. We who remain are hard to kill. But I know of one other who has passed, only weeks ago. It has been two years since I last met a kinsman, and they have been harsh years. But worse are to follow. Come. With luck, Lonas will have judged as well about the stables he recommended to us."

They found a number of suitable draft horses, though they did not purchase any of them, but did not have as much luck locating riding horses. Talon had also wanted to buy some other provisions. Aras apparently realized he hesitated only because he did not have the coin and was reluctant to ask; unbidden, he held out his entire purse for Talon, telling him to purchase what he needed and to return the rest. They added nuts, dried fruit, dried vegetables, two flasks of oil, and bandages to their supplies, the latter which might double as torch cloth. Although Talon was in desperate need of clothes, the ones from Gower now torn and bloodied and travel stained, and the borrowed ones he now wore likely to suffer a similar fate all too soon, he refused to spend his friend's coin for that. It was early evening by the time they returned to the inn.

When they knocked on Rion's door, he bade them enter, his voice sounding surprisingly happy and excited. When they came in, Talon was impressed by the change in the formerly spacious room. It looked like a miniature bazaar now, with bolts of cloth, cases of jewelry, rare foodstuffs, worked metals, and other things displayed to good advantage about the room.

Tarrell was sitting in a chair in front of a box, checking off some sort of list using his left hand, and he smiled up at them as they entered. Talon, who'd been in a dark mood, smiled back, pleased to see him out of bed.

Rion appeared from behind a stack of small crates. "Talon! I was right! The Guards recovered everything for us, just as I'd hoped they might! I had spoken to Lonas about it, and he assured me Captain Vincent was an honorable man. The other four wagonloads were brought late this afternoon, our two wagons and all we'd offloaded from the two-and-a-half we'd emptied. Lonas is storing most of everything for us at a fair price; this is mostly our display, although it's all of the jewelry and smaller things. He had a similar arrangement with Oberas in the past. Did you have any luck finding guardsmen for us?"

Rion's enthusiasm made Talon smile again. "More luck than we had finding riding horses. We did find some good draft horses for you to choose from; we've not purchased them yet. I thought it best to wait until we had a better idea of the number of wagons you'd have. It looks like you'll be needing additional horses now, unless you sell a considerable amount." He hesitated but then added, "Aras had to pay an advance commission of twenty gold for the men...."

Rion hit himself in the forehead with the palm of his hand. "I never thought of that!" He reached into a thin purse at his side and took out twenty gold and handed it to Aras.

"You need not reimburse me, Rion. My purse is yet full," Aras said, looking in apparent surprise and concern at Rion's thin purse.

Rion laughed. "Don't worry! I haven't lost it or spent it. After you told me last night what Talon told you about walking around with so much, it sounded wise to me to heed your advice. Before now I never carried enough coin to have to worry about such things, but I'm a much easier mark than Oberas was. So I've hidden the rest. By the way, Lonas is putting the cost of your room and meals as well as mine on account, and I insist on paying both, for the aid you've been. As near as we were, we'd never have made it to the City without your help."

Rion looked at Tarrell with open affection, and then back at Talon. "Tarrell's agreed to be my guardian. I'm going to teach him to trade, and he's already helping me with the inventories. He'll see that I'm not cheated, too. But even with him and the new guards, we could sorely use your company for the trip. Are you sure you can't come west with us? Whatever business you have, couldn't you do it in Gosa?"

Talon looked at him fondly. "I'm afraid not, Rion. But we're not going just yet. Vargas is finding the guards for us, but I still have to test them for you. Vargas has a practice yard behind his shop, which should be perfect for that."

Rion looked from his face to his arm and back again, although the bandages were concealed by his sleeve.

Talon smiled. "Believe me, I've fought far fiercer foes while far worse injured than this. I've even been eating and sleeping. I'll be getting soft, if this keeps up."

Then Talon's face clouded over, and he clenched the sheathed sword in his hand tightly.

"About the horses," Rion said in a rush, into the uneasy quiet. "I thought it would only be fair if you took Kaldahar and Janahar, since Aras told me you won't let me pay you for helping me. I'll be driving one of the wagons and Tarrell will be driving another. Most or all of our new guards will likely have their own horses. Tarrell also has more information for you, about what's happening in the southeast. I hope it will make you change your mind and come with us. I'm afraid I know the answer to that, but maybe it might help you stay safe, at least."

Suddenly Rion looked as if he might burst into tears. Talon reached out a hand and tousled his hair as an older brother might. "I shall miss you when I go, but I am not gone yet." He turned to Tarrell. "All the detail you can remember."

Tarrell had heard much more than Rion, and the details he gave were even more grim. Many cities had already fallen. The southeast was infested with Incuban's dark servants: Revenants, animated corpses, and sometimes even fusions of Man or Dwarf and beast. There were chimaera as well; as with the Revenants, Tarrell called them by name. Apparently, Oberas had known the names of all the Enemy's minions and had warned his guards about the true dangers they might face as they fled from Ardock.

Talon cursed himself again for not speaking to Oberas at length six years ago when he first met him. He would never know, now, what experiences he might have had in the Dwarven Lands, that he was so familiar with such evil. Although perhaps Lonas, the innkeeper, might know at least something of it, and possibly even as much. He would need to speak with him. He would even risk using the King's Voice, if necessary, to learn all he could.

Talon feared for Elanara, Elavar, Eladar, their parents, and their people. Riviera and Loatia were too close to the darkness, on the wrong side of the Velmar and Coroden Mountains for safety. They would be the first of the Elven Kingdoms to fall. The Enemy advanced quickly, too quickly. They were out of time.

Tarrell started to look a little gray after a while, and Talon said, "Forgive me. I forgot you need your rest. You've strained yourself. Let me check your arm. I've bought some new medicines that might help it heal better. I'll see that Lonas sends up dinner for you."

Tarrell walked wearily to the bed and lay down. Talon checked the injury and marveled again how quickly Aras had recovered under such harsh conditions. Thoughts of Aras reminded him again of his offer of the dagger. He had been moved beyond words.

He had suspected he would be risking Aras's life by bringing him here. It hurt, knowing he had done so. And Vargas.... It was for men such as Vargas that he would risk his own life, and his friend's. Not one man in ten thousand would have refused such a blade. Any Elven blade would be treasured amongst Men, and a blade of pallenteum could ransom a town, but a coming-of-age gift from an Elven King was beyond price.

Tarrell settled more comfortably onto the bed, and Talon told him to sleep, if he could. Rion said he'd stay with him and see that he did. Talon looked up, catching

Aras unawares. There was a look of such grief and loss and agony on Aras's face, he felt for a moment he was staring into the face of one of his own kin.

ARAS looked at his taciturn friend in concern. Talon was feeling a great loss at the death of his kinsman. Aras had no idea what he might say to console his friend. He had felt similar pain before at the death of friends, all too often in his short life. Each death hurt as much or even more than the last. Each friend lost was as agonizing to bear. It never got any easier. He would not want it to hurt less. Such irreplaceable losses should hurt. Aras realized Talon was looking at him and quickly turned away.

Talon said, "Come, Aras, let us check on the horses Rion has gifted to us."

Aras nodded, looking gratefully at him. He had not wanted Talon to ask what was wrong. He could not have told him yet, and he did not want to lie to his friend any more than he had to.

Aras followed Talon to the stable. Kaldahar and Janahar seemed pleased to see them. They were both exceptional mounts. Janahar whickered at Aras and nudged her nose under his hand to be petted, as if sensing his distress and knowing the contact would sooth him.

Her perceptive attempt at comforting him reminded him painfully of Aerlyr, his favorite mount, a far different beast. Aerlyr had left on a mating flight only days before the completion of his training, in spite of the danger of doing so. Aras wondered if he had been successful in his search for a mate, if they had found a safe place to roost, if even now their offspring might be gestating. He wondered what the Gryphon who honored him with his friendship had thought if he had already returned, only to find him gone.

Aras was confident Aerlyr would not be so foolish as to go to Nalea in search of him. Aerlyr was well aware that his father's people did not know of the continued existence of the Gryphon. They were blissfully unaware of the Isle of Gryph and the Player who dwelt there. They did not even know about the Game. The Aerta and Oceana had thought all the Gryphon lost with the Homeland, burnt to death with the Aerie and the Faeren. They had not mourned their passing. The Gryphon were yet grievously maligned for their former ties to the Aerie who had created them long ago, merging the essence of pumar and eagles.

TALON examined the saddles and bridles. They were worn but of good quality. Kaldahar butted him hard in the chest with her head, making it clear that she did not like to be ignored, and Talon laughed and lavished affection upon her as he planned his next move. He needed to go to the nearest of the Markers, to as many of them as he could, to leave warnings to his kinsmen about Incuban's change of strategy, that he was coming from the south now, not the east.

The thought burned like fire. Farad had died for nothing! He had left twelve years ago for the Dwarven Kingdoms, to unite them against Incuban's advance, and had somehow died there, and it was all for naught. "I am impatient to be away."

"It will not be such a bad thing to have given your arm a few days to heal," Aras said softly.

"I could heal as well on the road. But I will not leave Rion and Tarrell unprotected. We will stay, but only as long as we must." They left the stable. Talon was in a dark and restless mood the rest of the evening.

ARAS took dinner with Rion and Tarrell, while Talon ate elsewhere. Aras knew his friend was scouring the City for information about the attacks to the southeast.

Aras yearned to be off as well, in spite of his fondness for Rion and Tarrell and all he was learning from them as they spoke together at length while Talon roamed the City. There were no growing things in this City of Man. He missed the trees, though he was not weakened by their absence as others of his people would be. His bond to Aranas, the youngest Tree of the Lords' Grove, sustained him.

The following day, Talon spent much of the time away in other areas of the City as well. Aras missed his friend fiercely. He distracted himself by helping Rion and Tarrell as much as he was able. The two Men sold a considerable amount of their wares at excellent profit, and also picked up things they thought would sell well in distant Gosa.

When Aras tended to Tarrell's arm, he was pleased to see that Tarrell was able to move his fingers slightly now. Aras was relieved that it looked like he would keep his arm, for he'd had disturbing visions of his young friend with a missing sleeve like the one Vargas sported. Aras took advantage of the time to get to know Janahar better, and to speak further with Rion and Tarrell about Talon and the world of Men.

Chapter 5
Fourteen Good Men

JARGAS paid for his mead and sighed. That had been the last of his coin. There would be no lunch today, or dinner, but at least he had paid for his spot on the floor of the common room here at the Westgate Inn in advance for the night. He would not be forced to sleep in an alleyway. But he needed work.

The swordsman to his right was at least somewhat drunk and had been annoying Jargas for some time with his loud conversation, but it had suddenly taken an interesting turn, and he began to listen intently.

"I tell you, it'll be an easy fee. There's nothing but a single range of mountains and a few rivers between here and Gosa. The trouble is all to the south and east, not the west. Why not work for a rich merchant for a change?" the man argued.

He was speaking of work that Jargas could do, and Gosa was the nearest City of Man to his home. He wouldn't have to delay his return by first finding employment to finance his journey. His employment would bring him close to home and provide for him at the same time.

The man's friend was responding. "A single range of mountains, he says! Balark, you imbecile, you're talking of the Coroden Mountains! There are obearn in the foothills and ogres in those mountains that would as soon eat you as look at you! And the land around both those rivers beyond that is nothing but swamp, now. If the snakes don't kill you, the thrice-blasted insects will. Unless you mean to ask the Elves for safe journey across their cursed Wood? And that's just for starters. I'd rather fight a nice clean war, thank you, defending some poor city, where all I have to worry about is having my guts spilled. You go to the Bloodhand tomorrow if you want, but you'll go alone." He stood then, slamming his empty stein down for emphasis, and stomped off. His drunken friend stumbled out after him.

Jargas looked at his hand, which completely encased the large metal stein, thoughtfully. He'd never yet held one his fingers could actually grip the handle of. He took his second and last swig from the stein and licked the last trace of the sticky brew from his lips.

"Excuse me," he called out to the innkeeper, who came over.

"Another, sir?" the innkeeper asked respectfully. Most men spoke respectfully to him, those that valued their lives. He was again grateful for the physique he had been born with, for poor travelers did not often receive such courtesy, and the innkeeper must suspect he was at least low on coin.

"No, thanks just the same," Jargas answered politely. "I was wondering, maybe you can help me? I'm supposed to meet someone at the Bloodhand here in Athanark, but I only received part of the message, and I only just got into your City and haven't had much time to explore it yet. Do you know of it? Is it near here?"

"Sure! It's not far from here: Bloodhand Blades, on Archer Street. Vargas the Sword Master runs it, though Lonas and I are the only two who call him that nowadays. We traveled together, long ago, when I was just a lad." A look of pain passed over the man's face, and he cleared his throat. "Best weapons shop in the City, if you're looking for a blade," he added, his voice suddenly more gruff.

He'd thought the Bloodhand was a tavern. A weapons shop sounded more promising. "I'm not, but my friend is. Thanks. I'd be much obliged if you could tell me how to get there."

The man did, and Jargas thanked him and left. He'd go there now and see what he might find out, perhaps get a jump on the competition.

Jargas found the shop easily enough; the image on the wooden sign had been freshly repainted, a bloody hand holding a dripping sword. There was a wooden door and no windows. He opened the door, then ducked his head and turned sideways to enter. There were swords on racks everywhere within. A young man with a blade at his side, too young to be a sword master, eyed him appraisingly. "May I help you, sir?" he asked politely.

He stood before a giant with a quarterstaff in hand, yet there was no challenge in his voice, no fear, no bravado. He was well trained, Jargas thought. Many men quailed at the sight of him, while others felt obligated to hide their fear and prove their manhood by challenging him.

"My name is Jargas. I'm looking for Vargas the Sword Master. I understand a merchant will be hiring guards tomorrow for a trip to Gosa. I thought I'd apply today."

"Ah. Vargas is eating his lunch right now. I'll go fetch him for you."

"I can come back, then. I wouldn't want to interrupt a man's meal." Jargas didn't need a mark against him before he'd begun.

"It's no trouble, I assure you," the man said and ducked through a curtain to what must be a back room. Jargas eyed the contents of the counter. Daggers, all kinds of them. He looked up at the wall by the curtain. A sword hung there, proudly displayed. A second set of brackets above the first lay empty, and Jargas wondered what might have happened to that blade. Likely someone had purchased it and the store owner had yet to replace it with one of similar quality.

The younger man reappeared with an older man in tow. Jargas liked the look of him instantly. He was stout, all of his bulk muscle. His hair and eyes were gray, and his face grizzled, with a long white scar running from ear to jaw on his left cheek. His left arm was missing, but he still wore a sword. "I'm Vargas. Jargas, is it? I'm not familiar with you. Who referenced you to me?" He was studying Jargas's face intently.

"I heard about the opening from Balark," Jargas said, skirting on the edge of truth. He hoped it wouldn't be a mistake to mention the name, for he had not been impressed by that man at all, but if it was references Vargas was seeking, it was the best he could do. Farad had left him a week ago, and he didn't know anyone in Athanark.

"Balark, hmm? I don't know the name. Do you know who he heard about it from?"

"No, I don't," Jargas admitted and quickly changed the subject. "Look, I know my trade and you can tell by looking at me that I'm fit enough for the trip. You can feel free to test me if you like, both of you. And I know the way to Gosa. Ogres, obearn, bandits, rockslides, snakes, and swamp: it's all the same to me. I've never yet met a foe my staff or my head couldn't handle."

Vargas looked at him appraisingly. "Can you ride?"

Jargas nodded. "When I can find a horse strong enough to carry me."

"What was your last work?" Vargas asked.

"I traveled with a man named Hunter, back from the Malar Kingdom in the Dwarven Lands, across the Fromer Mountains. It wasn't a paid position. It was to our mutual advantage: we both survived the crossing."

"The Dwarven Lands?" Vargas asked, pain lashing his face. Now Jargas realized the focus of his intense scrutiny before had been his beard. Perhaps he knew people from one of the Kingdoms, or had even visited one sometime in the past, and was trying to determine whether Jargas was from one he was familiar with. That would explain the look of pain. If it had been even only one or two decades ago, it was unlikely those he knew yet lived.

Vargas rubbed the seam over his missing arm absently and then stiffened, glaring at his hand as if it had betrayed him. He dropped it to his side. "Could Hunter provide a reference for you, then?" Vargas pressed, his voice suddenly cold and hard.

Jargas sighed. "No, he's already gone. And I think you'd like the looks of him even less than you like the looks of me. I'm sorry to have kept you from your lunch." Jargas turned to go.

"Wait. Forgive me my tone. It's not you I'm angered at. They're looking for men with references, so I can't promise you anything, but be here at sunup tomorrow morning. They're looking for fourteen guards, and I've promised them twenty to choose from. You make the twenty-first, and there might be one or two more by tomorrow."

Jargas turned back to him in surprise and looked at him intently. "Thank you, Sword Master. You'll not regret it, nor will they." Then he left.

THE next day, Tarrell and Rion accompanied Talon and Aras to the Bloodhand. Tarrell was now dressed in the same type of rich, brightly colored merchant's clothes as Rion. Tarrell fidgeted, obviously uncomfortable in the new clothes Rion had bought for him. Rion empathized with him, remembering how awkward he had first felt in such attire until he'd gotten used to it. They walked slowly, for Tarrell's sake, but Rion was concerned to see he was pale and drawn by the time they reached the weapons shop.

Vargas the Sword Master greeted them warmly, apparently much more favorably impressed by him and Tarrell than he had been by Talon and Aras on their first meeting, from what Aras had told them. Aras again wore his hood and carried his staff.

"I'm Sword Master Vargas. I've twenty-three good men for you to choose your fourteen from. They're waiting in the practice yard."

"Excellent! I am Rion, and this is my guardian, Swordsman Tarrell. This, then, is for the three extra men," he said, extending his hand with three gold, lest Aras do so first.

"Nay, lad. I'll not take your coin," Vargas said, instead holding out two ten-gold pieces to Rion. "I'd not have taken it before, had I known the men were for you. Talon hadn't mentioned your name to me. But then Lonas came to see me after the burial, and—I'd have gone, too, but...." He began clearing his throat and blinking rapidly.

He continued on in a voice gruff with emotion. "The least I can do, the only thing left I can do for Oberas, is to see you safely guarded, lad. Now then, why don't you come into the back and have some refreshment with me, before we begin? It's a long, dusty walk from the Brightwater, and I can see your new boots must be quite uncomfortable."

Rion was touched by Vargas's loyalty to Oberas and also greatly relieved, for he had seen that Tarrell should rest for a few minutes but hadn't known how to go about it without hurting his feelings.

They went through the curtain and saw a room with two doors. One door was open and led to the practice yard. The closed one likely led to his living quarters. The back room had a table and four chairs. Everyone but Aras sat as Vargas brought glasses, a pitcher of juice, and a plate of sliced melon.

Rion teased Tarrell gently, playing into Vargas's insight as he saw Tarrell squirm in his new clothes. "You think I'm uncomfortable in my new boots? Tarrell wanted to wear his old livery, but it is important these men see him as their employer from the start. They will respect his orders, where they might question mine."

"You just wanted to be sure I couldn't help test them. I can fight with my left hand, when I have need, and my arm heals well," Tarrell said defensively.

"And I'd like to see it heal fully. Besides, I think Talon chafes at inaction as much as you do and welcomes this chance to fight. Would you take that from him, after all the kindness he has shown us?" He turned to Talon. "Just go easy enough on them that some might pass your test."

Talon, who had been silent and brooding, smiled slightly. "Actually, Sword Master, I've a favor to ask. I'd like to borrow one of your blades for the test. To use my own would give me unfair advantage."

"Then come, select one," Vargas said, and the two left for the display room.

When they returned, Rion said, "If you wouldn't mind, Sword Master, this table and these chairs would come in handy outside, for Tarrell and I plan to take notes, to be sure we keep everyone straight." He did not think Tarrell could stand for any length of time.

Tarrell said, "You see, he thinks like a merchant and would inventory the men."

Rion blushed, but he was relieved to see Tarrell was up to teasing him.

"This will prove to be interesting," Vargas said, as he helped them with the table. "It will quite confuse my neighbors." They exited through the back door and soon understood the comment. The yard was as wide as the shop and three times as long, and faces peered out of doorways and from rooftops all along it. "I bought up their five yards years ago, to expand my own, and they get the added value of free entertainment. I suspect today shall be a rare treat for them."

The men were grouped together in twos and threes for the most part, in a rough line, with a few exceptions. They eyed the newcomers curiously. Rion noticed that Aras received several sharp glances and mutters. Having the advantage of standing so close and being able to see his face in spite of the cloak, Rion realized that Aras was smiling in apparent glee under his hood.

JARGAS considered the four critically: a swordsman, a wizard, and two merchants. The swordsman was tall, not as tall as him, of course, but as tall as Farad, and they shared the same build, long of leg and arm and leanly muscled. His eyes were blue rather than brown, though, and instead of dead, they were intense. Those eyes had seen much and missed little. His face looked younger than Farad's as well. It was a good face, strong of character. He'd be a good man to have at your back on the road.

Jargas viewed the wizard suspiciously. He wouldn't have come if he'd known about the wizard. Still, he was here now. He could tell little about him. He carried a staff, as did all his kind, and he was tall and thin, but he wore an oddly mottled brown cloak which covered much, and his hooded face was in shadow.

Jargas looked at the two merchants next. Neither of the two was old enough to know his trade. He hoped the wages would be secure. The older one had the look of illness about him too. No, not illness: injury. His right arm couldn't bend; it was useless to him. If he'd sustained such an injury, perhaps the sword at his side was not just for show, then. The hilt did look more functional than pretty, now that he looked at it. He didn't usually pay much attention to blades. He was intrigued. The other was still a boy in size and build, but he had the eyes of a man. And he was confident, but did not appear arrogant. An interesting party.

WHEN Tarrell and Rion were settled at the table, with Aras and Talon standing, Vargas asked all the men to get more fully in line, and they did so.

Vargas said, "They can all ride. At least those I don't know personally say they can. Although some ride better than others, and some fight better afoot."

Talon nodded. "My name is Talon," he called out to the men. "This is Aras, Master Rion, and his guardian, Swordsman Tarrell. We seek fourteen men to guard a merchant caravan to far Gosa, in the west. Aras and I will not be coming with you. You have all learned of the wolven-riders that have been plaguing the Road to

Athanark. This is some of what you will face. There will be mountains to cross and rivers to ford, as well as ogres, obearn, bandits, and other dark things to fight ere you reach Gosa. You will be paid five silver per day and a twenty-gold bonus upon reaching Gosa."

Talon had discussed the question of pay with Rion, to ensure he could afford so many men without leaving himself a pauper. The high bonus was to encourage the men to stay for the duration of the long journey. There was a pleased murmur: the wages were fair and the bonus was high. "There, four of you of his choosing will stay with Master Rion, until his business is concluded, and he may keep you on from there, if you've an interest in steady work."

Tarrell spoke. "I am Swordsman Tarrell, guardian of Master Rion. You will take your orders from me and from Master Rion."

One of the men muttered something under his breath, but Talon could not make it out, nor even be sure who had spoken. He looked coldly in the general direction of the sound, hoping the man might fidget nervously under his gaze, so he would at least know who the potential troublemaker was.

Aras's keen ears, however, were apparently up to the task, and his clear, strong voice piped up from under the hood. "Then you, in the blue and gray, we do not want you. Leave now," he said, pointing to the speaker, and he said it in a tone of command and with a presence that Talon had never heard from him before. Talon, and the others also, eyed him keenly, unsure of what had just happened.

Aras continued, "And any others of you who won't take orders from Master Rion may leave now as well."

Talon smiled to himself, thinking how the others must now think Aras might be reading the doubts in their minds, as well as hearing their softest whispers. This would be yet another test of their mettle.

There was a nervous mutter, but no one else moved. The man Aras had indicated cursed and stomped his feet, pushing past the others to the door. Vargas glared at him and followed him, no doubt to make sure he left without trouble and to relock the door to the shop behind him.

"Now, first we would know more of you," Rion said and pointed to the first man in the line. He asked him to give his name, the weapons he was skilled with, the length of time he'd worked as a guard and in what capacity, and surprisingly, whether he knew anything of healing. Rion took careful notes as he spoke, with Tarrell commenting here and there. They questioned the others similarly and made a list of names and details as they went. Talon noticed Vargas watched the proceedings with obvious interest.

RION tried his best not to stare at the ninth man in line, who stepped forward when his turn came. He was huge, a giant of a man, more than a head taller than Talon, larger even than Elkrum had been, well over seven feet tall and almost twice as broad as a normal man. His black hair was oiled and hung down his back in a single long, intricate braid made of dozens of thinner ones woven together in a complex pattern, and his beard went nearly to his waist and was oiled as well and braided in two long similar braids, Dwarven style, even to the gold rings at the end of each braid. His legs were like tree trunks, and his bulging arms were hairy like a Dwarf's, covered in thick black curls, bare save for the bucklers on his forearms.

When he spoke, his voice thundered clearly through the yard. "My name is Jargas. I'm a staff master. I need no other weapons, though I know the use of many," he said, holding out his massive staff for emphasis. "I have wielded a staff since I was a lad. I killed both my first ogre and obearn at sixteen and my first Man at twenty. Much of my guard work has been for my own village, but I know the Roads between here and Gosa, I've traveled them, and I've gone to the Dwarven Lands and back again. I know nothing of healing, for my sister's a healer, and I seldom take injury in any case."

JARGAS saw Talon's face pique with sudden interest. "Which Dwarven Kingdoms and how recently?" he asked.

"Malar in the Fromer Mountains. I just returned from there," Jargas replied.

Talon looked as if he wanted to hear more, but he nodded and turned his attentions to the next man in line.

Jargas saw that some of the spectators drifted from their doors, and some of the men in line were impatient by the time the interviewing was done. He wondered if Rion and Tarrell noted that, too, on their list.

"NOW to the test," Talon said, pointing to the first Man and saying from memory, "Rarnak, son of Vornak, you are first." He walked to the center of the yard and faced off with him. Rarnak strode confidently into the center opposite him.

They drew their blades and the bout began. Talon exchanged blows with Rarnak, testing his skill with the blade, as if he were leading him through a series of exercises both had rehearsed.

It became apparent that Rarnak realized his foe was toying with him, and could disarm him easily at any moment, and he angered. But his ability increased rather than decreased, and Talon smiled. When Talon finally effortlessly slipped his blade under Rarnak's guard and disarmed him with a quick twist of his blade a few parries later, Rarnak's anger melted. "Well fought, my friend! It is a shame you will not be making the journey with us!"

Talon smiled again. Rarnak was one of the best swordsmen he'd ever crossed blades with. He was glad this was only a test and he had not had to slay him. Rarnak had told them he had guarded three caravans and worked for a few years in Lomas as a City Guard. He certainly had the experience, bravery, and strength of character they needed. He added a few of his own comments to those Rion and Tarrell noted, and

Vargas did as well. Talon noticed that there were more faces in the doorways again, now that the fighting had begun.

JARGAS stared at Talon, stunned, his breath held. It was him! He hadn't realized it until Talon had smiled. He'd been a fool not to have seen it, but it had been long enough ago and far enough away, and much had happened since. This man was one of the two whose faces Jargas had seen as a bright flash in Farad's mind. He was one of the two living men Farad yet loved. Chosen or not, he would have a talk with Talon.

Man after man, each swordsman was tested. After the eighth in line, it was Jargas's turn. Jargas noted that the doorways were a sea of faces now, and that there were many people lining the rooftops on each side of the yard, as well. Jargas held up his staff. "As I told you earlier, this is my only weapon."

TALON thought he was old for a guard, perhaps forty, though he was a mountain of muscle and sinew and bone.

Jargas said, "A sword would be an unfair test and I would not wish to break your blade."

Jargas's eyes bored into his own, as if he were trying to view his core, but he felt no wave of Power. It was silly of him even to think it. Still, Talon wondered at the look, but he smiled. "But this sword is only borrowed, and I will pay Sword Master Vargas for it if you damage it. I must test you this way, for most of the foes you face will face you with swords, so I must see how you would fare against one."

Jargas nodded then and approached. They faced off and began.

For the first time, Talon faced a true challenge. Talon leapt and danced expertly away from each blow, but Jargas was astonishingly agile for one of his size, and Talon could get nowhere near him with his blade. For a good while neither could gain the upper hand. But Jargas was fresh, and Talon had already fought long duels with eight, and he was just an instant too slow to move his sword. Jargas's mighty staff cracked against the flat of the blade and sheared a full foot of steel off the tip. The blade fell from Talon's numbed hand as pain shot up the length of his wounded arm.

Aras stepped forward in concern, but Talon waved him away and picked up the sword in his other hand. "I would continue. I have fought with a broken blade before, and my left arm serves me as well as my right."

But Jargas shook his head, planting the end of his staff firmly on the ground. "I did not know you were already injured until I saw your face. But I'll not fight you further, sword to staff, even if it means I'll not be hired. You've seen I can defend myself against you, and it's not a fair test of my ability."

Aras called out then, his voice alight with mischief. "Then will you fight staff to staff, Mount Jargas?"

Jargas eyed Aras suspiciously. "My staff is only made of wood, Master Wizard. I'll not match it with yours."

Aras laughed and his eyes twinkled as he tossed off his cloak and leapt over to him like a deer. There was a gasp from the rooftops as the word "Elf" was echoed across them, and a cheer rang out. "My staff is of plain wood, as is your own. Or do you fear your fleet feet are no match for mine?"

Jargas smiled. "I have often wanted to pit my skill against one of your kind," he said. And they began. At first, they fought standard style, and their staffs cracked against each other as loud as thunderclaps. Talon's heartbeat quickened as he watched their deadly dance, at the thought of what one of those blows might do to his fair friend if ever he faltered. Slowly and deliberately, he crossed to one of the empty chairs and sat, putting his feet up on the table as if he were bored by the display. He would not risk distracting Aras and leading him to disaster.

With a gleam in his eye, Aras danced back and began to twirl his staff until the air hummed. A grin broke upon Jargas's face and he began to twirl his as well. They attacked again, and were again matched blow for blow. It appeared they could continue thus for the entire rest of the day, with neither gaining the upper hand.

"Hold!" Talon cried and rose from his chair, and the two parted instantly.

"I think you are well tested, Staff Master Jargas," Talon decreed. There were loud cheers from the rooftops, as well as from the line of men in front of them, and thunderous applause.

Aras grinned and bowed to them as if he were a street performer. Then he turned to Jargas, whose smile matched his own. "Well met, Staff Master Jargas!"

"Well met indeed, Staff Master Aras."

Vargas called a short break as Argo produced water for the combatants and Vargas selected a new blade for Talon. Then Talon called the next man in line.

One by one the others were tested individually by sword until the seventeenth man was called, Ronamark of Ogaten. The seventeenth, eighteenth, nineteenth, and twentieth stepped forward as one, as the name was called. The first spoke.

"I am Ronamark, and I speak for myself as well as my brothers. My brothers and I are all willing to be tested individually. You already know our weapons. You will find Garamark and Vanamark are not quite as skilled as Rarnak with a blade, but they excel at the bow. Aramark and I are equals to Rarnak with the blade, and while not as skilled as our brothers with the bow, we are still better than most. But, as Jargas requested a true test of his ability, we request one also. We would have you select any seven of the men you have already tested and are impressed with to join you in attacking the four of us as a group. Further, we ask that Aras or another you name stand in our center, for we would show you how well we can guard another from attack even against twice our number of skilled warriors."

Talon looked at Ronamark with interest.

Rion stood up. "Then you will guard me, as you would on the road."

Tarrell started to object, but Talon said, "Done. First I will test each of you individually, and then as you described."

Talon proceeded, and found to his delight that Ronamark had undervalued his own skill with the blade, for he was even better than Rarnak, almost his own equal. And Ronamark had judged his brothers' sword skills accurately.

Talon said, "Now then to the test you proposed. You and your opponents will lose favor with me if you actually draw blood. You must show the utmost control, for I will not have anyone harmed."

He saw the surprise on many of their faces and was certain that few of them had realized before that he had been holding back on his attacks, though they knew it now, and none of them had held back on their own.

"If an opponent is touched by a blade, he is considered out of combat and must fall and lie where he falls: Aras, Rarnak, Jathran, Rennon, Oldar, Lerdon, and Vekran, if you would be willing?"

Aras leapt forward silently, and the six others let out a hearty "Aye!" as they stepped forward proudly. Some of the others muttered to one another, for they now knew that Talon favored the other six in his choice for guards, although there were still four slots left open, even if the brothers pleased him. Jargas, who had not been chosen and might have expected to be, gave no sign of his thoughts.

JARGAS saw that when Rion made to move forward, Talon stopped him and bent and whispered something in his ear. Rion looked intent for a moment and then nodded. Then Talon went over to Aras and whispered something to him in what might have been Elvish, from the odd sound of the trace of it he could hear. Aras nodded.

Rion went to stand with the four brothers. Instantly they enveloped him in a box made of their bodies, each of them facing outward in opposite directions. Their assailants formed up outside the box, on all sides. "Begin," Talon commanded.

There was a flash of blades. Aras used both his swords. It soon became apparent that Talon was holding his blade back, keeping himself in reserve to intervene if any needed his aid to avoid injury. He let Aras perform his attacks for him.

AFTER a few blows, Talon saw Vekran touched by Ronamark's blade, so lightly he did not think Vekran felt it, and indeed he did not fall. "Vekran, fall," Talon commanded, and Vekran looked surprised but did as commanded.

As Aras pressed his attack to make up for the lack of an ally's blade, Talon watched the brothers with interest. The four weaved back and forth. To his surprise, though they fought in pairs, as he had expected, they did not keep the same pairs, but bonded to one and then another free-form, as the fight required. Oldar and Rennon were both struck almost simultaneously and fell.

Then as he watched, his blade blocking a blow from Ronamark, Aras lunged for Garamark and Vanamark at the same time, but he appeared to stumble. One sword arced toward Vanamark, unrestrained, and the other was heading for Rion. There was a shout of alarm from Tarrell and Vargas and gasps from the roof, and some of the other swordsmen surged forward, but all were too far away to help.

Garamark had dodged from the blade aimed at him, but in so doing had moved too far away to aid Vanamark, whom he had been partnered with. Vanamark had been caught off balance when Aras's attack went wild, accidentally dodging into the blade's path instead of away from it.

Talon saw Ronamark's and Aramark's eyes widen in horror, as both of them leapt to parry a blade, the same blade, the one that was coming for Rion, even as Rion fell to the ground. Just as suddenly Talon's blade was blocking Aras's blade to protect Vanamark, but as he hoped, there was no clang of metal on metal as the blow never fell. Ronamark and Aramark bent to check on Rion, and there were many shouts and utter chaos.

"**Hold!**" Talon shouted, his voice echoing across the yard, and everyone froze where they stood. "This was all part of the test. No one is hurt," he called out clearly, and then there was movement again, but calmer: the panic had evaporated.

JARGAS looked at Talon intently. He'd felt the wave of Power flow around him. Farad had used such a voice upon Gervan in Malar. The King's Voice, he'd called it. Talon used it here now on two dozen men or more, as if it were nothing to do so!

There was the buzz of confused, excited voices.

RION stood up and hugged Tarrell, who was at his side, white-faced and shaking. Rion spoke soothingly to him.

Ronamark and Aramark were pale and shaking as well, as they turned from Rion to Vanamark, eyeing him critically for injury and then hugging him fiercely. Garamark was trembling, forgotten for a moment, until Vanamark pulled away from his other brothers and embraced him.

Talon gave them a moment together before he spoke. "Forgive me for the test, but it was necessary. Your pattern worked well, but you are brothers, and it is obvious you truly love each other. I had to see what you might do when given the choice of saving your employer or your kinsman. I picked the youngest as victim and the oldest as potential rescuers on purpose. You kept to your pattern, though it would have cost Vanamark his life. Had you broken your pattern, you still would not have been able to save Vanamark, but were this not a test, Rion would have died when you tried."

Ronamark looked at Talon as if he were a demon.

"You asked me to test you. I have tested you. You have passed," Talon said solemnly.

"Were you to offer us the position, if you were to be coming with us, we would not take it," Ronamark swore.

Talon nodded. "I can understand that. But I want you to know that Vanamark was never in any danger, nor was Rion, despite how it might have looked. I had instructed both Rion and Aras in advance. I had Rion fall for safety's sake, and you saw that I moved to stop Aras's blade as a precaution, but that our blades did not even touch. Aras was in control the entire time, as I knew he would be."

"I hate you for it, still. We have always known one of us might die, that we might not be able to save him, but to experience it...." Ronamark's voice shook with the horror of it.

"Be thankful, then, that it was only a test. You all yet live. I know many men who would give anything to stand where you stand now, with your brothers still about you." Talon fought grief at the thought of Farad's lost brothers, at the thought of so many others who had fallen. Farad! Farad too was now gone. Dead, all dead, so many gone, entire families, entire Houses.

"We will take another break," he called out grimly, fighting his despair, fighting the urge to burn it away with the sun. He could not afford to appear weak to these men, nor to Aras, not again. "Testing will resume shortly." He turned and went inside the back room of the weapons shop. Aras followed.

After a brief respite, Talon emerged from the shop with Aras. Talon conducted the rest of the testing efficiently and emotionlessly.

ARAS judged the bow work of the six bowmen, four of whom were the Ogaten brothers. They all shot in teams of two against each other on the targets Vargas set out. Garamark and Vanamark indeed shot as well as Ronamark had claimed: each time they let loose a flight of arrows, they hit square on the mark, and Garamark and Vanamark's arrows were so tightly clustered in the center of the target they appeared to be a single thick shaft.

Impressed by the feat, Aras spoke to Talon softly. "I had not known Men could wield the bow as effectively as they do. I have heard there is a tribe of nomads in a land called Aralon who shoot almost as well as we Elves do, though I had doubted it. Might they be from there?"

Aras was alarmed to see pain flash across Talon's face at his innocent words.

MEMORY seized Talon, with the merciless force of an ogre's hand about his throat. He fought to breathe, to stand. Farad had used an Aralon bow, the one Lord Halon had gifted to him a century ago in Thenalon, during the War. Lord Halon had not survived the War, and now Farad was just as dead.

Talon shook his head and found his voice enough to choke out a single sentence. "Those are not their bows, nor their arrows, nor do they have the look of the Horsemen of Aralon."

He turned from Aras. He could not say more.

ARAS eyed his friend in concern. Talon was in grief, in agony. It was more than the recent loss of his kinsman Beryl. Something else was preying upon his spirit. If only

Talon would speak to him, confide in him, he might find some way to comfort him, to help him.

TALON called out that the testing was done. He, Aras, Rion, Tarrell, and Vargas compared their notes, and the fourteen men were chosen.

Talon called out the names of those who had not been chosen, and Rion gave each five silver for their time. That somewhat cheered them, and they left to drink to their loss with their day's wages.

The other fourteen were called: Rarnak, Jargas, the four Ogaten brothers, Lerdon, Jathran, and six others. Jargas was assigned as their Captain, as he had earned the respect of all the others. Each of them also received five silver for the test, except for Jargas, who received eight for his new rank. They also all received an invitation to dinner at the Brightwater from Rion and were told to meet them again at the inn in the morning, where they would be measured for guardsmen's livery.

Dinner was a loud and festive affair. After it was done, the new guardsmen left for their homes or inns, all except Jargas, who lingered and asked if he might stay and drink with the four of them. They welcomed him heartily.

Jargas asked Talon how he'd injured his arm, and Talon told him. Then he asked why they wouldn't be traveling with them, and Talon lied and told him that he had business in the Dwarven Lands, across the Fromer Mountains, that he and Aras were headed to Dorolingas in a few days' time.

Jargas eyed him carefully. "Then I should tell you that the pass at Dorolingas has been sealed and save you from finding out on your own. Malar is still open, though."

Talon looked intrigued. "Then I would use the pass at Ironhand, for Malar is not to my liking."

Jargas sighed. "You'd be wasting your time there as well. Malar is the only way through, now. If King Balgar was what was keeping you from getting too close to Malar, you need not be so wary. His son, Valar, now rules, much to the betterment of the Kingdom."

"I find it curious that two of the three passes have so recently been sealed. Would you care to enlighten me on that?" Talon asked.

Jargas met his gaze evenly. "There's an Enemy who's fought His way across the Dwarven Lands, all the way from beyond the Deathshand Mountains. He's smashed Kingdom after Kingdom over the past two and a half centuries. If my people had banded together, they could have beaten Him long ago. They've finally seen it now, or it's been shown to them, at least. The last three Dwarven Kingdoms are banded together in an alliance. They've sealed two of the passes to funnel the Enemy toward the one remaining pass, where the three armies will wait for Him and His army. They've sworn to hold their Mountains to the last Dwarf or until the King comes with his army to join theirs."

"King? Which King?" Talon's voice was soft, his eyes riveted on Jargas's.

"The Lord of the Watch, Hunter's King. You know him," Jargas stated confidently, watching Talon just as carefully.

"Who, the King?" Talon said with a laugh, but his laugh sounded hollow, and he drank deeply from the mug in his hand.

"Aye, you well might. Hunter is the one I meant, though." Jargas was gazing at him shrewdly.

"I've known many men named Hunter. It's a common traveling name," Talon said casually, looking at him levelly.

Jargas would have believed he truly was unconcerned, save for what he'd seen before, in Talon's eyes and in Farad's mind. "Your eyes betrayed you, Talon. I read much from them at the name: shock, longing, anguish, despair. Why should one man's name mean so much to you?"

Jargas saw Aras's gaze lock on Talon, full of concern for his friend.

"You are mistaken," Talon said, and his voice was iron.

"You are as close-mouthed as he is, sitting there listening innocently to me speaking of the Enemy, wondering if five more Dwarven Kingdoms could all truly have fallen in the twelve years since you've seen Hunter. They have. Shall I describe Hunter to you? He's tall, like you, your build, too; his hair is dark and his eyes are brown. They are dead eyes, to those who don't know him, a predator's eyes, hard and pitiless. He has a scar that goes from temple to chin across his left eye, but he wasn't blinded by it. He dresses all in brown and has an unusually long bow of a strange white wood, and his arrows are overly long and fletched with eagle feathers. Like this one."

Pulling out the feather Hunter had given him from the buckler over his right forearm, he laid it gently on the table. He didn't yet reveal the band, which his buckler concealed. Farad had counseled him to keep it hidden in public, lest the Enemy's spies see it and target him because of it.

Talon had listened dispassionately to the description, until Jargas mentioned the eagle feathers. Jargas had seen the façade begin to crumble and had been surprised, but at the sight of the notched eagle feather a look of anguish crossed Talon's face, and the hand that reached for the feather trembled. Jargas slipped it back into his buckler. "If you would speak more of him, I would meet with you in private," he said, concerned now. Why should sight of the feather affect him so?

Talon's eyes searched his face, and Jargas caught glimpses of suspicion and fear and indecision. "Did he tell you his given name?" Talon asked, his voice gravelly.

Jargas nodded. "That and more besides."

"Then we must talk." He rose and Jargas did as well. But when Aras made to follow, Talon said, "I'm sorry, my friend, but these words are for my ears alone."

Jargas saw the look of concern in Aras's face replaced by one of hurt and wounded pride.

Talon called the innkeeper for a keg of mead, and they took it up to his room along with their two steins.

Once there, Talon said, "I would hear all you know of my kinsman, but first I would hear his given name and how you came to know it."

"His name is Farad, son of Jarad, Lord of House of Wolven, of Amontir."

Talon's eyes widened. "Why, even if he told you his given name, would he betray his true name and identity to you by revealing his father and his House?"

"Because he was lost to madness and could not help himself," Jargas answered honestly.

Talon collapsed onto his bed, as if a marionette whose strings had been cut. "Mad? Not dead as I thought, but mad? No, not that. Anything but that; even dead, but not mad. And he severed his bond to me, when I might have helped him? Two kinsmen lost, two Houses, one to madness and one to death? And the Dwarves await the King?"

Talon's eyes had taken on a wild look, and Jargas suddenly feared for him. Talon had shown none of the weakness before that Farad had. He had not dreamt the effect his words might have had upon Talon, or he would have chosen them more carefully. Jargas grabbed his shoulders and shook him. "Talon, he is not mad now. He is healed, he is well, as well as he can be and still be the man you know."

Jargas saw Talon try to calm himself. He drew great breaths, but there was fear on his face, turning to panic and then horror, as if he were being dragged over a cliff and could not escape. "It is too late, too much. I cannot stop it. The Sword is not strong enough; I am not strong enough." Talon tore off his gloves, his hands shaking violently.

Jargas saw Talon's eyes flare brightly, lit from behind with the same wild fire that had tried to consume Farad. Talon was drawing his sword against him, and the sword itself was glowing with a strange red fire. Jargas cracked Talon's wrist against his knee, and the sword went flying. Talon let out a bone-chilling cry of loss as the light left the sword.

Jargas tried to force himself into Talon's mind as he had forced himself into Farad's, but he reeled as a dark wave instead crashed against his own core, almost overwhelming it. He clung desperately to the strands that bound him to Jarina and Farad, terrified they would break, but they were like iron. He was fed by both of them and strengthened. He pinned Talon to the floor, but he controlled only his body; his mind was already lost. Jargas could not reach him, and still Talon battered against his core, like a storm lashing him.

The door to the room flew open and suddenly Aras was there with them.

"I'm trying to help him, not harm him," Jargas said desperately, afraid Aras would attack him and not see the true danger.

But Aras went to Talon's side and held Talon's head in his hands and their eyes locked. Jargas saw that Aras's eyes blazed with a silver light.

"You call and I come. There is no Madness, there is no panic, there is no terror, no failure, no helplessness, nor grief, nor sorrow, nor self-pity. All the torments that plague you flee from my light. I banish them for you. They are gone, all gone, and they will not come to you again, not while I am here to protect you, and I will never leave you. I will not die, I will not be captured, I will not be killed, I will not go mad. I am your anchor, I am your lifeline, I am your tie to self. None can harm you while I watch over you. You are well now, you are safe, you are healed."

Jargas saw the light leave Talon's eyes, and they were a clear, lucid blue again. The light left Aras's eyes as well, though it smoldered for a long moment, as if it would not be quenched so easily.

Talon looked at Aras in wonder. "How is it you can see with the King's Eyes when you are not kin to me, when you are not even an Amontir, but an Elf? How can you have such Power over my mind and heart?" Talon asked, incredulous. "Not even Arcanus could have done what you have just done."

Aras swallowed and looked at him in confusion and fear, all the earlier confidence and strength leached from his gaze. "I do not know. I do not understand what is happening to me. I cannot feel you bound to me, as I am bound to you. I am still alone. I have ever always only been alone. I do not want to be alone any longer, I did not think I would be now, bound to you as I am. Can you not feel me as I feel you? Can you not touch me?"

TALON stood and hugged Aras tightly, wrapping his strong arms around him as if he were a child, for all his Power. Aras was trembling violently. Talon turned his gaze inward and looked for the vine about his core, but instead found that a great tree had grown up around his core, encasing it completely. He could not even see his core anymore, but the thought did not frighten him as it should: the tree was more beautiful than any he had ever seen, silver barked and leafed, a tree of moonlight, of pallenteum.

"I cannot even try to reach you. You have sealed me away completely." He described his former bonds to his lost kinsmen, both how they had looked and how they had felt, and compared them to his earlier strange bond to Aras and this current one, which was unlike anything he had ever imagined.

"Arcanus will be able to explain it to us," Talon said, but it sounded hollow in his own ears. It was not just that he did not think Arcanus would be able to help him. Suddenly he felt that he did not want Arcanus to know, that he must not know about Aras, ever.

Talon felt eyes upon him then. He kept his arm about Aras and turned to Jargas. He had been so distracted by Aras's distress that he had forgotten Jargas was even in the room with them. "You also saw with the King's Eyes."

JARGAS nodded. "I am kin to you. I have that Power. I am bonded to Hunter by it, and to one other."

"How can you be? You are not kin to us. You cannot be. I know every surviving member of every House," Talon challenged.

"I wear the armband of House of Gryphon," Jargas said and removed the buckler that blocked it from sight about his wrist. He did not lie. He did not say he was Lord of that House, only that he wore the band. He knew that Talon would make the wrong assumption, as he must, for now. Jargas could not yet reveal himself. He must talk to Farad again before he did so.

Talon's eyes widened. "Then we have lost only one House, where I thought we had lost two, and we have regained a House long thought lost. Welcome Jargas, Lord of House of Gryphon. I would talk more to you, but later, for now Aras needs me. But first, I must be sure. You said Hunter is well? Despite what I felt, what I feared, he yet lives?"

"Aye. We parted only a week ago. We did not have an easy journey from Malar, and it took much longer than he had hoped. He was anxious to be on his way. I gave him the last of my coin, to speed him on his journey, and told him I would come here and find work to get me back home. He headed north. There is still much I would like to tell you, about what happened in Malar, and there is much I need to learn."

"On the morrow, Jargas," Talon said, his tone one of command, brooking no argument.

Jargas reluctantly agreed. "We will speak later." He left the two of them, wondering at all that had happened, all he had seen and heard. Talon had welcomed him as Lord of what he thought was his House, but Farad had told him only the Prince, the rightful King of the Amontir, could do so. Was Talon then Dewalaren, the King Farad had saved from Madness twelve years ago?

TALON felt pity for his people, that they were so desperate they would embrace him as their King, even knowing the Madness might claim him at any moment, that he might slay them all as his great grandsire had slain their forefathers. As he had once tried to slay them.

Aras looked at him, eyes alight with fear instead of Power. Talon could not think of himself now, not when Aras was in need.

Talon and Aras talked long into the night, but they knew no more when they finished than when they had begun.

Finally, Aras slept, but Talon stayed awake. Despite what Talon had told Jargas, he could not speak to Jargas, not when his core was trapped within the tree and he could not reach out to test Jargas's claim. Farad's token and Jargas's Power were not enough. An agent of the Enemy might be able to show the same evidence; they had been deceived more than once in the past with such a ruse. Yet if Jargas was a minion of the Enemy, it would mean that Farad was truly dead. After having been given a glimmer of hope that his cousin yet lived, he could no longer bear to accept that he might not. He loved his older cousin, he missed him fiercely, and he wished for the thousandth time that Farad had not left them.

Talon looked at Aras tenderly. He looked troubled even in his sleep. Talon wished he could ease his friend's fears better than he had been able. Talon stroked Aras's forehead, and the crease left Aras's brow as he nuzzled against Talon's hand in his sleep.

Talon was awash in memory of being young and afraid, with the Power still new inside him. Talon remembered how his father had first described his Power to him, when he was still a boy, only ten years of age, for his Power had been strong even then, too strong.

EVANAREN had looked at him intently and begun. "What you and I and all of those kin we call the Amontir share is something no others in all the lands of this world have. All those we once called Lesser Men, the Dwarves, and even the Elves do not share our gift. Their minds are like walnuts: small, cold, dark, and protected with a brittle shell," he said, showing Dewalaren a walnut in its shell for emphasis. "You can view their cores, but never touch them. At the slightest touch, this would happen." He took his heavy crystal paperweight and slammed it down upon the nut. The shell shattered and the nut meat and shards pulped together.

Dewalaren had jumped at the violent display. His father showed him the crystal, brushing off the nut meat. The crystal was no longer perfect: it was chipped and scarred where it had struck the nutshell.

"The mind you would touch would shatter, but you would damage yourself as well, though you might not even feel it. You might not realize it. If you did such things enough, you would eventually lead to your own destruction. It is perhaps nature's way of protecting the others of this world from us."

Dewalaren had nodded, imagining how he might turn someone into a drooling madman with the merest thought. It was terrifying.

"You may safely touch only the mind of another with the Power, Dewalaren. Only your kinsmen. To do so in a certain way forms a bond between your mind and the other person, a bond you can see, at least with your inner eye, and feel; it is like a metal thread, a wire, made of pyrenteum, the King's Metal, like the Sword you will one day wield. Children are born connected to their mothers by such bonds, while fathers gently forge them. You and I are connected by such a bond," he had said and had tugged lightly on the bond.

Dewalaren's eyes had widened. "I can see it! And I feel you!" he said, in wonder. A wave of warmth had flowed through the bond, and he had basked in the feeling of his father's love for him. His father had smiled at him in joy, and then his face had grown serious again.

"You can aid another through your bond. You can help him in times of need, offering your strength. But always you must take care. For the bond is fragile and easily broken. But also, you must never rely upon another for strength, even when it is offered, especially when it is offered. You can take too much. You can kill one you love in such a manner. It is why we refrain from touching the bond and feeling through it, except in times of greatest need," Evanaren had cautioned.

"Is that how Mother died?" Dewalaren had asked, with a child's innocence. He had only vague memories of his mother. He did not feel loss thinking of her, only curiosity. But he had felt agony then, for the first time in his young life, as fire had coursed down the length of the bond that touched him. He reacted without thinking, pulling back and striking at the pain. Suddenly the pain was gone, but everything else was gone as well; there was only blackness.

When he could see and feel and hear and think again, he discovered he was lying in a well-lit room, but one not his own. He recognized it; he had been here once before. He was in the House of Healing. He could hear hushed voices speaking.

"… can do for him. Even in his Madness, he is too powerful. I cannot reach him. We are fortunate his attack upon Dewalaren weakened him so greatly. What Power the boy must have had to have done so! Evanaren could have killed us all before we could restrain him, had it not been for his son. I had never thought to see the Madness in Evanaren. He had never before shown any sign of it, not even when his wife died." Dewalaren recognized the voice of Gefan, their Master Healer.

"What of Dewalaren?" a deep, grief-stricken voice asked, and Dewalaren recognized it as that of his uncle, Jarad, Lord of House of Wolven, Protector and Friend of his father, and his father's closest friend. "If Evanaren is lost to us, our hope lies with his son."

"I dare not try to reach Dewalaren. He shielded himself from his father's attack somehow. To try to penetrate the shield could kill him, or destroy his mind, if it is yet intact. I have never before been so helpless…." Gefan's voice faded out of the range of his hearing.

But his father had not attacked him! It had been memory only, the pain of loss. He saw his mother clearly now, through his father's memories of her, and understood what his innocent words had done. He saw the bond his parents had shared, a fierce, bright love that had joined them so closely.

His mother had died saving his father. His father had not taken her strength: she had thrust it upon him, leaving none for herself. His father had never forgiven himself for her death. He had survived the loss of his beloved wife only because of his son.

But Dewalaren had severed their bond and sealed himself away, and his father must have thought him dead, or worse, his mind shattered to pulp and shell like the walnut. He must find his father and repair the damage he had accidentally caused.

He left his bed and walked barefoot to the door. He opened the shield around his mind and instantly knew where to go. He walked down the hall, saw another door, and opened it. His father was there. He was bound to the bed, but not conscious.

One of the other healers, Alarson, was there. He turned, eyes widening in concern and something else when he saw Dewalaren standing there so silently. Fear. He was afraid of him!

"You should not be here, Dewalaren," Alarson said, approaching him.

"Stand aside. I command you to silence," Dewalaren said, meaning only to speak as a Prince. But he spoke with the King's Voice; he could feel the Power flow from him, and to his shock the healer was silenced, and he moved aside submissively, eyes glazed, entranced. Dewalaren swallowed and continued to the bed. He had done more than he meant to. It frightened him that he had done so.

He looked down at his father, wide-eyed. His father had always been a pillar of strength, but now he appeared weak and helpless. He was drugged; Dewalaren felt the cloud over his mind. And he was bound. Or he would not be helpless or weak. The drugs might make this difficult.

He touched his father's cheek. "Father, you must hear me. It is Dewalaren. I am not harmed, I am safe. But there is much only you can teach me. I cannot lose you so soon. I am frightened. I do not want to be alone."

He reached out with his mind, but his father could not hear him that way, either. His father's core was a jagged turmoil of thoughts, feelings, and memories. Linking to it might bring the Madness to him. But he had little choice. He must try to undo the damage he had done to the father he loved. He had never meant to harm him. If the cost of saving his father was his own sanity, or his life, so be it.

Dewalaren found the snarled, broken strand that had once bonded them and straightened it and extended it. He reached outward with it toward the ragged opposite end, which was protruding from his father's core. He touched the two ends together.

The Madness surged through the wire toward his core, but it met a wall of pyrenteum. The wall became a wave, pushing back down the length of the bond. The wave flowed over his father's core, as water churns over jagged rock; it slowly began to calm, in the way water wears away the jagged edges of stone over the centuries, turning it into smooth river rock. The Power coursed back and forth across his father's core, the ripples intersecting one another over and back again until finally they became still.

Can you hear me, Father? Dewalaren asked with his mind alone this time.

I hear you, my son, his father answered.

Forgive me! I did not understand my words. I did not realize I harmed you by them. I never meant to. I've tried to make you well again. Dewalaren felt a flow of something across their bond, something different: not warmth, but fear. *Why are you afraid of me?* Dewalaren asked, astonished and dismayed.

You cannot be so young, so untrained, yet so strong!

Please, you must not fear me. You must teach me more. You had only just begun. This Power frightens me. Dewalaren let his father feel his loneliness then, and his own fear, carefully, lest it overwhelm him. Suddenly the warmth he remembered, that he longed for, was back again.

I will help you, my son. A father can do no less. And you have saved me from the Madness. But you are so young to have touched it. I hope it will not prove ill for you. You must return to your own core now, Dewalaren. You must try to never again leave your own so fully. To outside eyes you will appear dead. The healers must not move your body, or you might never find yourself again.

Dewalaren left his father's core and followed the copper strand back to his own core. He stood looking at it. It was shiny, it gleamed of pallenteum, but it was dark, so very dark; it frightened him to see it so. He reached his hand toward it instinctively, not sure what he needed to do next.

Dewalaren's eyes opened. He had been slumped over his father's bed, but now he stood. Dewalaren sensed fear then, not from his father, but from behind him. He was being watched.

He turned slowly, doing his best to appear nonthreatening. There were six Lords in the room. Jarad was amongst them, and he had an arrow nocked against him. He saw Jarad swallow as he looked at him, but his hand did not waiver.

"You should not fear me, Jarad," Dewalaren said softly.

"Are you Dewalaren or Evanaren?" Jarad asked cautiously.

Dewalaren was surprised. "You think my father has stolen my body because his own is bound and drugged? No, Uncle, it is truly me."

Jarad was not reassured. "Let Alarson go, Dewalaren."

Dewalaren turned and looked at the healer. His Voice still held him prisoner, even while he'd been helping his father. "Of course. Forgive me, Alarson. I had only meant to command you as your Prince. I had not meant to seize your will," he said as he carefully released his hold upon him.

Once Alarson could move of his own free will again, he drew quickly away, trembling.

Evanaren's eyes opened and Dewalaren gazed at him in love and joy and then looked intently at Jarad. "I am not mad, Jarad, nor is my father, at least, not any longer. I have cured him of his Madness. I have repaired the damage I did to him. I hadn't meant to hurt him. I'm sorry I frightened you all. Please, I humbly ask that you see for yourselves, that you untie him, once you feel it is safe to do so." He made sure his words held no Power this time, not even the power of his station.

Gefan approached the bed. He raised his hand and moved it toward Evanaren. "With his Highness's permission?" he asked. Evanaren nodded, and Gefan touched his face.

His eyes took on a distant cast as he focused them inwards. He stepped back a moment later, exhaling in relief. "Evanaren is well," he confirmed. Two of the Lords stepped forward to begin severing the ropes that bound him, but Jarad still did not lower his bow.

"Wait. You must test Dewalaren as well," Jarad insisted.

"Test me? Oh, of course."

Gefan touched his face and Dewalaren felt a gentle breeze blow across his core, nothing more. Then the healer removed his hand. "His mind is too powerful. It is closed to me," Gefan said, and there was fear in his voice. The Lords shifted uneasily.

"Do not fear my son," Evanaren said, speaking for the first time since waking. "He will not harm you. He had not meant to harm me. It was my own fault that he did so. I harmed him first, without meaning to, when I should have been more careful. 'Carelessness can kill even the most seasoned warrior.' How well I know that proverb, but I've also learned it can harm those you love. Dewalaren is young for such Power, but his youth gives him innocence as well. His heart knows only love, and that is what it returns. I wish he could remain always so."

His father had known even then; he had seen it. As the world touched him with its darkness, as he saw pain and death dealt to those around him, as he learned to inflict it himself, his core was altered by it.

The Madness had first come to claim him twelve years ago. He'd wielded the King's Sword for decades, but he'd never needed its true Power until that fateful day, when the Madness had come. It had seized him so suddenly. Kathalanar had flamed to Power, it had burned with red light, but the fire in it had quickly died. Without the

King's Ring to power it, the Sword was no match for the raging Power that consumed him from within.

Dewalaren had attacked his kin, Sword still in hand, as they tried desperately to restrain him. Fortunately his Power was flowing so wildly he could not focus it to harm them. But his Sword was an extension of his hand; he needed no rational thought to wield it to deadly effect, and no other blade could stand for long against it. His kin desperately parried his attack, but they would not attack him themselves. All except Farad.

Farad had overpowered both of his Guard, taken one's bow, nocked an arrow, and promptly driven it into the wrist of Dewalaren's sword hand. When he still did not release the blade, Farad drove two other arrows into his forearm, the third aimed so carefully it avoided bone and drove clear through the soft meat of his arm, pinning his arm to the back of the wooden chair beside him. The Sword had fallen from his hand then, and half the Lords had leapt forward and further pinned him, calling for rope to bind him.

The other Lords came for Farad, for his attack upon the Prince. But incredibly, Farad spoke with the Power of the King's Voice. **"You will not bind me. Stand aside so I might help him."** And entranced, all had obeyed. Then Farad had taken Dewalaren's head into his hands, forcing him to look into his dead brown eyes. And his eyes had changed.

Dewalaren saw the red-gold light of Power blaze from behind them. But it was more than the light. He saw Farad's heart in his eyes. He saw all the anguish the coldness masked: the love for his father and his mother and three brothers, who had been tortured to death by the Enemy to torment him. He saw love in those terrible eyes, for all those he had lost, but also for his Prince, in his anguish. And Farad's Voice was of steel melting in the forge as he spoke to him; it was not the words he spoke, but the Voice. Dewalaren felt the warmth and then the heat. And the light from Farad's Eyes and the heat from his Voice had burned the Madness away. But Farad had done more. He warded Dewalaren against further harm and did not break the link that now bonded their cores together.

When he was done, Farad released the Lords. They welcomed their Prince back in relief and joy. That day, Dewalaren named his cousin Farad Heir to the Throne, should he fall, for he had no son, and all had seen that the King's blood ran true in him.

But there were many dark mutterings outside of Dewalaren's hearing, for of all of them, only Dewalaren did not fear their cold cousin, and the Lords now had much more to fear between Farad's newly revealed Power, and the power of the throne he might one day inherit. Dewalaren learned of their fear too late from Lunahr, his twelve-year-old cousin, after Farad was already gone in his self-imposed exile.

Farad must have seen their fear, or felt it. Farad had left without a word to any of them, only a letter to Dewalaren that stated he was going as an envoy to the Dwarven Lands, to unite the Dwarven Kingdoms. And in the twelve long years that had followed, there had been no word from him.

Then, six years ago, the Madness had come again. This time, Farad was not there to save him; the bond was not broken, yet he did not come across it to aid him when he might have. But aid had come to him again, from an even less likely source: Lunahr, who was but a boy, only eighteen.

The Amontir aged far more slowly than other Men. Lunahr had not yet come-of-age; he would come-of-age at twenty-five. He should never have had Power enough to save him at such a young age, not when Dewalaren had Power unequaled in all their long history. But Lunahr, with his soothing eyes of green alight with laughter and hope and love, had come to him, singing; he was seldom without a song on his lips.

Dewalaren had been writhing and screaming on the floor alone this time, fighting against the Madness, trying not to harm anyone but himself. He had barely heard the song at first, but the words and the melody washed over him, cooling the fire of his Madness.

Lunahr had healed him with his song so gently, lovingly, and warded him against further Madness with it, at least for a time. He now knew that such efforts could not last for long. When he'd come to himself again, Lunahr's arms were about him, not restraining him, but hugging him, in love and in joy that he was well again.

The Lords did not fear Lunahr as they had feared Farad. They loved him, they had always loved him; everyone loved him. He was like a younger brother to all of them, a foster brother, for his parents, Lord and Lady of House of Eagles, were dead. Lunahr had been too young to be named Lord of his House when his parents died, though he was the last of the Eagles. Dewalaren's mother and Farad's had both been of Eagles, but they had died even before Lunahr was born.

Dewalaren named Lunahr Lord then. He placed the band of House of Eagles about his arm and named him Heir to the Throne, after Farad, should Farad fail to reappear, or fall. It hurt knowing the other Lords hoped Farad would die in the Dwarven Lands, that many of them were convinced he already had.

It hurt further to send Lunahr away. He had been the one spot of brightness in their lives, of joy and laughter and song. But they could not risk him falling into the Enemy's hands, ever. He was last of his House and King's Heir besides. But he was so much more: he was their last child, their spirit, their heart. They sent him to Riviera, Jewel of the River Kingdoms, to the Elves, to safety.

TALON returned painfully to the present. He had not sent his young cousin to safety, as he had hoped. He had sent him to his death. It had taken six years, but the Enemy had found him and killed him. He supposed he should be grateful, knowing Lunahr had died fighting a horde of mindless Revenants who did not understand his importance, that he would have been so mutilated by their attack that even his body would be worthless to the Enemy. If the Enemy himself had found Lunahr, it would have been so much worse, terribly worse, horrifyingly worse.

Aras tossed and moaned in his sleep, as if Talon's dark thoughts were haunting him as well. Gently he stroked Aras's face again. Aras was so young, so innocent: he reminded Talon of Eladar, Elanara's younger brother. It had been such an unbearably long time since he'd seen Elanara in Erenia, since he'd been with her.

He felt the fear building again. If Lunahr had been killed, had Riviera been overrun? What if Elanara had been there, instead of still in Erenia? Had she been killed as well? He shuddered at the thought of what the Revenants would have done to her. *Idare, please let her have died quickly, even by her own hand. Please don't let them have tortured and defiled her,* he prayed silently. It was a futile prayer, he knew. Whatever her fate had been, it was already long past. She either lived or not, had been tortured and raped or not.

Talon jerked back in surprise at the feeling of arms around him. He had not seen Aras waken. He had not expected his embrace.

Aras looked hurt by his reaction. "I only sought to comfort you. You are in such turmoil I cannot sleep. I should be able to help you, but I don't know how."

Aras's voice was so young, so lost, so filled with pain, that Talon's heart immediately went out to him. He hugged Aras back. "It is all right, Aras. Forgive me. You startled me, that is all. I did not realize my thoughts were intruding upon your rest. I did not realize they could. Your bond to me is so strange. I did not realize that you protect me from harm, yet can be harmed by me."

Talon felt the tension in Aras ease as he found comfort in his arms. "Please come to bed, Talon. We've a long ride ahead of us, and you might fall ill again if you do not rest."

Talon sighed. "Still you do not believe me. I do not take ill as other Men do. I have had many sleepless nights, hundreds. It is easier for me to count the nights I have ever slept than those I have not. But I would not make you ill, either, and if in order for you to rest, I must, then so be it, I will." He lay down beside Aras then and felt Aras relax further. "Though I have little idea how I am to still my thoughts so that I might sleep," Talon said softly.

"I can help you sleep," Aras said. To Talon's surprise, Aras began to sing, softly, sweetly. Only one other he knew had such a beautiful voice, and the thought of Lunahr, which had only moments ago brought anguish to him, brought only joy and love and comfort now. Talon's eyes slowly closed as his mind drifted away on Aras's song.

ARAS made sure Talon was fully asleep before he ended his song. It had not been an easy thing to layer his Power into the song so subtly that Talon did not realize he was using it upon him. The thought troubled him only for a moment. Talon's face was so peaceful now. Aras smiled at Talon in joy and love and drifted off to sleep as well, his arm protectively over Talon's chest.

IN THE morning, Talon and Aras knocked on Rion and Tarrell's door and told them they would be leaving after breakfast. Rion was dismayed they planned to leave already, though not surprised. He and Tarrell had been concerned about them both the previous night, when Talon had been so upset about Hunter and then failed to reappear after leaving to speak with Jargas, and Aras had appeared so bereft before excusing himself only moments later.

Talon asked that they give Jargas his apologies, and that they tell Jargas he could not stay and speak with him further, as he had originally intended.

To Rion, it seemed it was not because Talon was in a hurry to leave, but, conversely, he might be leaving so abruptly specifically to avoid Jargas. Yet Talon did not warn them against Jargas, so it could not be that Jargas was any sort of potential threat to them. But was he perhaps a danger to Talon, somehow? Or a threat to his friend Hunter? Rion was more than a little curious, but he would not ask. They owed Talon and Aras their lives. They were certainly entitled to their privacy, if they wished to keep their own counsel.

Rion told Talon and Aras that once their guards were outfitted with livery and horses were found for the four who had none, they would be ready to travel. He assured them that their trading was exceeding their expectations. They had learned that they were the first merchants in two months to have gotten through to the City and were selling their merchandise to excellent profit.

Though they were converting much of their capital to coin, there were also certain goods here they could not pass up, for they knew they would fetch high prices in the west, from all they had learned from Oberas. Rion told Talon and Aras that when they left, they would have fourteen guards and only two wagons of goods and provisions, so they would stand an excellent chance of faring well in an attack. He wanted to ensure that neither Talon nor Aras felt guilty about leaving. He and Tarrell did not want to add to whatever burdens their new friends were carrying by having them worry about them as well.

Rion was particularly concerned about Aras. Talon had been taciturn and moody since he had first met him, on the Road and what little he had seen of him since, but Aras had been far different during their long talks, friendly, warmhearted, and guileless, with a child's eagerness and open curiosity over everything he saw, heard, and learned. Now Aras looked so unlike the Elf they'd come to know, sad and even frightened, quiet and withdrawn.

They asked Talon and Aras to stop by their room again after they ate, before leaving. They had some parting gifts they wanted to give their friends before they left.

TALON and Aras ate in their room, quickly and with little appetite. Talon thought about bathing again before leaving, but realized it was a pointless waste of time, considering he only had the single wearable set of clothes that had belonged to one of the fallen guards. He knew he'd have to ask Aras to lend him coin so that he might buy some before they left, and he knew Aras would do so gladly, but it hurt his pride to have to ask his young friend. But then he smiled fondly, in memory of Aras's gift of song to him last night. The smile quickly faded, as darker thoughts prevailed. He sighed.

"Come, Aras. I hate long good-byes. I dislike good-byes of any kind, but we promised Rion and Tarrell." Talon was worried when Aras merely nodded, without speaking. He was eager to be on the road once more, to leave Athanark far behind. They went again to Rion and Tarrell's room.

"I know you are eager to be off. Thank you for seeing us again, before leaving. We hadn't wanted you to go without a chance to show you how much we value your friendship, how grateful we are to you for it and for all your aid," Rion said sincerely, handing Aras a wrapped bundle and a dozen arrows. The arrows were fletched in white, long and straight. Aras ran a fingertip lightly along the smooth shaft of one, and his face lit with joy.

"The bundle is a second dozen, wrapped in down so the feathers won't be crushed. They're made and used by the Horsemen of Aralon. I'm told that, next to Elven arrows, none fly so true." Rion grinned at Aras. Talon was relieved beyond measure to see the smile blossom upon Aras's face, and incredibly grateful to Rion and Tarrell for it.

"I had not thought to find such as these so far from home and did not have the means to make my own. I thank you for this precious gift," Aras said, as he slid the unwrapped dozen neatly into his quiver next to his own six remaining arrows.

Next, Rion handed Aras a set of clothes, which Aras regarded in equal surprise. "I think you'll find the fabric isn't quite so inferior as Man's usual weave, and I had them made especially for you, so they should fit you well. Besides, they will be less conspicuous than your own, of which Talon will certainly approve," Rion said conspiratorially, laughing as he said it. Aras fingered the soft cloth and thanked them again, smiling.

"And this is our last gift to you. Oberas had a case of this. I gave the rest to Lonas, in thanks for all his many kindnesses since we have come, but this is for you." Rion handed Aras a corked glass bottle. "This wine is from Thenalon. It is older than I am. I think it will be to your liking. Oberas was a connoisseur, and he was saving this to celebrate our new home," Rion said, clearing his throat and blinking rapidly. But then Aras's face lit with such delight that Rion grinned back at him.

"You both move me beyond words. I will miss our time together, but I will cherish it always, for I am gifted most by knowing you." Rion's eyes wet with tears in earnest then, as did Tarrell's, but they smiled at him.

Then Rion turned to Talon, and Talon looked at them so suspiciously Rion laughed again. Rion held out his hand and gave Talon a small but heavy purse. "This is for you: twenty-two gold, one for each of the men you tested, akin to the commission Vargas would have received, minus the man who left early. I wanted to give you much more, but Tarrell and Aras both warned me you wouldn't accept any of it then, and you earned this. I gave Aras one piece, also, for testing Jargas in addition to your test of him, and Aras didn't refuse it, although his purse is heavier even than mine, and I am now suddenly a trader of rather large means."

Talon gratefully accepted the purse. His own was woefully empty. He might buy some new clothes to replace the ones he wore, and now he would not need to rely on charity from Aras for other things he might need. But Rion was not done.

Rion handed him folded garments. "This cloak is for you, and these clothes. When I asked Aras what I might buy for you, Aras told me the clothes you were wearing when I first saw you weren't your own either, and that you could use some new things. Though he laughed and said I didn't have to worry they looked too new, that within a day you'd look like you'd slept in them for a month in a ditch, that you'd see to it."

Talon looked at them both in consternation, and Rion laughed at the expression upon his face. Then he examined the black pants, deep blue shirt, undergarments, socks, and the black cloak and had to smile. The fabrics were soft and strong, and he was weary of looking like a beggar. But Rion was not finished. He handed him a second set of pants and a shirt. "He also told us the story of how you first met, as he'd promised to, and described the shirt you made the bandages from." The pants were soft, a midnight blue, and the shirt was of Thenalonese silk, the color of moonlight, such a faint blue-white it almost glowed. "He said you'd play the part of noble Lord in that, when you might have the need."

"My friend has developed quite a loose tongue in my absence," Talon said, but without heat as he accepted the gifts and thanked him.

"Ah, but I am not finished, and you would not want to miss this last gift, I think," Rion said, his voice gently teasing.

Talon could not think what else Rion might possibly give him and was puzzled when he held up a large well-stuffed leather pouch, until his nose caught the faintest whiff of something impossible. It could not be *bacara!* He took the pouch, opened the drawstring, and inhaled deeply, eyes closing for a moment in delight. "But where did you find this? I have searched high and low in the City for it since we arrived, in vain!" None of the herbalists or other merchants had any. He would not have had the coin to purchase it, had he found it, but for this he would have swallowed his pride and asked Aras to pay.

It had been many, many months since he had last known the relaxing comfort of his pipe. The smell of the dried leaves alone brought back fond memories of far less desperate times, when his kin were yet around him, before they had left the dubious shelter of the Dwarven Lands for the Lands of Men.

"Oberas acquired a taste for *bacara* in the Dwarven Lands, many years ago," Rion confided. "He brought a supply of it with him from Ardock. I saw you fingering your pipe last night. It looked very similar to the one Oberas used, though he used it seldom. I hadn't known before that you smoked, or I'd have given it to you earlier. I was hoping you'd be pleased," Rion said, grinning.

"Pleased? I am overwhelmed! I will miss you and Tarrell greatly. You make it very hard to part with you. But perhaps my travels will take me to Gosa again someday."

"We'll miss you both also," Rion said, his voice choked with emotion.

The four of them clasped arms with one another warmly, and no one was embarrassed by the tears in his eyes, for each had eyes as bright.

TALON and Aras left, first going back to their room so that they might change. Talon even delayed their departure long enough that they each might bathe, for despite Aras's words, he did not want to sully such fine clothes until there was need.

They would not be going southeast toward the Enemy now. After all that had happened, especially the strange tree that formed their bond, they were heading north, to Nalea, where the Elf Lords dwelled, protected by the armed forces of the Seven Kingdoms. Talon thought that if there were answers to all of their many questions, that would be where they might be found. Aras had hesitantly agreed.

Talon suspected that Aras must have only recently graduated from there and was therefore not eager to return. Aras was reluctant to speak of his past. Talon still did not know which of the four Wood Kingdoms he was from, whether he called Loatia, Erenia, Lysenia, or Mytheria home. He hoped it wasn't Loatia. Both Riviera and Loatia were in grave danger now, if they yet stood.

Chapter 6
Friends and Enemies

IN THE stable, Talon watched Aras curiously as he mounted Janahar without benefit of saddle or bridle. "You give yourself away, Aras. Even the Horsemen of Aralon use saddle and bridle."

"If I must," Aras said as he dismounted. He saddled Janahar, who eyed Talon resentfully.

"Forgive me, Janahar, but it is necessary," Talon said, and Janahar snorted and tossed her proud head as if scoffing at his opinion.

Aras laughed and slipped on the bridle, then petted her as he remounted.

Talon was relieved to see that Rion and Tarrell's kindness seemed to have released Aras from his sorrow.

THEY headed out of the stable and down the street to the City Gate and then turned northeastwards. They rode in companionable silence for a long time, finally stopping late in the afternoon for lunch.

"It is a hard life you lead, my friend," Aras said softly. "How is it you can make such friends and leave them after only a few days? How can that be enough? The people I know I have always known and will know always. Centuries will pass, yet they will change little."

"Our friendships are all the more precious for their briefness," Talon explained. "We can learn much from each other in a short time, knowing those days are numbered. And time dims our memory, so we do not miss them so sorely when they are gone. Even when one tries to walk alone, it is hard not to be touched by extraordinary men. It is a gift when one sees them again and a curse to know they are gone forever. I have lived long for a Man; I am far older than I look. And I have been too little gifted and too often cursed." Talon's hand stroked the hilt of his fallen kinsman's sword, which was tied to his saddle.

"Then it is my duty to see that I do not add to your burden, when I seek to help you carry it," Aras solemnly asserted.

Talon's mood, which had seemed to threaten to become dark again, brightened with Aras's words, and he actually smiled. Aras felt his own heart lift. He had not exaggerated in Gower when he spoke about the effect of Talon's smile upon him. It truly did bring joy to his heart.

They mounted and rode again, but Aras noticed curiously that Talon looked to the east more than once with a wistful gaze, and he saw something he'd seldom seen on his friend's face before: indecision. "I go where you lead, Talon. The answers to my questions will take time to find in any case, and I truly doubt any of them can be found in Nalea. If something draws you east then there is nothing to stop us from changing our course."

Talon sighed. "It is my talk with Jargas. I missed my kinsman Hunter by only a week. I know Hunter must be well northeast of us now for having those days to draw ahead, but I am sure he travels on foot and therefore slower than we do. I hate to have passed so close and not seen him. It has been twelve long years, and he is now even stronger in my thoughts than he was before. And he may have left signs of his passing. I cannot say more, but still, I am drawn east to find out, though the route we now take is more direct for Nalea. It would cost us a full day, half a day there and back again." He fingered the lonely sword at his saddle again, with such a look of loss and longing and hope that it was painful to see.

"You must go where you are drawn to go," Aras said, and he turned Janahar toward the east. Aras turned in his saddle. "If you are to lead, you must ride in front, or at least at my side," Aras gently urged.

Talon nodded seriously, but then the sadness clouding his features lifted and he smiled in gratitude and perhaps more. "Then I would ride at your side, my friend." Kaldahar's pace quickened as she eagerly caught up with her friend Janahar.

DARKNESS fell when they were still some distance from the Marker Talon sought. He was reluctant to make camp, but it would be dangerous for both them and the horses to continue to ride through the woods without light to see by. They made camp, but even the cozy fire did little to cheer Talon's melancholy mood, which had correspondingly darkened with the setting of the sun.

Aras pulled the wine bottle from his pack and uncorked it. He inhaled the scent of the wine deeply, and a look of utter contentment lit his face. He looked so like a happy cat that Talon would not have been surprised to hear him purr in pleasure. Talon could not help but feel his mood lift just a little at the sight.

Then Aras's lips touched the mouth of the bottle, and Talon felt his breath catch and his heart begin to race as he watched him drink. He envied the glass those lips caressed and the ribbon of wine that flowed across Aras's tongue. Aras unconsciously moaned in appreciation and Talon shifted his position on the hard ground, trying to cover his reaction, as his manhood instantly stiffened in response to the sound of sensual delight. Talon's eyes were riveted to Aras's mouth, and then his throat as he swallowed, as he imagined those lips upon him.

"I did not know Men knew the art of winemaking so well as this," Aras said appreciatively, fortunately oblivious to both Talon's arousal and his discomfort. Aras passed the bottle to him. "Drink with me, my friend."

Talon would not sully such a fine vintage by pouring it into his metal cup and risk looking like an uncouth savage, nor insulting Aras by doing so, though he knew it would be a mistake to drink from the bottle. Resolutely, he thanked Aras as he took the bottle and drank from it anyway, marching eagerly to his doom. Talon almost moaned as well when, as he both hoped and feared, he felt the warmth of Aras's mouth still upon the glass. He barely tasted the wine, when it deserved to be savored.

As he righted the bottle, a single amber drip trailed from the lip of the bottle down the neck. Without thinking, Talon caught it with his tongue. He heard a sharp gasp of awareness as Aras belatedly recognized the phallic symbolism of the bottle's neck.

"An excellent vintage," Talon said, setting the bottle down upon the ground, purposefully neither looking into Aras's face nor risking their hands touching by handing the bottle back to him. He tried to feign casualness as he reached into his pack and pulled out the *bacara* and then pretended to have to root around for his pipe. He made a production of lighting it with a twig he dipped into the fire, relieved to see that his hand wasn't shaking in syncopation with his racing heart. By the time he was done with the ritual and risked glancing at Aras, Aras had safely reclaimed the bottle and was drinking deeply from it, apparently just as eager to appear unaffected by the incident as Talon.

Talon sucked long and deeply on the stem of his pipe, and then leaned back and closed his eyes. He held the warm billows of the smoke he had inhaled in his lungs, letting it work its healing calm upon him. When he finally opened his eyes and exhaled, he blew intricate curls and circles of smoke from his mouth.

Aras was watching him again, not in lust or need this time, but in curiosity and puzzlement and then in a child's fascination and delight, sniffing tentatively at the warm, woodsy scent of the pipe smoke. "May I try it?"

Talon nodded and passed him the pipe. "Do not inhale so deeply, though. It is an acquired ability."

ARAS placed his lips on the pipe stem and his face crinkled. "The taste is nothing like the smell." He inhaled carefully and began coughing violently, yanking the pipe from his mouth and thrusting it at Talon. "It is… it is not what I expected!"

The aroma of the smoke had reminded Aras much of Talon's own tantalizing scent, and he had been eager to taste Talon's lips again, as he had tasted them upon the lip of the bottle they had shared, but the reality was far different. The taste of the pipe was completely vile, and the smoke polluting his lungs was horrible.

He could do nothing to clear his lungs other than breathe, but he took a long draw from his water pouch to rinse the taste from his mouth. He could not rid himself of the foul taste fast enough, but he would not waste the wine. He could hardly drink himself into a stupor with a single bottle, nor would he ever leave himself so vulnerable, but that second deeper drink had definitely helped calm him when he was in desperate need of its aid.

He realized belatedly that Talon's earlier actions had apparently been unintentional, rather than the flirtation they had at first appeared to be. For the briefest moment, Aras had thought Talon might have shared his desire, that the attraction he had felt might have been reciprocated. There had been a musky scent on the breeze and Aras had mistakenly thought it might be Talon's arousal, but now he realized it must instead have been his own, merely tainted by the woodsmoke of their fire.

He was a fool to have hoped otherwise. Surely, if Talon had truly felt a similar desire kindle, he would have acted upon it? Aras might be an innocent, but he knew Talon must not be. Someone so desirable would have no shortage of pleasure loves. Jealousy again flared when he thought of Talon's earlier comment about thrashing in his sleep and who might have told him such a thing. But even if he had indulged in bed play as Aras had yet to, had Talon ever truly known the touch of love? Not merely temporary slaking of lust, but the meeting of hearts, of minds, of spirits of true lovers? Talon deserved to be loved, to be treasured and protected as well as pleasured. Aras felt shame, knowing that he hoped Talon had not been. He certainly wanted his friend to know such happiness, but he was selfish enough to want it to be with him.

His foolish hopes for such things were truly mad. He would be lucky to survive what was to come. He well might die, and he knew full well that, even if he survived, he would certainly be changed. Even if not physically maimed, his mind and spirit could well be all but destroyed. They should be. One should not be able to take a single life, let alone three, without suffering horribly for it. The thought that one of his intended victims was his own mother should have increased the horror of it a thousandfold, but it did not. In fact, he felt just the opposite: as her only child, it was his duty to rid the world of the murderous, heartless evil of the one who'd borne him.

"Where did you acquire such a strange habit?" Aras asked, desperate to break the silence before his thoughts either drove him mad or sent him into the sanctuary of Talon's arms, where he might confess all his secrets.

"I have not smoked for a very long time. My kin and I developed a taste for *bacara* in the Dwarven Lands," Talon said, an unusual look of contentment upon his face. "No City of Man I've ever found sells *bacara* for smoking, though I still check every city I come to for it, as some herbalist shops do sell it, for use in medicines. Although I've never found a medicinal use for the leaves, other than as a relaxing smoke upon burning."

"I am afraid I don't share your fondness for it, although I actually still do like the smell from a comfortable distance such as this," Aras said, relieved for the distraction and truly pleased to see his friend so relaxed and content. "For myself, I will stick with the wine, although I have had more than enough." He recorked the bottle and returned it to his pack.

Talon eyed him in surprise. "You show remarkable restraint, my friend."

"It has been over a month since I've tasted the wines of Lysenia. I would make such a precious gift last. Also, I find I am unused to traveling by horseback and wearied. I think perhaps I will go to bed early tonight," Aras dissembled. The truth was that his thoughts were yet in a turmoil, and he was feeling increasingly uncomfortable concealing so much from his friend. Desperate as he was for Talon's company, he did not want to fill the next few hours with half-truths and outright deception.

He could not understand why, after so many years of hiding the truth from all who might learn it, it was so hard to lie to this one Man he had met only scant weeks ago. The hold Talon already held upon his heart confused and frightened him as much as it excited him. He was tempted almost beyond all reason to tell Talon the truth, to lay all his secrets bare about everything: himself, Arcanus, Incuban, and even his mother.

An astonishing thought flashed across his mind. Could it be love he felt? Different than his love for Jarnath, but just as crucial? A selfless desire for honesty at any price. An overwhelming need to protect another even at risk of your own life. But he already was dangerously vulnerable, for his love of Jarnath and even of the father who despised him. And why, then, did he hold no love in his heart for his mother? Because his father only wished he were dead, while his mother consciously engineered his death, planned for it, worked toward it every waking moment from even before his conception?

Talon would not want to be loved, were he to endanger Aras by it. Aras might be ignorant of the ways of both Men and of love, but that much he knew for certain. Still, what he would not give to be able to lose himself in the warm safety of Talon's arms, to feel his embrace, to share his hopes, his dreams, even his machinations, as he shared his bed, his body. Even the thought of doing so set his heart racing. If only he was selfish enough to act upon his heart's desire!

"Then I will leave you to your slumber. As for me, the sky is clear, the stars bright, and the woods here are peaceful. I will stay up a while longer, I think, and indulge in the beauty of the night and the contentment of the *bacara*. I doubt I will have such an opportunity again for many long nights to come. Sleep well, my friend."

How could Talon's soft-spoken goodnight wishes feel as painful as a physical blow, or worse, as a mortal wound? How could it feel like a rejection of everything he was and everything he strove to be, when Talon did not even know he was desired?

How could Talon, who was so incredibly perceptive in all other things, not know? He should be relieved that Talon did not realize the influence he held upon Aras. One day soon, the other Players would learn of Aras, of the threat he was to them all. Incuban, Arcanus, and his mother certainly must never learn how important Talon was to him. His friend was already in incredible danger, for being an Amontir. He would become a target beyond any other in this world if they learned the rest.

He must begin to distance himself from Talon, the way he had distanced himself from all of those in Nalea who had dared befriend him, even from Jarnath and Meloneth, in his need to protect them from his father. Talon must be protected at all costs from this much greater potential danger he might one day face. Gradually, so Talon would not suspect anything was amiss, he would become as cold and aloof as his people were known to be, so that by the time they parted company, Talon would be relieved to be rid of him.

IDARE, give me strength! Talon prayed silently as he stared into their fire. The temptation was too great. He could not continue to travel with Aras. He must see him safely to Nalea as quickly as possible and part company with him there.

On the morrow, he would begin distancing himself from Aras. He would do it slowly, gently, so as not to wound Aras's heart by what he would certainly perceive as rejection if Talon did not take the utmost care. It would be unconscionably cruel of him to do otherwise. Even were Talon not betrothed to Elanara, he would not be free to act upon his feelings. Aras was not a woman, and his duty was to his people, to his House: he must sire an heir to both. He should sire as many children as he was physically able; they all must, if their people were to survive.

He ruthlessly fought down the knowledge that they would not, that they could not. It was already too late. Only eighteen survived. They were doomed as a people. They should be, for having led Incuban to the Dwarven Kingdoms, to their destruction. They had never meant to, but the fault was theirs, the blame must be theirs. The blood and torment of hundreds of thousands was on their hands. They should just gather together and surrender to the Enemy and end it. But it was too late. Incuban was already amongst the others. He would not stop with their deaths.

No, he could not allow himself to believe that his people were at fault. That path led to madness. He forced himself to acknowledge the truth as he had so many times before: had they allowed every child of every House to be massacred back in Amontir, in his unquenchable, rapacious hunger, Incuban would have still gone forth and attacked the Dwarves, the Elves, Men. They could not truly blame themselves for Incuban's depredations, though each of them often did.

Enough! He would go mad were he to dwell on it. His eyes instinctively sought Aras for comfort, and he yanked his gaze back to the fire with a muffled curse. Since when had he ever sought anything above the fire at night for comfort? *Since you met Aras. Even in the bright light of day you turn to him. The sun cannot sooth your core and heal your spirit as he can.*

The gentle whisper in his mind chilled him until he recognized the thought as his own. Idare help him, it was true! He was truly cursed, completely and utterly doomed, that he must distance himself from the one man who might save him.

In resignation, he began the familiar meditation Arcanus had taught him, knowing it could no longer aid him as it once had, that the words no longer held any Power over his core. But he chanted anyway, if only to break the silence of the night, if only to drown out the siren call of Aras's gentle breath as his friend slept, cradled by his youth, his innocence, unencumbered by the harsh responsibilities Talon faced.

THE next morning they were both eager to be off, neither hungry for breakfast. They rode through the morning in silence until they reached a small stream, where they dismounted to water the horses and refill their water skin and pouch. Talon surprised Aras by saying, "I must ask that you wait here for me, Aras. I will be as quick as I can, but it will take some time. You should eat while I am gone."

"I cannot come with you?" Aras asked, careful to ensure his face betrayed only curiosity, but belatedly realizing his tone had sounded wounded.

"I must go alone," Talon confirmed, seeming unusually oblivious to his hurt.

"There is a village near here?" Aras asked, hoping to find out more.

Talon scowled and shook his head.

"Then I will wait for you," Aras said with a sigh.

Without further word, Talon walked quickly away, heading south.

Aras was surprised at how suddenly and completely he disappeared amongst the trees. He watched the spot long after Talon had gone and then resolutely began to groom the horses, much to their delight. He began to sing as he cared for them, unable to bear the silence, and the horses flicked back their ears and nickered as they listened and luxuriated in the feel of the brush.

AS SOON as he was well out of sight, Talon headed northeast instead of south, until he intersected the stream again, taking care not to leave tracks even an Elf could follow. Aras's bond to him was so strange, he did not know if he might be able to perceive his location through it, as the Amontir could. He might not be able to deceive him, but he had to try. Besides, Aras was apparently new to his Power and untrained. Talon entered the stream and walked sure-footedly along the slippery stones, thankful that his worn leather boots were still watertight.

It was not that he did not trust Aras, or thought that he might follow him, but his steps led him to one of his people's secret Markers and Caches, and their very existence was a closely guarded secret amongst the Amontir. It was here that they left messages and supplies for each other. Even the messages were simple marks in a complex code, so any who stumbled across a Marker might only be puzzled by the ancient and more recent markings they found. Most were just indicators that a Knight or Captain of the Watch had passed this way, and when, but some were messages, mostly warnings. And the key to where the Cache was buried was marked there also, in code, so the location would not be known to any other.

Talon walked quickly until he spotted the crucial tree amongst a forest of others effortlessly, even though he had last passed here six years ago. His eyes scanned the bark eagerly for Farad's mark. He saw it, fresh and new. He saw to his surprise that there was a message beside it as well: *Farad going to Dewalaren's aid in Nalea. All others go to War Council in Caramore.* Talon stared at the message in confusion. His breath caught as he traced the mark above it in disbelief and then growing horror.

There were many dozens of marks here, others invisible where the bark had long ago sealed the wounds to the tree. His own mark from six years ago was still easily read. The horror came from the mark just above Farad's. It was also his mark, and it indicated a date over a week ago. Only he had left no such mark; he had not been here. The enormity of it stole his breath. Someone else had used his mark. And worse, they did not simply indicate his passage, but they had left a coded message in his name: *Dewalaren, urgent help Nalea.*

His mark might have been copied by a stranger, but a quick check of the tree showed none of the other symbols in the message had been used here. No kinsman would use a mark not his own. But the Markers' locations, their very existence, and the codes were known only to his people.

The conclusion was inescapable. One of their own number had betrayed them. Worse still, someone was trying to lure one or more of them to Nalea in his name. And Farad had been here; he had read the false message and was faithfully rushing to assist him. That a trap for his kin be set in his name and snare Farad! If Farad escaped, he would brand him a traitor in their midst. When they again met, Farad would confront him. Once Farad discovered he could no longer view his core, for the tree that surrounded it, he would think him a Resemblant.

There was a reason Farad was called Hunter. His cousin was everything his traveling name implied: an expert tracker, relentless and tireless, an efficient killer. And utterly ruthless when pursuing an enemy. If the Amontir could no longer trust their own brothers! Chaos! Ruin!

And a War Council in Caramore! He had called no such Council. Could that be a trap as well? Caramore had been compromised and abandoned six years ago; they'd assumed it destroyed. Who amongst them would not know that? He had sent a message to Farad across their bond, telling him of the Enemy's attack and their narrow escape, thanks to the timely warning and intervention of Arcanus's children, Magus and Circe.

Had one of their number they had long thought dead fallen to the Enemy instead? How long had the Enemy known of the Markers and Caches and not betrayed his knowledge? Had he used them before, to quietly lead some of his kinsmen to their deaths? Or had he learned only recently?

Who was lost but not burnt upon a pyre? Could it be Archer, Desmond, Lord of House of Serpents? He had inexplicably vanished almost ninety years ago. No, the Markers were not so old as that. Talon was the one who had thought to create them. Nor could Jarad or Alaria or any of Farad's brothers have betrayed them before they died. They had all died a century ago.

A sudden thought chilled his blood: Lunahr? No, it could not be. Could it? No. He refused to even think it. Lunahr was dead. Dead was bad enough. If he had instead somehow survived the battle and been captured, tortured and—no! He would drive himself mad again to even begin to think otherwise.

He wracked his brain for another name, another possible explanation, but there was none. He could not begin to fathom this, and it did not matter for the moment. The danger to Farad was what was now paramount.

He was on horseback and Farad would be on foot. He had to go to Nalea and spring the trap himself, before Farad might reach it, and hope to survive it. But first, he would be sure there was no clue here as to who the traitor might be. He carefully unsealed the Cache and probed it with his sword, expecting to spring a trap, but it was as empty as it had been six years ago. He surveyed the ground for tracks, but there had been rain recently, and there were none.

He could not leave this Marker here with its false message. He could cut away the marks, but more might be placed here. He wished for the flasks of oil on his saddle but could not leave this treachery here. Would that he had led Aras here! He could not even call to him through the strange link. He had never before felt so powerless. But he had his flint and steel with him; he carried them always to ensure he was never without the means of creating the flames he relied upon so desperately for his very sanity.

Talon gathered tinder and brush and pinecones, surrounded the tree with it, piling it high, to where the marks were. The fire kindled nicely. The tree was ancient and had served them well. He could not let the fire climb too high; he did not want to set fire to the entire woods. The fire burned slowly at first, the healthy bark loath to catch fire. But then the resin released and ran down the bark, catching fire as well. Suddenly the flames leapt higher, the fire burning more fiercely and more brightly. The blaze grew too quickly.

Talon cursed, whipping off his cloak and emptying his water skin onto it, and began beating at the blaze. There was smoke, too much smoke: it announced his location to any who might be watching. He cursed again, but there was nothing he could do to stop it. He worked furiously to save the tree before the whole forest caught fire from it.

ARAS had brushed the horses thoroughly and was becoming bored. He realized that was foolish. He loved the woods, and these trees were perfect for climbing. From the top of one of these trees, he might see far. He climbed quickly and expertly and scanned the treetops about him. He was on a small rise and the view was beautiful. But then, to the northeast, he saw smoke, too much for some traveler's campfire. Trees were burning! The rest of the woods might catch!

He climbed down quickly and leapt onto Janahar, urging her forward. Kaldahar made to follow, but Aras told her to wait for Talon, and she reluctantly obeyed. Aras rode quickly through the trees, trusting Janahar not to injure either of them. He had taken a good bearing and was sure he would be able to find the blaze. He knew that Talon would be able to track their trail easily when he returned from wherever he had gone. Aras wondered who might have set a fire here and why. Was it an accident, carelessness on the part of some traveler, or was this a deliberate act of evil? These proud trees should not be burned!

TALON heard hoof beats and spun around, Sword drawn, ready to face attack from an unknown foe. But it was Aras on Janahar. Aras stared at him, dumbfounded, and Talon cursed. "Why did you follow me?" he yelled in anger. More treachery, more betrayal!

"I DID not follow you. You went south. What are you doing here?" Aras stared at the remains of the pile of burnt kindling and the blackened trunk in shock. Although the fire was out, the bark still smoldered. Talon's new cloak lay smoldering on the ground at the base of the tree. Aras saw to his relief that only this single tree had burned, but such a tree! His eyes filled with tears to see it. "Why would you do such a thing? What harm has this King of Trees ever done to you, that you would burn him?"

"What harm? This tree may have cost me the life of my cousin, my friend! This tree may cost me a price too terrible to pay! Everything has gone wrong. You should not be here!" Talon was so enraged he shook, his hand clenched tightly around the hilt of his still-raised sword.

Janahar took a step back from Talon and pawed the ground nervously, ready to defend Aras if need be. Aras looked at his friend in disbelief. "You would seek to kill me for discovering your secret when I don't even understand what I have found?" he asked softly.

Talon looked at him in confusion and then looked at the bared blade he held so menacingly. He roared in frustration, slamming his blade back into its sheath and flinging himself to the ground, head in his hands. "Go away. I cannot think with you here! I am undone."

Aras saw then that the arms of Talon's shirt were burnt as well, and his left hand was raw and red. Aras turned Janahar and rode away, back the way he had come, without another word.

TALON sat without moving, listening to the hoofbeats fade. Then he cursed both the tree and his unknown kinsman, for he feared he had lost another friend.

A short while later, there were two sets of hoofbeats, approaching quickly. Talon swore softly as he rose and slipped between the trees. But it was only Aras on Janahar, with Kaldahar beside him.

When Aras saw his friend gone, he cried out in dismay and leapt from Janahar's back, eyes intent on the ground, looking for tracks where Talon had left none.

Talon did not know whether he should reveal himself or not. Aras must be able to sense his presence through their bond, mustn't he? Or did the tree about his core protect him even from Aras's strange Power?

"Talon? Talon!" Aras looked about in dismay, almost frantically. When he spoke again, his voice was heavy with self-recrimination and despair. "I did not think to find you gone! Would you leave me and Kaldahar behind and travel alone and injured and ill-supplied? I should not have left! I have failed you when you needed me most."

He looked so tortured, so distraught, that Talon could not bear to see it and stay hidden. He sheathed Kathalanar and slipped quietly from the trees. "I am still here, Aras," he said softly.

Aras turned and gave him such a look of relief and devotion it shamed him for having raised his voice in anger to his friend. "I only went because you told me to go. And you needed time to calm yourself, and I needed to get your medicines for you." When Talon looked at him, puzzled, he explained, "You have burnt your hand."

Talon looked at his hands and saw that he had burnt the left one. He had not even felt it, or noticed. But seeing the injury, now he felt it, and the pain was very sharp.

"The tree was too eager to burn in the end. I almost could not stop the blaze. I was afraid the whole forest would alight."

"Then I am a fool and you are not the one who burned him, but the one who saved him." Aras took the medicines and bandages out and began cleaning his hand with water from his water skin.

"No, you were aright from the first. I both burned and saved the tree. But the damage has already been done. It is my friend Hunter who may be killed, and I will be blamed for treachery." Slowly and hesitantly, he admitted, "Hunter is a Captain of the Watch." Even more reluctantly he betrayed their most closely guarded secret, "And I am Lord of the Watch."

Aras's eyes widened. "You are their King? I knew you were of the Watch; I have known for a while now. I saw your band, when you were ill, although the significance of it escaped me at first. When I realized, I knew you were an Amontiri Lord, a Captain, but I had not guessed you were their King." He looked curiously at Talon's blade. "Of course, you never let me see the true nature of your weapon before today. I never guessed it was the King's Sword, the Sword of Amontir."

Talon's eyes widened. He had forgotten all about the gloves. Aras had seen his unmasked Sword, the pyrenteum blade! Talon's heart began hammering in renewed fear. Aras gently spread ointment onto his reddened hand, his touch as light as a butterfly's wing, although it still hurt. He looked Talon in the eye. "I will not betray your secret, Talon. I would never betray you. Please, tell me how this tree could harm your friend."

Talon looked at Aras, suddenly understanding the Lords' fear of Farad. Aras was stronger than he was. He radiated Power, while his own core was now held helpless in the tree that bound it. Aras could force him to tell him, to betray another of their most closely guarded secrets. But he had not. Instead, he merely asked. Talon sighed deeply.

Trust did not come easily to his people, and to him seldom at all. It took an effort of will, but Talon explained about the Markers and the coded messages they bore. If the Markers had been compromised, the secret was useless now in any case. They were less than worthless: they were now tools of the Enemy. And that meant, of all his kinsmen, he could now trust only one, Farad, until he discovered who had betrayed them, and Farad was now most likely to be one of the first to fall. He must reach Nalea before him!

Aras finished bandaging his hand. "Then we must ride to Nalea as fast as we can," he said, unknowingly echoing Talon's unvoiced thoughts.

ARAS'S heart was in turmoil. He did not want to return to Nalea, not now, not yet, when he had only just begun to find himself, when he had already learned so much in so short a time, when he'd realized how much more he had yet to learn. He had hoped before to divert Talon to head to Logareth or Fenemal or elsewhere. But he would never allow Talon to set foot in Nalea without being at his side to protect him.

A sudden realization struck him with the force and pain of a blade: if Talon was the Lord of the Watch, then he was the one who was now betrothed to King Laranela's daughter, Elanara! No wonder Talon had not acted upon the desire they had both been fighting. He would never do something so dishonorable.

Aras's spirits plummeted. Talon was already lost to him. He yet traveled by his side, but it could only be briefly. Soon Talon would leave him, for his people, for his bride, his new Queen. Talon had lain with her already, in Erenia. Aras had read the reports his father's spies had sent about the betrothal being consummated. His heart tore in two, his nascent hopes shattered.

Aras carefully hid all indications of his heartbreak from Talon, when he would have fallen to his knees and wept. Talon had far greater concerns than the foolish dreams of a pathetic child.

"THERE is one more Marker between here and Nalea. We will see if it yet bears Hunter's mark. But first, tell me, if you did not follow me, how you came to be here," Talon challenged. Aras told him and he was again ashamed that he had not trusted his friend.

Talon gathered up his cloak, and they mounted and rode quickly through the trees, heading for the Southern Road so they could ride at far greater speed. As soon as they reached the Road, they urged their horses to a gallop. Their mounts would not be able to run the entire distance, of course, but the mares sensed their riders' need for speed and were more than eager to indulge it. He made sure the horses slowed their gait, alternating their pace so they would not become winded nor made lame.

They did not make camp that night until the moon's light faded and it was no longer safe to travel, even upon the Road. Tonight there was no wine or *bacara* or contentment. But neither could Talon sleep. He told Aras tales then, of the deeds of Farad, though he did not reveal his given name. He talked long into the night. But he could not speak of Lunahr, not yet. The pain of his loss was still too fresh, too keen. He finally settled into weary sleep only a short while before dawn.

With the sun's first rays, they rode again. And so three days passed, with little time lost for food or rest. Talon's thoughts dwelt always on who amongst them could have betrayed them. It might have been any of the other seventeen who remained, in addition to him and Farad. Eighteen others, with Jargas, but he would not know of the Markers unless Farad had revealed them to him and Farad would not have, until Talon had recognized him and his House. Who else might now be lost? They were already too few. How could they lose another? Dead! Lunahr was dead! He mourned the loss anew.

ARAS had never seen his friend in such a somber mood for so long a time. But there was nothing he could say or do to console him. So he rode in silence, afraid he would watch his friend become consumed by his despair.

THEY were traveling along the Western Road now. Just before dusk on the fourth day they turned into the woods at a landmark Talon had kept a careful eye out for. They found the Marker, and Talon was out of his saddle and at the tree before Kaldahar came to a stop. Talon cursed when he saw his own mark and the false message was there again, and Farad's as well.

"Hunter has traveled far and fast, as I feared. He runs blindly to my aid. I fear his loyalty will be rewarded by his death. But I will not have this foul treachery spread." Talon tied his scorched cloak about the tree above the marks and emptied his water skin onto it. Then he took one of the flasks of oil, held it against the bark, and slashed it with his sword, and the oil gushed across the marked face of the tree.

He saw Aras stiffen, but his friend did not interfere as he laid fire to it. The bark burned hot and bright.

Once the deceptive marks were completely obliterated, he and Aras extinguished the burnt bark with soil from around the tree, and Talon removed his ruined cloak.

The sky tonight was thick with clouds, and Talon cursed, for there would be no moon to ride by. "Come, let us leave this foul place. I will not make camp in the shadow of such treachery. But at least, seeing it scarred by fire when all about it is whole, none of my kin will approach it again, fearing the hand of the Enemy."

They rode on a short distance and came upon a cool stream and made camp there, refilling their water skin and pouch. They slept in shifts, one always on guard, for Talon's uneasiness grew as he neared Nalea.

DAWN broke and he and Aras rose with it. "I need to clear my thoughts. It has been too long since I've ridden like this. I need to stretch my legs. I think best when I walk. I will be back soon."

Aras nodded, and Talon headed back toward the Marker. He had forgotten to probe the Cache in his haste to burn the tree and his reluctance to reveal the existence of those, as well, to Aras, when there had been no need. But he had automatically noted its location before burning the notation. He should check it, if for nothing else than to be sure he left this part of the trap at least safely disarmed.

He was lost in thought and incautious. He was at the base of the tree, fully exposed, before he felt eyes upon him. He turned quickly, hand on the hilt of Kathalanar, and was shocked to see Farad. But his brief relief at seeing his cousin alive and well vanished, and his blood ran cold. Farad was viewing him with a hunter's eyes and stood with an arrow nocked against him, bowstring pulled taut beside his cheek as he emerged from the cover of the trees. But he did not release his arrow yet.

Talon carefully removed his hand from the hilt of the Sword. "I am not the Enemy, cousin," he said softly in Amontirin, knowing even as he said it that Farad might well view him as one, now.

"Yet the tree is burned and your sleeves are burned and you walk in my Enemy's footsteps. And the Man I knew would not have been caught off his guard." Farad's voice was achingly familiar but cold, and his eyes hard, and the scar on his face was vivid against his cheek. His face had not been scarred when he had left for the Dwarven Lands.

"I am no Resemblant, cousin," Talon said, with a confidence he did not feel. It chilled him, what Farad might think if he tried to view or touch his core. What would he make of the great silver tree that surrounded it? "It has been twelve long years since last I saw you. I have changed, as have you, but not so much that you do not know me."

There was a flicker of something across Farad's face. The bow did not waver, but he still did not release his arrow.

"My kinsman travels alone. I would know who you ride with," Farad said coolly.

Talon dared not answer, for to show any who was not kin a Marker was treachery, and this Marker had been burned. Yet he might name another of their kin whom Farad might know was dead, or elsewhere.

Suddenly Talon feared for Aras, for if he were dead, Farad would approach and Aras would neither see nor hear him, or worse, Aras would hear Farad and think Talon came with his own quiet steps. "I ride with Jargas, that his strong staff may aid me as he aided you," Talon lied. He did not know if it was the hesitation or that Farad sensed it was a lie. But he saw Farad's eyes narrow as his fingers loosed the arrow, and he knew he was dead.

But miraculously, the arrow never came, and the bow dropped from Farad's hand before he could nock and loose another. Talon was amazed but acted instantly. He leapt upon Farad and grabbed him by the collar and dealt him a single mighty blow to his face. Farad sagged limply in his hand. Talon looked up and saw a gray-fletched arrow had shattered Farad's own in midflight, and a second had driven straight through his wrist and was protruding from either side. Nothing less would have made Farad drop his bow.

Aras appeared, a third arrow nocked and pointed downward. Talon cut Farad's bowstring and partially hogtied him with it, binding his uninjured hand to his feet behind his body. He searched Farad for weapons and removed a knife, a wickedly barbed blade with a carved antler hilt and an oddly down-turned handguard. Talon wondered how and when he had lost his own knife, the pallenteum blade Talon had gifted to him so long ago. Only then did he release his grip and Aras un-nock his arrow.

"And how did you come to be here in my time of need this time?" Talon asked wearily. Could Aras trace him through their bond after all? The bond! He had forgotten, Jargas had said he was bonded to Farad. Farad would have sensed Jargas was nowhere near. No wonder he had attacked him! Were it not for Aras, his carelessness would have cost him his life. It might yet cost him a price too agonizing to pay.

"I thought better of letting you walk alone and followed you. Unfortunately, I saw him no sooner than you. When he did not immediately release his arrow and I heard the depth of emotion in your voice when you spoke to him, I realized neither of you truly wished to see the other harmed. So I waited with drawn bow amongst the trees, in case your words did not satisfy him, though I could not understand them, for your words are as powerful as your sword, and I was loath to injure one you cared for. I have dealt a most grievous injury to a bowman, but I could not disarm him otherwise. May you both forgive me for it. I will get the horses and see what magicks your medicines can work this time." Aras leapt into the woods, as fast and silent as a rabbit.

Talon cut the shaft of the arrow that had wounded Farad and pulled the arrow from the wound, then held his cousin's wrist tightly to staunch the flow of blood. Talon looked down at his bound and wounded kinsman and wondered how he could ever regain his trust. "Farad, my cousin, my friend, this is not how I wanted to meet! I rode fast and hard trying to overtake you ere you reached Nalea and sprang the traitor's trap. But I did not think to find you here when you should already be gone."

Aras returned with the horses. Talon told Aras to hold his knife at Farad's throat, lest he awaken and catch them unawares, though he thought with such a blow he could not yet. He replaced the bowstring with rope from their packs, binding his cousin's feet and uninjured arm securely to the trunk of a tree, knowing it might only bring them a few extra moments if Farad awoke and sought to attack them. Then he treated his injury with medicines and bound it, then bound Farad's fingers in bandages as well, and his arm to his chest, so he could not free himself easily, although Talon well knew no knot could hold Farad for long. The arrow had missed much in its flight. A hair's breadth to either side and the blood would have flowed too fast to quench. He only hoped the tendons and bones had fared so well. He marveled again at the skill of his friend with the bow; for even an Elf to have made two such shots was a feat.

Talon searched Farad thoroughly for messages and found none. But he saw other new scars, so many brutal scars, in addition to the one on his face. The past twelve years had been more harsh to his cousin than they had been to him.

"Now we must wait for him to awaken. And even bound and injured, we must watch him carefully. He may sleep for only a few moments more or for far longer. I had to strike him hard, though I have tried not to kill him. I have felled men with a single blow many times. It is far harder to render them unconscious with little injury than it is to kill them. And I know not what trials may have made him weaker than I might have thought." Farad was no longer lean, he was gaunt, a small step from emaciated.

Talon looked at his hand, now covered in Farad's blood, as if it were his Enemy. "I do not want to kill him. I wanted only to warn him and help him. I need him. He is the only one of my kin that I can now trust, for the traitor could be any of the rest. A curse upon whoever has used my own mark against me! How many Markers has he defiled with his false message? We have destroyed but two. What doom awaits those who go to Nalea? How can I warn my kin that the Markers are tools of the Enemy now? His arsenal ever grows as ours weakens. We cannot make haste to Nalea with Hunter bound here, nor take him with us to be a knife in our backs when we ride to face an unknown enemy and the perils that might await us there. But I fear the traitor amongst us might do much harm to your people, ere we can stop him." Talon's voice was dark with anguish and despair.

Farad's eyes opened and he spoke in Amontirin, his eyes widening slightly upon sight of the Elf at his side. "Give me your wrist and look me in the eye, Dewalaren, and tell me your story, and do not lie to me this time."

He gave a glad cry, for Farad had feigned sleep as he expected he might, as he would have done in his place, but he'd seen no sign of it. He had heard some of their words, at least. And he had spoken his given name! It had been so long since anyone had actually called him by his real name that it was odd to hear it. He had been Talon for so long to so many that he never even thought of himself as Dewalaren any longer. His earlier memories of his distant childhood had not been sufficient to change that. But the Power of his true name filled him now, it seized him, it engulfed him, strengthening his sense of self when he desperately needed it to.

Dewalaren cut the rope binding Farad's hand and held out his wrist, knowing what Farad meant to do. Farad put his fingers to his pulse, and he told Farad that he had met Jargas in Athanark and had spoken with him, learning Farad lived, when he had feared him dead. He told Farad he had arranged for Jargas to head safely over the Coroden as the Captain of the Guard of a merchant caravan, with strong men at his side. Hearing he'd only just missed seeing Farad, he had been eager to at least see his mark. Then he told him the rest, all that he had done, and all that he had guessed and why he had spoken the lie that had almost been his undoing. Farad listened, with eyes that bore into his own, and he remained silent ere he was done. Dewalaren was again afraid Farad might seek to renew his bond to him, to test him, but he did not.

"Then all is not lost, for you are still the Man I know; you are not lost to us as I feared. Of all of us, you are the only one we cannot lose. I am indebted to your friend for saving you from me. If it were not for his arrow, I would have slain you and become a tool of the Enemy all unknowing. Unbind my feet as well, cousin, for there is no need to act against you now. I do not wish to betray my unique ability to your friend and I have my own tale to add to yours."

Dewalaren saw from his eyes and face that he truly believed him, that he did not seek to deceive him. He gave a glad cry and cut the remaining ropes and hugged his cousin, careful of his injured arm. He cut the extra bandages that bound his arm to his chest and carefully unwound those at his fingers.

"Now for my own tale," Farad said. "I have completed the mission I set for myself in the Dwarven Lands, as well as I was able. Five more Kingdoms have fallen, in spite of my efforts to save them. At my urging, two of the three that remain had banded together as allies, Ironhand and Dorolingas, both of them mighty. But Malar had rotted from within and the Enemy's hand was strong there when I came. I was wrongfully imprisoned and mistreated almost to the point of death, which is why I severed my link to you. But I was rescued by the Dwarf you met, our kinsman from a lost House. He is Stephan's heir, Jargas, Lord of House of Gryphon. He told you the story of his House?"

Dewalaren shook his head. "Much has been happening here in the Lands of Men as well. There was no time to speak at length before we left."

Farad continued his report. "Prince Rowanar and the ten Houses he led made the crossing of the Deathshand, but far to the south and west of where they should have been. They came through a pass near the Great Marsh, one that's now sealed by rock. Stephan alone survived the avalanche that claimed the rest of our kin; the Enemy brought a mountain down upon the rest. But Stephan lost his memory. Jargas had been searching for the key to his maternal grandsire's past for decades.

"As for Malar, the old King is dead and his son Valar now rules in his stead, much to the betterment of the Kingdom. Malar now stands with Ironhand and Dorolingas against the darkness. After Jargas and I left the Dwarven Lands, we went to Thenalon and Aralon both. I found no trace of Aramis or Rolin in either, nor had the rift between the two been healed. I sent Jargas on to Athanark, parting with him east of there. I am glad you saw him so safely away.

"For my part, I have been leaving notices upon all the Markers I passed of a War Council at Caramore. I had not expected the city itself to yet stand, after the warning you sent me six years ago across our bond of the Enemy's attack upon it, but because of that, I hoped it would be the one place our Enemy would least think to find us gathered. I was shocked to find it yet intact and deserted when I scouted it only six months ago, before entering Malar. We will plot there to bring about the Enemy's ruin. It is well placed strategically for what is to come, near both Nalea and the three remaining Dwarven Kingdoms, as well as the Watchtower, and I was not certain whether the latter is yet unknown to the Enemy. I knew that, had it been discovered, it would be the ideal location for a trap, so I dared not attempt to scout it alone. Also, if he did not yet know of it, I was concerned I might somehow lead him to it, and I dared not risk compromising it, were it yet secure.

"Now that the three last Dwarven Kingdoms are united, and after what I've seen in Thenalon and Aralon since my return, we can no longer hope to find the Knife and Ring. We'll have to do our best to defeat the Enemy without them. I know Arcanus has insisted the Ring is necessary, that only the Sword charged with the Ring's Power is strong enough to slay the Enemy, but I think he speaks out of fear, that he has let it overcome his judgment. In any case, this is our only possible option for victory: once the Dwarves are dead and gone, Men and certainly the Elves will fall all too quickly.

"So I came to the Marker south of this one, but when I went to leave my mark, I saw your own and urgent request for aid. I had never known you to leave such a message and knew that your peril or that of the Elves must be great indeed. I left my own mark with the message that I went to your aid and my own message about the War Council and then made haste to reach the next Marker. There again I saw the mark and message and again left my own.

"I knew I could make greater speed upon the Western Road, so although I usually shun Roads, I cut through the forest to this one. But I traveled along it only a short distance when I heard the sounds of battle up ahead. I resolved to look only, for I could not delay, or risk injury in helping some stranger, but I thought it might be you, in need of aid, although you should be many days ahead of me, from the date upon your message.

"I saw then to my rage that it was a lone Elf on horseback besieged by savage men, riding upon the backs of enormous wolven, who could only be the Enemy's minions. Many of the beasts and their riders lay slain at his feet, but others yet surrounded him and it was clear he could not survive the attack much longer. My bow sang to his aid until my arrows were spent. But ere I could reach him to aid him further with my knife, his horse was felled and him with it.

"I slew the four foes that remained: they had not expected me to be able to counter their sword strikes with only a knife and were overconfident and incautious. Though I know little of healing, I hoped to at least bind the Elf's wounds, but when I knelt to help him I found him already slain, though he spoke two words with his dying breath. They were two of the few I knew in Elvish: the words were 'death' and 'Watch'. Then he was gone. His words troubled me greatly, for although he might have been speaking of any of our kin, I feared it most likely he spoke of your death, for your message.

"I thought that he might bear a written message, so I searched him. Though it was well concealed, I found the letter he bore. Upon it was a seal I'd never seen before. I know scant few words of Elvish and could not decipher the name, but I recognized the words 'King' and 'Tanieria.' Anxious for news of you, I broke the seal and opened the letter, but could only read a few words: 'Watch' and 'War' and 'death'. Then I knew I could not go to Nalea, for I needs must be the new bearer of this message to the King of Tanieria; there could be no delay, if it spoke of us and war and death, particularly if it spoke of yours. So I headed back down the Road.

"I came here, intending to leave a new message of my changed destination and the reason for it, fearing Nalea itself might somehow have been destroyed. But when I came and saw the Marker burnt and then saw you, I could not believe my eyes. I have felt such horror only a few times in my life. I had to confront you, to learn what I might, though I feared I was too late to save you. Still, I knew I must behead the monster I'd feared you'd become, lest the Enemy use your corpse against us again. The rest you know."

"But you carry no letter! I searched you everywhere for a message," Dewalaren said, baffled.

"I hid it well amongst the trees when I saw you, a few dozen paces from where you saw me. I did not want it to fall into the hands of the Enemy if you proved to be his pawn and if you somehow overcame me. I am surprised you travel with an Elf, when you have always traveled alone. Who is he who travels with you? Is this Eladar, Elanara's brother? He does not have the look of a River Elf."

"No, he is Aras. He has yet to tell me his Kingdom, though he has mentioned both Riviera and Lysenia, so it might be either Loatia or Lysenia. I came upon him northwest of here. I will tell you that tale, there is much you need to hear, but first, show me this letter."

Farad led Dewalaren to where he had hidden the letter, with Aras and the horses trailing behind them. Farad unearthed the message and handed it to Dewalaren, who opened it and translated it into Amontirin and read it aloud for Farad, even the cryptic portion at the top, his voice catching more than once and shaking with horror before he was done.

Date PA 07-17-3013 DA
Order 1-3.1-4-4/PL=MLRA/TC=1-Red-M-1B-1D;11-Black

King Elwyth of Tanieria,

    I speak with High-King Laedrin's voice and write with his hand, for he is near death and can do neither, and as previously reported, his son and heir is already dead.
    Captain of the Watch Beryl has turned assassin. He has mortally wounded our High-King with a blade poisoned by foul magicks. Our healers cannot aid him. Only the wizards might yet save him. If any of The Three are in your Kingdom, send them immediately to our aid. We are sending similar messages to the six other Kingdoms.
    We are enraged. We do as we should have done long ago and make our isolation complete.
    Martial Law is declared. Every Reservist in your Kingdom is hereby called to active duty. We declare War on the Watch and any who succor them. You are commanded to seal your borders against them and to slay any you find.
    If a wizard is to come, he or she must come quickly, for the High-King's time is nearly spent.

Acting Regent Lord of the Guard Ahrnad of Nalea

"Lunahr would never do such a thing!" Farad denied, stunned. "He could not slay any Elf, for his love of them, let alone the Elven High-King! And he would be truly mad to do so, when the River Elves of Riviera yet shelter him."

Dewalaren walked to Kaldahar and pulled Lunahr's sheathed sword from his saddle and handed it to Farad, his hand shaking in horror and renewed grief.

Farad's eyes widened in disbelief as he saw the familiar hilt. He half drew the sword from its sheath, exposing the brutal truth of the blade. "Why do you carry Lunahr's sword Loruthanar?" he asked, his voice sepulchral, knowing there could only be two answers.

Dewalaren was numb with the enormity of it. "I thought him dead. I thought no pain could be greater. But captured! I did not think that any of us could fall alive into the Enemy's hands any longer, to have his mind shredded, all our secrets torn from him, to have his body defiled, to become a Resemblant."

Tears streamed down his face. "I bought the blade in Athanark, from a crippled sword master who knew what he sold. It had been recovered from a battlefield outside the ruins of Alridge in the south. Over a fortnight before I discovered and reclaimed it, I had a vision of Lunahr's death, and I knew, if he were alive, the blade would not have strayed from his hand. To have Lunahr lost to us, the Elves lost to us, at war with us; our defenses lie in ruins! Even the Markers are compromised, our lines of communication broken. The Enemy has crippled us!" He sank to his knees.

Aras was at his side, clasping his arms and shaking him. "Talon, tell me what has happened, that I may help you!" Aras pleaded in Elvish. Talon shook his head, for Aras could not help, no one could. They were doomed, all of them, their people, the Elves, everyone.

Aras plucked the letter from his unresisting hand. He glanced at the seal, his eyes showing surprise, and then he scanned the letter, and his eyes widened in horror and confusion and desperation. "But I am not dead! And if I am not, then is this entire message false, a ruse of some sort? You told me Beryl was already dead, that he died far south of here. But this is written in Ahrnad's hand, and the order number is authentic, the verification coding correct, so it must be genuine. Is my father truly dying? Tell me what I am to believe," Aras begged in Elvish, dropping the letter, his arms gripping Dewalaren's shoulders and shaking him, so powerfully and violently that Dewalaren thought he might well break even his strong bones without realizing it, for he had the strength of his grief, on top of the strength of his kind. But his words broke through Dewalaren's crippling despair, and he looked intently at Aras.

"You are the High-Prince of Nalea? You are Laedrin's son and heir?" Talon asked in Elvish in sudden frantic hope.

Aras nodded, eyes stricken.

"Then perhaps this War on the Watch can be ended before it is begun and the breach can be sealed!" He snatched the letter off the ground and turned to Farad, who was eyeing them both in frustration. Farad knew none of their words, but he could see hope had rekindled in Dewalaren's face.

Dewalaren spoke in Common now, so both Aras and Farad would understand. "Hunter, you must ride Kaldahar to King Elwyth in Tanieria and deliver this written message to him, with a verbal one of my own. Tell him High-Prince Aras is not dead, that Talon, the Lord of the Watch, rides with him to Nalea. They must take no action against us."

ARAS mastered himself with an effort of will, forcing his terror down. He could not afford such weakness. "They will never believe such a thing without proof, and the other Kingdoms will yet be a danger to you, if the messengers that must have been dispatched to them were not intercepted by the Enemy as well. Give me the letter, Talon, and I will write one of my own upon the back of it," Aras commanded in Common.

He knew the letter was genuine. The order number might possibly have been forged, but the message had not been. He had used his Power to ensure it and had nearly been felled by the rage, the murderous intent of Ahrnad, which permeated the missive.

Talon took the letter back from Hunter and handed it to Aras, without question.

Aras turned to Hunter. "Greetings, Hunter. Forgive me my injury of you, but I had no choice. I could not allow you to slay Talon. The barbed head of an arrow is not the proper form of introduction to any ally, so forgive me for my presumption and the abruptness of my request, but do you have pen and ink I might borrow, or an artist's lead? Neither Talon nor I carry them, although I can improvise both of the former, if I've the need."

"I would give my life to save Talon, so were I to lose the use of my arm or lose it entirely, it is a small price and one I would gladly pay. I do not have what you seek. I did not think I would have need of them," Hunter replied.

Aras nodded and took his pack from Janahar. He pulled out the bottle of Thenalonese wine and uncorked it and then set the pack against the trunk of a fallen tree, to use it as a writing desk. "I must draw my dagger, Hunter, but be assured that I threaten neither you nor Talon by my action. I seek only to use it as a pen," Aras said, looking into Hunter's eyes once more, to be sure he understood. Then he deliberately sat and slowly and carefully drew his pallenteum dagger from its sheath, holding the blade parallel to the ground in his left hand, in a non-threatening manner.

He poured a thin stream of wine over the end of the dagger, turning it to ensure it was completely covered, cupping his right hand under it as he did so, to catch the wine. He let the dagger tip sit in the pool in his hand for a few moments, as Talon and Hunter watched, perplexed. He poured the wine from his hand and carefully cut his cupped palm, allowing the blood to pool in his hand, where the wine had been.

Talon started to protest in alarm, but Aras quickly silenced him. "It is a small wound and I sterilized both the blade and my hand with the wine to minimize the risk of infection. The tip of the dagger is sharp enough that it might suffice as a quill. Although blood is not my ink of choice, I did not see any berries nearby, and it is an acceptable substitute." He did not tell them that he had performed this ritual before as a child, more than once, under his mother's direction, when blood was specifically called for in lieu of ink, for the Power it added.

"Now please, I must concentrate, lest I make a mistake in the coding within the order number. I cannot risk doing so, for there must be no doubt that this second message is in my hand and is as genuine as the first. And I must take care with the wording, for the same reason."

> *Date PA 07-19-3013 DM*
> *Order 9-2.1-4-4/PL=MLRA/TC=1-Gray; 2.1-Green;*
> *10-Black; 11-White*
>
>
> *King Elwyth of Tanieria:*
>
>
> *I speak with my father High-King Laedrin's voice and write with his hand, for from this letter I learn he has been felled and can do neither. The earlier report of my death was incorrect. I live and as I am next in rank in the chain of command will act as Regent until my father is healed. I head with utmost speed for Nalea and should reach there in approximately five days.*

I hereby rescind the Declaration of War against the Watch which was enacted due to incomplete intelligence. I travel in the company of and under the protection of Talon, Lord of the Watch. It is thanks to the aid of the Watch that I yet live, when I should be dead. Neither Prince Talon nor his people are to be harmed or impeded in any way. You are to show the bearer of this message, Captain Hunter of the Watch, and any other member of the Watch you encounter all courtesy and are hereby ordered to offer them all possible aid and assistance: food, clothes, shelter, medical aid, coin, supplies, mounts, even troops, if they require them.

But I reaffirm the Declaration of Martial Law and order the Reservists to be activated, not against the Watch, but against our true Enemy and theirs, Incuban and His minions. I provide crucial intelligence as well. Incuban and His forces have bypassed the last of the Dwarven Kingdoms and instead advance up the Methris River from the southern coast. A number of Cities of Men have already fallen, and Riviera and Loatia are in immediate grave danger, if they yet stand. Reinforcements must be dispatched from every Kingdom at once and sent to their aid.

I command you to copy this message and send it with your fastest messengers with armed escort to each of the six other Kingdoms, including Riviera and Loatia. Be advised that the bearer of this original message was slain by the forces of the Enemy. You must ensure your copies of my message get through at all costs.

Once he was done he handed it to Talon and said in Common, "Please read this so I can be sure I have not overlooked anything of vital import before I sign it. I would have you translate it for your kinsman Hunter, as well, into either Common or Amontirin, so he might also offer his counsel. Just be careful not to smudge it, for it is not yet fully dry. I will bandage my hand once you assure me it is complete and I have signed it."

Talon took the letter and read it aloud in Amontirin to Hunter, and then he and Hunter conversed in the same language. Talon turned to Aras. "It covers all the crucial points admirably. But if you would add a line of message for your people to relay to my kin, in my name, I would be in your debt. They must be warned that our Marker and Cache system has been compromised, and that they are to avoid them at all costs, for any of them may now bear false messages or traps. Also, they are commanded in my name to head to Caramore at once, for a War Council."

Aras nodded and added the suggested text and then signed it "Acting Regent High-Prince Aras."

"Please, Aras, now that you are done, Hunter will hold the message while it dries so it does not smear. You must allow me to treat and bandage your hand."

Aras acceded to Talon's need to tend to him, after carefully cleaning his blood from the blade with more of the wine. It would be dangerous to leave his blood upon it, were he to work his Power through the pallenteum blade in the future. He was already leery of the blood upon the paper, but he could not instruct King Elwyth to burn the message after reading it without arousing their suspicions even further than they might already be by the broken seal and two such contradictory messages, the second written in blood.

"THE blood has dried," Farad said.

Dewalaren turned to him. "Then you must make haste to Tanieria. I will ride with Aras on Janahar. Take Kaldahar. She is an exceptional mount and will serve you well." He turned to the mare. "Forgive me, Kaldahar, but you must part from Janahar for a time. Hunter has need of you. Please serve him as selflessly as you have served me, and be gentle and patient. He is injured and I think it likely he has not ridden for a long time." Dewalaren did not consciously and overtly use his Power upon the mare, but still he felt the blood of House of Horses, which flowed through his body from his grandmother, call to the horse as he spoke. She nickered a gentle good-bye to Janahar, and they touched noses before she moved to stand by Farad of her own accord.

Farad looked from the horse to Dewalaren in surprise. "Would that I had your blood in my veins! But I am fortunate beyond reason that I do not have it upon my hands. That is more than enough." He embraced Dewalaren. "May Idare and the Elves keep you safe. Come to Caramore as quickly as you can, cousin."

"I have missed you, cousin! When next we meet, I hope it might be for longer and in better circumstances, though the latter appears unlikely. Take care. Stay safe. Be well." It was an effort almost beyond his ability to release Farad. After thinking him dead, it was hard to let him head once more to danger.

But Dewalaren resolutely turned to Aras. "Come, Aras. I would take you home."

Aras turned to Janahar and removed the bridle, eyeing it in loathing, but packed it carefully in the bag strapped to the saddle. He brushed Janahar's cheek softly with his hand, whispering to her. Janahar nickered and stamped the ground in excitement. Dewalaren tied his bedroll and Lunahr's sword behind Aras's on Janahar's saddle. Aras mounted in a leap, and Dewalaren was behind him in an instant, arms about his narrow waist. Aras whispered in Janahar's ear again, and they were off, heading back to the Western Road to go east before turning north through the woods.

FARAD watched them go. Aras had not been surprised when Dewalaren had stated he was the Lord of the Watch. Aras had apparently already known. It could not be that he did not understand the significance of what he had heard, for he had called him Prince in the letter as well. It appeared he might indeed truly be the High-Prince, and Dewalaren did not doubt it. He only hoped that Aras might also be the benevolent protector he appeared to be. He did not trust anyone he did not know with Dewalaren's safety and few enough that he did, but this time he had no choice.

Farad did not restring his bow with his spare string, although he had retrieved half of his arrows from the bodies of the wolven and the riders he had slain. He would not be able to use the bow again for some time. Now he had only the horse and his knife to see him to the safety of Tanieria. He had seldom before been rendered so helpless by an injury, but he was glad for it. He had almost killed Dewalaren. The thought chilled him. He knew the memory would haunt his dreams for a long time to come.

And Lunahr! He concentrated on the pain in his arm to spur him onward when that in his heart would cripple him. He could not cry for Lunahr, not until he knew the horror he had become was gone, cleansed by fire, until his body was reduced to ash to join all the others he had ever loved, save for Dewalaren. Dewalaren headed toward danger also, to death, if Aras could not keep him safe. But death was everywhere.

Farad clenched his teeth, mounted Kaldahar, and headed for the Western Road. He would be traveling west upon it through the Gelthor Pass in the Coroden Mountains and then across the wilds to Tanieria.

ARAS was in turmoil. His father lay dying, his people thought him dead, and they had declared War upon the Watch. How had so much chaos closed around him so suddenly?

He was not home where he should have been to see his father and people through their time of need. The reason he was not there left him cold. He had left home because he had been compelled to go, against his own heart, against his father's command. He had thought that destiny had drawn him to Talon in his time of need. But now he was not so sure. Now it looked as if perhaps a darker hand had brought him away so that his father would be more vulnerable.

No, he would not allow himself to believe that. Otherwise it would mean that Incuban already knew he was a threat. His only hope for victory, for life, lay in his continuing ability to conceal himself from the rest of the Players.

His people had declared death to the Watch, and now he was bringing one to them: the Lord of the Watch himself, the very Man the Enemy most desired. Aras knew his orders might sway King Elwyth, but he feared Ahrnad would not be so easily commanded. Ahrnad might even refuse to acknowledge his authority; he might seek to retain the position of Acting Regent. Aras knew his position in the eyes of the King's Guard would be tenuous, at best, after deserting his post. It was quite possible his father might have also issued an order for his arrest upon his return. Possibly even an order for his execution, though he was loath to even consider that his father might truly hate him so much. In any case, he feared he brought Talon to great danger, though he had little choice and could not even warn him of the danger without betraying too much. He had wanted to be a blade at his friend's side, not a knife in his back.

DEWALAREN could feel the tension in Aras. It was as if he were a bowstring drawn so tight a breath of wind would snap it. And he could do nothing to help his friend. Aras's father would live or die. The fact that Laedrin had survived the attack at all was astonishing.

He shuddered again at the thought of Lunahr in the hands of the Enemy, raped and tortured until his mind was torn from him. Now his body would be dead as well, at the hands of the Elves he had so loved. Their one hope lay in the fact that Aras was alive, and Dewalaren was the one who had saved the High-Prince. But Dewalaren knew that Elves did not think as Men, and much would yet depend upon whether their High-King lived or died.

They reached the Road, and once Janahar's hooves were upon it, it was as if she sprouted wings and flew. It was then that Dewalaren knew for certain that the blood of the steeds of Aralon must run in her veins. She was carrying close to five hundred pounds between her two riders; though Amontiri bones were not as dense as an Elf's, they were certainly heavier than the bones of other Men. But Janahar would not be able to keep to such a pace forever.

If his estimation of her ability was correct and they were careful with her, alternating her gait and resting her for a half hour or so for every four they rode, if she had a single rider, here on the Road, she could travel one hundred miles or so in seventeen and a half hours. The moon would be bright enough to travel the Road safely at least for the first few hours of the night. But as she carried both of them, her speed and the distance she could travel would be reduced. She could cover perhaps seventy miles. Nalea was almost two hundred miles from here and the final fifty would be along the riverbank and through dense woods, which would slow her pace considerably. If they slept for six and a half hours and began fresh again each morning, it should take them just over three days, quicker than Aras's earlier estimate, thanks to Janahar. They should arrive the morning of the fourth day.

ARAS had no idea how long they'd ridden before Talon's soft voice jarred him from his grim thoughts. "Aras, you must tell Janahar to slow or she will run herself to death for you, and we will reach your father no sooner. We can reach Nalea in just over three days without harming her or ourselves if we follow a careful schedule, alternating her pace and resting periodically. I can estimate time efficiently using the sun and later the moon and the stars, and I know how much distance we yet have to travel and the route we need to take."

Aras felt Janahar's sweaty shoulder and along her neck. She was yet sound, but Talon was right; she could not maintain her current pace without injury. He leaned over and whispered in her ear, but Janahar tossed her head defiantly. He whispered again, and Janahar reluctantly slowed her gait to a walk. "She has agreed to walk for a while," he said, stroking her proud neck. "I was distracted by my thoughts. I am glad you are here, even if I bring you to danger." Aras was unable to keep the desolation and despair from his voice.

"Danger follows me wherever I go, my friend."

Aras nodded. "You have lost Beryl a second time, even more terribly than the last. Please, can you not speak about him, to ease the pain in your heart?"

"NOTHING can ease the pain, but I will speak in honor of him, of the man he once was," Dewalaren said, and his voice broke. "Of the man he would have become, for he was still only a boy. His given name was Lunahr. He was Lord of House of Eagles, for all he was only twenty-four, not yet a man by our custom, when he died. We had sent him to Riviera six years ago for safety, so he might live to grow to manhood, so he might at least live long enough to sire an heir before following all the rest to oblivion.

"How can he have been slain? Where was Elanara? She was his guardian. She swore she would protect him with her life! Is Riviera destroyed? Is my love dead as well?" Dewalaren asked in agony that he might have lost two he loved, when even the first loss was more than he could bear.

He spoke Elanara's given name without hesitation, knowing now that Aras already knew it. He had not known the name of the High-Prince who had been engaged to wed Elanara before Arcanus convinced King Laranela and High-King Laedrin to alter the betrothal. He felt guilty for even mentioning her to Aras. Had Aras loved her? Arcanus had convinced him he had not, that it would not matter which Elven Princess the High-Prince wed. But surely, had Aras met her, had he known her, he would have loved her. How could anyone meet her and not? Lunahr had loved her, but she had taken care to ensure it would only be as a brother loves a sister. Dead, Lunahr was dead!

"How can our youngest cousin be gone? He was as a brother to all of us. He was called Beryl because his eyes were the color of Elfstones, and his hair was as long and golden as one of your people. He was a friend to the Elves and so like one of your own in form and temperament we used to tease him about his misshapen ears, which were the rounded ears of Man. And he would laugh with us. His voice was pure and sweet, and when he sang, his voice could warm the coldest heart. He spoke Elvish as well as I, although he was far younger. I know of no other who could have learned it so well in so short a time; your language is far more complex and subtle than Common. His temperament was gentle and generous. He was filled with joy over all life, but he had a special love for the woods, and those who dwelt in them. And for music, especially song. Meloneth himself could not have ever sung so sweetly.

"Even so young he could almost match sword to mine and he could almost match bow to Hunter. Gentle as he was, he was trained to kill efficiently, but he would only ever have done so in necessity, never in anger. When I found his sword in Athanark and thought he had fallen in battle, I did not think any pain could be worse.

"But knowing now that he must instead have been captured, to have been raped and tortured so viciously and brutally that he betrayed all our secrets. Then to have some vile thing use his body to commit regicide, the act most abhorrent to all of us. They have defiled him as no other in all our tragic history! To know that he is not only dead, but we have lost even the memory of him: he will be reviled as much as Ebonar by all our kin. To have the Elves as an enemy, instead of our allies! My very heart breaks.

"My only hope is that when your kinsmen see you still live, and know that I have returned you safely to them, they will falter in their thirst for vengeance against my people. In spite of the letter you sent, I know we are yet all endangered. Even if your people do not declare war upon us anew, I fear we have yet lost an ally we could ill afford to lose."

"I DO not deny it. Even if King Elwyth follows my commands, and he sends my message to the other Kingdoms, we will likely not be received well in Nalea itself. I will do all I can to protect you from the King's Guard's wrath, but my father and I did not part well when I left. We have never been close, as a father and son should be, far from it, but when I left we exchanged heated words, and he did not understand my leaving nor forgive it.

"I would never have left had I known! I should never have left. I was compelled to go, and it frightens me. I had thought something within me made me go, that destiny was choosing my path for me. But now I fear I was led away so that my father and I would each be more vulnerable. And we each found a Lord, but I found you and he found Beryl. I wish... I wish it would have been otherwise, that my father lived in your protection, and that I am the one who died at Beryl's hand." Aras shook with grief and sobbed.

As much as he had tried to sustain hope, he could not imagine that his father might yet live. He had read the detail in the coding within the order that the message itself had not revealed. Ahrnad wrote that his father's death was imminent, that it would be within a day and the message had been sent nearly two full days earlier.

All his dreams that someday his father might truly love him as much as he loved his father crumbled to dust. He wrapped his arms around Janahar's neck and wept. Janahar nickered softly, attempting to console him.

Talon tightened his hold about his waist, and Aras felt a flood of compassion laced with grief just as sharp. Talon knew the loss he felt. He too grieved; he had lost one who was as a brother to him.

Aras drew strength from both Janahar's and Talon's support. He wished it was Aerlyr that he rode, but he would not have traded Talon's embrace for anyone's, not even Jarnath's or Meloneth's. Aras's sobs subsided. Janahar whinnied and tossed her head, demanding he allow her to run, and Aras did not have the heart to deny her.

They continued onward, periodically resting, as Talon had recommended, in spite of Janahar's impatience, which mirrored his own. They ensured Janahar had time to drink and to graze. It was long after sunset that they made camp. Talon prepared dinner, but Aras could not eat. Talon tried to get him to partake of some of the wine, but he would not. His father would never eat nor drink nor breathe again. He had failed him utterly and completely. His disastrous decision to leave, his incompetence, had finally killed him. He could have protected his father from Beryl, sensed the danger, detected the monster he had become, stopped the attack, or at least healed his father from it, but he was not there.

He ached to cry again, to release all the tears he had refused to shed as a child, to pour his heartbreak into his blanket until it was sodden with his tears, but he was a man, not a child. Tears accomplished nothing. He would not shame the memory of his father further by showing such weakness again. He was mortified that he had wept before. He certainly knew better. Soldiers do not cry. His father's harsh words had drilled that lesson into him for decades.

Tears were only to be used as a weapon against his mother, to make him appear weak and helpless before her. But he was neither weak nor helpless. Incuban would pay for murdering his father, for assassinating their High-King and the many hundreds of thousands of others he and his minions had slain. His mother would pay for wounding his father's heart decades before, for slaying what little had remained of his spirit. And Arcanus would pay for whatever heinous crimes he had committed against his mother in their Homeland that helped turn her into the heartless, spiritless monster she had been, instead of the nurturing, loving mother he had longed for her to be.

FINALLY, after a long, restless night, dawn broke and they were off again. They met no other travelers, but they did not expect to. Heading east, this Road only led near Nalea and to the pass near the Kingdom of Malar in the Dwarven Lands. They rode through the second day. When they stopped for the night, Talon again urged Aras to eat, and he finally did so, out of duty rather than hunger. He must stay strong so he could slay his enemies. The thought was so cold and heartless, so foreign to him, so like something his father might say that it both chilled him to the bone and made him want to weep anew for what he had lost, for what he had never had. He did not mourn his father so much as he mourned what might have been, what now never could be.

When it became apparent he would not be able to sleep, Talon offered to show him the meditation techniques Arcanus had taught him so that he might at least rest his body and his mind. Aras seized eagerly on the opportunity to learn even such a minute fragment of intelligence about the techniques of one of his enemies. He felt awash in shame when he felt a flow of relief from Talon, that he had found a way to help his friend. Talon loved Arcanus almost as a second father, from all Aras had seen and heard, and here he was, attempting to twist that love, to warp it, to use it to destroy Arcanus.

He was no less a monster than his mother, than Incuban, than Arcanus! He knew firsthand the monster his mother was, and he'd seen volumes of evidence of Incuban's crimes. Arcanus was a monster as well; he'd known it from the start. Although... there had been no overt evidence of his crimes as there was of Incuban's. Then how had he known it? His mother had told him. His mother, who was truly and completely insane, as cold and cruelly mad as Incuban.

A revelation shook Aras to his core. What if Arcanus was in reality not the monster he had been led to believe? What if he fought Aethelia and Incuban for the same reason Aras did, out of necessity, out of self-preservation and the need to protect those he loved? He had never even thought to question before what Arcanus might be fighting for, what his motivation might be! Was it purely to protect the Amontir? Could he actually be the benevolent guardian he appeared to them?

"Aras? Please tell me what I might say, what I might do to help you. If I am so powerless to aid someone who is yet beside me, how can I hope to aid those who are so far away?"

Aras had been so self-absorbed he had failed to detect the turmoil building in Talon. He was becoming distraught, sliding into a black pit of despair, and from there, it would be a short step to madness.

Aras poured every ounce of love and reassurance and protection he felt for Talon into the tree that sheltered his friend's core, hoping Talon might somehow feel it.

The transformation was nothing short of miraculous. A smile of such relief and joy and wonder lit Talon's face that his own doubts and despair and anguish fled from it as shadows receding before the sun.

"I have not felt so warm, so safe, so loved since the last time my father hugged me! No, not since the last time Lunahr...." Talon gasped in agony, fighting to breathe as a look of anguish, of unbearable loss, ripped across his face. Aras knew it would have slashed his core to bloody tatters had his tree not embraced it.

Aras wrapped his flesh and blood arms around Talon as well, forcing Talon's ear to his chest, over his heart. "Do not listen to any of it. Hear only my heartbeat. I am alive, you are alive, you are safe, we are together, always. I will never leave you. I have told you, and you must know it to be true. I will protect you, comfort you, cherish you, calm you, always."

DEWALAREN gasped raggedly, inhaling the breath that moments before would not come, and then a second and a third breath as the wild hammering of his heart that had nearly shattered his core calmed and steadied to a familiar rhythm. It was then that he realized to his humiliation that he was clinging to Aras in desperation, not like a lover or even a father, but as a child. A moment later the feeling vanished, washed away by waves of warmth and understanding.

But he should not be so dependent upon another! He was a King. He was the one others should lean upon. His head knew he should pull from Aras's embrace, but his heart, having found the solace it so desperately needed, refused to hear it. He was certain he would shatter into a million fragments if he even tried to pull away.

"We are both equally fragile, both physically, mentally, and emotionally drained," Aras assured him. "We both need to sleep, to rest. I swear to you that Janahar will alert me to any danger that might appear in time for us to react to it, to survive it. If you would not be adverse to it, I ask to lie in your arms tonight, as a comrade, as a friend, so that we might draw comfort from one another's heartbeats, from the warmth of one another's arms."

There would be no danger in doing so, not tonight, and every danger in trying to survive the night alone. Dewalaren nodded, not wanting to speak, wanting his memory of Aras's voice to fill the silence of the night.

"Janahar, please guard us. Awaken us if there is any danger," Aras commanded.

Janahar whickered in acknowledgement and strode a few paces away from the fire, toward the perimeter of their camp.

"And you must sleep, my friend. May your dreams only be pleasant ones," Aras said gently.

His body surrounded by the warmth of Aras's body, and his core surrounded by the warmth of the pallenteum tree that protected it, Dewalaren fell quickly and easily to sleep, and Aras soon followed.

DEWALAREN awoke in Aras's arms with the first light of dawn after one of the most restful nights of sleep he had ever experienced. For the moment Aras's face was as relaxed and peaceful as his own felt. Idare, what would it be like, to go to sleep in the comfort of this man's arms every night and to awaken like this every morning? The contentment he had been feeling instantly transformed to completely inappropriate desire. No, he must not even imagine such a thing!

Resolutely, he instead replaced Aras's face with Elanara's in his mind's eye, his leanly muscled warrior's body with her soft curves. The effect was just as dramatic. It was as if he were hugging a block of ice, shriveling his heart, his manhood, his desire, his very core.

Aras jerked upright in his arms, his eyes flashing silver for a moment as he looked wildly about for danger, before morphing instantly back to their familiar, soothing green when he found none. "Did you have a nightmare?" Aras asked, still looking carefully about.

Dewalaren snatched the ready-made explanation like a lifeline. "I must have, though I do not remember it. I sense nothing amiss, now that I am awake and Janahar is still on guard. Even Fennel, Lord of House of Horses, would be envious of your skill with her, my friend."

"You spoke to her with no less skill. I doubt she would have pulled a wagon or left Kaldahar's side were any other Man to have requested it of her," Aras countered.

Dewalaren smiled, relieved at the effectiveness of the misdirection. "That is because I requested it of her, rather than commanded it. Noble ladies are proud and willful. They balk at commands." A sudden revelation seized him. Could that be why Elanara despised him? Had her father commanded her to marry him against her will? Just as quickly, the nascent hope that he understood her died stillborn. Laranela would never do such a thing. He was a loving father who cherished each of his children. He would never act against his daughter's wishes.

ARAS saw Talon's brow crease in concentration or perhaps inspiration, but it was fleeting. Whatever he had been thinking, he had dismissed it almost immediately. He did not ask. It was clearly something upsetting. He would not return Talon's core to the sudden jangled turmoil that had overwhelmed it only moments before without warning. He had awoken terrified that Talon had somehow come to harm while he slept, in spite of Janahar's alertness. He wished for the twentieth time that he had not given the gem-battery to Audra, much as she had needed it, when Talon was apparently in need of its protection after all. He would have used it last night to ward the camp instead of relying only upon Janahar's vigilance and his own keen senses.

They broke their night's fast and then resumed their journey. They left the Western Road and entered the woods, soon emerging on the banks of the Tahir River. Their pace was by necessity slower as Janahar was forced to pick her way cautiously. They crossed sandy banks in some places, treacherously smooth river rocks in others, and often found themselves amongst the trees, where Janahar carefully stepped over protruding roots and other hazards as they remained alert for low hanging branches that might unseat them. He and Talon watched constantly for patrols, lest the soldiers discover them first.

As Talon had calculated, they were yet short of Nalea when it became too dark to see, the moon's light blocked by the canopy of branches above them. That night he and Talon sought sanctuary in the branches of one of the trees. They would not light a fire, not here within these woods; they would not reveal their presence prematurely. They took turns on watch. They dared not risk both sleeping; Janahar would likely not recognize one of the Guard or King's Guard as a threat until it was too late.

WHEN dawn finally broke, they left their sheltering tree eagerly. Aras changed into his Elven clothes, the ones Millicent and Audra had mended for him. It seemed so long ago, so distant now, as if in a different lifetime, a more innocent and carefree time, for all the dangers he had faced. He felt Talon's eyes upon him as he disrobed and then dressed, but he was careful not to acknowledge it. When he finished, he turned and saw Talon was also changing his clothes, to the fine silks Rion had tailored for him to Aras's specifications. Aras's breath hitched at the sight of the delicate fabric lovingly embracing every muscle.

Talon turned and their eyes locked in mutual appreciation. Just as quickly they both turned away. "Come, we've still a bit of a distance to travel," Talon encouraged.

The way along the riverbank grew a little easier as the morning progressed. They were yet a distance from Nalea when they heard the sound of fighting up ahead. Janahar picked her way gingerly and silently through the trees toward the conflict as bravely as if she were a trained war-horse.

There were the shouts of Men and the clash of swords. Through a break in the trees, they saw some thirty Men with gleaming blades fighting three Elves at close quarters. Bodies of both peoples littered the ground. Aras recognized the look of the Men instantly, in dismay. Since when were they at war with the Hill People?

Even as they approached, one of the Elves fell, and the other two stood back to back against fifteen times their number. The Elves were unable to use their bows in such close quarters, but Aras was not so constrained. His bow began to sing as Talon leapt from Janahar and ran to the left, engaging three foes simultaneously.

Aras emptied his quiver of all sixteen arrows, his own four and the dozen from Aralon. But this time, he did not shoot to kill. Each arrow pierced the wrist of a swordsman, and each Man dropped his blade.

Talon was still laying about expertly with his blade, at the moment fighting four men at once. The beleaguered Elves had instantly rallied, turning from defense to offense. After downing his four foes, Talon leapt to the aid of one of the Elves, not a moment too soon. The Elf had been driven to one knee and disarmed, and a sword was arcing down for his head, but Dewalaren parried the blow and then felled his attacker with a slash from his blade.

One of the Hill People called out a guttural command, and suddenly their foe fled back through the trees, toward the River.

Aras ran to Talon's side, in case their warriors turned about and attacked again unexpectedly, instead of retreating, as it appeared.

"Well met, cousin!" the Guard Talon had succored said to Aras, rising to his feet again, retrieving and cleaning his sword.

The other Guard eyed both Aras and Talon coolly and suspiciously, and yet held his blade at the ready. "Do not judge so quickly, Leonas. This tree hugger did not slay our foes, and we do not bring Men into our woods."

Aras winced at the racial slur, though it was one of the more mild ones the Oceana could have used.

Talon cleaned and sheathed his own blade and turned his back on the Elf. "Five of your number lie wounded, and I would sooner help them than bicker with you."

The Guard stared at him, stunned, for Talon had also spoken in Elvish. The Guard tensed, but the other soldier grabbed his arm and said, "We are not yet at war with all Men, Nolas." Aras thought he sounded bitter at the prospect that they soon might be. "This Man saved my life." He turned to Talon. "For your aid in our time of need you have the protection of Captain Leonas of the Guard."

Aras knelt by one of the fallen. "For him, we are too late."

"Varyl was the first to fall," Leonas said, his voice tinged with loss. "We were ambushed."

"When I left, we were not at war with the Hill People nor the Watch. I did not think to find my home so changed," Aras said sadly.

"Then alas, I must bring you tidings of far worse. High-Prince Aras was slain nearly a month ago." Leonas's brave voice broke and his eyes glistened with unshed tears.

It touched Aras deeply that those in the Navy still loved him, after all they had suffered because of him.

"Then, while the City still lay stunned in grief and mourning, an assassin struck High-King Laedrin, and he lies near death." Leonas said the last as if it mattered little, compared to Aras's death.

Aras was poleaxed. His father yet lived? "Still alive! Then you have given me most joyous news, Captain Leonas, for I feared my father had succumbed days ago!

And I return some small measure of joy to you, for I have not been slain, although I would still hear the details of my death so I might understand why my people mourn me."

Leonas stepped back in surprise and stared at his face. Then his eyes widened in recognition, and he fell to his knees at his feet and kowtowed before him, bow raised in his outstretched hands. "Forgive me, Highness, for not recognizing you and for bringing you to danger! My bow is ever at your service!"

Nolas spun around and stared from one to the other, and then also fell to his knees, as did the three wounded who could stand. "Forgive me my harsh words, Highness," Nolas apologized, worshipfulness replacing the former arrogance of his tone.

"They are forgiven. Arise, all of you. Now tell me, my father is recovering?" Aras asked, his voice hopeful.

Now Leonas looked grieved. "No, Highness. His life hangs by a thread. The healers have tried all they can, but he was struck by a poison blade and our most skillful arts are almost powerless to work against it. They have only slowed the poison in its work. He was felled six days ago."

"Then I must go to him at once. Help me with your wounded." They sat the one who could not walk upon Janahar, and the dead Elf, Varyl, was slung over Janahar's back behind him. Aras gave the Elf with the injured leg his staff. Nolas helped the one whose head was bandaged. The one who had his arm in a sling was able to walk unaided.

"We delay you, Highness. You would go more quickly with only Captain Leonas and Nolas to guard you," the one with the staff said.

"I will not leave you so vulnerable. But I would have you run ahead, Captain Leonas, and report this attack and bring us aid. Then find me, when your duty is done."

"At once, Highness," Leonas said, and he was off like a deer.

The Elf with the injured arm said, "The Hill People think to find us vulnerable without our High-King and our High-Prince, but Lord of the Guard Ahrnad and Commander Daras are not to be trifled with. Still, we have been without war for so long, I would face one foe at a time."

Aras nodded. As they marched onward at their plodding pace, constantly scanning the forest for new dangers, Aras learned the names of the other Guardsmen, and they spoke of all they knew regarding the War with the Hill People. They were only halfway to their goal when twelve bowmen broke from the cover of the trees, catching them completely by surprise, but hands were quickly lowered from weapons when they saw that they were Naval Guardsmen.

"Nolas! What happened? Was it Hill People?" their Captain asked, scanning the faces of the mobile injured and the two on the horse critically, paling. "Where is your Captain, Leonas?" he asked anxiously.

"Fear not, Captain Gaius! Captain Leonas yet lives," Nolas said, with compassion he had not betrayed before. "Though it was a close thing. These were no lone scouts nor small raiding parties this time. We were ambushed by a well-armed and well-trained war party of forty. We would have perished but for the High-Prince. High-Prince Aras is not dead; he has returned to us!"

Gaius looked at Aras closely then and fell to his knees, and his men quickly followed suit. "Highness!" they cried, as one.

"Rise, all of you. Captain Gaius, I would have you send six of your men back with Nolas to lead them to the site of the battle, to recover any of the enemy wounded who might yet live to be taken prisoner. The rest of your men I would have escort our own wounded and the fallen to the Healers' Hall. We have already sent Captain Leonas ahead with news of the attack. Now that the wounded are safe, I would ride to the City to be at my father's side."

"Of course, Highness!" Gaius said, and then he commanded his men as Aras had outlined. The nonambulatory wounded Elf and Varyl's body were removed from Janahar's back. As soon as they were free of the saddle, Aras and Talon mounted and were off.

They found that fleet-footed Leonas had reached the City before them. They were met by a mounted honor guard of the Guard and escorted directly to the Palace. But at the steps, they were blocked by Lord of the Guard Ahrnad and twenty-four of the King's Guard.

"Lord Ahrnad, would you block my way when my father lies inside?" Aras asked.

"No, Highness. But I would have you come closer so I can make sure it truly is you, for we thought you dead," Ahrnad challenged.

Aras dismounted and came up the stairs toward him. Ahrnad looked him up and down intently. "It is the High-Prince. NOW!" he ordered, and he grabbed Aras and dove between the line of bowmen. Twenty-four arrows trained upon Talon's position. But Talon was no longer there. He had leapt behind Janahar. Leonas interposed himself between the King's Guard and both Man and horse, arms out, crying, "Hold!"

Aras echoed his cry, his voice ringing with Power. The King's Guard were frozen where they stood. Aras struggled from Ahrnad's grasp.

"Highness, you bring an assassin to your father! I recognize him. This is Talon, Lord of the Watch! He has come to complete the job his subordinate left unfinished."

"No. Talon is my friend and protector, and he has saved my life and returned me safely to Nalea. I trust him with my life, and my father's. As your High-Prince and Acting Regent, until my father recovers, I order you and your men to stand down and draw no further weapon against him," Aras commanded, releasing the hold of his Wizard's Voice upon the men only after Ahrnad so ordered them. Talon walked cautiously out from behind Janahar, apologizing softly to her for using her as a shield. Janahar snorted and butted him in the chest with her nose in reprimand.

"Come, Talon." Aras said, turning for the door.

"Highness, no!" Ahrnad argued. "He cannot enter the Palace! Your father lies helpless."

"You forget yourself, Lord Ahrnad. Your High-Prince has commanded you. Stand aside." Aras's voice held no Power now save the power of his station. It was the voice of ultimate authority and not to be disobeyed. Ahrnad stood aside, but with a look of venom in his eyes directed toward Talon.

They entered the Palace, the King's Guard following closely behind them. They walked through marble corridors to an ornate, guarded door.

"I would see my father. Stand aside," Aras commanded the King's Guard at the door, and they immediately obeyed.

FOUR healers turned to them as they entered the room, and Dewalaren saw they stared wide-eyed at their High-Prince. Aras passed them unseeing, his eyes on the bed before him. His father lay as pale and still as death, a bandage wrapped around his left arm from wrist to shoulder. His face was creased in pain though he was not conscious. Aras knelt beside his bed and touched his father's noble brow and spoke words of love to him that he could not hear, and cried for what he had not yet lost.

One of the healers had eyes only for Aras. His eyes were bright with unshed tears. Aras rose then and turned to him. "Jarnath, my mentor, tell me what happened."

Dewalaren looked at the Elf in surprise. Why would this healer be named after the God of Healing Men followed? The Elves did not worship any Gods. They did not even worship their ancestors, as the Amontir did.

Jarnath told Aras in a hushed voice that the wound had been the faintest of scratches on Laedrin's wrist, but it had been enough. The blade was poisoned with some dark magic and beyond their power to heal. They were only able to delay the progress of the decay it brought, for a time, but the wound was festering and growing and consuming him. The poison would eventually reach his heart.

By the time they realized the severity of what they faced, it was beyond their skills to combat. It was too late even to amputate his arm, a drastic action seldom even considered. The High-King was far too weak; the shock would have killed him. Jarnath told him they had sent an urgent call to all the Kingdoms for aid from any of the three wizards, but feared it would come too late.

"Can you tell us what you know of the attack? There may perhaps be some clue there as to how to save him," Dewalaren said in Elvish.

Jarnath looked at him in surprise. "You should know more of it than I, if what Ahrnad told me is true. Are you not the one who ordered the attack?"

Dewalaren was shocked that this Elf thought so, yet was speaking to him so calmly. If it were King Laranela lying in that bed, every one of his subjects would want to slay him with his or her bare hands. There must not have been any love lost between this healer and the High-King, however much he might love the High-King's son. Which meant he might not be aiding Laedrin to the best of his ability. Were the three others healers?

ARAS replied angrily, "Talon did not order the attack. This was an act of the Enemy. Neither Talon nor Beryl is to blame for it."

"Forgive me, Aras! Please do not look at me like that when I have been grieving for you for so long. My heart is not strong enough to bear it," Jarnath said softly.

Aras looked at his teacher in sudden concern. He truly looked ill, old, and frail. "Jarnath, please forgive me! Much has happened. I....."

"Hush, Aras. Forgive me. I should not have said that to you. Do not worry. My heart is strong again, it sings now that I see you are alive and well."

JARNATH turned to Talon. "You have asked me to tell you of the attack, and I shall. Captain of the Watch, Lord Beryl, came to see the High-King six days ago. He is well spoken of by King Laranela of Riviera, and we saw the band of his House, so he was trusted. He sought word with the High-King in private. Audience was granted. But Laedrin has always had his audience chambers watched. And since Aras's... death... the High-King's wariness has grown. None knew it at the time, but he had taken to wearing the pallenteum chain mail vest he had not worn since... that he has not worn in a long time, under his clothes." Jarnath was appalled. Lord of the Watch or not, no Man must ever hear of the War, and here he had almost mentioned it to him! He still had not recovered from the shock of seeing Aras alive, when he had known him to be dead for so long.

"When they were alone, Lord Beryl spoke only three words. He said, 'You cannot move,' and somehow his words froze not only Laedrin, but the concealed King's Guard as well. Then Lord Beryl drew a knife and lunged at Laedrin. All who saw said he had a look of wild glee upon his face as he stabbed Laedrin in the heart with the dagger. But the vest turned the blade, saving him, though the knife scored Laedrin's arm.

"As Lord Beryl fell off balance in surprise, Laedrin and the others were suddenly free of the foul spell of his voice. Laedrin ordered, 'Do not kill him! We must question...,' but then he shuddered and fell and spoke no more.

"The King's Guard released their arrows from the concealed arrow slits in the chamber walls, felling Lord Beryl, but they followed the High-King's order and did not slay him. Then they rushed into the room and secured the prisoner. Even with multiple injuries, Lord Beryl fought like a demon to be free, doing further harm to himself and injuring a number of the King's Guard, until he was rendered unconscious. They bound him and carried him to the dungeon and chained him there. We were summoned first to the High-King's aid and then to Lord Beryl's, to treat his wounds, so he might be strong enough for the King's Guard to question him.

"The High-King has not wakened. He has not moved nor spoken since. We have been able to prolong his life, but not save it. After we healed Lord Beryl, when he awoke, he claimed ignorance of all that happened. He pretended not to know where he was, or how he came to be here. And nothing we have done to him since has loosened his tongue. But still we try, because as he felled the High-King, he alone might know how to heal him."

"BERYL is your prisoner? You question him still? He yet lives?" Dewalaren asked in desperate hope. He had thought Lunahr would have been instantly slain for his crime. He knew the Elves would not show mercy to an assassin, but they had obeyed the High-King's final order. Jarnath's calm words of his torture chilled him, though. As with all their other works, Elves had developed torture into an art, although a dark one that they fortunately seldom used.

"Aras, if he still lives, I must see him! I must know what the Enemy has done to him," Dewalaren pleaded. "He must be a Resemblant, I'm almost sure of it, but still… Incuban is so vile, He might have kept him a Man, just to torment Hunter. There is no one else left save for me that He could use to such effect against him."

"Then we will go to the dungeon," Aras said. He ordered Ahrnad to take them to the prisoner.

Ahrnad seethed, but obeyed.

JARNATH'S eyes followed Aras as he left, and his heart went with him, even as he kept his place by Laedrin's side. He had already done everything in his Power to see that the father Aras had loved lived, for the good of the Seven Kingdoms. Laedrin was cold and bigoted and selectively cruel, but Ahrnad was a hundred times worse.

Ahrnad was the one who had urged Laedrin to declare war on the Hill People and as Acting Regent had all too eagerly declared war upon the Watch as well. He had activated the Reservists and been ready to declare war upon every City of Man. Praise Aralyn and Ragnar both that Aras yet lived and that he had the strength of will to wrest the Regency from Ahrnad! Perhaps now both the Seven Kingdoms and the Cities of Man might yet survive this latest calamity.

LORD AHRNAD led them to the dungeon. They descended the cold, granite stairs. As they walked past empty cells toward the light in the corridor ahead, they heard the sound of sobbing in the dark.

Dewalaren clenched his jaw and reminded himself of what Lunahr had done, of what he probably was. But he still was not prepared for what he found when they entered the lone occupied cell.

It was Lunahr. At one glance, he knew it was truly him, not merely his shell, but the boy he loved. He could tell from his eyes it was truly still him, and the thought repelled him. Lunahr could not commit regicide! None of them could, but his gentle, sweet cousin? He especially could never kill an Elf, let alone the High-King.

Lunahr was almost unrecognizable. He was not bruised nor burnt nor beaten, but he was chained to the wall, his eyes were red from crying, and his face and body were twisted in agony, as some vile liquid was forced down his throat. He was choking and sobbing and begging for mercy.

"STOP!" Aras commanded. The two interrogators turned and backed away cautiously when they saw Ahrnad but then recognized Aras and stared at him in awe and joy. Aras was horrified when he recognized them as two of the Naval Guard he'd secretly befriended as a child, ones that had not been discovered by his father. They had looked so hard and cruelly at their prisoner as they tortured him, but now he saw guilt and revulsion and pity in their eyes that marked them as the men he had known, for they were just as tortured as their prisoner by what they were doing.

Beryl sagged and lay dangling by his wrists in the chains that glowed silver in the semidark room: pallenteum chains that would not bend or break. The shackles were caked with old blood and sticky with fresh blood where the skin about his wrists and ankles had torn from his struggles. His eyes were closed and he was panting.

"I WOULD speak with him," Dewalaren said, and his voice broke.

Aras nodded his consent.

"Lunahr, it's Laren," he said softly, in Amontirin.

Lunahr's head shot up and his eyes were wild with fear as he saw him. "No! Laren, they'll kill you! They've gone mad! They think I tried to assassinate the High-King!" he cried, in the same language.

"Tell me what truly happened," Dewalaren begged.

"I don't know what happened!" Lunahr swore. "I've told them that, over and over again, but they won't believe me! The pain! Idare, it hurts, it's endless!

"King Laranela feared Riviera would not be safe for much longer. He knew Elanara was still safely in Erenia. He sent Queen Naraena first to Tanieria and then to Salenia and then later sent Elavar to Salenia to join her. Eladar never came home after his training. His father knew how much I'd missed him, but he sent him off without telling me where he was going or why. What kind of King makes sure his own family is safe when he knows the rest of his people aren't?

"When he tried to send me away as well I refused to go. I told him I would not leave him and his people alone to face the Enemy. I was a Captain of the Watch and would fight beside them. But he scoffed at my offer of aid. He thought I was a helpless child.

"It's your fault! King Laranela told me that you had told him I must not be risked in battle, that my House must live at any cost. He ordered me to join Elavar or Elanara in safety, when he knew it was Eladar I most wanted to see. But I had my duty as part of the Watch. I knew I could gather vital intelligence, that I could help save Riviera and Loatia when Laranela was too fearful to send his own scouts as he should. So I lied to him. I told him I would ride to join Elanara. But instead I rode down the Methris, to see what I could learn about the Enemy's plans and movements so that I might keep Loatia and Riviera safe.

"It was horrible, all the things I saw! There were so many refugees coming up the Methris, many of them with nothing but the clothes on their backs, ragged and hungry and dirty, bandaged and limping, and their eyes, Idare, their eyes! There was terror and despair. They had lost their homes, their villages or cities, sometimes even their entire families. I learned all I could about the Enemy's forces and then I headed back for Riviera.

"But I misjudged how fast they were and how strong. I was caught just outside of Alridge. The city was overrun so suddenly! Revenants, Laren, so terrifying! Worse than anything you or Farad ever told me of. I fought them, Idare, I fought so hard, but there were too many! They wounded me in a dozen places. I was dying, I knew I was dying, and that's when you touched me. When I most needed my strength, your touch weakened me. I had to keep you safe, I had to sever our link to save you from Him. Oh Laren, how could you make me break our link? I was so afraid to die alone! I remember the blood and the teeth and the knife and the pain.

"Then suddenly I woke up here. They tell me I am in Nalea, many leagues to the north of where I was. They say I've knifed and poisoned their High-King. And they're torturing me for it. They won't stop until I tell them everything I know. But I can't tell them about their High-King. I don't know who attacked him. And even though you exiled me, I won't betray my kin.

"They want to know all our true names, and how we contact each other, where we are and where our refuges are, all our strengths and our weaknesses, so they can hunt us down and kill us. Laren, have mercy! I'm on fire! They are worse than the Enemy, they are so cruel! Please make them stop!" His body convulsed in agony.

Dewalaren could not help himself, even knowing Lunahr had attacked the High-King, hearing how tainted his words had been against Laranela and even him, for he loved Lunahr still. He embraced Lunahr, feeling every tendon in his young cousin's body stretched to the breaking point. In that instant, Lunahr suddenly went limp in his arms.

Dewalaren was terrified that he might have succumbed to the tortures and died, but then suddenly Lunahr's hand snaked out and looped one of his chains around Dewalaren's neck and drew it tight. Dewalaren was taken completely off guard by the unexpected attack. His eyes met Lunahr's in disbelief, and to his horror he saw Lunahr's eyes were wild with madness, terrible eyes. Dewalaren's fingers clawed desperately at his throat as little points of light filled his vision, as the world began to disappear in a red haze, as he fought to breathe.

Aras and Ahrnad and the interrogators were pulling at Lunahr's arms to no avail, but then Ahrnad cracked Lunahr across the face and he fell limp.

Aras unwound the chain from Dewalaren's neck and pulled him to safety, his eyes frantic with fear until he saw his windpipe was not crushed, that he could yet breathe.

Dewalaren stood gasping, his hand at his bruised throat, looking at his young cousin with horror-filled eyes. Lunahr was indeed lost to them; not a Resemblant, something even worse. He was completely mad, not the King's Madness, something unspeakably vile. He was twisted beyond all redemption. Killing him would be a mercy. They would never find out about the poison from him.

The interrogators drew the chains taut, stretching Lunahr so tightly against the wall that his shoulders bulged out as if they would tear his arms from their sockets. Lunahr moaned then, and roused, and Dewalaren drew back from him.

"Laren! Laren, please, don't leave me here! Please, as you love me, help me!" Lunahr begged. "Why are you looking at me like that?"

Dewalaren realized Lunahr had no knowledge of what he had done. He stumbled out of the room, shaking, unable to reconcile the creature in the cell with the boy he still loved.

Ahrnad and Aras followed. There was a scream from the room behind them and Dewalaren staggered as if he were the one in such pain.

"Tell me everything he said to you," Ahrnad demanded, grabbing Dewalaren by the shoulders.

"Release him!" Aras commanded, and Ahrnad obeyed.

"Talon, please. Forgive me, but we must know what he told you," Aras said, his voice warm with compassion.

It hurt to talk and his voice sounded gravelly, but Dewalaren told him everything Lunahr had said, except about the interrogation concerning the Watch, clenching his fist so tightly against the sound of the screams that echoed from the walls that his palm bled from the pressure of his own nails. Then suddenly, the screams ended. Oh, Idare, what had the Enemy done to him? The Elves had tortured him for six days like this, and he had not broken.

Dewalaren felt Aras's strong hand clutch his shoulder, and he pressed his hand to Aras's, desperate for the warmth of the contact as his eyes streamed with tears. He would have collapsed in his grief, his despair, were Aras not with him.

"THEN there truly is no hope," Aras said, as devastated by the knowledge that his father was going to die and he was powerless to save him as he was to know that Incuban had destroyed someone Talon loved as a son.

A comforting, fatherly voice drifted to them from around the corner, down the hall. "Where there is life, there is always hope."

"Arcanus!" Talon said, his head jerking up, sudden hope shining in eyes that were yet wet with tears.

Aras felt the skin on the back of his neck crawl and his heart began slamming in his chest in fear as he braced for battle. Arcanus was here! No! He was not ready! He drew upon Aranas's strength, increasing the Power of the shield that masked his core tenfold. Arcanus must not discover him, he must not learn of his Power, not now, not yet!

"I understand the High-Prince is down here. I need his help. They won't let me in to see the High-King without him," Arcanus said as he came around the corner.

Aras fought for his expression to be one of eager hope instead of shock and surprise. Arcanus was nothing like he had expected. Arcanus had adopted the form of an elderly Man, though his masking spell was so weak it was easily visible to one with his level of Power. Arcanus's image wavered and coruscated, the wrinkles on his face fading in and out of existence, his waist length hair shimmering from brittle white to gleaming burnt sienna and back again, even as his gray eyes darkened to the color of blood before fading once more to the color of weathered slate. So at least that much of what his mother had told him about Arcanus was true: he truly appeared to be Faeren.

ARCANUS was careful to look at Dewalaren in fatherly concern, concealing his consternation as he clutched the staff in his hands, truly leaning upon it for support. He had been shocked to hear Dewalaren's voice. He had come here to see the High-Prince. He had not known Dewalaren was here. He had not expected to see him yet. He was not prepared. He had planned to channel more Power into his masking spell before he did so, but it was too long since he had fed sufficiently. The Watch must not see him so weakened, let alone the Lord of the Watch, lest they manage to pierce the veil he had so carefully concealed himself under these three millennia.

It disturbed him greatly that he had been surprised by his presence. He should have sensed Dewalaren's core as soon as he had arrived in Nalea. But he could not detect it, even now as Dewalaren stood before him. He had thought he either had not yet arrived, or that he had already been slain by the soldiers of Nalea. For a moment he feared the Enemy might have taken him, but this was no Resemblant. He'd have been able to sense it if he were. And he had such a haunted, tortured look upon his face, the look of one yet hunted. It must truly be him. He must speak with Dewalaren.

But now the High-Prince was speaking to him, his voice painfully young and eager. "Arcanus! You have answered the summons!"

"No. I am merely here by fortunate accident. I was both astonished and relieved to hear that my pupil Magus had made a grievous mistake in his scry of you, High-Prince. Now that I am here, however, I think I can help your father."

ARAS did not want to let Arcanus anywhere near his father. But if he did not allow it, the King's Guard would think he did so to ensure his father would die. They would be convinced he committed treason and regicide; they would think he sought to steal his father's throne. "I will take you to him at once," Aras replied, cloaking his reluctance in layers of false enthusiasm.

On the way to the High-King, Arcanus asked questions about the attack, and Lord Ahrnad told the same story Jarnath had told them.

Just before they reached the Palace, a King's Guardsman ran up to them. "Lord Ahrnad, we need you in the Wood." Ahrnad looked torn between his High-King and his other duties.

"Go. My father is safe," Aras commanded. To his relief, Ahrnad nodded and departed. Now he would be able to focus all his attention on Arcanus, the greater potential threat.

They entered the Palace and Aras led them to his father. Jarnath looked up from his father, and Aras was almost felled as a double wave of amazement, joy, relief, hope, guilt, and terror unexpectedly slammed into him from two sides: the emotions of both Jarnath and Arcanus almost overwhelming even his reinforced defenses.

"**LEAVE US. ALL OF YOU SAVE JARNATH**," Arcanus commanded. "I must consult with him and examine the High-King in private."

Aras felt Arcanus's Wizard's Voice deflect harmlessly off his shielded core, but it bathed the entire room and even through the walls beyond to all the observation rooms. Everyone in the room and within range of his Voice began to obey without question, heading into the hallway, distancing themselves from the door to the room. Aras realized to do otherwise would arouse suspicion he could ill afford.

He exited with the first few. He was hesitant to leave Talon in the corridor, but he was afraid if he used his Power to spy upon Arcanus and Jarnath, he would be discovered, and he would not leave Jarnath and his father in potential danger, though astonishingly, Arcanus seemed far from an enemy to his mentor. Aras darted into one of the recently vacated observation chambers.

"… truly be you?" Jarnath asked, his eyes bright with tears.

The masking spell about Arcanus sputtered and extinguished, and a burnt-sienna-haired, blood-eyed stranger stood in Arcanus's place. The staff in his hands fell to the floor, and he swayed and began to fall.

"Escolier!" Jarnath cried in panic, catching him without hesitation as he collapsed.

To Aras's horror he saw his mentor pale and begin to falter. *No!* he screamed silently, but his cry was echoed aloud from within the room, from the Faeren Jarnath held. Before Aras could blast through the wall to save Jarnath, the Faeren that had been Arcanus paled and appeared to weaken as he tore himself away from Jarnath's embrace, a look of horror upon his face.

"Forgive me, old friend! Please, tell me I have not harmed you, that I restored all I took," the Faeren cried, anguish in his voice. "You cannot touch me. I drained myself dangerously using my Voice upon so many, and it was already too long since I have fed. Now my need is too great. I could not control it, especially when I felt the offer within your heart." He swayed again and Jarnath embraced him immediately, despite the apparent danger.

"Do you think I did not feel your need? Have you forgotten who and what I am? I again offer my strength freely to you. Your need is not so great that you will slay me, not with the trees and the thousands of other lives around us to strengthen me. Especially not when my heart sings to see you! Tell me, are there others who have been in hiding with you? No, do not speak their names, not here. Forgive me for speaking your own!" Jarnath said, appalled at the realization. "Tell me your Voice has protected you, that it has protected us both."

"Do not worry, Jarnath. None are within the range of hearing. I wish I could speak other names to you, but there are none to say. I thought I was the last; I thought no others had survived. Jarnath is such a common name, I had no idea you were the Lord, the healer, of whom all speak so highly! No wonder Men thought you divine and named you their God of Healing! But tell me, I must in turn know, are there others you shelter?"

"Please, Escolier, do not lightly speak such blasphemy. Have you forgotten I am also a priest? As to your query, there are others, but none we knew. A new generation has arisen from the ashes of the old. A precious few, but some," Jarnath replied.

Aras listened in astonishment, confusion, and awe. He had no idea what they were speaking of! How could Jarnath be a priest? His people worshipped no Gods, they never had. And he would never have dreamt that Jarnath was part of some great millennia-old conspiracy. Were these the secrets he had been so careful to protect? Was Aras a fool for not ripping the knowledge from Jarnath's mind years ago? Surely he could not also be a Player, part of the sick, twisted Game, a mad monster like the others? Or did this mean his earlier doubts were true, that perhaps Arcanus, Escolier, was not the monster he feared? His name! He was certain he now knew Arcanus's given name!

The Faeren Escolier had spoken of feeding, and it was clear that he had fed off of Jarnath, draining his strength. Jarnath in turn had casually mentioned feeding off the people of Nalea, as well as the trees. Aras's heart slammed in sudden fear for the Grove. Surely he had not meant the Trees? Not the Lords' Grove? No, he could not have. They would have sensed the danger, defended themselves from him, wouldn't they have? Yet they were so weak. Aras felt renewed horror. Were they so weak, not because of the land and the water, but because of Jarnath? Was his mentor slowly killing the Trees of the Grove? Killing Aranas?

A wave of warmth and reassurance cascaded through his bond to Aranas and with it came knowledge and understanding and wonder. Jarnath was not endangering the Trees of the Lords' Grove at all! He instead saved them! He was the reason they survived, in spite of the poor soil, the weak water. They drew their strength from the people of Nalea through Jarnath and his bond to Aranath. Not enough to harm any one man or woman, yet enough to keep the Trees alive.

Were the Trees of the Grove then evil? No, of course not. Were they, they could have manipulated Jarnath to drain the soldiers around him of their very lives. Aras's head was reeling with all he was learning, but he must hear everything and his fears had distracted him.

"… know of the royal family of Riviera: Laranela, Naraena, Elavar, and Eladar?" Escolier was asking. Aras was intrigued. Why did he did not mention Elanara? Why only her parents and brothers?

Jarnath nodded and then looked toward the bed, at the prostrate High-King. "Laedrin knows of them as well. He has watched them all carefully, these past centuries."

Aras felt as astonished as Escolier looked. His father knew of this conspiracy?

"Laedrin knows and they yet live?" Escolier asked, shocked. "Then he knows of you, as well? I have been hiding for nothing? No, not for nothing. After what happened, that I am Faeren, fire personified, is enough for him to want me dead, and he has far greater reason. That is why I revealed that much of the Enemy to him. I described how he appeared, feigning confusion and innocence, that he was an Elf, beautiful in form and feature beyond all imagining, yet with red-orange hair and eyes. Meanwhile, I have worked hard to preserve my own disguise as a Man, though these days it weakens me greatly to sustain the illusion."

"I knew nothing of that! But how could you betray one of us to Laedrin, even to that limited extent? And how could you doom a fellow Faeren, when I fear there are only two of you left in all the world? Until today I thought you all extinct, sacrificed along with the Aerie and the Gryphon to save those of us you could. Why would you…?"

Jarnath paled, his eyes widening, a look of abject horror upon his face. "Blessed Aralyn, save us! Not Him? Please tell me the Enemy is not that madman, the one who began the War, the one who betrayed us all, who slaughtered millions in a single act! He cannot have survived!" Jarnath cried, grabbing Escolier by the arms and shaking him with astonishing violence. "No! He is dead! He must be dead! How could He not be dead? Even a Faeren could not possibly stand in the equivalent of the heart of a star and live! He vaporized an entire continent in the blink of an eye! Tell me He is dead! He must be dead!"

Escolier, who had looked restored to health by Jarnath's aid, far stronger than before, looked suddenly ill again. "Ragnar forgive me, it is He, the monster you fear. I will not risk saying His given name or even His other name aloud, when it might draw Him to us, even here." Escolier's voice was scarcely above a sepulchral whisper, as if even saying so much was either dangerous or unbearable.

"He was my greatest creation, my greatest mistake, and only one of many, many sins against Ragnar and Aralyn, may they someday forgive me for them. I understood so little, back then, when I thought I knew so much; in my hubris, I thought I knew all. I have been trying to do penance for it, Jarnath, these three millennia past. I have tried to use the aftermath of the death and destruction to help, to heal.

"It was the catena subdere. He turned the sklabos colier into a weapon, forgetting it too was my creation. It survived the blast even as it absorbed the essence of all it destroyed: it saved us both when all around us perished. But the part of the ocean that had not instantly transmuted to steam came thundering in to fill the void of the continent that had been vaporized. As the water rushed toward us, I told him I understood, that I loved him, that he was my lythenia, that we would finally be together in death when we were forbidden to be in life. I told him all that he had always wanted to hear, and then as the waters rose around us, drowning us, I summoned the gem-battery and the mechanisms it was bound to and rose through many leagues of water and fled to safety, leaving him to drown. I could not die mired in such sin, without repentance, penance, and absolution. And so I flew."

Escolier sighed heavily. "I was a fool. I am still a fool. I still do not know how he survived, but as I live, so does he, though it took him over two and three quarters millennia to find me. I shudder to think where he has been all this time, who he has harmed, what other races might have been sacrificed to the altar of his madness, his lust, and my stupidity.

"He was so strong when next I saw him, two and a half centuries ago. I fell immediately under his Power, all unknowing. I would be under it still, only he wanted me to see how he controlled me, and in his mad jealousy, he wanted me to watch those I shepherded, those that I loved as my children, tortured and destroyed before my very eyes. Fortunately, he did not understand the Power of the gem-battery at my beck and call. I barely escaped from him, gathering those I could save and fleeing into the night. The rest you know. He has all but decimated the Dwarven Lands, and now he comes here, to your own.

"I was thrilled when I crossed the mountains to find some of the Aerta and Oceana had indeed survived, that our final great sacrifice was not entirely in vain. I will fight with my last breath to see that no more of you draw your own."

"If he is truly that powerful, could He have heard me speak your given name, even here?" Jarnath asked, horrified.

Escolier sighed. "I do not think he might, here in the heart of Nalea. But even so, it is not as if he did not know my name already. Though I have been Arcanus for so long, to so many, I truly almost forgot it myself until I heard you speak it. I must forget it. The man I once was is dead. I deserve to be dead, for what I unleashed upon us all, may Aralyn and Ragnar someday forgive me. I must die so that you all might live, yet for now, Arcanus remains," he said, and in so saying, physically he was Arcanus once more, an elderly, white-haired, gray-eyed Man, instead of a Faeren.

"We both must remain hidden. In answer to your earlier question, Laedrin does not suspect me," Jarnath said. He sighed. "I would have been long dead if he knew. He has only stayed his hand in acting against me for my other transgressions as long as he has because I alone of the healers am a Lord. He needs me. Though he might as well have slain me, for all the aid I have been able to give him this time. I've stayed the poison's course, but only for a time. It is beyond my skill to save him, even with the Trees to aid me. He cannot survive much longer."

"Would you not rejoice in Laedrin's death?" Arcanus asked.

Jarnath shook his head. "He is not to blame for what happened, nor truly to blame for what has come after. Do not forget, he was one of the few who supported our cause, at first. Were it not for the loss of his brother Hadrin, for our part in his death, I believe he would have ultimately fought with us, instead of against us. And it is thanks to him that so many ships were launched before the Annihilation. Had he not commandeered the flagship and nineteen other Great Ships of the Navy to aid in the Great Evacuation, the two thousand ships they escorted would have been unprotected and might all have been lost, instead of the many that were.

"And it is he who now stays Lord of the Guard Ahrnad's hand, and Ahrnad is only one of many. The bigotries of our Homeland haunt us still. Ahrnad has always been far more racist than Laedrin has recently become. Ahrnad despises both Men and Oceana alike. He would see the Seven Kingdoms plunge into war once more, against all Men, and do the Enemy's work for him, all unknowing. And when he was done, he might well turn the Aerta against the Oceana, when our peoples have seen enough genocide to last a thousand lifetimes.

"Besides, Aras truly loves his father in spite of all his faults, though Laedrin has many. Aras is the son-of-my-heart, the only son I will ever have, with Shiaera long lost to me, but he is Laedrin's son-by-blood. I would aid Laedrin if I could for the sake of his son, if for no other reason. But he has saved the last of us as well. Also, ultimately, I am still a healer, in spite of my part in the madness we unleashed upon the world. I would heal Laedrin because by my very nature I can do no less, though I am ashamed to admit I have been tempted sometimes, even in the recent past, to do otherwise, when I thought Aras lost because of him.

"You are an alchemist of the flesh greater than any other in our history, my friend. If I were to lend you my strength, and that of the Trees, could you save

Laedrin, heal him? You said you would see no more of us die. Surely that includes Laedrin? Particularly if I asked it of you on the strength of the past we share?"

Arcanus looked from the hope and compassion in Jarnath's face to the motionless form in the bed. He sighed heavily and then clasped Jarnath's shoulder. "I can but try. I will need to examine both his wound and the knife that was used to inflict it. And as you ask a boon of me, I ask one of you in return. I need to see Lord Beryl. And dependent upon what I find, I will need you to do everything in your power to save him for me. As Laedrin is precious to Aras, Beryl is precious both to me and to Talon, to all the Watch. I would save him if I could."

"I will do all I can," Jarnath swore.

"Then bring the blade to me, but take care not to touch it, even for a moment, even the hilt. Bring it to me on a stone tray. Cloth or metal won't be enough to protect you, if it is what I suspect it to be."

"No one has touched it since the High-King fell. We have already taken such precautions," Jarnath said.

"I must release my hold upon the others. It would be too draining to maintain it and yet do what I must. From now on, Jarnath, I must be only Arcanus to you, a respected wizard, nothing more. But I would speak more with you later, in private, when we have the opportunity to do so safely, both as priest and as friend, for I am sorely in need of both."

"Of course," Jarnath readily agreed.

Aras quickly slipped away to join the others in the hall before Jarnath could leave the room, in shock from the magnitude of all he had overheard but burying the knowledge, forcing the thoughts down, lest he betray himself.

Jarnath exited his father's room and headed down the corridor. Aras went to Talon's side and entered the room with him, once he saw the other healers made to do so, waiting until he knew they were no longer being held by the Power of Arcanus's Voice so he would not betray that he had been unaffected.

Aras fought impatience until Jarnath reentered the room with a box of the purest white alabaster, the lid carved with a relief of a stag with many-pronged antlers, so lifelike it seemed as if it would leap off the box at them.

Arcanus took the box and carefully laid it upon the table by the bed. "I'll need the use of a knife, but do not give me something you would want back."

One of the King's Guard volunteered his dagger. With the tip of the blade, Arcanus slowly and carefully opened the box. Inside on a ruined piece of silk was a knife. The interior of the box was green and black and glistened as if wet. Arcanus studied the blade and hilt without touching them. Then, with the tip of the knife, he turned the blade over in the box and scraped at the hilt with the knifepoint here and there. Then he shut the lid and made to gently pass his staff over the box, but the heavy box suddenly slid across the table as if gliding on ice; it shot off the edge and began to fall, opening as it did so.

Aras was too distracted to react quickly enough. It would have crashed to the ground, had Talon not sprung quickly and caught it in midair, slammed the lid shut, and gingerly placed it on the table in front of Arcanus, shaking his left hand in sudden pain.

Arcanus grabbed his hands and twisted them over so the palms showed, and he looked at them intently, particularly at Talon's bandaged left hand, and waved his staff over them and then released him with a sigh.

"It was only the corner of the box on the burn," Talon assured him.

"You took great risk, for the hilt bears its own dangers. Indeed it is to be feared far more than the blade, though both bear the mark of the Enemy's dark hand. And the inside of the box now bears the mark of both. You could have been lost to us with a single touch. The hilt resists me. But the blade tells me much." He turned to the healers. "Do you know, when he attacked, did Beryl wear gloves?"

Jarnath nodded. "I cut them from him when I treated the arrow wounds on his arms. I still have them."

Arcanus looked suddenly ill. "Then, Healer Jarnath, I'll need to see your hands." Aras heard fear behind his quiet request, and his own heart raced at the thought that Jarnath had somehow endangered himself so greatly that Arcanus might truly fear for him.

Jarnath nodded and showed him his hands. Arcanus examined his hands as he had Talon's, and sighed as if a great weight were lifted from him. "You are well. Take care not to touch them when you bring the gloves and never again use any tool you used upon them."

Jarnath nodded and left to get them as well.

DEWALAREN was puzzled. Lunahr did not wear gloves. None of them did, save him, and he had not worn his own since the Markers were burnt. But he was relieved, also, because Lunahr had carried the blade on his person and wielded it besides, and if the slightest touch would have lost him to them, then Lunahr would truly have been beyond saving. He did not think he could be saved even now, but he could not help but nurse the faintest glimmer of hope, for Arcanus had always symbolized hope to their people.

ARAS watched intently as Jarnath brought the gloves and Arcanus studied them carefully, nodding as if he found something he had expected. Then Arcanus turned to Laedrin and passed his staff over his arm, and his brows drew together in a frown. He passed it over him a second time, more slowly. He removed the bandages, and Aras paled. His father's wounded arm was blackened and greenish, oozing and festering. Dark lines ran up his arm along the shoulder, toward his father's neck. That once-strong arm had never embraced him. Not once had his father ever touched him in affection. Aras looked away.

"I will be able to treat him, I think. But it will not be easy, nor will it be safe for any of you to remain here. You must leave and not reenter, no matter what you might hear."

The King's Guard and the healers looked to Aras, and suddenly he was High-Prince again, and when he commanded everyone to go, none hesitated. But he paused and turned and kissed his father's brow before he left.

He closed the door behind him and then stood before it with his eyes locked upon it as if he might see through it, his face stricken with grief and longing. Aras only allowed Arcanus to treat his father out of desperation. He did not know how to cure such a malignant wound when even Jarnath was powerless. His father would die without aid. Fortunately, Arcanus did not yet suspect that Aras was his enemy as much as Incuban was.

Neither Incuban nor Arcanus knew of his mother. She had been biding her time, plotting her revenge against both of them. Now that he was an adult and his own Power was in full bloom, she would make her move soon. How was he to defeat all three?

DEWALAREN wanted to go to Aras, but he saw Jarnath watching Aras intently. He sensed the healer hung on a knife's edge of doing the same, and he held himself in check and instead leaned against the wall, watching them, with his ear to it so that he might listen to what transpired both inside and outside the room.

Jarnath approached Aras from behind and placed a hand on his shoulder, saying, "Aras, my boy." Dewalaren noted he had been the only one to use his given name since they arrived. Aras turned to Jarnath and saw the tears in his eyes and embraced him. "We thought you dead. How is it that you live? I was with Laedrin; I looked into the glass."

"Jarnath, my teacher, my friend, what glass? Why have the people of Nalea been mourning me? Arcanus said something about a scry. I still don't understand."

Jarnath took a few deep breaths, calming himself. "It happened over a month ago. Your father was very... upset... after you left. You hurt him greatly by leaving. He started to have dark dreams, always of you in danger. He thought them premonitions of coming disaster. He could neither eat nor sleep for a fortnight. He was too proud to send the King's Guard out after you. He commanded me to rid him of his dreams or... or he would execute me."

Aras was shocked that his father might make such a threat.

"I tried to aid him, but my medicines only made it worse. He was trapped in sleep, in his dream. I was desperate. Magus was here on an errand for Arcanus. I asked him to do a scry of you, to show the High-King you were well, to reassure him. Now I know he showed us a false vision and I am appalled by it."

"What did you see?" Aras asked.

"We went to your room. He bade us sit, and then he walked about the room, looking about, touching things gently with his fingertips here and there. He took the mirror from your wall, the one of silvered glass, and placed it on the table before us. He poured a thin film of water over the surface and spoke a few words, waving his staff. The water changed. It clouded and grew dark. So dark it was as if it turned to ink. He was surprised by that. He said you were in a place of great darkness, that he could not see you because of it.

"He spoke more words and the water rippled, as if a stone had been cast upon a lake. Then the center of the blackness grew lighter again, and it looked like the beginnings of a face. He was sweating from the strain and the hand on his staff was trembling. Then suddenly the image grew clear. It was your face we saw. But it was creased in pain, and pale, pale as moonlight. I felt Laedrin's hand clutch my arm as if he would crush it.

"The image grew to the edges of the mirror. You lay in a dark wood, so very far away, and we saw you were in the jaws of a monstrous wolven. Your injury was mortal, you lay dying, and you knew that you were dying. You were alone, far from help. I thought, were I there, I perhaps might save you still, but I could do nothing. It was as if I could hear what was in your heart, your fear, your love, thoughts of Nalea and your father and of me. I could see his face in your eyes and then my own. You asked for forgiveness and then you were gone. Then the mirror shattered, spraying glass everywhere, and we were flung to our knees.

"Laedrin said, 'My son is dead,' and he rose and walked out. But I could not believe it. I could not accept what I had seen. It was too unbearable. Magus was as certain as Laedrin, but he said he would try again the next day, when he had a chance to recover, for you were in an evil place which resisted his will and the scry had drained him. The next morning, he tried again, but this time he saw only darkness: no trace of you lingered. He said you were truly gone. Then he left to report to Arcanus.

"I cannot see how he could have had such a false vision, yet you are here and you are well. But even after all the agony I have endured these weeks, thinking you dead, my heart can now sing in joy, knowing you did not suffer such torment, that all I saw was some twisted shadow brought to life in a looking glass."

"Jarnath, my teacher, my friend. Your heart must be content to sing knowing only that I am alive and well now, for the torment you saw and the rest of your vision was very real." Aras unlaced his shirt at the neck and pulled it to the side, baring his chest and shoulder to him, exposing the web of faint scars from the wolven bite he had survived. Jarnath's eyes widened and his hand trembled as his fingertip traced the scars.

"But know that I would suffer so again, and gladly, for the treasure it brought me. The only flaw in Magus's vision was not his, but mine, in me, that I thought myself alone and far from help, only because I knew none of our people were near to save me. But I was found and rescued and healed not by an Elf, but by a Man, by Talon, the Lord of the Watch. I have been healed by him and have healed him, I have learned from him and taught him, I have walked and ridden and fought beside him, and I would die for him."

JARNATH looked from Aras to Talon. Talon was leaning against the wall with his eyes closed, as if asleep, a bedraggled traveler in once fine but bloodied and dirty clothes. Jarnath extended his Power but felt nothing special about him. But then Talon's eyes opened and he stood straight and tall and looked at them, as Jarnath watched, and suddenly he saw him as Aras must see him, and he beheld instead a King. Talon nodded to him, ever so slightly, then melted against the wall again, eyes closed, and became once more only a weary, dusty Man, asleep against the wall. "A treasure indeed, Aras. Guard him well." Then Jarnath hugged him and left to speak with his fellow healers.

ARAS turned back to the door and watched it, his mind in turmoil. He should not have survived long enough for Talon to come save him. He had wondered how he had, and now he knew. He had done something unforgiveable. He had been so weak at the time, dying, truly dying. He had not realized where the strength had come from that saved him. When he saw his father's face and Jarnath's, he had thought it had only been in his mind's eye, but it had not been. He had seen a third face. He had somehow viewed them as they had viewed him, through the scry.

He had wondered who the strange young River Elf was, why he might be having a vision of someone he had never met before as he died. Aras had known he couldn't have been one of the Navy: the Elf he'd seen was still a child. It had been Magus he had seen, Magus's touch he had felt, when he had instead only meant to touch the Elf to ease his fear and sorrow. He had guided Magus's hand to his aid through the mirror, somehow. He realized now in horror that it was Magus's life's energy he had somehow stolen.

He shivered. He had fed upon another, upon a child. He might have killed him! He was no better than his mother, than Incuban. Than Arcanus, who had fed upon Jarnath. A sudden realization seized him. Than Jarnath, who spoke of feeding upon all the people of Nalea. Jarnath was one of them. A fifth Player. And he had spoken of others. Even the Royal Family of Riviera was somehow part of this conspiracy of silence. The very Trees of the Grove were as well. He would go mad if he tried to decipher it all now! He focused instead upon his own crimes.

He looked at Talon in growing dread, and then denial. No, he had not fed upon Talon. He could not have. He had instead given him his own strength, so gently and carefully that Talon could not sense he did so. Talon must not know. Talon must never learn how truly powerful he was. If he realized, he would know he might also pose a threat to him, a deadly danger, and the fear would come again. Aras could not bear to think Talon might fear him, draw back from him, push him away.

He ached to go to Talon, to feel his strong arms about him again, to have him hold him, as he had in the inn. He felt so alone and afraid. He could no longer seek comfort from Jarnath, or even Aranas. He could no longer trust either of them. But the others were watching; they were always watching. He could not show such weakness.

His current position was tenuous enough. He must play his part. He had almost forgotten how stifling it was here, always forced to play a role he despised. For a single glorious month he had lived his life as he had always wanted to, but now he was again trapped.

And the mirror was destroyed. His heart hammered in terror. What would his mother think, the next time she tried to speak to him through it? He had been so careful to appear helpless to her, controlled by her. He was not ready to pit his Power against hers yet. She might think he was defying her. She might seek to punish him. She might come for him. He shuddered, remembering the last time she had held him in her arms, when he was eight, when he'd known that she was only using him as a tool to gain victory over her enemies, that she would someday kill him, without remorse or compassion, to achieve her goal.

If only he could tell Talon the truth about himself, about everything! He had told Jarnath once about the Game, as his mother called it, long ago. Jarnath had thought him mad. Or perhaps only pretended to. He could no longer trust anything Jarnath had ever said or done. Jarnath had kept so much from him! Talon would not think him mad. Talon would believe him. He would recoil from him in horror. He would loathe him the way he loathed Incuban. He would seek to destroy him, focusing all his Power to do so.

TIME dragged with infinite slowness as Arcanus worked in concealment behind the closed door. No sound emanated from the sealed room. Aras suspected Arcanus had completely warded it against all intrusion. At least half a day passed, but he, Talon, the healers, and the King's Guard kept their vigil, few partaking of the lunch that was brought to them.

Just before twilight there was suddenly a deafening boom, like a crack of thunder from within the room. Talon jumped back from the wall, which shook, and Aras leapt for the door, but Talon moved just as quickly and blocked his way. "You cannot enter. It could be dangerous for you, Arcanus, and your father. You must trust Arcanus. He has worked miracles before," Talon assured him, but there was doubt in his eyes, and his doubt made Aras fear more.

But then the door unexpectedly swung open. Arcanus was there, leaning heavily upon his staff, looking very old and tired. "That was harder than I expected," he said, and he swayed for a moment, even with his staff to support him, and leaned upon the doorframe as well.

"Are you all right?" Talon asked, his brow crinkled in concern.

"Don't worry. I'll be fine. But I must rest." Arcanus turned to Aras. "See to your father," he said, smiling warmly at Aras.

Aras went to his father's bed and stared, astonished. The bandages were gone. His father's arm looked completely healed, with only a faint scar twice the length of his thumb and the width of his nail at his wrist to indicate he had even been injured. And then his father's eyes opened and focused on his face. "Then I am dead at last, for the pain is gone and you are here," he said, and tears filled his eyes. Aras felt a wave of love wash over him: his father's thoughts of him were as warm and loving as Jarnath's.

Aras stared at his father in wonder, concealing the horror he felt with effort. This man was a stranger to him! He was the father he had always wished him to be. What had Arcanus done to him? He had healed him, but he had changed him somehow as well. He could not check his core now, not with Arcanus here. He must continue to play his part. He did not know whether he was strong enough to stand against Arcanus yet, especially now that Jarnath aided him.

Aras forced his plans into the back of his mind. He hugged his father tightly, and for the first time in memory, his father returned the embrace. "No, Father, we are both alive. And things will be right again," he swore, his voice rough with emotion, knowing that for them to be right, he must somehow undo the change Arcanus had wrought and thereby lose his father's love.

Aras heard Talon speak in the hallway, addressing the King's Guard. "Arcanus must rest. Is there a chamber where he may do so undisturbed?"

"A place has already been prepared for him," Captain Belreth said.

"Come, Talon. You will rest with me," Arcanus instructed.

Aras hid his fear. He did not want Talon to be alone with Arcanus. He was not sure the tree which embraced his core would be strong enough to protect Talon, and bound by it, Talon would be helpless to protect himself, even if he had the ability, the strength. But if he tried to prevent Talon from leaving, Arcanus would become suspicious.

"WE WILL escort you," the King's Guard Captain said, and Dewalaren held his arm out to steady Arcanus. He looked truly ancient. Dewalaren had never seen him look so old, so exhausted. It was an effort for Arcanus to walk even the short distance down the corridor to the chamber they had prepared for him.

Once they were in the room, Arcanus warded the door against intrusion. He nearly fell from the effort of the simple spell. He leaned heavily on Dewalaren as he walked to the bed and eased himself onto it slowly. "Once I've rested, tell me everything that has happened. There are foul magicks at work here. If it weren't for the power of the trees, I wouldn't have been able to counteract them to help the High-King. And Lunahr will prove a monumental challenge if what I suspect is true. I feared you were walking to your death here, you know; I should have known better, I suppose, but it looked very grim. I had no idea you had found the High-Prince. The time is drawing near now, nearer than you know. You must help me find him." He sighed heavily.

"You are making little sense," Dewalaren said gently.

"I must rest," Arcanus said, and in the next moment was already asleep.

Dewalaren looked at the door warily and tried to open it, but Arcanus's spell held fast, even in sleep. He saw there was food and drink set out for Arcanus, more than enough for two, but an image of Lunahr in his torment drove the desire for it from him. He too was tired, so very weary. He felt as old as Arcanus looked. It dawned on him that Arcanus had wanted him to rest, as well, and so had locked him in a place he might feel safe enough to do so.

Dewalaren was worried about Arcanus. He had never seen him so drained. Even great magicks had always come so easily to him, it had seemed. The Enemy's dark hand had stretched far to reach Nalea, yet still it was so strong!

He cast some cushions onto the floor and lay down, but his thoughts kept him awake long after his body willed him to sleep.

ARCANUS awoke feeling somewhat recovered, but still weak and incredibly hungry. Nalea teamed with life, not just the Elves, but the trees and the animals in the forest about the buildings. He could sense the energy all around him as he lay there, absorbing it like a sponge, restoring his strength. There were only seven other places of Power such as this left in the world, places where he could feed from so many at once without needing to physically touch any of them. His brow creased. Or five, if what he feared was true, and Riviera and Loatia had already fallen.

Marcus had been here. It was here he was last seen. He should not have been in danger in this place. He should not have disappeared. He must find him!

Dewalaren would aid his search. Arcanus sat up and stretched stiffly, eyes casting about for him. For a moment he thought Dewalaren had found some way out of the windowless room, but then he saw him asleep on the floor. He extended a link and reached for Dewalaren's core, to feed from him and monitor his thoughts, as he had done so many times in the past, without Dewalaren's knowledge.

He yanked back, astonished. There was a tree of pallenteum where his core should be! Such a shining tree was not his work, nor his pupils', nor the Enemy's, certainly. There was an unknown here, one with great Power, Power that rivaled his own. Another had robbed him of one of his greatest creations; a stranger now controlled Dewalaren. He must learn more!

"I do not like to be watched, not even by you, Arcanus," Dewalaren said, sitting up and scowling at him.

Arcanus faked a hearty laugh with practiced skill. "Then I shall try not to stare at you more than necessary." He must tread with care, now that Dewalaren was awake. He swung off the bed lightly onto his feet, slipping into his shoes. "Eat with me," he urged.

DEWALAREN sat with him but made no move to eat. "I would have you tell me why you came to find me. You said you had need of me."

Arcanus nodded and said between mouthfuls, "And so I do. But first, I would help Lunahr if I can."

Dewalaren said in despair, "No one can help him. He is—the Enemy has left nothing of him. Lunahr is dead, and a shadow talks with his voice."

Arcanus scowled at him. "Dewalaren, you cannot know that for certain. If after I have seen him I agree he is but a monster, then we must slay it and you may grieve for the Man he once was. But I will help him if I can."

"If there is even the slightest chance he can be saved...." Dewalaren's voice caught.

"I must see if the Elves have Loruthanar. Lunahr's blade might aid me, if it has not been too tainted."

Dewalaren's eyes widened. "I have it. I came across it in Athanark and recovered it to bury. I saw a vision of Lunahr's death, and from what I saw, I did not think there would be any remains left to burn."

"Then it was not captured with him? Excellent! Loruthanar may well be the key."

Dewalaren cursed. "I left Loruthanar on Aras's mare, Janahar. I do not even know where she is. We must find Aras."

Arcanus nodded and opened the door. "Take us to the High-Prince," Arcanus commanded the two soldiers standing on guard before it.

"Yes, sir," one of them replied. "We have been ordered to give you all assistance." They led them to Aras.

Aras smiled in joy at seeing them, and Dewalaren could not help but smile at him in return. Aras looked himself again. All the tension and pain was gone from his face. He looked every bit the High-Prince, as well: his worn and mended traveling clothes and cloak had been exchanged for Elven silks. He still wore his knife, but there was no sign of his swords or bow.

"It is good to see you smile again," Dewalaren said, and Aras beamed.

"IT IS good to be home. And to see my father well again." Aras was almost giddy with relief. He had felt Arcanus's futile attempt to touch Talon's core. Arcanus was so weak! To think he was someone he had once feared! If only his mother and Incuban were as powerless! But he must not become overconfident; he must play his role for now.

He turned to Arcanus. "We are in your debt, Arcanus." He said it in the mode of the royal "we," indicating that the debt was the crown's.

"It is no light thing, to be in debt to a wizard," Arcanus said carefully. "I would give you a chance to repay that debt."

Aras's face grew serious. "What is it you ask?"

"I would like to be given the chance to question your prisoner, Lord Beryl, and to heal him, if it is within my skill to do so. And if I find what I expect to, I would ask that you end your war with the Watch before blood has been spilt. The Watch is not your enemy."

Aras nodded. "I am well aware of that. I owe Talon my life, and I have no quarrel with his people. I have been trying to convince my father as well. He is willing to listen. He has charged me with finding the truth of the matter, as he does not feel he can be impartial. Although I love my father and should wish vengeance on the one who tried to slay him, Lord Beryl is kin to Talon and very dear to him, and Talon has told me much about him that is now hidden. As I already wish to see him healed and to stop a wrongful war, we are still in your debt."

ARCANUS nodded, smiling, but his thoughts belied the expression upon his face. He had an odd feeling that the son was more dangerous than the father. In spite of Jarnath's fondness for Aras, if he had the energy, he would alter him as well. But it would have to wait.

"WE HAVE need of Beryl's sword," Talon said. "It was still tied to Janahar's saddle."

Aras clasped his arm. "I have kept it safe for you. It is in my room with the rest of our things. Wait here. I will get it."

Aras left for his room. He was concerned for Beryl, as well as Talon. The Enemy had done enough damage to Beryl already. Now Arcanus would further harm him.

Aras had carefully and cautiously viewed his father's core after he'd confirmed that Arcanus was asleep, to determine what Arcanus had done to him. It was fortunate Aras had viewed his father's core so many times in the past. He was ashamed he had done so sometimes with the very thought of changing him, knowing that just a little difference here and there would make him into someone who might be able to return his love.

The thought repulsed him. He could not do such a thing to one he loved. He liked to think he could not even do so to an enemy. But because he was so intimately familiar with his father's core, it would be a relatively simple matter to restore it, to reverse the changes Arcanus had made. But Aras did not know Beryl as he was before the Enemy had taken him, had damaged him. How could he be sure he would not harm him further, when he sought to fix the damage Incuban and Arcanus had wrought?

He entered his room and retrieved Beryl's sword from the hidden, warded drawer in his bureau, holding it by the sheath, as he had before. He put his hand upon the hilt, intending to take a closer look at the blade. He gasped in astonishment. The sword still bore the image of Beryl, pure and unaltered. He extended his Power into the sword.

It was like finding a brother he had never known existed. Such a pure, clear image was upon the sword, his heart sang with the music that rang from the blade. What might he have found if he had viewed an instrument instead, if even Beryl's sword held such music? He must introduce him to Meloneth! But first he must be further harmed, before he might be healed. Aras desperately hoped Arcanus might truly only try to heal him, but he feared the worst.

Lunahr. Talon had revealed his cousin's given name, when speaking in memory of him. He must think of him by that name, if he was to help him. He imprinted the name deep into his core and then let Lunahr's spirit as it was overlain upon the blade etch deeply into his core as well, binding it to his name. No matter what Arcanus might now do to defile the sword, he would have a clear template with which to restore Lunahr.

He could stall no longer. He returned with Lunahr's sword.

"COME, I will show you the way to the dungeon," Aras said. Dewalaren noted that the four King's Guard who had been following him and Arcanus were joined by a dozen more.

Aras watched the King's Guard gather around him and sighed. "It is worse than before I left. But the Hill People are still a danger."

Dewalaren wondered if Aras believed his own words or had said so for his and Arcanus's benefit. They, or perhaps Lunahr, even chained, were surely viewed as a far greater threat.

They entered the dungeon, and Dewalaren felt suddenly cold. But there was no sound of sobbing this time, or screams. It was deathly silent, but the door to the cell was yet closed and guarded. Aras ordered it opened.

Lunahr was alone now, lying on the bed, staring at the ceiling; the chains had been loosened enough for it. He did not move when they entered, not even turning his head toward the sound of the opening door.

"I ordered the questioning stopped. His mind and body will be free of the elixirs now," Aras said. "There is food and water also, although it does not appear he has partaken of any of it. He was given only the barest minimum to ensure he survived before. Please see that he eats and drinks. I swear it will not harm him, but I don't blame him for not being able to trust our words, considering how he has been treated so far."

Arcanus nodded. "Excellent. I had worried I would have to wait until his body was free of the elixirs, and we will have need of the food and drink before this is done. Now, if you will leave me, I will get to work. The building is to be cleared, and I am not to be interrupted, no matter how long this takes, and it may take long, indeed. If I am gone a full week, only then may you come and see what has happened to me."

"I will so order it," Aras said.

Lunahr's voice rose from where he yet lay prone upon the bed. "You do not frighten me, Arcanus."

Arcanus said kindly, "I am not here to frighten you. I am here to help you."

Dewalaren stood silently. He did not think Lunahr knew he was there, but he could not bring himself to speak. He looked at his cousin one last time and then, without a word, he and Aras left, taking the King's Guard with them.

The main door to the dungeon was sealed, and Dewalaren took up vigil before it. Aras stayed for a while, then left to be with his father.

The King's Guards' eyes were constantly on Dewalaren and even outside he felt caged. The entire day passed, with no activity from inside that could be seen.

WHEN Aras came by in the evening, Talon was still standing where he had left him. Aras did not think he had moved from the spot at all. "Talon, the King's Guard will bring word. Please, come eat with me."

Talon shook his head. "I am not hungry. Dine with your father, Aras. He needs you right now more than I."

"Do you plan to sleep out here as well?" Aras asked, concerned.

"I will not sleep," Talon said, and Aras knew he meant it.

Aras left and returned in a little while, with Talon's bedroll and a tray of food for him. "In case you change your mind."

Talon thanked him.

"I will share your vigil, at least for a while, while my father sleeps. Do not worry, my friend. Beryl will be healed, I swear to you."

"I am worried about Arcanus, as well. I have never heard him speak as he did before. I fear he is taking on something too dangerous, this time. Powerful as he is, the Enemy's magic is far beyond any he wields."

Aras was disappointed to hear that. He had yet to pit himself directly against any of the three other Players, but what he had sensed of Arcanus so far had given him false hope that he might defeat the others more easily than he had feared. If Arcanus was truly the weakest, then who was next strongest? His mother or Incuban? The subtle deceptions he'd used on his mother in the past were in no way a test of her true Power. Where did he fit in? Might he truly be able to defeat all three? And what of Jarnath? And the Trees? Were either or both truly a danger? Would he need to fight them as well? Should he break his bond to Aranas, or continue to shield himself against him?

There was a soft, rustling whisper in his mind, from outside the shield, as of branches in a spring breeze gently rapping against a glass windowpane. Aras recognized Aranas's voice, but not the tone, at first. Then he realized Aranas was gently scolding him, the way Aerlyr sometimes did, the way Talon occasionally had, the way Jarnath did, the few times he gave his mentor cause, with warmth and love in his voice.

Aranas had heard him! His thoughts, his doubts, his fears! He had heard! And... and he had not attacked; he had not tried to breach Aras's carefully erected shield, when he suspected it might have shattered as easily as if truly made of glass, were Aranas ever to unleash an onslaught against him. Aranas had instead spoken with the gently chiding voice of a somewhat amused and exasperated parent of a recalcitrant child.

Aras's fears subsided for the moment. He did not remove his shield, but neither did he strengthen it.

"Forgive me. I am poor company," Talon apologized, and Aras realized he had been so distracted, he had been ignoring his friend when he was most needed.

"No, forgive me. Much is happening that I was not ready for. I am sorry for all that has transpired to bring you here, yet I am selfish enough to be glad that you are here with me, my friend," Aras said sincerely.

"As am I, with like reason," Talon assured him. "I stand here in the dark, yet I no longer fear the night. There is beauty in the moon, the stars, and peace. The whisper of leaves overhead is no longer the voice of the Enemy, the snap of a twig is not the tread of a foe's foot. The night passes slowly, and I worry for my friends, but I do not count the minutes until dawn in frantic desperation. But you must not spend all your time with me, Aras. Your father needs you as much as I, perhaps more so. You should go to him. I will be here for some time, I think."

"I can yet stay awhile," Aras said, Talon's words calming him, his own worries subsiding with the wisdom and warmth of them.

The night passed slowly, and the morning brought no change. Aras spent as much time with Talon as he could, but he was also taking advantage of the time with his father: he was both enjoying his father's attention, and using the opportunity to cement his position as his father's son in the eyes of the King's Guard. He could not repair the damage Arcanus had done until he left.

Two more days passed in the same manner. Talon stayed at the door to the dungeon almost the entire time and neither ate nor slept at all, though he did drink the water Aras brought to him and he did not sink into despair as he might have.

Finally, on the morning of the fourth day, shortly after dawn, the door to the dungeon opened and Arcanus emerged, blinking at the barely risen sun as if it were the brightness of midday. He looked ancient, frail, pale, and weak. He leaned heavily upon his staff and smiled tiredly. "It is done. I have done all I can. He is sleeping now. Only I can waken him. When he awakens, I will need you to test him, Talon."

Arcanus turned to Aras. "His cell may be guarded, if you feel it necessary, but none may enter, or even look upon him." He swayed and Talon steadied him. "Now, I must rest. I shall sleep a long time, this time, I think." Without another word, his legs folded under him, and Talon caught him as he collapsed. He was not conscious.

ARAS looked at Arcanus in wonder. He had weakened himself almost to death! With the slightest touch of his mind, Aras could finish it. He could eliminate one of the three Players while he was weak, while he was helpless. But first Aras must see what Arcanus had done to Lunahr. He must be sure he could reverse the damage unaided. Reluctantly, he let Talon leave with Arcanus in his arms.

DEWALAREN carried Arcanus to the bedchamber they had been assigned, escorted by the King's Guards. He was surprised by how heavy Arcanus was when he looked so thin, so frail. He felt as heavy as an Elf. Dewalaren could scarcely carry him unaided.

He closed the door firmly in the King's Guard's faces and wished for a lock. He laid the staff next to Arcanus on the bed, making sure his hand was upon it, not knowing whether that might help but knowing it could not harm. Then he sat beside him, holding his hand. Arcanus's hand felt cold. Dewalaren layered blankets over him.

Idare, he was all but done in himself. In spite of his words to Aras, he had been afraid to sleep before, afraid that something awful might happen to Lunahr or Arcanus or both if he wasn't vigilant, though he knew there was nothing he could do to aid either of them.

It sounded like Arcanus might sleep for a long while, and that Lunahr could not wake until he did. Perhaps it would be all right for him to sleep as well, now. He gathered up the single remaining blanket and then piled some cushions on the floor in front of the door, effectively blocking it from opening. He lay down upon them and covered himself with the blanket. He was afraid he might lie awake endlessly, worrying, but the blanket was scarcely drawn over him before he fell asleep.

ARAS entered the dungeon, but hesitated at Lunahr's cell door. Arcanus had said none might enter nor look upon Lunahr. Why? What would happen if he did so? Had Arcanus said it just to protect him because he knew he would be unconscious and unable to protect himself? Or was there truly some sort of danger? Had he warded the entrance? What might happen if he did not enter, if he viewed his core from here? The last thing he wanted to do was to further harm the cousin Talon so loved, but he must see what Arcanus had done to him.

Aras did not see how his gentle touch might harm him. Tentatively, he reached into the cell with his mind, and with the greatest of care touched Lunahr's core. He fell to his knees, sobbing, at what he found.

The music was gone. It was all burnt away, and what was in its place was too terrible to bear. Incuban had done such horrible things to Lunahr: to his body, his mind, his spirit. Incuban had warped and twisted Lunahr to truly love him. Lunahr would kill for him, commit any betrayal, even regicide. He would die for Incuban. Yet Lunahr still loved his kin, especially Talon, whom he called Laren, a loving abbreviation of his given name, Dewalaren. It was an odd name, but it suited his friend. Hunter, whose given name was Farad, also still burned brightly in Lunahr's thoughts. But his love for Incuban overrode all else. Incuban was cruel beyond measure for what he had done to Lunahr, and Lunahr was only one of the many hundreds of thousands Incuban had harmed over the centuries. He must destroy him!

But Arcanus… Arcanus had not harmed Lunahr. He had only tried to heal him as best as he could, pitting his own failing Power against the full force of his Enemy's might. The effort had nearly killed him. There was an echo of pain, compassion, even love of Arcanus for Lunahr and all his kin: the love of a father for a child, only many,

many generations removed. Aras had not expected to find love or compassion or pain in Arcanus.

Perhaps he was right and Arcanus was not the monster his mother had painted him to be. But Arcanus had harmed his father. Or at least changed him. People should not be changed in such a manner without their knowledge or consent. But was it truly so wrong to have a father who knew how to love again, who could finally love his own son?

Aras was not sure what to do. Arcanus was a danger to him, of that he was certain. He had seen past his façade earlier to know that much at least. But perhaps he was not a danger to Dewalaren and his kin, as he had thought.

Lunahr needed him. He must find a way to return Lunahr's music to him. But Lunahr's core was still so damaged and his love for Incuban unaltered. Aras was not trained for such subtleties; he was not trained at all. If he tried to work his Power upon Lunahr, he might further harm him. He might destroy his mind altogether or even kill him. Or, in removing his love for Incuban, he might remove his ability to love anyone. Death would be preferable.

Aras sighed. He could not easily help Lunahr, and he could not act against Arcanus, not now, at least. Arcanus had done as much as could be done, for now. Maybe the Trees of the Grove might be able to help Lunahr further. They were old and wise and powerful; they might possess Power and subtlety enough. But could he trust them, after what he had learned about them? He still did not know.

At the thought of the Trees he heard his own, Aranas, calling to him. He had yet to visit him since returning to Nalea. Aranas had been just as grieved at the thought of his death as Jarnath; he had suffered greatly. The entire Grove had mourned him, but the slender birch had been particularly despondent. Unlike Jarnath, though, Aranas had known he yet lived as soon as the darkness was washed from the woods by the rain.

It was foolish to delay further. It was time to act. He must go to Aranas, speak with him, discover what the Trees and Jarnath had been concealing from him. He could tell Dewalaren was sleeping soundly. There was nothing more he could do here for now. He left for the Grove, for the strength and wisdom of the Trees that might soon be pitted against him.

THREE more days passed while Arcanus slept. Dewalaren slept most of the first day, but had trouble sleeping thereafter. He forced himself to eat, though he consumed little, but he did not leave Arcanus's side. Unexpectedly, on the fourth morning, Arcanus's eyes snapped open and he sat bolt upright. Dewalaren jumped, startled. Arcanus smiled warmly at him, and Dewalaren saw to his relief that he looked himself again. Then Arcanus said gravely, "Now I must tell you what I have found and what I have done."

Dewalaren nodded, both eager and loath to hear.

"Lunahr was indeed captured by the Enemy, although he has no memory of it, at least none I could reach, so I cannot say for certain all that transpired. I could not find any hint as to what might have happened during that missing time. He was not lying when he told you he didn't know how he came to be in Nalea. But I was able to examine him and to determine that he is under two unbreakable compulsions: the first is to kill High-King Laedrin and the second is to kill any kinsman he meets. We must assume that the Enemy did not think he would survive after fulfilling one or more of the appointed tasks. So, he is a tool, but one the Enemy discarded even in using.

"It is possible the Enemy has captured others of your people and turned them as well. Lunahr will have revealed all the secrets he knew of the Watch to the Enemy. It has been decades since one of you was last captured, though many of you have fallen. From what Farad told us, his parents and his brothers Haranad, Sarad, and Alarad all died without being so compromised. The Enemy's focus was different at that time.

"As Lunahr broke his link to you, we cannot know all that happened to him. However, it is certain he would have been like an open book before the Enemy. He will know your identity, your true name, Dewalaren, after all the many decades we have kept it safely hidden from him. But he will know far more. He will know all your true names, your codes, your hiding places, your friends, and your sanctuaries. Some of the latter will still be safe havens from him for now, places of Power, which the Elves still hold, like Erenia.

"I fear Loatia and Riviera may have already fallen. That is what I must next learn. The Elves who remain must be warned not to stray from their Cities. I must remember to warn High-King Laedrin not to be tricked into taking the war with the Hill People to their valley.

"As I said, the compulsions are unbreakable, or at least not within my Power to break. But I have worked around this. I have used pallenteum and Elfstone and the very trees around us to place strong spells of binding about Lunahr. I have used his own sword for a spell of repulsion as well. I will need your aid in testing my spells. Lunahr is not able to fight against the compulsions. He will again try to kill you, but if I have done as well as I think, this time he won't be able to act against you. Nor will he be able to harm himself, for I have bound him against that as well.

"Had the Enemy captured his sword, I could not have used it, even had you found it. Lunahr is bound to his sword almost as much as you are to yours, as one of the two symbols of his House. It defines him and was the one thing left undefiled. As I have bound him to his sword, I have bound him here, to Nalea, to the trees. He will not be able to leave here as long as the Enemy lives. He is still one of the Watch by his nature, which was not changed by the foul magicks used against him, despite how it may appear. But he can no longer fight by your side. He must ever shun and be shunned by his kin."

"Then it would have been kinder to kill him," Dewalaren said, horrified by all Arcanus had told him.

"It would certainly have been easier," Arcanus said, and Dewalaren heard the weariness in Arcanus's voice that sleep had not, after all, erased. "He will not have an easy life here, and perhaps not a long one, although we must try our best to make the Elves understand. There are many who will fear and hate him regardless of our efforts, and others who might seek to kill him out of pity, as in his despair, he will almost certainly ask them to, as I have prevented him from being able to take his own life directly. He is no less the man he was for what has happened to him, or what he has done. You or even I would have fallen just as easily, if we faced the Enemy alone in his stronghold. It is vital that you understand that.

"And perhaps he may still be able to play a part in what is to come. Where there is life there is always hope. When we forget that, when we choose to deal out death rather than preserve life, no matter the cost, we will have become the Enemy we fear.

"Now come. This will not be easy for either of you, but I must be sure I have bound Lunahr as strongly as I think. I have never before woven so many complex and opposing spells so tightly together, to such desperate purpose. We wizards are known for our arrogance, and I am certainly no exception, as you well know, but we cannot afford overconfidence or failure here.

"Events are beginning to draw to a close. The smallest misstep will lead to ruin. And Lunahr's presence here may ultimately be used to our advantage. It may keep the Enemy's eye trained here while we work in secret elsewhere. We have much to discuss, but it must wait. Time passes too quickly."

But when they made to exit Arcanus's room, they were stopped by one of the King's Guard. "I'm sorry, Arcanus, but you must wait here. I was instructed to summon Lord of the Guard Ahrnad upon your waking."

Arcanus eyed him, but then sighed and said, "We will wait."

Two other King's Guard took places by the door, and Arcanus and Dewalaren went back inside.

AHRNAD and Aras entered a few minutes later. "You still haven't been eating and sleeping," Aras said critically, eyeing his friend in concern. Dewalaren nodded in admission.

Ahrnad said, "The High-Prince and I have come to learn what you found when you examined the prisoner, Arcanus."

Arcanus told them some of what he'd told Dewalaren, although not how the Watch had been compromised. Dewalaren's jaw was clenched tightly, and Aras's eyes never left him.

"You expect us to give sanctuary to this Man, after what he has done? Now that the High-King has recovered and we have learned all that we need know, his life is forfeit for his crimes! I will see to it personally, and I will be sure his death is not an easy one," Ahrnad said with relish, his voice hard.

"You will not harm him. He is under my protection," Arcanus said, the air around him all but crackling with Power, as if lightning was gathering and preparing to strike.

"And mine," Dewalaren said, as if he were stating a simple fact, without threat.

Aras stepped between them, facing Ahrnad. "My father ordered that Lord Beryl not be killed, and he has not rescinded that order. Further, you will not harm Lord Beryl by my command, under the authority granted to me by my father. The High-King has charged me with determining the truth of this matter. And if there is such a time that Lord Beryl is then condemned to death, it will be swift and merciful, and at my own hand or at his friends'."

"Yes, Highness," Ahrnad obeyed reluctantly, and his jaw clenched.

"Now, let us go see the prisoner," Aras commanded.

They walked to the dungeon, and Arcanus led them down the long, gray staircase, to the door of the cell. Arcanus waved his hand over the door, and it opened. They stepped inside.

Lunahr lay asleep on the cot in the cell, his face peaceful and free of pain. He was no longer bound by chains. The pallenteum chains had vanished, and in their place, around his wrists and ankles and neck, were narrow bands of pallenteum. Embedded in the band on his neck was a single perfect Elfstone, of the purest green, the size of a thumbnail. The cuts about his wrists and ankles were gone. His sheathed sword was at his side, and his right hand held the hilt lightly, even in sleep.

"Now, I will have you all stand against this wall. Only Talon is to approach him, and only when I tell him to," Arcanus commanded.

Ahrnad spun on Arcanus, appalled. "You cut his chains and you armed him!"

"He is still bound," Arcanus said.

"He will not be armed!" Ahrnad snapped and strode toward him, but was literally stopped in his tracks at a muttered word from Arcanus.

"He cannot be disarmed, by you or anyone. But to try might be dangerous to you. Now stand against the wall or remove yourself." Then Arcanus waved his hand and released him.

Ahrnad seethed, but Aras took his arm and pulled him back. Arcanus stepped slightly closer and waved his staff almost imperceptibly, his lips moving slightly.

Lunahr awakened. His eyes opened, and he cried out in dismay and sat up suddenly.

"Do you remember, Beryl?" Arcanus asked, his voice fatherly.

Lunahr looked at Arcanus and shuddered. "I remember. I had hoped it had all been a terrifying nightmare, but in my heart I knew it was real." He looked at Dewalaren, and his eyes filled with tears. "Forgive me! I attacked you. I would never wish to hurt you. And I've put you all, my kin, in such horrible danger."

Dewalaren's heart broke anew at seeing the cousin he loved so anguished. "None of this is your fault. Any of us would have been as vulnerable as you were. I forgive you everything that's happened, or that might yet happen because of it."

"Talon, I need you to approach Beryl slowly, now," Arcanus instructed. "The spells are set to trigger when you are in danger. If he had a bow instead of a sword, they would have triggered as soon as the door opened."

Dewalaren started to approach Lunahr, his jaw set. Lunahr shrank back on the bed, against the wall, fear naked on his face. "No! Please stop! Please don't make me do this!" Lunahr begged, but Dewalaren approached relentlessly.

Suddenly, when Dewalaren was six feet away, Lunahr sprang to his feet, drawing his sword, eyes dark with madness. Dewalaren drew his own blade, to ward off his attack, but Lunahr's sword never cleared the sheath. Instead, Lunahr curled into a ball, head bowed and ankles and wrists all drawn together, his face turning purple as the band about his neck constricted, choking him. At the same instant, even as Aras sprang between them to protect Dewalaren, Dewalaren was flung violently backward and slammed hard against the wall. Then just as suddenly Lunahr uncoiled and lay gasping, his fingers clawing at the collar about his neck, which expanded again so he might breathe.

"I seem to have outdone myself," Arcanus said in satisfaction. "If anything, the repulsion aspect is too strong."

Lunahr looked at the sword half drawn in his hand, then wide-eyed at Dewalaren, and then curled back up on the bed, of his own accord this time, and began sobbing.

Dewalaren stood helplessly, unable to even approach his young cousin to console him. Shaking with rage, he turned on Arcanus instead. "Was that necessary?" he snarled.

Arcanus turned on him and his eyes were suddenly hard. "Yes. And if you think it was brutal to experience and to watch, think how much more awful it was to have conceived and executed it."

Arcanus was trembling, Dewalaren saw, not in anger, but in pain. Dewalaren's anger melted at Arcanus's pain, and he clasped Arcanus's arm instead. "Forgive me, my friend. I sometimes forget you are still a Man, for all you are a wizard of such strength."

ARCANUS calmed as well. He was surprised at the depth of his own compassion for Lunahr. Lunahr reminded him so much of Marcus. Marcus! Had the Enemy discovered him, captured him, and tortured him as he had Lunahr? Had he turned Marcus against him? Might he have to kill him, or could he yet save him? And where was Selene? If she had found Marcus, why had she not returned?

There had been a link to Marcus, but he had been unable to use it. He had been too weak, and then it had been broken before he could regain his strength and follow it to Marcus. He feared they were both dead, or worse, turned against him, that the Enemy might make him the instrument of their deaths, or them of his. Dewalaren must help him find them!

ARAS sat on the bed beside Lunahr, softly murmuring words of comfort to him, his arm wrapped around the young Man as if he were a small child.

Ahrnad, who had been distracted by the argument, apparently suddenly realized the potential danger Aras was in. "Highness!" he cried in alarm.

Aras looked at him levelly. "I think it would be best if you left us alone for a while." It was not spoken as a request, but as a command. "All of you," he said more gently, looking at Dewalaren and Arcanus.

Jaw clenched, Ahrnad left.

Arcanus studied them for a moment, then nodded and departed.

Dewalaren opened his mouth as if to speak, but turned away in silence and left as well.

DEWALAREN stopped Arcanus in the hall. "Are you sure Aras is safe?"

Arcanus said, "Would the boy you know ever think to harm him?"

"No, of course not," Dewalaren said.

"Then you have answered your own question, Talon," he said, conscious of the King's Guard listening to them. "He is still Beryl, for all that his eyes cry now, instead of laugh. He will not harm Aras, and I think Aras might perhaps become his friend, from what I have seen. Beryl will have need of one. It is time for us to go, Talon. It is time for you to aid me, as I have aided him."

They left for the sanctuary of Arcanus's room, where he could insure no ears could overhear. Arcanus had expended far too much Power recently, with no way to safely recharge it. He could not touch Dewalaren to feed upon him. The Amontir were scattered everywhere, and there were less than twenty of them left. Now his two youngest children were both missing.

Jarnath had aided him greatly. It was Jarnath who had gifted him the warded and charged gem-battery that linked Lunahr to the trees. Only one who was both Aerta and Latent would have such ability. Arcanus had been able to use his Power upon the sword and upon the pallenteum chains, the latter of which he had crafted into the pallenteum bonds Lunahr now wore.

He had crafted them carefully, so that they did not look like catena subdere, lest Laedrin instantly make the connection upon seeing them. It helped that he had only the single gem-battery to work with: the wrist manacles and ankle fetters were unadorned by the gem-batteries that should have strengthened them. He could hardly have used any of his own few precious gem-batteries; those of the Faeren were of a distinctive ruby hue, and by the very nature of the carefully cultivated jewel, that was not something that could be masked.

The gem imbedded in the pallenteum King's Band Dewalaren wore upon his bicep was only a ruby. The original pyrenteum band it replaced was graced with a gem-battery, but it had vanished two and a half centuries ago with Prince Rowanar, along with the King's Ring and any hope they ever had of killing the Enemy.

How he longed for the Power of the Ring! With it, he had been akin to a God. He sighed heavily. That is why he had dared not wear it any longer. It was far too powerful, too tempting. He had barely recognized in time that he did not have the strength of character to wear it daily, to wield it at his merest whim. He might well have become the monster the Enemy was, had he continued to do so, in his spirit-shattering loneliness, his guilt, his despair.

The blood of millions was on his hands and in the stone of the Ring, the extinction of two races and the near complete extinction of five others. Some scant thousands of the Aerta and Oceana had survived, but only two Faeren, one a Houerfashang and one a Latent, and not a single Aerie or Gryphon remained.

The Faeren had sacrificed themselves, forming a living barrier between the onrushing devastation and the Evacuation Fleet, drawing what heat they could into their bodies in order to save those who fled, knowing the fire would overwhelm and destroy them. The Aerie and their proud Gryphon mounts had sacrificed themselves no less nobly, drawing the great plume of ash from the sky and driving it into the ocean, until in their exhaustion, they finally plummeted to their watery graves with the last of their burden. Those few Oceana of the Sea who had survived the boiling waters dispersed the ash into the benthic depths. To his knowledge they had all drowned doing so. But they and the Aerie had thereby ensured the sun would yet warm the distant shores that remained, that the swirling ocean currents would still team with life. The world would not be plunged into years of unending winter and ensuing starvation. They did so selflessly, in protection of all those who already dwelt upon those other lands, as well as of the refugees who escaped to them.

The Dwarves had been doomed because of the stone as well, of course, but they had drowned, their life's energy wasted to the water, instead of absorbed by the stone, save for the hundreds of thousands who had successfully evacuated their own doomed Homeland. They had come here, to this continent, and rebuilt their civilization, to an extent, though it was a fractured mockery of what it had once been. They cowered in isolation on their various mountaintops, behind their massive iron and stone doors, and thought themselves safe. But two hundred and fifty years ago, the Enemy had come.

In the two and a half centuries since, the Enemy had systematically waged a genocidal war against them in his hunger for Power, and likely, in his twisted need for vengeance against the race that had helped conceive him, though unknowingly and unwillingly. His madness, his capacity for hate, for revenge, knew no bounds, may Ragnar and Aralyn forgive them both.

No. Neither of them should be forgiven. They both deserved to burn in Ragnar's flame for what they had done. Yet they both survived when so many who were far more worthy had died, and neither of them had learned from his past mistakes. They both still played at being Gods: he was the God of Life, and the Enemy was the God of Death. He was the God of Reason, and his creation was the God of Madness. Sometimes it felt like he would be forever locked in an unending struggle, in eternal torment, with the beautiful monster he had unleashed upon the world.

For millennia he had denied the existence of Ragnar and Aralyn, with valid reason. Even a scant handful of years ago he had been confident and resolute in the validity of his arguments against them. Were they real, protective and nurturing of their children, how could they have allowed him to conduct his experiments? How could a true God and Goddess idly watch the systematic brutalization and exploitation of the resulting children he had crafted, and do nothing to save them? How could they have stood by and watched a continent teaming with life they had created vaporize? How could they justify betraying and drowning the Dwarves who worshipped them, who built Temples and shrines in their names?

He still could not fathom it. They must be as fatally flawed as he was. He neither loved nor worshipped the God and Goddess so blindly as Jarnath, in his foolishly misguided devotion to them. But he had finally accepted that Ragnar and Aralyn were real. They must be. They were the only hope left for the world.

His own Power was a pathetic shadow of what it once had been. The Dwarves were all but extinct, like the Aerie and Gryphon before them. The Aerta and Oceana would soon follow, and then all too quickly, Men would fall. The world was dying. And it could not.

What would it all have been for, if there was no one left to see it? Why create such a complex and beautiful world if there was no one to admire it, to appreciate it, to be awed by it, to seek to tame it, to improve it, to bend it to their will? What were Gods without worshippers, without those who trembled before them and begged and wept?

He might go mad thinking about it. Would that not be the ultimate irony? That he go mad as well? Perhaps that was the God's and Goddess's way of punishing him, for all his many sins against their children. For having the audacity to create his own children, as if he too were a God: first the Latents and the Houerfashang, in their blessed Homeland, then the Amontir, using the Power of the Ring, and then finally Marcus, by the simple act of laying with his all-too-willing mother. Marcus! He would not allow yet another life to be sacrificed upon the altar of his hubris. He must find him! He must save him! But he could not do it alone. The Power he had gained from Jarnath, his old comrade-in-arms, was only temporary. Once he left Nalea, he would use it all too quickly, especially with the search he must now conduct.

He turned to Dewalaren. "My pupil Magus has disappeared. He is young and overconfident. He worked a scry here, to find Aras, when he should not have. He ended up battling the Enemy for the knowledge, without realizing that was what he was doing. He called for help: Circe and I both heard him. She reached him first, and now she is also missing. I must find them both. I need you to help me," Arcanus said, the desperation in his voice genuine.

"Of course. Do not worry, Arcanus. We will find them," Dewalaren said confidently. "But before we go, I must make sure that this pointless war against my kin is truly ended. I must say good-bye to one who has grown very dear to me. I also need pen and ink and paper. I need to write a letter to a friend."

They did not find what they sought in the room, but it was quickly provided at Arcanus's request. Then Arcanus exited the room, leaving Dewalaren to his writing. He needed to visit Jarnath one last time, to speak to him and feed from him.

THE pen in Dewalaren's hand hovered over the inkwell for a long time as he planned out what he needed to say. This was the hardest missive he hoped ever to have to write. Finally, he dipped the pen in the ink and set pen to paper and began the letter to Lunahr in the bold script of the Amontir so no other might be able to read it, save for its intended recipient.

The letter was heartrendingly difficult and stained by more than one tear ere he was done. He sealed the letter with wax, using the seal that had been lent to him, and wrote the name "Beryl" in Elvish upon the outside of the folded paper. The door opened, and he looked up. Arcanus was already back. It must have taken far longer than he had realized.

"I need to say good-bye to Aras. I will join you at the stables," Dewalaren said.

Arcanus looked at him for a long moment as if he would deny him but then nodded. "Do not be long."

"I will be as quick as I can," Dewalaren promised. This parting would also be a difficult one, for all the briefness of their time together. He exited the room, and a pair of King's Guards were immediately at his heels. He swallowed a sigh and headed down the corridor. He had only walked a few dozen steps when Aras rounded the corner, heading in his direction, but as yet oblivious to him, looking seriously and sadly at the ground, followed by four King's Guards.

Dewalaren was suddenly anxious. Had his father not recovered fully as expected, or was something wrong with Lunahr? But then Aras's eyes lifted, as if sensing his distress, and he saw and hailed him. His smile was warm, and Dewalaren relaxed a little.

"Leave us," Aras commanded the six King's Guard that encircled them. The King's Guard hesitated. Aras looked at them coolly, and they bowed and left, but both Dewalaren and Aras noted that they went no further than their bows might reach.

Aras sighed as he stood looking at his friend. "Ahrnad cannot forgive himself for the attack upon my father. And he refuses to see you are not a danger to me. I will miss you greatly, but many will be relieved to see you go," Aras said wistfully.

Dewalaren looked at him in surprise. His friend already knew he was leaving.

Aras smiled warmly at him. "Arcanus warned me this morning he was taking you away with him. His need is most great, although he could not say more. I knew you would be coming to say good-bye. I thought if I spoke first, it might make it easier for you."

Idare, how he would miss his friend! He was a warm light in times of cold darkness.

"I have told the stables to expect you. It comforts me to know that Janahar will carry you. Arcanus may, of course, choose whichever mount he desires. At least you need not walk this time."

"I would take you with me if I could," Dewalaren said, unable to contain the wistfulness in his voice.

"And I would go with you if I could. But our duties lie apart for a while. Although I cannot help but feel our time together has only just begun. It makes it easier to part, knowing I will see you again." He reached out and they clasped arms, as warriors, as brothers.

Dewalaren was deeply moved. Of all the Elves he'd had dealings with, only Elavar had ever welcomed such physical contact. Elanara certainly had not. To his surprise, the confusion, longing, and despair thoughts of her usually brought were absent. Merely walking beside Aras made him feel complete, more at peace than she ever had. She had the opposite effect upon him. It was when he was with her that he felt most alienated by her, most alone. Would that Aras were the one he was to wed!

He instantly felt guilty for the forbidden desire. He had stolen Elanara from Aras, unintentionally though it might have been. And he was a King. He must have a

Queen, to bear heirs for his Kingdom, his House, his people to survive. He was unworthy of them, but still, he must try his best.

"WALK with me. We will get your things," Aras said, concerned to feel the despair growing inside Dewalaren, even as he yet walked beside him. He ached to send a wave of warmth and reassurance to him as he had done before, but he dared not use his Power so near Arcanus, now that he was strengthened by Jarnath.

He cautiously tested his bond to Dewalaren. He could not sense his presence as Dewalaren had told him he should be able to, but he would be able to sense danger to him, he was sure of it. Aras did not like the idea of Dewalaren leaving with Arcanus but could not think of a way to stop him without revealing too much. Lunahr needed him, and he was bound to Nalea. And he had yet to undo the damage to his father's core. He could not until Arcanus was safely gone. For now, he must remain here, in spite of what his heart urged.

Aras had been relieved to find Arcanus had indeed only sought to bind Lunahr here, that he had not worked further harm upon him. But Incuban had done much damage to him. He did not know if he would be able to heal him fully from it or not. He would proceed cautiously.

Aras handed Dewalaren a bedroll and pack that were not his own: they were new and clean, and the pack was large and full. Dewalaren hefted them and looked at Aras questioningly.

"I do not send you off so ill-supplied this time. You will be pleased at what you find." There was a light but warm cloak of the same waterproof material Aras's was made of and a blanket of the same fabric. There was a new set of clothes that would be difficult to tear and would shed dirt easily. There was food and drink that would sustain his friend far better than Man's fare and restore strength in ways the latter never could. And Elvish medicines, carefully packaged and labeled with their names and uses, in case Dewalaren was unfamiliar with any of them. He hoped they might help his friend on his long journey. And he had written a special note on one, as well, and smiled at the memory. It said, "For fever, for all that you never take ill, my friend. For, as our sheltering tree taught us, lightning may indeed sometimes strike twice." He hoped his words might brighten his spirits as well, in some future day of need.

Dewalaren thanked him and produced his letter. "I would have you give this to Beryl for me. I hope my poor words might provide some comfort to him in his lonely exile. I entrust you with his safekeeping. He has desperate need of a friend." He knew as well as Arcanus that merely binding Lunahr against harming himself would not be enough. It would be easy enough for him to let himself die.

"Do not worry for your cousin. I am releasing him from that dark hole today, once you are gone. Tensions would be too high with both of you on the loose at once. Already I have spoken words of comfort and friendship to him, and I will do far more. I will remind him how to smile, even how to laugh again, and I will teach him new songs and hear him sing them, so that, when you next see him, you will know him again."

Dewalaren unexpectedly embraced Aras. After a startled moment, Aras returned the hug. At the feeling of Dewalaren's strong arms around him, his heart began hammering. He could not say good-bye to him! He could not bear to, not when he felt that he had been born to be at his side, always. How could he let him go? Then he remembered all the many eyes upon him and quickly released him and backed out of Dewalaren's arms.

"Careful, my friend! You almost earned yourself an arrow in the back for that," Aras said, forcing a smile. Dewalaren smiled in return. His smile was so warm and full of love that Aras laughed in sheer joy, for he had not seen his friend happy for many days. Perhaps Dewalaren might fare well after all. "Until we meet again, my friend."

Dewalaren turned to go and Aras watched until he disappeared from his sight.

Chapter 7
Homeward Bound

"MASTER RION, we are approaching Logareth. It is the last City of Man before we reach the Gelthor Pass through the Coroden. We are still a long way from Gosa. I need to know how many of the men you are willing to lose to the mountains," Jargas asked.

"Lose? None of them!" Rion answered, sounding shocked he might even ask such a thing.

He responded with such vehemence that Jargas looked at him thoughtfully. "You have never traveled by caravan before, have you?"

"I have, once," Rion said defensively. "I traveled from Ardock to Athanark."

"Ah. And you would have lost few, if any, on that journey," Jargas said in understanding.

Rion paled and shook his head mutely.

Tarrell spoke up grimly. "We lost everyone, half a day out from Athanark: seventeen guards, Rion's master, and the four wagon drivers. Only Rion and I survived, and only because Talon and Aras saved us."

Jargas nodded and then spoke, choosing his words carefully. "In a crossing such as the one to Gosa, you must expect to lose half your guards. Fortune may smile upon you and you might lose less. Disaster may strike and none might live. But you must not expect all to live, for they will not."

Rion looked ill. "How can I bring such men to their deaths for me?"

"They knew the risks when they signed on, even if you did not realize. Each thinks he will live or he would not be a guard, nor have signed on for this trip. But he well knows his comrades might die," Jargas assured him.

"But Tarrell never thought that! Nor Hardred nor Alnas nor Elkrum, not any of them," Rion argued, looking at Tarrell for confirmation.

TARRELL was silent, though he knew Rion was wrong. Alnas had feared greatly for Hardred. He had been convinced Hardred could not possibly survive another caravan after already guarding so many. But Tarrell would not say either Hardred's or Alnas's name. Rion missed them both fiercely and feared for them. He worried that with only two of them, they might well have succumbed to an enemy like the wolven-riders, or other bandits.

He knew Rion feared finding their bodies along the route they took. They'd spoken about Rion's fears more than once on this journey, after making camp for the night. Rion desperately hoped he might somehow meet up with Hardred and Alnas again, but the two men had left weeks before them, on horseback, while he and Rion were traveling far more slowly, by wagon. Unless something delayed Alnas and Hardred, they'd not see their two friends again. And as the most likely delay would be serious injury and a need to recover from it, or the loss of one or both of their horses, he and Rion both hoped they did not see them, much as they longed for their company and their aid.

Tarrell hated being so helpless. Strangers now guarded Rion when he should be the one doing so. Although these new men were already fast becoming their friends, since spending a few days with them in Athanark gathering horses and supplies, and traveling alongside them for just under a fortnight.

Jargas continued with his explanation. "Before, you faced a two-hundred-mile journey, with only part of it through mountains and marsh. The trip you made was far shorter and easier and safer. This is nearly five times the distance, a nine-hundred-and-seventy-five-mile trip along rivers, through hills and mountains, swamps and woods, and we'll be facing ogres and obearn and thieves before we are done. Many of those you signed on have traveled by caravan before and are experienced in the risks. Any of them can tell you what they expect." He called Rarnak over.

"YES, Captain?" Rarnak said, wondering at the looks on Rion's and Tarrell's faces.

"You have made three such crossings as the one we're making. How many started in each and how many finished?" Jargas asked.

Rarnak looked at Rion and Tarrell with sudden understanding. "The first was the best or I'd have not tried a second, regardless of the wages or what I'd left behind. Sixteen of us set out from near Gosa and headed to Delthos. We lost four of the fourteen guards on the land portion. I was young, then, and didn't realize the true dangers. I thought us cursed when we were in fact fortunate. Then we sailed from Delthos to Seaview on a merchant ship. We lost none at sea, but I was ill nearly the entire time and decided to head overland back again. I'd gone for the adventure and the coin, like most, but I'd left a father and little sister behind that I'd planned to return to.

"The second trip was a disaster from start to finish, and the end was quick. We began in Seaview and were heading for Ardock. There were twenty-five of us. We did not even make it halfway. I alone survived to reach Lomas, and only just. Once I recovered, I did not think to leave Lomas ever, in spite of Talia and Father. I spent a few years there, as a City Guard, and was content enough just to be alive. But then the refugees started coming up the Methris from the coast, and I learned of the cities that had been burnt and the darkness that was coming.

"I joined a third caravan and made it over the Velmar Mountains and through the Feonoke Marshes to Athanark nearly three months ago. We had thought it would be far enough, safe enough. I expected half of us would fall, as is usual for such a journey, as I had finally learned, and indeed, of the fifteen of us who set out, seven survived, though we almost fared well. We had only lost three until savage men riding enormous wolven attacked us near Athanark. Four more fell then, and none of us would have survived their teeth and blades, for they use poison most foul upon their swords, but a patrol of the City Guard came when all hope was lost and helped us rout them. We lost none of the goods and only had the one merchant to protect, and he lived.

"I would not have left Athanark after that but for fear that the darkness might attack from the sea at Delthos or Meria as well and head inland, that my sister and father might be in danger from it, or that it might head west from here. Certainly no amount of coin could entice me to ever take such a journey again. Two such journeys is all most men ever take, except those who choose a guard's life, and a guard's life is usually a short one.

"I am almost twenty-five now, too old to be a guard. Such work is for younger men. I was fortunate you sought experience over youth, for few now would hire me. But I may yet get to see Talia and my father again, if Areth wills it."

Rion was looking at him wide-eyed. "It was you! Your caravan. Captain Vincent told me that the last caravan to make it through before ours had been two months earlier, and he said he had thought all the wolven-riders slain. Others attacked us, when only half a day's journey from the City. We lost—they all—how many will we lose this time?" he asked in a small voice.

Rarnak could see Rion was devastated by that journey. He looked to be fighting hard against tears. Rarnak was quick to reassure him without lying to him, smiling genuinely at him for his kindhearted nature, for caring about their fate. "Who's to say? But these are good, strong men, Master Rion, all of whom know their craft. I do not see it in any of them to run from danger nor betray you to it. They will all fight for you. Some of them will die for you, but not many."

Rion shook his head. "No. No more will die for me, ever. We will travel to Gosa and lose no one."

Rarnak said, "By Areth's grace, may your words hold the power of prophecy."

Rion asked Jargas, "Why did you ask me how many men I would be willing to lose to the mountains?"

"Because you seem generous for a merchant, but still, I do not know if you calculated all that this journey might cost you in men and coin before you are done," Jargas replied.

"I do not pay them enough for the risks they take for me, but nothing is enough. How can you value a man's life with coin?" Rion asked, his voice filled with pain.

JARGAS noticed the Ogaten brothers were listening silently. Their voices had risen too much. He had hoped to keep the conversation between the four of them. "I'm glad you believe so. We'll need to buy some things in Logareth if you expect to cross the mountains without losing any of the men or horses. We'll need to trade with the ogres for safe passage."

Rarnak looked at him as if he were mad. "Trade with the ogres? You might as well try to trade with wolven! Any fool knows the best way around the ogres is to sneak past them. But with three wagons and sixteen men, that won't be possible. The only way past them will be to fight our way through. We are fortunate Talon knew enough to choose all six bowmen, for that is the only way to avoid their rock. Few can go against an ogre's club with a sword and survive. Though the ogres are a cowardly enough lot that once one falls, the rest will flee. I've seen it. If we are quick enough and deadly enough, we will make it." His voice was loud, and the other men now had been drawn to their conversation and were listening.

Jargas said, "I can understand why you might think so. You would have encountered the ogres in the Holoren Mountains on your trip from Gosa to Delthos. It is possible to trade with them as well, though there are a large number of rogues infesting those mountains that would as soon eat you as look at you. But we are traveling through the Coroden Mountains. When I did so, the Rakakala controlled the Gelthor Pass. They were receptive to trade. If they still control the Pass, our crossing will be a relatively easy one. If not, then I'll have to earn my keep."

Rion looked surprised. "Ogres live in tribes?"

Jargas nodded. "Of a sort. Actually, more like extended families. The largest is about fifteen members. It's not possible to feed more than that. The ogress makes sure enough of the young males leave so it doesn't grow to be bigger than that. The rogue males are the ones that are the most dangerous, but you usually only come across them in the wilds, away from the roads and passes and river valleys. I suspect there are dozens of tribes over the length of the Coroden, if they're like the Holoren."

"And you expect me to trade with them?" Rion asked, wide-eyed.

Jargas looked at him seriously. "No, Master Rion. For this you must leave the trading to me. You, unfortunately, they'd view only as dinner. They'll see me with different eyes."

"I did not think ogres could talk. How do you expect to trade with them?" Rion pressed.

"They talk. They speak Common, after a fashion, though you might be hard-pressed to recognize it if you weren't used to listening to them speak it. They know maybe twenty words, and each tribe has different ones to a point, although 'food' and 'fight' and 'kill' are usually the same everywhere. I know the words the Rakakala use. Rakakala means Rock-killers. And there are gestures that can be understood by all."

"What is it I am supposed to buy?" Rion asked, clearly intrigued.

"Two oxen; two wheels of cheese, at least fifty pounds, the bigger the wheel and the more pungent the better; two casks of wine, at least twenty gallons; a gallon of honey; an obearn pelt; and a wagon," Jargas listed, ticking the items off on his fingers.

"BUT that will cost at least three hundred gold!" Rion said, shocked. "How can I expect to go all the way to Gosa if I am to spend such coin every leg of the journey?"

The men muttered uneasily. Rion realized everyone was listening, and he'd made a mistake to say such a thing in front of them. "Your wages are already set aside," he called out loudly, assuring them. "Even if I arrive in Gosa a pauper, you will not."

Jargas shook his head. "I can't think of coin like that you'll need to spend once we cross the mountains. Coin won't help you cross the rivers or slay the snakes or fight the bandits. Your men will do that for you, but they cannot if they are in the belly of an ogre, or crippled by a boulder thrown by one.

"Besides, it should not cost as much as you think. It need not be a good wagon, just one strong enough to travel for the few days we'll need it. The wine can be base as well. The oxen will need to be big and well fed, but they need not be in their prime. The obearn pelt should be old and worn, not new and sleek: that alone will save you plenty. If worse comes to worst, I'll have to leave the rest of you in the City while I go into the foothills and slay an obearn for one, for I lost my own in crossing the Fromer Mountains. But that would take time. The cheese will be costly, though, and the honey as well. If you bargain shrewdly enough, it might all cost you closer to one hundred gold than three."

"And if the ogres won't trade?" Tarrell asked.

"Then we fight, of course," Jargas said simply. "Did you think I was suggesting otherwise? I am just trying to do as Master Rion wishes and clear the mountains without losing any of the men. Even as we try to trade, the men must be ready to nock arrows to their bows and the horses must be ready to run. The men will be ordered not to fire unless I am slain. Not felled, for I've yet to keep my feet in such a battle, but slain," he said, looking around to be sure the others heard and understood.

"If the Rakakala do not control the Pass, and even if they do, I will likely need to battle at least one of the ogres. And although such battles have never before gone fully against me, I usually take at least one strong blow, which I hope to recover from. But poor luck sometimes overcomes skill, so who is to say what might happen this time?" Jargas said prosaically.

"How many ogres have you fought?" Rion asked, intrigued.

Jargas looked him in the eye. "Sixty-three."

There was another murmur, as those around them voiced their disbelief softly to one another. Only the Ogaten brothers said nothing. But Rarnak, who'd stayed silent and listened, had the courage to speak up. "Sixty-three? You claimed before to have slain your first ogre at sixteen, and now I'm to believe you've slain sixty-three?"

Jargas's eyes narrowed. "Nay. Master Rion asked me how many I'd fought, not slain. I have slain fifteen."

"Fifteen!" Rarnak scoffed. "Even then, I would have some proof of such a wild claim, for even if you are as old as you look, that means you have slain an ogre nearly every two years and fought four times as many, from sixteen to forty, which is not possible. Most men never face an ogre at all, and those who are unlucky enough to fight one are lucky to fight one in a lifetime and live!"

Jargas glared at Rarnak, and most of the men around him moved away uneasily as some hands strayed to sword hilts. The Ogaten brothers, however, moved two to either side of Rarnak and two to either side of Jargas, as if they planned to intercede to restrain them from each other if tensions worsened rather than eased.

"This is the first, last, and only time you will ever call me a liar, Rarnak, if you value your life. I make allowance only because you do not know me, nor my kin, nor my home, and of all of you, I am the only one who came unreferenced and unknown. I had thought I proved myself well enough to you at the combat trial, but I can see you fear these ogres, and I can tell from your eyes you fear them because you know them, you have faced them, you have seen comrades lost to them."

Rarnak paled at his words and watched him intently.

"But if it is proof you want, that I have. I would have worn it when we entered the mountains in any case. It is the custom of the ogres to wear trophies of those they have slain, and I always do so when I walk their lands."

Rion watched wide-eyed, wondering what horrible thing Jargas might produce. Jargas reached into his small pack and pulled out a long strand, holding it up. Rion swallowed. It was a necklace of teeth: they looked much like the teeth of Men, only too sharp and four times too large to be. Many of them were dark with age, shading from pale yellow to almost brown.

"These are the teeth of those I have slain: thirty teeth, fifteen pairs, for you string only the canines. You can see by the color I have done so over many years. You called me forty, but I have never claimed to be. I am eighty-three. My mother was a woman of Man, but my father is a Dwarf, and I get my longevity from him, though I've recently learned her people are remarkably long-lived as well. The Holoren Mountains, where my tribe lives, are infested with ogres. We keep the known tribes at our borders and aid them in driving off those who would challenge them. I'm the village Champion and, as you can see by looking at me, the most likely to survive such a contest."

RARNAK swallowed and faced Jargas bravely. It was not easy to say these next words in front of all the others, but he had spoken against Jargas before them, so he had little choice. "I apologize for my insult, for the words I spoke and the others I did not voice. For I see now that you have spoken truthfully to us, when I thought you had at the least exaggerated your feats. I saw seventeen good men die, once, because a comrade lied to us about his experience and led us falsely. You are right that I spoke out of ignorance of you and out of fear of the ogres, for they are creatures of nightmare and haunt my dreams still after five long years.

"I had thought myself too old to face them again. I have been dreading this part of the journey since I signed on with you, though I had sense enough until now to keep silent about it. But you have given me back my courage.

"We have a long trip ahead of us, and I'd rather undertake it as your friend than as your enemy. I will never again question your words or actions, for you have proven yourself to truly be a Captain, as well. Can you forgive me and trust me again as a comrade and perhaps even learn to accept me as a friend?"

Jargas studied Rarnak carefully, as if he were looking past his eyes into his mind and heart. Jargas nodded. "Aye, I can forgive you. You might doubt your own courage, but I do not, for few men have the courage to voice their doubts to me, and fewer still to make such an apology to any man in front of so many. I think you and I could indeed be friends, if you truly wish it."

THERE was a collective sigh of relief as the tension of the group eased, and the Ogaten brothers rejoined each other and spoke quietly amongst themselves in a language Rion did not recognize. Rion had thought that Rarnak would have to be replaced in Logareth, and that even so the party might be left fractious and divided by the altercation, but it looked now like all might be well. Rion spoke softly to Tarrell of his earlier concerns.

TARRELL agreed and was glad, for he liked Rarnak and would have hated to lose him. He was grateful to him, too, for he had not believed Jargas either. He was not so trusting as Rion, who had still seen too little of the world and been injured too little by it to have lost the naïveté of his youth.

The other men who had doubted Jargas also seemed to trust him now. Tarrell knew it was better that he had not been the one who had questioned Jargas, both for what Jargas might have thought of him, and for what Rion might have.

WHEN they reached Logareth, the men were pleased to be spending a night at an inn, more so because Rion paid them their wages for the journey so far and then also bought the first round of drinks for everyone. Rion was relieved they'd found a good place to stay. It had been difficult finding an inn with room for them all and a large enough stable. The city was swarming with refugees, though it looked like many of them wouldn't have the coin to stay in an inn.

Rion noted that Rarnak bought Jargas a drink after the first round, and then Jargas bought one for Rarnak. The Ogaten brothers were the only ones to drink only the first free round. Each man paid for his own dinner, but Rion surprised them all by paying for their lodging. They each had floor space in the common room below, while Rion and Tarrell shared a room above. Most of the men paid for the best dinners the inn offered, apparently already tired of trail fare, but Rion noticed the Ogaten brothers ate frugally.

After consulting with Tarrell, Rion arranged it so that four men guarded the wagons in the stable, and two the door to their room, each in shifts that Jargas coordinated so all got a decent amount of sleep. Rion told the men that the next morning, those who were off shift would be able to roam the City, with the understanding that they meet at noon at the inn for lunch, and then they would continue on their way. Jargas had agreed to go shopping with Rion and Tarrell, both to guard them and to make sure they bought exactly what was needed to appease the ogres. Normally they would have had two men protect them, but Jargas was both intimidating and competent enough that they could allow one more man to have some time on his own in the city.

The next morning, Rion, Tarrell, and Jargas were just finishing their breakfast when Gar came into the common room, spotted them, and headed for their table, a big grin on his face and a huge shaggy thing in his arms. "I hope this is what you had in mind, for I parted with five gold to get it, and my brothers won't easily forgive me for it if I made a mistake." He held it up triumphantly. It was an obearn hide, old and faded, moth-eaten and full of dust.

Jargas grinned widely. "It is perfect! A good one would go for a hundred, and I was hoping we'd be able to find one for maybe half that in a state much like this one. I'd all but resigned myself to the thought that I would have to hunt my own and cure it and drag it through the dirt to ruin it, but we've not even left to shop and you've done some of our work for us! Where did you find it?"

"In the stable," Gar said proudly. "You had assigned me to duty there last night, and I spent a good deal of time talking to Paran, the stable master. I plan to open my own stables someday. Paran invited me to his room for some kakla this morning. It was on the floor of his room. He was using it as a rug. I tried not to sound too eager about it and commented on it, and he said he's been meaning to get rid of it for years, that he'd rather have a rag rug than this thing, so I offered to buy it from him. Five gold sounded reasonable to me, so I'm glad it was."

Jargas handed it back to Gar. "You did well, very well. Put it in one of the wagons for now."

Rion handed Gar ten gold. Gar looked puzzled. "But I only paid five for it."

"The other five is a finder's fee, for you've shown initiative and saved us both time and coin," Rion said happily.

Gar grinned from ear to ear. "And here I thought Ron might give me a terrible tongue-lashing, and I'd have to listen to endless weeks of teasing over it from Ara and Van. Ha! This trip is starting out well for me at least."

"Let's just hope it goes as well for us from here on in," Rion said.

Rion, Tarrell, and Jargas went out into the City to do the rest of the shopping. On the way from Market to Lantern Street, they saw the Ogaten brothers enter the Temple of Elmoth. Ara was carrying a sword in his hands, one not his own, as his was still sheathed at his side. Rion was surprised. He knew only what his father's friend Cedric and Alnas and some of the other guards had told him of Elmoth when Oberas wasn't around to overhear. Elmoth was the God of Swordsmen and Bowmen. Most guards followed him, and offerings to him were usually in the form of weapons of one type or another, rather than the coin Laneth and some of the other Gods seemed to prefer. But swords were expensive: a new one of good quality cost around thirty gold. Ara or one or more of his brothers must be pretty devout.

Alnas was a follower of Elmoth. Had he and Hardred stopped at the Temple here, to make an offering, before continuing onward? Rion was tempted to go inside and describe his two friends, and ask the Priest and Acolytes inside if they'd seen them. But he wasn't sure about the protocols of doing so. He wasn't a follower of

Elmoth. And neither was Hardred. He didn't want to unintentionally insult or perhaps anger the God, or those who worshipped and served him, against him or his friends. And what if they'd been there, but no one remembered them? There were so many travelers, especially refugees, here in the City.

Rion was wary of how desperate some of the refugees looked and leery of leaving their goods with only Jargas and Tarrell to guard them, while he entered the Temple. To do so might prove too tempting to some of the men he saw. He belatedly realized they really should have brought more of the men with them, considering the burden of goods they had purchased. It would be better to return to the inn, now that they'd bought what they needed and it was loaded into the extra wagon they'd acquired. Reluctantly, Rion turned away from the Temple.

They returned to the inn and ate lunch. Though the Ogaten brothers were in a very festive mood, Rion was surprised to see that they still ate a frugal lunch, as if they didn't have the coin to buy better. They must have spent almost all their coin purchasing the sword they'd given to the God. He hoped the God looked favorably upon them, for their devotion. He was glad he'd given Gar the extra gold for the pelt. Even with the ten gold he'd spent for it, they'd bought everything they needed for only eighty-seven gold.

After lunch, they mounted up again, all except for Gar, who volunteered to drive the third wagon, the newer, more rickety one with their trade goods for the ogres. His horse was hitched behind Rion's wagon, lest the ogres get designs upon the animal as part of the trade. They were still far from the mountains at nightfall, when they made camp.

They awoke at dawn and set out again. They were nearly at the foothills when Rarnak rode up to Jargas and spoke to him for a moment. Jargas nodded and rode over to Rion's wagon.

"Master Rion, if it's all right with you, Rarnak would like to take a few moments to make an offering at the shrine we just passed," Jargas informed him. "He said his duty shift hadn't allowed him the opportunity to visit the Temple of Areth in Logareth, and he'd feel better about entering the Mountains if he had the chance to make an offering here. He'll only be a short while, and he can catch up with us easily enough. I recommend you allow it."

"Of course. Tell him that's fine. And make sure tonight at camp that the rest of the men know they're free to observe as well, as they see fit along this trip, as long as they don't abuse the privilege. You need not check with me about matters such as that, Jargas. I trust you as Captain to use your own judgment," Rion assured him.

Jargas smiled at him. "It pleases me to hear you say so." Then he went off to speak with Rarnak. Rarnak smiled at Rion and rode back to the shrine.

Rion was curious why Rarnak wanted to make an offering to Areth. He had mentioned her twice before, but Areth was the Goddess of the Harvest and Fertility, not of warriors. It was an odd choice for a trip such as this. Rion knew better than to ask Rarnak, though. Oberas had warned him to never speak about religion with anyone unless he was absolutely certain of their beliefs ahead of time. Oberas himself had hated Elmoth with a passion for an unbearable loss decades before that he blamed the God for.

Rion's father and uncle had been City Guards, but they'd worshipped Ragnar, as their parents had before them. Rion's father hadn't been very religious, but Uncle Farion had been pretty devout. He'd kept a shrine in his house for decades, with a consecrated flame that their mother had brought on pilgrimage from Logareth, and carefully replaced the candle every day.

Rion's mother had been a minstrel, so she followed Meloneth, but she'd always told him Meloneth liked to hear music rather than have people pray to him. Because of it, Rion had never even entered any of the Gods' Temples before. Rion always spoke respectfully of the Gods but didn't follow any of them himself. He was fascinated by the devotion of these men to their various deities and wondered anew whether he was missing something by not following any of them himself.

IT WAS late afternoon, still a long while until sunset, when Jargas surprised Rion by stopping beside an ancient, gnarled tree and calling the caravan to a halt. "I need some time to prepare, before we go further. Remember, you all need to keep your eyes out for obearn, in addition to the ogres, when we continue on. Their dens pepper these mountains, and they roam the hills freely. We're near enough the foothills now that one or more might be roaming about, so keep a sharp eye out. You can all stretch your legs for a short while here, and relieve yourselves if you've a need to, while I get dressed. We won't want to stop for anything once we enter the foothills, except camp at night, until we're well clear of the ogres. And there may be rogues or even a second tribe we come across before we're done, so don't get too confident."

Jargas dismounted from his horse and tied it to the back of the wagon Tarrell was driving, as Rion's already had Gar's horse tied to it. He went to the tree and eyed several of the branches, then grabbed the one nearest the ground in both hands and heaved. His mighty muscles bulged from the strain, and with a loud crack, the branch tore free.

Rion's eyes widened. He'd have thought only a man with an ax could have separated a branch that thick from a tree. Jargas snapped off the twigs that adhered to it and swung it about a few times as if it were a club, grunting in satisfaction. Rion observed him curiously, wondering what he was planning.

Jargas went to the back of the new wagon, carrying his pack, and set it down. He took off his guardsman's shirt and pants as Rion watched, puzzled, then changed into the pants he'd worn at the test. He remained bare-chested, however. Rion was amazed at the thick mass of hair that coated his back and chest and legs, in addition to his arms, which he'd seen before. Then Jargas's fingers were at his sleekly oiled and meticulously groomed hair. He began unbraiding the dozens of narrow braids, joined in an intricate weave to make up the single long braid that went down his back, and then combed his hair through with his fingers. He did the same with his double-braided beard, carefully putting the gold rings that had bound each into his purse.

Then he reached down into the dirt, pulled up great handfuls of it, and rubbed it all over his chest, drizzling it down his back as well. Jargas put more dirt into his hair and beard, grinding it in thoroughly. He put on his ogre-tooth necklace then took the obearn pelt and wrapped the two great forepaws with their six-inch black claws about his neck, the head flopping back against his back. He fastened it with a great broach he pulled from his pack, stepped back, and hefted the club over his shoulder.

Rion swallowed. Jargas looked fearsome, like a monster out of one of the stories his mother used to tell him at night. Rion glanced at Tarrell. He was smiling at Jargas. "All I can say is, I'm glad you're on our side. Though you give me at least a rough idea now of what it is we are facing."

"Nay! I'm far too short, scrawny, clean, and pretty," Jargas said, laughing heartily.

Rion swallowed again. Jargas was well over seven feet tall and at least half again as broad as some Men, twice as broad as many, and he looked ferocious and wild, like he might eat them alive.

Tarrell walked up to Rion and said softly, "Rion, you must try not to wear your heart on your sleeve. The men see your fear and it feeds their own."

Rion glanced around. At first, no one looked afraid to him. But then he realized how quiet they were and saw eyes that would not meet his and unsettled glances toward Jargas. He nodded and put on a brave face.

"Come, we've got a ways to go, now," Jargas said, and he started walking, leading them on foot. Gar followed in his wagon, and then Rion in his, and Tarrell came up last. Jargas's stride was so great they did not need to slow the horses' pace for him.

Night began to fall when they were still far from the mountains. A small stream ran along their path and Jargas signaled for the caravan to halt. "We'll camp here, near the water. We post double guards tonight and every night until we're through the pass and out of the hills on the other side. Keep the fire small and no singing."

The men nodded. Dinner was a solemn affair, and the men not on shift went to bed early. The night passed uneventfully.

TWO more days passed amidst the hills, and then they were through the foothills and in the mountain pass, the mountains towering on either side of them. Their path ran parallel to the stream, which had grown to be as wide as one of their wagons.

They continued on for an additional two days. At camp that night, Jargas told the men, "We're getting close to where I met the Rakakala when I crossed last time. There's a good chance we'll meet them tomorrow."

The men nodded. Rion heard Van say, "I'll be almost glad to meet them. This waiting is driving me mad."

"Don't be an idiot. We may still make the crossing without seeing them, if we have the luck," Ron chastised.

"Stop coddling him, Ron. You know as well as me that won't happen," Gar accused.

"Don't worry, Van," Ara said confidently. "Elmoth will watch over us as He has the rest of our trip."

"Just think about the coin. Once this trip is over, we'll be home and wealthy too," Gar said eagerly.

"I'd rather be poor and still in Athanark," Van said, eyeing the rock around them nervously.

"Not with those wolven you don't, and what was coming from the south. It's better we get through these mountains now, while the darkness is still another range away. Remember those stories Grandfather told us," Gar told him.

"All of you, get some sleep," Ron ordered. "We're second shift, and it's going to be a long night."

The brothers settled down.

Rion sat with Tarrell beside the fire. "You should get some sleep, Rion," Tarrell told him.

"What about you?" Rion asked.

"I'm not especially tired right now."

"Neither am I. But you're setting a bad example for the men if you don't sleep," Rion said with a faint smile.

Tarrell looked at him and grimaced. "You'd throw my own words back at me, then? Very well, I'll sleep, or try to, at least."

THE next day came and went, and there was still no sign of the ogres. The day after that passed without incident as well. Some of the men were starting to relax.

The following morning Jargas still strode in front. Rion was amazed at his stamina. He wondered how many days Jargas would be able to walk as he had been.

Suddenly, a loud crack shattered the thought, and a boulder crashed down beside Gar's wagon, narrowly missing it. Gar pulled hard on the yoke, stopping the oxen that drew it. Some of the horses shied and stamped their feet nervously.

"Bak!" Jargas roared in challenge and shook his club into the air, looking around at both sides of the mountains around him. The men eyed the rocks nervously as well, bows now at their sides, but arrows not yet nocked.

"Lata Jak!" There was a mighty roar, then a rumble, and a piece of the mountain slid free. For a moment, Rion thought an avalanche had been unleashed upon them, but then something rose and walked free of the sliding rock, and he realized it must be an ogre. It was enormous, over ten feet tall and half again as broad as Jargas. The club it carried looked to be fashioned out of a tree trunk, not a branch. It was mostly naked, save for a ragged scrap of hide across its loins and an obearn hide that made the one Jargas wore look like finery in comparison. The ogre was dirty and hairy and horrible.

The horses were panicked now, and some of the riders had to fight to stay mounted as their horses tried to rear and pull away from the nightmarish creature. The ogre raised its club over its head, towering above Jargas, and Rion saw Rarnak slam Orcan's bow out of his hands, the arrow he'd been about to fire hitting the ground harmlessly beside his horse. "Not unless he is slain!" Rarnak hissed. Orcan nodded, too afraid to retrieve his bow.

Rion heard the club hit and looked frantically back at Jargas. But the club had come down inches from Jargas, hitting the ground instead of him. Jargas likewise slammed his own club down next to the ogre. The ogre stared over Jargas's shoulder, then, at the others, and licked a great tongue over its lips.

"Fata," it said.

Jargas walked over to the wagon Gar was in and said softly, "Out. Don't run. Walk to your horse and mount it." Gar nodded, looking wide-eyed, and left the wagon slowly.

TARRELL couldn't hear what Jargas had said, but he saw Gar heading toward them, his brothers carefully watching, bows at the ready. Gar unhitched and mounted his horse.

Then Jargas pulled the oxen forward.

The ogre started to walk toward the other two wagons instead, and Jargas shook his head. "Na! Fata!" he said, gesturing at the food in the wagon before him. He showed the ogre the wine and said, "Hapa-wata." He gestured at the cheese and the honey, and then pointed toward the oxen and said, "Anma," while miming first drinking and then eating.

Two more rockslides came, and with them, ogres. Tarrell watched them warily. These two were somewhat smaller than the first, though not by much. One of them reached for one of the wine barrels.

The first ogre spun about and smacked his hand away.

The other glared and slapped him back.

"Faat!" the littler ogre yelled.

"Faat!" the first ogre roared back.

Jargas quickly backed out of their path as the two dropped their clubs to the rocky ground and lunged for one another. They started pounding on each other as the third ogre hooted and growled in what Tarrell realized in sick fascination must be laughter.

Tarrell backed his wagon away from them so Rion might back his, but Rion seemed frozen in place by the battle.

Many of the men still fought their panicked horses to remain in their saddles. Tarrell thought it was a good thing they weren't trying to battle the ogres, for with the horses so terrified, the men couldn't have spared a hand for sword or bow.

Ron's horse was better behaved, and Tarrell saw Ron lean over and speak to Rion. Rion looked over his shoulder at Tarrell. He looked terrified. But Tarrell saw him back his wagon.

Tarrell had thought Jargas might try to intervene in the fight, but he just watched, occasionally moving farther away as needed.

Then the second, smaller, ogre took a mighty blow to the head and dropped and lay still. The first prodded it with its foot.

It moaned, then rolled over and rose slowly to its feet.

"Haat?" the bigger ogre asked.

"Na," the other denied.

Jargas approached and pointed to the wagon. "Fata."

The ogre started for Tarrell's wagon, but Jargas stepped in front of it and firmly said, "Na!"

The ogre looked frustrated for a moment. It was pointing. Tarrell swallowed and paled. It was pointing at *him*. Jargas came over to him and indicated the horse tied to the back of Tarrell's wagon. "Anma fata?"

The ogre nodded eagerly and Tarrell nearly fainted in relief. The ogre apparently wanted to eat Jargas's horse, not him.

Jargas walked back over. "Na!"

The ogre looked frustrated. Then it looked toward the mountainside, and a look remarkably like inspiration crossed its face.

It pointed toward Rion and then at the horse. "Hama fata." It started to approach Rion, and Jargas stepped immediately into its path, even as the Ogaten brothers tensed. As they'd not lost control of their mounts, they still had bows in hand. The ogre pointed to the mountain and said, "Hama." Then it pointed to Rion and the mountain and enunciated slowly and carefully, "Hama fata."

"Na! Lata brada," Jargas said, pointing to Rion.

"Na!" the ogre said in frustration. Jargas apparently hadn't understood what it wanted. It was trying to express something it didn't have the words for. Then that look of inspiration appeared again and it looked at the ground around its feet, grunted in satisfaction, and picked up two rocks, a big one and a smaller one.

Tarrell was afraid it would throw them at Rion or Jargas. But it held the smaller one in its left hand and the larger one in its right. It pointed the left rock at Rion, then the right at the horse, and said, "Anma baga fata." It slowly moved its left hand with the rock from Rion toward the mountain and said, "Hama lata fata." It held the bigger rock in its right hand out to Jargas, and Jargas took it, a look of bewildered concentration on his face. Then the ogre held up the rock in its left hand, pointed to Rion and the mountain once more, and then held it out to Jargas, and Jargas took it as well. Then the ogre took the first rock from him. They had switched rocks. The ogre broke into a toothy grin, nodding. The smile was terrifying.

Jargas held out his arms to it in a gesture that Tarrell interpreted as, "Wait." Then Jargas called out to them in Common, "Can anyone figure out what it is Bak's trying to tell me? He said "animal big food" and "home little food." It looks to me like he's trying to get me to trade Rion for my horse, so he can take him home to their village on the mountain to eat him, but that makes no sense, and he's also said it isn't Rion he wants. He's got me completely stumped. I'd be eager to hear your thoughts."

A look of revelation flashed across Gar's face. "Oh Elmoth! I think I know what it's trying to tell you. I think it means it has a Man up at its home. They were going to eat him, but your horse looks bigger and tastier, and it's offering to trade that

Man for the horse. It's not about Rion at all. It was just using him to help explain what it wanted."

Jargas nodded thoughtfully. "I think you've gotten it, Gar." Jargas tested the theory through more gestures and words, and the ogre looked excited. "Ya," Jargas agreed. The ogre left with a big, toothy grin on its face while the other two stood there.

Rarnak slowly and carefully dismounted and climbed into the wagon next to Rion. Tarrell saw him put his arm around Rion, who leaned against him.

Jargas said, "Bak's going to get him for us. I only hope he's alive and that they haven't started to eat him already, whoever he is. Either way, I couldn't have said no. Bak wouldn't have let us leave without taking my horse in any case, poor beast."

"Rion, are you all right?" Tarrell called out softly.

Rarnak answered instead of Rion, "He's doing fine. Don't worry about him. Stay where you are. We may need to move quickly once Bak comes back." Lerdon held Rarnak's horse's reins.

A short while later, Bak's lumbering form loped and slid back down the mountain toward them. It was carrying a hooded and cloaked figure over its shoulder. It tossed him off its shoulder at Jargas, and Jargas caught him before he hit the ground. Then Bak started to approach the wagons.

The horses nearest him went mad, and their riders battled to calm them. Jargas ran in front of Bak and put the man down in the back of Tarrell's wagon. Then he untied his horse and pulled it toward Bak. The horse was fighting against him every step of the way. Jargas's muscles bulged as he pulled it, then he danced out of the way of its lashing hooves but still held the reins.

Bak reached out and grabbed the horse by the head. It kicked him in the right leg. Bak grunted, from his expression more in annoyance than pain, and slammed the horse's head down onto the ground. It collapsed, quivered, and then lay still. With a satisfied grunt, Bak lifted the massive animal, slung it over his shoulder as if it weighed nothing, and began walking toward the mountainside. The other two ogres dragged the wagon with the oxen behind them.

When they were well clear, Jargas got into the back of Rion's wagon, on top of the trade goods. "Ride as fast as you all can, but keep together, and don't stop until I tell you to."

Rarnak held the traces of the lead wagon and urged the horses forward. Rion was still leaning against him. Tarrell looked on anxiously but followed. Then he turned and looked over his shoulder at the slender man slumped lifelessly against the goods in the wagon. The man's head bobbed and swayed as he bounced along in the wagon. Tarrell's eyes widened as he saw a mass of long silver hair tumble out of the hood, at first thinking in shock that it was an old woman, until a gracefully upswept ear was revealed with the next bounce. It wasn't a Man at all! It was an Elf!

"I can't tell if he's still alive or not," Tarrell called out.

"He felt warm, but Bak was none too gentle with him. We can't stop to help him until we're further away. These ogres seem to favor horses over oxen. I wish I'd known that earlier. I don't want them deciding they want the rest of ours."

"Rion?" Tarrell called again, and Rarnak said something to Jargas. Jargas said, "He'll be fine, Tarrell. He was scared out of his wits. He froze in terror when he saw Bak coming for him. He passed out, that's all."

"I, for one, won't make him feel the worse for it," Gar said. "Bak scared me out of my wits too. Turning my back on him and walking those dozen steps from the wagon to my horse was the hardest thing I've ever done."

Tarrell nodded. He'd been frozen, too, when he'd thought Bak had pointed at him, not the horse.

A while later, Jargas judged they were safely enough away that they could stop. Rion walked over shakily to Tarrell and tried to smile but looked like he might cry instead. Tarrell embraced him. "It's all right. We're safe now and you were very brave. I'm proud of you."

Rion looked at the Elf and swallowed. "How is he?" The Elf was dirty and cut and scraped everywhere, as if he'd been dragged along the ground. He well might have been. "He's still alive. Lerdon, you told us you've some experience healing. Can you help him?"

"I'll do my best." Lerdon cut the Elf's clothes off of him, explaining he didn't want to risk injuring him further by undressing him. The Elf's entire body was a mass of black, purple, blue, and yellow bruises. "From what I can tell, his left leg and left arm are broken. Elves have strong bones, from what I know, so that might be worse for him than it sounds. Other than that, save for the scrapes and bruises, he looks all right to me, but he could be injured where it can't be seen. Jargas, I'll need you to help me set the bones. Just follow my directions, all right?"

Jargas nodded and did as instructed. After setting the bones, Lerdon washed and bandaged the Elf's arm and leg carefully. Then he washed the rest of him and used a salve and more bandages on the many scrapes. He'd just finished the last one when the Elf moaned, and then, unexpectedly, his eyes snapped open. He looked in confusion at the strange faces all around him. His eyes widened as he saw Jargas, and he reached for his side with his right hand, as if for a weapon, but touched bare skin.

Lerdon wrapped a blanket around him as Jargas said with surprising gentleness, "It's all right. I'm not going to eat you."

Rion held out his water skin to the Elf and spoke slowly and clearly in a strange lilting singsong. "*Sehla. Ha losha suhla.*"

The Elf looked at him in surprise, and Tarrell and Jargas looked at Rion in astonishment.

"Since when do you speak Elvish?" Tarrell asked, recognizing it from having heard Talon and Aras speak it in Athanark. "What did you say to him?"

Rion ignored Tarrell for the moment and said to the Elf, "*Ha losha fasehlana. Lata un hapo ya.*"

The Elf looked at Rion intently and said, "*Maya ya lar? Fota mae isa?*"

Rion looked sheepish and said in Common, "I'm sorry, but I can't understand you. I only know twelve phrases, and I've used four of those already." Then he turned to Tarrell. "I asked Aras to teach me some, and he taught me what he thought might be most useful on our journey."

"So what did you say to him?" Tarrell asked, intrigued.

"First I said, 'Hello. We offer you water,' and then I said, 'We offer friendship. Let us help you.' I'm afraid I don't know how to say 'We rescued you from the ogres,' or to ask him who he is, or how he got caught in the first place, or where he was going, or to tell him about his injuries. This is going to complicate things. Once we're out of the mountains, we'll need to bring him back to his people. Or at least to other Elves. There's no way for us to tell where he really belongs. I hope it's at least the west side of the mountains. But they'd be able to get him home safely, even if it's not. Jargas, do you know where the nearest Elven Kingdom is and how to get there?"

"Aye, I know of them, and roughly where to find them, but you can't even find the Kingdoms, let alone enter them, unless the Elves want you to. You must have heard about that: paths that just take you in circles, or you forget where you were heading in the first place, that sort of thing. The Elves don't really like Men, usually. Aras was an exception, Rion. They'll like me even less! Also, it might be dangerous for us too. The Elves might think he's our captive and that we're the ones who harmed him."

"But some of them must speak Common. We'll do the best we can to help them understand. Which is the nearest Kingdom?" Rion pressed.

"Erenia, we call it; I'm not sure if that's their name for it. They're Wood Elves there. I don't know whether he's a Wood Elf or a River Elf. I've heard they look the same. He could be either. There are two major rivers that this stream flows into, west of these mountains."

"How far is it to Erenia?" Rion asked.

"A few days extra journey by wagon, and we'll have to leave the Road. But if the Elves let us through their Wood, it would actually save a great deal of time and trouble. We'd be able to avoid the Kierness Marsh surrounding the Merdan River altogether and exit out only two days out from Falnor. There are poisonous water snakes and thousands of disease-bearing insects in that marsh, and the Road is often swallowed by it. That's actually the most dangerous portion of our journey, and the most time-consuming. But it's just not possible to enter the Falnor Woods without the Elves' permission."

"Perhaps having him with us will be enough," Rion said hopefully. "In any case, I'm glad he's alive and safe now, and that his injuries weren't worse. I'm sorry about your horse, Jargas, but at least you didn't have to fight the ogres after all."

"No, that young upstart's attack on Bak saved me more than a few bruises. I'll be glad to be out of these mountains so I can clean up again, although I can well imagine what our new friend's reaction will be when he sees me then! He'll like me as I usually appear even less than he likes me as a wild man, although my father has had some luck trading with the River Elves in Salenia. But as we might yet meet a second tribe or a rogue or two, I guess I'm stuck as I am for the next few days."

"He must be in pain, though he's hiding it from us. Lerdon, you should have something you can give him for it. Why haven't you?" Rion asked.

"I don't know if it's safe for him or not. From all I've heard, Elves have strong bones compared to us and heal faster, but they are as susceptible to poisons as we are. I've heard that some don't affect them, but it might also be that some medicines that are beneficial to us might be harmful to them. I don't want to risk it. I'm just glad I was able to set his arm and leg for him, with Jargas's aid. But once we get moving again, all that bouncing will certainly hurt."

Rion sighed and turned to Tarrell. "I wonder how Talon and Aras are doing. I wish they'd come with us from Athanark, that they were here to help us and so they might translate for us, so we could talk to him."

"I speak Common," the Elf said in that language.

Rion stared at him in astonishment. "Then why didn't you say so before?"

"So I could judge your intent and be sure you did not lie, for Men are often devious and treacherous," the Elf said. He smiled at Rion. "You speak Elvish poorly, Little One. I could scarcely understand you."

Rion bristled. "I don't like being called devious and treacherous or little or being insulted for trying to help you."

The Elf looked amused and Rion's face flushed.

"I told you Aras was an exception, Rion," Jargas said, scowling at the Elf. "Don't expect gratitude or even politeness from this one, for all that we saved his life. Perhaps he'd prefer to walk the rest of the way to his Kingdom, though his leg is broken, rather than surround himself with such poor company. Or we could always bring him back to Bak to eat, though it won't get me my horse back."

The Elf sighed. "I should have remained silent, for you were eager to help me before, but your favor has now turned against me. I was chosen for my fair tongue, and here I have stepped upon it!" He looked amused again, although this time his amusement seemed to be directed at himself. "He-who-is-my-brother would laugh to see me now, though he might have wept before. But as I cannot walk and I have no wish to be eaten, I needs must try again. Perhaps it is the smile? She-who-is-my-sister has warned me of it. I shall try to appear solemn then."

For a moment the smile almost left his face, but then he grinned. "No, I cannot, for solemn is aloof and aloof is worse. Besides, to ask me not to smile is like asking the sun not to shine upon the water."

He turned to Rion. "It is too vexing to talk to you. I think it is best that we both pretend I never spoke at all, that this is all but a dream. I will awaken again when we reach Erenia or the side of the Road, wherever it might be you decide to release me." With that he closed his eyes and pulled the blanket more fully over himself, as if he were going to sleep.

Rion laughed in spite of himself. "You are completely absurd! You still offer no apology, yet now I no longer feel slighted."

The Elf peeked through low-lidded eyes, and then opened them again. "Ah. My tongue is working aright again, so perhaps I am awake after all."

Lerdon spoke then. "As your tongue is working now, would you like me to give you something for the pain? Or is it you feel none? For I can't believe you can smile and speak so easily."

"I feel the pain all too well, yet pain sharpens the wit and medicine dulls it, so I will endure what I cannot change. We Elves have learned to endure much, for there is little we can change. Perhaps 'No, but thank you for your aid' would serve better, for

Man likes his words brief and unadorned. I was also chosen for my brevity of phrase, though I can see your ears have almost fallen asleep already: they have not the shape to embrace such prose. That is not meant as an insult, so please do not take it as one. 'No, thank you' might have been enough, I think. There. We Elves are slow to learn, but you have taught me something already."

Rion looked serious again. "I would also learn from you, if I could. Can I review the phrases I know with you, so you might correct my Elvish, so it is not so laughable? I did not know your smiles were both gifts and weapons, for I've seen now they can warm the heart, but also wound it."

"Well spoken, Child of Man! I am teaching you already," the Elf said, looking pleased.

"My name is Rion. You heard it. Why won't you use it?" Rion said, hurt again.

"You did not offer me your name. How can I speak what is not offered, what is only overhead? I did not say 'Little One' for I saw that it hurt you. 'Child of Man' was carefully chosen. Is it you really offer me your name, when we have only just spoken? But I cannot speak yours, for I cannot offer you my own," the Elf said, looking vexed.

"Oh. But Rion is not my given name. It is my nickname, my short name. Is there a nickname or perhaps a title I might call you by?" Rion asked.

"Truly? You are the first Men I have ever met, save for those of a single Kingdom, who understand the danger of revealing your given names. I will have to ponder what you might call me. I have gone by such a name only twice before, but neither suits me any longer. I can think of many unflattering things you might wish to call me, but my vanity should not be so bruised as my body," the Elf said with a smile.

Jargas spoke up. "Now that our thorn has been tended to, we must move on."

The Elf grinned. "Thorn! It is perfect. I am aptly named. Rion, you may call me Thorn. Now that it appears I will be traveling in your company for a time, might I trouble you for some clothes before we proceed onward? My own appear to have met with an unfortunate accident while I slept. Was my pack perchance rescued with me?" he asked, his voice hopeful.

"I'm sorry, but anything you might have had with you is lost, I'm afraid," Tarrell said. "But you and I appear to be a similar size, and I have a number of new items of clothing I've yet to wear, which should fit you passably well. My name is Tarrell."

"I would be most appreciative, Tarrell, if you would be so inclined," the Elf said politely.

Tarrell went to his pack and brought out one of the outfits that Rion had insisted he buy so that he look the part of trader instead of guard. He handed the clothes to Thorn, who accepted them and thanked him. But then he looked at his arm and leg and sighed.

"Would you like me to help you dress?" Lerdon offered.

"Feel free to cut the thread along the seam of the leg and sleeve, also. It can easily be mended afterward," Tarrell magnanimously offered.

"Your kindness and generosity are much appreciated," the Elf said, truly sounding grateful. With Lerdon's help, he dressed. "Might I sit beside the wagon driver on the bench? For this is none too comfortable a perch, even for a thorn," the Elf said with a smile.

RION grinned. "You can sit beside me. I drive the lead wagon."

The Elf looked pleased for a moment, but then frustrated once more. "Ah. But how am I to get there from here?"

Rion looked at Jargas, but then thought better of it, looking at the clean clothes and bandages. Jargas was still filthy. "Ron and Ara, could you lend a hand?" he called.

"Yes, Master Rion?" Ara said, coming up first.

"Could you and Ron carry Thorn to my seat?" Rion asked.

"Certainly. If you will permit our touch?" Ara asked politely.

"Ah, someone of refinement at last. Your touch will be permitted," Thorn said magnanimously.

Rion watched as Thorn was carried to the lead wagon. He went over to Gar and Van and asked in a low voice, "What was that all about?"

"Elves do not like to be touched by Man, or perhaps by anyone," Gar explained. "Our home is actually in the River Elf Kingdom of Salenia. Our grandfather was succored by them, long ago, and was given grace to live within their Kingdom, in the mill they built for him on the banks of the Merdan River. We've ground their grain and made flour for them ever since, and we've learned some of their customs. Thorn looks to be a River Elf: generally, River Elves have silver or white hair and blue eyes, and Wood Elves have blond hair and green eyes, although there are occasional exceptions. Regardless, River and Wood Elves differ little from each other in many regards."

"I would have you teach me all you know of them," Rion said eagerly.

"Certainly," Gar said.

Rion headed to his wagon, climbed onto the bench beside Thorn, and took up the traces. Jargas called for the caravan to move forward.

Rion expected Thorn to speak to him, but he was strangely silent and he was not smiling any longer. He saw Thorn's jaw twitch and realized Thorn had clenched his teeth against the pain, that the bumps and jolts Rion took in stride were agony to Thorn.

"Please, won't you let us give you something for the pain?" Rion entreated.

Thorn shook his head.

"Then may I talk to you to distract you from it?"

He nodded, a look of gratitude crossing his face.

Rion told him about their journey so far, everything since arriving in Athanark. It was too painful to speak of Ardock or Oberas, or Hardred and Alnas, or of the guards and drivers they'd lost. Thorn listened with interest and seemed particularly intent when he spoke of Aras and Talon.

It was a long bumpy ride until they made camp. Rion was able to assemble a dinner he thought Thorn might like from his and Tarrell's supplies, from what he knew of Aras's tastes. Thorn seemed truly grateful, but ate little, though he seemed to try. Thorn was exhausted from the ride and, to Rion's disappointment, fell asleep soon after dinner.

Rion approached Gar and Van and asked them about the River Elves. He overwhelmed them with his questions, and soon all four brothers were clustered about him, answering as much as they could. Rion wrote down all they said in his journal.

Gar laughed. "Our father would love to meet you, Rion, for few share your liking for Elves, and he is a kindred spirit to you in that, at least."

"You'll not introduce him to Father, Gar," Van protested. "Father would eat him alive!"

Ara laughed at him, "Don't say such things to him, after the ogres, Van, for he'll think you mean it literally!"

"Besides, you have yet to face Father's full wrath," Ron said. "You are fortunate that you are the youngest, Van."

Van scoffed at him. "Fortunate, am I? You think it is fortunate to have a brother such as you, and him besides?"

Rion laughed. "I think you've answered all you can and that I'd better bow out of the middle of this before I'm drawn into it."

Rion sought out Jargas. "Jargas, you said before that the ogres only speak twenty or so words. Would you mind teaching them to me? And anything you know about them, their customs, their lives."

Jargas looked at him in surprise. "Why would you want to know that?"

Rion shrugged. "I'm just fascinated by all of this: the Elves, Dwarves, ogres, all of it. Where I grew up in Ardock, there were only Men, though two of the Elven Kingdoms were near us. The master I was apprenticed to had limited interactions with the Elves and had visited the Dwarven Lands, but he never spoke of them. Next time I have to deal with strangers such as these, I might not be so fortunate as to have people like you and the Ogaten brothers around me. I might have to rely upon my own knowledge."

Jargas nodded. "I can see as how that makes sense. All right, if you truly want to know, I'll teach you what I can."

Rion made sure the ink was dry from everything he'd written about the Elves and then began a new page about the ogres, eagerly taking notes as Jargas talked. After he was done, Rion reread all he'd written about both the Elves and ogres, wishing he knew more about the Dwarves, too. He'd asked Jargas about them earlier in the trip, but he seemed much more reluctant to speak of his own people.

Rion flipped to the beginning of his journal and began to read about the journey from Ardock in sudden longing for his missing friends, the faces he'd never see again and the two who were so far away. But it was still too soon, too raw. He pictured their guards dead all around him and Oberas beside Elkrum. The thought of any of these men beside him now dying was unbearable.

He swallowed hard a number of times and stealthily wiped away his tears, hoping no one was watching. He packed his journal away and headed for his bedroll. He lay down and looked at the stars, trying to fill his mind with the quiet beauty of the night, but the faces of the missing and the dead haunted him. It was long into the night before he finally fell asleep.

THE next morning, Rion found it difficult to waken. Tarrell tried to rouse him more than once, finally enticing him out of bed with the promise of kakla before he reluctantly rose and dressed for the day. Rion was concerned that Thorn did not look well rested either and was relieved when he finally agreed to take medicine for the pain.

Thorn told Rion he needed to bathe in the stream before they left. Lerdon offered to cloth bathe him again instead, but Thorn politely and firmly refused. He insisted he needed to bathe in the stream.

Lerdon argued against it, as he'd need all his bandages changed again if he did so, and though the water was not deep nor the current strong, the rocks were slippery and he might bang his arm or leg against the rock, or slip and hit his head. Thorn was looking frustrated and agitated, and Rion was just about to intervene when the Ogaten brothers came up to them.

"We will assist Thorn in bathing and see that he is not injured. And we will take care of bandaging him, so you can focus on your other duties, Lerdon, or have some additional time to yourself," Ara volunteered. Both Ron and Ara had already shed their boots and socks and had rolled their pants up to their knees, apparently in preparation for assisting him, so their clothes wouldn't get wet. Lerdon was still reluctant, but they were determined, and in short order the brothers had convinced him.

Ron and Ara carried Thorn to the stream. Thorn undressed upon the bank, with their aid, and then they carried him into the stream and seated him in it. Rion watched curiously, as Thorn laid back and immersed himself fully in the shallow water. Rion waited for him to surface and was surprised and then concerned when he didn't as soon as Rion thought he should. He was either holding his breath for an astonishingly long period of time, or perhaps actually breathing the water. He would have feared Thorn had drowned, but the brothers were far too attentive and did not look at all alarmed.

But the thought of breathing the water made Rion's stomach lurch, and he quickly looked away, fighting down the memory of six years ago when he had been dragged into the shark tank in the Arena and breathed the water, when he had drowned. The memory would have been more horrible, only that was when he had first met Hardred. Hardred had saved him. He'd dived into the tank and pulled him out and then resuscitated him.

He worried about Hardred and Alnas anew. Were they still alive? Still safe? How would he ever know what happened to them? They could not write to him; they would not know where he was. He was supposed to have stayed in Athanark, with Oberas. At least he knew where they'd been headed: Meria, for Hardred's sister. Maybe when he got safely to Gosa, he'd send a letter to them. He'd find a caravan headed to Meria, or perhaps even pay a trustworthy messenger to take it, or maybe even go himself. He missed them both fiercely, and he'd never seen the ocean.

The thought of a body of salt water like the one he'd drowned in, but one that went on past the horizon, as far as the eye could see, was both terrifying and wondrous. How wide was the ocean? How deep? He should have asked Hardred when he had the chance, though perhaps he did not know.

He looked back at the stream. To his relief, Thorn surfaced, but only for a moment, and then he went under once more. He was not so much bathing as he was just submerging. Did that confirm that he was indeed a River Elf? Did he find the water somehow soothing, comforting? Did he need the water's embrace, the feel of something familiar, safe, while he was stranded here amongst strangers? He would ask Thorn about it later. He would not press him for an answer, but surely it could not hurt just to ask?

Thorn finished a while later and dressed, and the brothers brought him back to camp just in time to load him on the wagon for their journey. Thorn slept for much of the wagon ride that morning, and Rion was hard pressed to keep awake as well, for sleeping so poorly the night before. He yawned often, one arm around Thorn to keep him from falling over while he slept.

Lunch helped reenergize both of them, and he and Thorn spoke at length both during lunch and in the wagon that afternoon.

That evening Thorn began teaching Rion more Elvish, as he had promised, now that Rion was stationary and not in a bumping, jolting wagon and could write the words so he might be able to read them phonetically, so he would remember how to pronounce them properly. Thorn looked at his notes curiously and seemed both intrigued and amused by them.

Thorn had not revealed much about himself, but he had admitted that he was a River Elf, although he had actually been heading to Erenia, which he confirmed was a Wood Elf Kingdom. Rion was eager to hear how he had been captured but was reluctant to broach the topic because he didn't want to upset Thorn. He was surprised and pleased when Thorn volunteered the information.

Thorn told Rion he had been walking along a narrow ledge above the ogres, to avoid them, when the ledge had crumbled under his feet and he'd slid down the mountain right into their midst. "We Elves are not made for such slides as are the ogres. It was then I broke my leg and lost my bow and knife, and I could not escape them. One of them scooped me up and slung me over his shoulder rather roughly, and I must have passed out. When I came to, my arm was broken as well. Apparently he had flung me down none too gently while I slept." He laughed, and Rion wondered how he could be so cheerful about something so dreadful.

He realized he must have betrayed his thoughts by his expression, for Thorn's next words. "Believe me, I was not so jovial while I was their captive. But it is in the past, and I am relatively well now, so why dwell upon it? I think Men would be much happier if they just learned to endure, as we Elves endure, and then move forward. You waste much of your short lives bemoaning what you cannot change, consumed by your past instead of embracing the present. It is better to live for the moment, for the past is done, and who knows what the future might bring?"

Rion nodded, thoughtful. "My mother once told me something similar. I am learning much this trip that I did not realize I would be. I am sorry you came to us in the manner you did, but I am glad you travel with us. I wish your people weren't so insular and secretive. Men could learn much from you."

Thorn laughed. "Learn from us! Woe to us when we try to teach you! But I will try now, though I might regret it. Do you truly want to know how our kind sees you, and how your kind sees us?"

"Of course," Rion said eagerly.

Thorn laughed again. "You are children to us, all of you, regardless of your age, and poorly behaved ones at that. Is it a wonder, then, that we treat you as such? Men are loud and brash, rude and boorish, unrefined, undignified, ruled by passions, abrupt, argumentative, combative, arrogant, and full of self-importance." Rion opened his mouth, ready to argue the point, and Thorn laughed again. "Ah, I forgot to mention impatient, for you do not let me finish."

Rion flushed sheepishly.

Thorn continued. "As for us Elves, you think of us far differently than we see ourselves. What we see as pride, you see as vanity and arrogance. Our jealousies are ruinous. What we see as dignity, you see as stuffiness and aloofness. We are slow to learn, ponderous, trapped in ritual and tradition. We delight in intricate turns of phrase, while you wish us to speak bluntly. At best, we are tricksters and pranksters, vicious in little ways. You find our sense of humor appalling. We are so misunderstood by you!

"We were at one time often asked to take part in Men's affairs, but when we did so, we were viewed as manipulative and malicious. Then, when our kind clashed with yours, and we sought only to defend ourselves from you, you found our anger cold and purposeful. You thought us pitiless. If only you knew how much we hold war in contempt, how the very thought of such conflict is abhorrent to us, the act is agony for us. Our history would make you weep."

He shook his head. "But still, I am young and idealistic, and I sometimes wonder if your kind and mine are really so very different. I think, perhaps, that the real difference lies in such a simple thing as age. You live such short lives! Is it any wonder you are as wild as you are? How could you condense one thousand years of life into sixty and not lose so much by it? We Elves only just come-of-age at forty-nine. At forty-nine a Man is considered well past his prime and often well on his way into decay. We do not flaunt the fact, but young Elves often behave like Men, much to our embarrassment, until they mature and learn the dignity and restraint our kind are so known for." He grinned. "I am but just turned fifty myself, though she-who-is-my-sister still sees me as a child. It is why I was chosen as Ambassador, for I still think and act enough like a child that Men and even the Dwarves might understand me."

Thorn laughed. "Or perhaps just be vexed by me. Perhaps my people just tired of listening to me and thought to be rid of me for a while. There is little enough use for a second son, when so few now have even one," he said with an odd catch to his voice. Rion sensed there was truth and pain layered beneath his flippant words. "I liked that you called me absurd, for it reminds me of the many similar things she-who-is-my-sister has called me."

His face grew suddenly serious, and a pang of longing and sadness flashed across Thorn's face. It was so alien to the Elf he knew that Rion's heart was torn by it. "I had not thought to hear her sweet voice scold me again," Thorn said softly.

Rion wondered what it must be like to be an Elf, young and alone and afraid, so injured he could not even walk, in Man's world, dependent upon strangers for his very survival. Rion reassured him, "You will see her again soon. We will keep you safe."

Thorn suddenly smiled again. "I hope it is soon. For Men are often melancholy, and she would not recognize me were I to come home with anything less than a smile upon my face." He yawned then, and stretched with one arm. "I think I have instructed too much already for one night, for I can think of two things at least I should not have told you, and I could probably think of a host of others were my wits not so dulled. Sleep well, Rion."

"You also, Thorn," Rion said, and stretched and yawned himself, then curled up under his blanket.

THE following morning Jargas told them that by that night, if they traveled steadily, they should clear the mountains and enter the foothills on the other side. Everyone was eager to be through the Pass. Jargas saw that more than a few of them expressed annoyance when they saw that their Elven guest was again headed to the stream to bathe, aided by the Ogaten brothers.

Jargas resolutely headed to intercept them. "Ron, Ara, wait a moment. We don't have time for another bath. It might delay us enough that we might not clear the Pass by this evening. When one tarries, it takes that much more time to get the others moving."

"But I must bathe," Thorn said, his tone an odd mix of command and diplomacy, with a touch of anxiety mixed in.

Jargas said patiently, "I've seen your kind values cleanliness almost as much as mine, but surely one more day won't matter to you."

At the perplexed look on Thorn's face, Jargas laughed heartily, realizing how ludicrous it must have sounded for him to say such a thing, filthy as he was. "You've not yet seen me as I normally look. But as you Elves like riddles and puzzles and games so much, I'll give you a hint as to how I should appear. If you can figure it out from that single clue, then I'll let you take a quick dip." He reached into his purse, took out his three gold rings, and laid them in his palm for Thorn to see. "I should be wearing these," he said, grinning, expecting his words would only flummox Thorn further.

Thorn's eyes widened as he looked at the gold bands in Jargas's hand, and then he studied him from his toes on upward, his eyes sparkling in merriment. "Now I understand your comment when we first met, about your appearance and how I might react to it, although you leave me with even more questions than before. I think we might enjoy enlightening one another upon this trip, my labyrinthine friend," Thorn said, laughing at Jargas's consternation. Thorn had spoken to him in flawless yet oddly accented Dwarvish.

Jargas shook his head, returning the gold bands to his purse, but then he grinned in delight. "I think I did well indeed signing on with this particular caravan. We Dwarves enjoy puzzles no less than your own people. It should prove to make this little detour we are taking an enjoyable one. All right, you can take your bath, but make it a quick one," Jargas conceded.

"Thank you," Thorn said, again in Dwarvish. Then he and the brothers proceeded to the stream. Jargas glanced at it wistfully, but he could not clean himself yet, not until they were clear of the mountains. He headed back to the others to ensure they would be ready to go as soon as Thorn was done.

RION saw that Jargas intercepted Ron, Ara, and Thorn and was surprised when, after speaking with Thorn and showing him something, he allowed them to continue on their way. Rion was curious to know what they had said to one another, and what Jargas had shown him, but he had told Jargas that he was in charge of the men, and he didn't want Jargas to feel that he was spying upon him or questioning his decisions, so he kept silent. He hoped that Thorn might reveal what had convinced Jargas, later when they spoke in the wagon.

THEY headed out as soon as Thorn was done, at a quicker pace than before. After traveling for the whole morning and through the early part of the afternoon, they were just starting to look for a good spot to stop for lunch when, without warning, a boulder crashed down from the left side of the pass, crushing the hindquarters of Van's horse, Malnor. Malnor was felled, screaming in agony and kicking wildly with his forelegs, and Van was pinned under him. Van cried out in pain, but before his brothers could go to his aid, there was a shower of rock, and to Tarrell's horror an ogre slid into their midst, his left hand reaching for Rion and Thorn, and his right for Ron's horse, Raynor, which was nearest him.

Thorn pushed Rion, who was apparently frozen in fear, from the bench to the ground, but he could not get out of the ogre's reach. He was grabbed by a huge, grasping hand and lifted above the wagon. As the ogre squeezed him, Thorn cried out in agony and fell limp in its hand.

Tarrell ran toward them, awkwardly drawing and gripping his sword in his left hand. At the same time, Lerdon rode under the ogre's left arm and slashed with his sword along the underside of it, and the ogre dropped Thorn, who fell heavily onto the ground and lay still.

Tarrell saw Raynor rear from the grasping right hand in terror as Ron was firing his bow, and Ron was thrown from his horse. Ron's head cracked against the rock of the valley floor. His riderless horse galloped off through the Pass toward the hills, and Ron lay in a crumpled heap where he had fallen.

A flight of two arrows hit the ogre in the back. It bellowed in pain, but did not seem weakened by them. Jargas slammed his club into the ogre's chest, but the club broke from the impact, and Jargas was swatted aside with a great backhanded blow, as if he were an insect, while the rest of the men fought their panicked horses, unable to aid the others.

The ogre reached down for Rion, but finally Tarrell reached them. He dove in front of Rion, thrusting his sword upward at the large palm. The ogre yanked its left hand away reflexively, as if a thorn had pricked it.

Then the ogre grabbed Van's screaming horse with its right hand. As it pulled the animal off of him, Van yelled in agony, but his cry was suddenly cut short.

Tarrell stood protectively in front of Rion. He saw a second flight of arrows hit the ogre, one to no visible effect in its left arm, but the second found its left eye and it bellowed in pain and dropped Malnor, reaching for its ruined eye.

Rarnak leapt from his terrified horse, ran behind the ogre, and slashed with his sword along the back of its left leg, hamstringing it.

Lerdon leapt from his horse and stood over Thorn, sword in hand.

Jargas stood shakily and staggered for his quarterstaff, which was in Tarrell's wagon.

The ogre roared in rage, pounding its right fist onto the ground, narrowly missing Ron's prone form. A third flight of arrows hit, one harmlessly striking its right arm, but it was fully blinded when the other arrow hit its right eye.

Rarnak ran behind the ogre's right leg and hamstrung that as well. It crashed to its knees, crippled and blinded.

Jargas leapt at its head, and his quarterstaff cracked down upon it with the sound of a ripe melon bursting upon stone. The ogre collapsed, twitching, its right arm flailing out and pinning Rarnak as it fell.

Jargas pulled Rarnak out from under the fallen ogre, and Rarnak slashed the ogre's jugular with his sword, making sure it was truly dead.

Ara ran to Van, feeling for signs of life with shaking hands.

Gar ran to Ron's side, doing the same. Ron was deathly pale, and his hair was wet with blood. Gar collapsed to his knees and started to weep, cradling his older brother in his arms.

Tarrell spoke urgently to Rion, trying to waken him, and then called frantically for Lerdon, looking around desperately for him. Lerdon had been checking on Thorn, but ran to them.

The rest of their guards finally got their horses under control and secured Lerdon's and Rarnak's mounts, but Ron's horse was lost from their sight.

"We camp here to tend the wounded," Jargas said, swaying slightly and steadying himself upon Rarnak's strong shoulder. "I want six guards keeping their eyes on the mountainsides around us. This looks to be a rogue, but the sounds of battle might draw another." Jargas shook his head as if to clear it, then took his staff and put Malnor, who was crippled and struggling weakly in agony, out of his misery with a single quick blow to the head.

Lerdon was able to rouse Rion. "Rion's not badly hurt. He's lucky. He just had the wind knocked out of him when he was thrown from the wagon," Lerdon assured Tarrell, patting him reassuringly on the shoulder. "Thorn is in a bad way, though. I think I'll have to reset his arm and leg, but I'm afraid he's been hurt worse, where I can't see to help him. I have to see to the brothers next. Two of them look pretty bad."

Tarrell nodded and began comforting Rion, who was looking appalled and devastated by the fallen men around them.

LERDON knelt by Ron first. Gar moved back as Lerdon examined Ron and began cleaning the wound on the back of his head. "He's still alive, Gar. Scalp wounds tend to bleed profusely and he hit his head pretty hard, but it doesn't feel like the bone is broken. It's hard to feel that on the skull sometimes, though. If we're lucky, he'll awaken soon." He did not say, as he bandaged him, that Ron might never waken. "Bring his blanket. Be sure to keep him covered. He needs to stay warm." Gar nodded, eyes wide in his grief-stricken face.

Lerdon went to Ara and Van and examined Van. "Your brother was very lucky, Ara. He could easily have been crushed, but it looks like his horse mostly pinned him. It will be a while before he'll be able to put any weight on his right leg, but the bone doesn't appear to be broken, from what I can tell. It looks like he might have just passed out from the pain. He should come to soon. If we're lucky, that's the extent of his injuries. I'll know more once he wakens and I can speak to him."

"May Elmoth will it. How is Ron?" Ara asked, his voice laced with concern.

"He hit his head pretty hard. It's hard to say, but I hope he'll wake up soon."

Lerdon went back over to Thorn and called Jargas over to help him. He reset the bones and made sure Thorn was warm. Then he described everyone's injuries to Jargas.

JARGAS saw that Rion, who came over with Tarrell, was looking at Thorn with wide eyes. "He got hurt saving me when he could have saved himself. I just kept remembering last time, and I couldn't move or think, and then I felt him push me, and I saw it grab him and it squeezed him…." Rion was trembling.

"Rion, it's not your fault. Terrible things just happen sometimes," Tarrell soothed.

"Elves are stronger than they look. He'll be all right, you'll see," Jargas said, with a confidence he didn't feel. He was afraid Thorn wouldn't survive the additional injuries he'd sustained. He was all too aware of the crushing power of the ogre's tremendous hands.

Rarnak came over to them, limping slightly. "That was a very brave thing you did. I won't forget it," Jargas said.

"Maybe now I can sleep peacefully again. Maybe they won't haunt my dreams."

"How's your leg? Is there anything I can do?" Lerdon asked.

"No, I'll be fine. I'm in a lot better shape than I was on the last journey when I faced one of those rogue monsters. We were lucky to have had a gifted and well-trained healer with us, or I'd not have survived."

VAN moaned and Ara spoke to him urgently. "Van, can you hear me? It's me, Ara."

Van opened his eyes, and Ara hugged him in relief, but cautiously, lest he be injured worse than he appeared. "Are you all right? Other than your leg, does it hurt anywhere?"

Van shook his head. "No, just my leg. It doesn't feel too bad. I don't think it's broken, but I don't know that I'll be able to walk."

"Don't worry. We're not going anywhere. We're making camp here, for now, while the wounded are tended."

"Are Gar and Ron all right?" Van asked. When Ara gave him a pained look, Van grasped his arm. "Tell me what's happened to them!"

"It's all right, Van, calm down. Gar's fine. He wasn't injured. He's with Ron. Ron hit his head when Raynor threw him. Lerdon is hoping he'll wake up soon. I'll help you go to him."

Van nodded and limped to his oldest brother with Ara. Ara hugged him as he started to tremble when he saw Gar's tearstained face and the bloody bandage about Ron's head. They both sat down beside Ron and Gar.

Van gently brushed the hair from Ron's forehead, over the bandage. His hand was shaking. "He'll be all right, won't he? He has to be. I didn't mean what I said, about not wanting him for a brother." He started to cry, and Gar and Ara hugged him, murmuring reassurances to him.

TARRELL headed over to Jargas. "I don't think we should stay here, now that all the wounded have been treated. I think we'd better repack the wagons so Thorn and Ron can ride in one of them. I'm hoping Van can still ride, maybe ride double with one of his brothers. I'd like to make it into the hills. From what you've told me, the ogres seldom leave the mountains, and I don't want to risk facing any more of them. I'm afraid we'll fare far worse, if we try."

Jargas nodded. "Aye, I've been thinking the same." He called some men over, and they began unloading and repacking half of everything from one wagon into the other while the rest of the men stood watch. Fortunately they'd sold most of their goods in Athanark and had packed the two wagons low, to make river crossing and marsh travel easier. Tarrell was certain they'd be able to make room for the wounded without leaving any of the goods behind.

To his relief, Rion joined him to help rearrange the goods, and the guards did much of the manual labor. They'd repack it again for the river or marsh when they had a need to. Hopefully, by then the wounded would both be conscious and able to sit.

RON moaned, and his brothers clustered even more tightly around him. He came to with a start and tried to sit up, then winced and fell back.

"Take it easy, Ron," Ara urged.

"What happened? Is it dead?" Ron asked.

"Raynor threw you when the ogre grabbed for him. Yes, the ogre's dead. We all helped kill it," Aras said.

"Is Raynor all right?" Ron asked.

The brothers looked at him, suddenly sheepish, and Gar said, "We don't know. He ran off."

"Ran off! He cost thirty gold and weeks for you to train him, and you just let him run off and haven't gone after him? Some stable master you'll make, Gar!" Ron scolded.

Gar grinned in relief. "Well, he's abusing me again, so he must be all right. Don't worry, Ron, you stay put. Ara and I will go after Raynor, now that we know you're recovering."

Ara came to Gar's defense. "Gar shot the ogre in the eye with an arrow. What a shot! You should've seen it, Ron! And then he got it in the other one. He blinded it. We'd not have fared nearly so well if it wasn't for him. And he cried over you."

Gar glowered at Ara, but Ron said with surprising gentleness, "Forgive me, Gar. I didn't mean to scold you, nor to frighten you before. You should have known with my hard head I'd be all right."

"Just try to be more careful next time," Gar chastised. "What would Father say if we came home without you? Ara has no desire to be the eldest, trust me."

Ron's face creased as if he were suddenly in more pain. Van soothed him as Ara and Gar stood and then mounted their horses. They rode over to Jargas. "We're going to get Ron's horse, if that's all right?"

Jargas nodded. "Just be careful of obearn. We were fortunate not to run into any before, on the other side of the mountains. They like the taste of horseflesh. They're in the hills on this side of the mountain, too, though there aren't as many of them. The hunting and scavenging is not as good on this side because of the marsh."

Ara and Gar set off down the stream, toward the foothills.

"We'll wait here until they return," Jargas told the men. "Everyone should eat some lunch, but we'll do it in shifts. I want those on duty to be paying attention."

THE first shift of men ate, while their friends watched the terrain warily.

After he was done eating, Ron stood, testing himself, and was able to walk. He was concerned to see Van couldn't.

"It's all right, Ron. It's not serious. Lerdon told me I'll be fine. It's not broken or anything. I just can't put my weight on it for a while," Van reassured him. "I'm thankful to Elmoth you and I both escaped with so minor injury, considering what happened to poor Malnor. I'm grateful we were all spared, that no one was killed. We were wise to make such a generous offering to Elmoth in Logareth."

Ron made a small snort of derision under his breath and Van frowned.

"I know you don't believe as we do, Ron, but you must at least show the proper respect," Van said in Thenalonese, obviously not wanting the rest of the men to overhear and understand them.

"I'm not saying Elmoth isn't real. He and the other Gods very well might be. It would explain much," Ron conceded bitterly in the same tongue. "But even if they exist and are the all-powerful beings you and Ara and Gar believe them to be, that doesn't mean they are worthy of my respect. Respect is something that needs to be earned, and in my eyes, He and the others have failed miserably in that regard.

"Do you honestly expect me to respect a God who'd be so greedy and petty to actually care whether we spent the thirty gold to buy Him a sword, or only fifteen to buy Him a dagger? You're a fool if you do, Van, and Ara's a bigger one. We all survived because Gar has a better eye and arm than the rest of us, and his arrows flew true, and because, from what you told me, Rarnak and the others were brave enough to fight that monster with nothing more than their swords and wit, with their muscle and sinew and bone. Elmoth is supposed to be the protector of the innocent. Where was He when Rion sat too terrified to move and nearly died for it? Thorn is the one who saved Rion's life, not Elmoth. And in thanks for his selfless act of bravery, Thorn all but had the life squeezed from him. The Elves are strong, but they're not immortal. You and I both know he's not going to live to see Erenia."

"Ron! You mustn't say such things! You can't blame Elmoth for—" Van began, but Ron interrupted him.

"I can blame Him for plenty. Where was He when all those cities were burning? How many thousands of women and children died, Van? How many others were raped and killed by bandits as they fled, or died of their injuries on the road, or are even now starving to death? It's no different than what happened to Thenalon a hundred years ago! Where were Elmoth and the other Gods when she burned? And don't try to tell me those people weren't devout enough to be saved. Elmoth shouldn't care whether someone even worships Him. An innocent should be saved regardless."

The look of pain and sympathy Van gave him shamed and angered him further, but his youngest brother's soft-spoken words gutted him. "I know what's truly in your heart, Ron. You still blame Him for Mother. For our baby sister."

Ron kept silent. Van was too young to remember all he blamed Elmoth for. Three had nearly died that day. He forced the debilitating memories down and glared down the Pass and then at Van. "Where are those lazy, worthless brothers of yours? How long does it take two men to find a horse?"

As if his words had summoned them, Ron heard the sound of horses and he looked up the valley once more, expecting to see Gar and Ara returning with his horse, but there were only two horses headed for them. Ron recognized both horses, but to his horror he only saw Ara at first.

Ron ran to meet them. As they drew closer, he saw that Gar was slumped over the neck of his mount and his hands were tied about his horse's neck. Before he could reach them, Ara swayed and fell from his saddle onto his back on the ground. His horse, Aragar, stopped and touched him with his nose, huffing in concern. Then Ron was beside Ara and the other men ran to them as well.

Ron paled as he saw that Ara's shirt was drenched in blood. Ron picked Ara up and carried him to where Van sat. Lerdon ran over to him. He stripped off Ara's shirt. His chest was uninjured. Ron realized the blood must be Gar's, but then, when Lerdon turned him over, they saw that his back had been raked by claws from shoulder to waist. Lerdon started cleaning the grave wounds.

Jargas cursed. "Obearn! I warned them to be careful! I should have sent more men out with them."

Rion offered, "After you clean the wounds, I can bind them. I know how. You take care of Gar."

Lerdon nodded.

Ron turned to Gar, who some of the other men had carried over. His eyes widened in horror. Gar's head was swathed in blood-soaked makeshift bandages: his entire face, save for the bottom of his nose, was covered. His shirt was gone. Apparently it had been cut into strips to make the bandages. His torso was also bandaged. Ron felt gently for his heartbeat, hand shaking. He was still alive.

Lerdon turned from Ara and gently removed the bandages from Gar's face. Ron paled, horrified, as he looked at the ruin of Gar's face, and he heard the sound of at least three of the men retching behind him. Ron could scarcely even recognize the brother he loved. The obearn had slashed diagonally down from temple to waist. The claws had missed both eyes, but little else. Gar's cheeks were slashed open. He could see the white of his teeth and bone through the welling blood. Ron heard the faint whistle of his breath through his torn cheeks. His nose and chin were gouged, and his chest and stomach were raked, as Ara's back had been.

"He's still alive," Lerdon said grimly, and began cleaning the stomach-churning wounds.

"Will they live?" Ron asked in a ragged whisper, his face pale and drawn.

Lerdon swallowed. "With wounds such as this, it's hard to tell. They have bled much and such wounds often fester, despite medicines. But your brothers are young and were strong before, so they might yet survive their injuries."

Ron turned back to Ara. Van was beside Ara, talking softly to him, even though Ara was unconscious and couldn't hear him. Ron could see now that Van was one of the ones who had retched at the sight of Gar's face.

AFTER Rion finished bandaging Ara, he went over to Tarrell. Tarrell was proud of Rion, who'd freed Lerdon's hand to aid Gar, but he was angry at himself. He'd thought himself so disfigured, because of his arm. Gar had been fair of face, all the brothers were, but he'd been the most handsome. Now, even if he lived, no man or woman would ever look upon him again without revulsion or pity. He would live always in shadow, surrounded by his fair brothers.

Rion put his arm around Tarrell. "It's not your fault, Tarrell. Terrible things just happen, sometimes."

Tarrell hugged him tightly. "I'm glad you are with me." Rion returned the hug, but then started to tremble, and Tarrell pulled back and looked at him in concern. "No, please. I didn't mean to make you cry."

"I won't," Rion said bravely, and Tarrell saw he fought his tears back down. "I'll lay their bedrolls on the wagon."

RION saw there was an extra bedroll and pack tied to Ara's saddle and realized it must be Ron's. He wondered why, if they'd found Ron's horse, they hadn't brought him back with them. Perhaps the horse had broken his leg or his neck in his wild run.

"We should move out now," Jargas said. "I'll still be walking, but at a quicker pace than before. I won't slow us down. There's only one day of foothills on this side of the mountain, and from there on the land is flatter and safer. We'll be on the Road and then head south, to the Falnor Woods, to Erenia, if we can make it. Elves are known for their healing; perhaps they'll be willing to help Ara and Gar, since we've helped Thorn."

Rion went to Van and asked if he thought he'd be able to ride, and he said he could. Ron carried Ara to the wagon, and Jargas carried Gar. They laid them next to Thorn. Then Ron helped Van mount Gar's horse, Thenagar, and Ron mounted Ara's horse, Aragar. The caravan headed out, down the last of the pass, to the foothills.

They'd not been in the foothills very long when they came upon the site of a battle. Ron's horse, Raynor, lay dead and half eaten, and there was an obearn corpse as well. It was a small one, not fully grown. It would have stood perhaps seven feet tall when reared on its hind legs. There were no arrows in it; it appeared to have been slain by a blade. There were a jumble of hoofprints and footprints all around it.

At the sight of it, Ron leapt from his horse with a spine-tingling, roaring scream and drew his sword. He started hacking and plunging his blade into the dead beast, releasing his hatred upon it. Then he fell to his knees and started sobbing.

Van rode over to him, forcing Gar's skittish horse close to the two corpses, and slid awkwardly from the saddle, balancing on one leg. He sat beside Ron and held him as if he were Ron's father, not his younger brother, as Ron wept in his arms. "Please, Ron. I cannot bear to see you cry for them. Do not mourn them, when they yet live. You did not cry for Mother, as we did, even when we were children. I did not think you could cry. I cannot face this alone and injured. It is too awful. I need you to stay strong for me."

Ron hugged him tightly and drew deep shuddering breaths. "Not for the coin, not for the horse. What's it all for, without them? I can't have killed them, not for that."

Van began speaking softly to Ron in that odd-sounding language they used with one another, which Van had told him earlier was Thenalonese. Rion was grateful to see the other men pulled further away, as he did, even though they could not understand them, so they could have their privacy.

After a while, however, Jargas strode over to them. "Ron, Van, forgive me the interruption, but we cannot stay here. It's too dangerous. The smell of the fresh meat and the blood might attract more obearn. We need to get moving."

Ron nodded sepulchrally and stood and helped Van mount again, then mounted Aragar, and the caravan headed out. They pushed their pace and managed to clear the foothills by nightfall.

RION spoke to Jargas, who told him that they were only two days from the edge of the Falnor Woods, nearer than Rion had hoped to the Elves, who might help them. They made camp, and Jargas posted a double watch, for they were still near enough to the foothills that there might be a stray obearn drawn to them by the smell of the horses.

Rion checked on the injured. Ara and Gar were still unconscious, but Thorn was moaning and stirring. "Thorn, can you hear me?" Rion asked, hopefully.

Thorn moaned more, but did not wake. Rion tried to give him some water, but he coughed and choked on it and still slept. Rion saw Jargas speaking to Thorn just before dinner and was hopeful, until he realized Thorn didn't appear to be conscious.

The mood was somber at dinner, and the men ate with little appetite. All but those on watch went to bed, but few found sleep easily.

The next morning Rion checked on the wounded again, with Lerdon. Rion was concerned that they drink water, at least; he knew they must have water soon if they were to live. Ara lay on his chest, and Ron, who hadn't left his brothers' sides all night, turned Ara over. To their relief, Ara stiffened and his eyes opened. He hissed in pain but then focused on Ron's concerned face. "I made it back?" Ara whispered, and Ron nodded, unable to speak.

"Gar!" Ara said, trying to sit up, but he gasped and fell back into Ron's arms.

"He lives," Ron said, his voice sounding broken. "He lies beside you."

"Forgive me," Ara whispered, "I could not bring you Raynor. We went after him too late."

Ron looked angry and Ara paled. Ron hugged him. "I am not angry with you, Ara. How could I be? I am angry at myself for sending you into danger."

Ara looked relieved. "You have Father's temper and his tongue." His whisper sounded weaker. Rion could see Ara's words had hurt Ron, but Ara didn't seem to notice.

"You should not try to speak yet; you must rest and get strong again," Ron said, his voice gruff. "But first, you must drink."

Rion held the skin for him, and together he and Ron saw that Ara drank without choking. The simple effort exhausted Ara. He closed his eyes and Ron laid him back down.

Ron was very gentle with Gar when he tried to rouse him. Gar seemed semiconscious, and Ron and Rion tried to help him drink as well, but Gar only coughed. He could not drink, and they stopped trying, fearing they might drown him.

Rion looked away, toward Thorn, and saw to his relief that Thorn was awake and watching him. "You must drink also," he said, and Thorn nodded and tried, but drank little.

"You must drink more," Rion said, concerned.

Thorn was very pale and looked far worse than when they had first rescued him. Thorn shook his head. "I cannot," Thorn said weakly, squinting up at him as if it was hard for him to see. "Are we near Erenia?"

Rion swallowed. "We just cleared the foothills. We are two days away from the edge of the Wood. I don't know how deep into them we must go to find help."

Thorn looked at Gar and Ara. "The ogre?"

"No, an obearn. You were injured the worst by the ogre, though we at first feared we'd lost Ron, and Van, Rarnak, Jargas, and I were all injured. You saved my life, and have nearly died for it," Rion said, and his eyes filled with tears.

"You are worth saving." Thorn closed his eyes, and Rion feared he was unconscious again, but then he opened them. "I fear I might not be able to speak by the time we reach Erenia. Something is wrong inside me, I can feel it. I must teach you what you need to say in order to gain entry to the Wood. And you must also bear a message for me. It is vitally important, it is crucial. It is why I have come. But you cannot know what I say. I must tell you in Elvish and you must write it all down, the way you did before, in sounds you can read. Then I will help you practice speaking the two for as long as I am able."

Rion was concerned and frightened. "Your kin will be able to help you. Elves are skilled healers," he said, desperate for reassurance.

Thorn nodded. "But you must help me get there. Get pen and paper." His voice was already weaker.

Rion ran to his pack and got out his journal, pen, ink, and drying sand and hurried back.

Thorn said, "This is what you must say, as soon as you enter the grace of the trees. Call it out every few moments, as loudly as you can, to be sure that you are heard." He spoke a few sentences in Elvish, a word at a time, slowly and clearly, having Rion repeat each word to be sure he heard it properly. "Excellent. You are doing well, Rion. When an Elf appears, you must do whatever he or she commands, including eating or drinking whatever is offered to you. Then, when you are in the

City and they speak to you, you must relay this for me." Then he spoke for a much longer time.

Rion listened intently, repeated each word, and wrote all he heard. He recognized Aras's and Talon's names in surprise and wondered why they were in the message. No wonder Thorn had seemed so interested when he had spoken of them before! He wanted to ask about that part, but knew he couldn't. Thorn had already told him he couldn't know what the message said. Instead, he asked, despairing, "How can I learn to say all of that?"

"You may read it to them. You need not memorize it, but you must speak it all correctly for them to understand you. Elvish is a very tonal language, as I instructed you earlier. To misspeak a word can change its meaning entirely."

"But some of them must know Common as you do," Rion reasoned. "Can't I tell them that way?"

Thorn shook his head. "No, it must be in Elvish for them to know it is truly from me, and also, I say things a Man must not know. It is the only way."

"Then I will do it. I would do anything you ask of me. It is my fault you are hurt worse now than before," Rion said, swallowing hard and fighting against fresh tears.

Thorn shook his head. "I could not have escaped the ogre's hand, but at least I saw you safe, my friend." His voice was barely a whisper. "I must rest now. Practice what you must say. I will try to listen again, once I awaken." His eyes closed, and his breath came fast and shallow.

Tarrell came over. "Rion, we're ready to move out, but you haven't eaten yet."

"I'll eat later. I have to learn this now, while I can still hear his voice saying it."

"What is that?" Tarrell asked, with a puzzled look at the careful notes.

"It is our way to the Elves, and a message for them. It's all in Elvish. I just wrote it in the letters I know," Rion explained, realizing it must look like complete gibberish to Tarrell.

A short while later, they were underway once more. Rion studied his notes whenever he could, almost running his wagon off the Road a few times until Jargas took the lead from him and guided his team of horses. Other than that, the morning passed uneventfully.

They stopped briefly for lunch. Rion, Tarrell, and Jargas were all speaking quietly when Ron came over looking so upset that Rion was afraid that something unbearable had happened, that either Ara or Gar might have succumbed to his injuries.

"Forgive me for interrupting, but I need your assistance, Jargas. We need to bring Thorn to the stream. I'm strong enough to carry him unaided, but I'll need help lowering him into the water safely and making sure his head stays above water and his arm and leg aren't banged."

"Nay, I'll not move him when he's so injured. I'm surprised you even thought to. It can't matter to him right now whether he's clean or not," Jargas said adamantly.

"You don't understand. Cleanliness has nothing to do with it. He'll die without the stream. River Elves need water to live. They don't just need to drink it, they need to immerse in it as well. They weaken without the water, and they suffer physically as well: their skin dries and cracks and blisters, and their vision is affected. It's all the more important he immerse now because he's injured. Water doesn't just help them stay healthy, it helps them heal as well. We're not near a River Kingdom, or even a big river. I don't know if the water from the stream is actually potent enough to help heal him, but it certainly can help stop him from suffering for lack of water. I should have spoken to you sooner about it, but I was so worried about Ara and Gar I didn't even think about it until Van insisted I take a drink from his water skin. He was worried I was making myself ill worrying over the two of them, and that's when I realized."

"Why didn't Thorn tell us that? Why didn't you say something before the attack? Why didn't you tell us that's why he was so insistent about bathing?" Rion demanded, uncharacteristically angry. "He could have died and it would have been our fault!"

JARGAS noted that though the brothers had teased and complained about Ron's temper, he did not lose it now, even when he was upset over his brothers and Rion was provoking him. "I'm sure he thought he'd awaken again in time. Elves have few weaknesses, but they are understandably secretive about those they do possess. I was respecting his custom, his need for privacy."

"Ron's had concerns of his own," Jargas said, defending Ron, though he put his hand comfortingly on Rion's shoulder, nearly engulfing his entire upper arm with his palm. "You don't have siblings, Rion. You don't know what it's like, seeing one so gravely injured, and Ron's been watching over two of his three brothers."

RION'S eyes brightened with tears, and he looked from Ron to Jargas and then to Tarrell. "Forgive me. I'm not fortunate enough to have a brother, that's true, but Tarrell's as a brother to me, and other men have been as well, so I know...." He swallowed convulsively, fighting to keep from sobbing as memories of Tarrell's injury and the death of their guards and Oberas began to overwhelm him.

"There's nothing to forgive," Tarrell said gently, hugging him and pounding him twice on the back and then letting him go, so it was a man-to-man hug, rather than man-to-child, but it comforted Rion all the same. "You've scarcely gotten any sleep at all, Rion. Why don't you lie down for a while, while Jargas and Ron bathe Thorn?" Tarrell suggested.

Rion wiped determinedly at the tears leaking down his cheeks, trying to smile reassuringly. "No. No, I'm fine, really. I just need some kakla. I need to practice the message," Rion insisted, heading for his journal. He was nearly sixteen, nearly a man. He didn't have the luxury of acting like a child, not when his friends needed him.

He read the message intently, over and over again, out loud. No, that wasn't it at all! He could hear it sounded wrong, but he wasn't sure why. Perhaps it was because he was so worried, so upset. Everyone always spoke about how infuriatingly calm Elves were, even in the midst of disaster. Everything seemed to be a joke or a game to them. They didn't take anything seriously. Nothing bothered them. They moved through life and the world aloof and unperturbed. Aras hadn't been like that, or Thorn; they'd been wonderful. But they were both young.

He needed to speak slower, his voice more calm, to enunciate the words clearly but not sound so forced. Thorn had stressed to him that Elvish was a tonal language. He listened to the memories in his mind of their voices, the way Elvish had sounded when Aras and Thorn and even Talon spoke it, lilting and singsong, musical.

The thought made him think of his mother. She'd been the most gifted minstrel in all of Ardock. He'd listened to her sing for endless hours. Sometimes he and his father had sung with her. An Elf had even once sung to her: when she was dying, he'd fulfilled her fondest wish, so she might die in peace, fulfilled.

He read it again, hearing his mother singing it instead. That was it! He needed to think of the message more as a song than a letter. Calm, dignified, musical. He read it again, aloud, from start to finish, not trying to do it from memory, concentrating instead on tone and pitch and cadence. Better, much better! He curbed his excitement, channeled it. Aloof, calm, regal. He read it again. Better still. Then a third time, a fourth.

THORN still did not waken. Neither the water nor the changing of his bandages roused him. But Ara woke and drank and even ate a little. Ara told Ron what had happened in the hills. He and Gar had been following the tracks of Ron's horse and rounded a hill. Their horses had given them no warning; they must have been upwind. They found Raynor, but the obearn had found him first and was eating him. The creature reared and attacked them. Their horses went mad with fear. Gar was raked by the obearn's claws and fell from his horse, and Ara's horse threw him. Ara drew his sword and attacked the obearn, driving it away from Gar and injuring it while keeping clear of its claws. He was able to keep it at bay, wounding it further, until it grew so infuriated by its wounds that it leapt into his blade so it might reach him. It clawed his back even as it died.

Ara had seen that Gar was grievously injured but still alive. He tore his shirt into bandages and bound his wounds but could not reach his own to tend to them. He called their horses, and Gar's horse, Thenagar, came to him. He was able to mount him and set out to look for his own mount. Aragar had not run off very far. He rode back to Gar and put him onto Thenagar, tied Gar's arms about his horse's neck, and led them toward camp. Ara looked faint again, by the time he was done speaking.

"I'm very proud of you, Ara," Ron said. "Now please, you must rest. Do not worry. Van and I will take care of Gar."

Ara nodded and closed his eyes and instantly fell asleep again.

They rode on, reluctantly leaving their stream. But by nightfall, they had found a brook, and they made camp by it. Jargas washed himself in it enthusiastically and changed back into his livery. He took brushes and combs, a mirror, and a bottle of oil from his pack and began laboriously grooming himself, spending an amazingly long time putting his beard and hair back to rights again, combining dozens of braids into the intricate weave he'd sported when they'd first seen him in Athanark.

Rion tried to rouse Thorn, but he still could not wake him.

RION was relieved when Ara awoke and was able to eat and drink what he brought to him. Ara was looking a little stronger and even sat up for a while, stroking Gar's hair and talking to him.

Then Gar moaned, and his eyes opened. His eyes moved about, but when he turned his head slightly he moaned louder in pain.

"Gar, can you hear me? It's me, Ara," his brother said eagerly.

Gar's lips moved, but he did not speak. His hand moved weakly to his face, and he felt the bandages. His eyes looked frightened.

"Gar, you must try to drink some water. You've been injured, but you'll be fine," Ara lied, carefully pushed the water skin into his mouth and squirting water into it. Gar gagged and gasped, thrashing, pulling weakly at Ara's arm, as Rion watched, powerless to aid him. Ara pulled back, shaking, and Gar swallowed once, then again.

"Hurts," Gar mouthed, soundlessly.

"I know it hurts. I'm sorry, Gar. Can you drink more?"

Gar shook his head slightly and moaned again.

"All right, but you must try again later. Don't worry about anything. We'll take care of you. You must rest more, if you can. Perhaps you can have some broth later. You must have something for strength until you can eat again."

Gar's eyes closed and he slept.

Ara sank back weakly.

"You must rest too, Ara," Rion insisted, and Ara nodded and closed his eyes.

Rion felt helpless. He sat by the fire and practiced the two messages until he couldn't keep his eyes open.

THE caravan moved at first light. Those who could eat had eaten before dawn, by firelight. Ara, Gar, and Thorn still slept.

They pushed forward, stopping only for lunch. Ara was looking slightly better, but Gar and Thorn were both deathly pale. Ara ate again, with more appetite. Gar awoke long enough to choke down another mouthful of water Ron gave him, but he could not swallow more. Ron held his hand and talked to him until he fell asleep again. Rion tried once more to rouse Thorn, but he would not waken. Rion was starting to fear that he might never waken again.

They traveled onward. Finally, just as dusk approached, they reached the edge of the Elven Woods. There was a faint, narrow trail heading deep into the trees, like a path deer might have made. As there was no other entryway apparent, they pushed onward along it, wincing as the brush to either side crackled and snapped, flattened beneath the horses' hooves and wagon wheels. Still, they were relieved that, for now at least, there was room enough between the trees for the wagons, though it was slow going. The horses were skittish, and their unease fed the men's own fears. Each of them knew that the Elves might well seek vengeance for every leaf they crushed.

Rion tried not to let the hammering of his heart affect his voice as he began calling out his message. No, too fast. He must sound calm, aloof, cool, musical, dignified, singsong, lilting.

Rion kept repeating his first message, his voice loud and clear but somehow not nearly as intrusive sounding as it should have been in the eerily quiet woods. It was getting darker under the trees as the last of the sun's light faded, and the branches above shadowed the ground, but this part he knew by heart, word for word, every syllable and nuance.

Suddenly, silently, from behind the trees, twelve bowmen appeared. They were Elves, but unlike any Elves Rion had ever heard of. They wore the same odd, hooded, tree-bark-patterned cloaks Aras had worn, but underneath they wore silver armor: helmets, chest plates, and arm and leg guards that gleamed in the fading light of the sun. Their faces looked as hard as their armor. Four of their bows were pointed at Jargas, and the other eight at everyone else, moving from target to target as if choreographed.

"Don't anyone draw weapon against them," Rion reminded the men, and then he repeated the first message in Elvish so they would know he was the one who had been speaking it.

One of the Elves scanned his face in surprise, but then there was a sharp outcry from one of the other bowmen, and the man's gaze was drawn to the wagon, to Thorn. He must have been their leader, for he gestured, and one of the bowmen un-nocked his arrow and slung his bow so fast that Rion saw only a blur. Then he bent and lifted Thorn. After another silent command, the bowmen started pulling back. They had not spoken a word.

Rion realized in panic they were leaving. "Wait, stop, *alethia hapo un*, I have another message!" he called out frantically. They could not leave! They must help Gar and Ara, and he must tell them Thorn's message!

One by one they slipped between the trees and vanished from sight as Rion ran after them, calling out Thorn's second message.

Tarrell yelled, "Rion, no! Come back!"

Six arrows hit the ground around Rion's feet, encircling him. He stopped but continued to call out the second message.

To his relief, their leader reappeared, but now his face was hard and cruel. In the blink of Rion's eye, he nocked and drew back an arrow and held it aimed directly at Rion's heart. Rion instantly stopped speaking, staring at him wide-eyed with fear.

The Elf said something harsh sounding in Elvish to him.

"Don't hurt me, please! I'm sorry, I can't understand you. I'm only trying to help Thorn," Rion begged.

"Finish your message," the Elf demanded in Common, in a voice of ice and iron.

Rion swallowed and said bravely. "No, I can't. Please, first you must help us. One of our men is dying. You can save him."

The Elf snapped what sounded like an order in Elvish, and two of the others appeared, dragging Tarrell forward. They pushed him to his knees, and one of them held a gleaming sword at his throat. Rion was as terrified as Tarrell looked.

"Finish your message or he dies," the Elf commanded coldly.

"Don't hurt him! Please! I'll finish it! I... I can't remember it all. Wait, I have to read it!" He lifted his notes, but his hand was shaking so badly and the light was so dim he couldn't read them at all.

The Elf snatched the paper from him, peered at it, and then glared at him in disgust. He said something in Elvish.

The others from their party appeared, surrounded by Elves. Ron was carrying Gar, Ara was leaning heavily against Rarnak, and Lerdon was helping Van walk. Jargas's arms were tied behind his back, and his forehead was bleeding.

"Do whatever the Elves say. Don't resist them," Rion ordered, his voice shaking.

"I did not resist them before," Jargas muttered.

Four of the Elves began blindfolding them, and then a cloth dropped over Rion's eyes and was pulled tight. He was pushed roughly forward. He began feeling his way through the woods, stumbling over what must have been tree roots, scraping against rough bark, occasionally bashing a shoulder or an elbow into a tree trunk or other obstruction. He tripped and fell to his knees a number of times and was jerked roughly back to his feet each time. The journey felt endless to Rion.

Then Rion heard voices, the lilting singsong of Elvish the way Aras and Talon and Thorn had spoken it, soft and gentle. Abruptly Rion felt smooth hardness under his feet, instead of rotting leaves and forest loam and tripping roots. He suspected they might be bringing them into a dungeon, despite the voices, but when there were steps, they led up, not down, and oddly there was the sound of rushing water. Then his blindfold was removed.

He was relieved to see everyone else was still with him. They were in an impossible room, all of white alabaster, a room without corners, soft curves everywhere angles should have been. A crystal waterfall ran from the ceiling down one wall, cascading into a stream that ran along another wall, running over smooth river rock and then disappearing into the floor. There were brightly colored cushions of what looked like silk everywhere. There was a table laden with food and drink. Pale white light gleamed about them, as if the very stone were emitting it.

An Elf was there as well, but a woman, not a man. Rion thought she might be the sister Thorn had spoken of, for she looked so much like him. She took Rion's breath away, both by her beauty and by the look upon her face. She was dressed all in blue, a gossamer fabric that clung to every curve. Her hair was long and silver and fell loosely all the way to her sandaled feet. Her long tresses were interwoven here and there with blue flowers. Her eyes were of liquid sapphire, a blue more intense than eyes should ever be. She was a vision of loveliness, but her face was creased in pain, and seeing her perfect face distorted by pain made Rion want to weep for her.

She glided over to Rion. "Please, you have a message from my brother. I would hear it, for I cannot read it," she said in Common, and she held out the notes the other Elf had taken from him, her eyes searching his own.

Rion looked at his men, then back at her. "I will read it to you, I will do anything you ask, but please, can you help us? One of our men is dying and another is gravely injured. We had hoped you might be able to help them, perhaps even heal them."

"Of course we will aid you. I see some of you are injured and that much of the message I have heard from the King's Guard." She called out in a voice that tinkled like the ringing of silver bells. Another beautiful Elven maiden appeared. Thorn's sister spoke in a musical voice to her and she responded. Then his sister spoke to them again in Common. "Those in need follow her with your injured. She will take you to our healer. It is not far and he speaks this tongue as well and will help you."

Rarnak, Lerdon, and Ron left with Ara, Van, and Gar.

She turned to the others and said, "You are all tired and hungry and frightened. Please, you are safe here. Sit and eat and drink. You will not be harmed. This place has become as a second home to me, and even now the King's Guard follows my commands."

Tarrell and Jargas gestured the others to the table, but the two of them stood with Rion.

"Now, please, the message," she implored again.

Rion could not have resisted her had he wanted to. He nodded and swallowed and took a couple of deep breaths, then began to read, his voice sweet and clear and lilting again, as it was meant to sound, not stumbling and stuttering as he had been in the woods.

The Elf's eyes widened as she listened and unexpectedly swam with tears at the end of the message. Rion was startled. He had not known Elves could cry, but then he remembered what Thorn had said, that his brother might have wept to see him prisoner of the ogres.

"You speak Elvish very well, Rion," she told him, and he was surprised, for her words were the opposite of what Thorn had told him, yet her smile was so like his, it pained him to see it. She looked at him intently. "You do not know what it is you have said, do you?"

He shook his head. "I was taught a dozen phrases by Aras, another Elf I know, but Thorn said I mustn't know what I spoke, that you needed to know it was from him, but also I had to speak of things a Man must not hear."

She stiffened at his words but, sounding clearly puzzled, said only, "Thorn?"

"Your brother. I don't know his given name. Thorn is the name he chose to use with us. Please, do you know if your healers can help him? He is my friend. He was already hurt when we rescued him from the ogres who had captured him, but then he was much more gravely injured saving me from another ogre. I don't want him to die." Rion's eyes filled with tears, and he wiped them away in frustration. He did not want to appear a child to her.

She looked at him in wonder. "You cry for him as if he were your own brother." She touched a tear he had missed, one that had rolled down his cheek, and he shivered at her gentle touch as his skin tingled and every nerve in his body suddenly awoke.

"I do not know if he will be all right, but I also hope he might be. You are right in that our healers are very skilled, though I wish our mother was here to aid him. But you have both given me an important duty to perform. I must become the bearer of my brother's message now and deliver it.

"It is most timely. Much harm would have come to many had my brother not relayed it to you for us, or had you not been so insistent upon delivering it. I will be back as soon as I can and say more to you, for your message speaks of two I would hear more about. Please, eat and drink. You are in need of it, and you are safe here." Then she glided away, as if skating across ice, through the doorway.

Rion let out the breath he'd been holding since she touched him.

Tarrell hugged him and said, "I thought we were all dead."

"Aras, Thorn, and our hostess aside, I find I do not like Elves," Jargas said. "Though I had never before heard of ones such as those in the woods. I never knew Elves could be deadly."

"Something is very wrong," Rion said, his voice laced with concern. "She said 'even now' the King's Guard still obey her. And look at this room. It doesn't fit at all with what we saw in the woods. I was expecting to be brought to a dungeon after that. And I know that Thorn did not expect our reception either, from his words to me. He thought we would be brought to their City but made to sleep or have our wits addled by food or drink. He did not expect us to be abandoned in the woods, or blindfolded and pushed through it."

"Now we have lost the wagons and all our goods and even our horses and our packs, but I will be grateful if we might escape here with our lives," Tarrell said.

Rion nodded. "When I told the men I might arrive at Gosa a pauper but see them paid, I did not mean to be speaking prophecy. Still, if the Elves can help Gar, I will feel a wealthy man, even if I am a poor one, for I value him and his brothers as friends and would pay any price to see them happy and whole and together again. Perhaps the brothers might even teach me their trade."

"I'll not have you work as a guard, Rion, ever," Tarrell scolded. "We'll stop at the nearest city and pay the men for this part of the trip, then release them from our service and try to restock with what coin we have. We can buy enough to start over again, taking only small things of great value, whatever we can carry on horseback, perhaps with a single guard or two."

"My home is only some few leagues from Gosa. That is why I took this job. If I can find a horse strong enough to carry me, I will go with you," Jargas said.

Rion smiled at him gratefully as they walked to the table.

The men were eating and drinking with gusto. Jathran said enthusiastically, "You must try this! I have never tasted food nor wine like this, and perhaps never will again."

"I'm not really hungry," Rion said, but he sipped the wine and tasted some cake and soon found himself eating ravenously. Tarrell and Jargas ate just as enthusiastically. When they were too full to eat more, they stretched out on the cushions with the rest of the men and everyone soon fell asleep.

JARGAS awoke with an odd feeling of timeless slumber. He looked in sudden concern at the others, who slept soundly, remembering stories his father had told him. But the others were still as clean-shaven as they had been: they hadn't slept for weeks or months all unknowing. Still, there had been something not right about the food and wine. He had not meant to sleep. He had not even posted a guard.

He thought to go exploring and looked to where he had seen their hostess exit, but there was no door, nor even a sign that there had ever been one. He searched the wall, vexed, to no avail, unable to find a crack in the solid stone even with his innate ability to sense the thickness of the rock all around him. He walked to the other walls and searched along them carefully, with hand and eye, but they too appeared seamless. His eyes narrowed. So, despite its appearance, they were truly in a dungeon, then.

He tried to rouse Tarrell, but he would not waken. He realized then that his great size, or perhaps his Dwarven blood, must have protected him somewhat from whatever elixir had been in the food and wine. He felt suddenly thirsty at the thought of the wine and found himself at the table with a gold goblet of it in his hand before he realized what he was doing. He dashed it angrily to the table, and the red liquid flowed everywhere, staining the white cloth as if with blood.

Jargas shook his head, trying to clear it, and spotted the stream. He knelt by it and cupped his hands to the water. He smelled it, tentatively, and then tasted it. It was cool and clear. He drank deeply and his thirst vanished, and suddenly his mind felt sharper and clearer.

"I take it back. I only like Aras and Thorn. Our hostess has deceived us." He looked for his staff and wasn't surprised when he discovered it and all their other weapons had vanished, including his once-hidden knife. It was only then that he noticed that Rion was gone, and he cursed. He should have noticed before, but the wine had still clouded his mind.

Why would they have this stream here, when any might discover the power of its waters? But no one else stirred. No doubt he should not have been awake to do so.

He checked the walls again, with eye and hand, and this time, his head clear of the wine, found the smooth seam of a door where he'd thought it should be.

He went back to the waterfall with his fallen goblet and rinsed it thoroughly in the stream, then filled it with the water. He held Tarrell's head in one hand and poured the water into his mouth, forcing him to drink.

Tarrell did so and coughed and sputtered, and his eyes opened. "What are you doing?" Tarrell asked, struggling in his grip.

"Rousing you from your slumber. There's something in the food or wine, or both. You wouldn't wake up until I discovered the water from the stream works against it. Rion is gone, and all our weapons are missing as well."

Tarrell looked around at their sleeping guards, afraid. "Why would they take him?"

Jargas gritted his teeth. "I'm afraid it might have been to question him. Perhaps they're not sure he has given them the entire message, or some of it appears false, or they might think he knows more Elvish than he's let on and has changed it."

"HE'S just a boy! They wouldn't harm him…?" Tarrell's fear was naked in his voice. He already knew the answer. He remembered the blade at his throat too keenly. These Elves had no regard for the lives of Men, and their leader had not liked Rion. They were cold and hard and pitiless, and the thought of them possibly torturing Rion, who loved them and trusted them, terrified him. Rion had nothing more to tell them, but they would not believe him.

Jargas put a strong hand on his shoulder. "Let's rouse the men and then we'll plan. I should not have let them take the wounded from here. I don't know what game they are playing. I have heard much about Elves and their mischief, but this is beyond that. From what we saw in the woods, methinks these Elves are gearing up for war, and I'm not at all sure they mean to fight the Enemy in the Dwarven Lands."

RION slept dreamlessly. It was when he awoke that his dream began. There was a beautiful vision smiling down at him, her sapphire eyes warm and welcoming. He sat up and looked around curiously. He was not in the room they had been in before. He was alone with their hostess. This room was of wood, not stone, and it contained a single bed, which he was on. The walls and floors were ridged, not planed smooth, and he suddenly felt as if he were in the hollow of some great tree trunk. "Are we truly inside a tree?" Rion asked in astonishment, standing and feeling the wall.

The Elf laughed. "Even the Wood Elves of Erenia cannot grow a tree so big as that! Each of the walls is two trees: eight trees grow together to form this room."

Rion's eyes lit with joy and wonder as he tried to find where one might end and another might begin. Then he looked at her curiously. "You are not from here. Thorn said he was a River Elf, so you must be one as well, not a Wood Elf. Also, when you move, you do not walk, you flow like water, and there was the stream. Do the Wood Elves need trees in order to survive, the way you need running water?"

She laughed again. "Such questions! Even were that true, should I betray our peoples' natures or weaknesses to you?"

Rion looked suddenly concerned. "I didn't mean… I was only…."

She smiled again, and his anxiety washed away. "You are not like other Men, Rion. You do not ask why you were sleeping, or touch your face to feel for a beard to see how long it might have been, or ask where your friends are. Most Men would show fear, awakening in my bed."

Something in her tone made him blush darkly. She laughed again, but it did not hurt to hear; he grinned at her, as if she had shared a joke with him. "Why should I worry? You have told us we are safe here."

"And so you are. But many might not believe so. It is why your friends sleep. Even were things as they should be, and not as they are, we could not have you roam freely about the City." She sighed. "But things are not as they should be."

Rion nodded. "Those armored Elves in the Forest. They're not guards, they're soldiers. I didn't know Elves had soldiers. How can you have soldiers, after what Thorn told me about how you feel about war?"

Her eyes widened slightly.

He sensed she was truly shocked by his words but was an expert at concealing her expressions and reactions. He suspected were she not so worried about her brother and concerned about whatever wrongness there was here, he would not have seen her react at all.

"What did he say to you about war?" she asked, too casually.

"He said you hold war in contempt, that violence is so abhorrent to you, it even hurts you to commit it, and that you have a terrible history."

"Even my brother does not usually have so loose a tongue," she said and frowned, no longer even trying to be discreet.

"He was tired and in pain. I didn't mean to have him tell me too much, and he did stop himself. And he didn't tell me nearly as much as Aras did, and Aras had no excuse. He wasn't even injured any longer by the time I met him."

"I would hear what Aras said to you. I would know all you know of Aras and Talon. I need to know so much more than you will know, for you will not be able to tell me why Aras lives when he should be dead, or why Talon travels with him," she said, sounding almost desperate.

"But I do know why," Rion said, thrilled that he might be able to aid her, even a little, by enlightening her. He told her of the wolven attack and how Talon found Aras and healed him, and all about their friendship and their travels, sharing his knowledge of the many things Aras had spoken of to him, and sometimes to both him and Tarrell, during their long talks.

She looked at him in wonder. "You are a most dangerous Man, Rion, for my brother to speak so openly to you and Aras before him. What Power do you have that would make us betray our secrets to you? Did even Talon bare himself to you? Not entirely, for then you would know his given name. Or do you know it and not speak it?"

"No, I didn't realize Talon had a different name," Rion said, wondering now what it might be. He smiled, thinking of him. "If Aras was like an open book, Talon was one closed and locked and written in a different language. You know him?"

"Oh yes. Talon is known to me. He has also lain in this bed." Again, something in her tone of voice made him blush darkly.

She looked at him intently. "Tell me, did Talon look well to you?"

"Well, I told you about the wolven biting his arm."

"No, I mean, was he sad, upset, melancholy? He is sometimes afflicted by moods," she said, as if she wished to say more but would not.

"He was very taciturn. He could smile, but he was most often melancholy. He was devastated when he found his kinsman Beryl's sword, though Aras had said he had already known he was dead. Then, when Jargas spoke to him of Hunter, it was agony for him. I think Hunter might have died as well."

She was staring at him, openmouthed, the perfection of her face again distorted by pain. "But Beryl is not dead! It would have been better were he slain than for one of the Watch ever to… and Hunter cannot be dead! Without both Beryl and Hunter… agony, you said? Tell me, what did you see? Did Talon recover, did he leave, what happened to him?" She was intense, frighteningly so.

"When he left for his room with Jargas, he looked stricken. But the next morning, when he and Aras said good-bye to us, he looked well, more well than I had ever seen him, I think, except for his concern for Aras. Aras was the one who looked stricken then, although we made him smile more than once with our gifts to him before he left. Why should it frighten you to hear? Everyone suffers grief and loss, at one time or another, and Talon is strong. Such things would not consume him. Would they?" Rion asked, suddenly doubting his own confidence in the face of her continued concern.

"I do not know. I hope it might be so, that he might be strong enough, even alone."

"But he is not alone. Aras travels with him," Rion assured her.

She shook her head sadly. "In this, only a kinsman might aid him, and of them, there were only two who had that Power."

"You mean Beryl and Hunter were both kin to him? So then is Talon also part of the Watch? Tell me, what is the Watch? I had not heard the term before you spoke it."

"Did I truly say all of that to you? I have said too much as well!" she said, surprised.

"I'm sorry. I didn't mean to hear it. I will not speak to anyone about it, whatever it might mean," Rion promised.

"I should take you back."

"No, please. I don't want to sleep, I want to learn! Not secrets, just everything else. You haven't even told me how Thorn is, or Gar. Can't you at least tell me that? You were smiling before. I'd hoped Thorn might be healing. He misses you greatly. I could hear the longing in his voice when he spoke about you. I know you'd be near him if you thought he might awaken soon, but still…."

"Hush, Rion. You were like a smooth river stone, and now you are like a storm at sea." Her voice was soft and sweet and soothing. "I will not send you away or to sleep. Thorn is healing, but it will take time, for his injuries are grave and not easily mended. The one you have called Gar was much easier to heal: his wounds were all on the outside. He and his brothers are well."

"You mean Gar is already healed? How is that possible? Tell me, are... are the scars very horrible?" Rion asked, hoping they might not be too repulsive, for the Elves helping him.

"Scars?" she asked, as if she did not know that word in Common.

"The marks from the claws," Rion clarified.

"He is healed. The marks are gone," she said, sounding puzzled.

"No, I mean... here, like this. I cut myself here, when I was eight," Rion said, showing her the inch-long scar on his forearm.

"You did not fully heal," she said, her voice full of sympathy as her fingertip gently stroked the mark on his arm.

He felt that same strange thrill at her simple, gentle touch; his whole body tingled with it. He looked at her in astonishment. "You mean... you mean even with such grievous wounds, Gar does not have any scars?"

"No. Of course not. He has been healed."

Rion's face lit with a grin. But suddenly he was concerned again, but not for Gar. He swallowed. "Do you mean no Elf has scars?"

"Elves do not bear scars," she agreed.

"If... if an Elf had scars, would he suffer for it?" Rion asked hesitantly. "Would he be poorly treated, viewed with pity or revulsion, even if they were faint, even if they weren't on his face? Aras is scarred, on his shoulder, where the wolven bit him. He showed his scars to me, when he told me the story of how he and Talon met."

"Poor Aras. Yet another thing to set him apart from all the rest. But he will endure. He has learned to endure so much in his short life, though I have heard he has not let it weigh too heavily upon his heart. I know much about him, although we have yet to meet. Tell me, does he still smile like my brother? Is he still childlike, innocent, trusting in the goodness of all, even Men? Is he still full of joy? Other than before he left. You already spoke of that."

Rion nodded. "He smiled and laughed often. He was wonderful. I miss him terribly."

She smiled at Rion. "I am glad he has finally found friends, although it is sad that he had to leave his own people and almost die to do so. But Talon and you and perhaps your guardian have all befriended him. I am grateful to you for that. Though I might wish it were otherwise, I could never be his friend." She sighed.

"Why not, if he needed a friend so badly?" Rion asked, puzzled.

"Because he was still a boy and I was not yet allowed to spend time with him. It would not have been proper. He has only just come-of-age. Now it is not proper for a different reason. But I cannot speak of it. I have spoken too much already. And I must alert the Council about Beryl and Hunter and Talon and Aras. They will need to question you further. They will want to hear all you know. The King's Guard, the Army, will be there also. Do not let yourself be frightened by them, for I will be there as well, and no harm will come to you," she assured him.

Rion couldn't hide his fear in spite of her reassurances. The soldiers had been so cold, even cruel. The beautiful Elf looked at him in concern, and he wished he'd been better at concealing his fear. He did not want to look weak or afraid to her.

"I have said I will not send you back, nor make you sleep. But if you wait here alone, will you not become frightened?" she asked diplomatically.

"I am already frightened, by what you said," Rion admitted. He could not lie to her. "But I still would not sleep."

"Then I will give you a book to read, so your mind might be kept busy. You must take the greatest of care with it, for it was written by a Man who no longer lives and is very precious to one who yet does." She touched the wall beside her, and slowly the wood parted, revealing a hollow with a book inside. She handed it to him. The binding was simple and unadorned, but the book was massive, at least three inches thick and quite heavy.

He opened the cover, curious as to what a man might write that might be precious enough for an Elf to want to protect. The title page was written in a bold hand, the title apparently written in three different languages, two he did not know and Common. It read, *Understanding Elves: One Man's Perspective.* Rion smiled in delight. He was surprised that the author had not penned his own name below the title, as he would expect. Perhaps it was concealed in one of the other two lines? The first language was Common. He was almost certain the second was Elvish, from the elegant, flowing nature of the writing. But the third was a mystery. It seemed to have elements of both: more graceful than Common, yet more angular and rigid than Elvish.

"Now I must go," the Elf said.

"Wait, one last question," Rion said, before she could disappear. "Please, what might I call you?"

She smiled. "If my brother is a thorn, perhaps because he is at times a painful annoyance, should I then be a rose? For I am soft and sweet and beautiful." And she said it with an expression on her face that so matched the look Thorn had given him when at his most absurd, he had to laugh.

He shook his head. "No, not Rose. Not something pale and pink and delicate. How about Brook? For you are all blue and silver and you flash so brightly, like sunlight upon the water, and you are strong yet soothing, and speaking to you has refreshed my spirit."

She looked at him intently, and he thought perhaps he had said too much. But then she smiled and his heart stuttered wildly, knowing he had brought a smile to her face, even when she was so burdened by concerns.

"I had feared for a moment you might have lost your heart to me, but your heart is still your own. Still, I would caution you to guard it carefully, Rion, for it is a precious gift that may be given only once in one such as you. My heart is not mine to give, for I am already betrothed, for good or for ill, to a healer who is himself in need of healing, to a madman and a savior, to a Prince who should be King."

Rion looked at her, wide-eyed.

"What is your true name, Rion?" she asked unexpectedly. "Your given name, your father's name, and your birth city?"

"Alarion, son of Anorion of Ardock," Rion said, without hesitation.

"Many in your world speak such things freely when they should not. Never tell anyone who asks you again, Rion," she chastised. "There are those in this world who can wield your name against you like a blade. A true name may ever only be offered, not asked for, and if accepted, the one who accepts must state his or her own. Never state your true name to one you do not fully trust," she cautioned.

"But I trust you, and I do not ask you for yours. To me you will be Brook, if it pleases you, as your brother is Thorn. And he chose that name for himself."

"Was I ever so young? Was my heart ever as open as yours? It has been too long for me to remember. I give you a gift, Alarion, son of Anorion of Ardock. My true name is Princess Elanara, daughter of King Laranela of Riviera. Remember it well, for one day you might have need of it. Now I must go." She turned and touched the wall, and a doorway opened, then closed again.

Rion stared at the wood. She was a Princess of Elves? The room seemed dead and empty and dark with her gone, though the living trees still surrounded him, and strangely, there was light, where there should be none. He had not thought to feel her leave-taking so keenly.

Rion swallowed and opened the book, and then lost himself in it. The customs, the rituals, the language of the Elves: all were here at his fingertips. The Elvish words were written first in that beautiful flowing script that must be Elvish. Then the word was written phonetically in Common. The word was also written in its equivalent in Common, or defined when there was no direct equivalent. Then it appeared to be written in that third language, more graceful than Common but more bold than Elvish. That third word was also written phonetically in Common. And then it looked to be defined below it, in that same language. He could scarcely contain his excitement. This was not just a compendium of knowledge in three languages: this portion, at least, was a translator's dictionary! It looked like it would be possible to learn either of the other two languages, if one knew only one of the three. He wondered what that third language might be.

He flipped eagerly through the pages, looking for words he already knew how to pronounce in Elvish, ones Aras and Thorn had taught him, so he might see how they looked written in Elvish. But then he found a word he had not looked for. The translation leapt off the page at him: war. He sounded it out and gasped, for he realized he'd spoken it before, as part of the secret message Thorn had taught to him, the one Man must not know. He flipped away from the vocabulary. He would not betray Thorn's trust.

The next section was on Elven customs. It looked fascinating, but it was hard to concentrate upon it. If Elanara was an Elven Princess, then Thorn must be a Prince. No wonder the soldiers had reacted so strongly! A Prince of Elves should never lie helpless and injured in the hands of Man. Even if he were not heir to the throne of Riviera, for he had said he was the second son. Rion forced his attentions to the pages of the book, for he was still delving into secrets he had meant to let lie.

The entire book appeared to be written in all three languages, Common, Elvish, and that other language. He began reading. The section on Elven children was fascinating. The coming-of-age-ritual was so shrouded in mystery, the book's author had no knowledge of it, other than it happened when an Elf turned forty-nine, as Thorn had mentioned.

Rion read about guardians and began feeling guilty being away from Tarrell. But then he remembered that Tarrell would be asleep. He would not be frantic with worry about him as he would otherwise have been.

There was something on parents, which didn't look quite as interesting. He skipped over that part and began reading the section on ritual greetings and partings.

The wall split open suddenly, and he looked up eagerly. He had not thought Elanara would be back so soon. Then he shrank back on the bed, the welcoming smile dying upon his face. It was not Elanara. It was the soldier from the woods, the Elven commander, the one who despised him.

"You will come with me," the soldier demanded in Common.

Rion swallowed. "Where are you taking me?" Elanara expected him to stay here.

The soldier's eyes narrowed, and as fast as a snake striking, his right hand darted out and grasped Rion's shoulder as he seized his other wrist with his left hand and yanked and twisted. Rion fell from the bed to his knees, gasping in pain, and then there was a rope about his wrists, and his hands were tied tightly behind him. The rope was looped about his neck and knotted again, and he was yanked up by it. The book was knocked to the floor as Rion was pushed roughly forward. The Elf had moved so fast!

The wall opened again, and Rion was dragged from the room. Rion attempted to cooperate, afraid the rope would choke him otherwise. He tried to walk quickly, but the Elf's stride was long, and Rion stumbled often. Each time he was yanked forward roughly, as if a disobedient dog on a leash.

He was forced along a network of interwoven branches, downward, past other clusters of trees. Then they were on the ground, and a great hill of rock loomed before them. There were more soldiers in front of it. A door appeared from what had looked to be solid rock, swinging open. They entered and the door shut behind them with only a whisper of sound. It was cold and dark and silent here.

Rion was forced down an unadorned passageway to another door, also guarded by soldiers. This door opened for them as well. Rion was pushed roughly into a room.

There was a long, hollow, truncated oval table, almost U-shaped, although the ends curved inward. There were twenty-four chairs along the outer edge of the table, nine of them along the bottom curve of the "U" occupied with four Wood Elves and five of the armored soldiers. Rion was shoved toward the inner curve of the table. Bound as he was, he lost his balance and fell, his knees cracking hard on the stone floor. He barely kept from pitching forward and bashing his head upon it as well.

"I bring the prisoner," the Elven commander said in Common. Rion was surprised he still spoke Common to these other Elves.

"Why is he bound?" one of the soldiers asked in the same tongue.

"He did not come when called," the Elven commander said.

"But I...." Rion's nascent protest was cut off.

"Silence!" the Elf at his side barked and cracked him across the mouth for emphasis.

Rion pitched sideways, the left side of his head cracking hard against the floor. Then he was yanked back up to his knees by the rope. "You will speak only to answer our questions. And you will answer them, and truthfully. You will have no choice."

This must be the Council, Rion thought desperately. But Elanara was not here. She had said she would keep him safe. Where was she? He realized she must not know they'd taken him.

He was terrified of the Elf beside him. He desperately wished Tarrell was here to protect him, even as he realized he would be powerless to do so, not from the Elves, even were he awake and here.

The commander turned to the table and lifted a vessel of glass from it. There was something dark and oily looking in it. He started to approach Rion, a look of malicious anticipation upon his face.

"I demand my guardian, Princess Elanara, daughter of King Laranela of Riviera, be summoned to aid me!" Rion called out loudly, desperately, into the quiet room.

The commander glared and grabbed Rion's hair and yanked back his head.

He was going to force him to drink! Rion clenched his jaw, locking his mouth shut, as tears began to stream from his eyes.

One of the Elves called out in a voice of authority, something in Elvish this time, and amazingly, the commander stopped. He let go of Rion's hair. There was a heated exchange in Elvish amongst the soldiers and between them and the Wood Elves.

The same Elf who had asked before why he was bound asked Rion in Common, "Are you not a man?"

For the first time, Rion was glad to be so young. He shook his head. "No, I am not. I am only a boy, a child. Men come-of-age at sixteen and I am only fifteen. My parents are dead and my guardian is captive and asleep. Princess Elanara said she would protect me; that means she's offered to be my guardian while I am here. By your own laws you cannot keep us apart when I call for her aid. Please, summon her here!" Rion entreated. He began to sob, he could not help it. He was terrified of them.

The eyes of the soldier who'd spoken to him narrowed in anger, but he turned his glare to the commander beside him and said something harsh sounding in Elvish.

The commander stiffened and turned, shooting Rion a look of pure hatred as he passed. But to Rion's relief he headed toward the door. Rion risked glancing at the door and saw the commander leave. He took great shuddering breaths, trying to calm himself, hoping he'd soon see Elanara.

ELANARA entered her bedroom and stared in disbelief at the empty room. Then she saw Dewalaren's book upon the floor, lying face down and open, as if it had been carelessly dropped. The upper right corner of the front cover was dented inward, and some of the pages were bent. She retrieved the book, smoothed the pages with her hand, and closed it. She opened the cupboard and concealed the book safely inside once more. Then she ran through the open doorway, down the tree branch paths, toward the Council building, both angry and frightened.

They had taken Rion! They had deliberately tried to exclude her. They would hurt him. They would not be able to believe he was so guileless, so innocent, so loving, so trusting. She had promised him he would be safe and he would not be.

Rion reminded her painfully of Lunahr. He possessed the same gentleness of spirit, the same openness and curiosity and eagerness for knowledge. She fought back tears as so many memories of Lunahr surfaced. She had failed Lunahr. She had been separated from him, exiled here, and when he needed her protection most, she was not there to give it. He had been captured and tortured and turned into a monster. The boy she had loved like a brother was dead, though his body was yet being used as a weapon against them.

She finally reached the door to the Judicial Building, but it was shut and blocked by soldiers. "Let me pass," Elanara commanded, with all the cool authority of her station, fearing it would not be enough.

"No, Princess. None may enter until the Inquest is concluded," one of them replied, his voice adamant but respectful.

Elanara hid her fear. So this was not merely a hastily called Council Session, one portion of which would be dedicated toward questioning the bearer of her brother's messages. It was an official court of inquiry. "But I'm a member of the Council. I should have been summoned before the Council Inquiry convened," Elanara insisted.

"No, Princess. Do you forget that the Kingdoms are now under Martial Law? This is not a Council Inquiry. This is a Military Tribunal. You were not one of the four Council Members chosen to participate in the inquisition."

She paled, unable to fully conceal her fear. The presence of the four Council members was a mockery. The will of Laedrin's men, the King's Guard, would prevail: kill the prisoners, steal their memories, confine them in sleep until they were old and gray. All the stories of imagined atrocities Man had ever told leapt into her mind, yet this time, any one of them was possible. Elanara wished Eladar were awake to help her. He was the sneaky one, mischievous, devious, tricky. He would find a way inside.

The door unexpectedly opened from inside. It was Commander Fenrath, one of the most prejudiced and arrogant of the soldiers she had encountered. He glared at her. "You are summoned, Princess." It was far from the tone she would usually respond to, but she meekly followed him, for Rion's sake.

The Council Chamber door was closed and guarded, but it was opened for them, and they were allowed in. Elanara saw nine of the twenty-four chairs were filled. Someone was kneeling on the floor in front of them, his hands bound tightly behind him, and there was a rope about his neck as well. She recognized the clothes and hair instantly: it was Rion! She hurried to him, fighting the urge to run, already moving with far more haste than normal for one of her station. She saw him tense when he heard her steps, ducking his head down and lifting his shoulders, cowering as if expecting a blow, like a tortoise trying to protect himself from a perceived threat.

She circled him, so he would recognize her, and know himself safe. But when she passed in front of him, she saw his face was streaked with tears, his eyes were wide and frightened, and there was a thin stream of blood trailing from his nose to his lip.

All decorum and reserve was forgotten as she knelt in front of him and embraced him. She felt him shudder against her. "Hush. It's all right, Rion. I am here now. None will harm you again. None should have harmed you before."

She rose and turned to face the Tribunal and spoke in Elvish, her voice one of cool reprimand. "I would know why I am summoned late."

"You are not summoned as Councilor," General Ranyr said, his tone identical to her own, his eyes locked with hers. "The boy has spoken your true name and named you as his guardian within the City. He said you offered your protection because his own guardian is incapacitated. Do you assume that responsibility?"

Elanara was fiercely proud of Rion. He had found a way for her to enter here when otherwise she could not have. "Of course. I already did so when I offered him my protection," she said smoothly.

"We must question the prisoner and know he tells the truth. He must drink ekleetha so we know he speaks truly," the General said, his voice adamant but not challenging, as it could have been.

"You would do so, knowing that he is only a child, and if he resists, he would be permanently damaged by it?" She was aghast at the thought of what they intended.

Councilor Jelarath spoke up, his tone wheedling when she knew he would think he sounded conciliatory. He was not nearly the great diplomat he pictured himself to be. "But you are here and he trusts you. It will not hurt him to answer if he does not fight it, if you are the one to ask him."

The soldiers had been careful in their choice of Council Members. There were none here of great political power or strength of character.

"My father will hear of these proceedings." It was no light threat. Her father was second only to the High-King.

General Ranyr's voice grew cold. "High-King Laedrin would hear of them as well, were he not incapacitated, did he not lie near death for the treachery of Men. As your intended leads the Men who betrayed us, and as you are the guardian of Lord Beryl, the assassin who attacked him, you will forgive us for not believing all we have heard without confirming it for ourselves. That you are not already in chains and formally charged with conspiracy, sedition, and treason is in deference to your station. But the world changes, Highness, and you are no longer in Riviera. If you hope to survive, you had best learn silence, humility, and obeisance. Your King might allow such an arrogant tone of disrespect out of parental indulgence, but we do not."

Elanara paled, realizing she had badly misjudged her own culpability in their eyes, that her position was far more tenuous and fragile than she had realized. She was grateful to General Ranyr. He was not threatening her so much as he was warning her. Were the Commander to somehow become the ranking officer here, she would be imprisoned or possibly even killed immediately.

She kowtowed to the General, in complete obeisance and submission, for the first time acknowledging his overwhelming authority over her under Martial Law. "Forgive me, General Ranyr. I meant no disrespect. I am overwrought with concern over my younger brother, who has been so gravely injured, and for the rest of my family and all my people, as well as the people of Loatia, whom we protect, all of whom are in grave danger."

"Your apology is noted," the General said. Elanara knew he implied it would be officially recorded in the proceedings, including her statement regarding the perilous position of both Riviera and Loatia.

Their agent in Nalea, Commander Narenius, had accurately identified the General's position. He was not a friend of the Oceana, but neither was he an enemy. He merely performed his duty to the best of his ability, under the constraints of his station as imposed by High-King Laedrin.

"Rise," General Ranyr commanded. She stood and he looked her in the eye. "The boy will drink the ekleetha and you will ask him the questions we tell you to, and then we will know the truth. If you or this boy have lied to us, even your father will not be able to save you from our wrath."

Elanara turned back to Rion. The General might no longer be as open-minded as he once was, now that Laedrin had been attacked. She was truly afraid of him now, when she had tried hard not to be before. She was afraid of all of the King's Guard. She was not used to being afraid. She refused to reveal her fear to them. These soldiers saw fear as weakness. She was the daughter of the strongest King of the Oceana. Riviera was the Jewel of the Seven Kingdoms. She would be proud, but not arrogant or disrespectful.

She went to the end of the table, lifted two chairs, and brought them over to where Rion yet knelt. She helped him to his feet and pulled a slender knife from her sleeve, from the sheath hidden against her arm, and cut his ropes, dropping them to the floor.

"You bring her before us into the Council Chamber armed? No one but the King's Guard may bear arms here," General Ranyr said acidly, glaring at Commander Fenrath in reprimand. Then he turned his angry gaze to her. "You will surrender your knife to Commander Fenrath, and you will be searched."

She paled at the thought of them laying hands upon her. She had miscalculated again. She could not think clearly with Eladar so injured, Rion trembling before her, and Lunahr lost. She held the knife out to Fenrath, hilt first, proud to see her hand did not shake. But when he began to search her, and she felt his rough hands upon her, both over and under her clothes, she began trembling in outrage and humiliation. He was vilely thorough in his search. The four Councilors shifted uncomfortably but did not voice a protest at the indignity she was forced to endure.

"She is unarmed," the Commander said in smug satisfaction.

Elanara turned stiffly back to Rion. He was looking at her in helpless rage on her behalf, agonized. He was so brave! She drew strength from his courage and forced a smile to her face. "It is all right, Rion. They've only harmed my pride. Now, please sit. I'll be right here beside you."

Rion obediently sat, rubbing his wrists and neck, wincing in pain when his hand found the rope burn around his neck.

Elanara sat in the other chair and spoke to him further in Common. "Rion, the soldiers need to know you have spoken the truth." She did not say the Council. In spite of what she had told Rion before, it was now brutally apparent that it was not the Council who was in charge here. She drew a deep breath, to quell her anger and her fear for the moment, and continued. "In order for them to be sure, you will need to drink that," she said, pointing to the glass.

He looked scared, but not terrified. She could again see the effort he was making to be brave in the face of this new terror. She forced another smile for his benefit. He must not fight against the drink, if he was to survive the questioning intact. She would die before she saw another who trusted her come to harm.

"Rion, it is safe. As long as you do not try to lie, nor keep from answering, you will be fine. But if you try to lie, or do not answer, it will harm you. You will soon be forced to answer anyway, and to speak the truth, but you would still be damaged from having resisted it. Do you understand?"

Rion nodded, eyes wide with fear.

"Do you trust me?"

"Of course," Rion said, without hesitation.

"Then drink it, all of it, answer truthfully and quickly, and all will be well. No harm will come to you, or me, or your friends."

"Have I put you in danger, by naming you my guardian? I did not mean to," he said, sounding agonized.

"No, Rion, not by bringing me here now. And it is not because of you, at least not entirely. I was already in danger. I am afraid I cannot say more." She did not want to antagonize the General further against her. She lifted the glass and handed it to him.

Rion took the glass and drank from it. He shuddered, and she saw he almost retched, but he forced it down, swallowing the last of it.

"Very good. I'm very proud of you. Now I am going to count to twenty. Then we will begin," she said, and started to count. By five Rion's eyes looked glazed. By ten all expression had left his face.

It was strong: it was acting so quickly on him. He was not yet fully grown, yet they must have given him a dose for a man. Or perhaps it was because he was a Man, not an Aerta or Oceana. She feared anew that it might harm him, but there was nothing she could do about it now. She reached twenty.

"Have him state his true name," the General commanded.

She was furious Ranyr would ask Rion to do so when he was helpless to resist, after what she had warned him, but she repeated his command in Common.

Rion answered her, his voice monotone, completely lacking the vibrant life she had already begun to associate so closely with him.

The General told her to ask him whether Eladar had given him a message and if so, to repeat it as Eladar had spoken it to him.

"He knows my brother only as Thorn. He does not know his given name," she argued.

"Ask him as I spoke it," the General commanded.

She did so. Rion said he did not know anyone named Eladar, but Thorn had given him a message.

"Have him speak it," the General ordered. She repeated his command.

Rion spoke first in Common, then the two messages in Elvish, "In the woods, Thorn told me to say, '*I speak for Prince Eladar, son of King Laranela of Riviera. He is injured and calls for aid.*' Then Thorn said, 'When an Elf appears, do whatever he or she commands, including eating or drinking whatever is offered. Then, when you are in the City and they speak to you, you must relay this for me:

'*I bear a message from Prince Eladar, son of King Laranela of Riviera. I speak for him. Aid these Men as you would aid me. They rescued me from the ogres. It is not their fault I am injured or slain. They bear my message.*

'*I have learned that Nalea has sealed her borders and declared War on the Watch, and that High-King Laedrin is near death, supposedly at the hand of Lord Beryl, Captain of the Watch. But this Man, Rion, the one who speaks with my voice, has given me vital information. He has told me High-Prince Aras was wrongfully reported dead, that he survived the wolven attack and yet lives: he was rescued and healed by Prince Talon, Lord of the Watch, and travels with him. The details he has provided are irrefutable. You must hear what he has to say.*

'*Do not allow yourselves to play into the Enemy's hands. Riviera and Loatia are in grave danger. Your forces must concentrate upon reinforcing their defenses, not attacking innocent Men.*

'*Lord Beryl and his people are not responsible for the attempted assassination. They can still be our allies in this war, not our enemies. Truce must be called. Do not let my injury or death be in vain.*

'*And please, I beseech you; I have been so long away from my River, I have been so far from home. Please bring me home to Riviera, even if it is only to see me buried there, for the River yet moves my heart, even if my heart has been stilled.*'"

Hearing the message the second time was no easier than hearing it the first. Elanara fought the emotion that sought to overwhelm her, refusing to show such weakness before these men.

"Ask if he knows what he just said, the Elvish part," the General said, his tone surprisingly gentle, as if a heart perhaps still beat beneath his shining breastplate.

She relayed his message once more.

"I know only the words 'aid' and 'you' and 'war'. I did not know the word 'war' when I spoke the message in the woods. I learned that here."

"Ask him who taught that word to him here," the General said, eyeing Elanara keenly.

"I read it in the book Elanara gave me," Rion said.

The General's eyes narrowed, whatever trace of sympathy he might have felt obliterated by Rion's damning words, and Elanara's heart quickened. But Rion was not done speaking.

"I found it by accident. Thorn said Man must not know what was in the message. That is why he entrusted it to me only in Elvish. So I did not read any more vocabulary, once I realized what I had learned, for fear I might see what I should not."

Elanara was careful to keep her face calm, but her heart sang in triumph at Rion's words.

The General looked both surprised and impressed by Rion's integrity. "Ask him what he knows of the Watch," Ranyr ordered.

Elanara did so, nervously, for Rion had been too perceptive when she had spoken earlier.

"Beryl and Hunter and perhaps Talon are part of it, but I don't know what it is," Rion replied.

The General asked to hear more of Beryl, Hunter, and Talon, and Rion dutifully told him all he knew. He also questioned him at length about Aras in particular. It seemed the Inquest might never end. All Rion's answers matched exactly what he had told her before, and what she had told the Council.

Finally, Ranyr appeared finished. Whether he was satisfied with what he had heard remained to be seen. The General told her to leave with Rion. She did so without inquiry or comment. She had done all she could to see herself and her brother, Rion, his friends, and the Watch safe. All their fates were in Ranyr's hands now.

Rion followed her obediently to her bedroom, as if he were yet on a leash. She told him to lie down on her bed, and that she would count backward from twenty and he would sleep, and when he awoke, he would have forgotten all she had said to him after drinking the ekleetha and his mind would be free of the effects of it. She counted and he fell asleep.

She gently brushed the hair from his forehead and then impulsively kissed him on it, astonishing herself by doing so. His skin felt cold. She covered him in a blanket and watched him sleep. She would not leave his side, especially not when he was so vulnerable. He had done well, remarkably well. The Army would have to make what they could of what he had told them.

Elanara worried for Dewalaren and Aras and for all Dewalaren's kin. She wished again that she could love Dewalaren the way he needed to be loved, the way he deserved to be loved, despite how she had been forced into the betrothal to him. She knew Dewalaren had been unaware of the High-King's machinations at Arcanus's bidding. Dewalaren would have been horrified to learn that Laedrin had threatened to kill Eladar if her father did not agree to the betrothal. She had learned much about Dewalaren in their time together. He was also a remarkable Man. But unlike Rion, he frightened her. He was so powerful yet so vulnerable, so terribly cursed.

She was relieved the situation had not been made unbearable. At least she had not loved Aras, nor he her. Laedrin would have altered the betrothal anyway. She thought he might even secretly take joy in breaking Aras's heart. He had tried for decades to crush his spirit and mold him into a pale reflection of himself.

She could not hate Dewalaren, but she hated Laedrin. Many hated him, many wished him dead. But not the Watch. They needed Laedrin and his Army and Navy.

Incuban had engineered this. Either Lunahr was a Resemblant, or he was so twisted by Incuban's tortures that he was no better than one. She remembered the gentle, beautiful, innocent boy with the long golden hair and laughing green eyes, with sunlight and songs in his heart. Dewalaren had sent Lunahr to Riviera to be safe. She had been his guardian; she was supposed to have protected him. She had loved him as a brother for six years. But she had been exiled and imprisoned, and tragedy had struck House of Eagles once more.

She almost hoped Farad was dead, as Rion suspected. Dewalaren had told her much about his eldest cousin. Farad had tried so hard not to love his young cousin: he saw each of his lost brothers in Lunahr. He was tormented by his memories of them. But still he loved Lunahr and now Lunahr was tortured and dead by the Enemy's hand, just like Farad's parents and brothers. And Eladar, her own beloved brother, just as innocent, had been hurt by the ogres and nearly slain. Poor Rion! What a brutal world for a young innocent to live in.

Rion stirred in the bed and his eyelids fluttered open. "Elanara? Are you all right?"

Elanara smiled, a true smile this time. "Am I all right? After what you have just gone through, you are concerned for me? Your heart is bottomless, Rion! I am the one who should ask you. Are you all right? I am so sorry they hurt you. I had not thought they might take you. It was a stroke of brilliance to summon me as your guardian. When I told you that you might need my true name, I had not thought you might need to use it so soon."

SHE sounded much better than she had looked when he awoke. The memory of the look upon her face as that Commander had searched her had incensed him. Rion smiled at her in relief. "I got the idea from the book you let me read. I read about Elven children and guardians and thought it might work." He was still embarrassed for having to resort to such a thing and upset for having endangered her, though she'd denied it. He did not want to seem a child to her. She was so wonderful. "Is the book safe? I didn't mean to drop it, but that soldier grabbed me and tied me and it fell."

"It is safe," she said, taking it out of the cabinet she had stowed it in. "I would like to ask you a great favor, Rion. I do not want Talon's book to remain here where the Army might decide to take it or even destroy it. You said when we questioned you that you were going to Gosa. That is very near the River Kingdom of Salenia. If I were to write a letter, would you take both the book and the letter there for me? I can tell you how to gain access to their Kingdom."

"Of course! I would do anything for you and for Talon. He saved my life. I hadn't known the book was his until now. But I cannot just leave you here. I am worried about you. It does not seem that you are safe here. Please, come with us."

"I CANNOT," she said sadly. "I am more prisoner here than you. Besides, I will not leave my brother. You are very sweet to worry so about me. But I will endure, I will survive. While Father and Mother yet live, I will be safe."

Loatia and Riviera were so vulnerable to attack, while the Army thought only of the Watch being a danger. She knew her mother was safe in Salenia, as her father had sent word to her of her mother's trip, but he and her elder brother Elavar were both yet in grave danger. They knew it, but they would not leave their people.

"As soon as the Army frees you, you must go. I will say my good-byes to you after I write the letter, for your parting will perhaps be abrupt." She sat on the bed and touched a spot on the wall, and a drawer appeared with pen and ink, drying sand and paper, silver wax and a seal.

She wrote quickly in the loose, flowing hand he recognized as Elvish from the book. Then she folded the letter, melted the end of the wax and let a few drops splash upon the paper, and stamped her seal upon it, the image of a swan.

"When you get to Salenia, ask for River. This letter is for her." She tucked the letter into the center of the book and the book into a pack she pulled from a concealed drawer in the wall.

She fervently hoped the Army would not find the book and confiscate it, or worse still, find the letter. If they did, Rion and his friends would be in great danger, and she would be in a far less gilded cage than the one she currently was trapped in. But her mother must learn of the danger she and Eladar were in here. She was the one in the best position to come to their aid.

"For as long as Talon's book is in your possession, you may read it, any and all of it. Men must be strangers to us no longer. War is coming to claim us all."

"I will guard Talon's book with my life," Rion swore. "I thank you for allowing me to read it. It is a precious gift you give me and means much to me. But I am gifted most by knowing you."

She looked into his intent, guileless blue eyes and almost warned him about the danger of the letter, but bit back the warning. Rion might be an innocent, but he was smart, he was a survivor. He might still be part boy, but there was already much of the man he would soon become in him. He was upon the very cusp of coming-of-age. He reminded her so much of Eladar, only a few years before. The thought was comforting: Rion would find his way out of the danger, if put in it.

She smiled. "Still, I will not see you and those you travel with leave here worse off than when you came. You should not suffer for your kindness to my brother." She reached into her dress and pulled out a small pouch. "This is for your friend, Jargas, to repay him for the horse he sacrificed. It is worth far more than the horse, yet far less than the life of the one he exchanged his horse for." She handed him a gem-battery, so green it almost glowed. It was an Aerta stone, not Oceana, or it would have been of the deepest sapphire blue, or so her mother had told her. She had never seen an Oceana gem-battery. She did not think any still existed. They no longer had the Power to craft such wonders. She had little enough else to give him. She only wished she had the Power to ward it as her mother would have, to see him and his friends safe.

His eyes widened almost reverently as he accepted the gift. "Can I see Thorn before I go?" Rion asked hopefully.

"Yes, although only in sleep, for he must sleep until he is well. But you may yet meet him again, Rion, for you seem destined to play a part in what is to come, to your good or your ill, I cannot say, though I hope it is the former. Come. I will take you back to your healed friends and to the others who sleep, so you may help me wake them."

ELANARA led Rion to the Healers' Hall. The four brothers and Rarnak and Lerdon were all sleeping, as was Thorn. But while the others looked well, Thorn was still pale, although he looked like he slept easily and painlessly.

Rion told Thorn good-bye quickly. It felt odd seeing him like that. But when he looked closely at the others, he could not help but stare in awe at Gar. It was true. He was completely healed: not a trace of the grievous wounds marred his fair face. His nose and chin and cheeks were as perfect as they had been before the attack. And the other brothers looked well also.

Elanara handed Rion a cup and instructed him to aid them in drinking from it. Even in sleep they did so. Rion awoke Rarnak first, then Lerdon, then Ron and the others.

They stretched lazily, looking about as if puzzled as to where they were. Then Ron's eyes widened upon seeing Gar. "Your face!" he said. Gar looked suddenly frightened and touched his face, but Ron was grinning and ran to him, Ara let out a whoop of delight, and Van ran to him with a look of pure joy on his face.

Gar could not believe their joy upon seeing him until they showed him his reflection in a mirror of silvered glass Elanara produced. He touched his face, staring at his features in awe.

"Gar is not the only one fully healed. My back no longer pains me," Ara said, amazed.

"Nor my head," Ron said, unable to take his eyes off Gar and Ara.

"And I can walk again and feel as if I could run," Van said excitedly.

Gar simply stared at himself in the mirror of silvered glass. His astonished look turned to one of joy. Then he looked from one brother to the next and rose from his bed, and then knelt before Elanara, his hands outstretched, palms up. The other three quickly followed suit. *"Isa nera meh flaeya na ya,"* they said as one.

Rion was startled, for they spoke one of the few phrases he knew, one Aras had taught him, in case he ever owed an Elf a debt of gratitude or might seek to curry the favor of one, or sway one to his aid. They had said, "I pledge my sword to you."

Elanara smiled at them and to his surprise Rion felt a pang of jealousy at the warmth of it. His face flushed. It was a good thing he was leaving soon, before his heart might betray him to this Elven Princess.

"Arise, one and all. I accept your pledge, for I may have need of it someday. Where do you dwell?"

Ron spoke for them, "In the mill outside Ogaten, upon the riverbank, within the River Kingdom of Salenia. Our family has been friend to the Elves there for three generations. We will do anything you ask of us, for you have given our brother back to us, whole and well again, when we had thought him lost to us, even had he lived."

"Then I will tell you my true name, and those of my two brothers, to share with your brothers, and I would hear your own." She whispered to Ron, and he to her, and it was well that she did not smile at Ron, for Rion could not look away from the tableau. But then she turned to Rion and smiled at him, and his jealousy was forgotten.

The seven of them were in good spirits as they traveled with Elanara to the room where the others were being held in sleep. But when Elanara opened the door, they found their friends were not asleep at all, and far from looking well rested, they looked angry and afraid. The brothers instantly formed a protective square about Elanara, although they bore no weapons. Jargas glared at them.

Elanara scolded the Men in the room. "You've awakened too soon and now you are angry when there is no need to be."

"No need?" Tarrell said, outraged. "You tricked us and drugged us and took Rion while we slept," he said, his voice breaking. He was staring intently at Rion.

Rion looked away, unable to meet Tarrell's intense gaze.

"And his face is bruised, and his neck is burnt by rope, and there is the memory of fear in his eyes. He's but a child, and you have hurt him," Tarrell said, his voice so filled with pain and anger that he was shaking.

Rion stepped forward. "Tarrell, listen to me. Brook has not hurt me. She has kept me safe. She has kept all of us safe, endangering herself to do so. The soldiers would as soon see us all dead, I think. They are at war. They needed to question me, and I answered them. We are yet to be judged. Brook is wielding what power she can in our defense. She has healed our injured. Look at Gar, Tarrell. Look at him! How can you be angry with her? We had come to waken you all."

"She has ensorcelled you. She has stolen your heart," Tarrell said, his voice filled with hopelessness.

Rion blushed, for his words were so nearly true. "No, Tarrell, she has not, she cannot, she would not." He hugged Tarrell and muttered, "You are still guardian of my heart, Tarrell. You still keep it safe for me."

Tarrell hugged him back, at first gently and then fiercely. Rion held him just as tightly, all his earlier tension draining from him. He was confident now that he truly would be able to leave Erenia and not leave his heart behind.

TARRELL looked up and his eyes unexpectedly locked with the Elf's. He saw relief and a flicker of loss and longing in her eyes and knew then that Rion's heart had not been the only one in danger. To his surprise, she put her fingers to her lips.

He nodded slightly. He realized she was trying to impart a silent message to him. Rion must never know how close he had come to winning her heart.

"Now that we are all together again, we want our weapons returned to us," Jargas said.

ELANARA sighed. "They will be, if it is decided you are free to go." And if not, she thought, for she would not let them die without the hope of at least defending themselves. "I think it is best if I go now. Unfortunately, you will not yet be able to leave this room, so please do not try. There are safeguards here which you have yet to discover, which would be quite deadly, I am afraid." She knew that, had they tried to force the door before, they would have already released the water snakes and there would have been only bodies here. She left the room.

TARRELL wanted to know all that had happened to Rion, and Rion told him what he could of it. Rion didn't remember anything that had happened from the time he drank that awful liquid and Elanara had started counting until he woke up in her bed. Just the thought of it being her bed made him blush. Then he remembered the Elfstone Elanara had given him for Jargas. "Jargas, this is for you," he said, holding it out to him. "Brook said it is because of the horse you lost, in exchange for her brother Thorn."

Jargas shook his head. "He might have started out a thorn, but he was jewel enough, in the end. And I want no gifts from his sister. You keep it, Rion."

"Thank you," Rion said, tucking it carefully away. Now, at least once the book was gone, he would still have something of hers, to hold when he thought of her. And of Thorn. For now, the weight of the book in the pack on his back was a comfort.

The door opened suddenly and there were soldiers in the doorway; they poured in like water, hands to their mouths. Jargas fell soundlessly, and then all four of the Ogaten brothers almost simultaneously. Rion spun to face Tarrell in fear, but Tarell's hand went to his throat and then he too fell without a word. Rion saw something needle thin and shiny sticking out of Tarrell's throat. He heard the soft thuds of the others falling to the floor and looked up in terror, opening his mouth to beg them to stop, but then there was sharp pain and oblivion.

RION awoke to the feel of a soft blanket upon him and a gentle hand at his wrist, and the sound of Lerdon's voice. He could feel and hear, but he could not move or speak when he tried.

"… heart is still strong, Tarrell. I am sure he will waken soon," Lerdon assured him. "It's just that he weighs at least thirty pounds less than the least of us, yet it appears they gave him a dose for a man. Jargas was the one I worried for, for they got him with four of those darts. Perhaps they knew it was safe to do so, for him being a Dwarf, or so large. Perhaps not. I understand the Elves and Dwarves are often at odds with one another."

"I still say we leave, in case they change their minds," Jargas said. "We can load Rion in the wagon."

"Not until I'm sure he's all right," Tarrell argued. "The Elves might need to heal him."

Rion tried to open his eyes, but the effort was somehow beyond his ability. He concentrated hard on trying to speak instead, so he could reassure everyone.

"Look! I think I saw his lips move a little," Lerdon said. "Rion, if you can hear me, relax, you're safe. You've been drugged. It takes a while to wear off, but you'll be fine."

Rion felt a hand squeeze his own gently. "I'm here, Rion. I'll stay with you until you can move again," Tarrell swore.

It was frustrating, not being able to move or even speak. Time seemed to pass very slowly. So, the soldiers had not come to kill them, but to free them. But they were drugged, perhaps so they would not know the way back. Jargas had mentioned a wagon, and he was sure he heard more than one horse. Had the Elves returned all their horses and both wagons?

Rion felt the sun on his face, instead of the shade of trees overhead, and it did not sound like they were in the woods anymore. He wondered if they'd been let out where they entered. If so, they'd still have the whole marsh to cross.

How could he not even manage to open his eyes? He focused all his will on what should have been the simplest of tasks, and his eyelids lifted and he could finally see.

Tarrell was looking at him in concern but the frown on his face suddenly turned into a smile of relief. "Rion! Can you speak, can you move?"

"I'm all right," Rion said, or tried to, but though his lips moved, he made no sound.

Tarrell held a water skin to his lips. "Drink. It will help, although it's just regular water, not that stuff from the stream. Although you don't know about that yet, do you?"

Rion drank eagerly. He hadn't realized how thirsty he was until he started.

"Hey, go slowly! I won't take it away until you're done," Tarrell assured him.

When he finished, Rion tried to speak again, and this time he succeeded. "I still can't even turn my head," he said, concerned.

"It's all right. It was like that for all of us. The Elves drugged us again," Tarrell explained.

"The needles, they blew them somehow. I saw one of them in your neck when you fell. I thought they were killing us. But they freed us instead. I hear horses, and Jargas spoke of a wagon. Have we gotten all the horses back? And both wagons? Have we regained all we lost?"

Tarrell nodded. "And more. The sun and the trees aren't where they should be in relation to one another. Jargas says we're on the other end of the forest from where we entered. We've bypassed all one hundred twenty-five miles of marsh because of it. We're less than fifty miles from Falnor. It's saved us at least five weeks off our journey, and likely far more, and much of the danger we'd expected to face."

Rion smiled. "That must have been Brook. Or maybe even the General. He was stern, but he seemed fair. He was angry at the one who...," then he stopped, for he had not told Tarrell even what little he remembered of what had happened when he was brought to the Council for questioning. He hadn't wanted to upset him further.

"It's all right, Rion. You're right not to tell me. It's all in the past in any case. We should look to the future," Tarrell said.

Rion grinned. "Thorn would have been pleased to hear you say that. I wish I could have really said good-bye to him when he was awake," he added wistfully. "Brook knew we might leave abruptly, so we at least got a chance to say our good-byes. I shall miss them both. Hey, I think I can move my arm," Rion said, and he could tell Tarrell was relieved.

A little while later, they mounted up, Gar riding double with Van and Ara riding double with Ron. Jargas was still on foot. They'd be able to buy new horses for the three of them in Falnor.

They continued their journey to Gosa. That evening and every other for the rest of the journey, Rion lost himself amongst the pages of the book of Elves until he fell asleep, learning all he could about them while he taught himself Elvish and that other odd language. And every night he saw Elanara in his dreams.

Chapter 8
Lords' Grove

AFTER Dewalaren and Arcanus left, Aras checked on his preparations for Lunahr's release and, in a lighthearted mood, left for the dungeon. It was very quiet inside. When he nodded to the four King's Guardsmen in front of the cell door, he saw that they shifted uneasily and looked downward, avoiding his eyes as they let him pass. With a sudden lurch of foreboding, he opened the door and entered.

Lunahr lay sprawled on the floor. Aras ran over to him. The right side of Lunahr's face was a mass of bruises, his right eye was swollen shut, and his breath was coming in short gasps. His sword arm was bent at an unnatural angle, obviously broken, though his sword was yet sheathed at his side.

"What happened?" Aras asked, checking his chest for broken ribs. Lunahr stiffened and winced everywhere his fingers touched, though he was gentle.

"I seem to have fallen," Lunahr said without a smile.

"Who beat you?" Aras demanded to know, but Lunahr turned from him.

"Can you stand?" Aras asked.

"I haven't tried," Lunahr admitted, though Aras suspected he'd intended to stay silent.

Aras thought better of moving him. "I will only be gone a moment."

Aras exited the cell and spun on the guards in a cold fury. "Who did this?"

The highest-ranking member of the King's Guard who was present responded. "I cannot say, Highness."

Aras eyed him coldly. "You will answer your High-Prince. Did you strike him?"

The soldier swallowed. "No, Highness."

"Then which of your men did?" he demanded, furious.

"None of us, Highness. It was… it was Lord of the Guard Ahrnad, Highness. He was beside himself. He entered the cell and said that no prisoner of his would lie unchained and bear a sword. He commanded the prisoner to surrender it. The prisoner laughed at him, Highness. He told him if he wanted it, he should take it. We saw the Lord grasp the hilt, but then suddenly he was flung back against the wall. It enraged him. He leapt at the prisoner and began striking him. Then he grasped his arm and struck and broke it, and the prisoner just stood there, laughing, as if he wanted Lord Ahrnad to kill him. And he kept striking the prisoner.

"We feared he would kill him, and we knew the orders, so the four of us tried to subdue him. But his strength was greater than our own. But then the Lord suddenly stopped of his own accord; there was a look of horror on his face, and he fled the cell. We didn't know what to do. He's our commander. But the prisoner did not look so hurt that he might die, so we waited. Forgive us for failing you."

Aras seethed. "Ahrnad did this after I gave him personal command that he not harm the prisoner!"

The King's Guardsman paled then. Aras realized he must have known only of the general order that the prisoner not be killed. This man had not realized his commander had committed a treasonous act by striking the prisoner even once, and he had struck him many times.

"You will fetch a healer and you will report to Commander Alwen. You will tell him that Lord of the Guard Ahrnad is to be stripped of his command and weapons and is to be locked and chained in the cell adjacent to this one. He is to remain there until I or my father release him. You will locate one of the Guardsmen, named Leonas, and you will bring him to me. Then the four of you will be locked in the remaining cell, although not chained, until I can decide what is to befall you. Is that understood?"

The King's Guardsman was visibly shaken. "Yes, Highness." He and his men disappeared quickly down the hall.

Aras breathed deeply for a moment, striving for calm, then reentered the cell. Lunahr still lay where he had left him. He was eyeing Aras from the floor. "You deliberately provoked Ahrnad. You hoped he would kill you," Aras accused.

"I do not deny it. They stopped him too soon. The sword played an unexpected part. I knew he could not take it from me, but I did not expect it to resist so strongly. It is better to die than to live like this, a collared animal, alone in the dark," Lunahr said, and his voice was very weary and laced with pain.

Tears of frustration filled Aras's eyes. "You aren't staying in here. I'd come to bring you back into the sun. I promised Talon I would see you safe, and he's been gone only a short time, and you are already almost slain."

Lunahr seemed to wither, then. "Laren is gone? I had hoped to see him again. There is much I wished to say. But no, it is better this way."

LUNAHR remembered Laren's face, full of horror and revulsion when he left him to suffer. Then the torturers came no more, but the pain of that look was worse than any of their art. He had known days of hurt and confusion, but still not despair, until Arcanus had come and tested him, and he had failed. Arcanus had told him he had been captured and had become a tool of the Enemy. That he had betrayed their most precious secrets. He told Lunahr of his attack on High-King Laedrin and, impossibly, on Laren. Arcanus said he was under compulsions that stole mind and will and memory from him.

Then he understood the look Laren had given him, and he knew he must be slain. But Arcanus was merciless in his pity and instead bound him with a few words so he could not move. Arcanus fashioned fetters of pallenteum. Lunahr saw the metal flow as if liquid, but it was not hot as it wrapped itself about his wrists and ankles and neck, and hardened. Arcanus told him he must be so bound until the very Enemy himself was slain. Arcanus returned Lunahr's sword to him, even as he worked his arts upon it. He told him he was further bound, by his sword and the very trees around him. He could draw his sword still, but never against the High-King or fellow kinsman, although he would try, if ever he saw them.

He could not even harm himself, lest he give in to despair. He was bound to Nalea by its trees and could roam no more, and his kin must ever shun him. Then Arcanus said that where there is life, there is always hope, but he saw none. Arcanus looked at him with kindly eyes, but Lunahr felt only guilt and despair. Arcanus's eyes grew sad, and he spoke soft words and all thought left him.

When he awoke, Laren was there, but only to test him. Laren had approached him with cold, pitiless eyes, and Lunahr's mind fled. When it returned, he lay gasping, tearing at the cursed collar at his throat with one hand, and to his horror, he saw his sword half-drawn in his other. He saw he had hurt his cousin, his King. He saw anger in Laren's eyes, and then, worse than any of the terrible things that had befallen him, Laren looked at him and there was only pity in his eyes. He had wept then, lost in despair. And Laren had left, without a single word of comfort. Now Laren was gone, forever lost to him.

Aras spoke again, drawing Lunahr away from his dark thoughts. His voice was kind. "Talon could not say good-bye to you in person. But he entrusted me with this for you." He held out a letter to him.

Lunahr took it and saw his traveling name written in Elvish. He traced each pen stroke with his fingertip, for the hand was one he knew and loved still. He sat up then, and although it hurt his body to do so, he almost did not feel it for the pain in his heart. He was afraid; nothing had ever frightened him so much as the thought of what Laren might now say. But he broke the seal awkwardly with one hand, and his hand shook as he opened the paper.

His eyes widened as he saw the first words in bold Amontiri script and then filled with tears as he read the words of love and hope.

Dearest Lunahr, beloved cousin, brother-of-my-heart,

> *You must not blame yourself for what has happened and you must not surrender to despair. You must eat and you must sleep. You must stay strong for me, for I cannot lose you again. Of all our kin, I have always loved you most, and I love you still.*

> *I would see you smile again, and I would hear you laugh, and sing. It grieves me beyond bearing that I cannot comfort you in your time of direst need. I cannot even stay. But I leave you with a friend, I think, and I charge you with his safekeeping, as I charge him with yours.*

> *Be well, my dearest cousin. This evil business draws to a close, and these dark days will seem but a terrible dream*

in the days to come. Live in hope, live in light, live in song. I
will not fail you, and I will return to you. I will see you free.
You must be there to greet me. I am trusting in you.

With ever my love,
Laren

Lunahr clutched the letter to his chest and sobbed. "Oh, Laren, I am such a proud fool! I almost betrayed your trust again, all unknowing." He slid the letter under his shirt, and held it against his heart. He saw Aras's eyes search his face, and he saw only pain and concern, and of a wonder, friendship on his face, toward the Man who had almost slain his father, his King, and he felt ashamed.

"Forgive me. I had not realized I could hurt you still, and I had not thought I could hurt Laren worse." His eyes filled with tears but he did not sob. "You said I might see the sun again. And the trees? I have missed them." Lunahr stood and Aras smiled at him, and Aras's smile was sunlight enough.

"Can you walk?" Aras asked.

"Walk? With Laren's love, I can fly."

ARAS grinned and clasped Lunahr's good arm and led him from the cell. Four new King's Guard were there. Aras eyed them carefully and said, "Lord Beryl is prisoner no longer. He is a Guest-of-my-House and not to be watched or followed or harmed. Any who do so will answer to me. Relay my orders to Alwen at once and tell him to report to me immediately."

"Yes, Highness!" they said as one and left in haste to do his bidding.

Aras and Lunahr walked toward the stairs slowly, for despite Lunahr's words, it was obvious that walking was an effort and he was in pain.

Lunahr sighed. "Do not judge Lord Ahrnad too harshly. He entered with intent only to disarm me, for he perceived me a threat. Arcanus is as much to blame, for the spell he cast on the sword, or me, for I provoked Lord Ahrnad most effectively, even when he might still have stayed his hand. I encouraged him to continue, when he might have stopped after a single blow. He acted out of frustration and powerlessness, for he sought to protect you from me when you would not be protected. He is not my enemy that I might wish to see him destroyed. Yet I used him as a tool to my own ends, even as the Enemy uses me."

They climbed the stairs, and Aras saw it took no small effort and caused Lunahr pain. Aras looked at him in wonder for his words. "Ahrnad will not love you for speaking well of him. I gave personal order not to harm you, and yet he struck you not once, but many times. So, his act was one of treason, but I realize now it was treason driven by loyalty. He must be punished, but perhaps not in the way I first thought. And you, for your part, have been punished more than enough, I think."

They emerged from the building, and Lunahr squinted against the sunlight which fell softly between the leaves, as if he stared at the naked sun at noon. He gave a glad cry as he saw the towering trees everywhere, above and around them.

One of the King's Guard returned with Jarnath at his side. The King's Guard watched them both nervously.

Jarnath observed Lunahr critically. "You should not be walking, I think. Your arm is broken and it hurts you even to breathe."

Lunahr nodded. "I fear I have cracked a few ribs, although fortunately I do not think I have broken them entirely."

"I spoke with Arcanus before he departed. He feared you might suffer further injury while amongst us and wanted to be sure I would help you to my full ability. I will aid you now with far greater enthusiasm for my work than I felt when I healed you days ago, though I am not sure you were aware of my aid. Then I healed your wounds so you might be strong enough to withstand the foul elixirs I prepared, as I was commanded, to force you to tell us what we needed to know. I took no joy in harming you. It will ease my conscience to know that I can in some small way make amends for the pain I have caused you. Since you are now free from your cell, and able to walk, I would ask you to accompany me so I may examine you fully, and treat you."

"Of course," Lunahr said, looking toward Aras, an expression of hopeful curiosity on his face.

"Go with him now. I will meet you there in a little while. I must wait here for Ahrnad and Leonas," Aras said.

"Thank you," Lunahr said, looking relieved. He left with Jarnath, walking slowly, his eyes fixed on the treetops above.

The King's Guardsman shifted his feet nervously. Aras sighed, but did not speak to him.

A short while later, Alwen approached with Ahrnad at his side. Aras saw that Ahrnad was unarmed. Alwen said, "I wish to inform you, Highness, that Ahrnad surrendered himself to me earlier this morning and reported that he had committed treason before the King's Guardsmen came to arrest him. I was still questioning him regarding the details when they reported your orders to me. Ahrnad is ready to report to a cell. Though he has not asked me to speak for him, Highness, I must. He acted rashly and inappropriately, but he acted out of loyalty and concern for you and your father. He has been overcome by recent events. Not in chains, Highness! Strip him of his command and his weapons, even his freedom if you must, but do not shackle him like an animal for his service to you."

Aras turned to Ahrnad. "You disobeyed my personal command, but I do not believe you did so deliberately. Lord Beryl has spoken on your behalf for leniency, stating that he provoked you. I see now that you have been overwhelmed. You are demoted to Commander, second-in-command of the Combined Guard. You will be locked in a cell for five days. You will be shackled for one day. You will know how it feels to be a helpless prisoner, so you might learn restraint when dealing with others so confined, in the future.

"But I will have you know that Lord Beryl had already been pardoned by my father and me for his attack, and that when you attacked him, he was Guest-of-my-House. I would hear you pledge your loyalty to me, so that I know you will never again disobey my commands." He gestured to the King's Guardsman for his bow, and gave it to Ahrnad.

Ahrnad took it and knelt before him and swore himself to his service. Then Aras took the bow from him and had one of the King's Guardsman escort him to his cell.

He turned to Alwen. "Commander Alwen, you are hereby promoted to Lord of the Guard. There will be a formal ceremony later today, before the Combined Guard, instating you in your new position. Congratulations. You are dismissed."

Lord Alwen hesitated for a moment, as if he wished to speak further, but then bowed stiffly and departed.

Aras stood looking at the trees, pointedly ignoring the King's Guardsmen beside him, who grew more nervous as time passed. Finally, the three other King's Guardsmen came with Leonas in their midst.

LEONAS bowed and said, "Highness, have I done ought wrong? The King's Guard told me I was summoned." He was nervous, for his friend Gaius had overheard some of the King's Guardsmen talking that the High-Prince was in a fell mood, and the dungeon was filling rapidly with King's Guardsmen this morning. As one of the Guard, he had no wish to be incarcerated amongst those of the King's Guard. They were far from friends at the best of times, and they had not forgiven him for standing against them, blocking their target, when they sought to attack the High-Prince's friend, Prince Talon. Aras had always been a friend to the Guard before he left and had seemed just as devoted to them in the woods.

Leonas was relieved when the High-Prince smiled reassuringly at him. Then Aras eyed the four culpable King's Guardsmen around him coolly and told them to report to their cell. They were told they were to remain there for two days, so they might better learn the helplessness of a prisoner, and so they might learn to recognize when one needed their aid.

When they were gone, Aras smiled at Leonas again. "Walk with me," he said and headed toward the Palace and the Healers' Hall.

Aras told Leonas what had transpired earlier. "Lord Beryl needs a bodyguard and a companion. I will also serve as both, but I cannot always be with him. He is kin to Talon, the Man who saved your life and whom you swore to protect in gratitude. Beryl is of the same mettle. He is also cursed under foul wizardry, but also bound by wizardry, now, against doing further harm. He has been pardoned for his crimes by my father and is Guest-of-my-House. Can you be companion and guard to him?"

Leonas considered carefully for a moment. "What of my other duties?"

"There are many who can protect us from the Hill People, but only the two of us to protect Lord Beryl. You will be in my service, as his personal guard. This elevates you above the others in the Guard, for now, and you will be answerable only to me, not even to Lord of the Guard Alwen. I trust that you won't abuse that trust?"

"No, Highness. I am honored by your trust in me. I will guard Lord Beryl with my life," Leonas swore.

Aras smiled again. "Beryl and I will be living in the Guest House from now on, for the foreseeable future. Gather your effects, for you will live there as well."

Leonas bowed and went to do so.

Aras continued on to the Healers' Hall. He saw that the healers had bathed Lunahr as well as treated him. His hair was wet, and he looked and smelled clean. For the first time, Aras began to see the Man Talon had described to him. Lunahr's arm was bound by bandages to his side, and his chest was wrapped and his shirt off. Everywhere large blue and purple bruises covered him. Aras began to think he might have gone too easy on Ahrnad after all.

Lunahr fastened the band of his House about his bicep and slowly struggled into a loose shirt of soft green as Aras watched. The healers had given him new clothes to replace the ones he had been captured in. Aras saw him tuck Talon's letter under the bandages. His empty sleeve hung limply at his side.

"Jarnath is a most skilled healer. He is frustrated with me that I will not allow him to make me sleep until my bruises and ribs and arm heal. But I know the toll that such a healing takes upon the healer. I will not cause him pain. I will not see another suffer for my mistake."

Aras looked at him in silent concern, unsure what to say. Lunahr's personality was so fragile now, his core so badly damaged. He knew he must tread lightly.

"Do not look so serious, Highness. I suffered far worse injury than this when I was captured in the south, and recovered from it, though I remember only the injury. I will try to be more careful in the future."

Aras was both concerned and encouraged. Lunahr was not recovered at all from his earlier injuries. Far from it. His core was far more injured than even his body appeared now. But at least he no longer appeared to be suicidal. Hopefully, with the aid of the Trees and Meloneth and Jarnath, Aras would be able to see Lunahr truly well again. Although it yet remained to be seen whether the Trees and Jarnath could still be trusted.

"If you are finished here, I would like to take you to your new... dwelling." Aras knew it was not "home" to him. "And, on the way, I have such Trees to show you that you needs must smile."

LUNAHR eagerly set out. They exited the Healers' Hall and walked past the Palace, through the gardens, toward the outskirts of the City and the edge of the forest that surrounded it. There was a large clearing carpeted with meadow grass and fragrant flowers in every color of the rainbow, but Lunahr passed them by almost unseeing, so riveted was his gaze to the stand of trees in its center: they were tall and strong, half again as tall as any others he had ever seen of those species. And he had thought the rest of the trees here magnificent! They paled beside these ageless beauties.

ARAS saw the look of rapturous wonder on Lunahr's face and could not help but feel the same. "We call this the Lords' Grove," he said in Elvish, and he spoke with reverence. "Each of us, the thirty-three Lords and Ladies of the Aerta, those you would call *Wood Elves*, has a tree here that we are especially attuned to, although there are thirty-seven trees: they are oak, fir, cedar, birch, maple, elm, ash, sycamore, beech, and chestnut. They were planted millennia ago, when this was still one of our colonies, before our Homeland...." Aras paused awkwardly. He had almost said, "Before our Homeland was destroyed." His father would have his head if ever he spoke those words to a Man.

He sighed and touched his father's tree, a massive oak, gently. "Each of the thirty-three has a name; they are named for the one they are bonded to. This one is Arandrin. He is my father's, the King amongst them." He showed Lunahr Jarnath's cedar, and told Lunahr he was named Aranath, but did not touch him. Then he showed Lunahr the four that were unnamed: they were ash, sycamore, beech, and fir.

LUNAHR was stunned that these trees might be as old as the High-Prince claimed. They should have only lived for hundreds of years, perhaps, were they fortunate enough to, not millennia. But as astonishing as it sounded, he could not doubt Aras's claim. The very air seemed different here, thick with wisdom and age, Power and serenity.

The fir drew Lunahr's eye. Every other tree here was a specimen of perfection of its kind. But the fir was different. Two-thirds of the way up, there was a great burl: the bark was gnarled and twisted, and the trunk had withered and died there. But one of the branches had grown beyond the burl, reaching up toward the sun, past the deformity, and thickened and formed a new trunk with branches of its own, which reached as tall as the other trunks in the Grove.

Lunahr's heart went out to the proud tree as the needles rustled softly in the breeze. But Aras was calling to him, and he tore himself away.

Aras was on the outskirts of the Grove, standing before a slender white birch, smaller than the others and set somewhat apart from them, but no less magnificent. This one he caressed and his face lit with love and joy. "And this one is mine: Aranas. I have missed him." Then he looked pointedly at Lunahr and said, "Touch him."

Lunahr did so, knowing from what Aras had said and what he had seen that he was being granted a great honor, for he thought it might be that normally only a Lord might touch his own tree. He ran his finger lightly along the smooth, white bark.

The leaves of the branches above fluttered slightly, and for a moment, Lunahr thought the tree whispered to him. He smiled at his flight of fancy, but still, he thought, *Thank you, Prince of Trees, for allowing my touch,* before stepping away.

"It is very peaceful here, and very private. You will always be welcome here."

Lunahr thanked Aras, for he knew that Aras had given him a precious gift.

They left the Grove, but Lunahr was surprised to see that they walked toward the forest, for he had thought the High-Prince was leading him to a dwelling. They passed flower-filled gardens and trellises and came to another large stand of trees that Lunahr at first thought was the start of the woods, until he spied a stone building amongst the trees with a stream beside it.

"This we call the Guest House. But as my father does not encourage visitors, we have had none for a long time. You will stay here, as will I, and Leonas, a new friend that you have yet to meet."

Lunahr smiled at the thought of living in such beauty and that he might have not one friend here, but two.

They walked inside. There was a living room with a fire pit in the center, with a hole in the ceiling above that the smoke could exit through. The room was open and airy and uncluttered. There were live plants everywhere and little in the way of furniture. Brightly colored cushions were scattered about a low table, on which a glass wine bottle and two glasses sat. That room opened up into a second, a dining area, with a table laden with food and drink.

Aras showed him the kitchen and the bath and his own room and Leonas's. Lunahr's room was across the hall from Aras's. There were other rooms, too, but they were empty and unassigned.

But his room! There were instruments! Amongst them were a lyre, a mountain dulcimer, a flute, a set of pipes, a mandolin, and even a harpsichord. There was also a writing desk with what looked to be two full quires of paper, and pens and ink and drying sand. There was even a wardrobe full of clothes. It was as if someone who knew him well had put everything here he thought he might wish to have. Lunahr could not help but smile, for it suddenly felt as if he were truly home.

"I am glad you are pleased. Now, will you come eat with me?" Aras asked, sounding hopeful.

Lunahr joined him eagerly. But when they sat at the table, Lunahr looked at the table laden with food and the smile fled his face. He realized he must look as stricken as he felt when Aras asked him what was wrong, the concern naked on his face. "I... I was just remembering. I— there was not much given to me... before. I am overwhelmed."

Aras clasped Lunahr's arm. "Then let me show you the true hospitality of my House. You have experienced us at our worst. Now see us for our best."

Lunahr nodded and tried to eat, but found he could only eat sparingly, although he delighted in the honeyed nectar laid out to drink for them.

"You will recover your strength and your appetite, once your injuries heal," Aras assured him.

Lunahr nodded and managed to eat a little more, for Aras's sake.

"Come, let us walk in the garden," Aras said, and Lunahr rose from the table in relief.

Lunahr thought that the other gardens he had seen were all lovely, but the garden behind the Guest House was beautiful beyond words. They spent the rest of the day there, talking a little, but for the most part in quiet camaraderie. Lunahr felt like a plant himself, one that had been denied sunlight and water for so long it had wilted, but then recovered at the touch of the sun and feel of the rain. Just being there amongst the great beauty renewed his spirit.

As dusk approached, they went inside. The food from lunch had been cleared away and new food brought, and the fare was even more sumptuous than before. Lunahr noted that the table was set for three instead of two, although no one else joined them.

After dinner, Aras led him to the living room and lit a fire. Aras poured wine for them, and Lunahr saw there was a third glass he left empty. He wondered about this other Elf, Leonas, who he might be, and why he might choose to befriend himself to an outcast.

The fire drew his eye. It reminded him of Laren, of all the fires he'd used as a focus for his meditations over the years. Incredible longing and worry should have surged over him, at the thought of Laren. He used to be bound to Laren: for six years he had known the warm reassurance of his presence, and more importantly, he had kept Laren safe. Through his bond he had helped Laren keep the Madness at bay. But they were bound no longer. He should have been frantic with worry for his cousin, his King. Why wasn't he? He felt only a ghost of those feelings. Mostly he just felt empty, numb.

Was it because of everything he had survived, in so short a time? Or was there something wrong with him? Had the Enemy permanently harmed him in some way, other than the compulsion to harm Laren and the others? Had the Enemy done something worse? He knew the thought should frighten him, but it didn't. Instead he felt a horrible, empty void; almost breath-stopping loneliness. He was not sure at all whom he was longing to see, to touch, to taste, but he knew it was not Laren.

A wave of foreign, yet achingly familiar, emotion and sensation rocked Lunahr to his core: terror and delight, panic and joy, pain and pleasure, and burning, all-consuming need and desire. Lunahr leaned closer to the fire, mesmerized by it, drawn like a moth to the glorious blaze. It was so beautiful: the oranges and reds, dancing in a flickering, sinuous pattern, tongues of flame caressing the wood like a lover, the log scorching under the fire's touch until it was ultimately consumed by it, fulfilling its only true purpose, to be fuel for the ravenous flame.

A loud knock on the door shattered the moment of clarity. Lunahr sprang to his feet, a wave of shame and guilt and eager desire cascading over him, his hand reflexively going to Loruthanar's hilt.

With the feel of the warm, familiar leather binding of the hilt in his hand, his pounding heart calmed and his head cleared. He was with Aras, surrounded and protected by the entire might of the Elven Army and Navy. He was not in danger.

ARAS was relieved for the knock. Lunahr had been looking and acting oddly, but he'd not been sure what to do or say. The knock seemed to have broken whatever fell spell he might have been under. Still, he must proceed cautiously, as always.

He extended his senses out beyond the door before opening it and was delighted and relieved to sense a familiar presence: Leonas. He opened the door eagerly and greeted him warmly. "You need not knock, Leonas. This is your house now, as well as ours."

Leonas looked sheepish at the gentle teasing.

"Leonas, this is Lord Beryl, Captain of the Watch. Beryl, this is Captain Leonas, Guardsman, on detached duty from the Navy in service to my House. Come, the night is yet young, and the wine bottle is still full."

THEY sat, and Leonas and Beryl surreptitiously studied each other. Leonas thought that by the look of him, Beryl desperately needed a bodyguard, although he could not imagine him not being able to defend himself with at least some prowess and still be kin to Talon. Their eyes locked unintentionally. Leonas smiled, and it looked like some of the tension drained from Beryl. He seemed to relax at least a little and smiled slightly in return.

"We missed you at dinner," Aras said.

"Forgive me, but my Commander, Daras, needed to speak with me one last time about the Hill People's attack. Lord of the Guard Ahrnad had been very upset with my patrol for not… securing… the prisoners, before leaving." He had actually been angered that they had left the area without slaying the foe to a Man, but he did not think it appropriate to say so in front of Beryl.

"His successor, Lord Alwen, was no more pleased. I was required to explain to him the exact course of events, as I'd reported it before to former Lord of the Guard Ahrnad. Commander Daras is in a bad position because the Hill People had doubled back after we left and retrieved their fallen and their wounded and their weapons, so when Nolas and the others had arrived, there was little left to recover. But, we have not even seen scouts since that attack, so I think perhaps it is best; they have seen us now in fuller force and find we are not the easy target they thought. We won't be surprised in ambush like that again."

He saw that Beryl was watching him intently now, and wondered if perhaps this was the first he was hearing of the war with the Hill People.

Aras sighed. "So they both fault me for wounding sixteen Men when I could as easily have slain them?"

"No, Highness. I mean, I wasn't really sure what the state of the enemy was at the time, or exactly what you or Prince Talon had done, other than you hurt them enough to drive them off, and there were certainly more fallen than my patrol accounted for. But I made it clear that we left under your orders while you were hastening to your father's side, and it was not our place to delay you."

Leonas saw Beryl tense at the mention of Prince Talon and then pale at the mention of the High-King, and he winced at his incautious tongue. He turned to Beryl. "My patrol was ambushed in the woods, by a war party over four times our number, the day that the High-Prince and your kinsman, Prince Talon, came. They came upon us on the brink of defeat and succored us. Prince Talon blocked a blade that would have been my death. I owe my life to him. I did what I could to repay my debt to him while he was here." He smiled at the memory, which was a source of pride.

"Leonas placed himself between Talon and twenty-four King's Guards' arrows," Aras said wryly, and then sipped from his glass.

"I am surprised they did not shoot through you to get to Talon," Beryl said, and his voice was bitter.

"I think they did so in deference more to the High-Prince's horse, who also shielded him, than to me," Leonas said with a laugh. "Also, my High-Prince's tongue was faster than their hands." He grew sober. "But I fear I have made the King's Guard my enemy, and there is little enough love between the Army and the Navy in any case." He swallowed heavily for saying so, for he had been so intent upon Lord Beryl, he had forgotten for a moment that the High-Prince was there as well.

But Aras nodded as if not surprised to hear such a thing. "I have been troubled by what I have observed since my return. Relations between the two have become even more antagonistic. I would speak with you more of these things, later."

Leonas nodded, wishing he had managed to miss the wine as well as dinner. He was still intimidated at having been singled out by the High-Prince.

Aras studied Beryl, whose attention seemed to be elsewhere, in apparent concern. "Come, we have all had a long day. I think it is time for sleep."

Leonas thought the High-Prince might be as uncomfortable as he was at the turn of their conversation. Leonas rose quickly, glad to be removed from the awkward position he had put himself in.

The High-Prince showed him to the room where his belongings had already been moved, with Beryl trailing after them. He bowed good-night to them both and then closed the door in relief, though he did not seal it all the way. He kept it open a crack so he might better be able to hear if there was need for him for any reason during the night.

Leonas looked about the room and wondered again how he had managed to get himself drafted into personal service to the High-Prince. Being in the Navy was dangerous enough without having been singled out for friendship by the High-Prince. He was painfully aware such friends in the past had the habit of dying in short order.

He sighed. If it was his fate to die for Aras, he would, in a heartbeat. Were it not for him, Laedrin might have done far worse to the Navy. Things had gone from bad to worse in the High-Prince's absence. It had seemed to them that the High-King was punishing them all for his son leaving.

LUNAHR was not eager for bed at all. He bade Aras good-night and closed his door resolutely. He left the lamp lit and took off his boots. The thought of stripping off his clothes set his heart racing for some reason. When he tried to unlace his shirt anyway, his hand began shaking so violently he could not even grasp the lace, let alone undo the simple bow.

He lay down fully clothed and stared at the ceiling, willing his eyes to close. He tried to find calm, breathing slowly, thinking of the garden, the trees, the Lords' Grove. Sleep had never in the past held terror for him. It should not now. He was no longer in that dark hole, although he was still in pain. Jarnath had been very insistent he take something for it, but he had accepted only the most mild treatment. He needed his mind to be clear.

He pictured the Grove and imagined himself under the branches of those great trees again. His breath steadied, and he dared to close his eyes.

ARAS had fallen asleep easily, the relaxed sleep of one who has successfully completed a number of difficult and satisfying tasks and is finally home. But his sleep was abruptly interrupted by the sound of screaming. Lunahr!

Aras snatched up his swords, tore open his door, and darted across the hall to Lunahr's room. He cast caution to the winds and flung the door open using his Power so he could instantly attack whatever was assaulting Lunahr. But Lunahr was alone, sitting up in his bed, wide-eyed and terrified, clutching his chest in pain and shaking violently.

Leonas ran into the room only a moment after Aras, his sword also drawn, but he stopped upon seeing the two of them were not in any danger.

Aras waved him away and Leonas obeyed and left without question.

Aras laid down his blades and cautiously sat next to Lunahr upon the bed, unsure what to do or say to calm him. He had comforted Lunahr in the cell by holding him. Aras remembered the feeling of Talon's strong arms around him, comforting him when he had been in need, and that he had likewise soothed Talon. He hesitantly held open his arms, unsure how Lunahr might react to him now, and was relieved when Lunahr dove into his embrace, until he began sobbing violently.

Aras patted his back, awkwardly at first, but it felt so right, so natural to comfort Lunahr, to hold him. Lunahr was desperate for the physical contact. Lunahr drew great, shuddering breaths, hissing in pain with each one as his cracked ribs protested.

Aras wanted to heal him, both his body and his spirit, but he was leery of using his Power when Lunahr's core was in such turmoil, afraid he might do something wrong, that he might harm him due to his inexperience. "You are safe here. None will harm you, I swear it."

When Lunahr calmed enough that he could speak, between gasping breaths, he told Aras he had fallen asleep and had a dream. He could not remember it, only that it had been dark and horrible, that he had awoken with the feeling of being a hunted animal that had been trapped and about to die.

"In... in the cell... it was like this, also... the few times they would let me sleep.... I still would try not to... because always I would sleep a little... and waken screaming. When my body was so tired it would betray me with sleep, I even hoped they would come with their tortures, for with the pain, I could think of nothing else. I had hoped here I would not—and now it hurts even to scream, and I am so very tired.

I only slept that unnatural sleep that Arcanus afflicted me with… and Laren would have me promise sleep to him, but I cannot sleep! I will never sleep again!"

Aras asked Lunahr if the healers had not given him something for the pain, and he nodded. Aras told him that it would also help him sleep, but Lunahr shook his head violently.

"No, it is dangerous for me. The Watch has learned to live with pain. Pain is sometimes a friend. It keeps your wits sharper in times of danger. Even in sleep, we can sense danger and waken in time to fight it. Such medicines dull the pain, but also the senses and the mind. And something searches for me in my dreams. Something hunts for me. Arcanus said the Enemy cannot reach into this place, that it is safe for me here. But I think the Enemy tries. I will not sleep. Perhaps in daylight, under the sun and the trees, I may find rest, but not here. Go back to your rest, Highness. I will not waken you again tonight with my screams."

Aras shook his head. "I will not leave you alone in the darkness, even awake in a lit room. Come, let us rekindle the fire. I will tell you stories of Talon, and stories of Hunter, what I remember of them from what Talon told me."

LUNAHR gazed at him in relief and gratitude, for he had not wanted to stand alone against the darkness. When they opened the door, Leonas's door opened as well, and he looked out at them.

"Beryl cannot sleep. We are going to light a fire," Aras said.

Leonas looked at a loss for a moment.

"Come, join us," Aras invited.

Lunahr stiffened, but then he saw Leonas smile. "Please join us," he echoed, for he did not like to show his weakness, but he liked Leonas already, and this might strengthen their budding friendship.

ARAS lit the fire while Leonas poured the wine.

"I wish I could offer you *bacara* to help relax you," Aras said. "But I did not think to ask Talon for any before he left, although he is at the moment quite well supplied."

"No, thank you. I prefer air I can breathe," Lunahr said, and the face he made was so like the way Aras had felt when he tried it that he had to laugh.

At his laughter, Lunahr relaxed, just a little.

"But Talon told me all your kin smoke it, although he said few outside the Dwarven Lands do."

Lunahr sighed. "At the time I left, they would not allow it for my age, though I had tried it in secret, of course. I was told by Heather that all of them did so, at least once, and often many times, before they came-of-age. But unlike the rest, I grew violently ill from only the very first lungful. It was only one of the ways in which I differed from the rest.

"I would not eat meat, even as a small child. I refused to cut my hair. I preferred learning to play instruments to learning to fight with the sword or bow. Fa… Hunter used to tell me that was why I excelled at both at such a young age: he said I knew I must get proficient quickly, so I would have more time to spend learning the dulcimer and the flute. They used to tease me for my eccentricity. Yet another example of my Elvish ways." He grew more melancholy, at the thought of happier days amongst his kin.

"Come, you promised me stories of my kin. I would like to hear them. It will make me feel they are still close to me when they are so far away."

Aras told Lunahr briefly of his travels the first two weeks, when he traveled alone. He described the village of Men he avoided, which he said he later learned was called Gower. He told them of the wolven attack and his battle against them, and both Lunahr and Leonas were completely enraptured. But when Aras told of his awakening and described the Man who tended him in brutal detail, eyes alight with the memory, Lunahr actually laughed. Aras saw him transformed as amusement lit his face and his eyes danced.

"Poor Talon! He has low enough opinion of himself sometimes." Then the light left his eyes and the laughter died, but there was still a fond smile on his face.

Aras continued his tale, but started to skip over the part of Dewalaren's illness, as he himself had done in telling the tale in Gower. But Lunahr noticed and was upset by it.

"There is more that you are not telling me. Don't you trust me to hear it?"

Aras studied his face and said, "Of course I trust you. I had thought it might upset you to hear." Then he described his cousin's illness and healing, and Lunahr indeed looked disturbed.

"But that doesn't make any sense. Talon doesn't get sick," Lunahr argued.

"That is what he tried to tell me when we both could see otherwise," Aras said, with a wry smile.

But Lunahr persisted. "No, I mean, he has never been sick. Talon is far older than he looks, and in all his many decades, he has never once taken ill. We did not think he could. Though the Amontir are a hearty breed, each of us has, at one time or another, fallen ill, except for Talon, even during the plague that claimed my parents and so many others. We did not think illness could touch him, because of…." He trailed off awkwardly.

Aras thought he knew what Lunahr had been about to say, although he was not monitoring his thoughts. Talon's Power, and possibly the King's Sword, protected him.

"Then perhaps it truly was the rain. Talon told me that when he was out in the storm, it changed at one point: the wind blew from the east and the air grew much colder, and the clouds went from gray to green, and the rain stung like hail. He said he took shelter after a few drops hit him, even though he was already drenched, and had felt the urge to do so sooner. He later thought that there was something unnatural about that storm."

"Then it was fortunate for both your sakes you found one another when you did. For the wolven or the storm or both might have overcome him," Lunahr said, and he sounded serious and brooding again.

Aras clasped his arm in concern. "Curse my tongue! I was afraid it might upset you, but I did not realize how much. I almost wish now that I'd kept silent, except that you remembered yourself for a moment and laughed, and it brought my heart great joy to see it."

Lunahr made an obvious effort and smiled again. "Please, dawn is still so far away. Forgive me for being such poor company. Please tell me more." His eyes were pleading, now.

Aras sighed and continued, leaving out nothing, but tempering his words, especially regarding finding his sword and what had transpired at the two Markers, lest what Lunahr heard further upset him. By the time he was done, dawn was just breaking. With the rising of the sun, some of the tension left Lunahr.

THERE was a knock upon the front door and breakfast was brought in for them. Leonas busied himself laying it out for them, relieved to feel useful, even for a moment. He had done little more than offer his presence to the aid of the High-Prince and Lord Beryl. Leonas marveled that so much had happened to his High-Prince in such a short time. Time seemed to pass more quickly outside their Wood.

They all ate and then changed clothes for the day. Beryl said he would like to go for a walk. The High-Prince said he needed to go to the Palace for a while and that Leonas should accompany Lord Beryl wherever he went.

They left the house, and Leonas let Lord Beryl take the lead. But when Leonas saw that Lord Beryl headed for the Lords' Grove, he was nervous, for he knew that it was a place sacred to the Lords and forbidden to all others, save the King's Guard. But Lord Beryl strode with such purpose, Leonas did not speak against it until they were almost under the Trees. "Forgive me, Lord Beryl, but we cannot enter here. These Trees are special. We call it the Lords' Grove. Only the Lords and some of the King's Guard may enter here."

"Ah," Beryl said. "I suspected as much when Aras brought me here yesterday. He told me it was a special place, a peaceful one, but he also said I might come here when I wished. I take it that is a rare privilege?"

Leonas nodded. "Sometimes, very rarely, an honored guest comes here, and is allowed to enter. And the High-Prince has named you Guest-of-his-House."

"He also named three of the trees for me, and asked me to touch his own." Beryl seemed to be eyeing him carefully for his reaction.

Leonas stared at him, unable to hide his amazement. "But in all our history, no one has ever touched a named Tree that is not named for him! I did not think the Trees would allow it."

"I have need of the peace of the Grove, Leonas. I think Aras knows that, and he told you to come with me."

"I have always wanted to be so honored, but I knew as one of the Navy I never could. My father is Aerta, what you would call a *Wood Elf*, but my mother is Oceana, a *River Elf*," Leonas admitted, fierce pride mixed with shame upon his face at his mixed parentage. "The Army would not have me for my mixed blood, although the Wood has always called to me more loudly than the River."

"Then walk with me now," Beryl said and went on.

Leonas swallowed and followed him. They both walked worshipfully amongst the Trees.

LUNAHR stood before the unnamed fir again, studying it for a long time in all its beauty and deformity. Then he whispered to it softly. "I am Lunahr, son of Quilahr, Lord of House of Eagles, of Amontir. I would like to lie here, if you'll allow it."

The slightest of breezes rustled the needles at the very top of the tree as Lunahr watched and listened. He smiled and lay down at the base of the tree and folded his arms under his head and was asleep within moments.

Lunahr awoke at dusk, not remembering when he had felt so rested. He had no memory of dreams, either foul or fair. As he stood, he realized that Leonas had apparently sat watch over him the entire time he slept, and his face flushed. "I'm sorry. I thought you might have gone. I have never before been able to sleep when someone watches me, but I slept well indeed. You have missed your lunch and must have been very bored."

But Leonas shook his head and smiled. "I have waited my whole life to be here. I could sit and watch these Trees forever."

Lunahr smiled at him and then thanked the Tree softly. They both headed back to the Guest House.

Chapter 9
The Avatar

DEWALAREN met up with Arcanus after leaving Aras, and they headed for the stables together. When they entered the stable yard, Dewalaren saw that Janahar was at the back end of a paddock that adjoined it. She came galloping up when she saw him, and to his delight, she cleared the fence that separated them effortlessly in a graceful, perfectly executed jump and nickered a greeting, bumping her head into his arm, demanding to be caressed. Dewalaren laughed at the welcome, all his concerns thrust aside for the moment as he greeted her just as warmly, whispering to her.

The stable master approached them. The serious expression on his face softened at the obvious affection between the mare and Man. "Welcome, Prince Talon. The High-Prince told us you would be departing today and were to be given his horse for your mount. She has been fed and watered and groomed and is ready for you. He mentioned that you might also like the *saddle* and *bridle*?" He pronounced the Common words carefully and without negative inflection, though Dewalaren knew he must find them both offensive and repulsive. There were no Elven equivalents for the tack Men burdened their mounts with, both of which were crafted of leather.

"Yes, thank you. I am very pleased to hear the *bridle* is here as well. I had not thought to ask the High-Prince for it. If you show me where they and the *saddle* blanket are, I can put them on Janahar. I apologize for causing objects made of animal hide to be brought into your stables. I certainly would not want you to have to endure touching them and apologize if you were required to handle them earlier."

The Elf seemed surprised and pleased at his consideration.

"I trust the High-Prince might have mentioned that I will also require a mount? I need your fastest, strongest steed," Arcanus interjected.

The stable master hesitated. "When I spoke with the High-Prince, I had thought to give you Moonshadow. But now I do not know which horse to give you, Honored One. Our finest steed is Stormcloud. He has only just returned to us, but he has been ill-used and is in a foul temper. He has attacked all who have tried to touch him. We regret that he does not seem fit for you to ride, for he is exceptional, even for our stables. We had lent him to your compatriot, the Wizard Magus."

ARCANUS eyed him sharply. "When did Magus ride him?"

"When he left us, weeks ago, the day after we were told the High-Prince had been killed. He said he needed our fastest steed. I told him Stormcloud was our finest messenger but was also trained as a war-horse and had a temper. But Stormcloud accepted him as a rider easily enough, and they left at a gallop. That was the last we saw of Stormcloud until this morning, when he returned to us riderless. He is in the open yard beyond the paddock. He eagerly accepted food and water, but only when laid out for him. He will not let any approach. We have been unable to check him for injury or to groom him."

"Take us to him," Arcanus commanded. He might be able to learn what had happened to Marcus, if he had been felled while on the horse. Perhaps the horse might even lead them to where Marcus had last been, before they were separated. All he had known before was that Marcus had been east of the Coroden near a river. He felt a sudden flare of hope.

They were only able to get within thirty feet of Stormcloud before he shied away from them. "Leave us," Arcanus commanded the stable master. The Elf did so with a final look at the horse.

"Dewalaren, you have the blood of the House of Horses in you, from your grandmother. You have no small talent with horses. Can you calm him so we might approach? We might learn much if only I could touch him."

"OF COURSE," Dewalaren said. He began speaking softly in Elvish to the horse, weaving his Power carefully into the words. Stormcloud tossed his head and shied away from him, as if he sensed what he was trying to do. He was surprised that Stormcloud fought him. It was as if he had felt such Power before, and it held terror for him. Dewalaren spoke more firmly and layered his Power more heavily into his words.

"I will not harm you, King of Horses. I wish only to speak with you, and to ride you, if you will allow it. You need not fear me. I would see no harm come to one such as you, ever," Dewalaren soothed. He felt the horse begin to calm. He approached him slowly, wishing he had thought to obtain a treat for him from the stable master. But perhaps the touch of his hand would be enough. Or better, of a brush.

"If you have a brush or a comb in your pack, Arcanus, I might use it upon him. I think it would help," Dewalaren said, keeping his tone soft and even so as not to startle Stormcloud. He approached slowly, trying to appear nonthreatening, hoping to stroke him with his hand until Arcanus produced the brush. Stormcloud watched him warily but allowed his approach. Dewalaren was only feet from him when he shied away again. Dewalaren was impressed by the horse's will, that he could resist his Power. He was truly a magnificent animal.

Arcanus handed him his brush, and patiently, Dewalaren began again. On his fourth try, he finally reached Stormcloud. He stroked him gently and felt him tremble under his touch. But he began to calm as Dewalaren began to brush him, removing the burs and brambles that had adhered to him on his journey back to the Elves. All the while, he continued to speak to the animal, using his Power sparingly.

"I think it would be safe for you to approach, if you do so slowly and nonthreateningly," he told Arcanus.

ARCANUS approached them both, forcing himself to do so slowly as Dewalaren recommended when he wanted to pounce upon the horse and rip the information he sought from his mind. This beast must tell him where Marcus was! He followed Dewalaren's continued instructions and was soon touching Stormcloud. He directed his Power toward the horse. He sensed the shadow Marcus had left upon the horse's bare back: desperation and fear turned first to confusion, then to panic and despair, and finally to sheer terror, so strong he was driven to his knees by it. Dewalaren's strong hands caught him as he fell, and Stormcloud shied away from them again.

"We must... we must get him to lead us to where Magus was," Arcanus said, fighting to get to his feet. Instinctively, he reached for Dewalaren to renew his strength, drawing back from the shield surrounding him just in time. He must not try to penetrate that shield again until he knew more. "We must ride. Do you think you can tame Stormcloud enough to accept you as rider? I do not think he would tolerate me."

DEWALAREN nodded, reluctant though he was to have Arcanus ride Janahar. He wondered at his reluctance. Aras had entrusted his mare to him, yet surely Arcanus would do her no harm?

After some more patient attention, Dewalaren was able to get Stormcloud to allow him to mount. He was surprised when Arcanus mounted Janahar bareback. He had never seen Arcanus ride without saddle or bridle before. He had not known he could. "Instruct him to retrace his path and return to where he parted from Magus," Arcanus commanded.

"I will try. He seems remarkably intelligent. But I do not know how successful we will be."

Dewalaren set a slow, steady pace. He wanted to conserve Stormcloud's strength. He did not know how well or poorly he had eaten these past weeks, left to forage on his own. At least he'd not had a bit in his mouth to hamper his feeding.

Dewalaren was surprised when, instead of turning left, as he expected, at the juncture of the Sarashen River with the Tahir River in the Elven Wood, Stormcloud headed right, up the Tahir. When Arcanus questioned him, Dewalaren assured him that Stormcloud was adamant as to the direction he had come from. He made sure Stormcloud would not bolt and then dismounted, casting about for tracks in the soft riverbank. He found the hoofprints he sought more easily than he expected. "It truly appears he might have come this way. Let's ride on for a while, and I'll check for his tracks periodically to ensure he remembers correctly." They rode on, angling further and further north.

"But why would Magus have gone this way?" Arcanus questioned. "It makes no sense for him to have... confusion. Magus's confusion, which I sensed when I touched Stormcloud. The Enemy was already attacking him, even here, in their Wood, so close to Nalea, influencing him, leading him astray."

Dewalaren shivered. "Are you certain? If He was so powerful, could He not instead be leading us astray or influencing Stormcloud now? No, there are the tracks clearly marking his return. Still, the thought is unsettling." Although there was the pallenteum tree surrounding his core; Aras was protecting him. But surely Aras would not be powerful enough to protect him from Incuban himself? He was an Elf, not a wizard.

How could Aras protect him at all? Or bond to him? Dewalaren opened his mouth to ask Arcanus about it, but the question died stillborn upon his lips. No. Better not to speak of it now when Arcanus was already so agitated. At times his mentor had an impressive temper, though he seldom displayed it, and he was under much stress. There would be time to speak of it later.

They continued along the riverbank of the Tahir for the rest of the day. Stormcloud showed no signs of tiring, and Janahar paced him effortlessly. But once night fell, with the tree branches shading the ground from the moonlight, it was too dangerous to continue. Dewalaren called for a rest, and Arcanus reluctantly agreed.

Dewalaren dismounted and took his pack off his back, wishing for Janahar's absent saddle and saddlebags as he stretched the aching muscles in his shoulders and back. His pack was heavier than he was recently accustomed to carrying, and he seldom rode. He opened it, excavating for what they would need to make camp and eat dinner, and he was grateful for the supplies Aras had generously included. There were nuts and dried vegetables, in addition to a full half-dozen loaves of *raeta*. They had provisions for weeks. There were thankfully also four full water pouches. They had been drinking from Arcanus's and refilling it from the river periodically as he studied the tracks in different locations. They ate a late, cold dinner, and then Arcanus went to sleep, at Dewalaren's urging, while he stayed up and groomed and fed the horses and then kept watch.

He was worried about Arcanus. He had never seen such desperation in him before. His thoughts strayed to Aras. He had only just left him, but he already missed him fiercely. Inevitably, his thoughts turned to Lunahr, as he had last seen him, sobbing in despair in the cell. But he would not be in the cell now. Aras had promised to free him, to do more, to care for him, even to heal him. Dewalaren feared Lunahr might never be healed, that he might live and die bound by the Wood about Nalea, unable to leave, unable ever again to see his kin without being driven to madness. He forced those thoughts away lest they paralyze him. He wanted nothing more than to mount Janahar and ride back to them both, but he could not. His duty lay here, with Arcanus. He expected to need the solace of a fire but was relieved when he did not. The warmth and light of Aras's tree was, for the moment at least, enough.

They were on the move again at first light. They rode the entire day at a steady pace, speaking little, stopping only long enough for the horses to graze and to eat lunch themselves. Once they emerged from the Elven Wood onto the grasslands, they were able to make better time, though Dewalaren was careful not to push their horses. Both had undergone long journeys recently.

Finally, in the early evening, they came upon the juncture with the Methris River. Stormcloud headed left, downriver. They continued to ride along this new riverbank. Dusk approached and night fell. This time, they kept riding by moonlight, until Dewalaren insisted they must all rest once more. At first he thought Arcanus was going to argue the point. In fact, for a moment, he thought his mentor might fly into a rage, but he restrained himself and agreed Dewalaren's suggestion was the only rational course.

They ate a cold dinner again, and again Arcanus slept, though fitfully, it seemed. Dewalaren both could and would not, not when they were seeking one whom the Enemy had already claimed. They might well be riding into a trap.

Dewalaren longed for Aras's company as he kept watch. He would much rather be in Nalea, in Aras's arms, in his bed. He was a fool to think so, even for a moment. It should be Elanara he pined for, that he longed to see. But it was not her embrace he missed, her smiles, her laughter. She had done little enough of all three when they were together. She had been nothing like the sister Elavar had spoken so fondly of.

Elavar. Was he still alive? Were his parents? Or had Riviera already fallen? From what Lunahr had told them, he had not been in Riviera when he was captured, but by now, the Enemy might certainly have advanced so far. But surely those in Nalea would know if Riviera and Loatia had fallen. Wouldn't they? Aras had certainly tried to mobilize aid, through his letter to the King of Tanieria. But would it come too late? Had Aras or his father sent troops from Nalea to reinforce the two endangered Kingdoms? He had not thought to ask Aras before he left and he had been distracted while there, by Lunahr, by Arcanus.

Something hot and wet brushed the back of his neck, and he leapt clear and drew Kathalanar, expecting to see a host of Revenants had somehow snuck up on him while he was distracted. Janahar snorted and huffed accusingly at him, and he almost fell to his knees in relief. She had been the one to touch him. It was her lips upon his neck he'd felt. She'd sensed his distress and come to comfort him, and he'd drawn against her. He shook his head in disgust at himself and sheathed the Sword, thankful he had not cried out and wakened Arcanus, and that he had not already been awake to witness it. "Forgive me, Beautiful One. Come here and allow me to return your gesture," he said, holding out his hand.

She walked to him and butted him hard in the shoulder with her nose, nearly knocking him to the ground, and he laughed softly. "I am suitably chastised, Lady." He began stroking her affectionately, lavishing all the warmth and attention upon her that he was in need of himself, and to his joy, she whickered and nuzzled against him and lipped his hair affectionately. "I am glad you are with me, and that you are not jealous of my riding Stormcloud instead of you. If it were my choice, I would choose you, though he is quite magnificent as well. He would be a good mate for you, did you not have eyes only for Kandahar."

At her friend's name, she let out a huff of air that sounded poignantly and surprisingly like a sigh.

"Forgive me for reminding you that she is not at your side where she belongs, and for separating the two of you in the first place. I would not have, had the need not been so great. But I promise you, I will see you reunited with her, though it might take a while."

She nuzzled him again, as if she understood every word. He thought she well might, if she truly was of Aralon. The steeds of Aralon were as remarkable as those of the Elves for their intelligence and demeanor. Rolin had been in Aralon. Was he there still? Did he yet live? Both Farad and Lunahr lived, when he'd thought both lost. He only hoped his other kinsmen also survived and that they had endured far less horror than either of them.

Janahar butted his other shoulder and he smiled. "You are right. I have no right to be so melancholy and grim when you are here. Forgive me again. Allow me to groom you, to make up for my earlier lack of attention." Janahar nickered in contentment, and he dug out his brush and began grooming her as promised. When he was done, he gave Stormcloud the same attention, even as he kept an eye out for trouble.

THEY set out again the next morning. But they only traveled for a few miles when Stormcloud stopped abruptly and would go no further. Dewalaren used his Power to ascertain why and told Arcanus in surprise, "This is the spot. This is where he left Magus, where he last saw him. There is an image in his mind. It is so strong even I can see it. Magus is lying upon the Road." He looked over at Arcanus, compassion in his eyes, and swallowed hard. "He is screaming." He dismounted and walked to the spot, and Arcanus joined him.

ARCANUS knelt in the dust, placing both hands palm downward on the ground. His eyes welled with tears, which flowed unchecked down his face. He sensed Marcus with painful clarity: his terror, revulsion, ecstasy, agony, and horror. He knew for certain now that the Enemy had taken him. Marcus had been attacked over and over, weakened almost to the point of death. And Selene. She was here as well.

He sensed her terror, desperation, lust, hunger, and then her unnatural strength, the flare of Power, and the imprint of four Men. She'd fed upon them, all of them, and that was not the worst. She had not done so as he would have, but as Pyrfier would have. He collapsed into the dust, sobbing. He was too late. Both Marcus and Selene were lost to him.

DEWALAREN witnessed Arcanus's collapse in dread and reached for him. "Arcanus, please, what have you seen? Tell me how I might help you!"

Arcanus's voice, when he spoke, was chilling, broken and gravelly. "We are too late. My pupils were my one hope for the future, but now they are gone. There is only one way you might help me now. I am old, Dewalaren, and my Power is waning. I have been battling Incuban for two and a half centuries now. I will not lose, I must not lose. But I have drained myself dangerously aiding Lunahr because I know what he means to you, not only as a Man, but also to you as the King. Lunahr is next in line for your throne, after Farad, unless you bear heirs. And Farad will not survive much longer. He has been too damaged, too many times. His core is terrible to look upon. He is nearly spent."

Dewalaren wanted to argue with him, but he could not. He had not seen Farad's core, even when they had been bound together; Farad had always kept him at a distance. And outside of Athanark, he could not view it, for Aras's tree that bound him.

"How might I aid you? What do you need from me? You need only ask," Dewalaren urged.

"Honesty," Arcanus replied curtly.

Dewalaren was taken aback. "I have never been other than honest with you."

"You must tell me of the tree that binds your core, that blinds me to you."

Dewalaren was surprised. How could Arcanus know of the tree, unless he had viewed his core? But he would not have done so without first obtaining permission, would he? Dewalaren felt sudden fear. "What is it you are asking?"

"You have given yourself to another, Dewalaren. You have sealed yourself off from my aid, my protection. You have put yourself and all your people in danger. **WHO HOLDS YOU IN HIS POWER**?" Arcanus demanded to know, his gaze intent upon Dewalaren's face as he wove his Power into his words.

"I... I am not held," Dewalaren denied, as unbeknownst to him, Arcanus's Power battered against the tree that sheltered his core. The terror in his heart was turning to dread. He was held, he was bound, he was helpless. No, he was safe, safer than he had ever been. He was in no danger from Aras. Aras would never hurt him. Would he?

Doubt crept into his mind again. Aras had forged the first link, the vine, while he slept, while he was helpless. He had feared it at first, but moments later he had accepted it. Why? What did he know of Aras that would make him trust Aras so? He had not even known he was the High-Prince, until Farad's stolen message had forced his hand and he had revealed himself as such. Aras had been bringing him to Nalea, without Dewalaren knowing whose company he rode in, while all the while Aras knew how much his father hated all Men.

When the tree had encased his core, his first thought had been that Arcanus might aid them. Yet again, moments later, his mind had changed. Arcanus had suddenly seemed to be the danger, then. Arcanus, who had been known and trusted for centuries, advisor and protector to him, his father, and his father's father, back to at least seven generations of Kings before them.

How old is Arcanus? a soft voice whispered in his mind. The thought sent a sudden chill through him. Arcanus could not be so old! Ten generations? Ten lifetimes? Amontiri lifetimes? That would mean Arcanus was at least two thousand years old, perhaps two thousand five hundred! Even the Elves did not live so long! Why had his father never questioned it?

Your father was never safe from him, the voice whispered.

Safe? Safe from Arcanus? But Arcanus was not the Enemy! And there was a voice now, in his mind, where there should be none. It was the voice that should be feared! The Enemy, Incuban, worked through such means.

Why had Aras been in the woods for him to save, so far from his home? Why had he himself fallen ill for two days? Had Aras drained his life from him, almost to death, as Incuban did when he fed upon his captives? Had Aras raped his core, instead of his body? Like Incuban would have, had Aras so twisted him that he would love Aras, when he should revile and despise him?

Dewalaren was trembling now; he could not stop it. He fell to his knees as knives of fire lanced his temple. He was not safe! He clutched his head in agony. It felt as if it would split in two.

DEWALAREN was oblivious to the soft thuds as Stormcloud and Janahar both fell lifelessly to the ground under Arcanus's hands as he drained them of their life to fuel his Power so he could fight against the one who held Dewalaren in his thrall.

"The wizard who holds you in his Power fears me, Dewalaren. He sees I will free you from him. He would rather see you dead than release his hold upon you. A name, Dewalaren! **I MUST HAVE HIS NAME, HIS TRUE NAME, IF I AM TO SAVE YOU.**" Arcanus's voice echoed with Power.

Dewalaren did not see Arcanus's eyes burn with crimson fire as he fought for control of him, nor feel the strong arms gripping him. He could feel nothing beyond the agony in his head. Dewalaren could scarcely breathe as the name was forced from his tongue. "High-Prince Aras, son of High-King Laedrin of Nalea," he gasped.

Arcanus was momentarily surprised, but then his eyes blazed with victory. Aras was in Nalea, two day's journey from Dewalaren, and he did not know Arcanus's true name.

Arcanus focused the full force of his Power, drawing upon the lives he had drained from the horses and the strength he'd stolen from Dewalaren to add to what he had gotten from Jarnath in Nalea. He aimed a great gout of flame at the pallenteum tree surrounding Dewalaren's core, channeling it down the trunk to the roots so it might burn along the lengths of them and incinerate the one they led to.

But his fire unexpectedly met a funnel of wind that effortlessly sucked the fire from about the tree and snuffed it out. Then the tornado ripped through Arcanus's wards, through all his age-old defenses, carving a great gash down the center of his core.

A terrifying voice ridiculed Arcanus in his agony, in his terror. *"Foolish One! That is not my true name, Escolier!"*

In a blind panic, Arcanus tore his hands away from Dewalaren, who collapsed into the dirt. Arcanus stumbled back from him and leapt into the air in a cascade of lightning, using his remaining strength to fly, to flee as far from Dewalaren as he could.

DEWALAREN heard Arcanus's screams of agony fade into the distance as he lay upon the cold ground trembling, as weak as a newborn kitten. He had heard the battle. The frightening voice was Aras's. He'd recognized it. Aras had tricked him and tortured him and driven Arcanus away.

The agony was gone, but in its place was terrifying weakness. He had scarcely enough strength left to breathe. After all the many times he had battled to live, it was not fair that he should die alone, in the middle of nowhere, betrayed by one he had loved.

A warm, soft breeze blew against his abused core, a gentle whisper upon it. *Do not fear me, Dewalaren. I will not harm you. I have not, I would not. You have been deceived, but not by me. Your father, Arcanus, has been King of Lies since long before Incuban came. I have learned much while his defenses were breached. He created the Amontir, combining his own essence with that of trees and beasts and Men, nearly three thousand years ago out of his loneliness, but also so that he might feed upon you, if ever the Power of the Ring waned. You, who draw your Power from the very sun itself. Then Incuban came and stole the Ring from him through Ebonar. But it was stolen in turn by your grandfather Idare and then lost to all. Now Arcanus's need is great, his fear is great. Arcanus has sired Marcus to feed upon, for your people are almost spent. Let me restore what he has taken from you.*

Who are you? Dewalaren gasped in his mind. He did not have strength enough even to give voice to the question, were the disembodied voice here.

I am Aras, your friend. One who loves you, the voice said, somehow managing to sound hurt, even as it vibrated with strength.

Dewalaren would have shaken his head if he had the strength to. *No. If Arcanus and Incuban both are King of Lies, you are Prince of Lies. Even your name is a lie. I want nothing from you.*

I have never lied to you, Dewalaren. I would not. I told you Aras was not my given name, but only what those who hold my trust call me. Not even my own father knows my name, though he does not suspect that he does not. Please, Dewalaren, you must let me help you. The cold, distant voice changed. A new chord entered it. No, not new, achingly familiar. The voice sounded young, unsure, and afraid. *"Please. I did not think he would harm you so. I would not have let you leave with him. I would have betrayed myself to warn you, had I known. He has taken too much from you. You must believe me! You are too weak to survive without my aid.*

I am strong enough to fight you, Dewalaren lied.

If I remove the tree that shelters you, if I gift you with my true name, will you then trust me to help you? Aras asked, his voice thick with desperation.

Only if I may read your core, to see you do not deceive me. Only if you bare all your secrets to me.

I will come to you, Aras said without hesitation.

The voice was gone. Dewalaren lay where he had fallen, the left side of his face in the dirt. He felt grains of grit in his mouth but did not have the strength to turn his cheek from the ground or even to wet his lips with his tongue. A lot might happen in two days. It was such a struggle even to breathe. Would he be able to survive until Aras came? He would, he must.

What if someone else came upon him first? Bandits might come. Travelers might think him only a pile of cloth upon the ground and ride their wagon over him, crushing him. Only they were far north of Fenemal, north even of Gower. Few, if any, Men would venture so far. They were only fifty or so miles from the mountains of the north. That range was enormous and unexplored; it was not even named.

Where were Janahar and Stormcloud? He could not call to them with his voice or mind. He could not even see them. He could only see what was right in front of his right eye. His left lay closed against the dirt. He ached to have Janahar whicker at him and lip his hair. It worried him that she did not come. He feared she had been frightened away by the battle, that she might run afoul of obearn or wolven or even ogres if she headed north. He hoped Stormcloud was with her, that they both might make it back to Nalea safely.

The Ring! With all that had happened, he had not had the chance to tell Arcanus about the King's Ring. Farad had told him where Rowanar had died. The Ring must be there, in the pass, buried by rock these two and a half centuries past. He was sure of it. He would have laughed at the absurdity of it all if he had the strength. Arcanus had so robbed him of his strength he might die, when he could have regained the Ring.

Lunahr! Lunahr was so vulnerable, in greater danger than ever before. Aras might harm him. The thought that his young cousin might suffer further harm chilled him.

Arcanus had helped Lunahr, as much as he was able. How could Arcanus be evil, as Aras implied, when he had done so much for them for so long?

He was fortunate it was yet morning, and that the sun, which was already shining brightly, would burn more brightly still for a time. But night would come long before Aras did. He would go mad lying here helplessly, only able to think, once the sun finally set. But at least if he did, he would not have the strength, this time, to harm anyone, not even himself. He was beyond harm. He was dying. He would not still be alive when night came. He would not live even until noon, to see the sun burn brightly overhead. Already he was fighting for every breath he drew. No! It could not end like this!

There was a strange sound, like the flapping of wings, only far too strong to be a bird, much louder than a bird's wings should ever be. A huge shadow crossed over him and his heart began hammering in terror. A chimaera! Incuban had found him while he lay helpless in the dirt. At long last he had come to claim him. The Sword! Incuban must not get Kathalanar! He would destroy the Sword, and then his kin would be doomed.

Dewalaren focused all his will upon his hand, urging it to move, to grasp the hilt, to draw the Sword against Him. His hand barely made it to the Sword. There was still some small amount of Power in the Sword, he could feel it. But there was no strength in his hand. He grasped the hilt, but he could not even draw the Sword from its scabbard. He felt despair overwhelm him as the creature descended and landed in front of him.

But then he knew confusion. It was not a chimaera. He stared in shock and awe as he saw the forelegs of a great eagle and the hind legs of a pumar. It was a gryphon! But it could not be! They were dead, all dead. The last of them had died centuries ago. Stephan himself had mourned the passing of the last of their kind before King Albinar was slain. The magnificent beast bore a rider. He saw the booted leg as the man dismounted.

"Guard us," a familiar, impossible voice said in Elvish. The creature took to the air again, leaving the rider on the ground. He had recognized the voice. But it could not be. How could it be?

Aras knelt by his side. It was truly him. His eyes were filled with fear, his face was lined with concern. "I came as fast as I could." Dewalaren's hand tightened on Kathalanar's hilt. Aras reached a hand toward his face and he found the strength to flinch from his touch.

Aras's face showed agony. "Please, Dewalaren! I must touch you to remove the tree that shelters you, as I have promised I would. I will not harm you. I would never harm you. You must know I could not."

Dewalaren clenched his jaw and nodded ever so slightly. But the touch upon his cheek was unexpectedly warm and soft and gentle. He felt something strange and his eye turned inward. A crack had formed along the trunk of the great tree, from root to branch. He could see his core through the crack. His core was so dark! The tree had not sheltered him; it had fed upon his light!

"No, my friend. You were well until Arcanus attacked you. You will soon be able to believe me," Aras assured him. The bark began to shed from the tree, and the leaves began to fall. Dewalaren felt a wave of immeasurable sadness wash over him as he saw them fall, as if he was losing something precious and irreplaceable. He fought the feeling. Then the last of the bark and leaves were gone, and the branches and trunk began to flake away as well. His core was visible again, pure and untarnished, but he could scarcely see any light. It was as if the flame of a single small candle burned within. He felt a stab of fear, like a sword thrust through his heart. He had been right: he truly was dying.

"You will not die, Talon. I will not let you. The tree is gone, as you have commanded. Now, as promised, I gift my true name to you: I am Aeras, son of Aviatrix Aethelia of the Aerie." He said it as if he expected lightning to strike him at the mention of his name.

He let out his breath in a big sigh. "Please link with me, Dewalaren, so I might lend you my strength to replenish your own. So I may bare myself to you so you know you have nothing to fear from me."

Dewalaren concentrated. He strained. Such a simple act, forming the strand for a bond. When he was ten years old he had done so easily, yet now it took all the will he had. The strand reached out toward Aras. It was greeted by a blaze of light, as if the sun itself were imprisoned in Aras's body. The strand was drawn toward the impossible glare and touched it. Dewalaren expected to feel flame, to feel pain. How could he touch such a blazing Power and not be burnt by it? But he felt not heat, but warmth. The breadth and depth of Aras's love for him stole his breath away.

There was memory as well. A flood of images threatened to overwhelm him, until they drew back and Aras displayed them to him one at a time, so he might view them and comprehend what he was seeing. There was the memory of Aras awakening in the hollow tree, when they first had met, followed by all the memories of the time they had shared thereafter. Dewalaren felt Aras's wariness turn into curiosity and then joy. He felt the first tenuous rays of love being born and then grow until they permeated him completely. All the memories were as he himself remembered them, but from Aras's point of view, with his feelings and thoughts, instead of his own. There was no duplicity, no betrayal. But there was fear. There were secrets carefully kept, Power cautiously hidden.

Dewalaren probed deeper. To memories of life in Nalea before Aras left, memories of his father, of his childhood. Dewalaren felt Aras's loneliness and confusion and sorrow at his father's utter and complete rejection of him. He felt Aras's anguish for the friends his father had sent to their deaths, and the triumph and joy over those he had saved in secret, once he realized the danger his friendship represented to them. He felt his love for the healer, Jarnath, who had so shaped and guided him. He saw Aras's cruel mother, witnessed her manipulations. He shuddered. What pitiless creature of darkness might Aras have become, had he only had his father's and mother's influences upon him, had Jarnath not shaped him with his love and kindness and healing spirit?

He felt Aras wince at his fear of him. Then he felt Aras's own fear. That he would be lost to him, either through death or through fear; that he might recoil from him.

Dewalaren fought the urge to reassure him. Not yet, he could not go to him yet, as much as his own heart warred with him to. First he must view the recent past. All that had happened since their arrival in Nalea.

Dewalaren was appalled at what he found. Aras and Arcanus had been quietly waging war against one another since Arcanus had arrived in Nalea! And they had almost used Lunahr as a battleground! Yet they both cared for Lunahr, they both sought to see him safe, for their own very different reasons.

Aras had spared Arcanus's life in Nalea when he might have killed him easily. Knowing that Arcanus ultimately must die, he had not killed him when given the chance. Then when Dewalaren had gone, he had been terrified he had made a grievous mistake when he felt Arcanus's attack upon him, when he arrived in time to battle for him, but the battle itself almost cost Dewalaren his life.

Arcanus had tortured Dewalaren; he had tricked him into betraying Aras's true name, or what he had thought it had been. Arcanus had tried to kill Aras. He had sent the wave of fire to burn him. Yet even then, when Aras casually defeated Arcanus's attack, he had not killed Arcanus. Even infuriated, shaking with a need for vengeance for the harm Arcanus had done to him, Aras had let Arcanus flee. Why?

Because of Magus. Because he hoped Arcanus might still aid him. Because Magus was a child, a pawn working for Arcanus, yet still an innocent. One Aras had harmed without ever meaning to, without even knowing what he had done until he heard of the scry. Aras had fed upon Magus! But he had done so unwittingly, and he had been horrified to learn he had done so, repulsed by it, so filled with self-revulsion he'd been ill from it. Incuban hunted and fed upon every person he found. Arcanus had created the Amontir and then Magus and succored Circe, to feed upon. Aras's mother, Aethelia, had created Aras to feed upon. Of all of them, Aras alone did not feed upon any, though he had learned to his horror that he had the ability to. Where then did his great Power come from, other than from within?

The Grove! It was the Trees that sustained Aras, that gave him the Power he wielded, all trees, any trees, but particularly those of the Lords' Grove. His mother had bred him for just such a purpose. She had mated with Laedrin, one of the Lords of the Wood Elves, one with great potential for Power, but limited Power of his own, so that she could tap into the ability to get strength from the trees.

But the Trees of the Lords' Grove were like no others in all the lands. They were the last thirty-seven surviving trees from the Homeland of the Elves. They were all but immortal. They thought, they felt, once they had even moved. They had Power of their own.

But there was something more about the Trees, and about the Elven Homeland itself. There was something dark and terrible, horrific and hidden about it.

Dewalaren felt his heart beat faster. He fought a wave of dizziness. He could not breathe deeply enough, quickly enough, with his heart beating faster.

"Dewalaren, please! Enough! It must be enough for now. Please let me help you! It is almost too late! Your light is fading! I will not be able to rekindle it if you let it grow fully dark!"

There was panic in Aras's voice, his thoughts now. Terror. Pain. Aras was in agony for him.

"Please, Dewalaren, you cannot die! Not when you finally are beginning to understand. Not when you have seen so much, yet still do not shun me. I beg you, let me help you!" Aras was sobbing, but Dewalaren could barely hear him. Dewalaren could barely feel Aras's arms around him or feel the splash of Aras's tears upon his face.

You may help me, Dewalaren whispered across the bond. The wave of relief and love that roared across the link would have overwhelmed him, would have snuffed out the sputtering flicker of his core, did it not carry such Power with it.

Dewalaren felt himself replenished. He felt himself grow strong again. The Power continued to pour into his core, as if a dam had burst and all the water were being released at once. Power cascaded toward him as he grew stronger than he thought possible, as he felt he too might begin to glow bright as the sun.

"Stop!" Dewalaren pleaded, sitting up and grasping Aras by the arms, shaking him. "I'll not have you sacrifice yourself for me as Mother did for Father!" He did not think Aras would be able to hear him over the roar of Power, but the flow slowed and quieted, although it did not stop. It continued in a steady stream.

"Do not worry, Dewalaren," he heard Aras say, using his given name aloud for the first time, though he had already known it. Dewalaren had heard it in Aras's thoughts. Aras could learn anything he wished to know, now that they were bonded like this, but the thought did not frighten him anymore. He was relieved beyond measure to hear Aras's voice was still warm, still strong.

"This is what I was born to do, although not for you. Mother would not be pleased at all were she to find out what I am doing. She had thought I would be born only with raw Power and the ability to obtain more from the trees of this world. She never dreamt I might learn to focus it, to channel it as she does.

"She left me as she did, so young, to ensure that I would be weak and helpless until I matured, until she could use me. She did not foresee I would find Men at the age of twelve, outsmart my Father at the age of fourteen, and wage a battle of wits with him thereafter for the lives of my friends. Father never guessed how many of those he had thought he had sent to their deaths I fought beside, how many I saved in secret.

"Neither Mother nor Father knew that Jarnath would nurture me as he did. You are right: I owe him much. I must remember to tell him again of my love for him. Jarnath has always been as a father to me. He has earned both my trust and my love daily for decades with his actions. How could I have ever thought that what I have recently learned might change that?"

Aras stood and Dewalaren stood with him. "Please, Dewalaren, you should not know any more. Arcanus does not yet even know of my mother. Even Incuban does not. And you not only know of her, you know her given name, now, as part of my true name. But there are other truths involving her too nightmarish to think about, too cruel to bear." Aras's voice was haunted.

"I have seen enough, Aras. I can trust you again."

Aras did not look at all relieved. "I did not view your core as you viewed mine. I already knew your given name, though I did not speak it to you before, but I could not help but hear your true name as well, your core called it out so loudly to me, though all your other secrets are still hidden from me. But there is one thing I must know."

The Ring! The thought leapt out and Dewalaren slammed it back violently.

"You are hiding something from me. You are frightened of me again." Aras's voice was laced with pain and despair. "I do not wish to know your secrets, Dewalaren. I want only to know the truth.

"When you chose the tree to shelter me, you saved my life. Magus's power was not enough; I'd bled most of it away during the night. I fed from the tree as well, so weakening it that when lightning struck it the second time, it fell and was destroyed. But what I do not know, what I must know but only you can tell me: did I feed upon you, as well as upon Magus? Unknowingly, while you tended me, did I weaken you, so I might become strong? Is that why you succumbed to the rain, to illness?" Aras's voice was haunted and his eyes held fear. Dewalaren sensed his very heart might stop were the truth what he feared it to be.

Dewalaren drew back carefully and viewed his core, then viewed the memories a second time to be sure. "No," he said honestly. "I find no sign you did so. You did not harm me, Aras. You have never harmed me. You have ever only aided me."

Dewalaren saw fear and doubt and disbelief change to overwhelming relief and then pure joy. "I thought... I'd feared... I'd not dared hope...," Aras began, then wrapped his arms about Dewalaren and hugged him. "I need to go now, Dewalaren. We know enough for now, all we each safely can, I think. You must sever your bond to me, now, quickly. It is so hard for me not to hear your secret." Aras's voice was quaking with loss, even as he begged him.

Dewalaren hesitated. Breaking this bond would be even harder than watching the sheltering tree vanish. But he had little choice. Dewalaren broke it, and they both cried out in loss. Only their external embrace allowed them to bear the severing of the link.

Aras was the first to pull away. "You must go, Dewalaren. You must follow your secret. I hope that you travel safely."

Aras's eyes welled with tears as he walked to where Janahar had fallen. He petted her lifeless body gently. "I had wanted her to carry you, to protect you. I knew she might die for you, but I did not think it might be so soon. Had she not been here, Arcanus would not have stopped himself in time. He would have killed you instead. I know it, yet still I will grieve for Janahar. I will mourn that her proud heart has been forever stilled."

Dewalaren stared in horror at Janahar and saw Stormcloud also lying far too still upon the ground. "Arcanus did this?" he asked, voice breaking. He stumbled as he joined Aras by Janahar's side. His hand shook as he touched her, and tears slid freely down his cheeks.

Aras stroked his face, his fingertips smearing the dirt mixed with tears upon his cheek. "My father has always told me my heart is too soft. I had wondered, what would he say were he to see me now, crying for a horse? Yet you mourn her too, as a friend. I will see that she is laid to rest in a meadow. I will bury her in a place that knows the warmth of the sun. Stormcloud deserves no less respect, but Aerlyr cannot carry them both." At his words, with a strong beat of wings, the gryphon alighted beside them. Dewalaren stared in stunned awe at the fierce, magnificent creature who stood proudly beside his friend, as if he belonged at his side.

"Be well, my friend, and return to me when you can. I will keep Lunahr safe from harm. I will see him well again for you." Then Aras mounted the gryphon, who wrapped the great clawed talons of his forefeet around Janahar carefully, as if respectfully, tenderly, and then he rose from the ground, his powerful wings beating against the air. They flew upward and over the trees, heading southeast, and soon disappeared from sight.

Dewalaren swallowed hard, once and then again, against further tears. The tree was gone as well as the newly forged link, but his core hummed with Power. The brilliance of it all but blinded him. So why did he feel so cold, so alone? Why did it seem so dark with Aras gone, as if the very sun, which still shone brightly, had fallen from the sky?

Dewalaren took steadying breaths and forced himself to peace. His march would be a long, lonely one. He must get started now, in the bright light of day, and travel far before he abandoned it without beginning, lest he run back to Nalea instead, to be with those he loved.

He eyed Stormcloud sadly, one last time, and resolutely turned south to begin his long journey.

Chapter 10
The Awakening

LUNAHR spent his days sleeping in the Lords' Grove, while Leonas watched over him, and his nights with Leonas in the Guest House. Aras had left after that first night, and they had seen no more of him. Leonas and Lunahr got to know one another better and became friends, although Lunahr sometimes went for walks through the wondrous woods of Nalea unaccompanied during the bright light of day, those times he was not sleeping. The morning of the sixth day after being released from his cell found him in the Lords' Grove once more.

Lunahr's bruises were healing, and he moved with less pain. He was even able to use the hand of his bandaged arm a little. But though he had been thrilled to be gifted the instruments and the paper and ink, he found to his growing dismay that he could neither play nor write. He could not even sing, though he tried. It was as if all the music inside of him had somehow vanished. The thought of never singing or playing again chilled him. He tried to convince himself that his music would return as his body healed.

How could he live without his music when he had already lost so much: his innocence, his freedom, his kin, his friends? Farad, Elanara, Elavar, and Eladar were all gone; they'd all abandoned him. No. Laren and Laedrin had sent them away. It was their fault. They must pay, as Laranela had…. He jumped and bit back a yelp, his chain of thought broken, as the pinecone that had fallen upon his head rolled onto the ground.

"Beryl? Are you all right?" Leonas asked in concern, seeing him startle and looking relieved once he saw the reason for it.

Lunahr smiled sheepishly at Leonas as he rubbed the sore spot on his head, secretly thrilling at the silken feel of his hair against his fingertips in exquisite contrast to the bite of pain beneath. "I'm fine. I've certainly been hurt far worse. I'm sorry to have alarmed you." Lunahr settled again beneath his fir, Aranahr.

He wasn't entirely without friends. Leonas had been wonderful. It might be his duty to protect him, but he had done far more, and Lunahr suspected he'd protect him now regardless of Aras's orders. He grew wistful at the thought of Aras. He desperately wished Aras would return to them, but there was as yet no further sign of him. He knew he should be worrying about Laren and his other distant kin, but the only emotion he felt was relief that they were not here, where he might harm them.

The only peace he found was here in the Lords' Grove, beneath the fir tree that sheltered him. Nalea did not seem as much a prison when he was with Aranahr. The peace and calm of the Grove filled him and he drifted off to sleep.

Lunahr was rudely awakened from his sleep by an indignant roar.

"What are you doing here? I come to the Lords' Grove to find peace after five days in the hole you put me in, after being chained, and I find you here, defiling even this place!" Ahrnad was seething with rage. He lunged at Lunahr even as Leonas sprang between them.

Ahrnad tried to reach past Leonas to grab Lunahr, but he tripped upon a protruding root and fell. He reached out his hand to catch himself, and found the trunk of the fir Tree Lunahr had lain under. He cursed and snatched his hand away from the bark, revealing a cut and bleeding palm. He stared, appalled, at the bloody mark upon the bark of the Tree.

"Beryl, go quickly! I will try to calm him!" Leonas ordered.

Lunahr knew his continued presence would only make things worse, so he obeyed Leonas and ran. He headed back to the Guest House, but he did not stop there as he had meant to. His calm shattered, an irrational blind panic seized him. He needed the trees. The trees would keep him safe!

He headed for the woods beyond the Guest House and ran into the woods, deeper and deeper, until each breath became an agony as his lungs fought against his cracked ribs. He was gasping for breath like a fish out of water, but he could not get enough air. He collapsed and tried to catch himself, but his bound arm betrayed him. He fell hard, his injured arm striking against a rock that thrust up from underneath the soft bed of leaves. There was a bright red flash of pain and then nothing.

LEONAS cursed himself. He'd been a fool to let his guard down! But he had not thought anyone would break the solitude of the Grove so completely. He had hoped Ahrnad would regain his composure and control with Beryl gone. But, although Ahrnad had been dazed by seeing his blood on the tree, when Beryl fled, he had turned to pursue him, like a pumar in pursuit of a hare. When Leonas had blocked his pursuit, Ahrnad had turned his fury upon him.

Even as they fought, Leonas reminded Ahrnad of the High-Prince's order concerning harming Lord Beryl. He tried to explain that he was on special service to Beryl and had been granted access to the Grove.

But Ahrnad was enraged. He said the High-Prince had been ensorcelled by outsiders and other fell things, and Leonas knew then that his reason had entirely fled. Leonas feared Ahrnad would draw his blade against him, but he did not.

Leonas had been hardened by patrolling the borders in the Guard, and Ahrnad had been too long in a position of privilege in the King's Guard. Ahrnad was the one who was finally laid out unconscious upon the ground when their battle ceased, although Leonas was not without injury.

Leonas left the Grove in search of Beryl, hoping he was not too agitated by what had transpired. But though Beryl had headed off in the direction of it, he was not in the Guest House. Leonas backtracked to the Grove and saw Ahrnad had gone. At first he feared he had set out after Beryl, that he might be tracking him, but he saw to his relief from his tracks that he had not. He had instead headed back the way he had come.

Leonas found to his surprise that Beryl's tracks were almost impossible to find and follow, until they passed the Guest House: then suddenly, they were vivid, and Leonas worried at the change. But when he entered the woods, all trace of him vanished, as if the very forest were hiding him. Leonas looked everywhere for signs of him, but there were none.

He grew truly afraid for him. He followed along the direction he had taken upon entering and ventured deep into the woods. He began fanning back and forth, backward along his own tracks, hoping to find Beryl, and he began calling for him as well.

Leonas was beginning to despair of ever finding Beryl, thinking it was time to notify the Guard to begin searching, when he suddenly saw something move to the right, out of the corner of his eye. Turning his head, he saw a branch swaying slightly. It was a fir tree.

He ran to the spot, knowing it must be some small animal he had startled, but still he checked. There was nothing there, but as his eyes cast about hopelessly, left and right, yards away, hidden amongst the trees, he saw corn silk where there should only be green and brown and ran over.

It was Beryl! He lay prone upon the ground, his face ashen gray, but his eyes were open and he was looking at him lucidly. "Leonas," Beryl whispered.

"I am here, my friend. I will help you." Leonas picked Beryl up as if he were a child, though he was heavier than he thought he might be, for being a Man and a slightly built one at that. He carried him through the woods to the Guest House. He started when he entered, for someone was inside. But it was only the female cadet with their lunch, and he was greatly relieved. "Go quickly, fetch Healer Jarnath. And send word to the High-Prince that his friend, Beryl, has been injured."

She looked at him wide-eyed in surprise but obeyed.

Leonas carried Beryl to his room and laid him on the bed, covering him. He knew that he had to keep him warm, lest shock set in, but he did not know what else to do for him. He knew the same basic first aid skills all cadets were taught, how to slow bleeding and bandage wounds and splint limbs, but Beryl's arm had already been set and wrapped and his cracked ribs had been wrapped as well.

"Water," Beryl whispered, and Leonas brought some and helped him drink it.

"Forgive me for letting you get hurt again," Leonas said, anguished.

"My fault," Beryl whispered.

Time passed with agonizing slowness, but finally Leonas heard the door of the Guest House open. He went out into the hall and, to his relief, saw Jarnath and called to him.

Jarnath glared at him. "What have you done to yourself?"

"I'm fine. It's Beryl. He fell." Leonas brought Jarnath to him.

Jarnath began questioning Beryl. He carefully cut the bandages from Beryl's arm and chest and examined him and then sighed, as if the weight of the Seven Kingdoms were upon his shoulders. "Fell indeed. You've misaligned the bone in your arm. I'll have to reset it. And I'll need to rebind your ribs, as well. Both will hurt worse than now, I'm afraid. Drink this, all of it," he commanded, pulling a small flask from his shirt.

It was a sign of the severity of his pain that Beryl didn't argue, but drank. When he was done, Jarnath instructed Leonas to hold him still, showing him where to hold him. Then, with expert hands, Jarnath realigned the bones of his arm. Beryl passed out midgasp. Jarnath bandaged his arm and his chest again. "Now that he is unconscious and will not be able to refuse my services, I will begin to heal him in earnest, as soon as I've tended to your own injuries."

Leonas shook his head. "I am fine. My injuries are trivial, though painful, so you will not suffer for me because I was too slow to escape every blow Commander Ahrnad directed at me. I am only fortunate in that, as I have been reassigned to report directly to Aras, I am now outside the chain of command and cannot be imprisoned or slain for attacking a superior officer." Ahrnad had attacked him, and he had only been defending himself, but such details did not matter when one was a Guard and the officer was a King's Guard.

Jarnath took in Leonas's solemn, cut and bleeding face and suddenly lost control. He turned upon him in helpless rage. "You people are all mad! You and him and Ahrnad, all of you! You waste my time re-treating the same injuries and making more. Aren't the Hill People doing enough? Three score wounded and four more dead in five days' time, many of them less than a hundred years old!"

Aras's soft voice came from the doorway, "Jarnath, my mentor, this is not their fault. They don't even know about any of the rest."

Leonas turned in surprise. To Leonas's concerned eye, Aras looked older, worn and exhausted. Aras hugged Jarnath, and the healer took a deep breath and calmed himself. "How is Beryl?" Aras asked, eyeing him in concern.

Jarnath sighed. "He will recover, if you can keep Ahrnad away from him. I was about to heal him."

"No, Jarnath. He would never forgive himself for it. Instead you must rest or you will soon give the other healers a new patient," Aras cautioned.

"Do not worry so over me, Aras. Your heart is burdened enough," Jarnath replied, sighing heavily again. "Very well. But call me if you've need of me again, and I will come. And I will try not to make you regret that you requested my aid." He managed a ghost of a smile that faded almost as quickly as it appeared, and then he was gone.

ARAS sat and leaned back in the writing desk chair and closed his eyes. "Tell me what happened," Aras commanded wearily.

"Highness, what did Jarnath mean? What haven't you told us?" Leonas asked, his voice thick with concern.

Aras sighed, as loudly and hopelessly as Jarnath. He had not told poor Leonas so many, many things. It was so hard to keep playing his part, with Dewalaren gone and most likely heading into grave danger with none to aid him. Aras would be lost, were it not for Jarnath and Aranas and especially Aerlyr's support, for his unexpectedly early return from his mating flight, in Aras's hour of greatest need. He never would have been able to reach Dewalaren in time to save him were it not for

Aerlyr. But the Hill People were exacting a surprisingly devastating toll upon their forces with their well-planned, lightning-quick, brutal raids.

"I'm afraid you were too optimistic in your earlier assessment of the Hill People forces. The Hill People haven't been idle. There have been more raids, more large parties. They have learned to fight well amongst our trees. Jarnath is beside himself. There have been five dead in a few weeks' time and eighty-nine injured besides.

"We can't keep fighting them this way. I hadn't wanted either you or Beryl to know about it, at least not yet. I need you here for Beryl, and you would want to return to patrolling the Wood to aid your friends. Beryl would want to help, but he can't, not until he recovers. And I've been busy with all this and worse, and now I've managed to let Beryl come to harm a second time. Talon chose poorly in his confidence in me. But I never thought that Ahrnad might go to the Grove or that Beryl would be there when he did, or that Ahrnad would dare disturb the Trees in such a manner."

"But why have the Hill People chosen now to attack us in force?" Leonas asked.

"I wish I knew," Aras said in frustration. "We have never been friends with them, but we have never done any ill against them that they might wish to engage in war upon us. They may not defeat us, for they are too few, I think, and our bows give us the advantage when we are not completely taken by surprise and ambushed, but they do weaken us. When the Enemy strikes, he will find us that much more vulnerable, because of them.

"But that is yet a problem for another day. My present concern beyond the Hill People is Beryl. I had wanted to be here for him. I should be here when he needs me so. Tell me, has he been eating and sleeping?"

Leonas nodded. "He eats well. He will not sleep at night, but in the daylight we go to the Lords' Grove and he sleeps there, under one of the Trees."

"I am glad my Tree shelters him."

"Forgive me, Highness, but it does not. He sleeps under one of the unnamed Trees. He showed me the four you showed to him. He sleeps under the great fir Tree, the one that was afflicted but recovered. I think seeing it gives him hope. But more than that, somehow, it gives him strength."

Aras was intrigued. Did Leonas mean that literally? Physically? He had not known any but the Lords of the Aerta amongst them could draw strength from the Trees. Could the special Trees of the Grove give their strength to anyone? If that were true, no wonder his father guarded them so jealously!

He already knew that each Lord depended upon a Tree of the Grove for his continued longevity. He wondered again if someone without a significant ability to retain and wield Power might not live as long as a Lord, simply by the grace of one of the Trees.

Regardless, from what he had learned, it sounded like both the Tree and all the Aerta Lords and Ladies in actuality owed their lives to Jarnath, though of course, they must never learn of it. But Leonas was still speaking, and he must pay attention.

"… always I watch over him. He says he cannot usually sleep when watched, but my attention does not disturb him. I never thought harm could come to him there, until Ahrnad came." Leonas told Aras all that had transpired in his absence.

Aras sighed. "We are all stretched too thin. Too much is happening too fast, and we are too slow in adapting to it. It is hard to learn to live in Man-time. But one Man lives with us and others fight us. We would be far better served to have those Men as allies at our border in the war to come." His voice was wistful. "But I have left you alone for too long to watch over Beryl, though it could not be helped. Now you must get some rest, and I will stay with him."

"Yes, Highness."

Aras corrected him. "We are beyond that, Leonas. In private, at least, I would have you call me Aras, as my friends do, for you are one of them."

Leonas looked at him with worshipful eyes and said, "I will try." Then he left the room after executing a precise, military bow.

Aras returned to Lunahr's side. Aras watched Lunahr as he tried to work through the turmoil in his own mind.

Suddenly, Lunahr began moaning and thrashing, as if he were caught in a bad dream he could not wake from. Aras remembered Lunahr's words of being hunted in his sleep and feared for him. He shook Lunahr, calling to him, and took his hand. But Lunahr would not waken, and Aras feared that Jarnath had given him something to make him sleep.

He squeezed Lunahr's hand and shook him harder, calling to him again. He was about to risk potentially exposing himself to Incuban, if Lunahr was truly under attack, by reaching for his core, when unexpectedly Lunahr squeezed his hand back, as if in a death grip, crushing his fingers and pulling upon them as a drowning man pulls himself along a rope to the surface. Lunahr's eyes snapped open and in them was a look of such pure terror that Aras feared he'd gone mad again. But then Lunahr's eyes found focus on his face and Lunahr hugged him and began to weep.

Aras spoke to Lunahr as he had in the cell, stroking his back and holding him as if he were a child. With painful slowness, Lunahr started to return to himself again. He finally looked up at Aras. "I saw the face of the Enemy. And he was speaking to me. I heard his voice, but I could not understand his words. He was reaching out to touch me, and I knew that if he did, I would understand him and then I would be lost. But I heard your voice too. I felt your hand touch me instead, and you pulled me away from him." Lunahr was shaking, but he was looking at him even more worshipfully than Leonas had.

"You pulled yourself away. I was only your anchor." Aras felt it was important that Lunahr know that if Incuban was truly hunting him even here.

"I remember now. I have seen his face before and heard his voice." He shuddered and whispered, "And felt his touch. Then it was a nightmare, too, but a waking one. And no less real than this time." Lunahr could not stop shaking. Aras hugged him tightly so he might feel his strong arms about him and feel safe.

"The Enemy has been looking for me, but I think he can only speak to me in my sleep. He had not found me again, until now, but he has finally learned I sleep during the day. When I am under the Trees, they hide me, they protect me. He cannot penetrate their shield, at least not yet. But he is so strong!" Lunahr's voice was intense, bordering on panic. "Please, I need to go back to the Grove, to my Tree! I am safe there. When I am there, I hear only the rustle of the needles and leaves and see only the Trees in my slumber."

"Then I will take you there. I will be back in a moment." Aras went to his room to get his swords, though he already carried his knife. He would not walk poorly armed with Incuban's attention potentially focused here and the Hill People such a threat, though neither had yet to come close to the City.

He returned to Lunahr's side and helped him to his feet. Lunahr leaned on him heavily for support as they walked slowly and carefully to the Grove.

Lunahr's steps quickened at the sight of the Trees. He walked up to the fir, and before Aras realized what he intended, he reached out his trembling hand and touched it. He jerked back his hand, as if the Tree had bitten him, eyes wide, clutching it in the armpit of his other shoulder, as if in pain.

"Did you cut yourself?" Aras took him by the wrist and examined his palm, but there was no wound on his hand. "Beryl, for all you love this Tree, it is not yours. It cannot be. You must not try to touch it if it does not wish to be touched." Aras's voice was full of compassion, but firm, for he knew it would be a hard thing for Lunahr to hear.

Lunahr shook his head. "Aranahr would never harm me. He has chosen me already. He is in pain; that is what I felt. Something burns him, like fire." He reached out his hand and gently touched along the bark of the trunk, probing here and there.

Aras saw Lunahr's teeth clench against the effort and beads of sweat form upon his brow. Lunahr's hand stopped near a discolored area on the bark, which he was careful not to touch, though he circled it with his fingers. When Lunahr let go, his hand was trembling again. Unexpectedly, he drew his sword in a single smooth motion.

Aras leapt back from him, eyes wide with surprise, drawing his own blades defensively. "Beryl, what are you doing?" He did not think he would be answered with words, but when Lunahr turned to him, he lowered his blade and his eyes were a clear, lucid green, although his gaze was intense.

"I am not going to hurt you, Aras, nor am I going to hurt Aranahr. I am helping him, as he has asked me to. I don't understand why, but where Ahrnad touched him, where he cut his hand, it burns Aranahr. He needs me to remove that piece of bark and whatever wood underneath may be damaged. Aras, I must! It is already far larger than where he touched and I fear it will grow until it consumes Aranahr. The pain from the cut I must make will be as nothing compared to this. It is like those elixirs in the cell: it is like fire. It is unbearable!"

Aras was impressed that Lunahr would have held his hand to the Tree for so long with the memory of that other pain, were that truly so. But this pain could not be real.

The needles of the fir overhead began rustling and Lunahr nodded. "He would have you touch him, so you might believe me. But I warn you, you will feel his pain."

Aras sheathed his swords, his eyes on Lunahr's face, and pressed his hand to the bark near the discoloration. It would have hurt less to reach his hand into a fire and pick up a glowing coal and hold it. He endured it, reaching out with his Power to the Tree, trying to hear him, but he could hear nothing. He let go, cradling his arm, then looked at his hand, unable to believe it would be whole, but it was undamaged. The pain had fled as soon as he let go, although the memory of the pain still burned brightly.

"I felt it, just as you described. I tried, but I could not hear him. I believe you now. But do not use your sword. Arcanus has tied his magicks to it and the blade might be damaged to ill effect we cannot foresee. Swords are not for wood." Aras drew his slender dagger and held it out to him. "This blade is well-forged and of pallenteum, which might aid you."

Lunahr thanked him and took off his cloak and laid it flat under the tree, against the trunk. Then he scored the trunk a full thumb length of healthy bark around the discolored spot. Then, working quickly, he cut deeply, angling the blade inward toward the center of the discolored mass. He sliced a thick section of bark off the trunk all in one piece. It fell away onto the cloak, as if the Tree was eager to shed it.

In the center of the bare patch, the underlying wood which had been revealed was blackened, in an area the size of a twenty-gold piece. This was solid wood and far harder to cut. Aras was relieved that it was the fir that had been afflicted and not his father's oak or one of the others. Pine was a far softer wood. Lunahr carved curls of wood until he found undamaged wood below, and then a little bit further, the curls falling onto his cloak. Then he laid the knife upon the cloak, careful not to touch the blade. "May I have one of your swords? Even though you might never be able to use it again?" Lunahr asked.

Aras handed it to him without hesitation. He would be able to ascertain whether or not it might be safe to use later, and perhaps cleanse it, if necessary.

It was far more difficult for Lunahr to wield the sword for such a task than the dagger with only one hand, and though finely forged, the metal was far inferior, but he peeled off a single final curl and handed the blade back. "Do not sheath it. I think the sword is still safe, but it might be better to discard it as well. I needed to be sure there was not a trace of the other blade's mark, as the taint might have been upon it. I am no wizard, and I do not lightly play with foul magicks."

Aras nodded and held the sword, pointed downward, not sheathing it. Then he aided Lunahr in carefully wrapping all the excised parts and the knife in the cloak, as it was an awkward job with only the use of one arm, and then Aras picked up the bundle.

Lunahr placed his hand on the trunk of the Tree again, and this time a smile of pure joy lit his face. He reached out and embraced the fir with his good arm, laying his cheek against the trunk, as the needles rustled softly overhead. Then to Aras's astonishment, one of the lower branches bent toward Lunahr and wrapped about him in a gentle embrace.

Lunahr stood like that for a few moments and then released the Tree, and the branch withdrew. When he turned to Aras, there were tears of joy on his cheeks, and his face was lit with a beatific smile. "He will be well, now. He thanks you for the aid. He says Aranas chose wisely in you."

"Beryl, we must remove these things from the Grove and we must talk," Aras said, trying to conceal the depth of his shock and amazement.

Lunahr nodded. "I will be safe doing so. He has strengthened me again. The darkness cannot touch me, for a time." With a parting caress, he left. "I could not hear him clearly until I touched him, and I had never before dared to until now. I knew these Trees are aware, that they could speak, but I had no idea they could actually move. I was so startled when he hugged me!"

Aras swallowed. "Beryl, they cannot move. I mean, they should not be able to. I could not believe it when I saw it. It has been over a thousand years since even Arandrin last moved, and he was the last Tree to do so. The soil here is different from the soil of our Homeland. The Trees' Power has been slowly fading for millennia." He did not tell Lunahr what he had only recently learned, that they would have been stilled long before had it not been for the Power Jarnath funneled to them. But as their people weakened in Power, so too did the Power Jarnath could safely draw from them and impart to the Trees.

"Few of us now can hear them when they speak, they speak so faintly. I think you have awakened them. Or rather, Arcanus has, through you. I think he forgot that when you bind something, the binding also holds the thing it is anchored to. He did not just bind you to the trees of Nalea: he bound the trees to you, all the trees, even these. And now the Trees of the Grove begin to waken and even move again."

Aras did not think Arcanus could have done such a thing without Jarnath's help, not if he was Faeren. That the Trees of the Grove allowed it, or perhaps even encouraged it, was both astonishing and troubling. The Lords and Ladies depended upon the trees for their very lives, but especially the Trees of the Grove. Did the Trees know Arcanus was one of Aras's enemies? Once it came to a confrontation, would they take sides? What if they chose to aid Arcanus against him?

He should not dare think such things while within the Grove. His shields were firmly in place, as always, but he was linked to Aranas. If only he had someone to confide in, to share his thoughts and fears with! His heart ached for Dewalaren, for his wisdom, his compassion, his counsel, his warm reassurance. But he was already far away. It might be weeks or months or even years before they saw one another again.

No. Dewalaren would come sooner, for Lunahr's sake if not for his own. "Come, I must go to my father."

Lunahr shook his head, wide-eyed. "You cannot take me to him. I would attack him again. I do not wish to harm him. I never wished to harm anyone, but I cannot prevent it." His voice was but a whisper, thick with fear and shame.

Aras clasped him gently by both shoulders, a warrior's embrace. "I know. But I need you to come with me to the Healers' Hall to speak with Jarnath while I speak to my father. I need to know what Arcanus may have told Jarnath about the assassin's blade. Arcanus was afraid for him and for Dewalaren, thinking either might have touched it. Fortunately he did not find what he feared in their hands. But someone put the knife into that box and Ahrnad was not there when Arcanus spoke to us, warning us of the dangers of the knife.

"Ahrnad was in the room after my father was attacked, and he has been acting as if his will is not his own. I think he might have held the knife, not realizing the hilt was more dangerous than the blade. Why else would his blood burn the tree? The knife may have been another trap the Enemy set, one we did not see until now. I must tell my father that Ahrnad must be located and captured and held until Arcanus can help him. I fear he has become a tool of the Enemy, and as such, he is a much greater danger to us all than you, even were you not bound."

"I think you are right. I must accompany you." They began heading to the Palace. "I have seen the torment on Ahrnad's face, the hate conflicting with his duty and his loyalty, but I did not see it for what it was." Then he gave Aras an odd look, one of curiosity and speculation and contemplation. He opened his mouth as if to speak, but closed it again.

Aras stopped walking. "Is something wrong? Please, Beryl, speak your mind."

Lunahr looked at him appraisingly and then appeared to come to a decision. "Just now, when you were speaking, you did not say Talon. You spoke Laren's given name. No one save for our people and the Royal Family of Riviera has ever known it. His name is our most closely guarded secret, lest the Enemy learn it." His face darkened in shame and humiliation, and he whispered. "Or it was. Until I betrayed him, until I betrayed all my kin, though I would sooner have gone to my own death than brought them to danger."

"You think I am a threat, a danger to your cousin, your Prince?" Aras could not keep the devastation from his voice that Lunahr might think such a thing, knowing that someday Dewalaren might again view him with eyes filled with fear, instead of the love he so ached to see.

"No! Of course not!" Lunahr denied. His voice was filled with such shock and vehemence that Aras was certain it could not possibly be faked. "How could you even think such a thing? You saved his life when he was ill. You traveled with him and kept him safe, when I and the rest of my kin were so far from him, when we could not. It is not that at all. I just—I wondered how close you two became, on your journey. I—never mind," Lunahr said. He was blushing darkly now.

Aras's eyes widened. Surely Lunahr could not know that they had bonded to one another, even for so short a time? No, that was not what he was asking, or he would not blush as if.... Revelation dawned clear and bright. Lunahr was asking if they had become lovers. Why might he wish to know? Could he be jealous?

No, there was no accusation, no anger in his words. And there was that dark blush of innocence that should no longer be possible for him, that would not be, had Incuban not blocked all the memories of what he had endured. Lunahr had remembered nothing from his time of captivity, and now only a little, it seemed, though that veil of false innocence must be torn away if he was ever to truly heal, if he could be healed.

"We became friends, close friends. How could it be otherwise, when one is a traveling companion to such a remarkable individual? There is such strength yet gentleness about him, such wisdom yet understanding, such solemnity yet humor, such patience, warmth, self-sacrifice, and humility. He is my teacher, my mentor, my friend. He is as a father or a brother to me," Aras added, realizing he might have betrayed too much, that the love he felt might have shown from his eyes, or in his voice.

"You love him," Lunahr said simply.

Aras was about to deny it, in panic, when Lunahr smiled, a look of warmth and relief upon his face. "We all love him, all his kin. I was concerned you might harbor some resentment against him, or perhaps even secretly hate him, for his betrothal to Elanara. She was to have been your wife, until Arcanus intervened. But you wear your heart upon your sleeve. I am relieved that you instead love him as we do. Laren so desperately needs to be loved. He loves Elanara with such devotion it is a joy to see. From the moment he first saw her, he loved her. There could never be another for him. I am thankful you were not harmed by it."

Aras almost fell to his knees at the declaration, though he knew Lunahr had not meant to be cruel. Lunahr could not know how his words burnt his heart, far worse than the pain of the Tree had burned his hand, for his love of Dewalaren, not Elanara.

But then the joy in Lunahr's eyes vanished, first replaced by infinite sadness, wistfulness, and then, shockingly, with a burning red rage. When he spoke, his words were all the more chilling for the whisper in which they were delivered. "I knew such a love, once. But I was betrayed. I pray Elanara's tainted blood might not betray her, that she might remain faithful to Laren, and that the perfidy of her father and brother do not manifest in her as well."

Aras was appalled by his words. From all he had heard, Lunahr had loved the King and Queen of Riviera as if they were his parents, and they had shared his love. Their children had been as siblings to Lunahr. This must be further evidence of Incuban's influence upon Lunahr. He could be delayed and distracted no longer. As soon as he enlightened his father about the Trees, Lunahr must become his number one priority.

He silently cursed. No, Lunahr must yet be second to the threat of the Hill People. But even so, he must begin working in depth to discover exactly what Incuban had done to Lunahr, to find a way to heal the damage. He wished he could enlist Jarnath's aid, but he could not trust one who was so closely tied to one of the other Players, to Arcanus, someone as steeped in lies and treachery as Incuban. He had trusted Jarnath, and the healer had betrayed his trust. In spite of his words to Dewalaren, he had not been able to forgive his mentor so easily. He sighed. Yet he had lied to Jarnath from the start no less than Jarnath had lied to him. Aras had known his mother's secrets for decades, yet had not revealed them to Jarnath or to his father or to anyone. Was he any less of a traitor to his people? And what of the Trees? He feared he would need their aid to heal Lunahr, but he did not trust them anymore either. He feared he might go mad, and his heart ached for Dewalaren anew.

"Aras? Aras, are you all right? Forgive me! I am such a fool. Of course you loved her. How could you not have? I did not mean to open an old wound. But please, do not blame Laren. Do not hate him," Lunahr entreated.

Lunahr's pain and despair drew him from his own. "No, Beryl. You must forgive me. I was not thinking of Elanara. You were right before. I do not love her. I have yet to even meet her. We were kept apart, as I had not yet come-of-age. I am thankful now we did not meet.

"I do not hate Dewalaren. I could never hate him. He is the best friend I have ever had. I would die to see him happy, to see him safe." He said so with conviction. If Dewalaren found happiness with Elanara, he would find some measure of joy in his own heartbreak, knowing Dewalaren was loved as he deserved to be, even if he was not the one blessed to be with him.

They began walking again to the Healers' Hall, each now lost in his own thoughts.

Aras saw Lunahr safely to Jarnath, then went to find his father and tell him about the Trees and Ahrnad. He and his father had developed a new, stronger bond in the days since his return, since Arcanus had worked his magicks upon him. He still had not undone the change Arcanus had made in his father. Yet another task he must undertake. But unlike his eagerness to aid Lunahr, he was reluctant to heal his father and thereby lose the love he had so desperately yearned for all these long, lonely decades.

But his father of old returned when he tried to tell him about the Trees. Laedrin would not believe one of them would speak to a Man, or would attune to one, and he shook with rage and roared that no other Tree might move when his no longer could. All his father's thoughts and emotions battered Aras as if he were caught in a river valley in a flash flood. In wonder, for the first time Aras sensed his father's pain. He had not known his father could feel pain. But he saw it all so clearly, now.

Laedrin had survived the destruction of their Homeland, the death of all but a handful of his people. He had clung to the fragments of his life for millennia and done what he could to help the survivors of the Annihilation, to preserve what he could of their culture. He had taken the battle-scarred troops from the War, the remnants of the Army and Navy, and gone into exile with them in Nalea so that the Seven Kingdoms might be free of their dark influence, yet might stay strong in case of future attack. Laedrin had seen that every Aerta and Oceana trained for five years to be prepared to join the armed forces, if ever there was a need, in defense of their new lands.

But the soils of these lands were different from the soils of home. In spite of all Laedrin had done, they began to die. They no longer lived ten thousand years as they once had in their Homeland. The refugees died after only a few centuries, and the colonial Elves who were born upon this soil and the progeny of the refugees who joined them lived a scant thousand years. Only the thirty-three Aerta Lords and Ladies lived as long as they should, because of their Trees. The few River Elf Lords and Ladies who were born died as prematurely as the rest.

Laedrin's heart had finally died the day Arandrin had been lost to him, the day his voice had sunk to a whisper and he could no longer move, the day that, for all his force of will and physical might, Laedrin was unable to aid him. His heart had already grown cold, and it was a small step from cold to cruel.

It was in that moment that Aras understood what Arcanus had done to him. He had not altered his heart. He had freed his heart. He had awakened it again. He had returned to Laedrin his ability to feel compassion, to feel love. He had healed him.

Aras had spared Arcanus's life because of Magus, but now he owed him a debt of gratitude for enabling him to see, to understand. He had to remind himself that Arcanus had tried to kill him, ruthlessly, that he had nearly killed Dewalaren, though he had not intended to. He must be just as ruthless when next he met Arcanus. Yet still, if he could somehow become his ally, instead of his enemy, when he already had two powerful enemies he faced alone.... He forced the thought aside. For now, he must concentrate on convincing his father to go to the Grove. His father would not believe Ahrnad capable of treachery if he would not hear the truth about the Trees.

Reluctantly, he wove his Power into his argument and subtly commanded his father to go to the Grove and speak with Arandrin. Aras made sure a full dozen of the King's Guard accompanied him and that none of them were those whom Ahrnad had favored. Then he sought Lunahr and Jarnath. They both looked grim.

Jarnath said, "I know no more than what you heard, about the blade, and we can only treat what lies in the cloak in the same manner until the wizards can advise us. But you need to know that I no longer have the assassin's blade. After Arcanus left, Ahrnad came for it. I gave it to him, still in the box, cautioning him not to open it. He was Lord of the Guard. I had no idea of the ill I did giving it to him. I was more right than I knew when I called him mad before, although I labeled Leonas and Beryl unfairly. Your father must summon Arcanus again. This is beyond my ability to heal."

Aras admitted, "I am almost relieved you gave it to him. For I believe he had already handled it and been tainted by it and that, had you denied him, Ahrnad would have killed you and taken it anyway. We must go to my father in the Grove. Lord Alwen is Ahrnad's friend and Ahrnad has been telling him fell things and spreading stories amongst the King's Guard that I am the one being controlled by outsiders. Alwen might warn Ahrnad rather than capture him. But he will listen to my father and believe him."

"I will come with you. The High-King may hear even my words more clearly than the words of his son." Jarnath sighed. "It has been a great sorrow to me that it has always been so."

"You have always been there to hear me, Jarnath," Aras said. "You are as a father to me, though I love him still. I had never thought to say it to you, for I thought you knew, as you well might, but also I thought time would be endless enough to say such words. But I am learning that such things should not wait."

"You have always been as a son to me," Jarnath said. His voice was choked with emotion. They embraced and Aras looked at Jarnath with love in his eyes, and the love in Jarnath's eyes was reflected in his own. It emanated from Jarnath's core in warm, gentle waves. Whoever Jarnath was and whatever he had done, millennia ago, how could Aras have ever doubted him?

The three of them headed to the Lords' Grove. Lunahr stopped when they were yet many paces from the Grove. "I cannot approach the High-King. I will wait here." Aras nodded and squeezed his arm in reassurance.

Laedrin was in the Grove, his arms about Arandrin, but to his amazement, Aras could scarcely see him for the great branches that held him in their embrace. The King's Guardsmen were looking at him in concern and shifting nervously, eyeing the Trees around them as if they might pull up their great roots and walk, as they had done millennia ago as saplings in their Homeland.

The leaves overhead rustled and Laedrin stepped back. He turned and saw Aras, and there were tears in his eyes. "He is awake. He not only speaks to me loud enough for me to hear, but he can move again. I would endure all that has passed these many weeks over again and would gladly have given my arm to receive such a gift.

"As for Ahrnad, from what Arandrin and you have told me, he must be found and either captured or killed. He has served me faithfully for these many centuries, otherwise I would order only his death, for he is a great threat. The order must be spread quickly. He will be capable of great harm to us all if he is not found."

Aras and Laedrin left the Grove. Lunahr saw the High-King and began backing further away. But Laedrin saw him as well and called out. "Lord Beryl! I would have you come to me. Stand at twenty paces so that I may speak to you. Arcanus has seen that it is safe for us, even at half that distance, but I think we would all be more comfortable thus."

Lunahr shifted nervously, but Aras urged him forward, and reluctantly he approached, holding his hands tightly clasped before him, to show they were free of weapons. The King's Guard tensed, as he approached and knelt before Laedrin.

"I am sorry, Majesty, for all the harm I have done to you and to Ahrnad. I ask that you show him what mercy you can, for he does not deserve his fate."

The High-King nodded. "Arise, Lord Beryl. You have done me great harm, but you were not in control of your faculties when you did so. You are not to blame. I have already forgiven you for the attack upon my person, and you have been named Guest-of-my-House. My son values you as his friend. And now, because of you and Arcanus, the Trees are awake; their voices are strong and they move again. I hereby grant you the title of Lord of the Grove, and charge you as Protector of the Trees. From this moment forth, you are responsible for their safekeeping. You are an outsider no longer. Nalea will ever be home to you, for as long as you have need of us."

Lunahr's eyes were bright with tears. "Thank you, Majesty. I will keep the trust you have bestowed upon me."

"Come with us now to the safety of the Palace. Until Ahrnad is captured, we may all be targets for his dark hand."

Aras dropped back to accompany Lunahr as he walked behind the rest. "Welcome home, my friend," he said softly. Aras could see that Lunahr could not speak, he was so moved.

LEONAS was brought to the safety of the Palace as well. The King's Guard and the Guard were alerted, and the City and entire outlying Wood were searched, but Ahrnad could not be found. There was no sign of him.

Chapter 11

The Enchantress

SELENE looked back frantically as she ran. She could not see the dogs, but she could hear them, baying and barking. She faced forward again, and a branch raked across her cheek, tearing through the thin, opaque veil, barely missing her eye. She jerked her face away and stumbled on a tree root, flailing arms catching at twigs as she fell. She was down for only a moment and then on her feet and running again, but even though she was uninjured, the brief fall was disaster. The dogs were closer now: they were going to catch her, to tear her apart! She was going to die!

Her heart was hammering in her chest and her lungs were burning. Then, unexpectedly, she broke through the trees and found herself on a Road. She was not alone. She almost screamed, thinking the farmers had gotten in front of her somehow. But these Men were different. They were armed, but with swords and bows. They were mounted, they wore uniforms, they were soldiers. Then she saw the wagons, the men in rich clothing, and realized the uniformed men were guards, the Men merchants. She'd come across a caravan. Hope flared.

She ran for the closest wagon, crying out desperately, "Help me! Please help me! They're going to kill me!"

A boy was driving the wagon, dressed in the same shade of blue Marcus wore. He was almost a man, with a handsome face and light-brown hair. Her violet eyes found his blue ones and their gazes locked. His eyes were bright and warm, filled with surprise but also intelligence, compassion, and strength. She felt the hunger surge over her and tore her eyes from his, lest he see beyond the terror to the insatiable desire within her.

RION stared, stunned. They'd heard the hunting dogs, so he had expected a fox or a deer might leap out of the trees onto the Road. He was prepared to rein in his team of horses, if they were startled. But a girl! He saw only her eyes, and a hint of her face. She was cloaked and veiled, but those eyes! They were the color of the twilight sky, and they were terrified. Then she looked away, and he leapt from the wagon, drawing his new sword, calling out, "Ron, Ara, Gar, Van, guard her!"

The four brothers leapt from their horses and formed a square around her, as they had formed one around Rion when they were tested so long ago in Athanark, and as they had about Elanara in Erenia. "The rest of you, protect the horses!" Rion called out. Then suddenly the dogs were upon them.

There were at least a dozen, snarling and barking, lunging onto the Road, ignoring the guards and the horses, intent on their prey. They leapt at the brothers guarding the girl. They were met with bared blades. Six fell, some whimpering and writhing, while others lay still. The rest broke off, some running for the trees, tails between their legs, others backing away, hackles raised and growling. Rion caught a glimpse of Tarrell. He'd dropped the traces and scrambled to the top of his wagon, shaking. He'd leapt to stand between Rion and a rampaging ogre, but after having barely lived through the wolven attack, the dogs terrified him.

There were sharp whistles from the trees, and the rest of the dogs ran into the woods, some of the injured ones on the ground futilely straining to rise. Eight men broke through the cover of the trees onto the Road.

They stopped at the edge of the Road and eyed the caravan angrily, pitchforks and staves and axes in hand. The tallest, a man with a staff, said, "You'd no call to kill our dogs! They wouldn't have hurt you. They only wanted the demon."

"What demon? Who are you? Why are you chasing this poor girl?" Rion asked, vexed.

The man laughed, but it was a harsh and bitter laugh, without joy. "Poor girl? You call that thing a girl? She's deceiving you. She's a walking nightmare! You wouldn't feel so kindly toward her if you saw poor Rowan, lying pale as death in his father's arms. You'd best be careful whom you succor, boy. She likes them young and innocent so they can't fight against her. I've heard of her kind. She's looked at you, hasn't she, boy? She's already cast her sights on you as her next victim, even while still fleeing for her life."

SELENE saw the look of indignation on the young man's face at being called a boy by the farmer, but she saw a look of doubt cross his face as well, and the faces of the four uniformed guardsmen around her. The youngest of the guards shifted a little away from her.

She had regained her breath and wits enough. She had to convince them the farmers were wrong about her. "I had nothing to do with Rowan's illness, I swear! His family offered me kindness. They took me in last night, gave me dinner, and let me sleep in their barn. I'm far from home, and I had nowhere else to go. They shook me awake this morning, screaming at me that their son was ill. They said I'd done it, but I did nothing, I swear it!"

"You repaid their kindness by seducing their son and sucking the life from him, you vile nightwhore!" the one with the staff said and started approaching angrily.

"You'll watch your tongue or I'll remove it for you," a towering giant who but for his size looked to be one of her mother's people said, stepping in front of the farmer.

Selene's eyes widened. She had been so terrified, and there had been so many men and the horses, she hadn't had time to see everyone clearly at first, but now as she looked closely at him, she saw his hair and beard were braided in the distinctive pattern of those of Malar, with only a single bold variation from that familiar pattern.

"Are you truly one of us? How can you be here, so far from our Lands, to save me in my hour of greatest need?" she asked in Dwarvish.

"You are far from the safety of your Mountain, Lady. Who are your people, that they would let you travel from it without an escort to guard you?" he asked reproachfully in the same language.

"I am Circe of Armsguard. My Kingdom and my people are no more," she admitted sadly.

"Then I will be your protector. I am Prince Jargas, son of King Rongas of Malar in Holoren. I will guide you to the Saravan Mountains, where you may yet find kin, for many of those from what Men call the Lost Kingdoms yet survive and dwell there."

He had just spoken his true name to her! The thought terrified and excited her, that he would unknowingly give her such power over him. Then his other words belatedly registered. Malar in Holoren, not Fromer? What could he mean? Surely there could not be a second Kingdom of Malar? And survivors of the Lost Kingdoms in the Saravan! Were there truly other Kingdoms, in addition to the three surviving ones in the Fromer? The very thought astonished her.

Jargas spoke in Common to the Man before him. "The Lady is under my protection. Take your dogs and go. You'll not harm her."

The man fumed. "Lady? I promised Aaron I'd bring that creature to him. I'll not leave without her."

Jargas's eyes narrowed. "We've sixteen trained men to your eight, double your number, better trained and better armed."

RION glowed with pride. Jargas had counted him amongst the men!

Some of the men around the one with the staff spoke to him quietly and he cursed. "All right, take her, then. But mark my words: you'll regret it by morning when that rich boy of yours is lying dead at her feet." The men scooped up their wounded dogs and left back through the woods.

Rion turned to the girl, who blushed darkly; he could see her cheek through the tear in her veil.

"Thank you, all of you, for your kindness."

Rion walked over to her and the brothers parted. "Did they hurt you? You're bleeding!" he realized in concern.

SELENE touched her hand to her face and adjusted the veil, covering her cheek. "It's just a scratch, a branch from one of the trees. The dogs didn't get close enough to harm me." She was trembling. He was so close to her; he looked so delicious.

She was horrified. How could she be so hungry again already? And they'd almost fought over her, good men, all of them. They might have died for her. The thought both repelled and excited her.

"YOU should sit and rest. I know how terrifying it is to be chased like that," Rion said soothingly, remembering the wolven outside Athanark and seeing her tremble. He reached his hand toward her and was surprised when Jargas's hand restrained his wrist.

"You cannot touch her, Rion. A Dwarven Lady can only be touched by her husband or her family. Those ignorant fools had no idea what they were saying."

"Dwarven? But she can't be!" Rion said in surprise.

Jargas looked at him, curious. "Why would you say that?"

"Well, she doesn't look anything like a Dwarf!" She was perhaps five-and-a-half feet tall, at least a foot taller than a Dwarf would be, from all he had ever heard of them, save for Jargas. Even with the veil, Rion could see her face was fine boned, and from what he could tell, under the cloak she seemed thin, petite.

"And what do you think she should look like?" Jargas asked, puzzled.

"Well… um… stockier and, uh…." From what little he'd heard in the cities, people said Dwarven women looked exactly like the men, down to the beards, and he suddenly realized how ridiculous that was. From what he saw, she was breathtakingly beautiful, and he realized Dwarves might guard their women as jealously as their other treasures, that few Men might ever have seen one, and that those they'd honored enough to might not have spoken of it. Rion turned to face her again. He could not see her mouth, but her eyes were laughing, as if she'd heard his thoughts. He blushed.

"Do you always wear a veil?" Rion asked, changing the subject. "Dwarven women, I mean."

"Of course, except for in private, in front of our families," she said properly, but there was a hint of amusement in her voice that reflected a fraction of what he had seen in her eyes.

"We're lucky to have Jargas with us. With customs so different, it's no wonder they viewed you so strangely. But we've already learned much about ogres and Elves on this trip. It's only fitting we'd get to learn more about Dwarves as well. Would you like to sit next to me in my wagon? I mean, um, if that's all right. I…."

Her eyes smiled again. "Of course. May I ask where you are heading? It is truly near the Saravan Mountains, or is Jargas going terribly out of his way for me?"

"We're heading to Gosa. We're about a week from there," Rion replied.

Jargas added, "The Saravan Mountains aren't far from there, only two hundred miles or so. But even were they a thousand leagues from Gosa, I'd not have you make the journey without me to guard you."

GOSA was a large city. She'd disappear from them there. Cold stone could no longer warm her. She needed men: only they had the heat, the fire, she needed. She'd be safer there. She could feed for a time without arousing suspicion. Men often disappeared in such cities. Even were she to lose all control and kill her victim, and his body be found, the City Guard would likely assume he'd fallen to bandits or other unsavory Men.

She bit back a whimper of fear and projected her thoughts outward. *Oh Marcus, what am I becoming? Where are you, where is Arcanus? Please hurry. You must find me. Please stop me before I kill someone.*

"What's wrong?" the young merchant asked in concern.

Selene realized he'd been able to see her fear. He was so perceptive, so sweet, so vulnerable. She mustn't touch him. He might be like Rowan. Rowan had seemed so strong, at first. Could he truly have been so weakened by her? Jargas was tremendous. He could satiate her hunger. She could feast upon him without fear. But the boy's blue eyes called to her.

"You are right. I must rest. It was so terrifying...." She climbed onto the bench and he scrambled up beside her.

He had almost offered his hand, but had withdrawn it at the last moment, careful not to touch her. "My name is Rion. May I ask you your name?"

Surely he wasn't asking her true name, when he had not offered his own? Then she realized why he asked. "Ah, that is right, I was speaking Dwarvish. It is Circe."

"Circe. It's beautiful," Rion said, then blushed and looked away.

She smiled at him, though he couldn't see it for her veil, a genuine smile of warmth, as if she were any woman and he a man who might win her favor.

The caravan moved off again, and Rion began chattering about who they all were and where they'd been. She realized he was trying to put her at ease, and she tried to relax. But there were so many lean, hard bodies all around her.

She forced herself to listen to his words and closed herself off to those around her. To Rion, it appeared as if she hung onto his every word.

RON eyed Circe carefully and looked toward his brothers. Neither Gar nor Ara seemed overly interested in her. Van, though, was watching her, but his expression was one of suspicion. Ron rode up and said softly, "You're betraying your thoughts, Van. Don't let Rion catch you looking at her like that."

"I'll try, Ron, but her eyes! She was staring at me and our eyes met for an instant and... even the ogre didn't scare me so much!" He shivered.

Ron wondered whether Tarrell shared his concern and saw to his surprise that Tarrell's gaze was shifting from Rion to Jargas and back again. Ron realized Jargas was watching Rion too, but the expression on his face was far from protective.

Rarnak rode up to Ron. "You've seen it, too?" he asked, softly. "That girl is trouble, whether or not she is what they said she is. We've only a week left of the journey, but it looks to be a long week."

Ron nodded and kept an eye upon her.

THEY rode until dusk and made camp. Selene was pleased to see how solicitous Rion was being. When they made dinner, Rion brought her a plate, but she ate almost nothing, barely able to choke down what little she did consume. Such food was no longer what she needed to sustain her.

RION'S heart quickened as she removed the veil to eat and he saw her face. It was as perfect as he had imagined it would be. Her rosy lips were full and inviting. He realized he was staring and was about to look away when she smiled warmly at him. He grinned back at her.

She reminded him of Elanara, in a way. She was as exotically beautiful, but dark not fair, and hot not warm. Those violet eyes were incredible. He had not known eyes could be so blue before Elanara, but he had not even known eyes could be violet at all.

"Who is she, this woman you compare me to?" Circe asked him, and her voice was deep, almost husky, where Elanara's was high and light.

"Brook. She is a River Elf I met in Erenia," Rion said and then started. "I mean, I'm not comparing you, I…." How could his wit be so addled that he say that and then not be able to explain himself?

Circe laughed, and her laugh was rich and warm, enveloping him in velvet, instead of sweet and cool, rippling over him like water.

"River Elves do not dwell in Erenia. It is the only Wood Elf Kingdom without River Elves to protect it," Circe corrected him.

"But she is a River Elf, from Riviera. She was only a… guest… there. What do you mean, protect Wood Elves? Why would any Elves need protecting?" His thought turned to the armored soldiers he'd seen. "Do River Elf Kingdoms have great armies, then?"

Circe laughed. "So many questions! Let me see. First, if she is from Riviera, she is indeed a River Elf, though far from home. The way you said 'guest' I might almost think her a prisoner there, except that Elves never imprison their own kind."

Rion shifted uncomfortably and her eyes widened in surprise. He was afraid she might ask more, but to his relief she continued. "As to River Elves protecting Wood Elves, how better to extinguish fire than with water? As for armies of Elves," she said, and the smile left her face and her voice grew quieter. "It has been three thousand years since the Elves have had armies or needed them. If they had armies now, it might mean they were ready to destroy the world again, only this time, there would be nowhere left for them to flee to."

Rion paled. He heard Thorn's voice again, speaking of war, and how abhorrent it was. "Our history would make you weep," Thorn had said. Rion asked, "Did the Elves really have a war? Did they really destroy their world and come here to escape it? How is it you know about it?"

"Oh yes, the Elves had a most terrible war, The War of the Wind. My teacher taught me their history. I will tell you, if you'd like to hear, but that was long ago. You need not look so frightened."

"Please, tell me. It's important I hear," Rion urged.

SELENE told him the story, as Arcanus had taught it to her. "The Seven Kingdoms, four Wood Elf Kingdoms and three River Elf Kingdoms, are but a pale reflection, a dying shadow of the glory the Elves once knew. How could they be more, when only two of the four races of Elves yet live? In the Elven Homeland, there had been four races: *Aerta, Oceana, Faeren,* and *Aerie.*

"The *Aerta* or Elves of the Earth held a love for all life, for growing things, plants and animals, but especially for the forests of the Elven Homeland, and drew their Power from the Trees. The Trees of those woods are not like the poor specimens in these lands. The Trees of the Homeland were sentient beings: they could think and speak and even move, and they were able to wield great Power, what you would call magicks. But the Trees are all dead, and the Wood Elves of these lands are but the shadowy remnants of the *Aerta.*

"The *Oceana* or Elves of the Water dwelt in every river and lake, even in the great ocean surrounding the Homeland. They drew their Power from the crystal waters. The River Elves are all that remains of them.

"The *Faeren* or Elves of Fire dwelt in the *faeraelen,* the mountains of fire of the Homeland. There are none here in these lands; you have no word for the mountains that sustained them. There were few of the *Faeren,* for there were few mountains of fire, even in the Homeland. But they were hardy and strong. The story of the destruction of the *Faeren* would make the strongest heart weep.

"The fourth race, the *Aerie* or Elves of the Air, those most hated, most reviled, once dwelt on the highest mountaintops of the Homeland. They began the War that destroyed the Elves' world. The mountains were not high enough for them. They were so aloof that they sought to remove themselves from the world below completely. They sought true flight, more than flight; they sought a way to put their great strongholds into the very air.

"They began chopping down the forests, to create the charcoal they needed to melt the ores they dug from the earth. They rent the land with fantastic tools, great creations of metal, like waterwheels or windmills, but powered not by water and wind but by wood and charcoal and then oil and coal and things for which I know no Common name. They poisoned the waters with their mining, with their building. They dammed many of the rivers, to drive their great waterwheels, leaving huge tracts of land to shrivel up and die. They poisoned the very air all the Elves breathed with smoke from their great machines. They even harnessed the power of the few *faeraelen* of the Homeland, using the tremendous heat of the molten rock within to drive their mad devices. They built great wings of metal which they thrust into the sky. They finally achieved their dream, but it had come at a high price.

"The *Aerta*, the *Oceana,* and especially the *Faeren* had begun dying by the thousands, by the tens of thousands, without the trees and waters and *faeraelen* they each needed to sustain them. The *Aerie* had turned a deaf ear to all their pleas. They were cold and aloof and cared not that their cousins perished. It was the *Faeren* that finally found the strength of spirit to challenge them. If they would not listen to words, to reason, they must be made to listen, by force of arms.

"That was the beginning of the War of the Wind. The *Faeren* begged the *Aerta* and *Oceana* to aid them. But their will was weak. They instead decided to flee the Homeland. Centuries earlier, the *Oceana* had begun crossing the great oceans with ships of deadwood they had built. They already had small colonies upon these lands. They decided to all leave, and the *Aerta* decided to go with them.

"The *Faeren* realized that such an exodus would take time. They told the *Oceana* and *Aerta* they would protect them from the *Aerie*, so they might evacuate into enough ships to reach the safety of this New Land. And so they fought, all alone against a great Army of the Air. They fought bravely, valiantly, but they finally realized they were losing.

"They feared for their cousins, for the *Aerie* had so spoiled the Homeland with their devices of smoke and metal and the ravages of their War that even they now sought a New Land, with clean, clear air they might breathe and water they might drink. And new forests to chop down and new rivers to dam, new lands to lay to waste.

"The remnants of the *Faeren* Army realized what they must do, the noble sacrifice they must make to save all the rest. They had been working upon a great weapon of flame, to be used only if all was lost. A weapon that would obliterate the Homeland and themselves with it, but a weapon of such great power it would reach into the very sky and smite the *Aerie*. And that is what they did. For the sake of the *Aerta* and the *Oceana*, the *Faeren* perished as a race. They died proudly, knowing that their Enemy, the *Aerie*, died with them, and those that remained might know peace and life." Selene's voice sank to a whisper as she finished.

Rion was staring at her, mesmerized.

Selene smiled sadly. "It is the fate of the good, the valiant, the noble, to die for their cause when faced with such an enemy. When I first heard that story, I thought myself safe, thinking that the enemy had been eliminated from the world long before I was born. What a foolish child I was to think so! The enemy is not dead. The enemy can never be dead. There is always some new terror to replace the old."

RION swallowed. He was about to tell her about the Elven soldiers they'd seen when Jargas came over to them and spoke in Common. "If you'll excuse me, Lady, I would welcome the chance to speak with you. It has been a while since I've had the chance to use our tongue."

Rion looked up at Jargas in annoyance. He realized he and Tarrell had been rather lax this trip observing the traditional employer and hireling boundaries with their guards, but Jargas had never before taken advantage of the fact. "Shouldn't you be setting up the watch for the evening or something?" Rion asked dismissively. He hadn't meant it to sound quite the way it did. But he and Circe were talking of the end of the world, both the Elves' old home and perhaps now even their new one. All their lives might be in danger, and Jargas was only interested in flirting with her.

"I've already done so, which you might have noticed if you'd not been taking advantage of her needing to eat. It goes well beyond rude to stare so at her uncovered face. If you'd done so in one of the Kingdoms, you'd be lucky to escape with your head," Jargas chastised with surprising heat.

"Well, in case you haven't noticed, we're not in the Dwarven Lands," Rion retorted with equal heat. "I wouldn't dream of insulting a Lady, but as she smiled at me for looking at her, I take it she might like me looking at her," Rion retorted, emphasizing the "me."

Tarrell, Rarnak, and Ron were all coming up behind Jargas. Rion's temper flared. "Stay out of this, Tarrell! Jargas works for me and he'll answer to me," Rion snapped.

Tarrell stopped, looking stunned by Rion's words and tone.

Then suddenly Circe was between them, laughing softly. "Gentlemen, please! I do not wish to be the cause of discord between you." She had pulled her veil back on. "I am tired. I'm sure you understand. I'll be more than happy to speak with both of you in the morning, once I've had a chance to rest. If you'll excuse me?"

"Of course. Why don't you use the wagon? There's a blanket there," Rion offered solicitously. It would be more proper than the ground, and more comfortable. The wagon was still packed in the same manner as when the wounded had used it as a bed. They'd not had to cross any marshes or ford any rivers after all, thanks to the Elves.

"Sleep well, Lady," Jargas said and then with a final glare at Rion, he turned and headed for the perimeter of the camp.

Rion watched as Circe climbed into the back of the wagon and covered herself with the blanket.

RON, Tarrell, and Rarnak sat down by the fire and began talking softly. Rarnak spoke first. "I don't like the game that little harlot is playing."

Ron agreed. "Did you see her face as she watched the two of them fighting over her? She was reveling in it! She only stepped in when she saw we were about to, and poor Rion thinks she's a heroine for it."

"What can I do?" Tarrell said in frustration and hurt. "You heard Rion. He wasn't just chastising Jargas, he was slighting me, too. He doesn't want my help."

"Want it or not, he needs it," Ron insisted. "We have to keep a close eye on the three of them and do our best to keep the two of them from being hurt by her, or each other. And I thought the tough part of the trip was over! I don't want to know what Jargas might be like when he is truly angered. I don't want to ever have to face him as an enemy."

SELENE lay down and pretended to fall immediately to sleep, all the while listening to the guards' soft whispers, her keen Dwarven hearing making it ludicrously easy to eavesdrop on them, in spite of their pathetic attempts at secrecy. She would be careful not to feed tonight. It was important that she lull them into a false sense of security, so it would be safer when she unleashed her hunger. Her hunger truly was like a living thing, a voracious beast fighting to escape the cage of her will.

Thoughts of Rion pinned helplessly beneath her, buried deep inside her, at her mercy, kept springing into her mind's eye unbidden. Unable to stem her need, she tried to picture Jargas underneath her instead, but it was no use. It was Rion she hungered for, his sweet innocence and beauty.

She ached to pleasure herself with him. She fought the urge to writhe in her need, to tear off her blanket and her dress and pounce upon him, to use his youthful fire to temporarily hold her unquenchable desire at bay.

She must not. She would kill him all too easily. He could not slake her hunger. No single man could. Save for Jargas, perhaps. Now there was a feast! He was so large, so strong. She could perhaps take him half a dozen times before he would lay spent. But not tonight. It was too soon, too dangerous to attempt it.

RION lay awake, thinking of all Circe had told him. It had sounded so awful. He had been disappointed to hear that the Wood Elves and River Elves had fled their Homeland rather than fought to save it. Though he wondered about that.

Surely some of them must have fought? There must have been soldiers there as well, mustn't there, if there were soldiers here? Or had they only become soldiers once they'd gotten here and found the lands already occupied by Men and Dwarves, when they'd realized there was nowhere left to run to, and that they must someday fight for their homes, if they meant to keep them? He was eager to speak more with Circe. Would morning never come?

SELENE awoke, amazed that she had managed to sleep at all. She immediately saw that some of the Men who hadn't been on guard duty looked tired and realized they'd stayed awake out of fear of her, lest the farmers' words prove true. Rion's guardian, Tarrell, looked exhausted. The ones she'd heard called Ron and Van looked tired as well, but Ara and Gar appeared fresh. Rarnak was tired.

Jargas did not look tired, but he had not slept either, she knew. He had come and stood staring at her while she pretended to sleep last night. She wondered what he'd been thinking.

When the caravan mounted up, Selene sat beside Rion again. Rion looked as if he had slept poorly, if at all, but from the way he greeted her so enthusiastically, she knew it wasn't from fear of her. Had he been dreaming of her, as she had dreamt of him, naked and sweaty and begging beneath her? She suppressed the image, lest it overwhelm her.

RION had had horrific dreams last night, after he finally had fallen into an exhausted sleep: dreams of mad creations of metal, dead trees, blackened waters and a smoke-filled sky, and everywhere the pale, bloated, rotting corpses of Elves. He could not bear to hear any more talk of the Elven War. Instead he began the conversation on a different tack entirely. He and Circe spent the morning talking about the various cities they'd been to, and the unique customs within them.

RION was a breath of fresh air, of innocence. He seemed eager to learn about everything. They spoke at length about cities and peoples of the Lands of Men, but then of Dwarven customs as well. To Selene's surprise, Rion asked if she might begin to teach him Dwarvish.

"I've asked Jargas to teach me. He taught me Ogrish well enough, but he doesn't seem to want me to know about his people."

Selene smiled. "Dwarves are like that. Even knowledge can be treasured and hoarded, though it does not impoverish the one with knowledge to share it. I would be happy to teach you."

Selene was surprised. She found she genuinely enjoyed teaching Rion. He was such an apt pupil. He seemed to have a talent for languages: he learned vocabulary quickly, and his pronunciation was excellent after only a few repetitions.

Selene felt herself again, as if the past weeks had just been some terrible nightmare, as if it were over. She almost believed it, but then they stopped for lunch. She couldn't eat, not anything. Food just did not hold an appeal for her: she was truly repulsed by it. She tried to force herself to eat anyway, then ran between the trees and fell to her knees and was violently ill upon the ground.

Jargas came to her. He was worried for her. He wanted to know what Rion had given her to eat, as if it were his fault. He was being fatherly or brotherly, she suddenly realized. She would have laughed if she didn't feel so sick. Here she thought she'd done such a good job of getting him to want her, and he was only interested in protecting her! She started to cry, then. She was completely mortified, but she threw herself into Jargas's arms, desperate for him to hold her, even in a fatherly embrace, especially in one. Jargas stiffened at her touch, and she was ready to draw away, realizing she shamed them both, when he unexpectedly wrapped his great arms around her, embracing her.

She looked up at his face and was surprised at the look she saw: longing, so intense, so long unfulfilled, that it was turned to pain. "I've dreamt of you, Lady," he said in Dwarvish. Then his face flushed darkly and he tried to pull away. But she would not let go. She hadn't visited his dreams last night. She'd been careful not to.

"Last night?" she asked, fearing she had lost all control.

His eyes met hers, his large brown ones withstanding her violet gaze. "Aye, and every night of my life."

Her eyes widened. She saw his hunger then, so like her own, only he fought his desire nightly, while she succumbed to her own. It gave her strength, just looking at him, holding him.

RION stood at the edge of the trees watching them. He'd been such a fool! Circe was standing in Jargas's arms, gazing up at him in adoration. Of course she'd choose Jargas over him! He could have saved himself the pain of it if he had just beheld himself in a looking glass. How could he hope to compete with Jargas for her? She'd just been humoring him before, or perhaps just being kind, lest she hurt the "poor boy's" feelings.

SELENE let Jargas go but still watched him. "You are like no other of our people I have ever met. Why do you travel alone in the Lands of Men?" she asked Jargas in Dwarvish.

"I was on a mission to my great-grandsire's homeland. Now I am returning home. My great-grandsire was from Malar, in the Fromer Mountains. He and many of his people left the Dwarven Lands seven centuries ago and settled in the Holoren Mountains to the west. My father is their King. My mother was Chieftess of the Varash, a tribe of Men that live in our mountains. We did not even know of the many Kingdoms in the Saravan Mountains until some decades ago a group of refugees headed there found us by mistake. We figured out the error they'd made and led them to where they meant to go, and spoke with those we found there. We had not even known of the war in the Dwarven Lands until then. We'd had no contact at all with them since we left, and the war only started two and a half centuries ago."

So many questions answered! But so many more took their place. She must learn all she could from Jargas about the Dwarves of the Holoren and Saravan. But first she would satisfy her curiosity about him. "So you are both a Prince and the son of a Chieftess, yet you work as a common guard? Why?"

He laughed and pulled aside the buckler on his wrist, revealing a distinctively familiar band that had been concealed beneath it. "I'm also a Lord."

She stared at the pallenteum band etched with the image of a gryphon, fighting to hide her shock and panic. "You are a Captain of the Watch? That at least explains why you disguise yourself as a mere guard!"

"I thought you might know of the Watch, for they have done much in aid of our kind. Though it interests me to see that impresses you more than my being a Prince and son of a Chieftess."

Selene was in turmoil and trying hard not to show it. Jargas was a Captain of the Watch! He was banded the Lord of House of Gryphon. But Gryphon was a dead House, a lost House! Could Jargas truly be Amontir? The Lords were the most powerful of each House. If he were truly a Lord, he might have the Power to read her thoughts, to know her heart. It was fortunate she had not fed upon him last night!

She must leave tonight, under cover of darkness. But if she could feed upon him first and then go…. The thought was too seductive to resist. If the blood and Power of the Amontir, and through them of Arcanus himself, flowed within his veins, with Power such as his, from both his body and mind, she might actually be satiated. She might finally be able to stop this madness, to find her center again. At the least, she might have the strength to call Arcanus and Marcus to her for help, without fear of attracting Incuban's attention. She realized Jargas was watching her.

"I knew you were a great man when first I beheld you. I had no idea how great. I am indeed fortunate to have found your caravan, Jargas. But we should perhaps head back. The others might worry that we are so long absent." He nodded and they turned toward camp.

Selene saw Rion was standing nearby, watching them, but he turned without a word and headed back to camp as well.

TARRELL had been watching Rion's back. He was at the edge of the trees. He figured Circe must be there, though he hadn't seen her leave. He didn't know why Rion went no further. Tarrell almost went to him, but he was glad he hadn't when Rion turned and he saw his face. Rion went back to his seat, dumped his lunch on the ground, and began to pack his gear.

Tarrell saw Circe exit the trees, with Jargas in tow as if he were a great mastiff on a leash. Tarrell saw Ron and Rarnak eyeing them as well. Circe walked past them as if oblivious to them. Jargas turned and headed for his own gear.

SELENE approached Rion alone. "I am feeling better now," she said.

Rion nodded.

"May I still sit with you in the wagon?" she asked contritely.

"Of course. I'll not make a woman walk when she might ride," Rion said coolly.

"Do not be angry with Jargas. He only seeks to protect me," Selene assured him.

"I think he is the one who needs protecting," Rion said sullenly.

"Why would you say such a thing?" Selene asked, concerned that he had.

Rion stopped packing for a moment and looked her in the eye. "Because you are using him, as you are using me. But I am not so naïve as you had thought, nor so blind as my friends fear. When I first saw you, I thought there was much more to you than there is. But you are made of glass, cold and hard and transparent, and you will cut me if I do not handle you carefully enough."

Selene looked at him, wide-eyed. And she had thought Jargas might be a danger to her! Rion knew. Somehow he knew her for what she was. Her eyes filled with sudden tears. "But I am so much more than what you see, I swear! I am truly in need of helping. If you only knew how desperately in need I am." Somehow she kept the hunger out of her voice and let only the loneliness and fear show through. She reached her hand toward his face, knowing he might pull away from her. Their eyes met and her hand gently touched his cheek.

HER touch sent a thrill through him. Rion's whole body tingled the way it had when Elanara touched him, but even more so.

Rion looked at her in concern. "You are not lying. You are in great danger. You are truly afraid. Can you not tell me what frightens you, Lady, so I might help you?"

"NO, I cannot, not yet. Please, just let me travel with you as before. Do not sit in silence beside me. Talk to me, I beg you. Your stories remind me of who I truly am. Teaching you reminds me. I need you, Rion. You cannot imagine what it is that I face. Do not make me face it alone." And this time there was no sense of hunger to quench; she meant every word.

"I will do anything I can to help you, Circe. You need only ask it of me."

"Selene. My true name is Selene, daughter of Arcanus, of Armsguard," Selene lied. "I want you to know it; I need you to know it. Please say my given name, let me hear your lips speak it to me."

"Selene," Rion said in wonder. "You offer me your true name, yet you do not ask me mine? I have done you a great injustice, Selene! I have wronged you with my thoughts of you. I have misjudged you. Forgive me. I am Alarion, son of Anorion, of Ardock. I will do whatever you ask of me, Selene."

Selene was astonished, both by his words and her own. She had him eating out of her hand again! When she heard herself speak her given name, she had been shocked, even though she had not revealed her actual true name. But now that Rion had offered her his own, she had ultimate power over him. "For now, all I ask is that you sit beside me and speak with me," she said, smiling smugly beneath her veil.

TARRELL cursed as he saw Rion lead her to the wagon. He had seen Rion confront her and had thought Rion free of her, but now he appeared more lost to her than before. He would not let her hurt Rion. He had been afraid Rion might lose his heart to Brook, and instead this Dwarven enchantress had snared him. They were only six days from Gosa. Jargas had told her he'd escort her to the Saravan Mountains afterward. But it would be too late for Rion. Tarrell feared it was already too late.

The caravan started forward again. Rion and Circe had their heads together and were talking intently. Jargas glowered at them as he walked, but they appeared oblivious to it.

At camp that night, Rion did not eat, as Circe did not. They talked until time for bed.

Jargas was on the night watch with Ara, Gar, and Lerdon. Ron, Van, and Rarnak were exhausted and fell soundly asleep. Tarrell fought sleep as long as he could, but finally succumbed to it.

RION lay awake, staring up at the stars. He could not sleep again tonight, but for a far different reason. He squirmed uncomfortably under his blanket.

Out of the corner of his eye, he saw unexpected movement, and he turned his head surreptitiously. He saw Selene rise from her wagon. At first, he thought she might be going off to relieve herself, but she was acting oddly, looking about and moving quietly, as if she were concerned that she not be seen. Then she picked up her blanket and headed for the edge of camp, and his heart sank.

He noted the direction she took, and after a moment's hesitation, he rose and followed her. Jargas had only spoken with her a few moments today, but it had apparently been enough. Rion feared she was on her way to an assignation with Jargas. He did not know why he was following her. No, he knew too well. He had to see the beginnings of their lover's tryst, in order to force his heart to believe she might do such a thing. Apparently Dwarven Ladies were only virtuous when someone was watching.

The moon was bright. He could see well enough to follow her without losing sight of her. To his confusion, he saw her approach Ara and Gar, who had apparently stopped to talk for a moment as they made their rounds. Maybe she was out here for a different reason after all? Hope flared. But then, as they turned toward her, they suddenly fell at her feet.

Rion stared in horror as she walked on, as if nothing odd had happened. She turned abruptly west and began to circle around camp in the opposite direction and disappeared into the trees.

Rion's heart was hammering. His sword was back at camp. Rion ran to Gar, feeling for the pulse of his blood at his throat, terrified. He was alive! Rion had thought she'd somehow killed them both. He checked Ara and to his relief found he was alive as well. But when he shook Gar, he would not awaken. Even when in desperation and growing fear he slapped him in the face, hard, he wouldn't.

Rion took Gar's sword and went into the trees after her. He knew he should waken the camp, rouse the rest of the guards, but he felt a sense of urgency. He'd lost sight of her. She could be anywhere, doing anything!

He pressed further into the woods. It was far harder to see now, with the tree canopy overhead blocking most of the moonlight. He strained to see ahead.

He was a fool! He should head back and get help, more men with torches to search. Then he stumbled. He'd tripped over something. He looked down and realized to his horror it was a man. He knelt and saw it was Lerdon. He felt frantically for his heartbeat, and found it.

Where was Selene, or Circe? Neither might be her name. He'd been a fool to betray his own!

He realized in sudden panic that he was no longer sure which way camp was. If he called out she might come to him, out of the night, and the thought terrified him. Rion crept slowly forward, searching, sword out and at the ready, though he was fearful if he tripped again he might impale himself upon it.

He heard a moan to his left and moved cautiously toward the sound, trying to stay hidden, to move quietly.

Moonlight fell in a little glade. He could see far more clearly. There was someone on the ground, lying still. From the size and shape it could only be Jargas, though the person standing over him, straddling him, shadowed him. It was Selene!

She was naked. Her long black hair hung to her waist and her pale skin glowed in the moonlight. She lowered herself down onto him.

"Get away from him!" Rion yelled, enraged and terrified, running toward them, sword at the ready. Selene stood and spun to face him, but Jargas did not move.

"**STOP, ALARION**," she commanded, her voice sounding frightful and husky, almost growling, and suddenly Rion could not move. She had somehow frozen him with her voice. She sashayed toward him, slender hips swinging back and forth as she walked.

He felt his head bow of its own volition: he could not control it. His eyes traveled from her feet to her groin and hovered there, then finally moved to her chest and then her face. Her smile was terrifying. "Do you like what you see, Alarion? Do you hunger for me as I hunger for you?"

Her hand reached out and took the sword from his frozen fingers and cast it aside. Her touch upon his hand sent a wave of desire thundering through him that aroused his body, though his mind fought desperately against it.

"I wanted you so badly, Alarion, but it was safer to feed upon Jargas instead. I was afraid for you. But you have come to me, and seen me, and you know me now. Now I think I will take you first. You will be a snack, an appetizer for me. Then I will dine upon him. I will finally eat my fill." Her fingers traced up his arm to his chest, then down his stomach to his waist and lower still. He stood gasping at the sensations that tore through him, on fire from her touch as she began to unlace his pants. He wanted to scream, to run, to fight, but he was helpless before her.

But suddenly there was a brilliant flash of blue light, a crackling sound, and a thundering, commanding voice boomed. "Selene, release them!"

Selene turned, and as she still controlled his movements, Rion turned as well to face what she saw.

A Man with long white hair and gray eyes, old but somehow ageless, in a robe of red, was suspended in the air, sinking slowly to the ground. He was held around the waist by a male Elf in a robe of blue, his long silver hair whipping about him and blue lightning arcing out from his fingertips and coruscating around them both. His face was as beautiful as Elanara's, but it was contorted in pain. Wizards! They must be wizards!

Selene faltered and then screeched. "**NO! YOU MUST NOT SEE ME LIKE THIS!**"

The two wizards were tossed back against the trees. Rion could suddenly move again. Either Selene did not have the strength to hold him while she attacked them, or she had merely forgotten about him. It didn't matter. All that mattered was he could see Gar's sword on the ground, and he ran toward it. His hand closed about the hilt and he rose and lunged for her. She seemed oblivious to his attack, but the two wizards were not.

"**NO, DON'T HURT HER!**" a different voice cried, frantic and youthful and filled with panic and pain. The sword was wrenched from Rion's hand, as if by the voice itself, and it flew spinning to the ground. The Elf screamed, in agony and terror.

"Marcus?" Selene cried, her voice sounding suddenly young and afraid.

The wizard who had spoken in command before begged now. "Selene, come quickly! You must help him as you did before. Don't let Incuban have him! I beg you, daughter, save your brother."

Selene ran, stumbling toward them. "Marcus!" She fell to her knees and hugged the Elven wizard in blue tightly, sobbing.

"It's all right, I'm here. Take my Power, Marcus, take all of it! I don't want it. Oh, Marcus, please! I can't lose you! Look at me! Look at what I've done to myself to save you. Please don't let it be for naught."

Rion knew he should run while he could, or hide, or try to save Jargas, anything but stand here where they could see him, but he could not move. His own heart, this time, held him fast.

The older wizard said, "I warned him not to use his Power again, not after flying us here. The risk was too great. But I cannot use mine and she did not see the danger." He looked at Rion then, and his eyes held no accusation, only infinite sadness.

Rion was horrified that the young wizard had been hurt because of him, when he'd been trying to protect him. "I'm so sorry! I was trying to help you. She was fighting you. I didn't understand. I still don't understand. How can she be his sister, your daughter, when she is a Dwarf, and he is an Elf, and you are a Man? How can she be so good, yet so evil?"

The Man before him sighed. "We can, each of us, only do the best we can with what we are given. Selene lost herself, sacrificed herself, saving her brother's life. We have been trying to find her since then, following the trail of pain she has caused. So far she has not killed any of her victims. That she helps us now means we are yet in time to save her. I apologize for whatever harm she has caused here."

He looked toward Jargas in concern. "The Dwarf has not risen." He walked to Jargas and knelt by his side. "He is still breathing," he said, and his voice shook with relief. "So she still has not killed."

"She attacked three other guards also. They only seem asleep, but I could not wake any of them," Rion said, afraid for them. "Will they waken on their own? Will the spell or magic or whatever she did to them wear off, or must she waken them? If she gives her brother all her Power...."

"The four of them will awaken. You are the one that concerns me," the older wizard said. "You have seen and heard too much. The Enemy might learn of our weakness through you, and you have heard their given names. If I could wield my Power, I could make you forget everything that has happened here. But I cannot. You are a danger to me and to my children." His voice was filled with infinite sadness, but his eyes.... Rion swallowed and began backing away from him.

"No, Father. I will not let you harm him," Selene said from behind Rion. He turned. She was still naked, but no longer looked threatening. She looked completely different, warm and strong and sweet.

"Rion saved my life when the farmers would have killed me. More than that, he has spent the past two days reminding me of much of myself I had almost forgotten. I might have truly been lost were it not for him.

"But also, he has told me much. You cannot harm him for the part he plays. Though he is barely a man and does not wield the Power of the Amontir, he wields a power of heart that has touched all he has met. Already he is a friend of Aras and Dewalaren, and Eladar and Elanara. He has given me knowledge of the Elven soldiers in Erenia and the corruption of Lunahr and the attempted assassination of High-King Laedrin. He is somehow a lynchpin, a keystone of this world. Even though he has been through such terrible trials, his heart has remained pure. There are so many playing pieces he has yet to meet, Father. You might spoil the Game and unravel the world all unknowing if you harm him now."

Rion looked at her, stunned. Did she truly mean what she said? That he was somehow important? Him? He remembered Elanara's words. She had said something similar to him. But he was just a merchant and they were Princesses and Princes and Kings and wizards. How could he be important?

"Marcus is well?" the older wizard asked.

Selene looked suddenly vulnerable and scared. "I have channeled as much Power as I could to him. It was barely enough."

Marcus himself came over, looking pale and weak. He held Selene's gray dress and cloak in his hands. "Sister, you have insisted upon walking around cloaked and veiled your entire life. I'll not stand idly by while you prance around naked now," he said, handing her them.

She had the grace to blush. "I forgot," she admitted, and slipped them on. "Brother, I have need of an Elfstone."

"Whatever for?" Marcus asked, puzzled.

"I need to waken Jargas when we are safely away from here. The others will awaken without my aid. I'm going to charm the stone and have Rion use it. I saved just enough Power to do so. For, aside from being a giant, and a great warrior, and a Prince of Dwarves, and the son of a Chieftess, my dinner is also a Lord of the Amontir, a banded Captain of the Watch. After what I have done, I have no doubt he would kill me the second he saw me, even with Arcanus standing beside me, even were he able to wield his Power to defend me. I have touched his core, and his Power is nearly equal to that of Dewalaren."

"He cannot be," the older wizard denied. "He is unknown to me."

"He is Lord of House of Gryphon, a lost House. And I have much more to tell. There are Dwarven Kingdoms here as well, in both the Holoren and Saravan Mountains. But first, I need the Elfstone."

Marcus swallowed. "I do not have an Elfstone."

"But you must! You always do. How can you not?" Selene asked, vexed.

Marcus said defensively, "Do you have any idea how many weeks, how many hundreds of leagues we've traveled looking for you?"

"Um, excuse me," Rion said, digging into his purse, only finding the courage to say anything because they sounded so much like any other brother and sister bickering. They looked at him. He opened the tiny bag he pulled from his purse. "I have an Elfstone." He held out the stone Elanara had given him to Selene sheepishly.

Selene smiled at him then, a smile of warmth and friendship. "Of course you do. I should have known you might. I am again in your debt." She held the stone, stared intently at it for a moment, muttering a single word, then handed it back to him. "When we leave, you must count to six hundred, to ensure we are far enough away, and then place this upon Jargas's forehead, and let go of it. It will glow. Once it stops glowing, remove it. Then gently waken him."

Rion looked at the stone, curiously. "You mean that's it? It's got the magic in it already? But you only spoke a single word and you didn't do anything...."

She gazed levelly at him.

"Oh. And none of you are carrying staves, either. You mean it's all for show? All the words, or most of them, and all the gestures and staves and...." He swallowed and looked anxiously at the older wizard. "And I swear, I won't tell anybody, ever! Really, you can trust me. I've kept other secrets. It's just that I don't know that half of what I hear are secrets, until somebody tells me. I don't mean to understand so much."

"Father, Marcus, I'd like to say good-bye to Rion in private."

They eyed her appraisingly and reluctantly walked an appropriate distance away.

Selene smiled at Rion. "I'm going to miss you, Rion. I wish you could have met me weeks ago. You'd have thought much better of me. I hope I can get well again, so that I might meet you sometime in the future."

She peered at him intently, and the smile left her face. Her voice lowered to a whisper. "But if you do see me again, be careful, Rion. I might not be at all who you are hoping to see. Don't regret you almost used your sword upon me tonight, Rion. You were right to. Marcus was a fool to stop you, I think.

"Be careful of him, too, for Incuban has touched him, and he may already be lost to us, despite how he appears. Marcus's wizard name is Magus. I already spoke my two names to you: Circe and Selene. In that at least I did not lie. Our father is only ever Arcanus. Even we do not know another name for him. Any of us might be changed, Rion, or might show our true natures. Trust in the Dwarves, Rion, not the Elves. I have told you their history. Do not love them so blindly.

"Farewell, Rion. Try your best to stay pure and untainted by what you see and hear. It is all that might save you. It is once you start down the path to darkness that you will be lost to it."

She kissed him on the forehead then, startling him. "I'm glad I did not hurt you. Don't ever let a woman hurt you. We're far more dangerous than you might ever guess. Take care of yourself." Then she put her mouth to his ear and whispered, "I will keep your true name safe from them, I swear it. And if ever you see Talon, Dewalaren, the King, again, you must tell him that Arcanus must never again hold the Ring. He will understand. Shh, it's a secret, for his ears alone." Then she backed away from him and walked to her father and brother, and they left, walking amongst the trees.

RION eyed the trees nervously. Their camp was unguarded; their guards were all still in that unnatural magical sleep she had cast upon them. He looked down at Jargas. He did not have the look of one entranced; he looked only asleep. Rion flushed and bent down and laced his pants and shirt for him. He wondered at Selene's words of him. Was Jargas truly all she had said? A Dwarven Prince and the son of a Chieftess and a Captain of the Watch? Like Talon, Dewalaren she'd called him, and Beryl and Hunter? And a Lord? Where was Amontir? He'd never heard of that Kingdom. It sounded like the Watch were from there, from what Selene had said. And Talon was a King! Who was Incuban? Was he a wizard as well, an evil one? If Arcanus was a good one, he never wanted to meet an evil one! His kindly voice, sorry he had to kill him.

Rion shuddered and clutched the hilt of Gar's sword more tightly and belatedly started to count. But he only made it to fifty when he stopped. She'd told him to count to six hundred, but he couldn't wait any longer. He placed the Elfstone on Jargas's forehead and held his breath. It glowed green. Jargas's face looked odd in the light. Then the light was gone. But Jargas did not need to be shaken awake. His eyes snapped open and glowed with golden fire. Rion stumbled back from him in fear, as

Jargas leapt to his feet. Selene had tricked him! She'd done something to Jargas! Jargas was going to kill him!

"Where are you, you bitch? Show yourself so we can burn you!" Jargas roared, looking about. He saw Rion then, cowering at his feet, the sword on the ground by his side.

"Where is she?" he roared at him.

"G-g-gone," Rion stuttered in terror.

Jargas started cursing, in Common, then in what sounded like Dwarvish from what Rion had heard him speak of it before, and then some other language entirely. "You need not grovel, Rion. You're not the one I'm angered at. I've always liked you for not being afraid of me, though you could have shown me more respect in the past few days," Jargas said, his voice more normal, now.

"Your... your eyes! They're b-burning!" Rion said, shaking.

Jargas cursed again, closed his eyes, and breathed deeply, inhaling and exhaling slowly and purposefully five times. He opened his eyes again, and they were only brown. "There, did it work? Hunter says it should. I'm sorry, I forgot about the eyes. I remember how that looked when I first saw the fire in Hunter's eyes. I didn't stop to think mine would burn as well. What are you doing here?"

Rion stared at Jargas, still fearful of him. "I f-followed Circe. I was s-suspicious. I saw her f-fell Ara and Gar. I tried to wake them, but I couldn't, so I took Gar's sword. I was afraid for you and Lerdon. I found Lerdon and then you. She was with you, she was going to... hurt you," he finished lamely, face flushing.

"You saw what she was yet you came after her yourself? Why didn't you go for help?" Jargas asked, incredulously.

"I didn't realize she was so dangerous, what she was doing. By then I was afraid there wasn't time. I didn't think I'd be able to find camp fast enough," Rion admitted.

"So you went after a demon with a sword? It's no surprise she got away, but it's a wonder we're not both dead. Come, we'd best go back to camp."

Rion nodded, relieved that Jargas seemed all right. But his eyes! He bent to retrieve Gar's sword and saw the glint of the Elfstone and quickly palmed it. He was not about to tell Jargas any of the rest of what had happened. "I'm sorry for before, Jargas, for what I said, and how I said it. I had no right to talk down to you like that."

"I'm sorry too, Rion. That nightwhore got into my head. My tongue was not my own. It was a brave thing you did, trying to help me: foolish, but brave. I'm glad she didn't hurt you. Which way is camp? I can't remember a thing after she touched me," Jargas said, looking about.

Rion thought she must have spoken to Jargas before she'd entranced him, for him to know what she was. He looked around. "I think I came from that way," he said, doubtfully.

They headed in that direction. Jargas's eyes were on the ground. "Aye, there are your tracks. And there are mine and hers, the bitch." They followed his tracks back to Lerdon. Jargas tried to rouse him, and this time he awoke easily.

"Jargas! What happened? Why am I on the ground?" Lerdon asked, confused.

"You were attacked by that vile nightwhore we've been traveling with, same as I was. Rion chased her off."

"If we keep following my tracks, we'll find Ara and Gar, too," Rion said, relieved Lerdon had awakened so easily.

They didn't make it that far, though. Tarrell and Rarnak and a quarter of the remaining guards bearing torches met them before they got there.

"Rion! Thank Elmoth you're all right!" Tarrell said, relief naked upon his face. "Where's Circe? Have you seen her? She wasn't in camp, and you were gone as well. I woke everyone, and we split up to look for you. Ron was with us, but we found Ara and Gar. We thought they were dead at first, but they were only sleeping, though we haven't been able to waken them. We left Ron with them, and we went on ahead."

"Circe's gone," Rion said truthfully, worried that Ara and Gar weren't waking.

"Rion scared her off," Jargas said. "She had me under her spell, but Rion saved me from her. The farmers were right. She's a nightwhore. She revealed herself to me as such before she felled me. I was a fool for thinking otherwise."

They backtracked to Ara and Gar. Rion was greatly relieved to see they were on their feet and looked all right. Rion handed Gar his sword. "Gar, this is yours. I borrowed it. I'd left the one Tarrell had gifted to me in camp, and I needed one."

"Thank Elmoth!" Gar said fervently. "I wondered what use she might have had for it. I've been going mad thinking what she might have done with it." He returned it to the scabbard at his side.

There were more questions as they headed back to camp. Rion omitted all mention of the other wizards. It would have been too hard to explain, yet keep the secrets he'd sworn to. The other guards were informed to call off the search. Jargas posted double guards around the camp, and no one slept. At first light, the caravan moved onward.

TARRELL kept a careful eye on Rion, but he seemed all right. And he was relieved to see that Rion no longer seemed to be at odds with Jargas, either. If anything, he seemed to have found new respect for Jargas, and likewise, Jargas for him as well.

They were only days from Gosa. Soon they would be safe. They would pay off most of their guards, settle in their new city, and build a new life for themselves.

Tarrell smiled fondly at Rion. He'd seen him grow to be a man on this trip. More than just turning sixteen on the journey, he'd truly come-of-age. He felt as proud of him as if Rion were his son.

RION saw Tarrell smiling at him and grinned in return. He was anxious to reach Gosa. Though he knew enough now to know that anything might happen in the last few days of their journey, he was confident that they would all reach the city safely. They had already survived ogres and obearn and Elves and wizards. What greater danger could they possibly face?

It would hurt to see his new friends leave them, but at least this time they would yet live so that he might see them again. He hoped at least some of the guards would be willing to stay and work for him and Tarrell in the new shop they would set up in Gosa.

RON was anxious to be home. They'd thought when they left that they might only be gone a year, and here they'd been gone almost two. It would be good to be home again, to see the mill and the River, and especially Lisandra. He'd missed her dreadfully this trip. He hoped she was all right, that Father had not been too harsh to her while they were gone.

He looked around at his brothers, proud of them, of all they had accomplished. Ara had laid grandfather's bow to rest, as he'd promised. And he and Ara had saved enough coin and learned enough from Rion and Tarrell that they would soon be able to begin their new trade as merchants.

Gar still had two of the four stallions they'd acquired in Thenalon for breeding, for the stables he planned to open, and he had found two mares in Falnor to replace the two horses they'd lost. They'd ridden them on the remainder of the journey, and both were of exceptional stock.

Van had grown to be a man on the journey and saved enough to build the inn he had dreamed of.

It had been touch and go more than once, but it looked like their trials were over.

RARNAK was looking forward to going home. The farm was only two days out from Gosa. He'd never thought he'd ever be eager to till the soil, but after five years working as a guard, he'd welcome the quiet life of the farm. And he could not wait to see Talia again. She'd been but a child when he left. She'd be a grown woman now.

He wondered if she'd married and left the farm. He was worried that his father might have been left to tend it all by himself. He was getting old for such work. Now that he was so close to home, he missed his father and his sister fiercely. He'd begun to despair he'd never see either of them again.

JARGAS was anxious to be home and was thankful Gosa was so near to it. He needed to see Jarina, to hug her and his father again, to tell them he loved them. And there was so much more to tell them as well.

Then the preparations for the long march to war would begin. It brightened his heart to know his father would still lead them as their King, and that they would not be fighting the Enemy alone, as they'd feared. Both Malar in Holoren and Malar in Fromer had strong allies now, in Dorolingas and Ironhand. But they would not be their only allies. He would call all of the Dwarven Kingdoms of the Saravan to march along with them, to avenge the deaths of their people and reclaim their Lost Kingdoms. And the Amontir would fight by their side as well. From what Farad had told him, the Elves would, too, and perhaps even some of the Kingdoms of Men. He'd seen now, through Farad, what it was they would be fighting against. They faced a daunting foe. But they had the Power and the might to defeat him.

But before he faced Incuban, he had another foe to face. Jargas had liked Talon. He'd admired him and respected him from the first. It saddened him that, when next they met, it would be as enemies. He feared that Talon would not surrender his throne easily, but Jargas meant to claim his birthright, despite what it might cost them both.

When next he saw Talon, he would shed the band of House of Gryphon and reveal his true line. Jargas was the grandson of Crown Prince Rowanar, Lord of House of Obearn, and the rightful King of the Amontir, and he had the lost King's Band, Prince Rowanar's Armor, and the missing King's Ring to prove it.

The Beginning of the Story

DESCENT of KINGS Book 1

Prelude to War

Maria Albert

http://www.dreamspinnerpress.com

Coming Soon

DESCENT OF KINGS
BOOK THREE:
The Coming of the King

"The world is ending. It is a cruel place and perhaps it should end. But then, there is Rion and you, and the brothers, and Rarnak, and those like you, those I might still find reason to fight for. So I look for Jargas, so he might help me, for I can stand alone against the darkness no longer."

—Farad, Lord of House of Wolven

After risking all to come to the aid of Rion and his friends, Farad believes his only hope for sanity and survival lies with Jargas. Yet it is Jarina who will either destroy or save him, at the cost of a lifetime of faith and loyalty to Prince Talon.

Meanwhile, past the outskirts of Nalea, Aras and Leonas undertake a dangerous mission to parlay with the Hill People, never dreaming the fates of both their own people and Talon's rest upon the outcome. Ironically, consumed by suspicion and mistrust, believing Jargas to be the Enemy's minion and fearing Farad lost, Talon lashes out at Aras, with devastating results.

The Amontir see agents of the Enemy everywhere, where there are none, and fail to see those who are beside them, ready to strike.

Coming Soon

DESCENT OF KINGS
BOOK FOUR:
The Final Battle

"But I am just a Man! You all want so much of me! ...I am not a wizard. I am not even one of you. I have no magic. There is no fire in my eyes."

—Rion of Ardock

Rion wields a power of heart that touches all he meets. The wizard Circe once called him a lynchpin, a keystone of the world. When Rion is viciously attacked and maimed in Gosa, he believes Circe's family is retaliating for his betrayal of them to Crown Prince Elavar. Learning the horrific truth brings him to the brink of madness.

Rion's friends take him to the River Elves of Salenia for aid, but the Elves send them onward, to King Talon. The company's perilous journey to the Watchtower is fraught with danger and filled with tragedy and triumph, but their trials have just begun.

King Talon's army has been decimated by the Enemy's relentless attacks. After staggering losses, they are outnumbered ten to one and teeter on the brink of defeat— yet somehow their dwindling forces must overcome a being with the Power of a God.

MARIA ALBERT lives in California Bay Area with her two daughters and several dozen friends, most of the latter of whom are still confined in binders on her bookshelves. She looks forward to releasing many more of them in the coming months.

Also from MARIA ALBERT

http://www.dreamspinnerpress.com

Also from MARIA ALBERT

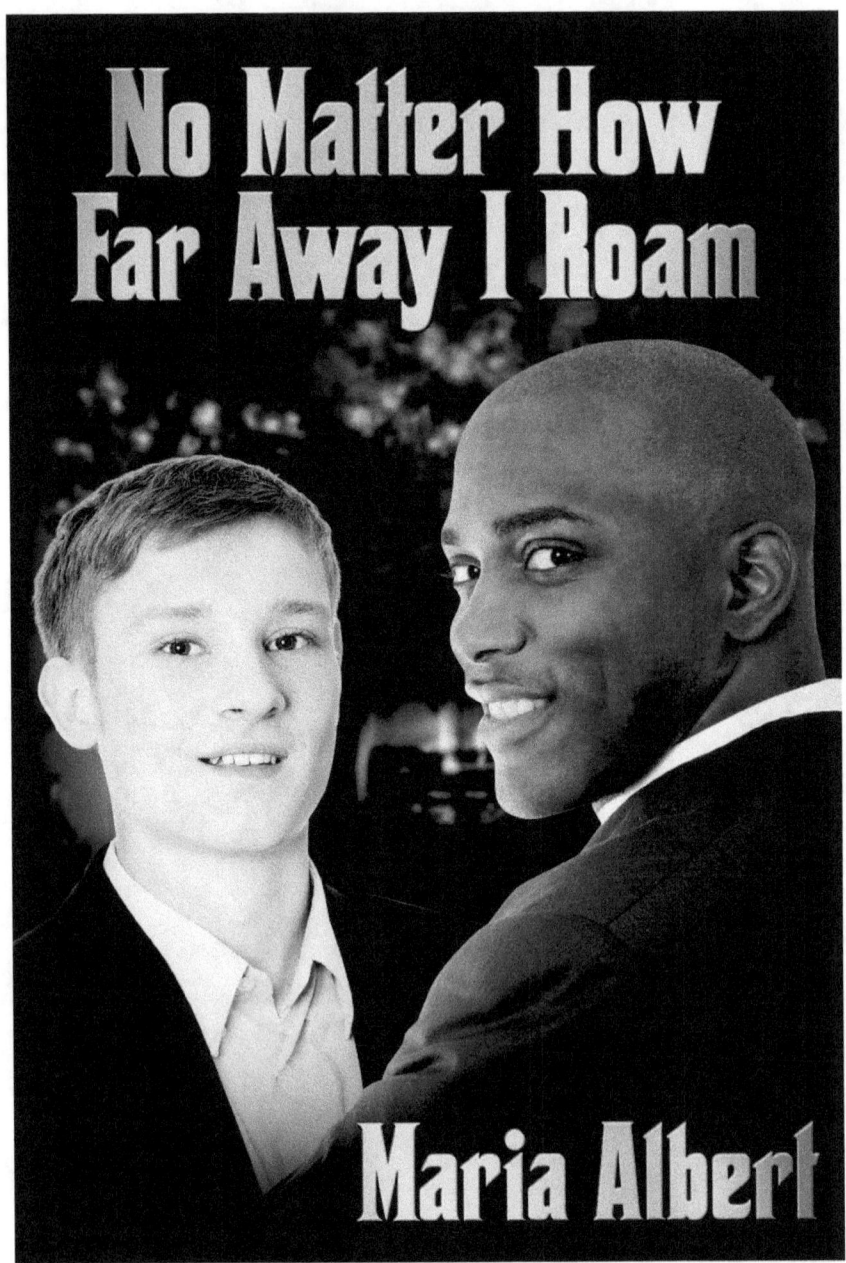

No Matter How Far Away I Roam

Maria Albert

http://www.dreamspinnerpress.com

Also from DREAMSPINNER PRESS

BOOK 1 OF PLEDGED TO MAGIC

Apprenticed to Pleasure

Brandon Fox

http://www.dreamspinnerpress.com

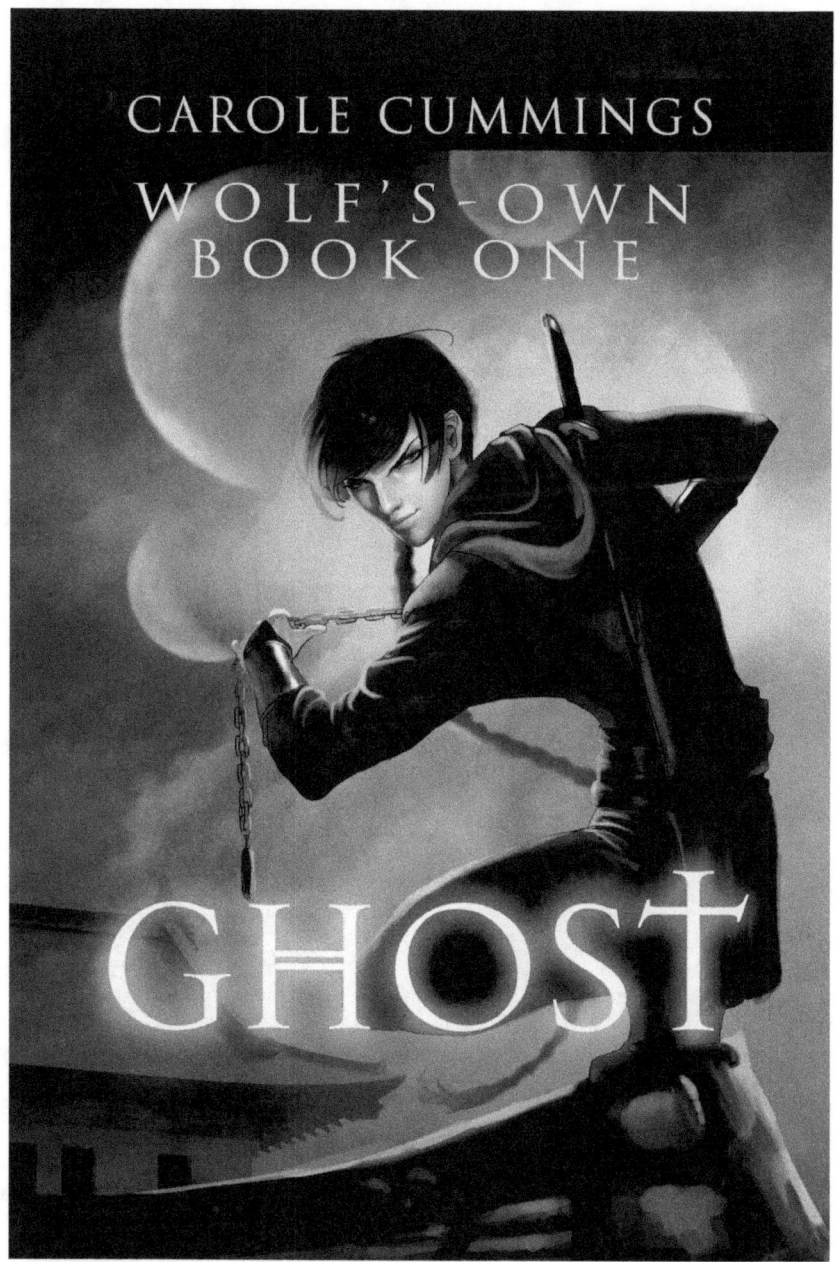

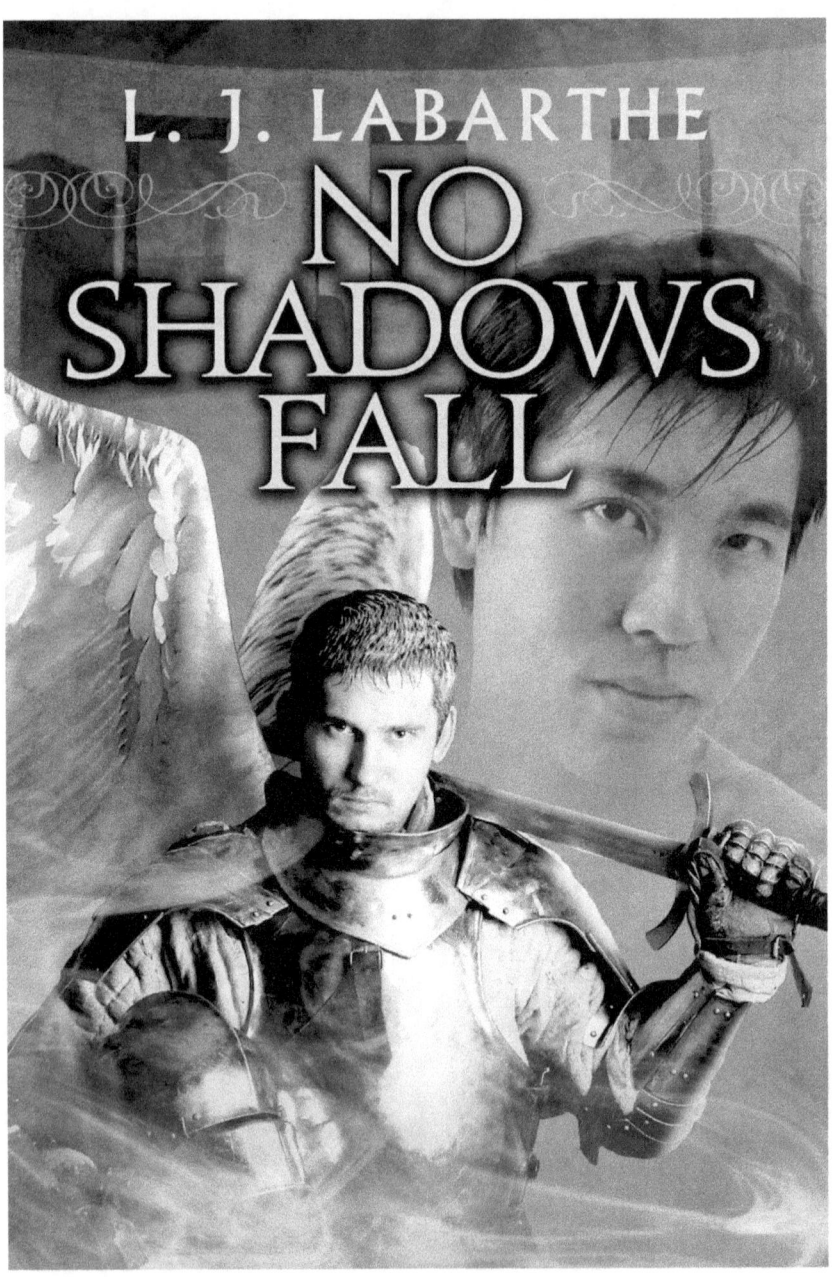